3.95

P9-DVF-355

BOOKS BY ROBERT H. PILPEL

TO
THE
HONOR
OF
THE
FLEET

TO THE HONOR OF THE FLEET

Robert H. Pilpel

NEW YORK   ATHENEUM

Map (pages x–xi) by Anita Karl and Jim Kemp

Charts (pages 324 and 326) by Marjorie Zaum

COPYRIGHT © 1979 BY ROBERT H. PILPEL
ALL RIGHTS RESERVED
PUBLISHED SIMULTANEOUSLY IN CANADA BY MC CLELLAND AND STEWART LTD.
PRINTED IN THE UNITED STATES OF AMERICA

BRENDAN ANTHONY ELLIOTT
1941–1973

Gentlemen, I propose the morrow's battle: for the glory of God, and to the honor of the fleet.

NORWAY

SWEDEN

Jutland
Bank
✕

JUTLAND

North
Sea

DENMARK

Copenhagen

Baltic Sea

Dogger
Bank
✕

Kiel

FRISIAN ISLANDS

Hamburg
Wilhelmshaven

GERMANY

Emden

Elbe R.

Berlin

Delfzijl

Ems R.

Rhine R.

Amsterdam

The Hague

NETHERLANDS

HOOK OF
HOLLAND

Kirkwall

MAINLAND

Antwerp

Scapa Flow

HOY

Brussels

BELGIUM

SOUTH
RONALDSAY

LUX.

Pentland Firth

FRANCE

SCAPA·
FLOW

Paris

A·Karl/J·Kemp

PROLOGUE

1916, 4TH JUNE—DUNFERMLINE, SCOTLAND

Admiral of the Fleet Lord Fisher of Kilverstone, seventy-five years old and sick at heart, sat reading his Bible. He had excluded the two American prisoners from his awareness. He had excluded the Royal Marine sentries outside, the breeze billowing the curtains, even the June sunlight dancing far below on the waters of the Firth of Forth. His mind was absorbed by the prophecies of Isaiah, and by a painful sense of their fulfillment:

> For the day of the Lord of hosts shall be upon every one that is proud and lofty, and upon every one that is lifted up; and he shall be brought low: and upon all the cedars of Lebanon, that are high and lifted up, and upon all the oaks of Bashan . . . and upon all the ships of Tarshish, and upon all pleasant pictures. . . .

Pleasant pictures of all the ships; it had been for these that Fisher had chosen this promontory as the site for an Admiralty wireless station. Here atop the hills behind Dunfermline town one could take in the entire southern horizon: Edinburgh, the Forth Bridge, the Water of Leith, and in the middle distance, Rosyth, anchorage of the fast Battle Squadron and Admiral Beatty's cruisers. Since his resignation as First Sea Lord one year before, a restless and resentful Fisher had come here frequently, deriving some consolation for his lack of office from the sight of those ultimate dreadnought battleships that he had conceived, designed, and built. Now three of the most beautiful lay at the bottom of the North Sea. And in vain, to no avail, for nothing.

The muffled noise of approaching automobiles impinged on the prophet's warnings, and Fisher listened as hurried footsteps and shouted orders confirmed his sense of rising anticipation. Lifting his eyes from Scripture, he turned his head toward the two Americans. The younger officer looked frightened, or perhaps tormented was closer to the mark. Contemptible! His companion, though, seemed complacently amused, and for him, in place of contempt, Fisher felt molten loathing.

There stood the saboteurs: a spineless schoolboy and a damnable Semite—two paragons of dishonor who had robbed Britain and the Royal Navy of the greatest seafaring triumph since Trafalgar: the destruction of the German Fleet! No retribution could be too harsh for crimes like theirs.

More noise from the driveway in front of the small frame building: automobiles skidding to a halt, fragments of greetings, car doors opening and slamming shut. And there was that hectic undertone peculiar to the former First Lord's comings and goings, that air of crisis, of momentous events impending. Though Fisher thought such mummery a bit pathetic given the new arrival's diminished stature in Parliament, he did not love him any the less for it. Thus when the man stormed in with all the inevitable self-generated tumult, the admiral had no trouble summoning up a smile. "Ah, Winston. You've made good time."

"Hello, Jack. Are these the two despoilers?"

"The jackals in sheep's clothing, more nearly."

Churchill grunted. "I've brought Reeves-Wadleigh with me."

"Good. I was thinking he ought to sit in myself."

Another grunt. Churchill walked up to the two Americans and glowered at each one in turn. "Commander Maltbie, if I'm not mistaken," he said to the younger man.

Maltbie swallowed visibly. "Yes sir."

Churchill stared at him a long time, then slowly shook his head.

A haggard British naval officer tapped lightly on the open door. "Come in, Wadleigh," said Fisher. "I'd like you to keep the record of these proceedings—enjoy the fruits of your labors."

"Rather bitter fruits, sir."

"Damn me if they aren't, Captain. But they're all the portion we're likely to get."

Churchill went to the door and addressed the marine standing just outside. "We'll want the building cleared, Sergeant, and no one allowed within fifty yards."

"Lor', sir. Are you goin' to set off a bomb then?"

Churchill smiled. "Perhaps, after a fashion. But with your cooperation not a soul will hear it. All right?"

"Right, sir. Will you be wanting a guard for the prisoners?"

"No. I think they've done all the damage they're likely to do for a while."

"Aye, aye, sir," said the sergeant, then saluted, faced about, and left.

The building grew silent. Churchill crossed to the long conference table in the middle of the room and sat down facing the two Americans. Fisher took a chair on his right. Reeves-Wadleigh seated himself at the end of the table where pads and pencils had been laid out. The three Britons exchanged brief affirmative nods, then Churchill spoke:

"Captain Gehlman, Commander Maltbie—this is an executive inquiry convened pursuant to the special supplementary articles of the Act for the Defence of the Realm. Our purpose here is twofold: first, to determine what role each of you played in affecting the outcome of the recent engagement between the fleets of Great Britain and Germany; second, to inquire into the circumstances surrounding your assignment to the British Fleet and into the nature and provenance of certain instructions you received from your superiors during your incumbency.

"This is a secret inquiry, gentlemen, not a judicial proceeding. Thus, although you will not be represented by counsel, neither will you be subject to criminal prosecution on the basis of your testimony here. Our only object in this investigation is to establish the facts and submit our findings to the Prime Minister. I must tell you, however, that the evidence already gathered by Captain Reeves-Wadleigh and his subordinates appears sufficient to convict each of you several times over on capital charges, and I warn you to be under no illusions that your status as naval officers of a neutral power will preserve you from the operation of British law. Even your status as Americans will afford you no shelter. Indeed, it will only magnify the enormity of your wrongdoing.

"Gentlemen, it is plain to us that you acted pursuant to orders from higher authority. We can but speculate, given the present limits of our knowledge, as to the motives—and the identity—of those who directed you. It seems indisputable, however, that one of two hypotheses must account for their actions. Either they were seeking to further some undisclosed, and to us unfathomable, national objective at our expense, or"—and here Churchill's voice seemed to drop half an octave—"they were undertaking to provide clandestine military assistance to the Central Powers, with whom we are at war."

The rustling of the window curtains accentuated the silence that closed around the room as Churchill paused.

"Gentlemen," he resumed finally, "this is an awful moment in the life of the English-speaking peoples. Two American officers, steeped in the traditions of honor so sacred to the naval service, have lifted their hands in treachery against the British seamen in whose ships they sailed as trusted guests. You have struck us a blow from behind, gentlemen, and left us grieved and uncomprehending in the midst of our already great travail. The bonds of honor, the ties of comradeship, even the ancient tablets of the Law, lie shattered irretrievably on the ground. It is, I say again, an awful moment."

Fisher kept his eyes fixed on the two officers. He was pleased to note that "honor," "travail," "treachery"—all of Churchill's carefully aimed salvos—were punching very respectable holes in Commander Maltbie's fragile self-control. The faint derisive smile on Captain Gehlman's face, by contrast, seemed to rule out any remorseful disclosures from that quarter. Fisher was glad that he had kept the two men separated since the fleet's return. Now Winston had only to keep pouring in the heavy ammunition and one of them, at least, would crumble.

"I cannot believe," Churchill continued, "that you acted in this matter otherwise than under the compulsion of obedience to orders. I am certain, as one who is half-American himself, that as a personal matter your acts were as repugnant to you as they were injurious to us. Alas, what's done cannot be undone, and we stand now on the verge of a truly serious rupture in Anglo-American relations. Gentlemen, where we cannot assign causes we must assign blame. Unless you can explain to us what other purpose than outright enmity your superiors had in sending you here, the consequences will be very grave, for you as well as your country—not to mention for us."

Good, Winston! thought Fisher. Now go for the kill.

"Captain Gehlman, Commander Maltbie, I implore you, though it is late in the day for such reflection, search your consciences. Surely your masters in preparing this scheme could not have intended that it should result in an open breach between Britain and the United States. We for our part, though sorely wounded and grievously distressed, still hope to avoid such a calamity. It lies with you to determine which way the balance will incline. You have fulfilled an obligation of duty to your country; will you not now reconsider its best interests—and your own—and fulfill an obligation of simple decency to us?"

Again there was silence. Churchill sat back heavily in his chair. Fisher thought he could detect a film of wetness over Maltbie's eyes, a slight tremor in his bearing. He judged that the moment had come to speak. "Commander Maltbie," he said in as gentle a tone as he could summon forth, "just tell us whatever you feel you can."

BOOK I

As far as Harris Maltbie was concerned, the self-conscious profusion
of nautical memorabilia in Franklin Roosevelt's office was a definitive comment on the personality of its occupant. The clipper ship
prints on the wall, the bronze sextant on the desk, and the ship's
clock on the bookcase all combined with the miscellaneous maritime
knickknacks displayed on the tables and shelves to mirror precisely
the sort of person who insisted on a seventeen-gun salute every time
he came aboard a navy ship. True, protocol could be cited to justify
the man's insistence, but the fact of his insistence diminished him in
Maltbie's eyes, just as did the over-frequent references to "Uncle
Teddy" and "my year at the helm of the *Crimson*."

And as if all this affectation weren't bad enough in itself, there
was also the matter of young F. D. Roosevelt's attire. Maltbie
thought the Assistant Secretary of the Navy looked like a coxcomb:
the pince-nez, stiff collar, and three-piece suit were all a little too
neat and elder-statesman for a man whose birth in 1882 had preceded
his by only twenty-seven days. As it was Maltbie's prime affliction,
moreover, to be thirty-two and look a decade younger, the sight of a
contemporary affecting to be middle-aged was doubly exasperating.

Still, on an objective level, he could sympathize with Roosevelt's
problem. There he was, number-two man in the Department, ordering around captains and admirals almost twice his age, and needing
very much to have himself taken seriously. So he dressed the part.
Maltbie wished that he were in a position to do something similar.
To have gunners' mates and turret captains treat him like an ensign
when he was a lieutenant commander with twelve years' commissioned service was absolutely maddening—and not Roosevelt's fault.
On reflection Maltbie decided that he did not really dislike the man
after all; and that was just as well, for they needed his help.

Tall and majestic, even sitting down, Captain William S. Sims of
the Atlantic Torpedo Flotilla was arguing their cause. "It's quite

simple, Mr. Secretary," he said. "We are frittering away the opportunity of the century."

"The century's only fourteen years old, Bill. I'd call it the opportunity of the decade."

"Then you agree with me?"

"I agree with you in principle. But what you're proposing is scandalously 'unneutral,' as you perfectly well know."

"That's why I came to you, sir, instead of Secretary Daniels."

"You fire-breathers seem to be doing a lot of that lately," said Roosevelt. "What do you think, Commander Maltbie? Is it fitting for Captain Sims here to be going under Mr. Daniels's head?"

Maltbie could have done without the condescension. "I wouldn't like to say, sir. I'm a party at interest."

"Oh? So you'd really like to sail the sea with the king's nay-vee?"

Maltbie decided he did really dislike the man after all. "Yes, sir. I would."

"Why?" Suddenly there was nothing jocular in Roosevelt's tone. Caught off balance, Maltbie looked to Sims for guidance, received only a nod of encouragement in return. He could feel the Assistant Secretary's eyes assessing him; the man might be a posturer, but he was no dolt.

"Well," said Maltbie, collecting himself, "from a purely personal standpoint I'd like to join Jellicoe for the excitement: the biggest navy in the world battling it out with the second biggest. From a professional standpoint there are dozens of considerations. First of all, gunnery. All the improvements Captain Sims and Admiral Fiske have made in our fleet would have taken years longer to conceive and apply without the work of Percy Scott, and Scott is now overseeing all director-firing for the British. We could learn a great deal in that area. Then there's damage control. None of our first-line ships has ever been tested in battle. The British, on the other hand, already have Coronel and Heligoland under their belts, and it looks likely that they'll soon be detaching a couple of battle cruisers to go after von Spee. There's just no way of knowing how your armor protection will hold up until you subject it to real shells. We can draw a lot of valuable inferences from British experience. Third, there's tactics. You remember how everybody pored over the reports about Tsushima and the other Russo-Japanese engagements. Well, we're as far from those mixed armament ships of '05 as Admiral Togo's cruisers were from three-masted frigates. Nobody knows what will happen when dreadnought types finally fight each other. If an American is there to see for himself, though, his reports might be worth two or three ships to us if we ever go to war. Finally, there's communications and engineering. Here again, a state of war necessitates all sorts of improvements which you just can't expect from peacetime, no matter how carefully you simulate actual battle conditions in your maneuvers. You need a war footing to show you what's really important and what's inessential. Radio range and interference, signaling, searchlights, engine endurance, speed under helm—everything from the bridge to the boiler room is tested in battle up to the limits of its capacity; and any navy that can discover those limits without risking its own ships in the process would have to be pretty damn fogbound not to take advantage of the opportunity."

Roosevelt laughed and slammed his hand down on the desk top. "By God, Commander Maltbie, you should have been an evangelist. You were right about this man, Bill. He knows his stuff."

Maltbie could feel his neck reddening. One more benediction from the throne and he was going to start getting rude.

Roosevelt picked up his telephone. "Essie, get me N Street, please." He held his hand over the mouthpiece and beamed at the two officers. "Gentlemen, it's providential you came to see me today as it just so happens we're having the British ambassador and Lady . . . Hello, Millicent? Let me speak to Mrs. Roosevelt, please. Thanks . . . We're having Ambassador Spring Rice to dinner tonight along with a couple of . . . Hello, Babs? Yes, I'm just about to leave. Listen, dear, Bill Sims is here with one of his staff officers and they're both tired of hardtack and salt beef. Can we do anything for them? Oh, splendid! You're a pearl of great price. We'll be there in half an hour or so. Yes, dear. Yes, I will. Bye."

Now Maltbie was really fuming. No invitation, no request; just this insufferable arrogance in taking it for granted that he and Sims would accommodate themselves to milord's wishes. Damn! Sims had stood up to Presidents in his time; why didn't he pin back this pipsqueak's ears?

Roosevelt put the receiver back on the hook, radiating satisfaction. "Let's walk, shall we? It looks like a beautiful evening."

"Fine." Sims nodded.

"I'll just have a word with my staff people and then we can leave. Be back in a minute."

After Roosevelt had left the office Sims turned to Maltbie with a frown. "Harry, sometimes I despair of you."

"Sir?"

"It doesn't matter a good goddamn to me whether you like Roosevelt, and it shouldn't matter a good goddamn to you either. This is business, Harry. We didn't come here to be pals with that man. We came here to get you posted to Jellicoe. Now we get a chance to discuss the whole project off the record with the British ambassador and you sit there as if you were being kept after school. I don't know what's eating you, son, but whatever it is I suggest you get your sights lined up on the right bearing, and pronto! Roosevelt is really sold on this idea, and I've gone to a lot of trouble to sell him on you too. Now don't you go fouling the lines for me. Just pack up all your little likes and dislikes and stow 'em for the evening, understand? Just behave yourself."

Maltbie burned with embarrassment, but finally was able to choke out, "Sorry, chief."

Sims smiled and shook his head. "Oh, for Lord's sake, Harry; now you look like you got caught robbing the poor box. Honestly! I wish just once I could chew you out properly without you ending up mortally wounded."

Maltbie kept his eyes on the floor, fought to retain his composure.

"Listen," said the older man, "just try to relax and enjoy yourself, will you. And try *not* to display every single one of your censorious judgments on that rubber-putty face of yours." He patted Maltbie on the arm. "After all, Harry, if things work out the way they ought to, you'll have to cultivate a little British reserve willy-nilly."

Leaving the Army and Navy Building the three men strolled through Lafayette and Farragut Squares and then up Connecticut Avenue to Eighteenth and N; 1733 N Street was a good-sized red-brick residence set a short distance back from the roadway. "My wife's uncle lived here while waiting for Mrs. McKinley to move out of the White House," Roosevelt declared.

"Your wife's uncle also began his career as Assistant Secretary of the Navy, if I remember right," Sims responded. Roosevelt shot him a slightly mistrustful look, but it was clear nevertheless that he was pleased. Sims's face gave nothing away, and it was only after Roosevelt stepped forward to open the door that the captain dispatched a furtive wink in Maltbie's direction, though he also had the good grace to look a little sheepish.

Inside, the two officers were introduced to Mrs. Roosevelt, who seemed kindly and a bit rattled, and to the Roosevelt children, none of whose names Maltbie remembered. The Assistant Secretary then proudly led them into the nursery for a glimpse of twelve-week-old Franklin, Jr., whose resemblance to his father immediately earned him Maltbie's vote as the single most repulsive-looking baby in Christendom. From the nursery Roosevelt ushered them out into the garden. It was gloriously warm, a second Indian summer. Some dusty Japanese lanterns cast a mellowing glow on the scene. Maltbie sipped his sherry and sniffed the smell of burning leaves that drifted over from a neighboring yard. A feeling of well-being began to suffuse his body, and after resisting it briefly, as if to preserve his bad temper, he finally let it wash over him.

Shortly after seven o'clock the other guests arrived. Maltbie heard them being welcomed at the front door and smiled at the sound of female voices exchanging delighted exclamations about the weather. Accompanied by Roosevelt, Ambassador Spring Rice was the first to step into the garden. He had a spade beard like Sims's, but was much shorter than the captain. To Maltbie he did not look English at all—Swiss, perhaps, or even German, but not Anglo-Saxon. He had a kindly professorial air about him, very courtly, but Maltbie sensed that he did not miss a thing, that the benign old-world facade concealed abnormal sensitivity. Two women followed the ambassador, the older of whom Maltbie guessed to be Lady Spring Rice. After them came Mrs. Roosevelt with a serious-looking man of about forty and a young lady no older than twenty-five. Introductions proved the man to be William Corey, Assistant Secretary of State, and the woman at Lady Spring Rice's side to be his wife, Caroline. The young lady was the ambassador's niece, a Miss Melina Bellamy.

All Maltbie had noticed about Miss Bellamy when she first appeared in the doorway was her smallness and delicacy of frame. The aura of fragility he projected onto her, however, was dispelled when he met her face to face. As she offered her hand she lifted two tigery eyes to meet his, eyes so innocently feral that Maltbie felt almost alarmed. But then she smiled, and her smile was so spritely, so knowing, and yet ultimately so demure that alarm gave way to captivation. Maltbie, as a reasonably personable young bachelor, had been the target for some fairly heavy-caliber smiles in his time, but none had had the impact of this. Quite suddenly, a seat next to Miss Bellamy at dinner that evening was as important to him as an assignment to Jellicoe's *Iron Duke*.

The canons of diplomatic precedence favored him. With the ambassador and Sims destined for the hostess's end of the table, and with Lady Spring Rice and Miss Bellamy destined for the host's right and left, Maltbie found himself sitting opposite Secretary Corey with Mrs. Roosevelt's social secretary, Lucy Mercer, on one side of him and the sparkling loveliness of Melina on the other. He could not have asked for a better arrangement, but in a transport of schoolboy shyness he devoted his entire attention to Miss Mercer, risking only the briefest gun-shy glances in the direction of his other dinner partner. The attention he withheld Roosevelt supplied in abundance, and Maltbie did not know whether to be grateful to him or wring his neck. After the main course was served, however, the question ceased to matter.

Miss Mercer having turned to the ambassador on her left, Maltbie was concentrating with absurd intensity on his roast beef when a low, velvety voice flowed over to him: "You know, Commander, you really must say *something* to me this evening, if only for appearance' sake." He turned to see Miss Bellamy fingering her wineglass, her eyes fixed solemnly on the centerpiece before her. "Forgive me," he said, blushing furiously, "I've been trying to think of something sensible to say."

Miss Bellamy turned and smiled at him, and he found he had to drop his gaze. Looking into her eyes was rather like having one's nose six inches from a catherine wheel: the sensation was spectacular, but one looked away for fear of flying sparks. "Tell me, Commander, is Harry really your Christian name?"

"Well, yes. Or no, actually. It's Harris, my mother's maiden name. Why do you ask?"

"Do you know Oscar Wilde's *The Importance of Being Earnest?*" Maltbie nodded. "Well, I've always felt that way about Harrys. Harrys are so sweet and helpless somehow, like you. The moment I saw you in the garden I was absolutely certain you were a Harry."

"And yet you asked if that was really my name."

"Yes. Because I wanted to find out whether you really were a Harry who was actually *named* Harry. It seemed too good to be true."

"Ah, then. There are Harrys and Harrys, it seems."

"Oh, of course. There are misnamed Harrys: men with no more

claim to the title than I have. Then there are unnamed Harrys: terribly sweet gentlemen who go around calling themselves Morris or Reginald or some such ludicrous thing. Last, and all too rarely, there are true Harrys: the genuine articles."

"What about Harrys named Harris?"

"Oh well, you're *called* Harry, aren't you. That's what matters."

"I'm glad to hear it," he said. And to tell the truth, he really was.

"But who are you, really, Commander?" Melina asked.

"Beg pardon?"

"Who *are* you? Whence comest thou, and whither dost thou go?" Her eyebrows were raised playfully, but Maltbie had the impression that there was a good deal more behind her questions than mere conversational chaff.

"Well," he said, "I come from a small place called Westport, in Connecticut; and whither I go is sort of undecided at the moment."

"Tell me about Westport."

"Well, it's on Long Island Sound. The people do some fishing and some farming. There's a ferry service across the Sound to Port Jefferson. And in the summer we get a lot of mothers up from New York City with their children, to avoid the polio."

Melina nodded. "And your parents?"

"My father was in the navy. He died of dysentery in the Philippines, during the Spanish War."

"You are wonderfully honest, Commander. You could have just said that he died, and left me to think it was a hero's death in battle."

Maltbie thrashed around in embarrassment for some appropriate response to this, without success. Melina speedily rescued him. "Forgive me, Commander; I interrupted you."

"Oh no, not at all. Uh . . ."

"Your mother . . . ?"

"Oh, yes. My mother. My mother died several years ago."

"How sad. She must have been still quite young."

"She was forty-eight," Maltbie said, wishing now that Miss Bellamy had not invested him with that onerous Order of Honesty. "She suffered from an illness—well, alcoholism. We had to . . . she lived in an institution." As always, he was furious with himself for feeling ashamed.

He felt Melina's hand fall lightly on his, then a brief moment of pressure before she turned the conversation to herself.

He learned that she had come to the United States only the week before, and that her parents were Sir Lloyd and Dame Margaret Bellamy, the celebrated team that had followed up on Schliemann's discoveries in Turkey and the Argolid. Melina herself had been conceived during the later excavations of Troy and born in a tent beside the Mycenaean digs. She owed her high color and sun-streaked auburn hair to a life lived almost entirely out of doors at various sites along the Aegean littoral. Her name—which described her perfectly —was the feminine diminutive of the Greek word for "honey."

She had had the advantage of being educated by her mother and father, and had concentrated her studies in the field of physical anthropology. More recently she had become fascinated with pre-Columbian civilizations. When she and her parents were obliged to return to England by the outbreak of the First Balkan War, Sir Lloyd had accepted an ad interim chair at Cambridge, and for the next two years Melina had assisted in the preparation of the three books he and Dame Margaret had completed as they waited forlornly for an opportunity to return to Greece. When it became clear that the conflict among the Great Powers would foreclose any fieldwork in the Mediterranean for a very long time to come, Melina had made the logical decision to pursue her pre-Columbian researches in the United States. After a few weeks of immersion in the materials at the Library of Congress and the Smithsonian Institution, she intended to set out for the Southwest; there, finally, to examine cliffdweller ruins and existing Indian settlements at first hand.

"By yourself?" Maltbie interjected with concern.

"Of course," she answered. "Your indigenous populations have been 'pacified,' have they not?"

"Well, yes. But that territory is still no place for an unescorted young lady."

"Oh, that's all right, Commander. I'm not much of a lady, I'm of age, and I'm seldom unescorted for long."

Maltbie did not find this reassuring. "But really, Miss Bellamy, there are some very rough people out there, very uncivilized."

He saw her bristle at the use of the word. "I'm aware of that, Commander. It's precisely because they're 'uncivilized' that I'm eager to share their society. All the civilized peoples I know of are engaged in the practice of slaughtering one another."

"Not quite all," he said in a conciliatory tone.

"Oh, you'll be involved soon enough," she answered with bitterness. "One can see how dead keen all of you are to be fighting, despite what President Wilson and Secretary Bryan say."

"But if we do become involved we'll surely enter in on England's side. So it will be all to the good."

Melina fixed him with an unforgettable look, at once outraged and solicitous. "Harry, this is an insufferably stupid war that we're fighting in Europe, a *totentanz*. It's poisoning our souls, and it will not be to anyone's good for you to join in the folly."

Taken together with her use of his given name, Melina's expression hit Maltbie like a fist, and he hardly noticed when Mrs. Roosevelt suggested that "the ladies retire." Melina's motion in rising from the table brought him out of his muddlement, however, and he shot to his feet to assist her with her chair. Had he needed further proof of the impact she had had on him, it was readily deducible from the strange bereft feeling he experienced as he watched her small figure depart from the room.

It required a real effort of will for him to shift his thoughts to the laconic masculine conversation that was soon in progress. The talk was of the war and of the latest news from London and the fronts. Sims asked Spring Rice if he had any details on the destruction of Admiral Cradock's squadron by Count von Spee off the coast of Chile.

"I'm afraid it was a question of indiscretion being the worst part of valor," said the ambassador. "Although we don't have all the facts yet, it appears the admiral was outgunned, outranged, and silhouetted against the sun. Nevertheless he attacked."

"It sounds like he feared to be thought afraid," Corey submitted.

"That would not be out of keeping with what I know of the Admiral's character."

"Kit Cradock feared nothing," Sims broke in with heat. "If he attacked it was because he was a born attacker and believed he could win."

Roosevelt laughed. "I should have warned you, Springy—Captain Sims here is one of our most ferocious anglophiles, and not quite rational when it comes to the Royal Navy."

Spring Rice appraised Sims with a genial smile. "Well, I never mind meeting ferocious anglophiles. We need all we can find nowadays."

"You must have been abroad when Bill stirred up that wasp's nest a few years ago," Roosevelt continued.

"Which wasp's nest was that?"

"Oh, a speech Bill made at the Guildhall while the Atlantic Fleet was paying you folks a visit. I guess it raised a much bigger ruckus here than it did in England. What was it you said, Bill? Something about us fighting to the last man and the last ship if England ever found herself at war with Germany."

"Something like that," said Sims complacently.

"Taft had a fit," Roosevelt added, obviously relishing the recollection.

"I don't repent of a word," Sims declared. "Sooner or later we'll be coming in on England's side. The only problem is that with Josephus Daniels and William Jennings Bryan running things at Navy and State we've got two teetotaling pacifist namby-pambies to contend with, and they just—"

Roosevelt threw up his hands in mock horror. "Captain, please! Decency forbids!"

"Well, I'm sorry to compromise you, Mr. Secretary—and you too, Mr. Corey—but facts are facts."

"Only some facts are facts, Captain," said Corey. "Others are propaganda."

"I don't follow you, sir."

"Franklin told me what you and Commander Maltbie have in mind, and it could be that you think Bryan and Daniels are namby-pambies only because you suspect they'll be against it."

"Now *I* don't follow you, Billy," said Spring Rice. "And I rather suspect that I'm intended to."

Roosevelt, Corey, and Sims eyed one another for a moment and then burst into laughter. "Damnit, Springy," Roosevelt yawped, "why can't you just jolly along with us once in a while? We go to so much trouble to broach things to you tactfully, you ought to show us a little consideration."

"You're both incorrigible scoundrels, and you merit no mercy," said the ambassador affectionately. "I reserve judgment on you, Captain, though you've clearly fallen into bad company. Now, what's this scheme you're all so busily priming me for?"

Roosevelt nodded in Sims's direction. "Go ahead, Bill. It's your baby."

Sims returned the nod. "Very well, Mr. Secretary." He turned to Spring Rice and cleared his throat. "Mr. Ambassador, I apologize for the way we beat around the bush, but this is such a damn touchy issue I just didn't know how to raise it. What I want to propose—get your opinion on, more precisely—is a plan for attaching an American observer to the British Fleet. Now I've known John Jellicoe for fifteen years—met him on the China Station—and I think I've got the right to call him friend. If I were to send him a letter suggesting that Commander Maltbie be attached to the fleet, I'm almost certain he would have no objection. He's already got a Russian and a Japanese up at Scapa, and old Pakenham sailed with Togo in '05, so there's good precedent for a neutral observer too. What concerns me, though, is that Jellicoe would have to clear the idea with the Admiralty, and with all his enormous responsibilities I don't want to load that extra work on him. Even if Fisher and Churchill accepted the proposal, they'd want to square it with the Foreign Office; the Foreign Office would want to make conditions; Jellicoe would have to explain why the conditions were unacceptable; the Admiralty would appeal to the Prime Minister; then *he* would probably want to make conditions; and a whole blizzard of extra paperwork would descend on poor Jellicoe's head."

"I must say, Captain, you haven't a very high opinion of our administrative hierarchy."

"I rate it roughly half again as efficient as our own, Mr. Ambassador," Sims replied.

"Order! Order!" said Roosevelt from the head of the table.

"My apologies, Mr. Secretary," said Sims. "I don't mean to be denigrating anyone's efficiency, but we all know how the bureaucracy functions. What I'm saying essentially is that unless one can prepare the way for this proposal—from above, so to speak—then the whole war will be over before a decision can be made about it, and Admiral Jellicoe will have been needlessly vexed."

"I take your point, Captain. But why are you so certain that Sir John would welcome an American to the fleet?"

"Simple common sense, sir. We've got the third largest navy in the world, and sooner or later we're going to be fighting that navy alongside your own. How quickly and effectively we coordinate our operations with yours when we do come in will depend to a large extent on how much advance liaison work we've had a chance to do. The best, and perhaps the only, way to get that liaison work started is to have an observer with your fleet."

Spring Rice mused silently for a few moments. "You take a very sanguine view of the trend in Anglo-American relations, Captain, and I don't doubt the sincerity of your assessment. As you yourself have pointed out, however, your Secretary of the Navy, your Secretary of State, and, to all appearances, your President have somewhat different notions. Do you really think it likely that they would assent to the plan you have in mind?"

"They wouldn't assent to it," Corey interjected, "but the President at least might not object to it."

"That was a very cryptic comment, Billy," said the ambassador.

Corey gave him a wintry smile. "I mean he might not oppose the plan, provided he wasn't obliged to approve it."

"You ask Billy Corey to clarify"—Roosevelt laughed—"and what you get is a second helping of murk."

Corey skeptically cocked an eyebrow. "Very well, gentlemen. In words of one syllable—if the whole thing could be done unofficially, and the President kept out of it, he might be glad to have it done."

"You mean if the whole thing could be done secretly," Sims suggested.

"No. It would have to be done secretly in any case. We couldn't let the Germans find out about it. By *unofficially* I mean in such a way that the President could disavow it, if he felt he had to."

"Hmmmm," said Spring Rice. "I'm not sure I should be listening to all this."

"Oh, come on, Springy," Roosevelt chided. "You're hardly well cast as the ingenue."

The ambassador smiled tolerantly. "No, perhaps not. But I'm in touch with Mr. Bryan almost daily, and unless I'm mistaken you're hatching a plot to circumvent him."

"A plot that won't succeed without your cooperation," said Corey.

Spring Rice was quiet for a long time. "All right," he said at last, "my advice is to explore the possibilities here before you write to Jellicoe. Then, if things look feasible, we might talk again, and I'll see what I can do about clearing a path for you in London."

There was a sudden air of relaxation around the table. Maltbie was surprised at the amount of tension that had accumulated so imperceptibly. The conversation became general, and soon—though not soon enough to Maltbie's way of thinking—Roosevelt suggested that they join the ladies.

Melina flashed him a smile as he entered the drawing room, but quickly looked down, as if something had upset her. He wanted to go to her immediately, but felt he had to observe the forms first. He chatted briefly with Lady Spring Rice and complimented Mrs. Roosevelt on a delicious dinner. Then, as soon as he decently could, he made his way over to where Melina was sitting. "Is something wrong?" he asked her.

"Is it true, Commander, as Mrs. Roosevelt tells me, that you return to Hampton Roads tomorrow morning?" Her remarkable eyes had all but lost their feline contours, and now looked wide and hurt.

"It's true. But Hampton Roads is only a few hours away from Washington, and I could return here within a week or so if you'd like to see me again."

The tiger eyes gleamed once more, sardonically. Maltbie took in Melina's smile and cursed himself for an imbecile. "I'm sorry. I meant if you would be willing to see me again, I would make every effort to get back here." The smile broadened. "Miss Bellamy, what I'm trying to say is, would you mind if, in the next week or so, I was able to get a few days' leave and come to Washington?" He ran that sentence over in his head and saw that it too left a great deal to be desired. "Forgive me, Miss Bellamy, what I mean is, may I write to you during the next few days?"

Melina laughed aloud, all elfin mischief. "Oh, Harry, with your gift for words, you may not *not* write to me." Still laughing, she stood up, leaned forward on her toes, and gave him a quick feathery kiss on the cheek. "You are the most delicious young lieutenant commander that I have ever set eyes on," she whispered, her closeness serving as a test of his equilibrium.

He spent what remained of the evening in a pleasurable daze. Around eleven o'clock Sims signaled him that it was time to go, and Melina bid him a lingering good night as they walked together to the door. Sims paused for a few minutes of intense conversation with Corey and then joined Maltbie in taking leave of their host and hostess.

The cab ride back to the Shoreham Hotel passed in total silence, with Sims shooting his junior an occasional questioning glance. Finally, through the haze of his euphoria, Maltbie began to wonder whether he had again caused the captain to be displeased with him, and he was genuinely concerned about it by the time they stopped to say good night in the lobby.

"You know, Harry," said Sims, "those were some pretty valuable discussions we had this evening."

Apprehensively Maltbie nodded agreement.

"Yes, Commander," Sims added, turning away almost too quickly for Maltbie to see his smile, "I only wish you could have been there."

1914, 26TH NOVEMBER—NEW YORK CITY

Colonel Edward Mandell House lay in his bed and listened to the weary clip-clops that marked the progress of the Fleischl's dairy wagon along Fifty-third Street. He had been awake for several minutes now, waiting for those measured hoofbeats that announced five o'clock each morning no less reliably than the chimes of St. Thomas Episcopal two blocks west. Sure enough, just as the clip-clops slowed to a halt in front of number 116 across the street, they were replaced by the faint sweet sound of a carillon, which jingled happily for several seconds and then gave way to the soft dullness of a single bell. The bell tolled five with a cadence so slow as to suggest misgivings about the earliness of the hour. In the face of so much darkness, it seemed strange that the day should now begin. But for the Colonel, at least, it was most certainly time to be stirring. In less than sixty minutes he would have the President at his door.

The Colonel rose and shuffled into the bathroom to relieve the pressure in his bladder. These impulsive visits of Wilson's were a strain: they placed everything too much in the realm of improvisation, left too much to chance. Having pulled the flush chain, House walked back to his bedside table with uncharacteristic haste. His bone-handled Galveston Colt was still there in the drawer along with the steel box containing forty-eight .45-caliber bullets.

The Colonel felt nauseated; the thought of something happening to the President always had that effect on him. He sat down on the edge of the bed for a moment to calm the fluttering in his stomach as an eruption of noise from the pantry downstairs announced that Mrs. Freitag was breaking out her pots and pans for breakfast. This daily commotion never lasted long, and the Colonel's home soon returned to that silence of prudence and moderation that he liked to think of as emblematic of his personal approach to life.

The Colonel's reticence was by now almost proverbial in the loud and blustering world of politics. In fact, he took nearly as much pride in his ability to perform his functions unstared-at by the public eye as he did in the nature of the functions themselves. Such pride was not misplaced, a truth that he sometimes came close to regretting. For with so much to be proud of, he stood in peril of pride itself, and he prayed each day for deliverance from its allure.

Or say, rather, he stood vigilant against it, being too prudent, and skeptical, to entrust his moral integrity to a divinity who might not exist and who, if extant, might have other things to do than answer prayers. Yes, keeping one's soul taut and well trimmed was too important a task to be left to God, especially when, to one who wore the mantle of "the President's adviser," each hour brought with it new and potent incitements to self-satisfaction. It was heady stuff, after all, to belong to Woodrow Wilson's inner circle and to share in the secrets of state. It was titillating to have the *Times* refer to one as "the President's silent partner," or to be called "the Texas Talleyrand" by the *World*. And it was downright intoxicating, on a certain level, to have one's innate reserve and long-renowned discretion turn one into a "man of mystery" in the nation's press. It was downright intoxicating, that is, if one drank it all in neat. But one did not. One was careful.

Of course, in the three years he had known Wilson it had long since become plain to House that the President himself was by no means free of pride. In fact, with his undisguised intolerance of human coarseness, his almost feminine sensitiveness to minor affronts, and his ofttimes suspicious thou-shalt-have-no-other-loyalties-before-me attitude, it could be said that the progress of the disease in Wilson's case was well advanced.

But then, Wilson was the President. And while his pride bore watching, it also gave him needed strength. House, therefore, though uncomfortable about condoning in one man an iniquity he condemned in every other, shrugged off his misgivings on the basis that the one man in this case was benevolently inspired.

Edward Mandell House had been as successful a backroom politician as it was possible to be without eventually coming to the fore. He had, moreover, all the earmarks of a gentleman. The only child of an upright Galveston shipowner, he had been raised in the roughneck East Texas of Fort Hood and Brazoria Counties and then been sent still farther east to Hopkins Grammar School and Cornell.

Since attaining manhood, he had traveled widely and regularly in Europe. He knew which fork to use for his salad, and never said "ain't" except for effect. He was at home at Sherry's, Delmonico's, the Ritz, and the Savoy. His wife, Loulie Hunter of Hunter, Texas, spoke softly, and seldom unless spoken to. His income of $25,000 a year from investments was large enough to be respectable but not so large—for a Democrat—as to cause offense. His stature was small, his features mousey, and his politics progressive. He had done well in the world, and now, with his house in order and his laurels still to be won, he wanted very badly to do good.

Guided by his credo of integrity, House as a young man in Houston had made his fortune by the decidedly quixotic method of building and running a Texas railroad without first bribing the legislators in Austin to float him bonds or buying off the sheriffs along the right-of-way to avoid harassment. Financed by the Old Colony Trust Company of Boston, Massachusetts—whose chairman was a friend from Hopkins Grammar—House brought the Trinity and Brazos Valley Railway into existence without a penny of public financing. He then proceeded to operate it so efficiently and honestly that juries in the towns it serviced actually found in its favor when the inevitable spurious tort suits were brought against it. After three years the railroad was so profitable an operation that House felt the challenge was gone. There was no lack of bidders, and when the line was purchased by the Sabine-East Texas Railroad Company he found himself a comfortably wealthy man.

He moved with Loulie to Austin, took up the burdens of a gentleman cotton farmer, and began to rub shoulders with the state capital's politicians on a daily, and nightly, basis. Soon, he was caught up in the 1892 reelection struggles of progressive Governor James S. Hogg. Despite House's comparative youth—he was thirty-three—his sharp political instincts together with his stoical acceptance of human nature and his not inconsiderable intelligence quickly made him the key figure orchestrating the incumbent's statewide campaign. Having a genuine disdain for celebrity, he was careful to avoid any official designation as Hogg's reelection chairman—but the governor saw to it that the man who had been so designated always secured House's advice before making any major decisions.

Hogg won in a walk, as did Charles Culberson in 1894 and '96, Joseph Sayers in 1898 and 1900, and William Lanham in 1902 and '04. In all these elections the one constant, pulling the strings from behind the scenes, was E. M. House, or rather, "Colonel" House, in conformance with the dubiously honorific title bestowed by Hogg as a token of his gubernatorial gratitude.

As House's importance in Texas politics increased, his circle of acquaintance in national Democratic politics widened. He became friends with Bryan and traveled widely on party matters, north and east. The first several years of the century were lean ones for Democrats, and on his travels the Colonel saw few signs of coming prosperity. In 1910, however, Theodore Roosevelt's increasingly public disenchantment with his chosen successor, Taft, spelled trouble in the Republican ranks, and 1912 loomed as the Democrats' first great national opportunity in twenty years.

As the man who would influence the votes of the large Texas delegation as much or more than even the incumbent governor, House felt a special responsibility to guide the delegates toward the optimum ultimate choice. He had come to the conclusion that, on paper at least, Governor Woodrow Wilson of New Jersey would be both the best candidate for the party and the best President for the nation. Bryan, among the alternatives, was a three-time loser and out of touch with the urban constituencies. House Speaker Champ Clark was a large amiable mouth without a bridle. Governor Harmon of Ohio was stolid at his most spritely and too malleable in the hands of the bosses. Congressman Oscar Underwood of Alabama was from Alabama.

Woodrow Wilson, by contrast, had a good brain, a northern coloration—though born and reared in the South—a fine combat record against New Jersey's Big Boss Smith, solid progressive credentials, and a certain something extra: a sort of evangelical rectitude that House sensed would quietly thrill the ladies (who influenced votes even though they couldn't cast them) and rather abash the men, who might vote for Wilson just to prove to themselves that they were still capable of high-minded deeds.

For several months House silently studied his candidate, both from a distance, in Austin, and from up close, as a part-time New York City resident. Wilson did not wither under scrutiny; in fact he took on added luster. So House began to round up support for him among the Texas rank and file.

Wilson and House shook hands for the first time in New York's Gotham Hotel on November 24, 1911, one day after Thanksgiving and seven months before the Democratic Convention was to be gaveled to order in the Fifth Regiment Armory, Baltimore, Maryland. House had liked Wilson almost immediately, which was a surprise as he had expected only to admire him. Though there couldn't have been any doubt in Wilson's mind that the Colonel was there to "look him over," he was as blithe and at ease as if their appointment had been for a friendly game of cards. Nor, House perceived, was this a pose; it was genuinely Wilson's way. The man not only had nothing to hide about himself, he also had a great deal he was glad to have known. His demeanor said: "Worldly ambition is all vanity, and my conscience is clear. Take me as I am or not at all, but in either case let us get on with our work."

House was captivated, so much so that he mistrusted his judgment and sought to play down in his own mind the impact that Wilson had had. He dwelt on the governor's unexpected gift of levity, brusquely ascribing it to a certain want of stature. "He is not the biggest man I have ever met," he wrote his brother-in-law dismissively. Then the demands of simple honesty compelled him to add: "but he is one of the pleasantest."

They met again on several occasions, and House's conversion was completed. Over and above his "pleasantness," Wilson had a truly elegant mind, sinewy and graceful in its workings. He also had a wide-eyed ingenuousness in the realm of practical politics that was both engaging to behold and hard to account for in one who had written the classic treatise on *Congressional Government*. House was highly flattered when he saw that Wilson regarded him as a professional politician who was also an honorable man—and not the least of the glory lay in the fact that up until their meeting the governor seemed to have doubted the existence of such a hybrid. House was flattered, too, at how readily Wilson took his advice on political matters—unquestioningly, with total trust. Of course he quickly perceived that on questions of policy and principle the governor welcomed prompting from no one, but he and Wilson were usually so much in accord on these questions that any prompting was superfluous.

They quickly found that they liked each other enormously.

Together with the governor's friend of thirty years' standing, the editor-publisher Walter Hines Page, House began to prepare the ground for a Wilson nomination. He judged that with so many men in the field it would be Bryan, the party leader, whose influence would ultimately tell. The Great Commoner stood ready to accept a draft, but otherwise did not actively seek—or really expect—a fourth chance at the White House. His foremost concern was that the party's nominee should be progressive, but as between Wilson and Champ Clark he declared himself neutral. House, therefore, quietly went about the business of persuading Bryan that Wilson at his most abandoned had cleaner hands and a purer heart than Clark at his most redeemed.

House's strategy was vindicated in Baltimore on June 28 when, on the tenth ballot of the convention, Tammany Boss Murphy switched New York's ninety votes from Harmon to Clark with the expectation that the swing would precipitate a landslide. His calculations were very narrowly in error, and that proved fatal for his man. Primed by House, Bryan now saw Clark as in league with the devils of Tammany Hall, and on June 29 he rocked the convention by breaking with the Nebraska delegation, which was pledged to Clark, and casting his individual vote for Wilson. Three days and thirty-six ballots later Wilson was acclaimed the nominee. Thirty-three days and one ballot after that, Theodore Roosevelt split Republican progressives off from Taft and the party machine by accepting the Bull Moose nomination. In doing so he gave Woodrow Wilson the election.

In the division of the spoils that followed this, the first Democratic victory in twenty years, Bryan was given the Department of State and Page the ambassadorship to Great Britain. House was offered any cabinet post he desired, but he declined all office, knowing that a portfolio would only interfere with his and the President's rapport. With Wilson's responsibilities now colossally magnified, he relied on the Colonel more and more to handle the political side of state matters, and he continued to consult him on policy as well. House kept New York as his base, both because it was there that he could do the President the most good and because his presence in Washington would render him far too conspicuous for his or Wilson's comfort.

In both his own and the President's mind, the Colonel's function was seen to be that of a "facilitator," to use Wilson's word. The need for such a functionary arose from the fact that the new President was not simply uninterested in the grosser political aspects of his duties, but regarded them with outright antipathy. He would speak to The People readily enough, and with some difficulty he could be persuaded to grant the odd congressman or senator an occasional audience. But when it came to pork barrels, horse trading, spoils systems, and patronage—in short, when it came to politicians —Wilson usually turned up his nose. He was aware, of course, of the importance of these vulgar matters in the overall scheme of things, and he was far too conscientious to disregard them. But since he had been blessed with so trustworthy and competent a political adviser as Edward House, it seemed only natural for him to deliver the less vital and edifying burdens into the Colonel's capable hands. House would bear those burdens far better than he ever could, and in doing so would leave him free to devote his energies to those great matters of policy and state that had led him to aspire to his office.

There was more to House's duties than mere political drudgery, however. Wilson valued the Colonel's opinion generally, and sought his counsel on matters of every description. Indeed, his confidence in House's judgment was so consistently justified by subsequent events that he began to regard the Colonel's advice on most issues of importance as indispensable, and began to invest him with more and more discretionary power.

The climax had come this past May, when the President had sent House across the Atlantic as his personal emissary. The purpose of House's trip to Europe was to probe the causes of the tensions mounting there and to see if there were any steps the United States might take toward reducing them. In Berlin he spent an evening listening to the Minister of the Marine, Grand Admiral von Tirpitz, dilate on the theme of *Perfide Albion*. He spent an afternoon at Tegel Airfield watching a transplanted Dutchman named Fokker perform thrilling aerial acrobatics in a new plane of his own design. Finally, thanks to a bit of diplomatic legerdemain on the part of Ambassador Gerard, he spent half an hour in private conversation with the Kaiser after the annual Whitmonday *Shcrippenfest* for the Household Battalion at Potsdam. The Colonel found Wilhelm mannerly, though a trifle overintense, and with breath that smelled of peppermint. The emperor went out of his way to disclaim any animosity toward England, even despite the systematic British failure to understand Germany's point of view. "The bayonets of Europe are pointed at us," he said. "We are menaced on every side." House suggested that England felt menaced herself by the ever expanding navy of a land power such as Germany, and he cited his conversation with von Tirpitz of two nights before. At the mention of the admiral's name the Kaiser's nostrils curled up as if he had been proffered offal. "The Marine Minister is entitled to his point of view. But speaking for Germany, I say that we desire nothing more from England than the recognition due us as a coequal world power seeking its rightful place in the sun. It grieves me that England should ally herself against us with Slavs and Latins when the only hope of advancing Christian civilization lies with our two empires and the United States." House conceded that friendship among the three nations was certainly a very desirable thing and said that he had come to Europe for the express purpose of promoting it. Wilhelm declared himself profoundly encouraged by such an initiative and concluded the interview by asking to be kept informed of House's forthcoming talks in London.

En route to Paris the next day the Colonel wondered whether anything at all had been accomplished by his visit to Berlin. On reflection he decided that the German outlook, while not pacific, was at least not bellicose either. That was a conclusion he could live with.

Paris, however, was a waste of time, a judgment that House interpreted as proof that he had become very dedicated or very old since his last visit there. Some months before his arrival, it seemed, the wife of Joseph Caillaux, a former premier and the incumbent leader of the Radical-Socialists, had walked into the office of the editor of *Le Figaro* and pumped six bullets into that busy journalist's stomach. Her grievance against *Le Figaro* had been its publication of some passionate love letters M. Caillaux had written her when both he and she had been married to third parties. *Le Figaro*'s grievance against M. Caillaux had been that he was pro-income tax and not anti-German. Mme. Caillaux, by killing the editor, had not only resolved one of the grievances outstanding but had also bestowed upon Paris one of its very best long-running scandals in years. Because her trial was about to begin the government was in crisis, and its leaders were far too preoccupied to discuss questions of war and peace with some itinerant crony of the American President. House waited for a week in virtual solitude and then resignedly went on his way to England.

London was having its most glorious Season in recent memory. The sun shone all day every day and, as the summer solstice was approaching, far into the evening as well. Chaliapin was singing *Prince Igor* at Covent Garden and Nijinsky and Karsavina were dancing there to the music of *Le Sacre du Printemps*. At the Palace Basil Hallam was starring in the hit musical review *The Passing Show of 1914*, and at His Majesty's Theatre Mrs. Patrick Campbell and Mr. Herbert Beerbohm Tree were squaring off in Shaw's *Pygmalion*. Theodore Roosevelt was in town, and House and Page had lunch with him at 6 Grosvenor Square (the home Page had rented at his own expense in the absence of any official United States residence, mission, or embassy, Congress regarding such establishments as decadent old world extravagancies). The Colonel met Henry James at dinner, John Singer Sargent at tea, and, a week after his arrival, Sir Edward Grey at lunch.

The Foreign Secretary impressed House immediately as a man with a formidable mind and a humane temperament. Grey listened with interest to the Colonel's account of his visit to Berlin and concurred generally in the conclusions House had drawn from it. He smiled ever so slightly, however, when the Colonel put forth the doctrine that nations should observe the same standards of conduct in their relations as individuals did in theirs. "Does that strike you as naive?" House asked him. "It strikes me as American," Grey replied in a friendly tone, "and therefore a little overwhelming in its sweep." "Naive, in other words," the Colonel persisted. "We deem ourselves very sophisticated on this side of the Atlantic," Grey said in an unhappy voice. "Given the difficulties that sophistication is now causing us, I believe an infusion of naiveté may be what we need."

House met Grey several more times and also dined with other members of the cabinet, such as the Chancellor of the Exchequer, Lloyd George, and the Prime Minister, Asquith. On the evening of June 28, strolling along the Mall in the evening cool, he saw the headlines announcing the assassination in Sarajevo.

The Colonel arrived back in America on July 28, the same day that Austria declared war on Serbia and started the dominoes falling. From his summer home on Boston's north shore he telephoned Wilson and received news much graver—in the strange universe of human perspective—than anything emanating from Europe: the President's wife was seriously ill with Bright's disease and tuberculosis of the kidney. Wilson said there was hope for recovery, but it was clear from his tone that it was a hope in conflict with conviction.

On the first of August, because the Czar had mobilized in support of Serbia, Germany declared war on Russia. On the third, Russia's ally France exchanged declarations with the Reich. On the fourth, in response to the German invasion of Belgium, England too plunged into the pit. On the sixth, Ellen Axson Wilson, greatly beloved, gentle of heart, passed away in her sleep.

With House's support and that of Navy Lieutenant Grayson, the White House physician, the President carried on. He sent an offer of mediation to the monarchs of the embattled states and exhorted Americans to be neutral "in thought and deed." Then, his day's work done, he would sit alone in the night hours and weep silently, stricken and inconsolable, until he gained a kind of sleep.

Ellen Wilson had been her husband's keel and rudder, an uncommonly sweet and self-effacing woman in whose love the President had sheltered for over thirty years. She had been a tree of life to him, he had clung to her, and she had died. House believed that Wilson might actually have gone mad with grief had not the events in Europe at the time of her death multiplied his work load to the point of near prostration. Even as it was, however, the President remained a desolate unquiet man, his own body uncongenial, his own company intolerable.

At Grayson's insistence Wilson left Washington at the end of August for his summer home in New Hampshire, where House joined him for several days. The President's restlessness did not diminish as autumn came on, however, and he began taking spur-of-the-moment trips to New York to visit the Colonel, often without notifying the Secret Service of his intentions. It was the imminence of such a visit that obliged House to be up and doing so early today.

At precisely five minutes to six the Colonel emerged from his room bathed, shaved, and neatly dressed in a dark gabardine suit. The smell of coffee and bacon floated into his nostrils as he descended the stairs. He felt calm and alert, ready to advise and console his great friend. On the table in the foyer lay the *Tribune*, the *Times*, and the *World*. The Colonel glanced at the lead stories: Carranza and Villa were still at daggers drawn in Mexico; Japan and England had agreed on a formula for dividing up Germany's Pacific possessions; the French and Germans were turning Joan of Arc's Lorraine into a cratered desert. House lifted his eyes from the cacophony of the headlines and listened. How wonderfully still his home was by comparison, the stillness of order and deliberation.

He went to the window. It was inky dark outside, the sidewalks deserted except for a scrawny stray dog sniffing warily at the base of a street lamp. The Colonel could see that the animal was shivering. Its ribs were prominent beneath a thin pelt, and there were livid welts on its hindquarters. It sniffed and sniffed round the lamp post but found nothing. In dejection it gave up the search and moved off down the street with a feeble lurching gait. "So much misery in the world," House sighed to himself. "So much pain."

Two sets of automobile headlamps turned left off Lexington Avenue and approached the Colonel's front door. He switched on the outside lights and stepped onto the sidewalk. The cars stopped and Wilson alighted from the rear seat of the first. "My dear friend. I cause you so much trouble."

"Come inside," said House, grasping the President's outstretched hand. "You must be tired after your journey."

"No, no. I enjoy sleeping on trains."

House took Wilson's coat and conducted him into the library, where the President hurried to the fireplace. He rubbed his hands together and then stood with his back to the flames. "Ah, that feels good," he said, persisting in a forced heartiness. "It's infernally damp and chill this morning, don't you think?"

"How are you?" asked the Colonel.

Wilson turned abruptly and faced the fire. It was some time before he replied, and when he did the forced heartiness was gone. "I hate my life, Edward. Each day since she died I hate it more. I work and work, like an automaton, and I try not to think about her. But at dinner last night it struck me that today would be Thanksgiving. A year ago we were all together, so happy. Now . . .

> "There was a time when meadow, grove, and stream,
> The earth, and every common sight,
> To me did seem
> Apparelled in celestial light,
> The glory and the freshness of a dream.
> It is not now as it hath been of yore;—
> Turn whereso'er I may
> By night and day
> The things which I have seen I now can see no more."

Wilson sighed heavily. "I miss my Ellen dreadfully Edward. I miss her so very very much."

"I know," said House. "You are bearing it with courage."

The two men ate breakfast in silence while outside the blackness modulated to a nacreous gray. They returned to the library for their coffee and sat looking out the French windows at the bleak November morning.

"Imagine what it must be like to face a day like this in the trenches now," said Wilson.

"I saw a poor starved cur limping along the sidewalk earlier—cold, terrified, hopeless. I imagine that's what it's like."

"Yes," said Wilson, staring down at the carpet. "Like that or worse."

"Page says it beggars the mind. He's spoken to officers of the BEF who've been at the front. Every soldier expects to be killed or maimed."

"It's too awful," said the President.

"Yes," said House. "Page's letter is in the safe, if you'd like to see it."

"Can you tell me what he says?"

"Nothing particularly new. Except—have you heard of Colonel Squier?"

"Squier? No. Not that I remember. Who is he?"

"Our military attaché in London."

"Ah."

"Yes. He attended your alma mater, Johns Hopkins, and he's something of an Edison, I understand. Has a real inventor's knack with radio and telegraphy. Page thinks very highly of him, and so, it seems, does His Majesty's Secretary of State for War."

"Kitchener?"

"Yes. Kitchener summoned Squier over to the War Office in great secrecy a couple of weeks ago and offered to let him visit the front."

"I thought they weren't letting anyone near the fighting."

"They aren't, officially. But they've made an exception for Squier. He's probably at their St. Omer headquarters already."

"Hmmmmm. What do you think they're up to?"

"Squier thinks they want to show us how to get organized, against the day . . ."

The President stiffened. "They're taking a great deal for granted, if that's what they have in mind."

"Yes, they are. But they're like that, some of them."

Wilson's jaw set. "I should hate to see us compromised."

House smiled at the President's severity. Though far from being an isolationist, Woodrow Wilson was so repelled by the notion of any sort of American involvement in the European war that he recoiled even from the discussion of tangential issues, such as America's military preparedness. Less than three weeks ago, in fact, when House as a matter of courtesy had passed along a request from Army Chief of Staff General Leonard Wood for permission to make a personal visit to the war zone, the President's dismissal of the idea had been so abrupt as to verge on rudeness.

House understood as well as anyone Wilson's reluctance to contemplate the unthinkable, and he didn't press the preparedness issue because, for the moment at least, serious danger seemed remote. The fact, however, was that the entire United States Army was probably less potent as a fighting unit than a single German brigade; and the United States Navy, while nominally the third strongest in the world, was also encrusted with obsolescence, backward in its organization, and dispersed over two oceans, the Caribbean, and the Gulf.

Knowing that Wilson would have to be brought along slowly, the Colonel had backed off and waited for a suitable opportunity for further discussion to arise. Page's letter about Squier had provided it, the more so because it arrived, coincidentally, on the same day as a report from Assistant Secretary Corey on an "off-the-record" observer proposal made by the Atlantic Flotilla's Captain Sims to the British ambassador.

"You know, of course," House said, "that we've had *six* officers sitting around in Berlin for the past three months waiting to have a look at the Germans in action. If Kitchener cooperates and Falkenhayn doesn't, I don't think that it's our responsibility."

"No, it isn't. Let's only hope that Kitchener recognizes that."

"Kitchener recognizes what it suits him to recognize, from all I've heard." The Colonel paused a moment before lowering the baited hook. "I think our official impartiality is pretty well established, however—at least as far as the land war is concerned."

Wilson bit. "What? Is there some question about it with respect to the sea war?"

"Not yet. But Assistant Secretary Corey tells me that Captain Sims—you know him?—canvassed Spring Rice about getting an American officer assigned to Jellicoe's fleet as an observer."

"What business is it of Sims's to canvass the British ambassador on such a matter?"

"None whatsoever. He appears to be cut from the same cloth as Kitchener."

"Hmph! And what was Spring Rice's reaction?"

"He seemed to think it could be done."

Wilson's brow furrowed, and House quickly weighed the advisability of pursuing the subject to the ultimate destination he had in mind. Well before he'd read Corey's report, he'd been aware of the many advantages that America would derive from placing observers with the belligerent forces. The difficulty with Sims's proposal, however, was that it ignored one of the principal belligerents. An American observer with the Royal Navy might look very sinister in Berlin in the absence of an American request to place an observer with the Kaiser's fleet as well. German suspicions would not be entirely allayed, moreover, even if such a request were made and turned down. The solution, therefore, seemed to lie in getting the Germans to say yes—and in this connection House had immediately thought of Oskar Gehlman's son.

The senior Gehlman, chairman of the Commercial Guaranty Trust Company, was German-born, and his two German brothers were highly respected pillars of the Central European financial community. Along with most of the other major *condottieri* of American banking, Gehlman had come into House's orbit during the struggle to get the Federal Reserve Act through Congress. He and the Colonel had conceived a liking for one another as they worked together to bring a national banking system into being, and on several occasions Gehlman had spoken to House with a sort of wistful pride about his son, Benjamin, who amazingly enough was a commander in the U.S. Navy. The Colonel initially had had to restrain himself from asking how the son of a Jewish-German financier came to be walking a quarterdeck, but he initiated discreet inquiries which revealed that the man had passed high from his class at Annapolis and was now considered one of the foremost gunnery experts in the service, second, perhaps, only to William Sims.

If there was anyone the Germans might find palatable as an observer—and the *if* was admittedly a big one—Benjamin Gehlman would certainly be the man.

Coming out of his reverie, the President said, "You don't suppose there's any connection between Sims and this Squier business, do you?"

The Colonel chuckled to himself. "That would involve imputing rather Byzantine motives to our English cousins, I think—and to our own armed forces as well. No, I believe these, uh, initiatives are both fairly innocent. Sims and Squier want to learn about modern warfare, and the British want to cultivate our goodwill. It doesn't seem all that nefarious."

"The Germans might disagree with you, if they found out about it."

That was the opening that House had been awaiting. "Well, as I said, they've had their chance to let us observe."

"On land," Wilson qualified, as if on cue.

"Yes!" said House, gratified. "So we'll ask them to allow us an observer with the High Seas Fleet too. Do you remember Oskar Gehlman?"

Wilson nodded.

"Well, he has a son in the navy who'd be the perfect candidate to propose. He's a senior officer, intelligent, and has influential relatives in the highest Berlin circles. What do you think? I rather doubt that there can be too much harm in trying."

Wilson let out a long breath as House waited expectantly for the verdict. "Very well, Edward," the President said at last. "But please keep a close watch on this business, will you. I don't want us getting entangled. And it would be terrible if we somehow lost a chance to mediate because we had too many soldiers and sailors scattered about among the combatants."

House reached over, smiling, and placed his hand on Wilson's arm. "It would be terrible if we lost such a chance for any reason," he said. "But so far as it's in my power, I can promise you that we won't."

1914, 1ST DECEMBER—LONDON

The First Sea Lord, Admiral of the Fleet Lord Fisher of Kilverstone —or "Jacky" as he was called by the men of the lower deck—rose every morning at four and walked from his home at Queen Anne's Gate to Westminster Abbey for half an hour's prayer. By five thirty he was at his desk at the Admiralty, where four hours earlier his First Lord, the nocturnal young Churchill, would have just finished dictating the last of the orders, minutes, and memoranda that were now heaped high on the admiral's desk. As Fisher began working through the pile of papers the petty officer on duty would bring in the old man's breakfast of a biscuit and a glass of lemonade. When Churchill arrived at ten he would find his output of the previous night back on his desk, each paper bearing Lord Fisher's initials along with annotations showing action taken, proposed, or, occasionally, not concurred in. Thus the work of His Majesty's Navy at war was carried on twenty hours of the twenty-four, seven days a week.

First Lord's Rooms   Admiralty, Whitehall
                                            30.XI.14

Jack:

During my conversation with Sir Edward Grey last night he passed along the following: Ambassador Spring Rice reports that he was approached "unofficially" by the younger Roosevelt and a certain Captain (Admiral?) Sims with a proposal to send an American observer to the Grand Fleet! They have in mind one Lt Com Maltbie. Spring Rice points out that pro-Allied, and particularly pro-British, feeling is strong in the U.S. Navy and shd be encouraged. The approach was "unofficial," however because of Navy Secretary Daniels' rigid pacifism.

A conspiracy!

Grey says the F.O. doesn't have to know anything about internecine struggles in the U.S. Navy Dept. and asks us to consider the Sims-Roosevelt idea on its merits, *viz*: do we want an American observer at sea with the Fleet, or do we not? Grey says the F.O. can manage the legal and diplomatic details for us, though neither of us could think of any precedent for a neutral observer on board a battleship at war except Pakenham on Togo's *Asahi*—and in that case of course there was our 1902 treaty with Japan in the background.

Grey feels, as does Spring Rice, and as do I, that on this question no circumvention of Daniels—and *a fortiori* of Bryan—would be possible without the cooperation of Colonel House, which for all intents and purposes is to say: the President. Of course any public request for an observer wd have generated charges of "unneutrality" and "entangling alliances" and such like from the Bryanists. We shd consider, therefore, whether this roundabout American approach to us is in the way of being a very tentative first step in the direction of de facto naval collaboration in the Atlantic. I realise I may be knitting a very long scarf from a very short thread, and that the Americans may simply be interested in enlarging their knowledge of naval tactics and technology. Grey thinks, and I think, however, that with all the resentment our North Sea blockade of Germany is causing in the United States, we ought to extend ourselves to cultivate American goodwill whenever suitable opportunities present themselves.

In other words, I'm disposed to let them have their observer.

What do you think?

W.

P.S. Do you suppose they are trying to place an observer with the German Fleet as well?

Admiralty, Whitehall
1.XII.14

First Lord:

I don't know much about Roosevelt *fils*—or is he some sort of nephew?—but Captain Sims is one of nature's noblemen. He is with us *totus porcus!* He came over here in 1906 when he was their Inspector of Target Practice and showed me an article he had written advocating *an all-big-gun ship!* He made all the arguments I ever made for the *Dreadnought* type, and he made them *better!* The article was so good I had it published in *Blackwood's Magazine* to silence the faint hearts and infidels who wanted to outlaw the twentieth century. I also—secretly—let Sims have a look at *Dreadnought,* which was doing her trials then. He was the first foreigner ever to board her! He went down to Portsmouth on Christmas Eve in civilian clothes and saw *everything*—keel to foretop, scupper to scupper. Then he went back to America with a report that convinced President Roosevelt *to build only dreadnoughts, WHICH WAS EXACTLY WHAT I HAD INTENDED!!!*

You know it and I know it; we've shared out the seas: the Mediterranean to France, the western Pacific to Japan (a piece of idiocy, that d———d treaty), and the rest of the

Pacific along with the western Atlantic *to the United States!* That's why I wanted America to start building dreadnoughts. You see how strained we are just holding down the Channel and the Western Approaches and the North Sea, and how thinly we're spread 'round Africa and India, and how narrow our margins are now that *Invincible* and *Inflexible* are gone to South America to hunt down von Spee. *Where would we be without the U.S. Navy patrolling the seas?* The Americans are on our side already—*THEY JUST DON'T KNOW IT!*

Another thing about Sims: he and Jellicoe have been friends for years. They're both gunnery maniacs! *Sims actually helped Jellicoe and Percy Scott develop our present system of fire control!* And you remember his Guildhall speech four years ago—"every American man, dollar, and drop of blood if England is in danger!" *Sims sublimis!* Did you know that he got a public reprimand from President Taft for his troubles?—*and he blew his nose in it!!!*

As to this Maltbie fellow—I met him in November '10, when I went to America to acquire my beautiful daughter-in-law. He was introduced to me by old Dewey as one of their brightest up and comers. I remember him because of the really stunning ideas he had about the potential of wireless telegraphy in naval operations. We should get Commander Maltbie over here *and pump him dry!*

Yes yes, we'll have to keep him away from the cypher books and the new director-firing apparatus, and we'll get Reeves-Wadleigh to have someone keep an eye on him. But you know how I feel about America, Winston: *She is Britain's destiny!* Remember your Bismarck: "The key fact in world politics is that Great Britain and the United States *speak the same language!*"

Bring on Lieutenant Commander Maltbie! I'm sure Jellicoe will be glad to have him. Any friend of Captain Sims, etc. *Vive l'Amérique!*

Fisher

P.S. There is about as much chance that Tirpitz would allow an American on a German battleship as there is that he would allow *ME!*

1914, 10TH DECEMBER—NEW YORK CITY

Commander Benjamin Gehlman, USN, a handsome, intelligent, rich, and unhappy bachelor of forty-one, strode through the vast cathedral of Pennsylvania Station, his mouth set in an angry line, his jaw muscles rippling. He hailed a southbound cab and directed the driver to take him to 10 Broad Street, better known as the Commercial Guaranty Trust Building.

The taxi swung east on Thirtieth Street and then right on Broadway, weaving its way downtown past horse-drawn vans, electric delivery trucks, Model T's, trolleys, and pushcarts. Wet snow was falling in the early evening darkness, falling on the rich and poor alike . . . except that the rich all seemed to be indoors this evening or in taxicabs, like Benjamin Gehlman, watching the wet snow fall on the poor.

It was, perhaps, an instructive spectacle—the poor being snowed on—but it was not a heartening one, and Gehlman in any case preferred to turn his gaze inward and concentrate on the snarling red anger that had brought him up from Washington so suddenly.

Less than six hours had elapsed since he'd first read the appalling message: "Your assignment to command of USS *Sterett*, Guantanamo Flotilla, is canceled. Pending publication of special orders you will continue to perform assigned duties at BurNav."

His High Episcopal office mate, Commander Simmons, had lost no time sprinkling salt on the wound, braying, "Do I again detect the unerring hand of your dear papaaaaahhhhh?" Gehlman was so enraged by the message, however, that it was only after he was out the door that he thought to yell back, "Go to hell!"

He'd gone directly to Admiral Boatwright's office, where he found what he regarded as conclusive evidence that Oskar was responsible: the instructions to cancel his assignment had been transmitted by no less an eminence than Woodrow Wilson's naval aide!

Without packing or leaving word with his superiors, he'd gone directly to Union Station. As luck would have it, he arrived there just in time to jump aboard the eleven thirty *Congressional Express*.

His father's secretary, Mr. Feiner, stood up obsequiously when

Gehlman appeared. "Good evening, Commander," he said. "What a pleasant surprise."

"Evening," said Gehlman. "I want to see my father."

Mr. Feiner's eyebrows rose and his hands fluttered to his cheeks in a travesty of consternation. "Oh, Commander, I'm so terribly sorry, but your father left an hour ago for Seventy-ninth Street to be with your poor mother. She's had another nervous attack, it grieves me to say."

Gehlman bristled and had a fierce longing to be away, to forgo his mission of reproach.

"Shall I telephone your father for you, sir?"

This was just like Feiner; ever the consummate lackey. Gehlman wheeled around and walked off down the corridor.

"Damn!" he thought, as the taxi made its way uptown. This grotesque pantomime his parents' marriage had become, this tawdry dumb show of perpetual expiation and revenge, was now in its *thirty-fourth year!* It had been in 1880 that his father—a remorseful slave to, as he put it, his "strong physical appetites"—had been surprised on his office couch by Gehlman's mother as he was effecting congress with Miss Selma Goldmark, Mrs. Gehlman's altogether superfluous "social secretary." Miss Goldmark had been scheming to turn a sinecure into a satrapy, Erna Gehlman being far too flabby a spaniel to keep up with sleek greyhounds like the Schiffs, the Lehmans, the Guggenheims, and the Warburgs, and Oskar Gehlman being obsessed to the point of frenzy by Selma's slablike breasts and great fleshy thighs. Her calculated but ill-timed submission to her employer eventually netted her ten thousand dollars, a good reference, and a fatal hemorrhage on a wooden table in an abortionist's office. It netted Benjamin Gehlman a neurasthenic invalid for a mother and ten suffocating years of pamperings, lecturings, and subtle emasculations designed to guarantee that he at least would never forsake her, as her husband had done, with some other woman. It netted Oskar Gehlman his son's undying, and unconscious, wrath and respect, the wrath because Oskar had not had the courage to rescue him from Erna's fetid embrace, the respect because he had had the good sense to be unfaithful to her in the first place.

There were side effects too. Oskar, his strong physical appetites unappeased, continued to satisfy them, but for discretion's sake he now did so only with the most accomplished professionals, beefy courtesans he maintained for his exclusive enjoyment in luxurious apartments scattered about the city in buildings he happened to own. Benjamin's introduction to sex at age fifteen was at the hands of one of these ladies, and as he was well on his way to misogyny by then, it confirmed him in his assumption that sex was just about all that a woman was good for. Oskar was a generous father (to the tune of $20,000 in annual trust income commencing on Benjamin's eighteenth birthday, the principal to vest on his thirty-first), so his son, whose tastes ran more to starved-looking urchin types, soon had a mistress of his own.

As Benjamin attained manhood he and Oskar enjoyed an increasing degree of intimacy with one another, and they could have been close friends but for one recurring source of friction: Oskar Gehlman was an aging apostate Jew with a sense of sin. It maddened Benjamin to see his father submit on an almost daily basis to the conscience-flaying rituals that his mother would devise. She would alternate hysteria and lassitude, sincerely believing herself to be suicidal one night, somnambulistic the next, and catatonic or autistic in the days that followed. Benjamin saw these recurring crises for what they, in part, were: a weak woman's petty revenge; and every time he was exposed to his mother's histrionics his contempt for her increased. Oskar, however, seemed to regard her perpetual puling as some form of divine judgment on his lechery, and in a continuing act of atonement he hurried to Erna's side at every whimper. Benjamin wanted to shake his father, scream at him, slap his face, awaken him *somehow* to the fraud that Erna was perpetrating. He thought her filthy, if only in some specifically female sense of the word, and he generalized this feeling into a hyperfastidiousness where women were concerned, so that now his mistresses were obliged to look diligently to their bathtubs, perfumes, and douches before their mouths and fingers were permitted to touch his skin.

As a boy, condemned to endure every summer in the purgatory of his mother's company on Cape Cod, Benjamin had taken refuge on the sea. He had had his first sailing lessons at age seven on Cape Cod Bay. By age ten he was master of his own skiff. At age fourteen, over Erna's wailing protests, he had been allowed to take a twelve-foot sailboat across to Martha's Vineyard by himself. That voyage, his first on his own on an ocean—or a part of one at any rate—had been decisive. As he tacked before a southwest breeze, alone on the waves in the sunlight, he had a firm and final sense that this was *right*. He,

Benjamin Gehlman, only son of a Hebrew banker, belonged on the sea; he drew strength from it, it made him whole; it was *clean.*

In his adolescent mind the sea of course meant the navy, and when he next was alone with his father he confided to him his new ambition. Oskar had smiled at the time, but three years later, with his son still adamant for Annapolis, he instructed Mr. Feiner to undertake some research. The results were predictably discomforting. In the years 1880–1890 the average graduating class at the Naval Academy had numbered forty-one; of the slightly more than four hundred passed midshipmen Annapolis had produced during the decade exactly *three* had been Jews, and of these three only one was still a serving officer. In addition, there had been fully *ten* Jews in the matriculating classes from 1876 to 1886, so the washout rate for Israelites was a solid seventy percent, as against twenty-five percent for Gentiles. As a final note there was the fact that in the more than one hundred years of the navy's existence only one Jew had ever risen to flag rank, Commodore Uriah Phillips Levy in 1860, and he had had to endure fifty-three years of official and unofficial naval anti-Semitism to achieve that distinction, even though his parents had been able to boast among their closest friends and neighbors one Mr. Thomas Jefferson of Monticello, Virginia.

Oskar presented these statistics to Benjamin not so much to dissuade him as to make sure that he understood the magnitude of the challenge he was confronting. Benjamin paid careful attention, gave the matter a few moments thought, and then reaffirmed his intention to make the navy his career. He was to reflect later, and often, that even if nothing else was right, he at least had been warned.

What he had not been prepared for, however, was the effect his progress, or lack of it, in the navy would have on his relationship with his father. In ways that Benjamin at first only suspected, but then more and more unmistakably, Oskar wielded his influence so as to make sure that his son's climb through the ranks proceeded at at least the same rate as that of his most promising contemporaries. He seemed altogether blind to the possibility that his son might regard such ex parte intercession as not simply unwarranted but pernicious and thick-headed as well. Benjamin, after all, was in no sense ambitious for an admiral's stripes; he had not joined the navy to rise in the world, but to steam away from it, and he was realistic enough to recognize the limitations his heritage imposed. Having little use for his brother officers—thus forestalling their having little use for *him*—

and having more money than most admirals would ever see in a lifetime, he had wisely chosen to stay as inconspicuous as possible, taking whatever subordinate positions he was offered and trusting to the
Navy List to yield promotions consistent with his time in grade. The
effect of his father's machinations, however, was to add to his sub-
stantive service identity of "Jew" the always cocked and pointed
epithet "pushy," and in the small ingrown navy of Cleveland and
McKinley's time, that was the kind of epithet that stuck.

Of course, given Benjamin's general disdain for the officers he
served with, he could easily have tolerated their enhanced hostility
had that been the only consequence of Oskar's meddlings. Unfortunately, though, there was a second consequence that stood well beyond the boundaries of the tolerable. This was the almost unbroken
string of shore assignments dictated by his father's professed conviction that Benjamin would be better off within the northeastern regions where the Gehlman influence could be made to tell most forcefully. At first he tried to restrain Oskar with gentle reproaches,
keeping his own anger in check with the assumption that his father
was only trying, albeit misguidedly, to do him some good. As time
passed, however, and Oskar's intrigues did not abate, a more sinister
explanation for his conduct took shape in Benjamin's mind. The evidence was all circumstantial, but the massed salvos of hysteria with
which Erna responded to every announcement that her darling Ben-
jie might be going away from her to sea must surely have had their
sequels in the form of bitter recriminations against Oskar for failing
to keep their only child near. Benjamin remembered that prior to his
departure on a long cruise in 1907, his mother had had to be physi-
cally restrained from harming herself, and that by the time he sailed
she had been under constant sedation for five solid weeks. How great
a toll had all that taken of Oskar's nerves? It was a chilling hypothesis to contemplate: his father, driven by guilt and self-delusion, delivering him again and again into his mother's unspeakable caress.

The mere possibility that Oskar might be engaged in this betrayal
was enough to enrage Benjamin, and at his first opportunity he instructed his father in violent language to cease all interference in his
affairs. Oskar complied for a while, but in the spring of 1910, when
Benjamin was assigned to America's first dreadnought, the *Michigan*,
he proved unequal to the fearsome pressure his wife unloosed. At the
last minute before the battleship was due to depart on its shakedown

cruise Benjamin was yanked out of his billet and ordered to the Naval War College at Newport, Rhode Island.

The immediate sequel to this sudden turn of events was a quarrel between Benjamin and Oskar so savage and protracted that they both doubted their relationship would ever recover. The later sequel was even unhappier, for Benjamin, taking a page from his mother's book, worked on his father's sense of contrition to win a promise that he would not only get sea duty when he had finished his year at the College, but sea duty in command of a ship. This promise cost Oskar upwards of $60,000 in sub rosa contributions to congressmen and navy bureaucrats, but in 1911 Benjamin got his gunboat.

While the sailors of the USS *Elcano* were relatively indifferent to their new captain's sectarian background, the same could not be said of the five commissioned officers aboard. Benjamin was temperamentally ill equipped to deal with their contemptuous disrespect, and when he tried to overbear them they ostracized him on his own ship. Of course, the *Elcano*'s performance suffered in consequence, and the responsible admiral was obliged to suggest to Benjamin, not without sympathy, that he request relief. Benjamin did so, and it was swiftly granted. From a seagoing command he was sent to a desk at the Bureau of Navigation just across West Executive Avenue from the totally landlocked White House. There he had sat with deadened spirits for three entire years—until two and one half weeks ago. Then, thanks to some string pulling he had done on his own, and to the fact that he had six years time-in-grade as a commander, he was notified by telegram that the Admiral Commanding Guantanamo intended to appoint him captain of the destroyer *Sterett*, on patrol off the eastward gates of the Panama Canal. Benjamin believed he had learned enough from the *Elcano* debacle to make his officers work for him now. There would only be three of them, and at any rate he would not make the same mistakes twice.

Poised as he was on the verge of getting his long-despaired-of second chance, he began to acknowledge to himself how very very badly he had wanted it. This morning, therefore, when the message canceling his assignment arrived, the blow had fallen particularly hard.

His taxi moved briskly up the Gold Coast of upper Fifth Avenue. On his right the French chateaux and Rhine castles of the overrich flashed by: John Jacob Astor, Mrs. Havemeyer, Benjamin Thaw, George J. Gould, the Tammany money man Thomas Fortune Ryan,

Mrs. Harriman, Samuel Thorne, Alfred Pell, Edward Harkness, Payne Whitney, Isaac Brokaw, and then, just south of Seventy-ninth Street, Oskar Gehlman. Here behind these facades, Benjamin judged, was the real filth of New York City, filth pestiferous enough to have made him a Socialist but for the fact that his contempt for men in general was only slightly less pronounced than his contempt for their "oppressors." True, he had been one of the almost 900,000 Americans who had voted for Eugene Debs in 1912, but he'd done that less out of conviction than out of a desire to infuriate his father. That desire had been abundantly satisfied, but as Benjamin got out of the cab in front of the family mansion, Oskar's fury of two years before seemed a very minor conflagration beside his own sense of indignation now.

He found his father reading to Erna in the downstairs sitting room. Walking in unannounced, he snatched the book out of Oskar's hands. It was a recent volume of E. A. Robinson's poetry, open to "Miniver Cheevy." He raised it to the light and began to recite: "'Benjamin Gehlman, child of scorn,/Grew lean while he assailed the seasons;/He wept that he was ever born,/And he had reasons.'" He looked down scornfully at his parents. "Ah ha!" he said. "My name scans perfectly, you see. What a coincidence. It's almost as if the poet knew me personally."

His mother and father glanced uneasily at him and then at each other. "Good evening, Benjamin," Oskar said at last. "This is a pleasant surprise." His voice bore just the trace of a German accent.

"That's exactly what your toad Feiner said when I came looking for you at your office."

Oskar reddened perceptibly.

"Your father tells me you may be going to Germany as an observer, dear," Erna put in. "You don't expect you'll actually go to sea, though, do you?"

Naval observer; so that was the new detour. Benjamin glared at his father for a moment, then fixed his mother with a gaze of patient contempt. "I expect nothing," he said. "I am without expectations."

Erna turned toward her husband, as if seeking a translation.

"You are without manners," said Oskar.

"You are without scruples," Benjamin spat back.

"Oh, please don't quarrel," Erna whimpered, weakly raising a hand to her forehead.

"We will not quarrel," said her husband, but she was already in tears.

Benjamin sat down, bestowing upon his mother a look of disgust. Unbidden, a lady's maid and a nurse emerged from the adjoining room and moved efficiently to Mrs. Gehlman's side. Oskar stared straight ahead, in silence. "Come, madam," said the nurse. "It's time you were in bed." Gently sobbing, Erna Gehlman was led away.

With an effort Oskar rose to his feet and walked stiffly to the sideboard where half a dozen bottles with yellowing labels stood next to a siphon and an ice bucket. "Brandy?"

Benjamin froze in his chair for a moment, then savagely flung the book away from him and snapped, "Yes. A large one."

"Do you enjoy causing your mother pain?" Oskar asked, pouring out two large snifters.

"Spare me."

"You seem to enjoy it. You seize every opportunity." He handed one of the glasses to his son.

"Shall we exchange recriminations then?" said Benjamin, taking a long sip.

"The pain I have caused your mother arose from weakness, not malice."

"And the pain you've caused me?"

"Such as it may be, it arose from my perceptions of your best interests."

"Damn your perceptions! And your hypocrisy."

"I am not a hypocrite."

"I'd been alerted to command a destroyer, do you know that? They were going to give me a second chance. I could have had a *ship!*"

"So? And what would you have done for a crew?"

Much of the truculence went out of Benjamin's demeanor. "The navy has changed in the last few years," he said lamely.

"Bah! And you? Have you changed? Are you no longer 'Jew' Gehlman as they so sportingly called you in the Academy yearbook? Are you a different officer to the one whose three months of sea command occasioned the only mutiny in the history of the navy?"

"It wasn't a mutiny, goddamnit!"

"No? What was it then? A boycott?—And kindly curb your language. The General Board didn't call it a mutiny because they were embarrassed and ashamed by it. But you and I knew what it was. *They* knew what it was."

"It was three years ago."

"Three years. And what is that? A geologic era?"

"To hell with you. Say it was yesterday if you like. It doesn't alter the fact that I could have had a ship but for your damnable interference."

Quivering with anger, Oskar took two swift steps forward and stood glowering over his son. "How dare you curse me!" he rasped, as Benjamin glared impenitently up at him.

A long moment passed, then Benjamin rose and went over to the bottles on the sideboard.

"All right, my proud young friend," said Oskar, hindered by his labored breathing. "You who wish your father to hell with such an easy air. Let us talk about my 'damnable interference,' as you call it. It was my damnable interference with President Harrison that got you an appointment to the Academy; it was my damnable interference with Navy Secretary Herbert that kept you from being dismissed on those trumped-up cheating charges; it was my damnable interference with half a dozen senators and bureau chiefs that let you keep your place on the Navy List when the bigots sought to block your promotion. Yes, my boy, and if you'll remember it was my damnable interference that *got you* your first ship three years ago, *my* warning that a Jew in command of Gentiles should tread softly, *my* prayers every night to God that you should be successful in your new position, *my* shame when you were not successful."

"Yes, father," Benjamin retorted. "And that's precisely the point. *You* have been the chief protagonist in *my* naval career."

"No, Benjamin. It is precisely the point that but for me you would not have *had* a naval career, the career *you* wanted, that you insisted upon."

"Oh, I insisted, did I?"

"Yes, you did. You were a very spoiled and headstrong boy, one accustomed to having his own way in all things."

"My father's son, in other words."

Oskar sighed wearily. "You are very hard with me when I have only sought your good."

"You deceive yourself."

"No! I swear to you, that has always been foremost in my thinking. Yes, they promised you another ship. You, a Jew of German de-

scent in an anti-Semitic anglophile navy. Very well, three years have
passed, things have changed. But have they changed for the better?
Yes, you may be older and wiser, but there is now the war. In England they drove Prince Louis of Battenberg from the Admiralty just
because he had German blood. And he was First Sea Lord! Don't
you see what they had in mind for you? Another ship, another . . .
unpleasantness, and your career would have been wrecked beyond
even my power to save it."

Benjamin shrugged impatiently. "It's my career, damnit! Mine to
make or break. Why can't you just stay the hell out of it!"

"I had no intention to interfere with you," Oskar replied in a
wounded tone. "You have made your wishes known for some time.
But on this occasion the initiative did not come from me. I was
approached by Colonel House. He knows the bank's connections in
Germany, and we have worked together often in the past. We have
an understanding."

"I don't doubt it, considering the colossal sums you contributed
toward his protégé's elevation."

Oskar shook his head sorrowfully. "You are ridiculous sometimes,
my son, with your preconceptions about the world. But as I say, we
have an understanding, and he called me. He said they were thinking
of proposing an American observer with the High Seas Fleet. He
asked me who among the Kaiser's retinue would be most friendly to
such an idea, who least. He asked me the best way to approach the
Kaiser himself on the subject. He asked a great many questions. Finally he inquired whether your designation as the American observer
might influence Tirpitz and the rest in a favorable sense. I was truly
surprised when he mentioned you, but I answered in all honesty that
I thought the Gehlman name might help. Later—and only later—it
occurred to me that an observer assignment might prove valuable for
your career."

"But it didn't occur to you to let me have some say in the matter."

"The Colonel spoke to me in confidence, Benjamin. To my
knowledge he has not even contacted the Kaiser yet. He said he
would wait for a favorable opportunity. And in any case there is no
certainty that the Germans will even let you come."

Benjamin regarded his father steadily. "And will you be bringing
my mother to Europe to visit me if they do?"

"Don't be an imbecile; there is the war. And your mother isn't
strong enough to travel."

"She's strong enough to move you around like a chessman's pawn. Why not herself?"

Oskar shook his head, as if refusing an hors d'oeuvre. "There is no point in our discussing this again."

"True. But then, is there any point in us discussing anything anymore?"

"You are my son, Benjamin."

There it was: the inevitable infuriating appeal to blood, infuriating because in some way it always struck home. "Damnit all!" Benjamin moaned. "Why won't you just leave me the hell alone!"

1914, 21ST DECEMBER—BERLIN

Admiral Georg Alexander von Müller had the genuine honor and dubious privilege of serving as Chief of Naval Cabinet to the All Highest War Lord, Wilhelm II of Hohenzollern. In this position, and by virtue of a slow-but-steady wisdom that the Kaiser had come to rely on, he had closer and more constant access to the Imperial ear than any other member of the naval establishment, Grand Admiral von Tirpitz especially included. On the debit side, he also had closer and more constant exposure to the Imperial mouth, from which streamed the whines and petulancies of a man whose capacities were proving more and more unequal to the times.

Admiral von Müller was in the act of doing something impulsive, which was not at all like him. Had the Foreign Office not stood directly across the Wilhelmplatz from the Hatzfeld Palace, the building leased by Ambassador Gerard to house the American Embassy, his usual conservatism would probably have deflected him from his course. But there the palace was: lights blazing in the early darkness of the war's first winter solstice, and the admiral had only to cross the square to give force to his convictions. So he began to walk.

After several paces he stopped. Impulsive was one thing, unprepared quite another. He reviewed in his mind his just concluded meeting with Under-Secretary Zimmermann at the Foreign Office. There was the cable from Colonel House in his breast pocket, given to him for transmission to the Kaiser. There was the Chief of the Naval Staff, Admiral von Pohl—and von Tirpitz, too, of course—beginning to badger Wilhelm for permission to unleash the submarines. There was the specter of America belligerent: 100 million people, inexhaustible resources and industries, the world's third navy—certain defeat for Germany in short. Von Müller felt with his fingers for the cable. Zimmermann was right of course; it would cause the Kaiser annoyance. Ambassador Gerard should have noticed that before sending it over. Of course Gerard had only done what von Müller was now *not* doing—serve as a faithful conduit for information. Even if protocol required that any message from House to Wilhelm go through the ambassador, the Foreign Office, and himself where naval matters were concerned, the message was still from one man to another and ought not to be tampered with. Even so, Gerard could have queried its wisdom or its phrasing in a cable back to House *before* he sent it to the Foreign Office; that would have been consistent with his duty. Well, what was he, von Müller, contemplating now? A simple recommendation that Gerard should do so afterwards. The admiral shook his head. He was tampering; there was no way around it. It was highly irregular. If Colonel House couldn't make his proposal for an American naval observer in a manner calculated to persuade the Kaiser, then that was just too bad. There was nothing to be done.

Von Müller began to turn away, but then stopped abruptly and stamped his foot. "No, by heaven," he said aloud, rather startling himself. Was one a thinking organism or not? Had one the power of choice or not? Well then, one must think and one must choose, not just mindlessly observe the forms. An American, especially a German-American like Gehlman, could if attached to the fleet be made to understand the Reich's naval point of view, and perhaps even espouse it. More important, he would stand as an earnest of Germany's good faith, a demonstration that the *Kriegsmarine* had nothing dark or shameful to hide. House was right about that, and right too that now was the time for America and Germany to strengthen their ties as much as possible so they would be strong enough to withstand the inevitable war-wrought strains to come. Commander Gehlman could be an important one of those ties. Was he to be flung away simply because of a few innocent blunders in a cablegram? Von Müller took a deep breath: Well! *If* I recommend some changes before delivering this to the Kaiser, and *if* Colonel House agrees to my recommendations, then I will have helped him say what he wishes to say in a manner the Kaiser will understand. I will have helped him and the Kaiser communicate with one another and avoid misunderstanding. I will have helped keep America's friendship. I will have helped Germany.

Von Müller laughed silently and shook his head: Well, well, old fellow, you certainly are eloquent in pleading your own cause.

The admiral sighed and, still shaking his head, resumed his course toward the Hatzfeld Palace.

A column of plaques outside the gates announced that the American Embassy was handling the affairs of France, Great Britain, and Russia in Berlin, as well as its own. Von Müller remembered those insanely jubilant days in August as one by one the Allies' ambassadors had come to the Foreign Office to request their passports and, having gotten them, then strode across the Wilhelmplatz and dumped everything else they had into poor Gerard's lap. Of course "poor" was not precisely the word to describe a man who could afford the Hatzfeld Palace as his home—"hard pressed" would be closer to the mark. But it was only a few minutes after von Müller presented his card that he was shown into the ambassador's office.

"Ah, Admiral," said Gerard, a small pudgy man with a bit of the dandy about him. "An unexpected pleasure."

"Good evening, your Excellency," said von Müller. "I hope I'm not causing you inconvenience."

"No indeed, no indeed. I'm delighted to have an excuse for a cocktail. Will you join me?"

"A . . . cocktail?"

Gerard brought his fingers to his mouth in an affectation of sudden distress. "Ah, forgive me. It's an Americanism for mixed drink: gin and vermouth, whiskey and vermouth, that sort of thing."

With an effort of will von Müller managed to conceal his revulsion. "No. No, thank you. I would enjoy a cognac though."

"A cognac? Certainly." Gerard opened the panels of a Louis Quinze escritoire to reveal a well-stocked bar. "Please sit down, Admiral," he said, and then paused with a bottle in one hand and a glass in the other. "I must confess I'm consumed with curiosity to know the purpose of your call. But I suppose it's really terrible form to bring that up. Isn't it?"

Yes, thought von Müller, it is. But he said, "Not at all. I have come to suggest a few . . . . clarifications in the message from Colonel House to the Kaiser."

Gerard's eyebrows shot up. "You mean it hasn't reached him yet? The Kaiser, I mean."

"I understand you. No, it has not reached him. I have just now received it from Herr Zimmermann."

Gerard put down glass and bottle and clasped his hands together in a gesture of thanksgiving. "Well, that *is* providential," he said elatedly.

"Sir?"

The ambassador wagged his head in silent laughter. "That message came through in cipher," he explained. "But Colonel House also sent a companion cable *en clair* which said—and I'm sure you'll find this rich—'In regard to my cable number such-and-such, suggest you consult with von Müller of *Marinekabinett* to ensure proper wording.' Or some such thing. Now, isn't that extraordinary?"

Inwardly von Müller gave a sigh of relief. His instinct had been right.

"The problem," Gerard continued, "is that I always attend to cipher cables first, because they're the most important. And sometimes, what with our insane workload these days, I fall a day or two behind on the *en clair* messages. So you can guess what happened. I sent Mr. House's letter over to Herr Zimmermann before I ever saw his covering instructions. I can tell you I was pretty upset about it too, because I distinctly remembered having some misgivings about the way the letter was phrased."

"Excuse me," said von Müller, taking a glass of cognac from the ambassador's hand. "But why wasn't Colonel House's second cable sent in cipher as well, if I may ask?"

Gerard lowered his voice conspiratorially. "You may ask. And well may you ask. And I'll tell you. Our damn-fool Congress gets periodically incensed over—quote—'waste and extravagance in the government'—unquote—so our damn-fool State Department has adopted a damn-fool rule which forbids us to use cipher for 'administrative' communications. Of course it's always some officious little twerp in the Cable Office who's responsible for enforcing this rule. So a message from Colonel House to the Kaiser goes enciphered, but a cable from Colonel House to me about how to transmit his message goes *en clair*. It's a wonderful system."

"Well," said von Müller, reflecting on the incredible *schlamperei* of American diplomacy, "at least no harm was done."

"Only thanks to your presence of mind, my dear Admiral. And you can be sure we'll be glad to make any changes you propose."

Von Müller shifted uneasily. Carte blanche was the last thing he wanted; he felt he was taking a great deal too much on himself as it was. "Thank you," he said, taking the message from his pocket. "I have only three suggestions."

Taking a writing tablet off his desk, Gerard sat down right beside the admiral, and von Müller had to force himself not to recoil from the ambassador's sudden unwelcome proximity. "May I?" Gerard said, reaching for the piece of paper. "We'll have to do the whole thing over, so I'll just go ahead and make the changes on this copy."

"Very well," said von Müller, aghast that an ambassador should openly undertake the duties of a secretary.

"Shoot!" said Gerard, beaming.

"Uh, yes. Well, you will have noticed that in the salutation Colonel House says, 'His Imperial Majesty, Emperor of Germany, King of Prussia.'"

"Yes?" said the ambassador, still smiling, pencil poised.

"Yes," replied von Müller, now somewhat at a loss. "Well, you see, it is a minor point, but as you know the Kaiser is not Emperor of Germany but German Emperor. The several kings and princes of the Reich specifically denied the first Kaiser's claim to the former title on the basis that it would demean their own status. Perhaps the difference in phrasing is not so significant in English?"

"Well, we don't have any kings or princes in America, so it doesn't really concern us," Gerard said.

"Yes," von Müller persisted. "However, His Majesty is very punctilious about such things, and he might take a mistaken appellation as a mark of offhandedness."

"German Emperor it is," said Gerard with a triumphant flourish of his pencil. "Next!"

Von Müller frowned. "Next" was an old pus-filled wound, and he did not relish the prospect of peeling the bandage off it. "Yes," he said after some deliberation. "Next is this sentence where the Colonel refers to the precedent of your Civil War general Sheridan having ridden as an observer with 'the Great Wilhelm' at Sedan in 1870." The admiral took a deep breath. "His Majesty is somewhat sensitive about references to his grandfather as 'the Great Wilhelm' inasmuch as they might be construed to imply an invidious comparison to himself. I would suggest, therefore, 'your Majesty's grandfather, Wilhelm the First' as being less susceptible to misinterpretation."

". . . grandfather, Wilhelm the First," the ambassador repeated as he wrote. "Done! And . . . ?"

God, but the man was forward! "The last suggestion I have pertains to the Colonel's reference to what he calls 'the destruction of Louvain' in August and our naval bombardment last week of, in his words, 'the ports' of Scarborough, Hartlepool, and Whitby. I understand that the Colonel has mentioned these things as examples of incidents where the presence of an American observer might have offset Allied propaganda about 'atrocities.' I submit, however, that the words 'destruction' and 'ports' unwittingly connote support for the Allied interpretation of these events, and I would suggest 'pacification of Belgium' and 'bombardment of British east coast installations' as phrases more—uh—neutral in their meaning."

Gerard scribbled furiously for some moments, then looked up and said, "Splendid! All's well that ends well."

"Yes," von Müller replied, now thoroughly desirous of taking his leave. "And I must no longer impose myself upon you. If you would be so kind as to have the modified letter sent to me directly, we could minimize the delay that has occurred."

"Of course," said Gerard. "May I ask, just for my own information, whether you think it likely that His Majesty and Admiral von Tirpitz will be disposed to regard the Colonel's proposal in a favorable light?"

Von Müller bristled; such colossal presumption. But he held himself in check. "I cannot speak for His Highness," he said. "But *if* Admiral von Tirpitz should be consulted on this matter, a negative response would, in my opinion, be a virtual certainty."

"Well, he won't hear about it from *us* in that case," the ambassador said jovially, escorting von Müller to the door. "Good night, Admiral," he added as they shook hands. "Many thanks for stopping by."

Dear God! thought von Müller as he walked past the guards at the gate. That the Fatherland's welfare should be dependent on the goodwill of such bumptious louts!

1914, 25TH DECEMBER—WASHINGTON, D.C.

Maltbie decided that he had no desire to sleep, and given the fact that he'd been lying awake in his bed for several hours now, the conclusion seemed a plausible one. Perhaps it was his status as a guest in the official residence of His Britannic Majesty's ambassador to the United States that worked to discourage slumber. Perhaps it was Melina's presence under the very same roof. And perhaps it was simply Christmas, a time of the year that Maltbie in general dreaded, but which this year seemed wreathed with enchantment.

Briefly, very briefly, he surveyed his ghosts of Christmas past: the years in Westport, alone with his mother, watching the pathetic, well-meaning, and ultimately futile efforts she made to derive from— and give to—the season the mood of easy merriment that she otherwise drew with less exertion from a bottle. Sweet, loving, and unhappy woman! Too shy, too slight, too submissive in every respect to carry off the feat of "marriage above one's station." Perhaps if she'd married a rich man, a lawyer or prosperous farmer, she might have been forgiven her humble background as a textile foreman's daughter. But Josiah Maltbie, a dead-end lieutenant commander, had not been rich at all; he'd been just barely middle class enough to afford some pretentious notions, the gaudiest among them being that his wife's lack of breeding was responsible for his own lack of consequence. The truth, hard to acknowledge and even harder to escape, was that Constance Harris was a better catch—humble background and all—than a man of Josiah Maltbie's defects was entitled to. And it was precisely this, her quality, that drove him to keep her down.

The task of sapping her self-respect was easily enough accomplished. Coming from the man one has sworn to love, honor, and obey, allegations that one's shortcomings greatly outweigh one's essential worth tend to take on the ring of authority after a certain number of repetitions. But how better to confound the critic than to prove him right! Hence, alcohol, degeneration, and, finally, the shame of an institution.

With one parent defined as inferior and the other—from a son's viewpoint—inferior from birth, Maltbie grew up with an urgent need to solicit and deserve approval from people he deemed his betters.

Because he was intelligent and good-natured, and because his fundamental humility was ineradicable, the approval he sought was readily forthcoming. Until he met Melina, though, he had always regarded such approval as being strictly contingent on his ability to work hard and do well. Melina, however, evinced little interest in his achievements, but still found much worth praising in his character. And as Melina, in his opinion, was as superior a creature as ever walked the earth, her assessment of him could not be totally incorrect.

For Maltbie, the six weeks that had passed since their first meeting existed in only two perspectives: time spent with her and time spent waiting to be with her. He had traveled to Washington as often as he could, which worked out to be almost weekly, given the avuncular indulgence with which Sims regarded his state of romantic hypertension. Once he got to Washington, the hours he spent with her were purely magical. Whether they took a walk or went to a concert or had lunch together in a restaurant, she always managed a stream of comment and observation that entranced him. The feel of her hand in the crook of his arm as they walked together and the sense of harmonious wholeness he derived from her company made him joyously giddy.

What she saw in him remained something of a mystery from his privatemost point of view, but the important thing was that she saw enough at least to warrant a continuing investment of her time. Of course, there were some indications that she saw a good deal more in him than he saw in himself. At all events, the invitation he'd received to be her guest at the embassy over the Christmas holidays gave him reason, or courage, to hope.

Softly, so softly that he doubted his hearing, there came a tapping sound in the midst of the darkness. He listened. It came again. He sat up and strained his ears. At first there was only the wind soughing through the naked trees in the embassy garden, then, three distinct taps on the door of his room. He swung himself quickly out of bed and wrestled on his robe. Fumbling in the darkness, his fingers found the handle of the door. He jerked it open and a small wraith-like apparition in white appeared before him. "Good *heavens* but you're a sound sleeper," it whispered.

"Melina! I wasn't even—"

"Hush!" she said gently, taking him by the hand and leading him down the hall.

They tiptoed along the upstairs corridor to the broad flight of marble steps that descended to the mansion's main entrance. The whole building was dark and silent, the only light the moonlight spilling through the wide front windows. As they reached the bottom of the stairs Maltbie caught a glimpse of the full lunar disk, well past its zenith. He guessed the time as four o'clock.

Melina led him through the reception area and into the grand ballroom. In the far corner loomed the embassy tree, its Star of Bethlehem barely an inch from the sixteen-foot-high ceiling. They crossed the dance floor to the window seat and sat down. The wind moaned and gusted, and Melina held Maltbie's hand very tightly in both of hers as the eddies whipped the tree limbs.

"Merry Christmas, Harry," she said at last in an excited whisper.

He looked at her, all white and shadow in the semidarkness—a faerie queen. "Merry Christmas," he answered.

They sat in silence for what seemed like a very long time; then Melina reached into a pocket of her dressing gown and pressed a small velvet box into Maltbie's hand.

"What is it?" he asked.

"Open it."

He lifted the box to the pale light and raised the lid. Inside was a chain and a medallion showing a boy astride a dolphin. Maltbie lifted the metal disk off its cushion; the weight confirmed that it was made of gold.

"My God, Melina!" he exhaled.

"Look at the reverse," she said, eyes shining.

Maltbie turned the medallion over and found an all-seeing eye with myriad lines of force radiating from its iris. "It . . . it's beautiful," he stammered.

"It's a talisman, Harry, for seafarers. It's very, very old and very, very potent, and you must promise me to wear it always, never to take it off."

"It'll make me stoop-shouldered," he protested jokingly.

"Promise me," Melina repeated with emphasis.

And Maltbie promised.

"Here," she said, "let me officially invest you." Maltbie felt a shock as her cold hand cleared a space between his neck and his robe and pajamas. Then she lifted the medallion into the air and placed it slowly over his head. "There. You are now under my protection. No harm can befall you."

Maltbie was moved, so moved that he could think of nothing

more eloquent to say than thank you, which struck him as utterly inadequate. In some embarrassment, therefore, he stood up abruptly and said, "Wait here."

"Why? Where are you going?"

"To get your present from my room."

Melina stood up too. "Oh no, Commander. I want my present now." She reached up, took his face in her hands, and drew his mouth down to hers. Then she kissed him with a sensuality and a thoroughness that were entirely novel in Maltbie's experience. "Oh, Harry," she said into his chest when she had finished, "do you think me terribly brazen and abandoned?"

"I think you lovelier than a summer night full of shooting stars," he replied with total conviction—and to his considerable astonishment. It had been a completely unpremeditated response, but he immediately felt mortified by it. He had never said anything like that in his life before, let alone meant it, and he was about to gabble some facetious disclaimer when he felt Melina's fingers on his lips.

"Don't!" she said, her voice husky. "Don't take it back. Don't question it. Please. Just keep on holding me and be still."

Maltbie obeyed, and as they stood there it suddenly came to him that his life henceforth would be a very unsatisfactory progression if Melina Bellamy were not a part of it. It also occurred to him that there was no other aspect of his existence—not even the navy—about which he could say the same thing. Thus he proceeded to the conclusion that he not only adored, but loved her, and, having reasoned it all out, he experienced such an intense surge of feeling for her that he was maddeningly at a loss for a way to express it. Then he perceived the obvious, and went down on one knee as though stricken.

Somewhat startled, Melina drew back a little and regarded him with a quizzical smile. "What are you doing down there, you silly man?"

"Please marry me," Maltbie answered, hoping he sounded as abjectly suppliant as he felt.

"Oh, Harry!"

"Please."

"Dear sweet Harry, you are already engaged to Admiral Jellicoe."

"Marry me," he repeated.

Melina looked down at him, caressed his cheek. "Darling Harry, I will never marry anyone else."

Though certainly not a refusal, this had a slightly equivocal ring to it that made Maltbie uneasy. "You accept?"

"Harry, I am going to New Mexico and you are going to Scapa Flow. We've known each other only six weeks. We've spent barely a fortnight together. We haven't tested each other at all."

"Tested each other? What do you mean?"

"I mean—oh, do get up off the floor, you great puppy—I mean that what unites two people is not simply love but common, or at least compatible, goals in life, as well as a conviction that despite all quarrels and misunderstandings each will accord the other unquestioning priority in time of need."

"I hereby swear to accord you unquestioning priority *all* the time."

Melina smiled. "I believe you, dear heart, but it's not you that I'm worried about."

"As far as that goes, I'd trust you with my life."

"You don't know me, Harry, any more than I know myself when it comes to this issue. Will you give me some time to study myself and my feelings before accepting you?"

Maltbie sensed that he ought to be content with that, and he tried to pretend that he was. "Very well. But I won't wait a day longer than ten years."

Melina did not smile as she again took his face in her hands. "I will never marry anyone else," she repeated, and then earnestly sought his lips.

1915, 5TH JANUARY—NEW YORK CITY

House had liked Lieutenant Commander Maltbie, and for the simple reason, he concluded, that Lieutenant Commander Maltbie was likable. The tall spare officer with the boyish face and somewhat flappy ears had been so plainly ecstatic—it was not too strong a word—about the Royal Navy's willingness to have him that the Colonel had forgone any formal briefing and chosen instead simply to draw the young man out. With twenty-five years in politics behind him he did not need the corrective lens of long acquaintance in order to read character. He could usually get a strong sense of personality right on the instant of meeting, and over the course of an hour he could refine his impressions down to a solid core of inference and observation. In Maltbie's case the refining process took rather less than fifteen minutes, not because the officer was shallow, but because he was uncomplicated. As he respectfully voiced his enthusiasm—for the navy, for Great Britain, for Captain Sims, for the English girl he hoped to marry—House put together the adjectives that best marked him out: intelligent, conventional, loyal, naive, conscientious, impressionable, honorable, earnest. And likable, eminently likable; so much so that when Maltbie burst out at the end of their interview: "I think sometimes that I must be dreaming, sir. I don't believe I've ever been so happy," House felt an unaccustomed surge of gladness on his behalf.

What a contrast with the testy and resentful man who now sat opposite him in his study on Fifty-third Street. But for the fact that "envious" was not a Maltbie adjective, Commander Gehlman seemed to have everything that someone in Maltbie's position might reasonably envy. Gehlman was rich, while Maltbie had no money at all. Gehlman came from a powerful and distinguished family; Maltbie's unconnected and unlucky parents were long dead. Gehlman was good-looking and magnetic, while Maltbie had average features and an appearance that, however engaging, was still somehow comical. Yet House, in assessing their more subtle endowments, had no doubt whatsoever as to which of the two men fortune had favored, and it was not Gehlman.

"I have the impression," he said, "that you aren't altogether enthusiastic about this assignment."

Gehlman made a sort of grimace which seemed to mix irritation over House's intrusion into his private thoughts with respect for the Colonel's deftness at divining them, though they were hardly well concealed. "I'm not altogether enthusiastic," he admitted. "I'd been alerted for an assignment to command a ship when this observer business supervened."

House noted the deprecatory petulance implicit in "business."

"Perhaps you're not aware of it," Gehlman continued, little short of outright insolence, "but seagoing commands are much sought after in the navy, and damn hard to come by."

The Colonel nodded attentively. "I can well imagine," he said in a sympathetic tone.

"Of course the navy can send me anywhere it wants to; I don't question that. It's just that I was disappointed about losing my ship. So near and yet so far. You understand."

"Of course, of course," said House, forbearing to bring up what his inquiries had revealed about Gehlman's previous experience of command. "To be quite honest with you, we had very little expectation that the Germans would permit an American observer to sail with them, even one with your unusually suitable qualifications. Had we nominated any other officer I seriously doubt they would have agreed to the arrangement. So at least you incurred your disappointment in a good cause."

House's display of forbearance in the face of Gehlman's surliness had its intended effect. "I'm sorry, sir," said the commander, shaking his head and nervously running his fingers through his hair. "I'm behaving like a child." He looked up at the Colonel with what seemed to be a plea for remission in his eyes, for a release from some private ordeal. "I know that this is a really worthwhile assignment, and I know that any other officer would give his eyeteeth to have it."

"You're upset, which is altogether natural under the circumstances. But I know you'll put your disappointment behind you and do an excellent job."

"Thank you, sir," said Gehlman. "I'll do my best."

"I don't doubt it. And I'd like to make a few suggestions, if I may, regarding your duties as an observer."

"Yes, sir. Please do."

"Well, given the volatility of our relations with the belligerents, you will constantly have to consider the diplomatic as well as the naval aspects of your position. Simply by virtue of your presence with the German Fleet on a day-to-day basis, you are going to acquire an immense store of valuable information from which our navy can't help but benefit. This being the case, you should avoid even the appearance of inquisitiveness. If you are told things, well and good. If you are shown things, better still. But on no account should you seek information on your own initiative. In doing so you would only jeopardize your standing with your hosts and risk causing us embarrassment here. The success of your mission will be measured not by how much intelligence you gather in Germany but by how well you fit in there and how long you stay. Please believe me, you are under *no* obligation to bring back any information other than that which the Germans freely make available."

"Very well, sir. I understand."

"Good. Now my second suggestion is more or less a corollary of the first. I have the feeling, though it is not much more than that, that there was a sharp difference of opinion in Berlin as to the advisability of permitting an American observer to join the German Fleet. This isn't surprising certainly, but it does dictate an attitude of extreme circumspection on your part about letting your presence become in any way conspicuous. You should therefore regard your mission as confidential in nature, wear your uniform as little as possible when ashore, and keep your social contacts to an absolute minimum, consistent only with what custom and usage may require. This may have the effect of making life rather dreary for you, but I'm sure you can see the reason for putting up with such an eventuality."

"Yes, sir. I can."

"Fair enough. Now all this leads up to my final suggestion. Given the fact that your coming is the occasion for some controversy in Berlin, there is a real possibility that the Kaiser may at any moment be persuaded to change his mind about letting you come. Thus the sooner you get to Germany the better. It will take more persuasion to have him eject you once you're there than it will to have him keep you from coming in the first place."

"I see that, sir, and I'd be more than happy to set off immediately, this evening even. There's nothing whatever to keep me here."

House was a bit taken aback by the undertone of bitterness, but the substance of the response was to his liking. "Good," he said. "The *Ancona* sails Thursday, and I'll cable our consul in Genoa to book rail passage for you from there to Berlin."

"Genoa, sir? Wouldn't it be faster if I went via Holland?"

"That would depend on whether or not the British stopped your ship on its way through the Channel, and on how long they stopped it for, and why. They keep changing the definition of conditional contraband every day, and if your ship's cargo were to turn up suspect in some manner you might find yourself shunted to England and obliged to change ships there. In such a case we would be hard pressed to provide the Germans with an acceptable explanation for the delay in your arrival, and if they were to discover that you'd come via England, well, I don't think your stay with their navy would be very protracted."

Gehlman accepted this at face value, and after a few more minutes of conversation took his leave. House did not feel at all comfortable about him, and he was by no means convinced of his fitness for an observer's role. The man had good instincts to be sure, but he was neurotic, and there were those unconsciously sneering inflections in his speech that betrayed the captious perverseness of immaturity. With fewer reservations about him House might have told Gehlman that the real reason he was being routed via Genoa was to prevent the British from getting wind of his mission. Of course, given the orders Gehlman had received not to discuss his assignment with anyone, he might just figure that out for himself.

BOOK II

1915, 17TH JANUARY–ZURICH

It was 6:30 A.M. in the dank and gelid Zurich Bahnhof. Barely twenty-four hours had elapsed since the American consul at Genoa had greeted Gehlman at the dock, steered him through customs and immigration, escorted him to the railway station, and sent him on his way. There had been a change of trains and a four-hour layover in Milan, then a long crawling climb in a heavy snowstorm up to the St. Gotthard Tunnel. Gehlman's compartment had been stifling, but if he opened the window more than a crack the blizzard roared in. It was an Italian train, so complaints to the conductor would have been fruitless. Left with a choice of evils, he had lain naked on his cramped and narrow berth and sweltered the hours away listening to the maddeningly slow *click-clang* of the wagon-lit wheels on the rails. It had been one of those interminable nights in which neither sleep nor dawn ever seems to get any closer. Around four Gehlman had given up and switched on the light. He had shaved and dressed, closed up his berth, and tried to read, but his tired eyes had watered and itched in the dim illumination. Finally he had turned off the overhead light and just sat gazing out the window at the dark shapes of winter's desolation, shapes punctuated now and then by snow-haloed lamp posts in empty depots or by mindlessly flashing warning signals at deserted crossings. It was a dead and cheerless world he had looked out on, and an empty sour feeling in his stomach added to the mood. Then, as too frequently happened when he was over-tired and underoccupied, a sense of aloneness began to claw into his entrails.

These attacks—for so he thought of them—would come on like Pacific rollers and break over him almost before he could sense their approach. They would begin as a tightening of the muscles in his neck and shoulders and would be followed by a vague feeling of constriction in his chest. If his conscious mind took warning from these threshold symptoms, he could, by forcing his body to relax, sometimes fend off the total syndrome. In most instances, however, he was well past the threshold by the time his brain sounded the alert, and then there was nothing to do but hold on.

Several bodily systems would seem to go haywire simultaneously. He would suffer an aguelike chill even as his skin began exuding a feverish sweat. His heart would pump like a trip-hammer, but all the pumping would seem unequal to the task of moving his blood, which felt silted, filthy, and thick. His joints would throb like catchments for tar, and his stomach would contract as if gripped in a vise. Over all this physical distress would float the stench of overwhelming fear, a sense of entrapment in isolation, of hopelessness, of futility, of childlike despair.

On this bleak morning Gehlman had managed to catch himself before the deluge hit. Beginning with his neck, he had sent impulses step by step down his body and forced his muscles to unflex. At the same time he had fixed his mind on the memory of a small *Konditorei* he knew just across the River Limmat from the Zurich station, a clean and cozy place where the owner's two pretty daughters served you *Kaffee mit Schlag* and fresh-baked croissants and powdered-sugar pastries filled with strawberry jam. The train would be half an hour changing engines in Zurich, he had recited to himself; there would be just enough time to nip across the Bahnhof Brücke, refortify his spirit in an orgy of self-indulgence, and get back on board.

Even before the train came to a complete stop he was out the door of his compartment and striding rapidly down the platform. The cold air was bracing, and it was bliss to be moving about freely after twelve purgatorial hours cooped up alone with his knotted soul. His mind was concentrated with almost desperate intensity on the croissants and pastries awaiting him across the Limmat, and at this time and place he certainly didn't expect to encounter anyone he knew. Thus when, on some level short of full awareness, his ears picked up the improbable sound of a voice calling out his name, the words did not register on his brain. It took several progressively nearer and louder repetitions to finally pierce his supposition of anonymity. Puzzled and a little irritated, he turned to see a short, round-faced man hurrying down the platform toward him. "Ahoy, Ben. It's me—Facchetti." Gehlman's stony visage burst into a delighted smile. "Wally!" he exclaimed as they clasped hands and vigorously pounded each other on the shoulder.

For Benjamin Gehlman, Walter Facchetti had been one of the few glimmers of light during four dark years at Annapolis. They had come to know each other, after a fashion, in December of Gehlman's first year, when Second Classman Facchetti had appeared in the plebe barracks to make an after-curfew inspection. As the son of an Italian immigrant, Facchetti had had to endure his share of snubs from such of his classmates as set excessive store by their Anglo-Saxon ancestry. But as a Christian, albeit a papist, he had been spared the near felonious persecution reserved for Jews. On entering the second-floor latrine that night he had found Gehlman lashed naked to one of the commodes while six giggling fellow plebes wielding old toothbrushes and jars of shoe polish crowded around him and daubed his body with Stars of David. Such humiliations were nothing new to Gehlman by that time, and by maintaining an outward appearance of passivity and indifference he usually managed to keep them from escalating into episodes of physical harm. They were something new to Facchetti, however, who watched in outraged silence for well over a minute before making his presence known.

The six young men had immediately frozen to attention, and they stood rigid as Facchetti moved silently among them, scrutinizing each of their faces in turn. His expression had suggested both intense professional interest and acute physical revulsion, as if he were a zoologist getting his first glimpse of some altogether new but repulsive species of slug. Turning his attention to Gehlman, Facchetti had looked for a long while at the ropes and black smudges on his body. At last, with a barely detectable irony, he had said, "These appear to be loop knots, gentlemen. Haven't you been taught to use a prolonge on a transverse spar?"

The six plebes had remained frozen, though faint flickers of motion around their eyes and lips indicated a hope that this upperclassman might be the sort to adjudge their antics good sport.

"And since when is quarter-inch cable authorized for premast restraint?" Facchetti had continued, his voice growing harder.

The plebes had begun to sense that their hope was fleeting.

"You've been here almost six months, gentlemen; haven't you learned *anything*? Anything, that is, apart from the elementary arithmetic that tells you that six can deal safely with one as long as they're prepared to behave like niggers and hid their brave exploits after curfew in latrines."

Facchetti's voice had become ominously gentle as he continued, "You will untie that gentleman. You will then return to your rooms, stand to at parade rest, and await further orders."

Gehlman had watched six pairs of hands fumbling frantically with the three or four knots that held him to the commode, and as he reached down to pick up his underwear off the floor he had seen six pairs of feet hasten out of the doorway. "Wash up and go to bed," Facchetti had said to him as soon as the two of them were alone. He had then shot him a sympathetic wink and gone off to bed himself, leaving Gehlman's tormentors to interpret reveille some six hours distant as the "further orders" to which they should respond. A night at parade rest with no sleep was a much rougher punishment than marching off demerits after all, especially as any demerits handed out for Jew-baiting would most probably have been marched off with a tic of a first classman's pencil in the Discipline Log.

Given Facchetti's two years of seniority as a midshipman, he and Gehlman had had almost as little contact with each other after their first encounter as before. Once Gehlman obtained his commission, though, their paths had crossed regularly, and several times over the next ten years they had shared pleasurable meals together or attended the theater as a threesome with Facchetti's petite and effervescent wife, Eileen. Then, in 1907, Gehlman was assigned as chief gunnery officer to the battleship *Connecticut* of the Great White Fleet, where his immediate superior, the ship's executive officer, was Commander Walter Facchetti.

The round-the-world cruise of the Great White Fleet under the command of Rear Admiral Robley Dunglison "Fighting Bob" Evans at the behest of President Roosevelt was a public relations bonanza for the United States and an extended nightmare for the United States Navy. Though the *Connecticut*, just recently commissioned, had fewer problems than many of the older ships, she still suffered her share of woe as the undermanned, undertrained, underexperienced, and underprovisioned armada limped across the seven seas. As executive officer—"ship's sheriff"—Facchetti filled the traditional role of captain's hatchet man and was, therefore, *ex officio*, friendless. Gehlman, of course, was his companion in isolation, and since the ship's guns were little more than ornaments on this topsy-turvy cruise, the two of them were able to socialize discreetly with one another without fear of compromising Facchetti's position; by the time the cruise ended in December 1908, they were close friends.

The anger and resentment Benjamin had felt in connection with his new assignment as observer had been tempered marginally by the knowledge that at least he would again see Walter, who was now a captain and the deputy U.S. naval attaché in Berlin. But he had not expected to see him so far from the Wilhelmstrasse. "What the hell are you doing in Zurich, if it isn't too disrespectful to ask?"

"I've come to head you off, old son. Now let's get your bags off that train."

"Head me off?"

"Heavy squalls, my boy, heavy squalls. All will be revealed shortly. But right now we have to hustle if we're going to catch the Hamburg train." He raised his palm to forestall further questions. "Yes, Hamburg. You're going straight to Wilhelmshaven without kissing the Kaiser's hand first. Now let's move it. We've only got five minutes."

Loaded down with Gehlman's luggage, they barely made it to the rear carriage of the Hansa express before the conductors slammed the doors. Then they had to struggle the length of the train to reach the compartment Facchetti had reserved. "Whew!" he said once they got there. "I'm done for." He closed the door, pulled the curtains, and plopped himself down on the seat. Gehlman stripped off his hat and overcoat and lifted his suitcases onto the overhead rack. Then he sat down facing his friend. "So?"

Facchetti gave him a big grin. "Welcome to the war zone," he said. "Would you like the whole story from the beginning?"

Gehlman nodded.

"Right then. You shall have it. The beginning is that whoever handled this thing in the States sure as hell knew what he was doing."

Gehlman permitted himself a sour smile. "Oh? How so?"

"He—or they—asked us to get Admiral von Müller in on the act, and he's just about the only man in Germany who could have sold the Kaiser on the idea of an American observer with the High Seas Fleet."

"Von Müller is Chief of Wilhelm's Naval Cabinet, right?"

"Right—and the one high-ranking naval officer who actually cares about staying on good terms with the U.S.A."

"There's only one?"

"Oh, there are a few admirals who don't mind being courteous to us as long as it doesn't involve any inconvenience, but Müller's the only one who thinks our friendship is a matter of importance."

"So Müller 'sold' the Kaiser?"

"He did a good deal more than that, *mein schatz*. He got Admiral Hipper to consent to your attachment to the scouting forces, he got

Wilhelm's approval for the assignment in writing, and he worked so quickly and quietly that nobody picked up the scent."

"Until . . . ?"

"Exactly. Until. Yesterday morning I arrive in my office. I find a message to call one of my friends at the State Marine *Amt*. He tells me, in muted tones, that Grand Admiral von Tirpitz has just heard about the observer plan and is in the process of hitting the ceiling and all four walls. So! I scurry down to see Ambassador Gerard. We plot and scheme. We hatch a plan. Disguised as a thick-coated land animal I am stealthily secreted aboard the two o'clock Alpen express. Sixteen hours later—*voilà!*"

"*Voilà* . . . what?"

"*Voilà*, you are now en route to Wilhelmshaven and the SMS *Seydlitz*. *Voilà*, you are no longer en route to Berlin, where the dreadful many-headed Tirpitz lies in wait."

Gehlman laughed.

"The ambassador and I figured it like this," Facchetti continued, patently pleased by the laughter. "If we don't head you off, Tirpitz will delay you in Berlin on any number of pretexts until he can get at the Kaiser, who always follows the advice of the person who's spoken to him most recently. *Sic finis* Operation Gehlman. If, on the other hand, we do head you off, we can get you to Hamburg on the day Tirpitz is laying his traps for you, and to Wilhelmshaven on the day he plans to spring them. In other words, we can *insert* you into the High Seas Fleet even as Tirpitz is plotting to keep you from it, and once you're inserted he won't be able to dislodge you except at the price of a diplomatic incident, which the Foreign Office won't let him pay."

"Very impressive," said Gehlman, deadpan. "And altogether devious and dishonorable."

Facchetti grinned broadly. "It is, isn't it? And they all take us for such hayseeds over here."

It was eight thirty at night when Gehlman and Facchetti arrived in Hamburg, and nine by the time they checked in at the Atlantic Hotel. They sent their hats and coats upstairs with their luggage and went directly in to dine. A light blue envelope had been awaiting Facchetti at the desk, and as soon as they were seated and had placed their orders he ripped it open and read the enclosure. Apparently satisfied, he then crumpled the letter into a ball and tossed it into the nearby fireplace, where it was rapidly consumed. "They haven't been idle at the embassy," he said in response to Gehlman's interrogative gaze. "They've gotten you the ideal billet."

"Billet? I thought I was going to the *Seydlitz?*"

"You are, *mon fils*, never fear. But you won't want to live on her."

Gehlman's brow furrowed. "I'm confused, frankly."

"Very crude accommodations on board. No *ton*. No *chic*."

"Oh, come on, Wally."

"I'm serious. The High Seas Fleet is fitted out for service in the North Sea and the Baltic—home waters. While we and the British are sailing around all over the planet, the officers of the German Navy are hardly ever more than a day or two from port. So when they're at sea everybody more or less roughs it. And when they're not at sea they live ashore, which is to say, in billets."

"Very sensible," said Gehlman, for some reason feeling a little uneasy at the prospect. "And you say they've gotten me a good one?"

"I said ideal, with an option on sublime. You are to be a guest in the house of—excuse me, in *one* of the houses of—Regina, Gräfin von Lutwitz zu Mecklenberg-Hagenau, widow and mother of Erzherzog Rudolph of Aachen, lady-in-waiting to the Empress Augusta Victoria, present wife of Fregattenkapitän Baron Sigismund von Tiel, millionairess several times over, proprietress of vast estates, thirty-seven years old, and one of the handsomest women I've ever gaped at with my mouth open whenever Eileen wasn't looking."

"I know the type," said Gehlman, almost managing to keep a straight face in the process. Facchetti bellowed with laughter.

"And her husband is in the navy?"

"Yes. Siggy von Tiel. Interesting character. His mother is English, it seems, and he studied at Cambridge for a couple of years after dazzling all his Herr Professors at Göttingen. He could have had an academic career, but he had his heart set on the navy, the fool. Anyway, he rose fast at first, but the pace seems to have slowed in recent years, and there's been talk that he's a little—you know—erratic. Seems his marriage to the Gräfin may have destabilized him a bit, as well it might."

"When did he marry her?"

"Oh, five, six years ago. But don't get me wrong. He's not foaming at the mouth or anything like that. If Hipper's kept him on as first gunnery officer on the *Seydlitz* he's got to be pretty steady. It's just that one hears talk."

"Perhaps Admiral Hipper doesn't listen when he hears it," said Gehlman, joking in an attempt to shake off a sudden eerie sensation of fear.

1915, 22D JANUARY—SOUTHAMPTON

Maltbie had an altogether unmilitary desire to sing as the *Mauretania* swung slowly to her berth at Southampton. To be back in England on such a winter's morning—clean twenty-knot wind whipping down from the northwest, sun gaudily flaring to the east, cold clear air and bird's-egg sky on all points of the compass—he almost doubted it could be the same England he had last seen four years before: gray, frigid, with that corrosive dampness that lodged in the joints of one's bones. Then he had been a lieutenant on the *Minnesota*, and his captain, William Sims, had just pledged Britain "every man, every dollar, every drop of blood of your kindred across the sea," in case the Hun attacked. Damned right! thought Maltbie now. And *I* am the first installment.

Lieutenant Colonel Squier was waiting at the dock—a prim, boyish-looking man whose military mustache, if anything, accentuated his boyishness. Maltbie too had experimented unsuccessfully with facial plumage in an effort to look his age, and he saw in Squier a kindred spirit. (Squier in turn thought Maltbie looked rather young.)

"Commander Symington sends his apologies," the colonel said, referring to the naval attaché. "He was invited to sit in on some prize court proceedings, and with the number of American ships being stopped these days, Ambassador Page thought he had better go."

"I'm sorry to miss him," Maltbie responded. "But it's a real honor meeting you."

Squier blushed vividly. "Yes . . . well . . ."

"I'm in signals myself so I knew about your radiotelegraph work. But then Colonel House told me you'd actually spent five weeks at the front and—"

"He shouldn't have told you that." Squier was frowning.

"No, no. He made it clear that it was confidential information. He

just thought you could give me some guidance on a foreign observer's role."

Squier's frown softened. "Oh, I see. Well . . . yes . . . I see. Look,
there's an embassy motor waiting to take us to London; do you mind
if we don't talk about it until we're under way?"

"No, of course not," said Maltbie, mortified to have put his foot
wrong so soon, but at a loss to understand wherein he had sinned.

"It takes a lot of getting used to," said Squier once they were on
the road. The partition was up between them and the driver, and
there was plenty of room between back seat and front. "You more or
less have to assume that you're being listened to when you're out in
public. You're not, of course, but the atmosphere here is so loaded,
and the spy danger is just plausible enough. So the better part of wisdom is extreme discretion."

"I see," said Maltbie. "I'm sorry."

"No, no. You couldn't have known. I don't think any American
can imagine how far things have gone here. It's madness really, the
hatred and suspicion—and something entirely new. I don't think
even the Civil War was this bitter."

"You make it sound grim."

"It *is* grim. At the front you get some respite from the hating because the front is such hell you don't think of it—and you know the
enemy is suffering just as much as you are. But among the civilians—
the 'home front,' as they're starting to call it—why, it's staggering the
venom people spit. Simply staggering. And now, with these zeppelin
raids . . ."

Squier lapsed into a gloomy silence and Maltbie gazed out at the
Hampshire countryside feeling uncomfortable and annoyed. Why
had they sent such a sour old crape hanger down to meet him anyway.

"Oh, yes," said the colonel suddenly. "Here's a letter that came
for you care of the embassy."

Maltbie had to restrain himself from snatching it out of Squier's
hand. It was postmarked Santa Fe, New Mexico, January 11. He
carefully prised it open.

11.1.15, Monday

Darling Harry,

Do you know that my eyes go all blurry whenever I write that—
darling Harry.

There! I've dried them and gotten a grip on myself. . . .

I had to stop then because I really started blubbering. Oh Harry, I shall never forgive you for not being with me these past few days! We went on horseback up to Taos and the Sangre de Cristo Mountains—myself, Professor Kidder, a Mr. Bridger (whose father was someone very famous in these parts, I'm told), Father Dessault (a wonderful old Dominican), and our guide, an Acoma Indian named Desmond Brown Bear, or Desmond Brown as he calls himself in Santa Fe, or Desmond B. Bear as he signs his name, or Des as he is referred to far and wide.

Taos was fascinating, but then we rode up into the mountains! I didn't know it could get so cold—or so breathtaking. We went to the site of an old cliff settlement high on a saddle between two peaks. We started before dawn and the men had icicles all over their beards, just from breathing, and Des made me wear a fur mask to keep my cheeks and nose from falling off. But Harry, the *experience!* We had to climb the last 200 feet with ropes and pickaxes, and just when we got to the ruins the sun came up over the near peak and we could see—forever. Mountains and pine forests and snow fields and then endless endless prairie stretching away to infinity. And the silence, Harry, the *silence!* No wind, no bird, no sound of man or nature—*nothing!* Oh, how I longed for you to be there with me. I started crying—and the tears froze! And one or two tears got my mask wet. Father Dessault—I've told him all about you—saw me snuffling and said, "Ah yes, it is not zee experience tzat is shared but zee sharing tzat is zee experience." And that made me cry even more.

I felt like such a fool, because I was really crying for joy—and for missing you. But now, darling Harry, there is a big black spot on my right cheek where my tears got my mask wet. Professor Kidder says that it's not serious but that it will leave a scar. I plan to call it the Harris Edward Maltbie Blubber Memorial, as you were responsible for it by your absence. (No you weren't, dear angel; I would have cried harder still if you had been there.)

My darling, I'm getting the paper wet again. I'm so happy and I miss you so terribly. Don't dare let anything happen to you—*and wear the talisman!*

All my love, always,
Melina

Maltbie looked up from the letter as though waking from a trance.

What had he done, he wondered, to merit the benison called Melina Bellamy. How and when had he stumbled into God's favor.

Other young women he'd known had been hobbled from birth by the dictates of respectability. Some had been bright and accomplished, others winsome and beguiling. But they'd all seemed deceitful and parasitic as Harry watched them prowl the shallow waters of petit-bourgeois society in search of young providers to replace their fathers. It wasn't like him to be so cynical, but having survived as a bachelor into his thirties, he'd seen too much of the mating ritual to discount its many hypocrisies. He'd lost count, for example, of the number of times he'd heard an eligible young lady vehemently disclaim any interest in marriage, only to send him a triumphal announcement of her engagement less than six months later. And he'd also noticed how young women famed for their abrasiveness and acerbity became progressively more docile and submissive with each birthday after the twenty-first, and how spinsters, losing hope, became progressively more militant about their chastity with each birthday after the thirtieth, as if to suggest that they'd *chosen* celibacy over the sordid indignities of the marital bed. Compared to these ladies, the prostitutes of Chefoo and Chemulpo that he had been with seemed far more honest, and in the long run far far less expensive. And even if he'd realized that his harsh assessment of women's motives had come straight from the mouth of his father, there would still have been enough of justice in his verdict to warrant vigilance and doubt.

Melina, however, seemed struck from a different mold. Her cheerful outspokenness, her fierce independence, and above all her candid sensuality set her apart in the annals of Maltbie's experience. She had never disclaimed interest in marriage, but she'd displayed an almost masculine suspicion of it. And as for the likelihood of her becoming more docile and submissive as she got older, Maltbie thought it far more likely that she would turn more piquant.

He was aware, of course, that Melina's parents were "comfortable," whereas most of the women he'd known had come from the ranks of the marginally genteel. Melina, in other words, was provided for, and didn't *need* a husband the way the others did. This, he was honest enough to acknowledge, might be a significant facet of her appeal. But then so, to a greater degree, was the fact that she didn't "need" a husband in any other manner either. She was all right on her own, and if she wanted a husband for any reason, Maltbie was confident that she could find one much better than him.

That fact, in the final analysis, was what made her so entrancingly desirable.

Number 6 Grosvenor Square was a neat four-story building of white limestone and red brick with a frontage of about forty feet. It stood in a row of houses of similar dimensions on the west side of the square, its only pretension to embassy-hood being a small portico over the front door supported by two fluted Doric pillars. The ambassador's office was on the second floor, and Maltbie was struck by how simple and small it was compared to Spring Rice's near-opulent quarters in Washington. The ambassador himself reminded Maltbie of Andy Gump, with his whisk-broom mustache and meager chin. But there was nothing Gumpish about Walter Page's personality, and the ambassador soon had Maltbie at his ease and talking animatedly about his mission, about Colonel House, about "home"— which Page appeared to miss sorely—and about the war. In connection with the latter subject, Maltbie mentioned that the captain of the *Mauretania* had flown American flags from her mainmast and ensign staff all the way up the Channel.

"I daresay he did," Page commented owlishly. "Wouldn't you have, in his place?"

"Well, sir, I don't know. I suppose it's a legitimate *ruse de guerre*, but what's the point of it? The Germans wouldn't deliberately sink a *passenger* ship."

"You think not?" said Page with a frown. "Well, God grant you're right. But I wouldn't put any money on it, especially after Tuesday's demonstration of German *Kultur* over Norfolk."

"You mean the zeppelin raids, sir? There was a bulletin about them in the ship's newspaper yesterday, but no details."

"Well, Commander, the details are that a squadron of German airships swept across the North Sea and dropped bombs on such menacing military bastions as Yarmouth, Sheringham, King's Lynn, Cromer, and Beeston, killing and wounding several dozen innocent civilians in the process. Having burnt Louvain to the ground and blasted Scarborough and Hartlepool from the sea, the Huns no doubt felt that their air service deserved its chance at an atrocity too."

Maltbie shook his head in dismay. "How can they do things like that? They must be mad."

"They're worse than mad, Commander—they're Prussian. They're so obsessed with the notion of primitive brute force that they actually believe that it can be used to intimidate entire nations. They have absolutely no understanding of the Anglo-Saxon mentality, no idea whatsoever of the spirit of defiance their bullying produces. And *that's* why I wouldn't feel safe for a second if I were the captain of a British ocean liner, and why I'd fly American flags from every davit and masthead on the ship."

"I see what you mean, sir," Maltbie said. "But from the American point of view, isn't flying the flag an infringement of our neutrality?"

Page's eyes narrowed slyly. "Yes, I suppose it is, if we know about it."

"Sir?"

"Are you familiar with the law, Commander Maltbie? I mean, the *Law*, with a capital 'L'?"

"No sir, not very."

"Me neither, but I've heard tell that there's a fundamental legal concept called 'notice.' Now, if I were officially on notice that the British were using our flag to disguise the nationality of their ships, I'd have to protest, and so would Washington. But no one has officially notified me yet, and no one short of the German Government is going to notify me either if I can help it. So I don't know about this *ruse de guerre* of theirs, and not knowing about it, I can't protest about it."

"But, sir, forgive me . . . but . . ."

Page smiled. "Go ahead, Commander. Speak your mind."

"Well sir, if the Allies use our flag and the Germans catch on to what they're doing, they'll start treating American merchantmen like Allied merchantmen, maybe even start sinking them."

"Good point, Commander. But before they do that, they'll *notify* us of what the Allies are doing, and we'll protest vociferously and put a stop to it."

Page sat back with a broad grin on his face as Maltbie struggled to look edified and enlightened. Finally he laughed and said, "I don't blame you for feeling uncomfortable about this masquerade, Commander. I sometimes do myself. But look at it another way. Let's say I protest now, before I have to. What will happen? Maybe nothing. Maybe England will stop using our flag and Germany *won't* start sinking her ships. But bear in mind that the *Mauretania,* the *Aqui-tania,* the *Lucitania,* the *Olympic,* the *Britannic,* and several dozen other liners are all subject to Admiralty control, and that provision has been made for them to be armed. Bear in mind too that these ships are as big and as fast as battle cruisers and could probably be converted to use as troop transports on only a few weeks' notice. Now, given the Germans' demonstrated concern for human life and their demonstrated respect for international law and morality, I'd say they have all the pretext they need to send one of these liners to the bottom, wouldn't you? And if they do sink one of them it's almost certain that a good many of the Americans who will be on board will die. And if a good many Americans die, a good many more Americans in Congress might vote to avenge them. And that is why I don't want to know about the ruse before I have to. If flying the Stars and Stripes helps keep these ships from being torpedoed, then I say long may it wave. Much as I'd like to see the Germans whipped, and much as I deplore Washington's niggling hair-splitting notions of neutrality, I still shudder at the thought of us being sucked into this awful conflagration. The longer you are over here, Commander, and the more you see and hear, the more you will thank God for putting the Atlantic Ocean between us and Europe."

"I don't doubt you're right, sir," said Maltbie. "A young British—uh—person of my acquaintance said that the war was a *totentanz,* a dance of death."

Page's features knitted together into a scowl. "I'm familiar with the phrase, Commander, and the sentiment. And I would be willing to wager that this 'person' you mentioned is related in some fashion to two noted British archaeologists."

Startled, Maltbie blushed. "Yes sir. But how did . . . ?"

"How did I know about you and Miss Bellamy? I knew because the young lady's uncle, Sir Cecil Spring Rice, thought it important for me to be aware that the newly designated American observer with the British Fleet was emotionally involved with the daughter of two of England's most prominent pacifists."

Maltbie sucked in his breath.

"You act surprised, Commander," said Page. "Didn't you know about Miss Bellamy's parents?"

"Well, yes sir. Meli—Miss Bellamy told me they were against the war. But I didn't realize they were opposing it politically."

"Oh, I wouldn't say they were opposing it. They're just rather vociferously not supporting it. They're in the Bertrand Russell camp down at Cambridge, and as a result have made themselves rather unpopular in many formerly adulatory academic circles. Fortunately, though, they haven't made much of an impression on public opinion as of yet. If they had done, I'm afraid your assignment to the Grand Fleet would have been in serious jeopardy."

Involuntarily, Maltbie winced.

"Even as it is," Page continued, "if Spring Rice had raised the subject with House or with someone at the State Department instead of with me, there'd almost certainly be some other officer sitting where you're sitting now. But since he's very fond of his niece—and apparently doesn't think too badly of you either—he confined himself to writing me privately about the miniature *entente cordiale* the two of you are involved in. He didn't want your relationship with Miss Bellamy to be clouded over with political complications, you see, but he felt that I had better know about it, especially in case you were planning to pay Sir Lloyd and Dame Margaret a call. . . . Were you?"

Feeling vaguely like a criminal, Maltbie for an instant considered lying. But then he admitted, "Yes, sir, I was—time permitting. But I assure you I had no idea . . ."

"Of course, of course," said Page in an understanding tone. "You had no way of knowing that visiting them might compromise your mission and embarrass your government. That's precisely why Ambassador Spring Rice wrote me as he did: so the danger could be avoided. He's as well aware as I am that the United States isn't all that popular over here at the moment, what with our constant complaints about Britain's maritime policies and our apparent blindness to the fact that she's fighting for her life against a militaristic juggernaut that threatens us almost as much as it does any of the Allies. Happily for all concerned, however, the British government values our friendship very highly and is bending over backward to respect our point of view in the face of adverse public opinion. But you can see how much more difficult its task would be if an American naval officer attached to His Majesty's Fleet were to be found consorting with a pair of well-known British pacifists."

Maltbie was a bit intimidated by how forcefully Page was driving the point home; and when he reflected on how close he'd come to making a travesty of his assignment he was intimidated a good bit more.

From Grosvenor Square Maltbie and Squier walked to Green Park, then past Buckingham Palace and along the Mall toward the Admiralty. The Colonel's advice on observer protocol seemed to boil down to: keep your mouth shut and your eyes and ears open, and Maltbie was fully inclined to heed it. His first few hours in England had convinced him that the smooth course he'd been sailing since he'd met Melina and gotten his new assignment was in fact a course through waters infested with hidden mines, and he intended henceforth to proceed very cautiously indeed.

Outside the Admiralty, Squier shook his hand and said, "This is where we surrender jurisdiction over you. From now on you're the property of the Royal Navy." He gave Maltbie what was probably intended to be a look of encouragement but which came across more as an expression of grave misgiving. Then he turned and walked off in the direction they had come.

Maltbie gave his name to the marine at the Admiralty gate, and another marine promptly arrived to escort him upstairs. One flight up the second marine was relieved by a dour civilian in a cutaway who said, "If you will be so good as to accompany me, the First Lord will be glad to receive you presently." Maltbie followed the somberly elegant figure down a long dark corridor which seemed colder by several degrees than the cold air outside. His escort stopped in front of an unmarked door and gave it one curt rap. "Your luggage is on its way from your embassy," he announced as they awaited some response from inside. "With your permission we shall see to its proper disposition." Maltbie meekly nodded assent.

The door was opened by a middle-aged woman who managed a cheerful smile despite an appearance of utter exhaustion. "Lieutenant Commander Maltbie, madam," the cutaway intoned.

"Thank you, Wade," the woman replied. "Come in, Commander. Mr. Churchill is just up from his nap and asked me to show you right in. . . . I'll take your hat and coat, thank you. Now, if you'll just step this way . . ." She opened another door and led him into an office where three secretaries sat at three typewriters making a clatter like a battery of machine pistols. Yet another door was opened before him. He passed through it and found himself in a large, map-littered room. Churchill's desk was at the far end. Maltbie recognized the First Lord from photographs he had seen: sparse sandy hair, sharp eyes, pouting mouth. Admiral Fisher, looking very much like his nickname, "the old Malay," and a gaunt-looking Royal

Navy commander were standing beside the young politician's desk.

"Welcome," said Churchill, extending his hand. "I believe you've already had the honor of Lord Fisher's acquaintance once before."

"Yes sir," said Maltbie, turning to the old admiral. "How do you do, sir?"

"Fine, fine," said Fisher brusquely, as if the social amenities were obstructions to business. "May I introduce Commander Montague Reeves-Wadleigh of our Naval Secretariat."

"Pleased to meet you," said Maltbie, startled on closer observation by the close resemblance the commander bore to portraits of the young unbearded Lincoln.

"My pleasure," said Reeves-Wadleigh.

"So," said Churchill, gesturing Maltbie to a chair. "Did you have a good crossing?" Fisher and Reeves-Wadleigh remained standing.

"Yes sir. Pretty smooth considering the season."

"And how does my good Captain Sims?" Fisher intruded.

"Very well, sir. He asked particularly that I convey you his respects."

"He's a brainy fellow, is our William Sims. Did he ever tell you about Christmas Eve, '06?"

For a moment Maltbie thought that Fisher was referring to the Christmas Eve just past, and he experienced some anxiety and confusion. Had he and Melina been observed? Was kissing a young lady in the British Embassy in some way a diplomatic affront? But then the "'06" registered. "Nineteen six, sir? Why, yes. You mean the *Dreadnought*, don't you?"

"I mean the *Dreadnought*. Did you know that Sims was the only foreigner to see that ship before it was commissioned?"

"Yes sir. The captain has often remarked on how honored he felt by the special confidence you reposed in him."

"Do you know *why* I let Sims see the ship?"

"Uh, no sir. Not specifically."

"Because you Americans and we British are the lost tribes of Israel. Please remember that."

There was silence. Maltbie looked at Churchill and Reeves-Wadleigh for some sign that Fisher was joking, or perhaps just giving rein to his notoriously eccentric habits of self-expression. Their faces revealed nothing, however, and their eyes continued to study him, politely but with a rather disconcerting intensity. At last Churchill resumed the conversation. "I'm afraid you're going to have to more or less look out for yourself once you join Admiral Jellicoe," he said. "There are no supernumeraries aboard in time of war, and everyone is awfully busy."

This at least was talk Maltbie could make sense of. "I understand completely, sir. I don't expect to be looked after and I don't want to add to the admiral's burdens in any way. Frankly, I'm so delighted to have this opportunity to sail with the British Fleet that I'd be content to ride along behind the *Iron Duke* in a dinghy."

The three Britons exchanged quick covert glances. "Yes, well, we're pleased to have you with us," said Churchill. "We wondered, incidentally, whether you might like to stop off at Rosyth on your way up to Scapa and have a look at the battle cruisers."

Maltbie's heart jumped. Admiral Beatty's famous "cats." "Yes *sir!* I certainly would."

"Splendid," said Churchill. "We thought you might. We'll put you up at the Coburg tonight, if that suits you, and you can catch the *Flying Scotsman* first thing tomorrow morning."

"Thank you, sir. That sounds perfect."

"Good. One of our duty officers will serve as your escort this evening, and tomorrow we'll send a car round to take you to King's Cross." The First Lord stood up. "It's been a pleasure. I wish you the best of luck."

Somewhat dazed, but happily so, Maltbie shook hands all around and was ushered out.

"He seems amiable enough," said Churchill, once the three Englishmen were alone.

"Yes," said Fisher. "I remember him as being a nice young fellow."

Churchill pondered a moment. "Monty, are any of your men serving up at Scapa?"

"Yes, sir," said Reeves-Wadleigh. "Half a dozen or so, plus an officer."

"Good. Arrange with Jellicoe's chief of staff, will you, to have one of them detailed to keep an eye on our American guest; for the time being at any rate, just to make assurance doubly sure."

1915, 23D JANUARY—WASHINGTON, D.C.

House and Wilson had decided that the Colonel should return to Europe to explore the possibilities for peace, and now he had come to the White House to say good-bye.

As soon as he entered the President's second-floor library it was obvious to him that Wilson was in a sour frame of mind. The President had become increasingly short-tempered in recent weeks, increasingly impatient with obstructive congressmen and importunate diplomats. Both House and Dr. Grayson—who along with Wilson's daughters were exempt from presidential spleen—looked on his surliness as an encouraging sign, a healthy symptom of a reviving emotional involvement in affairs of state. His spirit seemed to be recovering at last from the trauma of Ellen Wilson's death.

When House appeared Wilson was seated at his desk reading, his right hand on his brow, his left hand holding a sheaf of papers, and his mouth set in a narrow irritated line. But when he saw the Colonel standing in the doorway the tension immediately left his face. "Ah, there you are, my friend," he said, rising to take House's proffered hand.

"Good evening, Governor," said the Colonel, using the term of address that had persisted as a symbol of their special intimacy. "You appear troubled."

Wilson's lips came together again, this time in a look of muted disgust which seemed directed as much at himself as at the world at large. " 'Peeved,' though less flattering, would be a more accurate description of my appearance and mental state. I've been deluged with irritants like *these* all day." He brandished the papers in his left hand. "Have a look at the beginning paragraphs of this one from Gerard," he said, extracting one of the documents, "and this one from our friend at the British Foreign Office."

House took the decoded telegram from the ambassador in Berlin along with the immaculately typed communication on British Embassy stationery and seated himself opposite the President's chair. He found Gerard's message alarmist and annoyingly naive:

I do not think the people in America [by which, House

silently interpolated, he means, "You, Mr. President, and your advisers"] realize how excited the Germans have become on the question of America selling munitions of war to the Allies. A veritable campaign of hate has been commenced against America and Americans. Under Secretary Zimmermann showed me a long list, evidently obtained by an effective spy system, of orders placed with American concerns by the Allies. He said that perhaps it was as well to have the whole world against Germany, and that in case of trouble there were five hundred thousand trained Germans in America who would join the Irish and start a revolution.

Trained Germans?! Zimmermann must have been temporarily deranged to mouth such absurdities.

I thought he was joking, but he was actually serious. Impossible as it seems to us, it would not surprise me to see this maddened nation-in-arms go to lengths however extreme.

House shook his head. If Gerard could be bluffed so easily, Zimmermann would be well advised to stop threatening him and start playing poker with him.

The Colonel turned to the message from the British Embassy, which was a transcription of a cable from Foreign Secretary Grey to Spring Rice on the subject of House's mission to Europe.

It will give me great pleasure to see Colonel House and talk to him freely. Of course, he understands that all that can be promised here is that if Germany seriously and sincerely desires peace, I will consult our friends as to what terms of peace are acceptable.

Before, however, setting out on his journey, it is as well that he should be informed as to the state of public opinion here. I fear it is becoming unfavorably and deeply impressed by the trend of action taken by the United States Government and by its attitude toward Great Britain. What is felt here is that while Germany deliberately planned a war of pure aggression, has occupied and devastated large districts in Russia, Belgium, and France, inflicting great misery and wrong on innocent populations, the

only act of record on the part of the United States is a protest against our trade-with-the-enemy policy singling out
Great Britain as the only Power whose conduct is worthy of
reproach.

In the struggle for existence in which this country is at
stake, much store is set in England on the goodwill of the
United States; and people cannot believe that the United
States desires to paralyse the advantage which we derive
from our sea power, while leaving intact to Germany those
military and scientific advantages which are special to her.

I think it is only fair that Colonel House should be
warned that should people in England come to believe that
the dominant influence in United States politics is German-
oriented, it would tend to create an untoward state of public opinion which we should greatly regret.

House looked up at the President. "Whoever said that the peace-
makers would be blessed?"

Wilson laughed. "Precisely. But the way things are going Germany and England may yet bury their differences in order to unite
against *us* as their common enemy. They're both being remarkably
unreasonable, I think. And I must say, Edward, your mission is going
to be singularly unprofitable if these dispatches reflect their true attitudes."

House nodded in agreement. "Well, it certainly wouldn't do to
start out with any rosy notions about our prospects; that seems clear.
For one thing, the Germans are being a bit too eager about peace at
the moment for me to be satisfied of their sincerity. Of course, I
would be eager myself if I had Belgium, Luxembourg, and a large
chunk of France under my heel. Peace talk would suit me just fine.
If the enemy agreed to discussions I could parley from a position of
strength, and if the enemy wouldn't play my game I could point the
finger at him and claim he was responsible for prolonging the war."

"Another reason I'm suspicious of Germany is these damnable
zeppelin raids. I practically begged Ambassador Bernstorff when I
was down here last week to get Berlin to stop the attacks while our
peace initiatives were being pursued. I even offered him the use of
the State Department cable. Well, he said he saw my point and
agreed with me and would do everything he could, and this week's
raid on Norfolk was the result. If that sort of thing is symbolic of

Germany's bona fides, then this war is going to be with us for a very long time to come."

"What's your assessment of the Allied point of view?" Wilson asked.

"Well, in these exploratory phases I've pretty much limited myself to testing the ground with the British alone. They of course are as alert as I am to the advantages Germany could derive from any talk of peace during this period of military stalemate, so they're wary to begin with. In addition, they seem to be preparing some sort of naval stroke against Turkey in the Mediterranean, and they're continuing to build up Kitchener's 'Million Army' for an offensive in the spring. So they probably prefer their prospects on the battlefield at the moment to their long odds at the conference table."

"Our peace mission appears to have many of the qualities of a forlorn hope, Edward," said Wilson, almost reproachfully.

"Many of the qualities, and all of the defects," House acknowledged. "But there are two aspects of the situation that are potentially encouraging. First, all the belligerents do sincerely want an end to the fighting, even if only on their own terms, and all of them do pretty sincerely believe that the war was in one way or another forced on them by their foes. In other words, none of them likes the mess they're in and all of them would welcome a way out of it if a way they regarded as acceptable could be found. Secondly, Sir Edward Grey has committed himself to bring pressure to bear on France and Russia for a settlement if Germany agrees to withdraw from and compensate Belgium. With all respect to Sir Edward, I doubt he would have made that commitment if he had felt there was any chance of Germany's even considering a withdrawal. But he did make it, and it stands out as the first concrete precondition for peace that either side has enunciated to date. My thinking is that by going over to Europe now I can perhaps get both sides to enunciate just a little bit more, even if only in private conversation. As things stand today, all of them believe that their adversaries are intent on their total destruction. But if we can get them to start articulating their points of difference, we may start them thinking in other terms than total victory and total defeat."

Wilson looked dubious, but House could see that the doubts were uncongenial to him. "Well," he said after an interval of reflection, "I don't suppose it can hurt us to find out what's what over there, even if we don't accomplish anything more than that. I tell you frankly, though, if it were anyone but you who was going I wouldn't take the risk. When do you sail?"

"A week from today, on the *Lusitania.*"

"And you're going back to New York this evening?"

"Yes. In just under an hour, in fact. There's a lot of business that needs clearing up before I leave."

Wilson smiled sadly. "We'll miss you."

Both men quickly looked down at the floor in a reflex of shyness and embarrassment.

"Oh yes," the President said, reaching for an envelope on his desk. "Here's the letter you asked me for."

The envelope was unsealed. House took out the letter, and immediately on reading "Dear Colonel House:" he recognized the characters of Wilson's Hammond typewriter. "You typed this yourself?"

"You may keep it as an heirloom after it's served its purpose," Wilson replied playfully. Then in a more serious tone he added, "The fewer people who know the real reason you're going to Europe, the better. Don't you agree?"

"Certainly."

House read through what the President had written. It pleased him, the final paragraph in particular:

> If we can be instrumental in ascertaining for each side in the contest what is the real disposition, the real wish, the real purpose of the other with regard to a settlement, your mission and my whole desire in this matter will have been accomplished.

"It's not the most elegant set of credentials with which a presidential emissary has ever gone off to the wars," Wilson said, "but it should answer."

"It's fine," said the Colonel. "Just fine."

"Now let's see: you sail on the thirtieth, which means you'll be in London when?"

"Saturday, the sixth."

"And you'll be seeing Grey . . . ?"

"Monday probably, or possibly Sunday."

"So I can expect a cable Tuesday."

"At the latest."

"Good. Now we've got our cipher. Yes, here's my copy. And you've arranged with my secretary about your expenses."

"Yes, but—"

Wilson raised his hand. "Not another word. You're entitled to an allowance, and you shall have one. Be thankful I don't insist on your taking a salary as well."

House acquiesced with a nod of thanks.

"So. What else is there?"

The Colonel glanced at his watch and said, "Leave-taking, I'm afraid, if I'm to catch my train."

The two men rose and shook hands. "Your friendship has meant a great deal to me, Edward," Wilson said solemnly and without preamble. "I can never thank you enough for all you've done, and are doing, to help me. I know I've been terribly remiss in my duties since Ellen died, but if I hadn't had you and Grayson to rely on I would have broken down completely. I owe you more than I can say. You're the only person I can really confide in and always count on for support."

House found himself blinking rapidly, and for the first time in a long time he felt the need to express his private feelings to another human being. "Mr. President," he said, "I've searched all my life for someone with whom I could work out the ideals I feel so deeply, but until I met you I despaired of finding him, and I was sure my life had been a failure and that all I'd ever done was futile and vain. Your friendship has given me a purpose and a cause. It is I who am in your debt. It is you who are helping me."

House and Wilson looked into each other's eyes and then quickly down at their clasped hands. The Colonel could not remember when he had last been so moved.

How good it was to do good, he reflected, in this best of all possible worlds.

1915, 23D JANUARY—THE BATTLE CRUISER FORCE

The conductor punched Maltbie's Admiralty transport voucher and handed him a small printed handbill. "Welcome aboard the *Flying Scotsman*," it read. "For over fifty years the train in which you are now travelling has connected Britain's 'Athens of the North'—or

'Auld Reekie' as the Scots call their smoky capital—with the great metropolis of London. It was in 1862 that the first *Flying Scotsman* sped the 393 miles between King's Cross and Waverley Stations. The trip took ten-and-one-half hours then. But today, with modernised track and improved methods of steam locomotion, it takes barely eight. May you have a pleasant journey on this, one of the 'premier' express trains of the world."

"It's the American influence!" declared the other passenger in the compartment, a flushed-looking elderly gentleman whose expression suggested a lifetime's application to the taking of offense.

"Pardon?" said Maltbie in a meek voice.

"The American influence," the flushed-looking gentleman repeated angrily, waving his copy of the handbill as if it were a miniature U.S. flag he had caught flying from a British flagpole. "Drum beating! Tub thumping! Blowing one's own horn! As if I didn't already know what train I was traveling on. Monstrous presumption! It's the American influence!"

Maltbie nodded in agreement and smiled weakly, thankful he was in civilian clothes. But the elderly gentleman was squinting at him suspiciously, as if a nonverbal response to his expressed indignation was culpably lacking in spirit. Maltbie thrashed around in his brain for a British-sounding phrase of affirmation that could be uttered without revealing an American accent. Finally he came out with an emphatic, "Quite right!" which appeared to mollify his traveling companion.

But only somewhat.

Maltbie quickly buried his eyes in the illustrated magazines he had bought at the King's Cross newsagent's kiosk as the elderly gentleman continued to glare at him with bulging eyes. After several tense moments the man delivered himself of a final "Monstrous!" and snatched open his copy of *The Times*. Behind the redoubt of his own periodicals Maltbie let out a long sigh of relief.

Beatty and his battle cruisers seemed to be featured in every magazine Maltbie had bought, the admiral being one of the few popular heroes the war had generated who was not yet dead. Every feature extolled his courage in leading the *Lion*, the *Invincible*, the *Queen Mary*, the *Princess Royal*, and the *New Zealand* into the Heligoland Bight back in August. "That valorous charge into the very teeth of the German shore batteries," as one account put it, "spelled doom for three Hun cruisers, one Hun destroyer, and over a thousand Hun seamen."

Of course Maltbie, like every other naval officer in the world, already knew the Beatty story by heart: his gunboat exploits on the Nile in '96 and '98 during Kitchener's campaign against the Khalifa; his wounds sustained in the Boxer fighting during the relief of the Peking legations in 1900; his early promotions—to captain at twenty-nine and rear admiral at thirty-eight—unheard of since Nelson's time; his beautiful American wife, the daughter of Chicago's Marshall Field; and his receipt from Churchill of the Royal Navy's plum command—the battle cruisers, the *arme blanche*, the cavalry of the fleet. Even those navy men who disapproved of Beatty's somewhat swashbuckling style acknowledged his right to claim the four Nelsonic "aces": leadership, tactical imagination, openness to new ideas, and attacking spirit. Many British officers even shared Maltbie's tendency to think of him as already more than half a legend, and it gave Harry a slightly giddy feeling to know that he was soon going to meet the fabled admiral face to face. First, however, he had to get to Edinburgh without being exposed as an "American influence" by his atrabilious compartment-mate.

As the train pulled into York he saw that luck was with him. The red-faced gentleman rose abruptly, put on his overcoat as if he were punching holes in it, folded and refolded his *Times* as if he expected Maltbie to dispute possession, snatched up his briefcase, yanked open the door, nodded curtly, and stalked out.

The sudden drop in tension was almost palpable, and with the compartment to himself and only the gray winter landscape to divert him once the train pulled out of York, Maltbie dozed. It was dark outside the next time he opened his eyes, and the conductor was in the corridor calling, "Edinburgh."

Maltbie leaned out the window and watched as the train coughed its way into the grimy maw of Waverley Station. Yellowed light bulbs in wire frames secreted a grudging vapor of illumination over the platforms, and on every side he noticed grim-faced naval officers striding hurriedly, or in some cases running, in the direction of signs and arrows that read DALMENY—N. QUEENSFERRY VIA BRIDGE.

A sense of intense urgency immediately constricted his throat; officers did not run—except toward the rumor of battle. He snatched his overnight bag off the rack and was out the compartment door the moment the train's speed made it feasible to jump. He ran hard to the barrier, had his voucher punched, and looked around frantically for some sign of an escort. A tap on his shoulder made him start, and he spun around.

"Hi ho," said a small round RNVR lieutenant with a ruddy baby-fat face. "You're Lieutenant Commander Maltbie and I'm Morrison Waite." He spoke like someone supplying the answer to a hitherto insoluble riddle, and his blue eyes twinkled with complacent effrontery.

"Uh, yes," Maltbie responded. "Pleased to meet you. But how did you know who I was?"

"Well, a moment's glance at you suffices to reveal that you're American," Waite answered cheerily. (Recalling the red-faced gentleman, Maltbie cringed.) "And in all other respects you correspond to the description supplied us by the Admiralty."

"Oh, then you're from the *Lion?*"

"From the *Lion*'s mouth. I have the honor to serve—in an as yet unspecified capacity—on the staff of Acting Vice Admiral Sir David Beatty, KCB, DSO, MVO, who sends you his compliments together with my person and suggests that you repair aboard his flagship while the repairing is good, if you'll excuse the inelegancy of expression."

"I will," said Maltbie, amused but also a little taken aback by Waite's unmilitary bearing. "Show me the way."

They joined the crowd of officers streaming toward the Dalmeny platform. Maltbie ached to know what was going on, but after his experiences in London he was diffident about asking questions. His escort needed no prompting, however. "What you are witnessing here," said Waite with bland detachment, "is the last stage of the classic transition from a 'buzz' through a 'flap' to a 'panic.'"

"Oh?" said Maltbie, trying to sound only politely interested.

"Yes. The buzz got started about an hour ago when dense smoke was observed issuing from the funnels of the battle cruisers. The flap followed soon thereafter when inquiries at the North British and Caledonian Hotels revealed that a recall was in progress and that steam was in fact being raised. Now one can detect the near imminence of the panic, as sublieutenants and captains, paymasters and engineers alike, put aside the wanton indulgences of an Edinburgh Saturday afternoon and flock with anxious mien in the direction of Hawes Pier, each man tortured by private visions of missing his ship and thereby missing the show."

"You don't appear very tortured."

"Ah, but I *know*, my dear fellow. I know when and whether the Battle Cruiser Force will sail; and knowledge is the prime antidote for anxiety. Besides, Admiral Beatty could hardly set out to settle Fritz's hash without the services of one who has the honor to serve in an as yet unspecified capacity upon his staff."

"I'll take your word for it," said Maltbie with a grin; and he did feel somewhat reassured by the little lieutenant's cocky self-importance.

A train came and the officers crowded aboard. The twenty-minute trip to Dalmeny passed in almost total silence; even Waite seemed to bow to the tension in the air. Apparently "missing the show" was something one did not even talk about.

Hawes Pier presented a surreal picture on their arrival: a single electric light bulb set ten feet up a metal pole glared down on a cluster of dark-clad figures waiting soundlessly for transportation to their vessels. The megalithic girders of the Forth Bridge towered up behind the silent company, black against the blackness of the sky. Out in the channel searchlights blinked in random allusive patterns, and the smell of the North Sea ran cold and pungent from the east.

Maltbie was awestruck. Before him stood forty or fifty officers of the Battle Cruiser Force, stranded within hailing distance of their ships, knowing that each minute saw their prospects of getting aboard grow dimmer—yet silent, rock still, implacable, their will to battle flashing like furnace steel in the iron tongs of their self-control. He remembered other moments spent waiting for harbor craft: at Hampton Roads, Guantanamo, Bremerton, Mare Island, Balboa, Pearl Harbor, Wei-hai-wei, Cavite—but always there'd been chatter, either aimless banter about one's time ashore or, if the admiral was present, sober-sounding ruminations about such matters as the faulty generator on B Deck or the commendable accuracy of the new Schuette recording compass. Never before had he experienced this silence, this single-minded intensity of anticipation. There was a quality of compelling eloquence about it, a strong sense of the professional elite, that was uniquely Royal Navy. It was a feeling that Maltbie had missed with the less-than-prestigious naval service of the United States, and it thrilled him to be part of it now, thrilled him so deeply that even his love for Melina seemed muted by comparison. As the fellowship of arms settled over him he felt truly fulfilled, and he gave thanks to fate for having brought him so swiftly to the war.

The first steam pinnace to appear took off about a dozen officers for the light cruisers. The second carried away ten destroyer men. Maltbie and the other twenty or so officers destined for the battle cruisers now began consulting their watches with increasing agitation. "Damn!" said one eventually, breaking the spell, and "Bloody hell!" another. But "Steady on," came a low voice from behind them, and the four gold stripes on the speaker's sleeve brought silence again to the group on the pier.

At last the *Lion's* picket boat materialized out of the darkness. "Whew!" said Waite. "I was beginning to think the admiral had forgotten who the indispensables were." His tone revealed that he had been as anxious as everyone else.

The pinnace churned out into the Forth, and after about ten minutes hove to alongside a huge black silhouette, which Maltbie guessed to be a battle cruiser of the *Invincible* class. Several officers clambered over the side and disappeared up an accommodation ladder.

Next in line was an equally imposing profile with the name *New Zealand* discernible on its quarterdeck screen, and after that came an even larger ship, a *Lion* class superdreadnought, one of the "big cats."

Now the only passengers in the pinnace were Maltbie, Waite, and the deep-voiced captain who had uttered the "steady on." The captain had been darting furtive glances in Maltbie's direction since the boat left the quay. He seemed bashful and embarrassed, and rather conflicted as well. It was clear that he felt an obligation to speak to Maltbie, but it was equally clear that the prospect of gratuitously addressing a perfect stranger caused him considerable anguish. Finally, one could see, he made the mental resolve to subordinate his private comfort to the dictates of duty. "Would I be correct in assuming that you are the American naval officer the admiral is expecting?" he asked with a self-conscious smile that gave an engagingly boyish cast to his features.

"Yes sir," said Maltbie promptly, knowing from personal experience how painful an affliction shyness could be, and in fact *was* at that very moment. "Lieutenant Commander Harris Maltbie," he recited, and then, because it sounded British, somehow, "at your service."

It sounded silly, somehow.

The captain visibly suppressed a startled reaction to the incongruous turn of phrase. "Taylor's my name," he said. "Charles Taylor. I see to the BCF's engines."

There was an awkward silence, then Taylor resumed, "Just arrived from London?"

"Yes sir," said Maltbie, adding irrelevantly, "on the *Flying Scotsman*."

"Waite here looking after you properly?"

"Yes sir. Yes indeed. I've already learned the difference between a buzz, a flap, and a panic."

Taylor smiled broadly. "I'm not sure I know that myself, they come so often in their various forms. But perhaps this time there really will be a show."

"The admiral seems sure of it," Waite chipped in.

Taylor gave a small sigh and looked across the water. "Well, let's hope he's right," he said. Then, turning back to Maltbie, "As you may know, we've had five months of nothing but 'alarums and excursions' since the Heligoland action. I've lost track of the number of sweeps we've made over toward Jutland and up toward Norway only to learn in the end that the Germans were still skulking in the Jade. Even when they do come out they don't stand and fight. It's most irritating."

"I can imagine," said Maltbie truthfully.

"Well, now you're here, perhaps you'll change our luck."

"I certainly hope so, sir."

The pinnace drew up alongside another superdreadnought, and Taylor made ready to disembark. "Uh, by the way, Maltbie, I've asked Chatfield, the flag captain, to let you have my cabin on the *Lion*. Please make yourself at home there, and try some of the brandy in my sea chest if you start feeling the chill."

Maltbie was astonished. "Your cabin, sir? But I couldn't think of . . ."

Taylor jumped up onto the accommodation ladder, then bent down and shook Maltbie's hand. "Welcome to the fleet," he said, his craggy patriarchal features matching the warmth of his voice. "There's some not-bad claret too," he called over his shoulder as he disappeared up the clifflike side of the hull.

"Nice chap, Taylor," said Waite as the pinnace pulled away. "Engineer for the whole BCF. He's berthed on the *Tiger* at the moment because she just joined us in November and hasn't quite figured herself out. Plus she's got a very mixed bag of a crew. Plus also—*entre nous*—her captain's a bit of an ass."

"I see British engineer officers wear purple between their sleeve stripes," Maltbie said, carefully sidestepping Waite's tender of wardroom gossip.

"Yes," said the lieutenant, "and the paymasters wear white." He peered out into the darkness ahead of them. "But you'll never see an engineer or a paymaster in command of something like *that*."

Following Waite's gaze, Maltbie saw another monster silhouette looming out of the night, and as they drew nearer he could make out a red-and-white vice admiral's flag rippling gently at the foremast.

It was Beatty's *Lion*.

Even in the semidarkness of the compass platform Maltbie could tell who it was. Hat visor canted down over the right eye, hands flat inside the jacket pockets, thumbs out, elbows flaring rearward—the stance was unmistakable. He was not a very large figure, but in profile he had the aura of a hawk, and seen full face, his features eerily illuminated by the dim light of the binnacle, he radiated an almost Mephistophelian magnetism. Maltbie had met many men who were impressive because they were admirals, many fewer who were admirals because they were impressive. This man was unquestionably in the second category, and near the top of it.

All at once Beatty turned and shot him a look of frank appraisal. It was little short of concussive, and the smile that supplanted it was more like a mandrill's show of teeth. Like many young officers before him, Maltbie fell instantly under the spell. Here at last was one legendary hero who more than lived up to his billing.

"Second Battle Cruiser Squadron and attached destroyers report ready to proceed, sir," said the officer of the watch.

"That everybody?"

"Yes sir."

"Very well. Signal First and Second Battle Cruiser Squadrons to unmoor and shorten in to three shackles."

"Aye sir."

Beatty glanced at his wrist. "Signal all squadrons to proceed out of harbor at five thirty-five."

"Aye sir. Five thirty-five."

Maltbie looked at his own watch. It said 5:23.

For several minutes Beatty conversed in low murmurs with a somber-looking officer whom Waite had identified as Alfred Chatfield, the flag captain. Then, "Signal all squadrons to take W/T guard on wavelengths specified."

"Aye sir."

"All squadrons. Pass north of May Island, then steer one-oh-six degrees. Speed from outer gate seventeen knots."

"Aye sir. One-oh-six degrees. Seventeen knots."

There was a subtle but steadily perceptible increase in tension as the minutes passed. Maltbie consulted his watch again. It was time. "All right, Edwards," Beatty said at that instant, turning to the navigating commander at the compass. "Take us out—and don't knock over the bloody bridge."

There was a breath of laughter on the platform.

"Senior officer to all squadrons and ships in company," said the admiral. "Weigh!"

Maltbie heard the clanging as the order was relayed down to the *Lion*'s engine room and forward to her forecastle. The low background rumbling and vibration rapidly intensified beneath his feet.

Beatty gave his final order. "All squadrons, cease W/T communication except on replying to the admiral, or to report having the enemy in sight."

Once they were under weigh and clear of the Forth Bridge, Beatty walked over to Maltbie and stretched out his hand. "Welcome, welcome, Mr. Maltbie. I believe you've brought us luck."

Maltbie was not accustomed to shaking hands with vice admirals on first acquaintance, much less to having them credit him with supernatural virtues. Being addressed as "Mister" was disconcerting, too, even though Maltbie knew that lieutenant commanders in the Royal Navy didn't rate the "commander" form of address used in the U.S. fleet. He started to salute, thought better of it, and ended up rather jerkily extending his hand to encounter Sir David's. "Luck, sir? I mean, thank you, sir. It's an honor to be here."

"An honor! More like a ruddy miracle. Do you realize that if you'd arrived yesterday you'd now be en route to Scapa, and that if you'd arrived tomorrow there'd have been no one here to greet you? There was only one day in the whole wide calendar when you could have come to Rosyth at the right time to see the first big show of the war. And you came! Chatfield there says it's only a coincidence, but I say it's damned uncanny anyway. Don't you think so?"

"Well, yes sir, I suppose so. But I'm still a little in the dark about what exactly is going on."

Beatty gave him a conspiratorial smile. "Yes, I daresay you are." He reached into his jacket pocket. (Maltbie noted that the garment had the distinctive cut of Messrs. Gieves of Bond Street, Naval Outfitters, but only six brass buttons instead of the regulation eight. The stories about Beatty's maverick nature were apparently true.) The admiral took out what appeared to be a telegram. "If I show you this, will you promise not to tell Winston on me?"

"Mr. Churchill, sir? Uh—yes. Certainly."

"Very well then. Have a look."

Maltbie took the yellow piece of paper from Beatty's hand and unfolded it.

Adm^{ty}   23.I.15   2.17 p.m.

MOST IMMEDIATE

Four German battle cruisers, six light cruisers, and twenty-two destroyers will sail this evening to scout on the Dogger Bank, probably returning tomorrow evening. All available battle cruisers, light cruisers, and destroyers from Rosyth should proceed to a rendezvous in 55°13′N., 3°12′E., arriving at 7.0 a.m. tomorrow. Commodore (T) is to proceed with all available destroyers and light cruisers from Harwich to join Vice Admiral *Lion* at 7.0 a.m. at above rendezvous. W/T is not to be used unless absolutely necessary.

"My God!" said Maltbie, handing back the telegram. "Four battle cruisers is all the Germans have."

Beatty's eyes gleamed. "All the Germans *had*, Mr. Maltbie—as of tomorrow morning."

Waite led Maltbie down past the signal bridge and the searchlight platform to the main deck, where several dozen sailors detailed for the early watches were already either slinging their hammocks or asleep in them. The transition from the near-freezing night air of the compass platform to the stuffy malodorous swelter of the ship's interior had Maltbie perspiring, but the temperature began to drop again as they moved forward toward the officers' quarters.

The wardroom was deserted; its large shabby armchairs and dully glowing electric fire giving it the feel of a rather down-at-the-heels London club. It was as overilluminated as an operating theater, and every crack in the leather upholstery, every vent and pipe in the deckhead, every smudge of grease and stain of salt, stood out in bold relief against the off-whites, browns, and grays that supplied the dominant motif. Forward again was a softly lit corridor regularly punctuated on each side by red-curtained openings. To the left of each one, at eye level, was a number and a brass incised nameplate. Waite led Maltbie to the far end of the passageway, just aft of the admiral's quarters, and ushered him into the last cabin on the right, number 9. The doorplate read CHARLES G. TAYLOR, MVO, ENG. CAPT.

Maltbie looked around. There was a mirror, a wash basin, a narrow bunk bed, a wardrobe, and a small writing alcove. There was also, marvelously enough, his luggage, forwarded all the way from the Admiralty. A closer inspection revealed his uniforms hanging neatly in the wardrobe and a dozen or so books on a shelf above the bunk bed. They included a Bible, a hymnal, a copy of *England's Helicon*, bound Navy Lists for 1909 through 1914, three or four books on engineering, *Jane Eyre*, the latest edition of Brassey's *Naval Annual*, Herbert Spencer's *Social Statics*, and something entitled *Kaffirs, Fakirs, and Dromedaries* by Morrison Allardyce Waite.

"Is that *you?*" Maltbie gasped.

"Is what me?" said Waite. "Where are you . . . *Well!* Well well well well well. I'll be damned."

"It *is* you, isn't it?"

Waite smiled sheepishly and nodded. "How very, very flattering."

"So you're an author?"

"For my sins, old boy. For my sins."

"How many books have you written?"

"Only two: *Kaffirs* and another about Indo-China. I do feature articles mostly, newspaper and magazine stuff."

"How do you ever find the time?"

"How do I . . ." Waite caught Maltbie's meaning and laughed heartily. "Didn't you know I was an impostor, dear fellow? Didn't Admiral Fisher tell you? I only came on active service nine weeks ago."

Maltbie found this confusing.

"I'm in the Volunteer Reserve—you must have noticed that right away by the wavy sleeve stripes. Anyway, I've done Jacky Fisher and his liberal cronies a fair number of journalistic favors over the years, so back in November when I decided it was time to do a really first-rate firsthand book on the navy at war I went round to the Ad-

miralty and called in a few outstanding debts. Fisher arranged everything for me, and now I'm more or less the unofficial liaison between
him and Beatty. That's how *you* ended up being here, as a matter of
fact."

"Me!?"

"Well, it's a long story, but what happened was, Fisher told me
that you Americans were planning to send an observer to Scapa, and
I in passing happened to mention it to Beatty. Now, our David, like
every self-respecting vice admiral with a bit of Irish blood in him, is
just a wee tiny bit superstitious, and he periodically consults a rather
warty fortune-teller in Edinburgh by the name of Madame Dubois.
Of course, he doesn't actually consult her in person, you understand;
that would never do. But he does send members of his staff around
to peer at her entrails every so often and then report the auguries
back to him. Now, just about a week ago Madame Dubois interpreted a rumbling in her intestines as a sign that 'a sailor from the
New World,' as she put it, would help Beatty find Fritz and come to
close quarters with him. Well! The head scratching and brow fur-
rowing that went on in the admiral's quarters that evening was something to behold. Who could Madame have been talking about? Was
it someone from the *Canada*? But no, *Canada* was still fitting out
down at Elswick. Who then? The secretary brought out his anno-
tated Navy List; searching interrogatories flew from one end of the
table to the other; the admiral's patience showed signs of wearing
thin; brave men quailed; careers hung in the balance. Then, 'Ah ha!'
said Beatty. 'Didn't Waite tell me that there's an American going up
to Scapa?' All eyes turned accusingly in my direction. Within minutes I was drafting a telegram to Whitehall expressing the admiral's
sudden interest in the United States Navy and his rampant desire to
meet any American observers who might just be happening through
Rosyth on their way to visit Sir John Jellicoe's battle fleet. . . . So
here you are. And here you'll stay too, unless I'm very much mistaken, especially if we get hold of Fritz by the particulars tomorrow."

Maltbie changed into his uniform and then, guided by Waite,
went for a tour around the *Lion*. He was struck at first by how similar the ship's interior was to that of an American dreadnought, but
on reflection he decided the parallels were not all that surprising. A
dreadnought was just a seagoing gun platform, after all, and once
you added four or five double barbette turrets, six to twelve inches of
nickel-steel armor, a couple of dozen water-tube boilers, and a set of

three- or four-shaft triple expansion turbines to the two or three thousand tons of coal you needed to make the whole steel mountain move through the ocean at almost thirty miles per hour, you didn't have much latitude left in the arrangements you made for the care and feeding of more than one thousand human beings. The people were more or less an afterthought, a necessary evil you had to put up with in order to make your ultimate weapon function. So you squeezed them in wherever the weapon left you space to do so, squeezed them until, in places like the gun platforms where the weapon had its being, the people literally became numbered and interchangeable components of the machinery they worked.

Maltbie always found this blending of human and mechanical instrumentalities strangely exhilarating, and he had a moment of reflexive disappointment when Waite cut short their tour in order to get back to Beatty's quarters in time for supper.

There were some two dozen officers crowded into the admiral's mess that evening, and Maltbie was introduced to each one in turn by the admiral himself. Several men made an immediate impression. There was Beatty's secretary, Paymaster-Commander Frank Spickernell, or "Spick," as Beatty called him. He was Maltbie's age or younger, with kind intelligent eyes and a sly sense of humor, the sort of person whom one immediately marks out as a candidate for friendship. There was Flag Lieutenant Commander Ralph Seymour, Beatty's signal officer—"my little round flag lieutenant"—who matched Waite's chubby insouciance in so many ways that Maltbie could not help thinking of Tweedledum and Tweedledee when he saw them conversing together. There was the admiral's flag commander, a formidable-looking officer with the formidable-sounding name of Reginald A. R. Plunkett-Ernle-Erle-Drax. There was the navigating commander, Herbert Edwards, who had heeded Beatty's adjuration not to knock over the bloody bridge. There was Fleet Surgeon Alexander Maclean, and Major Francis J. W. Harvey, Royal Marines Light Infantry, the commander of "Q" turret amidships. The dour flag captain and chief of staff, Chatfield, whom Maltbie had seen earlier on the compass platform was not present; he was up on the conning tower, guiding the *Lion* through the night.

The mood of the officers Maltbie met was exuberant almost to the point of jubilation. Given the imminence of battle, they all managed, without any thumping of chests or bellowing of oaths, to convey a very British sense of celebration. More than that, they all seemed to share the intense conviction that the next day would be the grandest of their lives.

With supper eaten and the plates cleared, Maltbie noticed the admiral exchanging impish clandestine nods with several men of his staff. Beatty then raised his hand, and all conversation ceased. "Gentlemen," he intoned sententiously, "the King!"

Maltbie saw the men around him reach for their glasses and bend forward as if preparatory to standing up, and indeed there was never any question in his mind that a toast to the monarch would be drunk on one's feet. He therefore rose, and for several seconds did not really grasp the fact that everyone else had remained seated. When the stark truth came home to him and was reflected on his face, an enormous roar of laughter spilled over the room.

Smiling sheepishly, Maltbie sat back down in an agony of embarrassment.

"Please forgive us our little joke, Mr. Maltbie," Beatty said from the head of the table. "It's a friendly initiation we put all our outside visitors through. Drinking the king's health sitting down is one of the Royal Navy's most hallowed traditions, you see. It dates from that fateful day in 1832 when the sailor-king, William IV, rose in response to a toast aboard the old eighty-gun *Albion* and bonked his royal noggin on an overhanging beam." Affecting a tone of contrition, Beatty asked, "Can you find it in your heart to forgive us our prank, Mr. Maltbie?"

"I can, sir," Maltbie answered with mock solemnity. "But I reserve the right to get even at some future date."

This brought on another loud burst of laughter and a chorus of "hear, hear's."

As the noise subsided Beatty again raised his hand. "Gentlemen, now that Lieutenant Commander Maltbie is officially one of us, I can speak to you freely about tomorrow. As you are all well aware, our prize is at last in sight. After receiving the warning telegram this afternoon, I was asked by the Board of Admiralty whether I considered the Battle Cruiser Force in a fit state to engage in action. I replied to their lordships that Admiral Moore had taken over command of the Second Battle Cruiser Squadron only four days ago, that the *Queen Mary* was in dockyard hands undergoing refit, that *Tiger* had never yet fired her guns at a moving target, and that the installation of director-firing apparatus was complete in only one of our ships. Given these conditions, I advised them, there was only one conclusion that could possibly be drawn, to wit: that nothing short of an act of God could save the Germans if once we got abeam of them."

There was loud laughter, glasses were pounded on the table, "hear, hear's" came from all around the room.

"And so, gentlemen, I propose a toast . . . and on this occasion, Mr. Maltbie, you have my word that we shall all join you on your feet."

Everyone swiftly rose.

"I propose a toast made by another sailor in another war against another continental power—a toast made by Horatio, Viscount Nelson on the eve of Trafalgar. 'Gentlemen,' he said on that historic occasion, 'I propose the morrow's battle: for the glory of God, and to the honor of the fleet.'"

Almost with a shout, the mess responded, "To the honor of the fleet," and Maltbie's voice was as loud as any.

Later, in Captain Taylor's cabin, he tried to calm himself down. He carefully hung up his uniform in the wardrobe, shaved, and cleaned his teeth. Then he sat down at Taylor's desk and described his first two days in England to Melina—more precisely, his first forty hours, which now seemed more like a month. It was nearing midnight when he finished, and he had to turn out at five. Climbing into his narrow berth, he switched off the light. But he was far too keyed up to sleep. After half an hour of shifting and scratching, staring at the bulkhead, and kicking the bedclothes into a froth, he got up again, put on his uniform, and went up on deck.

There was a moderate wind blowing, no more than force two or three. The air was damp but not particularly cold. Maltbie glanced aft at the dim blue stern light by which *Tiger*, invisible two cables to the rear, kept station. *Lion*, steaming at the head of the line, churned forward into total night. Maltbie knew that the sea all around him was crowded with ships: there were the four great battle cruisers, the light cruiser screens on the wings, and the destroyers in night formation well astern. But in the misty darkness *Lion* seemed utterly without company, a lonely mastodon lurching blindly through the wild, cut off from the scent of its herd.

As the quarterdeck was traditionally the preserve of admirals and captains, Maltbie went forward to the forecastle and stood facing into the wind and spray while the two 13.5-inch muzzles of "A" tur-

ret gaped mutely at the back of his skull. He considered the high
pitch of excitement he was feeling with respect to the next day's battle, and he wondered to himself whether it partook at all of fear. Everyone else on the *Lion* appeared to regard the imminent clash as an
occasion as joyous as a boy's last day of school. Fear seemed to have
been completely overlooked by them, almost as if it were a relic, like
chain mail, of styles of war that were now passé. It was abnormal
somehow, Maltbie acknowledged, but he thought he could understand the feeling. On reflection, in fact, he thought he might share
it.

"They're out there, Maltbie."

Harry jumped. Beatty had materialized right next to him, his eyes
squinting ahead into the blackness.

"They're out there. *Seydlitz, Moltke, Derfflinger, Von der Tann.*
All four of them. And we're going to have their skins."

There was a pause, and when Beatty spoke again it was in a much
lighter tone of voice. "I hope you didn't mind that business about
the toast, Maltbie. It was completely without malicious intent, I assure you."

"Oh, I didn't mind it at all, sir, honestly. As initiations go, that
one was downright enjoyable."

Beatty flashed the mandrill smile. "But you still reserve the right
to get even."

They both laughed.

"I'll tell you something; you weren't the only one fooled by a toast
this evening."

"How's that, sir?"

Beatty gazed at him intently. "May I call you Harry, Mr. Maltbie?"

"Certainly, sir. Of course."

"Thank you. May I also ask you to serve as my confessor?"

"Your confessor, sir?"

Beatty's voice and features took on an aspect of mordant irony.
"What did you think of that toast of Nelson's I proposed after
dinner—for the glory of God, and to the honor of the etcetera?"

"I thought it was a perfect toast for the occasion, sir. It had just
the right spirit."

"That's what I thought too."

There was a very long silence. Then the admiral said, "I made it
up."

"Sir?" Maltbie's voice almost squeaked with incredulity.

"I made it up, Harry. I mean I made it up that Nelson ever said it. Nobody ever said it. I got it out of some silly novel I read years and years ago; I don't even remember the title. The hero was some Crusader sea captain fighting pirates and Turks. He was the one who said it, not Nelson."

Beatty ruminated on this rather fiercely for several moments. "It stuck in my mind," he resumed finally. "And after a while I got to thinking to myself, Nelson *should* have said it. And then tonight, on the eve of the first head-to-head dreadnought battle in history, I decided that, damnit all, he *had* said it, even if he bloody well hadn't."

The admiral seemed resentful, as if a part of himself that he favored was being scolded by another part that he disliked. But eventually he sighed and said, "I suppose it was really inexcusable." Then, with renewed truculence, "But it was in a good cause!"

It occurred to Maltbie to suggest, "Well sir, I'll bet that if Admiral Nelson were alive today, he'd have *wanted* you to say he said it—and been *proud* that you did, into the bargain."

"So you think the god of battles will forgive me, eh?"

"Provided his name isn't Heinrich or Wolfgang, I think he will, sir."

The admiral barked out a jubilant laugh. "Harry, you are a capital confessor, a true saver of troubled souls. If there were room for any more Americans around our navy, I'd have you impressed and make you my personal chaplain."

Pleased to the point of embarrassment, Maltbie parried the compliment with, "Americans around your navy, sir?"

"The upper echelons are infested with 'em, Harry; it's getting to be a scandal. There's my wife, Winston's mother, Fisher's daughter-in-law. Thank God, Jellicoe married Gwen Cayzer or there'd be rumors of a conspiracy running broadside."

Thinking he would have to add a postscript to the letter he'd just finished writing, Maltbie said, "Well, if it's of any relevance to the issue, the young lady I would like to marry happens to be English."

"You don't say so!"

"Yes sir."

"Well, on behalf of the British nation, let me say that I'm flattered. Where did you meet the lovely creature?"

"In Washington, about two months ago. She's your ambassador's niece."

"Oh? May I ask her name?"

"Miss Melina Bellamy."

Beatty's mouth dropped open in a very un-admiral-like expression of astonishment. "No!"

"Yes sir," Maltbie said, a little taken aback. "Do you know her?"

Beatty looked at him as if he simply couldn't be serious, but seeing that he was, he said, "Well, I'm damned."

"Sir?" said Maltbie, now greatly perplexed.

The admiral kept staring at him, then quite unexpectedly came out with a loud guffaw. "By God, Harry! Melina Bellamy is quite the most formidable little lady I have ever seen in my entire life."

"You *know* her, sir?"

"Well, we were introduced. But I don't think she took any notice of me."

Maltbie could not readily conceive of anyone, particularly a woman, taking no notice of David Beatty. Then the remembered gleam of a pair of tigery eyes rendered the notion less outlandish.

Beatty continued: "It was in the spring three years ago. We were all in Malta aboard the Admiralty yacht, *Enchantress*—myself, Winston, Prime Minister Asquith, Jacky Fisher, Prince Louis. Just a jolly old Mediterranean cruise for the ostensible purpose of inspecting our naval installations. I was along as Winston's naval secretary, and I hated every minute of it. The P.M. fancied himself a classical scholar, and every place we went he would whip out his Baedeker and disclaim upon the glory that was Rome. Winston, on the other hand, could talk of nothing but the sea and the navy, which was to his credit, I suppose, but left me weeping with boredom after the first few days. Prince Louis, poor fellow, was never known as a lively conversationalist, and chatting with Jacky Fisher was like playing with a live grenade. So it was pretty tedious going. Anyway, the Bellamys were in Malta on their way home from Greece because of the Balkan ruckus, and as they were *real* classical scholars, the P.M. had to have them to dinner. Well, here they came: a nice white-haired old gentleman, a nice gray-haired old lady—and this stunning little red-haired spitfire whom you propose to marry. No sooner have we sat down at table than she lights into Winston and Asquith as if it were question time at Westminster. Why have the Liberals re-neged on votes for women? she wants to know. Why have you be-trayed the female sex? That sort of thing. Well, the P.M., being a kindly courtly old fellow, fended her off with flattery for a little while, and when that didn't work he just sort of batted her arguments aside, like a horse whisking mayflies with its tail. Winston, however, charged in like an aggrieved rhinoceros. He'd taken an awful lot of abuse from the suffrage people over the years, and Miss Bellamy was getting under his skin. Well! Your young lady—all five feet and twenty-one years of her—sat there and went at it, hammer and tongs, no quarter given, with the First ruddy Lord of the whole British Admiralty. And they were *slugging,* let me tell you. Prince Louis was scandalized, the P.M. was nonplussed, I was awestruck, Jacky Fisher was tickled pink, and Sir Lloyd and Dame Margaret Bellamy sat there beaming, as if their little girl was reciting the Lord's Prayer at her first communion. I remember thinking to myself that I'd never seen so much high explosive packed into such a tiny projectile. . . . So all in all, Harry, I'd say you're going to have a very lively domestic life."

Maltbie laughed. "I imagine I will, sir. If Miss Bellamy will have me."

"Oh, she'll have you, Harry, don't you worry—roasted, basted, and with an apple in your mouth if she can't get you any other way. Believe me, if she let you fall in love with her, that means she'll have you. Young ladies with her spirit cast a very accurate net."

"I certainly hope you're right, sir," Maltbie said, reveling in Beatty's words.

"You wait and see. She'll marry you, you'll be deliriously happy, and you'll die young, completely worn out. Those are my predictions."

They both laughed loudly.

"Speaking of being completely worn out," the admiral said, glancing at his watch, "we've a battle to fight in the morning and it's time to get some rest."

He turned so that he was facing Maltbie and extended his hand. "Welcome aboard, Harry," he said warmly. "It's good to have you with us."

Back in his cabin, Maltbie felt excited still, but his excitement had a mellower tone. He undressed, got into bed, and closed his eyes. The hum and purr of the great ship relaxed him, the rise and fall of the hull on the waves becalmed his mind. He ran his fingers over the talisman resting on his chest, wished that he could always be so happy, and slept.

1915, 24TH JANUARY—DOGGER BANK

It was a new experience for Gehlman to be aboard a ship of war with fellow officers who did not despise him for being a Jew. His background was known, to be sure—thanks to his uncles in Hamburg and Frankfurt, the Gehlman name was almost as synonymous with German banking as the Krupp name was with German steel—but aboard the *Seydlitz* it was his family's national and not its religious identity that determined his social acceptability.

The war had effected a drastic change. Fregattenkapitän Baron von Tiel, the officer in whose house Gehlman lived, told him how in August the Kaiser for the first time in history had received a deputation of Reichstag members that included the Social Democrats. Previously the Socialists had been unwelcome at court, despite their standing as the largest single bloc in the Reichstag with 110 of 391 seats. With the coming of war, however, they were admitted unquestioningly into the Imperial presence, and Wilhelm had declared, "I no longer recognize parties, only Germans!"

He might have said much the same thing with respect to creeds. The German nation, not yet fifty years old, had been drawn together into a militantly inspired whole by the call to arms, and the German Navy, which in less than twenty years had grown from a small coast defense force into the second most powerful fleet in the world, was the proudest symbol of the new sense of national identity. It was Tirpitz who had said, "The navy is the melting pot of the German people," and Gehlman could see that he was right. Here was none of the Prussian rigidity and elitism that were known to infest the army's high command. Vice Admiral Franz Hipper, for example, was the jovial son of a shopkeeper from the small town of Weilheim in Bavaria. He had warmly welcomed Gehlman to his mess and immediately embarked on a spate of reminiscences about his 1902 visit to New York as a lieutenant aboard the Imperial yacht, *Hohenzollern*. Hipper's staff—von Egidy, Raeder, von der Lühe, Franz, Brutzer, Diffring—were also blessedly free of the Pomeranian *Blut-und-Eisen* mentality; they numbered among them a Swabian, two Hanoverians, a Hessian, and a Saxon.

Gehlman liked them; they were enthusiastic, dedicated, and cheerful, and they treated him not just politely but well. Of course he had an advantage in that prominent German-American Jews like Otto Kahn and Felix Warburg were openly supporting the cause of the Central Powers back in the United States. And even though Oskar Gehlman had not, as yet, joined in this teutophile chorus, his close business association with Kuhn, Loeb and the other Jewish-German banking houses made his son, for the first time, a popular man aboard a ship. Benjamin was surprised to find, in fact, that his popularity was considerably greater than that of his sponsor, Sigismund von Tiel.

Von Tiel was something of an enigma. Tall and slender with aristocratic good looks, he had impressed Gehlman at first as a fellow cynic. That impression had had to be modified after a couple of days, however, for von Tiel, though a cynic, was a cynic of an entirely different stripe. Unlike Gehlman, he did not despair of and berate mankind; he laughed at it. And where Gehlman was enraged by men's follies, von Tiel was entertained by them. Indeed, in his enjoyment of the havoc wrought by the human condition, there was something of the voluptuary's leer.

His brother officers regarded him with respect and with misgivings. They considered him little less than a genius when it came to gunnery, but they dreaded the jets of venom that frequently issued from his wit without warning or apparent reason, and left a blister prickling on the soul.

These toxic discharges were the only overt evidence of von Tiel's acknowledged involvement with alcohol—with brandy, to be precise. Gehlman had seen him consume half a liter in the space of an hour without slurring a word or fuzzing a line of thought. He had seen him down two bottles of the best Courvoisier over the course of a day, and it was a favorite jest of the baron's that Germany was fighting France for the sake of his thirst. Gehlman pondered the possible connection between von Tiel's drinking and his abnormal reticence with respect to his wife, whom he had referred to only once: as residing for the moment in Berlin. Gehlman also pondered when his turn would come to serve as the target for one of von Tiel's caustic gibes, and he stayed constantly on his guard, knowing his soul to be more easily bruised than most and less ready to forgive.

Apart from this wariness, however, his relations with his host were cordial, even warm. Von Tiel took considerable pains to see to his comfort, and was unfailingly considerate and polite. Although he and Gehlman were equal in rank, he was careful to ask permission before addressing him with the familiar *du,* and even after they got to be on a first-name basis he always maintained a nice balance between correctitude and bonhomie. Gehlman had the feeling that they were both holding back sincere impulses toward a bond of friendship, von Tiel out of diffidence and an excess of good manners, and he himself out of ingrained fear. But despite such inhibitions the professional interests they had in common steadily drew them together, and what drew them closest was their shared passion for the care and operation of heavy-caliber seagoing guns.

The *Seydlitz* carried a main armament of ten 11-inch cannon, and almost from the day of Gehlman's arrival von Tiel, in defiance of specific security directives emanating from Tirpitz's *Reichsmarineamt,* eagerly discussed with him the ways those guns were worked. Gehlman, for his part, relished the unfamiliar opportunity to talk shop with a fellow enthusiast, and gave unstintingly—and unneutrally—of his professional expertise. Colonel House had not said anything against *giving* information, after all, only seeking it, and Gehlman knew that no matter how much he gave he would get back double or triple his output every time he visited one of *Seydlitz's* turrets.

The *Seydlitz* was the first battle cruiser Gehlman had ever sailed in. He had been present in Washington back in '07 when the first reports about Admiral Fisher's new *Invincible* class of dreadnoughts had begun to filter in, and he remembered the great debate those reports had touched off among the design staff of the Bureau of Construction. With the *Invincibles* Fisher had sliced away from four to six inches of belt and turret armor protection and applied the resulting spare tonnage to the machinery of propulsion. The end product was a ship as big and powerful as a dreadnought, but with five knots more of speed. One camp in the design staff had vigorously applauded this pairing of swiftness and strength, arguing that speed, in addition to having offensive advantages, was also enough of a defense to make up for any skimping on armor. The other, and in the event prevailing, view was that any dreadnought-size ship fitted with dreadnought-size guns would sooner or later end up in the line of battle, there to confront other dreadnoughts whose weapons her armor would be inadequate to withstand. Even if the other dreadnoughts were themselves battle cruisers, the argument went on, the disparity between gun power and protection would remain a fatal flaw. One did not build capital units that could sink other capital units only at the cost of their own destruction. What one wanted was ships that could take it as well as dish it out; only after those prerequisites were assured did one bend all one's efforts toward speed.

And so America had built no battle cruisers. She had watched as Britain turned out the *Invincibles*, the *Indefatigables*, the *Lions*, and the *Tiger*; and as Germany turned out the *Von der Tann*, the *Moltkes*, the *Seydlitz*, and the *Derfflingers*. (Also, with considerable uneasiness, as Japan turned out the *Kongos*). She had witnessed the apparent vindication of the battle-cruiser concept when *Invincible* and *Inflexible* had destroyed von Spee at the Falkland Islands. She had observed the battle cruisers of the world's foremost navies grow bigger and stronger with each new design class until they were now, with the *Tiger* and the *Derfflinger*, the longest and largest warships on the seas. She had seen how readily these glamorous "naval greyhounds" had captured the public's imagination—in Tokyo, in London, in Berlin. What she had not yet seen, however, and what she and everyone else was waiting to see, was a clash of these titans head on.

The *Seydlitz* displaced some 25,000 tons on a waterline keel of 650 feet and a beam of 95. Her five twin 11-inch turrets manufactured at the Essen works of Friedrich Krupp, A.G. were disposed two abeam and three on the centerline, one forward and two aft. *Von der Tann* being in dockyard hands, she had sailed with *Moltke*, *Derfflinger*, and the slower armored cruiser *Blücher* from the Jade Bay the previous evening (the 23d), with orders to raid the British patrol screens on the Dogger Bank. Now she was well out in the North Sea, and von Tiel with Gehlman beside him was carefully inspecting her guns and their crews.

The inspection had begun at 5:00 A.M., and now, at 7:30, it was still not finished. Von Tiel had first taken a quick look at each of the fourteen 3.4-inch quick-firers ranged around the *Seydlitz*'s decks. These guns shot twenty-pound shells a maximum of 11,000 yards and were manned by four sailors apiece: one to aim and fire, one to load the shells, one to load the brass powder cartridges, and one to handle the breech. Von Tiel checked to make sure the shot-ready racks and cartridge racks were fully loaded and properly secured, and he had each gun crew go through a simulated load-and-fire.

He took more time with the twelve 5.9-inch casemate mounted guns of the secondary armament. These fired shells of 100 pounds a distance of up to 14,000 yards and were the *Seydlitz*'s main defense against destroyer torpedo attack. Their shells and cartridges were fed to them from thirty-six separate magazines deep in the hold, and each gun had a total complement of seventeen.

Satisfied that all was in order with the *Seydlitz*'s smaller-caliber weapons, von Tiel next turned his attention to the ship's firing control system. The system's command post was in the fore control, a heavily armored chamber of 14-inch-thick nickel steel situated in the rear of the conning tower just aft of Admiral Hipper's battle station. Here von Tiel would orchestrate the *Seydlitz*'s salvos in combat, assisted by two officers, a sublieutenant, three petty officers, two range-finder men, and a dozen messengers. There was a backup control station aft below the mainmast and a supplementary observer-controller in the circular steel fighting top sixty feet up the foremast. Far down in the hold, protected on both sides (like the magazines) with coal bunkers, were the transmitting stations, gunnery switchboards designed to maintain a smooth flow of observations and commands back and forth between the fore control and the several dozen gun and range-finder positions.

There was a 19½-foot-long Carl Zeiss stereoscopic range finder installed near each of the *Seydlitz*'s five turrets, a sixth one located at the fore control, and a seventh at the aft backup. All were electrically interconnected by the Bg. (or *Basis Gerät*) transmitter, which was situated right beside von Tiel's battle post. This device gave a constant readout for all seven instruments and an average-range reading as well. It also automatically transmitted the average range to all the turrets and casemates of the primary and secondary armaments.

Next to the Bg. transmitter were the deflection indicator and the director periscope. In battle the periscope was operated either by von Tiel himself or by a specially trained petty officer. It was electronically connected to calibrated indicators in each of the turrets. These indicators looked like thermometers with two small movable red triangles on their sides. The left triangle indicated where the director periscope was pointing and the right triangle indicated where the turret's guns were pointing. Thus, once the director periscope was pointed on target, the only thing the five turret officers had to do to get their guns pointed on target as well was align the red triangles on their indicators. At this point an adjustment for deflection was figured in using a specially designed calculator. With deflection established, all that remained was to get the range data (translated into angles of gun elevation) from the transmitting stations and match it triangle-to-triangle on an indicator exactly like that which was used to aim.

Gehlman found it an efficient system, but not significantly in advance of the American or the British, which were essentially similar. The Zeiss range finders constituted the one clearly superior element, and thanks to them the Germans would probably have an advantage in the opening stages of a battle. On the minus side, though, they still required their gun layers to compensate manually for the roll of the ship, whereas American dreadnoughts made use of a special sight mechanism, developed by Admiral Fiske, which allowed the guns to stay put at the elevation designated and then fired them when the ship's roll brought them onto the target. This yielded a somewhat slower rate of fire, to be sure, but it paid off in greatly increased accuracy.

When von Tiel had finished his inspection of the fire control system, he and Gehlman proceeded to the turrets, which from bow to stern had been christened Anna, Bertha, Caesar, Dora, and Emma. Each turret had five levels, and it was von Tiel's practice to start at the bottom and work his way up, the bottom in each case being the cartridge magazine.

Here if anywhere was every dreadnought's Achilles' heel—every warship's. To fling a quarter-ton steel-and-TNT projectile ten miles or more one needed a propellant. This was cordite, a blend of nitroglycerine and nitrocellulose, gelatinized with five percent vaseline to lubricate the gun barrel. Primed by a dozen pounds of black powder, a 250-pound charge of cordite, when ignited, would give the rapid burn and explosive release of incandescent gas needed to send a 600-pound shell spinning down the rifled grooves of the barrel and outward toward the enemy at 1,800 feet per second. This was fine as long as the cordite charge was ignited only inside the locked breech of the gun. But if it started burning outside, by accident or as a result of enemy fire, and if in burning it ignited the supply line of charges coming up from the cartridge magazine, then in the space of a very few seconds an entire ship could be blown to pieces.

In an attempt to deal with this danger, the cartridge magazines of all fighting ships were twice segregated from the gun platforms. On the level of the magazine itself there was an empty chamber between the main hoist and the cordite supply called the handing room. Only two cartridges at a time—one for each of the turret's guns—were allowed there, and only after they had been placed in the cage and sent up to the shell room on the next level could two more cartridges be handed out through the scuttle. Thus, if fire came down the trunk from the gun platform, one simply closed the scuttle to keep the flames away from the cordite—assuming of course that the flames didn't come too fast and hot.

Three levels up from the cartridge magazine, just below the level of the gun platform, was the second segregation stage, the working chamber. Here the main hoist terminated, thus foreclosing any direct route between the guns and the bottom-level cordite supply. Shells and cartridges on their arrival in the working chamber would be pushed out of the main cage by a set of rammers and into a gun-loading cage, which moved up an enclosed steel tube to the breech. This provided an effective shield against cordite flash from enemy shell hits on the gun house, but the problem of enemy shell hits on the working chamber itself remained unsolved, and possibly, given nine inches of barbette armor, academic.

Each turret had a crew of seventy: fourteen in the cartridge magazine, sixteen in the shell magazine, ten in the working chamber (where a spare crew of ten would be posted under actual battle conditions), twenty-five on the gun platform, and five in the switchroom, which was a cramped space between the working chamber and the shell magazine where all the turret's electrical and hydraulic equipment was monitored and maintained. Each time von Tiel came into a turret's switchroom with Gehlman he bent down to the voice tubes and gave the order "Battle stations!" This provoked a wild scramble on the two levels above and below him. Up on the gun platform the turret had to be sealed, breeches opened, rammers run out, and all gun positions manned; in the working chamber the main cage had to be sent down the hoist, the gun-loading cage made ready, and the rammers cocked; in the portside shell magazine one blue-and-yellow armor-piercing projectile had to be wheeled on a bogey to the hoist and another made ready with block and tackle; in the starboard shell magazine the same thing had to be done with the all yellow high-explosive trinitrotoluene (TNT) projectiles; in the cartridge magazine the main cage had to be down and open with one cartridge loaded in the tray, one waiting in the handing room, and another ready in the magazine itself. All these preparations had to be completed in the space of thirty seconds, each level reporting by voice tube to the turret officer when it was ready. In the switchroom von Tiel listened in, stopwatch in hand. Anna and Bertha took 28 seconds that morning, Caesar 31 the first time (a black mark for turret commander Oberleutnant Stosch) and 27 the second. Dora turret —generally acknowledged to be the sharpest on the ship—took only 24 seconds, and Emma a near-failing 29½.

With everyone at battle stations, von Tiel would reach over and flip off the turret's three main electrical circuits, plunging all five levels into total darkness. He would then call into the voice tubes, "Clear the turret!" and listen to the incredible racket and clatter that resulted as seventy men scrambled their way topside in utter blackness and flung themselves out of the turret through every possible aperture, including even the traps where empty cartridges were ejected. After the last man from the magazines had passed the switchroom level, von Tiel would snap on a flashlight and consult his stopwatch. The turret officer had to report "Turret clear" within 90 seconds. Anna took 81 that morning, Bertha 86, the slow-to-battle-stations Caesar 77 (prompting von Tiel to comment that Stosch's men clearly preferred running to fighting), Dora 79, and Emma 83.

The last step of the turret inspection was a simulated load-and-fire, first using electrical hoists and rammers, then chain hoists and hand-loading procedures. The gun platform was always a crowded place. Each gun had its captain, its layer, its trainer, and its sight setter, plus a number one man at the loading cage lever, a number two at the breech, a number three between the firing circuit and the magazine telegraph, a number four at the rammer, and a number five at the recoil cylinder. Supervising in the rear of the platform was a turret captain and his second, and in the soundproof control cabinet the turret officer, his midshipman assistant, and a signal rating on the navy phones.

All ten of *Seydlitz's* big guns were in order. The cages had come hissing up smoothly from the working chambers loaded with charge and shell, the rammers had shoved the lethal cylinders home into the breeches and then slid back, the breech blocks had been slammed shut by the number twos and the firing circuits closed by the number threes, all without a malfunction.

It was past eight when Gehlman and von Tiel stepped out of Emma onto the quarterdeck. They were joined there by Oberleutnants Radetzky and von Steifferberg, commanding Emma and Dora respectively. Johannes Radetzky was a good-natured officer, apelike in appearance, for whom von Tiel had an indifferently concealed contempt ("No one so ugly should have been given a commission"). Klaus von Steifferberg, by contrast, could almost have been called beautiful, with his dark eyes, classic features, and curly black hair. Von Tiel always referred to him as "our resident disillusioned anglophile," for von Steifferberg had been one of the first German Rhodes scholars, and at Oxford had fallen permanently under the English spell. He was one of the relatively few German officers Gehlman had met who took a personal interest in his men, and he now had the best turret crew on the ship as a result. His gunners had even unofficially rechristened Dora "the Steifferberg," in his honor. Their fierce affection for their lieutenant was regarded by most of the other officers on the *Seydlitz* as vaguely but decidedly subversive.

"I've never understood, Klaus," von Tiel was saying, "how you manage to reconcile the excellence of your turret with the fact that the more excellent it is, the more effectively it will blow up the English."

At first an expression much like anguish came over von Steifferberg's features, but knowing von Tiel's tendency toward malice he declined to be baited. "I often wonder about that myself," he said quietly, his face relaxing into a rueful smile. "And the conclusion I've come to is that such things can't be reconciled, so that one must choose between them."

"And have you chosen, my dear fellow?"

"England chose for me by choosing to join our enemies."

Von Tiel snorted. "You see, Ben, he even *talks* like a jilted lover."

Having some understanding of the young lieutenant's feelings, Gehlman limited himself to a noncommittal nod. He was tempted to ask von Tiel how *he* felt as the son of an English mother, but he judged that it would be inadvisable to raise the issue.

"I feel more bereaved than jilted," von Steifferberg said in a sad voice. "It's such a tragedy that they're fighting us. So unnecessary."

"Unnecessary?" Gehlman asked. He'd heard England's belligerency described as treacherous, selfish, perfidious, unforgivable, and so on, but unnecessary was new to him.

"If they'd only make it *clear* that Belgium would constitute a *casus belli*," the lieutenant said plaintively. "If only they hadn't been so vague about their intentions."

"Then what, my dear Steifferberg?" von Tiel brayed. "Would we have scrapped the Schlieffen Plan, given Alsace back to France, confined our attentions to the tsar?"

The lieutenant's composure slipped a little. "What has the Schlieffen Plan got us that was worth England's enmity?" he said in a rising voice. "The General Staff can't be such fools as to purchase a tactical advantage at the cost of a strategic calamity. If they'd known England would come in if we marched through Belgium, surely they would have acted differently."

"You believe that, my dear Lieutenant, because you like to think this whole war is just a misunderstanding between friends. You refuse to see that England was vague so that she could fight or not as it suited her, and that the General Staff *are* such fools that the enmity of the entire universe wouldn't have moved them to alter their battle plan. I marvel they didn't march through Switzerland and the Netherlands as well."

"I do not accept any of that," von Steifferberg snapped.

"Then accept my compliments instead, and resume your turret," said von Tiel, pointing over the lieutenant's shoulder at what appeared to be, but definitely were not, flickers of sheet lightning in the north-northwest. "It appears we are about to depart the realm of theory and put your unreconcilable choices to a practical test."

At that moment a sudden cacophonous burst of gongs, drums, and bugles signaled the call to battle stations.

"*Aurora's* engaged with Hipper's cruiser screen," said Waite, pointing out the faint flashes to the southeast.

Already Maltbie could sense the *Lion's* acceleration, the thrust of her prow toward the hunt. A *bataille!* he thought, only French seeming equal to the savage exultation he was feeling. A *bataille!*

"The admiral suggested the foretop as the best place from which to view the engagement," Waite added, "meaning we'd be least in anybody's way there."

Maltbie glanced up at the gray metal hut sixty feet above the deck. Yes! he thought, and to Waite said, "Let's go."

The way up was by a series of rungs welded onto the rear of the foremast, and with each rung the motion of the ship was more accentuated. The wind streamed icily through the rigging, and the two white ensign battle pennants snapped on the forestay like firecrackers. Looking aft for a moment, Maltbie saw the monstrous apparition of the *Tiger*, barely two cable lengths behind, heaving smoke from her funnels as though her entire inner structure were on fire. Behind her, and from Maltbie's point of view almost running up her stern, were *Princess Royal*, then *New Zealand*, then *Indomitable*, all four ships bobbing ponderously in formation, their masts making giddy patterns in perspective as they swayed in random rhythms from side to side.

Oh God! thought Maltbie. And then he simply had to shout it: "*A bataille!*"

Waite stopped climbing just above him, looked down with a condescending smile, and yelled "*Gesundheit!*"

They both laughed uproariously, like zanies on a high wire.

A set of flags went up the signal halyards. "What's that say?" Maltbie shouted, pulling on Waite's trouser cuff to get his attention.

Waite looked down to his right. "V-A-2-6," he read off. "He's calling for twenty-six knots, the bugger. *Indomitable*'s only designed for twenty-five."

"*A bataille?*" Maltbie queried with a big wide grin.

"*A bataille*," Waite agreed, and they shouted it and laughed again.

"What the devil are you two on about?" said Lieutenant Coyne, the spotter, as they squirmed through the lubber's hole into the foretop proper.

"See anything yet?" was Waite's response.

"Oh, this and that," said Coyne. "Those destroyers on the port quarter are Commodore (T) and the Harwich Force, and those smoke clouds on the beam are Commodore Goodenough and the light cruisers. That's about all there is, I guess, apart from those four black smudges fine on the bow, but they're just Admiral Hipper's battle cruisers."

Coyne and his signalman laughed raucously as Waite and Maltbie grabbed for their binoculars. Through the heavy lenses the four smudges were just barely resolvable into ships. Maltbie studied the profiles, estimated the range at sixteen miles, and guessed *Seydlitz*, *Moltke*, and *Derfflinger* from front to rear. The last ship in the line stumped him. "Who's number four?" he asked. "*Von der Tann?*"

"No sir," said the signalman. "It's an armored cruiser, the *Blücher* probably—and bloody doomed. That class can only steam twenty-three knots." He and Coyne exchanged carnivorous leers.

"You'll have to excuse Tredway's language," said the spotter. "The scent of Fritz brings out the savage in him."

Maltbie smiled politely and then glanced down at the signal bridge where Beatty and Flag Captain Chatfield had just stepped into view. Quite unexpectedly Beatty turned and looked up at him.

The mandrill grimace broke over his features, and for the briefest moment he raised his fist in a startling gesture of triumph—and of thanks.

"You see," said Waite. "He's giving you the credit."

Well, thought Maltbie, it isn't deserved, but it isn't stolen either. And aloud he said, "I'll take it."

Another set of flags went up the halyards. "Well done, *Indomitable*," Waite translated. "That must mean she's gotten her twenty-six knots."

The next signal needed no interpretation: "V-A-2-7."

Now, apart from the wind, all sense of motion seemed to dwindle away. The destroyers, the light cruisers, and Hipper's squadron in flight all sped southeastward with the *Lion*, so that to the naked eye their relative positions appeared to stay the same. In fact, however, the *Lion* was gaining ground. Maltbie calculated that given the nemesis bearing down on her, *Blücher* was capable of putting out twenty-four knots. That meant they should be closing on the Germans at about the rate a man walks, and assuming that Hipper was now only fifteen miles ahead, they should be within 20,000 yards of him within an hour—within range.

As if to corroborate Maltbie's estimate more flags rose up to the blocks: "V-A-2-8."

This was beyond the design speed of all the ships but *Tiger*, though *Princess Royal* had done 28.5 knots on her trials. Maltbie thought for a moment of Engineer Captain Taylor and the pride he must be feeling. He thought also of the black regions of the stokeholds and of the frenzied labor that was making possible such prodigious speeds. Under Sims he'd seen men burst blood vessels in the struggle to keep up steam—and that had been just in maneuvers! Now, with the real thing confronting them, he cringed to think of the stokers' spasms in the entrails of the ships.

Despite such efforts *Indomitable* and *New Zealand* were inexorably falling behind. "V-A-2-7" had been too much for them to cope with.

Facing forward again, Maltbie saw that *Lion* was steaming directly toward a swarm of several dozen small vessels, many of them under sail.

"Fishermen," Waite shouted. "Dutch or Danish. And right in our festering way."

With what Maltbie guessed was monumental reluctance, Beatty

altered a point to starboard so as not to plow the small boats under. Even given this shift, the cruisers passed close enough to the westernmost smacks for Maltbie to see the crewmen's faces. For the most part they presented a graphic study in bewilderment and irritation. It could not have been much more than a quarter of an hour since the Germans had bellowed past, and now here was this new herd of behemoths churning up the sea.

"Move yer bloody arses, yer gormless wogs!" Tredway bellowed as the nearest boats maneuvered frantically to turn their bows into the cruisers' wakes. One that was not quick enough capsized, and Maltbie winced at the thought of the freezing water.

"Serve 'em bloody right," yelled the signalman, causing Maltbie to shoot a look toward Waite, mutely seeking some explanation.

The chubby lieutenant responded to the appeal. "The rumor is that Fritz has rigged up some fishing boats to report on our ships' movements."

Maltbie acknowledged the explanation with a nod, relieved that there was some plausible motive for Tredway's display of ferocity.

But now the boats were gone. They had rolled up over the horizon, flashed by, and slipped away to the rear like raised dots on a rotating drum. Beatty signaled a point turn back to port and, to make up for the time they'd lost—or as a touch of the spur, more probably, since compliance was impossible—he sent up flags that read "V-A-2-9."

Slowly and majestically, the *Lion's* forward turrets began to train. Through his binoculars Maltbie could see the German ships in far greater detail than had been possible before, except that now the great clouds of black smoke pouring from their funnels often obscured the view. His concentration was such that a wolloping report from A turret took him completely by surprise, and he jumped at least a foot.

It was a ranging shot, and Maltbie, quickly regaining his equanimity, joined the others in the foretop in seeking to gauge its fall.

"One thousand short!" Coyne shouted down the voice tube, and Maltbie silently concurred. Only half a mile closer and they could start firing for effect.

Indomitable was a long long way astern now, and *New Zealand* too was distant. That meant it would be three British ships against four German when the shooting started in earnest. The threesome mounted twenty-four 13.5-inch guns between them, however, each gun firing a projectile weighing 1,250 pounds, and against their massed fifteen-ton salvos the ten 11-inch cannon of *Seydlitz* and *Moltke* plus the eight 12-inchers of *Derfflinger* could hurl back a broadside of only ten. The dozen 8.2-inch guns aboard *Blücher* were virtually inconsequential, all twelve of them packing less punch than a single *Lion* turret. Thus *Indomitable* and *New Zealand* would not be too sorely missed. If they were, however, their two-knot speed advantage over the German ships would have them back in the battle line in half an hour.

Maltbie glanced at his watch; it was just after 9:00 A.M. British time, 10:00 A.M. for the Germans. The forward turrets of *Lion*, *Tiger*, and *Princess Royal* trained balefully on the last desperate ship in the German line. Then with a bludgeoning rumble they opened fire. Great flash pans of flames spewed from the cannon's mouths and colossal brown billows stained the air. All three ships had let go within seconds; then silence, emergence from the smoke, and tense impatience while the projectiles flew. Through his binoculars Maltbie saw two mute fountains rise from the sea near the *Blücher*'s bow. "Left one!" Coyne shouted, as two more fountains well beyond the cruiser and four not far astern of her marked out the shells from *Tiger* and from *Princess Royal*. The *Lion* roared again, the *Tiger* bellowed, the *Princess Royal* howled abuse. After fifteen minutes of this, the Germans began to reply. Staccato flashes along the hulls of the fleeing ships announced the retaliatory fire. "My God! Look!" shouted Waite, and from out of the sky at vertiginous speed came four blurring hyphens, dead on the target, but long. Maltbie snapped his neck around and saw the shells strike the water three hundred yards to starboard. The sea heaved up in awesome gray-green geysers higher than the *Lion*'s mast, and just at that moment four more shells landed not fifty feet from the portside bow. The air took life with angry buzzings as metal splinters whirred and caromed off steel; then the foretop was full of water. The *Lion* emerged from the deluge with her own guns booming. "Good Christ, they ranged us quickly!" Waite exclaimed, and his observation was reconfirmed by four more shells exploding off the starboard quarter. The buzzing of the splinters came again, and then from the signalman Tredway a noise that began as a malediction but ended as a scream: "*Bloody FU-UUCK!!!*" A five-inch spike of metal had lodged in his right shoulder just below the collarbone; the flesh around it cooked and smoldered like sausage on a spit. Without thinking Maltbie reached out and yanked the splinter free. Tredway fainted and Waite looked on in awe as Maltbie prised the steel shard off against the foretop rim; it was red hot and had affixed itself to his fingers like a leech. The pain came later. "Down three! Right two!" Coyne shouted.

New Zealand had now attained the battle range, and Beatty ordered ship-for-ship fire against the German line. *Blücher*, clobbered and burning, was already losing speed. The *Lion*'s guns reached out for the *Seydlitz* as the blurred hyphens came thicker and heavier every moment. The sea around was never still. The secondary armaments of both battle lines were rapidly becoming engaged; the destroyer flotillas attempted to launch their torpedoes against a typhoon of 4- and 6-inch fire, then had to quit. Every second saw a shell land or a gun discharge, and there were screams now too, as the Germans had started to hit. One shell hit hard and the *Lion* seemed to stop dead. A great shuddering went through the hull and the foretop whipped back and forth like the pendulum on a metronome. The unconscious Tredway was almost flung out and lost. "Oh my Jesus!" Waite shouted, pointing at the signal bridge where Beatty, Chatfield, and the flag lieutenant had just been standing. "Up two! Up two! Up two!" Coyne hollered. Maltbie looked down at the bridge and felt his gorge rise. Three pulpy blue puddles was all he could see, three gold-buttoned overcoats covering who knew what shredded piles of flesh. The admiral! Then the admiral appeared, and the flag captain, and the flag lieutenant—and they seemed to be exchanging jokes! They were laughing and conversing with great animation at any rate, having shed their overcoats and left them where they fell. Gaping in astonishment, Maltbie noticed that he was feeling warm himself, despite being wet through. There were fires raging fore and aft; the funnels were almost molten; clouds of TNT from bursting German shells, the *Lion*'s own cordite and powder, the boilers and turbines at full extension, had all combined to banish winter from the air. What was that march they always played? Ah, yes—"The World Turned Upside Down."

The *Lion* resumed her forward momentum and was now firing full salvos from all eight cannon. Maltbie had his binoculars on the *Seydlitz* when a dull orange ball began to engulf her two aft turrets; then it blossomed into a monstrous explosion two or three times the height of the ship. "Oh, God," Maltbie whispered. "Oh, glorious death in battle." He decided later that it had been a prayer.

With his earphones on, Gehlman could hear Oberleutnant Weismer screaming in the foretop: *"Lieber Gott! Lieber GOTT!"*

"What is it, Weismer?" von Tiel shouted into the navy phones. Here in the fore control the only view outside was through the director periscope, and that was pointed out to starboard at the enemy. The British had been shooting poorly up to now, but a few seconds earlier Gehlman had felt or heard—he couldn't be sure—a faint rapid two-beat thud. Then Weismer had started screaming.

"Lieber Gott!" he wailed again.

"God *damn* you, Weismer!" von Tiel roared. "Tell me what you see!"

"Shell hits on Emma, sir. She and Dora have gone up in flames!"

Von Tiel flung off his earphones, leaped up to the front of the conning tower, and grabbed hold of Flag Captain von Egidy's arm. "Sir, you must flood Emma and Dora magazines *immediately.*"

It was clear von Egidy knew what that *"immediately"* meant. He paused for less than half a second, thinking perhaps of the magazine crews who would be trapped and drowned as the water came roaring in. Then he gave the order.

Von Tiel moved quickly back to his periscope. "Start counting seconds, Ben," he said. "If you make it to twenty, we won't blow up." Then, into the navy phones, "Deflection two left; rate four hundred closing; fourteen thousand; salvos—fire!"

There was a strangely feeble note to the din as Anna and Bertha let go. Caesar, on the port beam, could not bring her guns to bear on the British and so had been idle since the shooting began. But Dora and Emma had always joined in the salvos before. Now only two turrets had fired, and one could feel the reduced power of the broadside as the ship jerked on the recoil.

". . . seven . . . eight . . . nine . . . ten . . . eleven . . ." Gehlman counted off the seconds aloud as several messengers and signalmen watched him with frozen stares.

"Deflection two more left; down eight hundred; rate still four hundred closing." Von Tiel's voice was calm, conversational.

". . . twelve . . . thirteen . . . fourteen . . . fifteen . . . sixteen . . ."

The ship heeled, as the steersman had put the helm over hard to starboard on the second leg of a zigzag. A pair of binoculars fell off their peg and crashed on the metal grating with a loud clang. Everyone but von Tiel started at the noise.

". . . seventeen . . . eighteen . . . nineteen . . . *twenty!*"

Sixty men in the aft magazines would now be clawing and kicking vainly at the steel walls enclosing them, clawing and kicking and trying to scream in black pits filled with water.

"Salvos—fire!" said von Tiel.

Gehlman preferred to keep his mind off the magazine crews, so he moved forward to see if he could catch sight of the British line through one of the slits in the conning tower. He heard Hipper ask his flag lieutenant, von der Lühe, "Has the commander in chief replied yet to our call for assistance?"

"Yes sir. He replied *en clair*, strangely enough. Signal reads: 'High Seas Fleet coming out.'"

"Good!" said Hipper.

A signalman handed von der Lühe another slip of paper. The flag lieutenant read it, then did a sort of double take and read it again. "Excuse me, sir. Admiral von Ingenohl has sent a follow-on—in cipher."

"Well?"

"Signal reads: 'Coming out *as soon as possible.*'"

Hipper gave a mirthless grunt. "Very clever of the admiral. Now the British think he's coming out, and we know that he isn't."

Four colossal water spouts rose into the air just off the port bow.

"Somehow Admiral Beatty doesn't seem intimidated."

Blücher was now a blazing wreck drifting away to the northeast while doggedly firing what guns she had left. *Lion* had had all but two of her signal halyards shot away, but they served to direct *Indomitable* to administer the *Blücher*'s coup de grace. Coyne ripped off the earphones he had been wearing and flung them to the floor. "Bloody fucking Germans have knocked out all our bloody fucking dynamos!"

Now they were listing heavily to port. *Tiger* had already drawn abeam, and *Princess Royal* was closing fast astern. *Lion* was taking in water and losing speed. Two salvos struck her in quick succession. "Submarine off the starboard quarter!" Coyne screamed down the voice pipe. Maltbie could see nothing of a periscope's wash, but almost immediately the flags went up for "Compass P," a ninety-degree turn to port. This put them at right angles to Hipper's line of retreat, and the range opened rapidly. With his battle cruisers clear of the potential danger, Beatty sent up "Compass B" (course northeast) to carry them across the Germans' wake and clear of any mines they might have laid. "Compass R," the signal to resume the pursuit, would certainly be flying momentarily. *Lion* was now behind the rest of the battle force, however, and on the remaining halyard—instead of "Compass R"—rose the flag "A.F.": attack the rear of the enemy.

"Oh, no!" Maltbie cried when Waite had translated.

"What is it?"

"He's still got 'Compass B' flying."

Waite looked at the halyards again, stupefied, then at the *Blücher*, dead on a northeast bearing. Given the smoke of battle and the fact that the flagship was now floating far astern of the rest of the BCF, the four British dreadnoughts still in action had not yet seen and acknowledged "Compass B." But if now, in the course of maneuvering, they at last got a clear view of the *Lion*, they would read the two sets of flags on the halyards as a single signal. Instead of "Course northeast" followed by "Attack the rear of the enemy," they would see "Attack the rear of the enemy, bearing northeast"!

"But they'll know we sent *Indomitable* to finish *Blücher* off," Waite said pleadingly, as if Maltbie were somehow arbitrating the conduct of the battle. "Admiral Moore can't assume that Beatty wants him to let the other three ships escape. He just *can't!*"

But apparently, appallingly, he could and did assume just that. Priding himself, no doubt, on his exemplary obedience in the role of second-in-command, Admiral Moore on board the *New Zealand* led *Tiger* and *Princess Royal* on the *Indomitable*'s track toward the *Blücher*, while *Seydlitz*, *Moltke*, and *Derfflinger* raced away southward to safety. Maltbie trained his binoculars on the bridge and shivered at the wrath in Beatty's expression. "Compass B" and "A.F." having been hauled down, "74" (keep nearer the enemy) was sent up to the blocks. But by now it was much too late. *Lion* was out of the hunt and, indeed, out of the battle as well, without steam, without wireless, without motion.

Maltbie watched *Blücher* fight on tenaciously against four adversaries twice her size. After twenty minutes' pounding, however, she gave off a monumental sigh of smoke and cinders, rolled over smoothly, and sank. Beatty was making ready to transfer his flag to the destroyer *Attack*, hoping somehow to retrieve the situation. "Go get 'em, David!" Tredway shouted, having at last regained consciousness. "Finish the bastards off!" The sailors on deck were cheering too, but the admiral gave no sign he heard. Looking down from the foretop, Maltbie could see the toe of Beatty's half-boot tapping out a rhythm of murderous impatience on the slanting deck. At that moment the admiral seemed to sense the pressure of Maltbie's eyes, because he looked directly up at him and with a peremptory swing of his arm summoned him down.

"The admiral wants me," Maltbie called to his three companions as he jumped for the lubber's hole and started the long descent to the deck. He made it to the ladder and down the *Lion's* side just in time.

"I'm afraid we've spoiled the show for you, Harry," the admiral said as the *Attack* bucked along toward the *Princess Royal.*

"Can't we catch them, sir?"

Beatty didn't answer, just stared tight-lipped in the direction of the fleeing German dreadnoughts, his eyes full of bitterness and rage.

Dora turret was a catastrophe, a blistered hallucination out of a Goya cartoon. Twisted stalactites of blackened steel crisscrossed the semidarkness, bearing upon them malodorous goiters that had once had human form. One of the goiters had once had the form of Klaus von Steifferberg.

The British shell had smashed through the quarterdeck just starboard of Emma and pierced the turret's 9-inch barbette armor at the level of the working chamber. Perhaps a quarter of the projectile's bursting charge had exploded inside. This 250-pound blast of lyddite had killed most of the working chamber's crew and ignited two cordite cartridges that had just come up on the main hoist from the magazines. The resulting explosion had sent flashes of flame shooting up to the gun platform and down to the switchroom. In panic, the surviving crewmen of the working chamber had attempted to flee to safety in the Dora working chamber adjoining, but as soon as they opened the door the gluttonous fire had roared toward the scent of new air, blowing them through the hatchway like so many blazing rags. A few Dora crewmen had lived long enough to shield their eyes with their hands, and on the faces of these dead men one could see the clear outline of palm and fingers against the background of frizzled skin. The cartridges in Dora's working chamber had blown up immediately, setting off both powder and cartridges on the gun platform just above and producing a cataclysmic explosion. No more than fifteen seconds could have elapsed between initial impact and final detonation. No more than fifteen seconds more, absent von

Egidy's order, and the flames would have reached the magazines.

Gehlman and von Tiel had reached Dora's switchroom, having descended like cliff scalers with ropes around their waists. The fire had curled up the iron plating between the top three levels, and they could see all the way to the turret roof. It was like a huge, gutted mineshaft, all drooping cables and slanting beams. Water dripped from every overhang, and from every fissure came steamy fumes.

They pried open the bottom hatch of the switchroom and shone their lamps into the shell magazine. Three feet down the light reflected off the slowly receding water. There were bodies floating, some gaping skyward, others face down. On the ladder just below them was a seaman, his forehead resting on the top rung between his grease-stained hands. Struggling to escape, he had pressed the back of his skull up against the hatch cover, and the rivet bolts had left a pattern of indentations in his hair. His face downward, he had an attitude of profound sorrow about him, an air of weariness and grief. It was almost as if he were lamenting rather than dead.

"Good Christ!" Gehlman gasped, jerking suddenly backward.

"What is it?"

"I thought I saw someone . . ."

They lowered their lamps again and saw him, the light flashing strangely from his eyes. It was the magazine petty officer. Apparently he was floating on a barrel or some such object because his shoulder blades and his head, from the bridge of his nose upward, were above water. He looked homicidally enraged floating there, not blankly staring but ferociously intent on some unnamable revenge. It was only when they peered more closely at him that they saw that the top of his skull was gone.

Von Tiel made a sardonic barking sound. "Death is a joker," he said. "She likes to make us jump."

Gehlman was puzzled, because "death" in German is a masculine noun.

Maltbie was standing with Beatty on the compass platform of the *Princess Royal*. Night had come and with it an icy sleeting rain. The Battle Cruiser Force was on its way back to Rosyth, minus *Lion* of course, which was dead in the water, and minus *Indomitable*, which was going to try to tow her home.

Beatty had been very silent standing there, speaking only to acknowledge damage and casualty reports as they were brought to him.

The final figures had shown thirty-six BCF men wounded and fifteen men and one officer, on the *Tiger*, killed. For some reason the dead officer's identity had not been specified in the *Tiger's* summary, and Beatty had snarled at the signalman to "Get the bloody name."

The signalman was now on his way back to report. He came up beside the admiral, saluted, and handed him a slip of paper. Beatty squinted at it for several seconds, whispered, "*Damn!*" and handed it to Maltbie. In the dim light of the binnacle it was just barely possible to make out the words: "Engineer Captain C. G. Taylor."

Maltbie felt a cold shock of sorrow run through his chest. Again, as earlier in the day, he thought, Oh, glorious death in battle. But the sense of sorrow did not abate.

BOOK III

Admiral von Müller sighed to himself as Wilhelm II of Hohenzollern stormed around the room, his suspenders flapping around the
calves of his jodhpurs while the open buttons of his woolen singlet
revealed his not particularly imposing chest. There were times, the
admiral reflected, when the German Emperor cut a distinctly un-Im-
perial figure, and this was one of them. Von Müller knew—or had
known at one time—what an honor it was to be numbered among
the select few permitted to attend the Emperor dishabille, but the
person of the All Highest War Lord, no matter how exalted in
theory, was not a handsome object to behold. Stripped of the elegant
costumes contrived by the Imperial tailors, Wilhelm's scrawny phy-
sique and congenitally withered left arm evoked queasy images of a
carnival sideshow. Worse, they clashed sharply with the upturned
mustache and fierce gaze he relied on to convey the impression of
personal force.

It was not that von Müller was unsympathetic. Here it was, the
Kaiser's fifty-sixth birthday, and as a present from his navy there was
only Hipper and von Ingenohl's reports on the sinking of the
Blücher. From Berlin they had been forwarded here to Charleville in
the Ardennes Forest, Supreme Western Front Headquarters, and
they had arrived just as Wilhelm was returning in a predictably irate
condition from a visit to the Fifth Army sector near Verdun. The
Fifth Army was nominally commanded by his eldest son, the crown
prince, a man of thirty-two who grated on Wilhelm's nerves as only
the heir to one's own throne can. The crown prince had that morning assembled his personal regiment, the Death's Head Hussars, to
give his father three cheers on his birthday, but to Wilhelm's ears
the hurrahs had sounded inexcusably tepid. He chose to interpret the
soldiers' lack of enthusiasm as a personal affront, discounting the fact
that they had been standing in a freezing drizzle for over half an
hour by the time he arrived and had recently sustained over forty
percent casualties. The crown prince, having taken great pride in the

efficiency with which he had gathered together an entire regiment despite front-line transport limitations, took his father's surly expression of gratitude very much amiss, and a heated exchange ensued which ended with both men stalking off to their respective limousines. Back at Charleville the reports on the *Blücher* were the last straw.

"It's indefensible!" Wilhelm fumed, striding across the room. "Worse than that, it's insubordinate! Tell me, Müller, did we or did we not make it plain to von Ingenohl that no capital ships were to venture past Heligoland without a covering force available for their support?"

"Your Majesty's orders were quite clear about that, unquestionably," von Müller replied. If anything he was angrier at von Ingenohl than the Kaiser was. The admiral's bumbling had created precisely the situation von Müller had wanted to avoid. Now he was reduced to salvaging oddments from the wreckage. "In the admiral's defense," he said cautiously, "his assumption was that the battle cruisers' speed would protect them. And it would have, had they encountered any other force but Beatty's."

"But they didn't encounter any other force, did they?"

"No, your Majesty."

Von Müller calculated rapidly. He might hazard one more excuse for von Ingenohl without compromising his own position—but only one more. "Of course the admiral was terribly unlucky to have been without *Von der Tann* just when the weather cleared enough for the sortie. Had Hipper's scouting group been at full strength they could have left *Blücher* home, and then they would have had the heels of Beatty all the way back to the Jade."

Wilhelm glared at him. "Are you trying to say that the absence of *Von der Tann* explains away the loss of the *Blücher*?"

Von Müller had overstepped himself a little, and now the Kaiser was going to subject him to the humiliating process of catechism he invariably resorted to when annoyed with a member of his court.

"No, your Majesty."

"Would you like to make any more excuses for von Ingenohl, perhaps?"

Von Müller remained silent, hoping the sarcastic tone denoted a rhetorical question.

"Well?"

Alas, it didn't. "No, your Majesty."

"Then why don't I try my hand at some excuses for you. The Third Battle Squadron was absent in the Baltic. How's that? The tide was out in the Jade Roads. Yes? A stoker on the *König* had a head cold. The clocks were slow in Wilhelmshaven. The toilets on the *Markgraf* were clogged with shit. . . ." Wilhelm paused to catch his breath. "Have I left anything out, Müller?"

The catechism always ended with a yes-or-no question that could only be answered by asking for forgiveness.

"I apologize for overstating the case, your Majesty," von Müller said wearily. "Of course you have every reason to be displeased with Admiral von Ingenohl."

"Thank you, Müller," Wilhelm sneered. "That's most accommodating of you." He stomped over to his night table and poured himself a glass of schnapps. Then he whirled around, his finger pointing at the admiral. "And von Ingenohl isn't the only one I have every reason to be displeased with. There's his idiot chief of staff too, Eckermann."

This time von Müller was permitted to remain silent.

Wilhelm strode up and down the room with an air of extreme preoccupation. At last he halted and struck the rather truculent yet uncertain pose he affected whenever he came to a decision he was not fully comfortable with, but which he wanted no arguments about. "I have decided that von Ingenohl and Eckermann are to be relieved," he said.

Von Müller felt a knotting in his stomach. To this much he had by now resigned himself. But clearly there was to be more. The Kaiser's defensiveness was becoming more pronounced even as the admiral watched him, and that could only mean he had taken decisions more drastic than von Ingenohl's relief. "Yes, your Majesty," he murmured, shutting his eyes and waiting for the blow to fall.

"I don't want to lose any more of my ships, Georg."

"No, of course not," the admiral responded, feeling himself wince. Wilhelm addressed him by his Christian name only when set on a course of action he knew von Müller would disapprove of. It was the Kaiser's noblesse oblige way of trying to win him over, or at least soften his disapproval, which always unnerved and upset him no matter how deferentially expressed.

"I don't want the fleet making any more sorties out into the North Sea for the next few months," he said.

Von Müller maintained an icy silence. Here was a compounding of the criminally stupid "fleet-in-being" policy that refused to risk Germany's expendable battleships against England's indispensable ones.

"I'm going to give command to von Pohl," Wilhelm added with all the petulant defiance of a child.

Still von Müller said nothing.

The Kaiser clenched his fists in exasperation and his face took on an almost comical I-*refuse*-to-be-intimidated expression. "Furthermore," he declared, "I have decided that the time has come for us to see what we can do with our submarines."

1915, 6TH FEBRUARY—LIVERPOOL

The Cunard liner *Lusitania* glided regally along the surface of the Irish Sea on an easterly heading. In his stateroom on the promenade deck Colonel House contemplated the headline on that morning's edition of the ship's newspaper:

GERMANY DECLARES SEAS AROUND BRITAIN A "WAR ZONE"
All Allied Vessels Subject to Submarine Attack—Danger to Neutral Shipping as Well

The Colonel shook his head—the perfect end to a perfect voyage. Two days out they had run into a ferocious storm off the Newfoundland Banks, and the North Atlantic had tossed around the *Lusitania*'s 30,000 tons as if the ship had been made of cardboard. His wife, Loulie, and his secretary, Miss Denton, had been almost, but not quite, too terrified to be violently sick, and even Captain Dow and the ship's officers had confessed to anxiety. Then, yesterday, the captain had raised the American flag as they were steaming by Fastnet Rock south of Ireland, and he had kept it flying. Miss Denton had alerted the Colonel to what was going on, and that had been well and good. But the result was that House thereafter had had to restrict his movements when out on deck so as to avoid any sight of the Stars and Stripes. It was a nuisance, and it made him feel ridiculous, but when reporters asked him to comment on the captain's action he wanted to be able to say he only knew about it from hearsay and, therefore, could not discuss it. (Such, he reflected, were the clumsy subterfuges of high diplomacy.)

And now this morning, as Wallasey Rock Light off Liverpool was coming into view, there was this thoroughly unwelcome news of the German declaration.

It didn't really come as a surprise to the Colonel, but neither did it augur well for his peace mission. Ever since November, when England had declared the North Sea a "Military Area" subject to mining and announced that neutral ships entered "at their own peril," House had been expecting a German riposte. It was folly to assume that the Reich's leaders would submit tamely to an illegal British blockade, and the worst of it was that England had probably been hoping all along that they wouldn't submit. With Germany's fleet outnumbered and outgunned by the Royal Navy, the submarine was the Kaiser's only weapon of reprisal, but if he used it Britain would tighten the screws of her own blockade under cover of a worldwide outcry against German "barbarity."

Submarines were simply too slow and vulnerable to stop and search every possible target according to the rules of cruiser warfare. Even the most plodding unarmed freighters were capable of ramming and sinking a surfaced U-boat, and ships with any sort of artillery at all—even a single twelve-pounder gun—posed a serious threat to even the most advanced submarines. One shell hole, or several, in a surface ship could be tolerated after all; one shell hole in a submarine and it was *hors de combat*, at best.

Concealment and ambush were the tactics on which U-boats depended for their effectiveness and survival; warning and provision for the safety of noncombatants were the mandates of international law. House had little doubt as to which, the tactics or the mandates, would take precedence in this new phase of the war, and a quick reading of the German declaration confirmed his worst expectations.

Most ominous of all was the final paragraph: "Within this war zone neutral vessels are exposed to danger since, in view of the misuse of neutral flags ordered by the Government of Great Britain and of the hazards of naval warfare, neutral vessels cannot always be prevented from suffering from the attacks intended for enemy ships."

The Colonel felt a chill run along his neck and shoulders. If American passengers were killed, attacks on belligerent ships would be serious enough; attacks on American ships, however, whether intentional or not, would almost certainly doom the United States to war.

Ambassador Page was waiting to greet him at Albert Dock, and so —as House had foreseen—were half a dozen correspondents of the New York dailies. It was clear from the reporters' faces that they didn't expect much, as the Colonel was almost legendary for being bad copy. Grasping at a straw, one of the journalists suggested that House might prefer to have a meeting with them in London after he got settled and comfortable, rather than now when he was just off the boat. But the Colonel merely gave the man a sleepy smile and said, "We may as well talk here; I'll tell you as much now as I will at any other time." The reporters went through the motions of being amused and then lobbed three or four halfhearted questions in the Colonel's direction. One was about Captain Dow's use of the U.S. flag, which the Colonel—thanks to Miss Denton—had only "heard about"; the others concerned the purpose of his visit to England, which was "purely private and unofficial."

The reporters at last gave up, and the Colonel joined Page for the drive to Lime Street Station, where they transferred to the London train.

"This flag business is very dangerous," House said once they were alone in their compartment.

The ambassador gave him a sharp look. "You think, no doubt, I should have protested about it some time ago."

House sidestepped the combative tone in Page's voice. "Oh? Have they been doing it for 'some time'?"

"The Admiralty issued the official instructions a week ago, but some captains have been exercising their own initiative for several weeks."

The Colonel nodded judicially. "And were you unaware of their actions, or did you simply decide to look the other way?"

"You mean, am I a nincompoop, or a miscreant?"

House gave the smallest flicker of a smile. "Question withdrawn."

"In any case, it's all out in the open now, what with the German declaration, so I can leave it to Washington to make the necessary protests. . . . Can't I?"

The Colonel looked down at his hands. "Walter, the President asked me to remind you—and Gerard too, actually—that an attitude of partiality in this conflict tends to materially lessen an ambassador's influence, not just abroad, but more particularly at the State Department."

"The State Department!" Page snorted.

"Whatever you may think of them," House continued evenly, "both Bryan and Counselor Lansing are beginning to feel uncertain about your dispatches because of what they perceive to be a pro-British bias. And the President asked me to tell you that he feels very strongly about this, especially because of how much he depends on you to represent our interests here."

Page listened with his arms folded and an expression of sour amusement on his face. "Well, I was expecting some sort of reprimand, so I'm not surprised."

Almost mournfully, House shook his head. "There's no question of a reprimand, Walter; you know that perfectly well."

The ambassador leaned forward and gazed intently into the Colonel's eyes. "Let me tell you a story, Ed. Every day, several times a day, I get criticized by some Englishman or by some visiting American for being unforgivably *pro-German* as I try to represent 'our interests here.' And let me ask you a question. Is an ambassador a man sent abroad to maintain good relations with another government so that it can work amicably with our government to foster mutual interests, or is his business to snap and snarl and keep 'em irritated and get and give nothing?"

House gave a long sigh. "Walter, will you just bear the President's feelings in mind. You know how highly he regards you and how much he appreciates the job you're doing. He only wants you to keep the idea of neutrality foremost in your mind."

Page threw up his hands. "Well, don't you think that's what *I* want too? God knows it is. But you haven't been over here since the war began, Ed. You just don't know what it's like. The number of people who are thinking rationally grows smaller every day. You've got an appointment with Grey this evening and you'll see what I mean. He's one of the few sane men remaining, but even with him you'll find that there's damn little neutral ground left to stand on."

House was disturbed by the change in the Foreign Secretary's appearance since their previous meeting in June. He looked haggard, which was understandable, but there was also something forlorn about him, something distracted and unsure. His condition troubled the Colonel for a number of reasons, not all of them touching on matters of state. For one thing, House *liked* Sir Edward Grey, and respected him as one of the most decent and upright men he knew. He also had great admiration for the foreign secretary: for the quiet excellence of his diplomatic skills, for his tact, his broadmindedness, his humanity. Above all, the Colonel's anxiety over Grey's appearance stemmed from the fact that Page was undoubtedly right about him—he *was* one of the few sane people left, and as such his continued good health was of vital importance to the United States.

"Forgive me," said the Colonel during a pause in their conversation, "but I hope you're not letting the weight of your responsibilities lead you to neglect your health."

"My health?" said Grey lightly. "Oh, I'm remarkably fit. Indestructible. It's just . . ."

He hesitated, then appeared to come to a decision. "I'm going blind," he said in a matter-of-fact tone.

"Oh, *no!* My dear fellow!"

"Yes, I'm afraid so. Progressive retinal amaurosis, so they call it. A proper nuisance."

House felt as if he'd been struck a blow. "Isn't there anything that can be done?"

"They say not, the oculists. It's a question of a gradual decay of the blood vessels around the optic nerve. Quite irremediable."

"I'm so sorry."

The foreign secretary grinned ruefully. "It is bad luck, isn't it. But it's a very gradual process, a slow slow waning of the day. They tell me Milton lost his sight from the exact same cause, and he did some quite good work in the shadows: *Paradise Lost, Samson Agonistes—* pretty respectable efforts, don't you think?"

"Yes, pretty respectable. But he had Andrew Marvell to dictate to, and also a much easier government job."

Grey laughed. "Oh, I don't know. Latin secretary to Oliver Cromwell sounds like hard work to me."

"Not a tenth as hard as fighting this terrible war."

"Well, certainly not as costly," Grey said in a slightly affronted manner, as if a reversion to the subject of the war was somehow indelicate.

The two men sat for a moment in uneasy silence.

"Well," House said finally. "As to the submarine declaration; I don't imagine you're going to let it go unanswered."

Grey's face took on a somber expression. "No, we're not. And it will come as no surprise to you to learn that there is strong sentiment in Parliament for a total interdiction of *all* trade with Germany."

"That would be a very serious development," said House.

"I know. But I think I can promise you that provision will be made to safeguard neutral interests, however stern the measures taken against the Germans."

House felt a wave of discouragement wash over him. "And what happens when the Germans take their own stern measures in retaliation for yours?"

"I would have thought they had about exhausted their repertoire when it comes to savagery," Grey said in a placid voice.

"I would like to think that myself," House murmured. "But this war keeps uncovering new depths of inhuman ingenuity."

"Yes," said Grey. "Things that would have been totally unthinkable six months ago are now happening in Europe every day."

"Too true. Now tell me honestly, Sir Edward, do you really see *no* way out of this nightmare short of a fight to the finish?"

Grey sat silent for a while, gazing at the floor. Then he said, "Colonel, if Germany had not invaded Belgium, I doubt that even the total defeat of France and Russia would have moved this country to take part in the war. Even as it was, Morley and Burns resigned from the cabinet when our hand was forced in August, and many other ministers, including myself, faced up to our danger only with the greatest reluctance. But in the end there was no avoiding it. Quite apart from the moral issue that both we and Germany were treaty-bound guarantors of Belgian neutrality, there was the direct and immediate threat of Germany taking possession of Antwerp and standing astride the Channel. That was manifestly intolerable; it was then and it remains so now. The evacuation of Belgium is therefore *the* condition precedent to any peace negotiations as far as we are concerned."

"I understand that. But you also appear to insist that the Germans agree to an indemnity."

"No. An indemnity is a condition precedent to peace, not to peace negotiations."

House felt a sudden lifting of his spirits. "But that's splendid!" he said. "The Germans themselves have always denied any intention of remaining in Belgium permanently. You're nowhere near as far apart as I'd thought."

Grey wearily shook his head. "Will you forgive me if I speak very frankly, Colonel?"

"Of course," House replied, chilled by the dead hopelessness in the foreign secretary's tone.

"All right then. I must tell you that you are building castles in the air. For let us assume that we are prepared to talk with the Germans once Belgium is evacuated. Let us go further and assume that France is prepared to consider a peace in which Alsace-Lorraine becomes a sort of internationalized arms-free zone, and that Germany is prepared to consider betraying Turkey in order to let Russia have Constantinople. Already, you see, the edifice is teetering. Furthermore, there are the Balkans; how do we sort them out? And South Africa and Australia want to keep the German colonies they've confiscated. And so on and so on and so on. Now I know what you're going to say: one step at a time—and you're right, of course. But I'll grant you the favorable resolution of all these irreconcilable conflicts and then ask you, where will we all be then?"

"At peace!"

Grey shook his head emphatically. "No! We shall be back at Sarajevo. Do you not see, my dear Colonel; that is the real horror of this business. It has gotten out of hand, and we are all locked into the mechanism. What are *we* fighting about? The violation of Belgian neutrality. Why did Germany invade Belgium? To conquer France. Why conquer France? To be free to deal with Russia. Why deal with Russia? To support the Habsburgs. Why support the Habsburgs? Because Germany must have allies. Why? Because she is 'encircled' by the Entente. Why is she encircled? Because the Entente fears her. Why does the Entente fear her? Because she is a nation capable of invading Belgium to conquer France so as to be free to deal with Russia to support the Habsburgs to prevent herself from being encircled. You see? It's all nonsense, all Alice-in-Wonderland. Although every cog in the mechanism looked at in isolation seems eminently neat and functional, as soon as you flip the switch and start all the cogs moving together the mechanism starts to destroy itself. Likewise, every step taken last summer on the road to war was in response to a perfectly commensurate provocation. Yet the war as a whole is utterly incommensurable with any goal we, the Germans, or anybody else had in mind when we started fighting."

"Then you think it's all hopeless?"

Grey shrugged. "I can see only one possible way out of the impasse other than a military decision. . . ."

"Yes?"

"Until last summer we in Europe had managed to maintain a balance of sorts among the larger powers such that the interests of some could be adjusted, peacefully or martially, without seriously jeopardizing the interests of all. Now that balance is deranged, and only a new makeweight can restore the equilibrium."

"Such as?" House asked guardedly.

"Such as some supranational authority charged with mediating and guaranteeing a peace, an authority backed up by *all* the major powers in the world."

"Including the United States?"

"Especially the United States!"

The Colonel felt dejection settle on him. "But you know that's impossible. The keystone of our foreign policy since 1796 has been noninvolvement in European affairs."

Grey smiled resignedly. "Yes, Colonel, I know. America partakes of the mechanism too."

1915, 8TH FEBRUARY—WILHELMSHAVEN

Gehlman had begun to notice the change in von Tiel soon after the announcement that the Kaiser intended to visit Wilhelmshaven, and he saw in restrospect that even the Baron's initial reaction to the news had been abnormal. Von Tiel had behaved as if he'd been stung on the neck by a hornet but was trying to pretend it didn't hurt. He had also gone at his cognac with unaccustomed vigor in the evening, and Gehlman had had to have him carried unconscious to bed.

Both of them had been working to the point of exhaustion since the *Seydlitz* had limped back into port. It had not simply been a question of repairing Dora and Emma turrets at maximum speed, but of devising a completely new ammunition-handling system for the entire fleet. Before the battle no one had imagined that ships could engage effectively at ranges of almost 20,000 yards; now everyone treated the idea as a foregone conclusion. Of course, what had given the concept its force was the havoc wrought by a single British shell, a shell that had not come straight at the *Seydlitz's* armor-belted hull and broken up on impact as would have a shell fired at normal range, but which had followed the high arching trajectory required for maximum distances and gone *over* the armor belt, through the deck, and into a turret. It was the old mortar principle of lofting projectiles over battlements that were impervious to direct fire; but it was a totally new application of the principle: to a phase of modern warfare in which both the weapons and the targets were moving at high speeds and in constantly changing directions. All unnoticed, it seemed, gunnery technology had completely outstripped tactical theory, and having nearly lost a flagship in the process of discovering this fact, von Tiel and his colleagues were now faced with the urgent need to rethink all their old ideas about turret design, and to rethink them fast! (In this connection they were able to derive some small comfort from the knowledge that the British experience at Dogger Bank had probably not been such as to alert the Royal Navy to the existence of a similarly urgent need with respect to its own dreadnought squadrons.)

It was clear, to begin with, that the working chamber was a danger to the entire turret, not to mention the ship. So far from protecting against cordite flash, the chamber now stood revealed as a tinderbox. In fact the whole ammunition train, from magazine to breechblock, had been exposed as a veritable time bomb, and to defuse it von Tiel hurriedly designed a system of interlocking flash-tight doors at each stage of the loading cycle. Essentially the system worked on the basis that no door to a next higher stage could be opened until the door from a next lower stage had been closed. In addition, the number of cartridges permitted in any stage at one time was sharply limited, and, as a somber final note, the connecting doors between adjoining turrets were padlocked shut.

As to the guns themselves, von Tiel instituted one major modification: an increase in the angle of maximum elevation from 13½ to 16 degrees above the horizontal. This produced a corresponding increase in maximum range from 19,000 to 22,000 yards; for it was now plain to everyone that the worst one could do at long ranges was miss, and that if one granted one's adversary a monopoly of the early shooting, one might well be in no fit condition to fire if and when the ranges closed.

Throughout the feverish two weeks of post mortems, reevaluations, redesignings, and repairs that followed the return from Dogger Bank, Gehlman and von Tiel had been together on a round-the-clock basis. The pressure of work had swallowed them up completely, leaving only occasional two- or three-hour respites for sleep and the other bodily functions. The baron had solicited Gehlman's advice on all the modifications being planned, and had gratefully adopted a number of his suggestions. So close had been their collaboration, in fact, that some unknown party had complained about it to the *Reichsmarineamt*, prompting an admonitory letter to von Tiel from Admiral von Holtzendorff, the new chief of staff in Berlin, through Captain Michaelis, the new chief of staff of the fleet. "You see their inspired sense of priorities," the baron had said when he showed the letter to Gehlman. "The whole fleet has to be redesigned, and all they can do is bleat about my choice of friends."

That moment, three days ago, had been the high point of their relationship. Their common interests, their shared experience of combat, and their total absorption in the task of restructuring the turrets of the battle fleet had culminated in this, the first acknowledgment by either man that a friendship between them existed. Only a few hours later, however, the news had arrived that the Kaiser and Kaiserin would be coming to Wilhelmshaven to install von Pohl officially as the new commander in chief.

Gehlman had given little thought to the strangeness of von Tiel's initial reaction to the announcement, and he had discounted his heavy drinking in the evening as the product of overwork and fatigue. But the next day had found the baron unaccountably sullen and aloof, so much so that Gehlman, feeling a sharp twinge of rejection, had begun to cast about anxiously for an explanation. Perhaps the letter from Berlin had been the cause, or perhaps von Tiel had simply recoiled in embarrassment from the confession of friendship he had made the previous day. Gehlman struggled not to jump to conclusions. He waited and sought to contain his anxiety, wondering fretfully whether it was something he had said or done—or failed to say or neglected to do—that had prompted von Tiel to draw back and turn away.

The pace of work had slowed on the eve of Wilhelm's visit, and officers and men were granted some sorely needed time off in which to sleep, bathe, and prepare their uniforms for the scrutiny of the Imperial eye. For Gehlman it would be the first visit to dry land in over two weeks, but as the steam launch from the *Seydlitz* moved over the glassy surface of the Jade Basin he felt no great surge of anticipation. He stole a look at von Tiel, seated beside him in the stern sheets. Their relationship, it seemed, had regressed almost all the way back to the sterile formality with which it had begun, leaving Gehlman dismayed and baffled in the process. What was most exasperating about it all was the baron's impassive refusal to acknowledge the fact that any change had taken place. Every attempt that Gehlman had made to bridge the widening gap between them, or even discuss it, had been met with a languid smile and the bland assertion that no such gap existed. Now the two of them sat side by side in strained silence as the launch approached the dock of the von Lutwitz mansion, the place where their short-lived friendship had begun. Gehlman felt wretched and alone. While he more than half suspected that the blame for the change in von Tiel's manner did not rest with him, that thought afforded him little consolation. He did cling to a slim hope, though, that a bit of rest and return to dry-land comforts might reverse the unhappy trend in their relationship, or at least reveal the reasons it was turning sour.

The von Lutwitz mansion sat like a boulder on the Südstrand looming over the waters of the Jade Bay. From the outside it looked no different that evening: a great dark monolith with just the slightest suggestions of internal illumination visible here and there behind the blackout curtains. Before the Dogger Bank sortie Gehlman and von Tiel had lived there in comfortable bachelor informality, occupying a small section of the north wing and attended only by two manservants, a cook, and a scullery maid; the great vastnesses of the rest of the mansion had remained dark and empty. When they walked in the front door on this evening, though, they were greeted by a blaze of light and by the vision of footmen and chambermaids scurrying around in every direction, all of them, it seemed, as mindlessly intent on their domestic chores as the broom splinters of *The Sorcerer's Apprentice*. Gehlman caught the look on von Tiel's face: it reminded him of the wry resignation with which chronic gamblers watch their last assets being swept up by the croupier's rake. "It seems we have a visitation from my lady," the baron said, and immediately went off to get a drink.

At that moment a number of things began to become clearer to Gehlman. A visit from Wilhelm and the empress had naturally meant that von Tiel's wife might be coming from Berlin as well, in her capacity as one of the Kaiserin's ladies-in-waiting. Furthermore, whatever the reasons for von Tiel's extreme reticence about his spouse, it was reasonably apparent that his reluctance to talk about her was not the outgrowth of any husbandly affection or amorous rapport. Thus the prospect of seeing her was probably what had precipitated his standoffish behavior, not any act or omission on Gehlman's part. The questions remained, however, why such an innocuous cause should produce such a singular effect, and why such a singular effect should have Benjamin Gehlman as its target.

When Gehlman came down to dinner at seven forty-five he noted with some curiosity that four places had been set. He found von Tiel seated alone at the dining table, brandy snifter in hand. That the baron had already had a great deal to drink was clear from the rigidity of his posture and from the elaborate hieratical precision that went into every motion of his arms and hands. He acknowledged Gehlman's presence by slowly turning his head and curling his lips into a macabre travesty of a smile. "Commander Gehlman!" he said with effusive sarcasm. "So good of you to join us."

"Good evening, Siggy," Gehlman replied in as neutral a tone as he could manage.

"Siggy? *Siggy?!* Are we acquainted, Commander? Are we intimate friends?"

Gehlman poured himself a sherry and tried to keep rein on his feelings. "Forgive the presumption," he said drily.

Von Tiel flicked his wrist several times, as if idly shooing away a fly. Then he focused his semisomnolent gaze on the table. "Four for dinner," he announced.

"I noticed," said Gehlman. "Your wife?"

"My wife," he said, as if Gehlman's question had just reminded him that such a person existed. Then he opened his eyes wide and slammed his hands on the tabletop, making the silverware clatter and the crystal shake. "But there are *four* places, Commander. You, me, my lady wife, and . . . another. A mysterious unnamed other. Whom do you suppose it could be?"

"I couldn't imagine."

"Nonsense. Your race is famous for its imaginative reach. I entreat you to take a guess."

Gehlman shrugged in nervous irritation. He had seen von Tiel in action often enough to know when he was out for blood, and the not-so-casual reference to "your race" left little doubt as to whom he had chosen as his evening's prey. Gehlman attempted to fend him off with: "How can I guess? It could be anyone in the world."

Von Tiel arched his eyebrows. "Anyone in the world? Oh, no no no. It couldn't be just anyone. Tsar Nicholas, for example; it couldn't be him. Nor could it be Mr. Asquith, nor Monsieur Poincaré. And the teeming millions of the Orient; none of them would be asked to dinner here. Nor would the denizens of the African bush. But there, I'll be giving the whole game away if I go on like this. Perhaps you've guessed who it is already."

Gehlman took a sip of his sherry, said nothing.

"No? Well, let me give you a final hint."

Von Tiel lifted his butter plate to the light and began to examine it with theatrical absorption. "The person in question," he said, "is not of our sex. Yours and mine, that is. . . . Well?"

Even though he knew it was von Tiel's object to goad him into anger, Gehlman could not master his rising sense of aggravation sufficiently to keep back a sarcastic response. "You've brought me Berlin's most accomplished courtesan, perhaps."

Still gazing up at his butter plate, von Tiel began to quake with silent laughter. "Ah, Commander Gehlman," he said finally. "You have a comic nature."

Gehlman could feel his ears reddening. The laughter was abrasive, and von Tiel's continued ironic usage of a military title in place of the heretofore standard "Ben" was beginning to grate very harshly on his nerves. "Are we going to spend the whole evening in this disagreeable banter?" he asked, barely suppressing the impulse to add a snide "Kapitän."

Still staring upward, von Tiel replied, "Only if we wish to, Commander. Only if we wish to."

All at once the baiting was too much to abide any longer. "God *damn* it, Siggy! Stop talking to me as if I were a stranger!"

Von Tiel snapped his head around. "And how else should a gentleman address a Jew?" he said, whipping his butter plate downward and smashing it on the table's edge.

Gehlman recoiled in shock from the savagery in von Tiel's eyes. Bad as the words had been, he could sense the alcohol behind them. The eyes, though, were quite another matter; alcohol alone could not account for their ferocity.

They both noticed the countess was standing in the doorway. A male eye would have appraised her as voluptuous, a female eye as fleshy. She was approaching forty, and the corners of her corrupt-looking full-lipped mouth were beginning to sag ever so subtly downward into the beginnings of a jowl. Her eyes were hard and dark, bearing the same sort of predatory glint that made von Tiel's gaze so intimidating. She had, too, von Tiel's smile, bleak and humorless, and his air of inexpressible ennui. What she did not have, to all appearances, was his capricious instability; on the contrary, she seemed as fixed and inexorable as a gravestone. Whereas von Tiel might lash out blindly in all directions, she, Gehlman sensed, only struck after calculation, but struck hard.

With the shimmering luxuriance of her jet black hair piled high above her ears and neck, she was a formidable vision of a woman, a vision of patent carnality. And she had a subtler quality as well, something not readily definable that greatly magnified her impact. It was a certain mordant resignation, an insouciant disdain for comforting illusions that suggested large reserves of private courage behind the hard veneer.

It was clear that she had heard, and perhaps witnessed, the concluding phase of Gehlman and von Tiel's exchange, and that she credited herself with having a better understanding of its significance than they did. She measured the two of them with a frankly cynical smile, then trilled "Siggy!" with bogus enthusiasm and held her hand out to be kissed. Von Tiel took it as he rose from his chair, and applied his lips to the back of her wrist. "My angel," he said with equivalent insincerity.

She accepted his bow condescendingly and then turned her eyes toward Gehlman. "And who is this lovely gentleman, pray?"

Von Tiel smiled drowsily, as if her overtures toward other men were an old, rather threadbare, but still passably amusing game between them. "May I present Commander Benjamin Gehlman of the United States Navy, attached to the High Seas Fleet as an observer."

The Gräfin swept her eyes lewdly over Gehlman's body. "An observer!" she said, extending her hand toward him. "How sweet."

Gehlman went through the courtly motions with no great enthusiasm. He hadn't yet had a chance to recover his composure after von Tiel's stinging attack, and he didn't feel fully up to coping with this woman's carnivorous advances.

"You must be related to Oskar Gehlman," she said.

"I'm his son."

"Intimately related. How nice for you."

"Ma'am?"

"All those banks. Or are you one of those heirs expectant who affect a disdain for wealth?"

"I don't disdain money, your Ladyship; I just don't think about it much."

"The mark of a true patrician. Are you married, Commander?"

"No, ma'am."

"Oh? How odd at your age. Have you an aversion to women, perhaps?"

Gehlman stiffened. "Not that I'm aware of."

"A rather tepid denial. Siggy, has he an aversion to women?"

"Of course. Who doesn't?"

The countess made a little moue in von Tiel's direction, then turned back to Gehlman. "Have you an aversion to *me*, Commander?"

"I've only just met you, your Ladyship," Gehlman replied. He was fast tiring of this preciously risqué interrogation.

"Gallant to a fault. May I ask you how long it's been since you answered a yes-or-no question yes or no?"

"In my experience, your Ladyship, there are no yes-or-no questions."

The countess gave a satirical gasp of admiration. "Dear me! How very profound that sounded. It seems you've brought me a metaphysician, Siggy."

"I thought you might enjoy the novelty, my dear."

Gehlman bridled at the notion of being in some way "brought," particularly brought by von Tiel for the Gräfin's amusement.

"Your metaphysics aren't Platonic, I hope, Commander," she said, running her tongue across her lips to underscore the double entendre.

"As I said, your Ladyship, I'm not aware of any aversion to women."

"Well and good. But are you aware of any craving for them?"

"Now and then."

"How gratifying. I may yet hope, in other words."

"For what, your Ladyship?" Gehlman snapped.

"Why, for you, Commander," the countess replied with reptilian poise. "Whomever else?"

Gehlman was astounded by the brazenness of the response. Having embarked on his fifth decade of life, he was not unfamiliar with ladies of tarnished virtue; in fact he had occasionally done the tarnishing himself. But this woman was completely outside his experience. She seemed to take a literally perverse pride in her corruption and to be engaged, with her husband, in an appalling contest of degeneracy.

Quite unexpectedly, a new element now introduced itself into this seamy atmosphere—an exquisite little girl, eight or nine years old, with long, lustrously black hair, deep violet eyes, a petite nose, and small roseate cupid's bow lips. Standing in the doorway, hesitant and shy, she was far and away the most beautiful child Gehlman had ever seen, so much so that he experienced a constriction of his throat from merely looking at her.

"May I come in, please, Mama?" she asked in a soft faintly sibilant voice.

"Of course, my dear," the countess replied in a cool pro forma tone. Then, turning to Gehlman, "This is my daughter by my late husband, the archduke. Alis, this is Commander Benjamin Gehlman of the United States Navy."

The girl curtsied daintily and said, "How do you do, Commander Gehlman."

"How do you do, Fräulein," Gehlman said, bowing from the waist and extending his hand.

There was perhaps a quarter of a second's hesitation, even a hint of shrinking back, but then aristocratic conditioning took over, and the girl presented her slender wrist.

Gehlman had caught the fugitive symptom of—what was it? fear? revulsion?—and so checked an impulse to kiss the hand, limiting himself to a brief gentle pressure with his fingers. There was no avoiding the fact that he was very much taken with this ravishing child. Quite apart from her beauty, she had a compelling quality of forlornness that brought out all his protective instincts. He did not analyze the impression deeply enough to judge the extent to which it might be a reflection of his own feelings of marooned isolation. He did recognize, however, that his instantaneous and categorical designation of the girl as a companion-in-adversity might not be altogether objective.

"Alis will dine with us," the countess said. "I believe in exposing her early in life to the refinements of adult society. . . . Don't I, Siggy?"

Von Tiel, who had been staring fixedly at his stepdaughter,

seemed startled by the Gräfin's abrupt question. He reached out to steady himself, teetered slightly against the back of his chair, then made a weak in-flagrante-delicto grimace in his wife's direction. It suddenly dawned on Gehlman that Alis had not yet acknowledged the baron's presence in any way—and was still not acknowledging it, even though her mother had just addressed von Tiel by name. She stood with her eyes demurely downcast and her hands resting one over the other on the front of her dress. Gehlman had the half-conscious impression that she was somehow using her hands to shield the area of her genitals, but a sudden shocked realization of the subject of his musings brought him up short, and he immediately swept his mind clear.

Conversation at dinner was anything but general. Von Tiel drank in silence, ate nothing. Alis nibbled small portions of each course, solemnly, without pleasure. The countess seemed to regard her food as some sort of minor irritant, an obtrusion that could be banished only by persistent proddings with a knife and fork. It was plain that she wished to concentrate her entire attention on Gehlman, but he was so rattled by the rash of disconcerting stimuli he'd been subjected to that evening that he couldn't have returned her interest even if he'd wanted to, which, on principle at least, he did not. He was able to give only fitful attention to her continuous questions and frequently had to ask that she repeat what she'd just said. Before long a tone of asperity began to appear in her voice, and it had the effect of making all three of her dinner companions become rapidly more alert.

"I was asking, Commander," she drawled nastily, "whether American officers still carry a sword."

"A sword?" said Gehlman, still a little distracted. "Why, yes. Or rather, only on ceremonial occasions."

"Ah, I see. Then you needn't keep them sharp, need you?"

"We're not required to, certainly, but most of us like to maintain the tradition."

"How very ardent. We regrettably lack such spirit in our naval service."

"Oh?"

The countess's eyes narrowed. "Well, if Siggy is any indication, that is. Just imagine my dismay, Commander. There I was, a redeemed widow on the second wedding night of my life, feverishly awaiting a display of my new husband's expertly tempered blade. But what do you think I learned?"

Gehlman saw clearly enough in which direction her recital was moving, and he sought to head her off. "Your Ladyship, I don't think the intimacies of the marriage chamber are a proper subject for—"

"*What* do you think I learned, Commander?"

"I'm sorry, your Ladyship, but I have no interest in knowing."

The countess smirked at him. "I learned that my husband's sword was blunt, Commander, blunt as a barrel hoop and hardly big enough to fill a schoolgirl's scabbard."

Appalled, Gehlman glanced anxiously at Alis and then von Tiel. Surely the baron would put a stop to this, for the child's sake if not his own. But von Tiel sat motionless, rigid, studying his wife with a glazed expression that was a strange amalgam of both hatred and admiration. Alis stared empty-eyed at the plate in front of her.

"How I've prayed that one day he would get it sharpened," the countess resumed. "But to no avail, Commander, no avail."

"Madam," Gehlman said, sickened that such a conversation should be taking place in the presence of a little girl, "I know it's not my place to say so, but I strongly suggest to you that this kind of talk is totally improper and reckless of your daughter's welfare."

The countess looked at him for a moment with an expression very much like stunned surprise. But then she began to laugh, loudly and derisively, and her laughter continued to such a point that Gehlman felt obliged to get up from the table and walk out of the room.

He had packed in haste, wanting nothing more intensely than to be out of that house. The highborn Sigismund von Tiel had shown himself to be a degraded sot, and the higher-born Regina von Lutwitz stood revealed as a corrupting whore. He would go at once to the Nordsee Hotel. Many other officers were living there. His bags were packed and he would leave, right now, putting this hateful place and that hateful woman behind him.

But he sat for over an hour thinking about the girl. It was ludicrous, of course; she was none of his business. There was no plausible pretext in the world that would justify his intruding himself into her family life, no matter how pestilential it might be. But knowing what he knew, or rather, assuming what he assumed, about the moral climate in which Alis von Lutwitz lived, and captivated as he was by her mournful fragile loveliness, he couldn't simply walk away. No, as long as she stayed in Wilhelmshaven, he felt an obligation to remain in the von Lutwitz mansion. He didn't delude himself that there was anything much he could do for her, but however little it was, it would be more than if he were living somewhere else.

And so, feeling a little silly about his vacillation and about his new role as knight-errant, he was in the process of unpacking when the countess entered his room.

She had changed her clothes. She was wearing a silken white nightgown beneath a light blue peignoir. At her throat was a cameo hanging from a ribbon of black velvet that set off the smooth rosé color of her skin. Her nightgown was brazenly décolleté, revealing pendulous breasts that aroused Gehlman extravagantly, even despite the plainly visible tracery of wrinkles and liver spots in their cleft. The outlines of her nipples were prominent beneath the finespun crepe de chine of her garment, and the exaggerated rise and fall of her flesh as she breathed excited him in maddeningly direct proportion to his desire not to be excited.

"Why, Commander," she exclaimed, closing the door behind her, "packing your luggage by yourself! What *will* the servants think?"

Gehlman tried to bring all his resources of moral disapproval into his voice. "Actually, your Ladyship, I am unpacking."

"Then we haven't driven you off after all," she said as she sauntered around the room idly examining items of Gehlman's clothing and effects. "I'm so glad."

"No, madam, *you* haven't driven me off."

She paused in her meandering and cocked an eye at him. "You're very censorious, Commander. Do you know that? I wonder what gives you the right to be. Are you better than I am, do you think?"

"Do I need to be?"

" 'Let him who is without sin cast the first stone.' "

"That's in the New Testament, your Ladyship."

She gave a little exhalation of laughter. "Ah, so it is. But what about 'Judge not, lest ye be judged'?"

"That, too."

The countess shook her head in mock consternation. "Dear, dear. You're a difficult case, Commander; I suppose I'll have to allow you your reprobation of me. But as to your moral purity, isn't there an Old Testament commandment to the effect that one ought not to covet one's neighbor's wife?"

Gehlman could feel the tension welling up in his groin. "I don't see the relevance of that, your Ladyship."

The countess gave him a smile of lewd condescension, then cupped her hands caressingly beneath her breasts. "Do you not find me desirable, Commander?"

Gehlman stood frozen as the woman approached.

"Feel my breasts, Commander," she said, leaning against him. "Taste my mouth." Her hand dropped to his trouser leg. "You want me on your long sharp sword, Commander, I can feel the hardness of you wanting me."

Summoning up his last reserves of self-discipline, Gehlman roughly slapped her hand away. "My body wants you, Frau von Tiel. I myself despise you."

The countess lurched backward, her eyes flaring. "Your body is wiser than you are," she said angrily.

"I don't think so," Gehlman replied, trying to regain control of his breathing. His body had wanted her very badly indeed.

The countess took a few seconds to recover her composure, and then, with a wryly skeptical glance toward Gehlman, walked over to the settee near the fireplace and sat down. "I'll say this for you, Commander: you're less of a hypocrite than most men I've known." The customary tone of condescension had been banished from her voice.

"There are worse things than hypocrisy," Gehlman responded, sounding a bit pompous even to himself.

"Self-righteousness, for example?" the countess inquired coolly.

"You bring it out in people."

"Do I?"

"Your Ladyship, I don't expect you to understand this, but until a few days ago your husband and I were working on the foundations of a very promising friendship. Then he learned that you would probably be coming here, and the friendship withered. I see now that it withered because he must have known from bitter experience that you would seize on my presence here to humiliate and dishonor him. Now if it's self-righteous of me to deplore the behavior that destroyed my friendship with him, and if it's self-righteous of me to resent your assumption that I would join with you in such behavior, then so be it: self-righteous is what I am."

The countess gazed at him in silence. "I applaud you, Commander," she said finally. "You've made an intelligent analysis of the available information. I must inform you, however, that the available information is incomplete."

"Oh? How so?"

"Well, while it is true that the possibility of a visit from me was what caused my husband to change toward you, it is not true that he changed because he knew 'from bitter experience' that I would humiliate and dishonor him. He probably wants you to think that's why he changed, but that isn't the real reason."

Gehlman frowned. "No?"

"No. The real reason is that he *wants* me to humiliate and dishonor him, with your cooperation, of course."

"What!?"

"Yes, Commander. He wants you and me to fall upon each other like rutting leopards. He wants us to stain the sheets in this bedroom on a thrice-nightly basis at least."

Gehlman gave her an incredulous stare.

"He knew he could count on me to attempt your seduction," she went on. "I was notorious for that sort of thing even before he married me. But how could he get you, an obviously incorrigible moralist, to betray his friendship and give in to your baser instincts? Why, by spurning you, naturally, reviling you, casting you off, kicking you, for all practical purposes, into my lap."

Gehlman was by no means ready to accept what she was saying, but a strange sense of apprehension began to oppress him as he asked, "What possible reason could he have for wanting us to cuckold him?"

"Cuckold him *again*." The countess laughed. "You're hardly the first of my transgressions."

"Call it what you like. What reason could he have?"

"Can't you guess?"

A cluster of disjointed images tumbled fleetingly through Gehlman's mind, accentuating his feeling of uneasiness. "No," he answered.

The countess gave him a belittling smile. "Very well then. The reason is my daughter."

"Your daughter?"

"Yes, Commander. Siggy is in love with my daughter."

"But that's *monstrous!*"

"Love, monstrous? Not a bit of it."

"It's outrageous. It's . . . it's *infamous!*"

"Dear dear, Commander. If my husband can retrieve some fragment of his self-respect by means of an infatuation with a nine-year-old girl, why should there be any objection?"

"Why should there be any *objection?* A grown man forcing himself on your daughter, and you ask me why anyone should *object!*"

"Commander, Commander, please calm down. I never said anything about Siggy forcing himself on Alis. What do you take me for? I may be a libertine, but I'm not a monster."

"But you said that he's in love with her."

"And so he is. He worships her, adores her, but in a very Teutonic-knightly sort of way. He would never sully her with coarse sexuality."

"He doesn't have to 'sully' her to harm her, for God's sake! We are talking about a nine-year-old *child!*"

"Really, Commander, you must believe me when I tell you that my husband's fascination with Alis poses no threat to her, moral, physical, or otherwise."

"Why must I believe you?"

"Because I know Siggy and I know Alis, and if there were any danger I would not have brought her here."

"But why expose her to such a situation at all?"

The countess looked down at her hands and was silent for several moments. "You said that you were forging a friendship with my husband, Commander. As you came to know him, did you get the impression that he was a happy man?"

"He seemed prey to the same discontents that afflict all of us in one form or another."

The countess shook her head. "Not quite the same, Commander. Siggy and I married for love, you see. I even intended to abide by my wedding vows, outlandish as that may sound. We wanted children. We wanted . . . everything. And we were so besotted with one another that we actually decided to wait till our wedding night for the consummation of our marriage. Can you imagine such a thing? Siggy and I, two hardened veterans of the venereal wars, actually engaging in chastity. We should have known it would be fatal to us."

"The consummation never took place?"

"Precisely."

"Why not?"

The countess shrugged. "Who can say? Perhaps because Siggy had never before been to bed with a woman he loved. Perhaps because my reputation intimidated him. Perhaps because he associated sex with the base and low-born women he often bought it from. I don't know." Her face suddenly seemed hopeless and worn. "At first I didn't agonize too much about it, but after several weeks . . . I don't know. Perhaps, unconsciously, I began to lash out at him. Perhaps I . . . no, definitely I was hurt. I was very hurt. I had 'reformed' for his sake, and I found it very hard to forgive him. He, meanwhile, found it very hard not to hate me. He began to drink, and frequent other women, and not so gradually fall apart. He had to go on extended leave from the navy, to Bad Reichenhall, for a cure. When he came back, there was . . . nothing, nothing left between us. We thought."

She let out a long sigh. "Alis was only four then: lovely, but no lovelier than many other children that age. It was for her good, as we perceived it, that Siggy and I decided to keep up appearances. Of course, it was true that I was useful to him in his naval career, and that having a husband is always a convenience for a woman who 'goes about' in society. But Alis was the prime consideration. We, Siggy and I, both felt that, being a sensitive child and having already lost her real father, she should not be subjected to the distress of losing her stepfather as well. She was very fond of Siggy, and he was utterly devoted to her—properly devoted, I mean: in a fatherly way. It's only been recently . . ."

The countess lifted her eyes to Gehlman, and he was astonished to see in them the traces of a plea for sympathy. "It all happened very quickly. On her seventh birthday, three years ago this coming June, Alis was just a pretty little girl. But in July, all at once, she became . . . breathtaking. It was almost as if a witch had cast a spell on her. Her eyes became a darker blue, her face lost its residue of chubbiness, and all her features somehow fell abruptly into place— flawless, incomparable. Siggy had been away on a cruise since that March, and when he saw her for the first time on his return in August I thought he might faint. When we were alone later he said to me, 'She looks just like you must have looked, before the spoilage began.' "

The countess was silent for a long time.

"And . . . ?" Gehlman asked.

"And . . . here we are: hating each other, playing out our human comedy."

"And my role . . . ?"

The countess gazed at him compassionately. "I'm afraid, Commander, that you don't really have a role. You're not a player in this melodrama, but a prop. I use you to humiliate Siggy. Siggy uses you to help me humiliate him. We both use you in our struggles to convince ourselves that we're really no worse than anyone else. I can't commit adultery by myself, after all. And Siggy's guilty passion is simply a refined and exotic variant of the common lust that pervades and animates the world."

"And Alis?"

"Alis is a conduit. What Siggy couldn't give me he is forbidden to give her, so he cannot again be weighed in the balance and found wanting. He can love without fear and I can be loved, vicariously, without feeling cheated. It's a dead end for him and a pale substitute for me, but it sustains something between us, and that's what we seem to want."

"But surely it's not a very good idea for a nine-year-old child to be used as a 'conduit.'"

"I don't think Alis is particularly unique in that respect, do you? Most parents I've known deal with each other through their children, at least to some extent."

"Now that, if you'll forgive me, sounds a great deal like sophistry."

"Does it? Well, perhaps it is sophistical to a degree. But a child's innocence is what protects Alis. The purest metals make the best conductors; currents pass through them cleanly, without warping or discoloring them in any way."

"Alis is not a metal, your Ladyship, and she seems to be unhappy."

"She is a freak, Commander. At nine years of age beauty such as hers is no blessing. She is pawed and stared at by many of her elders, snubbed or ridiculed by many of her contemporaries. Her father is dead, her stepfather drinks, her mother has a 'reputation,' and she has no friends or companions with whom to share her troubles. She is sensitive, intelligent, creative, and aware, and the civilization she was born into is destroying itself all around her. You'll agree, I think, that she does not have cause for jubilation."

"No," said Gehlman. "I suppose not."

The countess rose and assessed him for a moment in silence. "I think I'll bid you good night now, Commander. I had originally intended to renew my advances, but satisfying your scruples seems to have drained me."

"I understand, your Ladyship," Gehlman said, feeling an odd mixture of relief and disappointment.

"It's only a reprieve, my dear moralist, not an amnesty. Tomorrow is another day—and I think I'll start calling you 'Benjamin' to commemorate it, if you'll permit me."

"Well, your husband has stopped doing so, so you may as well start."

The countess laughed cheerfully. "You have a sense of humor! That means there's hope for you. . . . And having struck that encouraging note, I shall now take my leave."

"Good night, your Ladyship," Gehlman said.

"My name is Regina, Commander. And good night to you too."

Gehlman watched her walk out the door, then let out a long breath and lay down on his bed. He felt depleted but wide awake, stimulated. Vexing as the notion was, he had to admit to himself that Regina von Lutwitz had very nearly won him over. It required a genuine mental effort, in fact, for him to reenumerate her moral imperfections in sufficient detail to revive his disapproval of her. It wasn't easy or pleasant work, but he managed.

1915, 24TH FEBRUARY—ABERDOUR

The admiral's barge churned across the Firth of Forth toward the sooty battlements of Rosyth Castle. Looking over his shoulder to the south, Maltbie could see the pale pink glow that marked the sun's losing effort to penetrate the leaden overcast. Though the time was not yet three o'clock, the lower fringes of the glow were already reddening as they lapped at the dun-colored haze on the horizon. In an hour it would be dusk; in two hours, night.

A gelid wind pierced all four layers of Maltbie's clothing—topcoat, tunic, woolens, and undershirt—and he reflected ruefully that this was what his friends on the flagship would refer to as "a spell of fine weather." He never ceased to marvel at how utterly impervious the British were to physical discomfort. It seemed to be some sort of ritual with them. The previous Saturday afternoon, for example, he had gone with Waite and Spickernell to see a traveling company perform *Man and Superman*. At the point in the third act where the Devil says, "An Englishman thinks he is being moral when he is only uncomfortable," Maltbie had rocked back and guffawed, finding the line delightfully apropos. It was with considerable embarrassment, however, that he heard his laughter reverberating through an almost silent theater, and though Waite and Spickernell made a comradely effort to pretend they enjoyed the epigram as much as he did, it was clear that they were very much at a loss to understand what it was that he had found so howlingly funny.

Now the two of them were seated opposite him and Beatty, with their overcoats unbuttoned and their gloves in their hands. The raw redness of the skin round their knuckles testified that their flesh was feeling the cold even if they weren't.

This afternoon had been set aside for a combination of celebrating and leave-taking. The cause for celebration was Beatty's promotion from acting to permanent vice admiral and the enlargement of his battle cruiser command to include *Invincible, Inflexible,* and *Indefatigable*.

Dogger Bank had been heralded as a great victory by the newspapers, while the escape of *Seydlitz, Moltke,* and *Derfflinger* had gone virtually unremarked. This wasn't so much the consequence of a journalistic assumption that the sinking of the *Blücher* made for better copy as it was of an Admiralty belief that very few details of the engagement could be released without supplying the Germans with information of military value. Thus what was recognized by people in naval circles as a wasted opportunity was regarded by the public at large as a splendid feat of arms, and as the Admiralty shared in the political benefits flowing from this popular misconception, Churchill was reluctant to foul his own nest with inquiries and recriminations.

All this Maltbie had heard from Waite, whose sources of inside information seemed inexhaustible. "Of course," the cherubic lieutenant had added, "no one has anything but praise for Beatty. It's Admiral Moore who's looked on as the culprit."

Admiral Fisher had made no bones about that when he came up to Rosyth after the battle. Maltbie, Waite, Chatfield, Drax, and Beatty had sat openmouthed as the old man stomped around the mess and thundered against the second-in-command's failure to pursue the fleeing Germans. "It was despicable!" he had said. "Both *Derfflinger* and *Seydlitz* were heavily damaged and on fire."

Beatty, having sunk his disappointment over the Germans' escape in the higher principle of loyalty to subordinates, had broken in with, "In his defense, Jack, there was the regrettable matter of the inexact signal. . . ."

Fisher had banged his fist down on the table. "No signal can justify throwing away a certain victory. If Moore had had the smallest grain of attacking spirit in him he would have pressed on regardless of signals, like Nelson at Copenhagen and St. Vincent. Why, the first principle of warfare is to disobey orders. Any *fool* can obey orders!"

And so Moore had been "promoted"—to command the 9th Cruiser Squadron in the Canary Islands.

There had been other changes as well. With the addition of the three *Invincibles* the Battle Cruiser Force had been reconstituted the Battle Cruiser Fleet, though it remained under Jellicoe's overall command. Organizationally it now consisted of fully ten capital ships disposed with supporting light cruisers and destroyers into three separate squadrons. Maltbie enjoyed imagining the fleet drawn up into line of battle. The hoary tradition-laden dreadnought names—*Lion, Tiger, Queen Mary, Princess Royal, New Zealand, Australia, Indomitable, Invincible, Inflexible, Indefatigable*—seemed sufficient by themselves to overawe any potential adversary. (Of course—and Waite said this was always the case—the battle cruisers were far from being at full strength. *Lion* was out of action until May, *Inflexible* was in the eastern Mediterranean serving as flagship for the newly launched Dardanelles campaign, *Indefatigable* was undergoing refit at Malta, *Australia* had only just arrived from the West Indies Station, and *Queen Mary* was still working up after a refit at Jarrow.)

The installation of director-firing had been accelerated after Dogger Bank, especially once the expenditure-of-ammunition reports had been tabulated. These revealed that of the 1,154 heavy shells *Lion* and her cohorts had fired at long range, only seven had been hits, and of these seven, fully four had been "doubtfuls." The Germans, by contrast, had registered twenty-two hits while firing roughly 200 fewer shells. (Part, but only part, of this disparity in marksmanship was attributable to the fact that *Tiger* had misinterpreted the distribution-of-fire signals, ignoring *Moltke*, which was her target, and joining *Lion*'s salvos at *Seydlitz*. In addition to leaving *Moltke* unmolested, *Tiger* further compounded her error by mistaking *Lion*'s accurate shooting for her own, which in fact was 3,000 yards over.)

A further measure had been the expansion of the signal book in order to prevent a recurrence of the Moore debacle. The new signals most directly in point were: "Engage enemy more closely" and "C in C transfers the command."

On a more domestic level, Beatty and his staff had shifted the BCF flag to the *Princess Royal* until the *Lion* could return to service. The *Princess Royal*, being *Lion's* sister, had an equal number of berths, but whereas on the *Lion* the admiral's staff had been integrated into the operational functions of the ship, on the *Princess Royal* there was a full complement of officers who could not efficiently be displaced. A certain amount of reshuffling had eased the initial overcrowding somewhat, but the presence of supernumeraries became increasingly difficult to justify. Waite was alert to the nuances of the situation, and having already gotten his taste of battle plus more than enough material for his book, he gracefully volunteered to forgo further active service and return to London.

Maltbie's situation was a bit more complicated. First of all, Beatty had become accustomed to the luxury of having a sympathetic outsider available to serve as his "confessor," and this, added to his conviction that Maltbie was good luck, made him extremely reluctant to part with this "Yankee confidant." Secondly, Jellicoe had been until recently in a hospital ship at Scapa undergoing surgical treatment for piles, and therefore in no condition to receive an official visitor. He had now returned to duty, however, and in a postscript to a telegram sent on the twenty-third he had requested Beatty to "forward our American colleague to the *Iron Duke*." Beatty, though regretful, had taken prompt steps to comply.

So Maltbie's bags were now packed and on their way, with Waite's, to Waverley Station, while he himself was bound for Admiralty House at Aberdour for a final afternoon of tennis with his host.

Aberdour was situated north and east of the Forth Bridge, no more than five miles from Rosyth and St. Margaret's Pier, opposite the battle cruisers' anchorage. Maltbie had gone there for the first time a week after Dogger Bank and had discovered to his surprise that Admiralty House was not a government building but a mansion Lady Beatty had purchased as an official residence for her husband. It was a huge drafty old place built around an enclosed central courtyard. In the middle of this skylit atrium Sir David had installed a glistening African mahogany tennis court. He had, he explained to

Maltbie, given up golf completely, even though it was the navy's sport in vogue. "Tennis is the thing," he declared. "It's exercise in concentrated form, and you don't waste valuable hours chasing a miserable helpless ball over the hills."

As played by Beatty, tennis certainly was exercise in concentrated form. It had begun that first afternoon with doubles: Flag Captain Chatfield and Flag Lieutenant Seymour against Maltbie and the admiral himself. Rank had prevailed in that set, despite Chatfield's and Seymour's vigorous refusal to defer to it in their play. Then Maltbie had teamed with Beatty's son Peter, age eight, against the admiral and ten-year-old David, Junior. As sibling rivalry had begun to show signs of boiling over, that set had been declared a draw with the score tied at six games apiece. Maltbie and Beatty had then squared off for a friendly game of singles—or what Maltbie thought was going to be a friendly game.

Beatty's tennis style savored more of the stokeholds than of the bridge, and it was clear to Maltbie—as it would have been to anyone who wasn't blind and deaf—that the admiral did not take kindly to the prospect of losing. This posed a problem of sorts, as Maltbie was by far the superior player and won the first set by an embarrassing six games to love. A second set was contested forthwith, with Beatty bearing down but losing again 6–2, while snorting ferocious imprecations into the air. These oaths caused Maltbie some moments of alarm; not because they were directed at him (the admiral never failed to show the most punctilious on-court courtesy to his opponents) but because they were uttered with such vehemence and in such stern tones of reprehension that the entire universe, Maltbie included, seemed called on to account. "See here, this won't do!" the admiral would say after a double fault, or, "Monstrous! Absolutely monstrous!" after finding the net, or, "Unpardonable!" after hitting a ground stroke wide.

The third set was a hard-fought 7–5 victory for Maltbie, who felt, now that the match was over, that he had sustained enough exercise in concentrated form to last him for several weeks. It was with stunned incomprehension, therefore, that he watched Beatty stride back out to the service line and announce implacably, "Best four out of seven."

Maltbie's legs were aching, and the splinter-burned flesh on his palm was beginning to throb beneath its padded bandage. A glance at Chatfield, Waite, and Seymour indicated he could expect no sympathy from that quarter. In fact, there was the trace of a malicious glint in their eyes. They seemed to be anticipating the imminent dismemberment of American presumption by British perseverance. Maltbie took a deep breath. So it was to be blood sport. Very well.

He decided that, tired as he was, an admiral twelve years his senior would be tireder still. His strategy, therefore, would be to keep the ball in play, avoid mistakes, and wear Beatty down.

It was a fine strategy, but it was based on a faulty premise. Beatty was not tireder than he was. Beatty was fresh as a colt. Beatty was keeping the ball in play, avoiding mistakes, and wearing *him* down. He saw at last that his best chance lay—or had lain—in using his superior skill to achieve a quick decision in set number four. But set number four was already beyond redemption; he was behind 5–2. So he let Beatty win the final game and resolved to seize the offensive in set number five. A forcing game combined with fatigue produced errors, however, and Beatty, playing prudently, won without visible strain 6–4. Set number six began shortly after four in steadily failing light. The electric fixtures around the courtyard did not begin to compensate for the waning of the day, and Beatty's night vision appeared to verge on the superhuman. He won the set 6–1.

For Maltbie the friendly game had long since turned into a Sisyphean ordeal. But he was damned if he was going to let a forty-three-year-old admiral take him four straight sets. He mustered his remaining energies and embarked with grim resolution upon set number seven.

Maltbie held service; so did Beatty. Maltbie broke service; Beatty broke back. Maltbie served at ad-in in the fifth game. Beatty rifled his return toward the corner of the deuce court. Maltbie lunged for it and managed to send a lob arching high up into the pallid twilight. He lost sight of it near the top of its upward trajectory. Beatty, having charged the net, scrambled back toward the baseline. There was a hollow *plup* as the ball landed, then a softer one as it came down from its bounce, then . . . silence. The admiral could be glimpsed stalking around in the encroaching darkness. "In or out?" Maltbie shouted. There was a growly rumbling, then an explosive "I couldn't see the bloody thing . . . and now I can't bloody find it!"

This brought great gusts of laughter from the sidelines, and by general consensus the match was declared over, and a draw. Beatty jogged out of the thick gloom looking jubilant. "By God, Harry!" he bellowed, pounding Maltbie on the back. "That was one of the best bloody matches I've ever had. Let's play again tomorrow."

And play they did—the next day, the day after, then regularly, whenever the war permitted.

Today there was time for only one set and tea, as Maltbie's train left for Inverness at four fifteen. Beatty guilefully proposed that the "stayers" should be matched against the "leavers," which meant—leaving the pun aside—that Maltbie was saddled with a partner, Waite, whose inaptitude was exceeded only by his antipathy to physical exertion. Spickernell, by contrast, although similarly nonproficient, was a demoniac competitor, made doubly hellbent on this occasion by the fact that he was playing with his admiral, for whom he would have cheerfully gargled strychnine. The stayers accordingly mauled the leavers by a score of six games to two, a result that Maltbie accepted philosophically and that Beatty unequivocally relished.

"I wish you weren't leaving us, Harry," he said as they toweled off. "It's like losing one of the family."

"I'm sorry to be going, sir," Maltbie responded, feeling a bit like a child leaving home for its first day of school.

Beatty smiled. "Well, well, Harry, we'll join forces again very soon; you wait and see. The next time Fritz pokes his nose out the whole fleet will rendezvous to get him, and when the BCF steams past the *Iron Duke* toward the head of the line I'll signal Jellicoe to send you over on a breeches buoy."

"That sounds like a lot of trouble." Maltbie grinned. "Why don't I just swim over?"

"What! And get your racquet wet! Out of the question!" said the admiral, and he and Maltbie shared a laugh.

There was more leave-taking at the station, as Waite's train was due to depart for London only half an hour after Maltbie's left for Inverness.

"Right then, you poor devil," the round-faced journalist said as they shook hands. "May you find truth and beauty amid the arctic splendors of February at Scapa Flow—and may you survive long enough to enjoy them."

"Thank you, Morrie," Maltbie said with a lame attempt at deadpan. "My only regret is that it'll soon be March, and winter will be over."

"Yes, that is cause for lamentation. When you come to the

months with daylight you're forced to actually look at the desolate regions they inhabit up there. It tries the soul."

Maltbie smiled. "I don't suppose I need to worry about your soul being tried in London."

"Oh, it'll be tried, I'll wager—and found wanting too, with any luck."

Maltbie laughed.

"Take care, Harry," Waite said with affection. "Please write me if I can be of any service."

"If you can't, may I write you anyway?"

"I'd be honored, dear fellow. And if you survive the life at Scapa, I shall expect you to call on me at Ashley Gardens."

"I'll do that, Morrie, thank you. Thanks for everything."

"Rubbish!" Waite snapped with what Maltbie sensed was not altogether bogus irritation. "You Americans are forever saying thank you to people who've done nothing whatsoever to deserve your gratitude. No wonder we in England always patronize you."

"I'm sorry, Morrie. I'll never say thank you for anything again."

"And you're always apologizing when you haven't done anything wrong. Utterly servile. No wonder we won't let you join in on our war."

"Young nations make mistakes, Morrie."

"Well, just remember what Disraeli said: 'Never apologize, never explain.'"

"And never say thank you, either."

Waite laughed heartily and clapped Maltbie on the back. "You'll do, Harris Edward. You'll do. Now you'd better get aboard, or the next person you'll be apologizing to will be Silent Jack Jellicoe when you show up a day late."

Maltbie glanced at his watch. "I guess you're right, Morrie. Goodbye. Take care of yourself."

"Good-bye, Harry. Godspeed."

They shook hands and exchanged a smile.

Maltbie walked to the barrier and presented his travel papers to the platform attendant, then turned and gave Waite a final wave. Just behind the lieutenant, Maltbie caught sight of a young seaman he recognized from the *Princess Royal* sprinting through the station in his direction. The sailor came to a ragged stop in front of him, saluted, and said in a breathless voice, "The admiral's compliments,

Mr. Maltbie, sir, and this letter just arrived for you from London."

Maltbie looked at the postmark and felt a thrill: Lordsburg, New Mexico, February 9.

"The admiral wished me to say, sir, that he thought you might like to have something to read on the train."

With a happy grin Maltbie replied, "Please thank the admiral for me. . . ." He thought for a second about Waite's diatribe against gratitude, then shrugged to himself and added in all sincerity, "And thank you very much indeed for getting this to me before I left."

"Right, sir." The seaman beamed, saluting again.

Maltbie returned the salute, waved one final time to Waite, and crossed the platform to his train.

He settled himself in his compartment and sat contemplating the letter from Melina with quiet joy. It had been some while since he'd heard from her, but here between his fingers was the taste and sense of her again. He lovingly inspected the envelope: the original postmark, the black cancellation stripes of the New York Maritime Post Office, the dark purple seal of the Royal Mails, and fourteen cents of salmon-colored U.S. postage bearing upon it the likeness of Benjamin Franklin.

Maltbie squeezed the envelope. It was thick—many pages of Melina to sink into, like a great pile of quilts. He turned the envelope over. On the rear flap was printed RIO GRANDE HOTEL, LORDSBURG, NEW MEXICO.

He waited for the train to start, feeling that only once it was under way would he have the sense of privacy and communion that he wanted. The compartment, blessedly, was empty except for him.

The train whistle blew. There was a lurch, then a slow slow gathering of speed. As the chuffing of the steam engine and the clicking of the wheels on the tracks settled into a steady drumming rhythm, and the train gradually lost itself in the misty dusk of the Scottish winter landscape, he inserted his thumbnail beneath the tip of the flap and ever so carefully prised the envelope open. There were five pages inside, all folded neatly together in the middle. He took them out, smelled the scent of rose water on them, folded them in reverse so they came straightened, and, with almost a touch of regret that the moments of anticipation were over, began with rapt absorption to read.

8.II.1915
Lordsburg, New Mexico

Darling Harry,

Thank God! Oh, thank God you're safe!

I was going mad with anxiety till I got your letter this morning. We'd come down out of the Gila River area four days ago, and in one of your b——y American newspapers there was this ridiculous excuse for an article that said there'd been a big battle in the North Sea with many casualties on both sides—and instead of giving any details the next paragraph turned out to be an advertisement for a certain Dr. Wigram's Truss! Oh, I could have *screamed!* I telegraphed right away to Uncle Springy, and do you know what he wired back? "Letter coming." He meant your letter naturally, but *I* didn't know that, and I imagined the most horrible things, and I couldn't sleep or eat and I had these weeping fits and, well, I was just a blithering monkey. Then this morning and your blessed blessed letter.

Oh Harry, there were times during the past few days when I was certain you'd been killed, and it felt like a big callused hand had reached up and yanked out all my insides. If I've never told you before that I love you I'm telling you now.

I love you.

Why is it that writing to you always reduces me to tears sooner or later? I had to put my pen down just then because I was—as my great-aunt was fond of saying—"overcome."

I feel so self-conscious all at once. Is this a very silly-sounding letter? Oh darling, thank God you're all right. Are you really all right? Are you, Harry? Are you keeping something from me? Were you wounded somehow? Were you? Oh God, I *know* you were! Oh Harry!

Tuesday morning

Darling Harry,

Professor Kidder has authorised me to say that it is entirely normal for a person who has been under great emotional strain to succumb to a (small) fit of hysterics. It seems I was "talking" to you as I was writing yesterday and was heard to become overagitated. Now I've had a very peaceful night's rest (thanks to Professor Kidder's medicaments) and I'm feeling thoroughly ashamed of myself.

I suppose one reason why I became so overwrought was my realisation that I want to accept your proposal of marriage. And yet the thought of marriage terrifies me. I'm not a domestic animal, Harry. Can you understand that? Oh, yes, I want to have your children and love you and take care of you and be yours, but I want so many other things too. Is that horribly selfish of me? Well, I can't help it. I don't even want to help it. That's the difficulty.

Another thing that troubles me is you, Harry, because you ascribe all sorts of celestial virtues to me that I don't possess. No, I'm not being modest—modesty is one of those c.v.'s I'm without—I'm just being truthful. I know myself pretty well, darling, and I'm not the world's nicest person. You *must* believe that I'm made of the same base clay as everybody else.

I'm saying all this because I believe we shall marry eventually, and I want you to know ahead of time what you're getting into. I'd marry you this minute, Harry, except that I want to think about us a little more calmly than I've been able to these past few days. I know that one can overanalyse one's feelings and dry them up, but there's no danger of that happening where my feelings for you are concerned. Please be patient with me just a little while longer. And please think over very carefully what I've said. I do so want our life together to be happy, so we must know exactly where we stand from the start, mustn't we?

> I love you, my darling Harry, my dear sweet
> darling darling Harry,
> *Melina*

Maltbie folded the letter and gazed off into space, smiling. Despite the caveats it contained, despite the equivocal meaning of "I *want* to accept . . . I *believe* we shall marry," his imagination was already busy conjuring up blissful visions of the future. He knew the images went against all reason and probability, but they were so rapturous, so haloed with enchantment, that he was unwilling to let them go. He thought of a small house in Newport News facing the James, with Melina writing treatises and raising children. There would be many children—three girls and two boys would be best—and all five of them would spend their summers in England, acquiring refinement from Melina's parents. He would take Melina once a month to Richmond, and three or four times a year to New York for second honeymoons. She would grow lovelier as they grew older, and she would be almost as happy as he was with the content of their lives. Her only serious complaint, in fact, would be that he was away too much at sea.

Yes . . . yes . . . it would all be idyllic and sublime—even though nothing ever was.

Feeling euphorically serene, he unfolded Melina's letter for the second time, sighed with contentment, and began again to read.

Washington Hotel
Curzon Street
London

February 25th, 1915

Dear Governor:

After three weeks here I have come to some general conclusions which I send you as a supplement to my other cables and letters.

First, as to Foreign Secretary Grey: he grows in my estimation with every meeting. If every belligerent had an Edward Grey at the head of its affairs, there would be no war; and if there were war, it would soon be ended upon lines broad enough to satisfy any excepting the prejudiced and the selfish. He has discussed everything with me with the utmost candor, taking me into his confidence to so great an extent that I feel complimented beyond measure. He is the one sane figure of consequence here, and I am proceeding with him on the basis that it is the part of wisdom to maintain the closest and most sympathetic rapport.

All this being said, the obstacles in the way of peace discussions continue formidable. Foremost among them are the apparent German belief that they are winning the war, and the countervailing British belief that the Allies are about to strike their most telling blows. Alas, there is ample justification for both points of view. The Germans, quite apart from their conquests in the west, have just recently routed the Russian Tenth Army near the Marsurian Lakes and have also stiffened Austrian resistance sufficiently in the southeastern sectors to produce a stalemate there. Allied offensives on the western front have accomplished little, and it is clear that the German strategy for 1915 will be to stand on the defensive in France and Flanders while mounting an all-out effort to crush Russia in the east. If this strategy of "one at a time" succeeds, Germany will dominate Europe, with consequences disturbing to contemplate. All signs indicate that the Germans are in fact preparing a massive enveloping movement behind their eastern lines, and it is most unlikely that they will welcome peace proposals while anticipating a major battlefield success.

The Allied point of view is similarly unreceptive to the idea of negotiating peace at this time. The Russian Minister of Finance and the French Minister for Foreign Affairs were here this week, for example, and told Sir Edward Grey that they preferred not to meet with me as they did not feel there was any point in attempting even to discuss negotiations. Britain and France set great store on the impending Dardanelles operation. They hope to force the straits in three to four weeks, thus opening a supply route to Russia and knocking Turkey out of the war. They also are greatly encouraged by word that Italian discussions with Austria are breaking down, and they talk now of Italy entering the Allied camp in a matter of weeks or months. What is perhaps of most significance is the Anglo-French conviction that they can confound the German "one at a time" strategy with the new armies they intend to throw against Falkenhayn in the west. If the Germans are sorely pressed in France and Flanders, they will have to draw on their eastern armies to prevent a serious reverse. This will relieve the pressure on Russia and turn the scales of attrition in the Allies' favor.

All this being true, I still feel we have an opportunity to "prepare the ground," so to speak. The Allies' minimum demands are (1) the evacuation of Belgium, (2) indemnification of Belgium, and (3) guarantees for permanent peace in the future. To an extent, these three points are but the tip of an iceberg, but regardless of all the myriad other demands—and counterdemands—that will be made, these three are the only points that have been declared absolutely *sine qua non* for the beginning of discussions. I have already suggested to Sir Edward Grey that the question of indemnification might reasonably be deferred or made the subject of arbitration, and in my correspondence with Under Secretary Zimmermann in Berlin I have indicated that the indemnity issue might for the moment be waived if it were to prove the sole obstacle in the way of negotiations. Thus we have a very rough consensus for a two-point program as the basis for peace talks: the evacuation of Belgium and guarantees for a lasting peace.

Of course, talking about peace is not the same thing as refraining from war, and at this stage, moreover, we are merely talking about talking. The prime difficulty, as I suggested above, is that each side at present entertains hopes of military success, and unless and until such hopes are proven false by events, no responsible figure in either camp is going to make any significant concessions.

More blood must be shed, in other words, before this terrible conflict can be resolved. But there are men on both sides who deplore the carnage as much as you and I, and as the prospects of military victory fade, these men will be able to exercise a moderating influence on the war factions that now dominate policy in all the major capitals. I hope, therefore, during my visits to Paris and Berlin next month—and during the remainder of my stay here—not only to establish the two-point program as the basis for eventual discussions, but also to cultivate interest in a plan for the freedom of the seas that will attract the moderates on both sides as well as ease our difficulties with the British and German blockades.

You will recall, no doubt, how we were able during the debate over the Federal Reserve to convince the bankers that the legislation would benefit them more than anybody else, as it has, while also convincing the farmers and small businessmen that it would subserve their particular interests, as it does. I believe a similar form of double-edged persuasion may be possible here. The notion that maritime commerce in war should proceed, pursuant to treaty or Hague Convention, with the same freedom from interference as maritime commerce in peace, would, if accepted, be of immense strategic benefit to Great Britain. Grey has acknowledged this, and it is, indeed, an inescapable conclusion. For an island nation dependent for its very life upon sea trade, the knowledge that the avenues of commerce are safeguarded by treaty must be a source of immeasurable comfort. For Germany, on the other hand, freedom of the seas would mean the banishment forever of the threat of British blockade. It would also supply a rationale for the evacuation of Belgium, as the Kaiser could say to his people that the Belgian coastline and ports were no longer needed now that England was "surrendering" her control of the oceans. As for us in America, absolute freedom of commerce would remove at a stroke the twin provocations of British highhandedness on the sea and German underhandedness beneath it.

So I am not discouraged. True, it grieves me that peace talks must await further bloodshed, but I also begin to discern that some good may yet come out of all this deplorable suffering, good not just for us and the belligerents, but for mankind as a whole. One thing that has struck me most forcibly since my arrival here is the strength of Sir Edward Grey's conviction that the only true guarantee of peace for the future lies in creating some form of permanent international conference specifically empowered to settle, or at least mediate, the disputes that arise among nations. I think it is a fine conception, and I assured him that the United States would applaud such an innovation as a great step forward in mankind's progress. He, of course, insisted that the United States should be a participant, and I, of course, repeated that it was not only our unwritten law but our fixed national policy not to become involved in European affairs. It was a very polite exchange, but I have the decided impression that Grey has no intention of letting the matter rest. (He was very appreciative, by the way, for the autographed copy of your book, and he is writing privately to thank you.)

I dined yesterday with Herbert Hoover, who is handling Belgian relief very adroitly, especially given the difficulties he has to contend with from the three governments involved.

I will be seeing Prime Minister Asquith again next week, and I will convey your message.

Page is still very partisan, but he's held in great esteem over here and, of course, is still the finest sort of fellow.

I think your "strict accountability" statement to the Germans about their new submarine blockade was splendid. It will make them think twice before embarking in earnest on such a pernicious form of warfare.

I hope, my great friend, that your health and spirits are good, and that you are following Dr. Grayson's advice.

Affectionately yours,
E. M. *House*

1915, 25TH FEBRUARY—LONDON

There were times when Commander Montague Reeves-Wadleigh thought he could feel the cancer. It was in his spleen, they said, or on it, and sometimes he experienced the sensation of a mindless knob-shaped slug poking at the outside of his stomach. It wasn't a painful sensation; it was just endlessly sinister.

They couldn't tell him much about the cancer: how long it had been growing, where exactly it was. "Inoperable" was the word they used to describe it, inoperable because of a "contamination of the lymphatics." Of course, they didn't know how extensive the contamination was. They didn't know if it had progressed beyond the spleen. They knew astonishingly little, he had found. All they could say for sure was that within three months to two years he would be dead.

The sensation in the well of his abdomen always seemed most pronounced when Reeves-Wadleigh was irritated or upset. The strongest surge had occurred just after he mentioned the feeling to the doctors and was told, rather sniffishly, that a tumor like his could not be "felt." The second strongest surge was occurring now, as he listened to Admiral Fisher catechizing Mr. Morrison Waite on the subject of the American observer.

Reeves-Wadleigh thought it was madness. It was bad enough that Commodore von Schoultz of the Imperial Russian Navy was aboard the *Hercules* and that Count Kendo of Japan was aboard the *Temeraire*—but at least those officers were allies. This Maltbie, by contrast, was the representative of an outspokenly neutral power, an outspokenly neutral power, moreover, that was almost as likely to end up in the enemy's camp as in England's. And as if his mere presence with the fleet weren't already folly enough, they were going to compound the insanity by posting him to the *Iron Duke!* Anglo-Saxon fraternity was meager compensation for the taking of such idiotic risks.

Reeves-Wadleigh shuddered. How many people knew about Room 40 in the Old Building, other than the few cryptographers who actually worked there? Fisher, of course, Churchill and the rest of the Board, the prime minister, Jellicoe, Beatty, he himself, and his immediate superior, Admiral Hall, the director of the War Staff Intelligence Division. Fourteen men. True, there had to be several dozen officers in the navy as a whole who were aware that the Admiralty was somehow deciphering German radio signals. But only fourteen people in the entire country knew about the drowned telegraphist the Russians had found aboard the wrecked German cruiser *Magdeburg* back in August, the loyal young sailor who had clutched the navy signal book to his breast as the waters of the Gulf of

Finland closed over him, thereby presenting to the Allies the single most important batch of intelligence yet to materialize during the war. Poor lad. He could hardly have suspected as the seawater exploded his lungs that his sinking ship would drift aground. He must have fairly glowed with patriotic ardor in those last few seconds before the final agony—he was taking the code book down with him! Reeves-Wadleigh smiled grimly to himself. It was one of those fine wintry ironies with which this war seemed increasingly to abound. Like his sister Moira's joyful reaction to the bitter news that he had been denied sea duty, her sallow-faced ecstasy, her spinster's rapture, over the fact that her dearest and only brother had been picked out by destiny to survive the war.

But there might well be finer ironies than the *Magdeburg's* code books in store, finer and more terrible. With this American aboard Jellicoe's flagship, what chance was there of keeping the secret of Room 40 OB? The man was capable of drawing inferences as well as anyone else, no doubt; otherwise he wouldn't have been chosen to come over here. And he was a signals specialist on top of that.

What utter lunacy.

Even granting the premise that he would refrain from dishonorable probing, how could he help but know what all the men around him knew: that the German Fleet never left harbor without the British Fleet's being forewarned? And there would inevitably be talk in the admiral's mess about the so-called Japanese telegrams that arrived magically from Whitehall whenever an action seemed imminent. It would require no great mentation on the American's part to draw the conclusion that the Germans were betraying themselves by their wireless transmissions. And once that conclusion was drawn, what guarantee was there that it would not be reported to Washington, or that once it was reported to Washington it would not reach the ears of an anglophobe or teutophile who would start it on its way to Berlin, or that once it reached Berlin it would not prompt Tirpitz to send the High Seas Fleet out with precise *written* instructions while transmitting decoy messages via wireless, thereby luring Jellicoe and Beatty into a lethal ambush of mines and submarines while the German dreadnoughts fell on the old *King Edward* class battleships in the Channel and severed the lifeline to France?

For want of a nail, for want of a nail. Miserere, miserere. And gentlemen in England now abed shall think themselves accurs'd. . . .

Reeves-Wadleigh did not like Morrison Waite. In fact, he actively disliked him, thought him a fop, a self-server, and a popinjay. He was the last man to whom the task of keeping watch on the American should have been entrusted. But they had been caught unprepared. They hadn't expected Lieutenant Commander Maltbie to spend more than a day with the battle cruisers. They hadn't expected Dogger Bank. The man they had designated to maintain surveillance was already with Jellicoe at Scapa. So Waite, who was already aboard the *Lion* and performing no duties of consequence, was recruited more or less by default. As Fisher questioned him, though, it was clear that he viewed his appointment as the inspired final outcome of a long and arduous process of selection.

Of course the information he was imparting was on the maddeningly worthless level of Lieutenant Commander Maltbie being a "good fellow," a "thoroughly trustworthy sort," a "man of honor," and so on. There weren't more than two or three scraps of hard information in his whole long self-satisfied report, and Fisher's questions elicited only a scant few more to go with them. A man with any sort of training at all would have presented more facts than these within two minutes of entering the room. Now, however, thanks to Waite's fatuity and incompetence, when the naval attaché's report on Maltbie's background arrived from Washington, there would be no body of data to check it against for discrepancies.

The cancer throbbed.

Waite concluded his recitation, Fisher thanked him, pleasantries were exchanged, and Waite left.

The old admiral leaned back in his chair and rubbed his eyes. Seventy-three was no age for a man to be running the world's largest navy at war. He was a titan, to be sure, and he was more than holding his own, but he was also, and increasingly, showing the strain.

"Well, Monty," he said, "what do you think?"

Reeves-Wadleigh made a small grimace. "I think, sir, that we're fortunate to have a good man waiting up at Scapa."

Fisher gave a snort, then cocked his head toward the door through which Waite had just departed. "I guess he wasn't much use, was he?"

"No, sir, he wasn't."

Fisher stretched and yawned, looked at his watch, shook his head. "Oh well, I daresay your man on the *Iron Duke* will make up for him."

He was silent for a moment, seemingly abstracted. "I know you're not comfortable with this whole arrangement, Monty," he said finally. "And I respect your misgivings. In fact, I'm grateful for them. Only try not to look so glum, will you?"

Reeves-Wadleigh forced out a cadaverous smile.

Fisher looked at him for a second or two, then rocked back in his chair and roared. "Oh, dear dear *dear*, Monty," he said between spasms of laughter. "Go back to looking glum. Immediately!"

Reeves-Wadleigh laughed too.

"I'll even give you something more to look glum about," Fisher said, wiping some wetness away from his eyes.

"Oh?" said Reeves-Wadleigh, immediately alert. "What's that, sir?"

"Me!" said Fisher bluntly.

"You, sir?"

"Yes, me. I don't know how much longer I can go on fighting with Winston over this Dardanelles adventure of his. It's going to bleed us white. I know it in my bones. But I can't convince him. He always outargues me. He's denuding us here in our home waters in order to maintain his Mediterranean sideshow, and if he keeps it up I'll have to resign."

"I hope not, sir," said Reeves-Wadleigh, who had never had any great opinion of Winston Churchill, despite the man's indisputable brilliance. He certainly wasn't a dilettante, as many charged, but perhaps it would have been better if he were. For he kept intruding himself into the operational realms that were the province of the professional seamen. Previous First Lords had properly confined themselves to the political side, leaving the Sea Lords to look after the sailors and the ships. Churchill, however, was all over the estate, and systematically "outargued" everybody. If Fisher resigned there would be no one left to stand up to him, assuming of course that he survived Fisher's resignation politically himself.

"Well, it may happen all the same," Fisher said. "And if it does, I'm counting on you to keep me informed—as we've discussed."

"I'll see to it, sir."

"You've started a file, have you, on the matters I'll want to keep up with?"

"Yes, sir."

"Good, Monty. And for your own peace of mind, make sure this Maltbie business is included in it."

"I'll do that, sir," Reeves-Wadleigh said; and the cancer throbbed and throbbed.

1915, 25TH FEBRUARY—WILHELMSHAVEN

Gehlman looked down at the countess sleeping naked beside him, snoring softly, her mouth hanging part way open. Although over two weeks had passed since he first succumbed to her, he still hadn't reconciled himself to the practice of adultery. Granted that virtue had reigned triumphant in the face of initial temptation, granted that von Tiel's role in the affair was one of virtual complicity, nevertheless . . . nevertheless . . .

Where, he wondered, had he come by such a lively sense of sin.

Of course, he had never had any use for rationalizations. At bottom he believed in the binary universe of his fathers: right-wrong, yes-no, done or forborne. He knew that one could rationalize anything; he assumed, therefore, that one ought not to, and only now and then did he get a glimmering that his morals might be better than his logic. In this specific case, for instance, it would have been easy enough to come up with extenuations. Von Tiel, after all, had virtually banished him from the *Seydlitz*, on the flimsy pretext that ongoing refinements of the director-firing systems were too secret and sensitive for Gehlman to see, at least during the installation phases. True, von Tiel had specific orders from Berlin that he could invoke as the reason for his actions, but he had received such directives before and ignored them. In any case, the refinements in question were of distinctly minor significance, and a number of them, moreover, had been recommended by Gehlman himself.

He certainly couldn't have protested his exclusion, even if he'd been disposed to. Colonel House's instructions to avoid both the substance and the appearance of inquisitiveness were still vivid in his mind, and there was, furthermore, the undeniable fact that he wanted to have as little to do with von Tiel as possible.

So he was beached—exposed to Regina von Lutwitz day after day. He had again considered moving out of the mansion to a hotel, but that still left Alis von Lutwitz out of the equation, so he stayed.

He looked again at the countess, lying there with one breast exposed, and wondered that he could desire her. Clearly there was something missing in him that he could have spent so many nights with her, and others, and still have awakened every morning with this feeling of clinical detachment floating, like a film of oil, on countless fathoms of disgust. To be driven to frenzy by creatures such as this, allured by their paints and fragrances, deranged by the touch of their bodies, reduced to the condition of a ravening boar—and for what? Only for them to transmute themselves beneath you as you chased your passion down, to see the paint dissolve beneath your kisses, the flesh go pulpy beneath your hands, the fragrance die in streams of acrid sweat.

And what were you left with? This gamine with a naked breast, sound asleep, insensible, this hoyden to whom you'd come for gratification, but whom, all unthinkingly, you had gratified, in return for a mere momentary spasm. You had set out to use, and you had been used. And your spoils, your trophy of the hunt: a sense of stickiness and enervation; while she, your captured prey, lay there like victory, smiling and replete.

It was endlessly puzzling; but always with her there had been something inevitable about it. She had come to his room several times after the first inconclusive night, but had not, to use her phrase, renewed her suit. They had talked: about von Tiel, about Alis, about her late husband, about Germany, America, the war, and he had found her conversation increasingly agreeable day by day. But as his pleasure in her company increased so did his already intense desire to possess her, and things quickly reached the point where, despite his scruples, the briefest touch or the softest summons would bring him instantly to her, if she still cared to have him come. She did, and his scruples went over the side like so much galley slops. She was adept, as he'd expected; but more than that, and something quite new in his experience, she was in control. He didn't think he liked that very much at all.

As for Alis, she remained exquisite: in manners, in beauty, in aloofness. She spoke almost not at all, and only with the utmost reluctance to anyone but her mother, her tutor, or her governess. The hint of revulsion that Gehlman had detected the first time he met her had proved to be one of the few regularly observable facets of her personality. It appeared whenever he tried to engage her in conversation, and if he chanced to approach her, he could see it grow in intensity and begin to modulate into fear. The countess had no explanation for this, though she admitted rather airily that other men had remarked on similar episodes in the past. Without having really reasoned it through, Gehlman formed the idea that Alis ought to be seen by a pediatrician, and he pressed the point so aggressively that he and the countess quarreled over it, forgoing two successive nights of copulation as an earnest of their anger. To Gehlman's considerable surprise, he ended up winning his point, which indicated, he guessed, that the countess too was concerned about her daughter's behavior. Thus the rather dowdy but plainly capable Frau Doktor Bauer had come to examine Alis and had pronounced her organically well and whole, though unusually shy. The matter rested there, resolved in the countess's mind, unresolved in Gehlman's, and copulation was resumed.

Gehlman looked at the clock on the dresser; it read a little after six. He eased himself out of bed and went into the bathroom to sponge himself and shave. The countess was still asleep when he reemerged and stayed asleep as he put on his clothes. He didn't wear a uniform these days; it would be too conspicuous now that he was confined to the shore. So his valet had laid out a three-piece brown tweed suit with bow tie and soft collar. Carrying his freshly shined oxblood boots in his hand, Gehlman slipped quietly out of the room and down the stairs. Once on the ground floor he pulled the boots on, then opened the front door and went outside.

It was a mild morning, very quiet, with a lacy damask of fog not quite thick enough to obscure the sky. He walked down to the strip of beach in front of the mansion and breathed in the wet air. He felt strangely tranquil, accepting, free of his customary aches and stresses. He even felt rather alert and energetic, hungry for breakfast, eager for the day. Why he felt so chipper he could not for the life of him imagine.

He heard, then saw, Hipper's barge making for the mansion's jetty. When it got near, the coxswain eased the motor back, and the boat glided smoothly in to the pier. A sailor jumped out and ran along the jetty and down the beach toward Gehlman. He stopped in front of him and saluted. "I am instructed by my Admiral Hipper to request the presence of Fregattenkapitän von Tiel aboard the flagship," he said.

Gehlman was taken aback. He had had no idea that von Tiel was ashore. But he returned the salute and said matter-of-factly, "I'll go and inform him."

He walked briskly back to the house and up the stairs. It must be fairly urgent for them to have sent the admiral's launch.

He knocked twice on von Tiel's door. There was no answer. He knocked again and pushed the door open. Alis was standing naked in a basin of water.

Something was wrong.

Von Tiel was kneeling beside her with a sponge in his hand. "Get *out!*" he slavered, his eyes bulging, his voice choked. Alis was standing rigid with her face averted. Gehlman could see that her fists were clenched and her eyes tightly shut.

"The admiral wants to see you immediately," he shouted, then reflexively jerked the door closed.

He stood there feeling dizzy and faint, prey to a dozen different impulses to action. One impulse quickly took hold of him, however. Lurching drunkenly, he rushed down the stairs and out of the door, wanting nothing more urgently at that moment than to be quit forever of the sight of that house.

1915, 25TH FEBRUARY—SCAPA FLOW

The fierce northeasterly wind battered the two-car train as it puffed its way north across the low hills of Caithness. In the rear car, empty except for himself and the guard, Maltbie sat gazing out at the angrily swirling rain. He shivered and drew his greatcoat closer around him. The train had been none too warm when it had pulled out of Inverness at lunchtime. Perhaps it was no colder now, but after four hours the chill had lodged in his bones, and the cheerless subarctic twilight added a desolate funereal quality to the already dismal surroundings.

This was the Zone of the Fleet: the entire northeastern tip of Scotland from Inverness to Durness and John O'Groats was, for all practical purposes, an Admiralty preserve governed under martial law. That was the main reason—apart from the railway schedules— why Maltbie had had to break his journey for a night at Inverness:

his travel papers had had to be telegraphically verified from both London and Scapa Flow.

His hotel room hadn't been much warmer than this train, he admitted to himself, but at least he'd had some blankets to bundle up in. Now he had only his clothes and Melina's letter, but not even that could relieve the painful numbness in his toes. Waite had been right: the north of Scotland in wintertime was not going to be any abode of bliss.

The train at last pulled into Thurso Station, which, so far as Maltbie could tell, was deserted. He felt more like an abandoned child every moment. Where was his escort? He went inside the waiting room and sat shivering in its barren gloominess as the elements hammered on the walls outside. He sat for what seemed a long uncomfortable time; then very gradually, and mercifully, he began to doze. . . .

"What's this?! Asleep in wartime?!"

Maltbie opened his eyes. Standing in front of him was what appeared to be a tall rain-soaked leprechaun in oilskins. The man had green eyes, red freckles, frizzy red hair that sprouted with particular profusion around his ears and eyebrows, a small turned-up nose, a sensitive mouth, and a chirpy tenor voice with such a preposterous Irish lilt to it that Maltbie almost doubted its authenticity.

"Lieutenant Commander Maltbie, is it?" the man said.

"Uh, yes."

The man whipped off his rain hat, saluted, clicked his heels, and bowed low from the waist, his right hand, bearing the sou'wester, sweeping around histrionically and coming to rest in courtly fashion against his left shoulder. "Corporal Terence Parnell Otley, RMA, at your service, sir. Sorry we weren't here to meet ye, but there's this bloody great storm blowin' in the Pentland Firth—if you'll excuse the profanity—and we had a time of it gettin' in at all, though we regret the tardiness for certain sure as our Terry here is detailed as your servant, ye see, as we've got a number of relatives in America is perhaps why. Ye don't by any chance happen to have any acquaintances by the name of Otley back there, do ye?"

"Uh, no," said Maltbie, who was a bit confused over the "we's" and over the reference to "our Terry." As the man standing before him was unaccompanied, Maltbie rather reluctantly drew the conclusion that it was the royal "we" he was hearing and that "Terry" was the diminutive name with which Corporal Otley referred to himself.

"Faith and it's just as well, 'cause our cousins and such are as scurvy a gang of rotters as you'd ever want to meet, which ye wouldn't. Which you'd rather join the Royal bloody Marines than meet in fact, like our Terry, to get away from the sods what *didn't* go to America, who weren't much of a bargain neither, if ye follow me."

Maltbie blinked a couple of times. "Excuse me, Corporal," he began, "but—"

"Beggin' your pardon, sir, but if ye wouldn't mind not addressin' us as 'Corporal' we'd consider it a great kindness, as we was a private for seven years, ye see, and don't like to think of ourselves as wearin' the boots of an overseer or such like and troddin' down on our brothers what's privates still, if it's all the same to ye. And we'd be pleased if ye could call us 'Terry' or 'Otley' if ye can manage it without inconveniencin' yourself or compromisin' your position as it might be."

"Terry it is," Maltbie agreed. "And I think I know how you feel, having been a lieutenant for eight years myself."

Otley beamed. "Well, that's all right then, and well concluded. And now we'd best be off, as Silent Jack will be awaitin' ye."

He replaced his hat, picked up Maltbie's suitcases, and moved a few steps toward the door. Then he stopped abruptly, stood motionless for a moment, wheeled around, and repeated the whole process in reverse. "If ye don't mind us sayin' so, sir, we're particularly pleased to be servin' an American officer; and if ye notice us now and then bein' a bit scanty with the courtesies of the service, ye should pay no attention whatsoever as it's just our way and no disrespect intended, if that strikes ye as fair speakin', sir."

"Fair spoken it strikes me." Maltbie laughed. "Fair spoken for fair."

Otley joined in the laughter, and soon worked himself up to the wildest guffaws. "Fair spoken for fair," he roared, picking up the suitcases once again and heading for the door. "Oh, but that's a lovely turn of phrase."

A bit staggered by the lustiness of Otley's mirth, Maltbie subsided into a bemused silence and meekly followed his new retainer out into the rain.

A motor coach took them to the harbor, where a small steamboat was loading. Maltbie looked out beyond the breakwater at the cold gray swell in the Pentland Firth. It was not going to be a smooth crossing.

It took three hours against the wind and tide rip to reach the lee of South Ronaldsay near the entrance to the Flow. Maltbie and Otley caromed around the passenger lounge like dice in a cup, and after an hour or so of violent exertions designed to ward off collisions with the bulkheads and each other they undertook to tie themselves down. Once they were secure Otley produced a half pint of brandy, and after another hour it was consumed. Slightly aglow, Maltbie relaxed and let the rope take the strain of his weight. He felt strangely disembodied, tossed and caught and whirled around in a little box of light while from outside came the howl of an all-engulfing darkness. Thank God for alcohol, he thought. And thank God for Corp—for Terry.

They were both asleep when the boat passed Flotta Island and entered Scapa Flow. Maltbie woke first with a change in the rhythm of the engine. He roused Otley, and they untied themselves and stepped on deck. The storm was blowing itself out, leaving the air clean and cold. A waning crescent moon shone brightly on the fleeing clouds, presenting Maltbie with his first glimpse of the Grand Fleet.

He had never seen anything like it, for the simple reason, he realized, that there *wasn't* anything like it: twenty-two dreadnought battleships, half a million tons of guns, turbines, and armor, the physical embodiment of Britain's sea power, drawn up into four silent lines, pearl gray in the moonlight. No other light shone anywhere, no human form moved. It was as if the fleet were deserted, or rather, enchanted, stolen by spirits and secreted here in this wild northern cove. The great guns gaped from their turrets and the clustered tripod foremasts thrust upward like gutted spires, pointing mutely at Rigel, Betelgeuse, and Bellatrix, the cold brilliants flashing round Orion's sword. Maltbie held his breath, as if one careless exhalation might dispel this luminous vision. Otley beside him let out a long, low whistle. "Sweet Mary and Joseph!" he said softly, as if he were seeing the Grand Fleet for the very first time. "Don't they all look bloody lovely!"

The steamboat turned to port and passed across the bows of the first two lines of battleships, then turned again and went down the channel that ran like a great boulevard between the two halves of the fleet. Maltbie read off the names that loomed and receded on either side of him, reciting to himself what particulars he knew: *Marl-borough, Hercules, Agincourt* (the gargantuan, almost grotesque, ship with fully seven turrets and fourteen 12-inch guns, built by Messrs. Armstrong for Brazil as the *Rio de Janeiro,* sold by Brazil to Turkey before commissioning as the *Sultan Osman I,* then expropriated and re-christened by England on the outbreak of the war), *Colossus, Neptune, St. Vincent, Collingwood* (carrying as a midshipman the king's son, Prince Albert), *Ajax, Centurion, Dreadnought* herself (the prototype for every capital ship in the world built since 1906), *Bellerophon, Superb, Temeraire, Orion* (the first of the "superdreadnoughts," mounting ten guns of 13.5-inch diameter and capable of broadsides aggregating seven tons), *Benbow, Vanguard, Monarch, Erin* (like *Agincourt,* commissioned originally—as the *Reshadieh*—for the Imperial Ottoman Navy), *Thunderer, King George V, Emperor of India,* and, down at the end of the line, the superdreadnought *Iron Duke,* named for Wellington and now flying the flag of John Rushworth Jellicoe, admiral and commander in chief.

The steamboat pulled up to the huge ship's ladder. "Ye go along, sir," said Otley. "We'll see to your luggage and quarters."

Maltbie went up the steps. At the top was a somber-looking man bearing rear admiral's stripes, and an aristocratically handsome younger officer. "Welcome, Mr. Maltbie," the admiral said. "I'm Charles Madden, Admiral Jellicoe's chief of staff, and this is Commander Salmond, our senior wireless officer." Hands were shaken all around. "Commander Salmond will see to it that you're introduced to everybody and shown around the ship and settled in. But if you wouldn't mind terribly, Admiral Jellicoe would like to welcome you aboard now, before he begins work on his evening telegrams."

"Of course," Maltbie said. "I'd be delighted."

The three of them walked briskly aft to the conning tower, descended one deck, and went aft again into admiral's country. Maltbie noted the busy signals room and the even busier printer's shop, where various operational and organizational orders were being set in type and reproduced on two loudly hissing presses. They passed offices with signs that read FLEET PAYMASTER, FLAG COMMANDER, FLAG CAPTAIN, and CAPTAIN OF THE FLEET, coming at last to Admiral Jellicoe's private sanctum.

The atmosphere inside the C in C's quarters was nothing like the electric exuberance one felt aboard the *Lion.* Here instead, among Jellicoe's subordinates, there was a sort of passionate serenity, like that displayed by the high priests of some especially sacred shrine. There was a sense of missionary zeal in the air, of total dedication to the work at hand; and though the atmosphere was cheerful, and in some ways even relaxed, it was also extremely intense. If Beatty's men had been a band of brothers, Jellicoe's were a conclave of disciples.

In the middle of all the intensity, seated at a small metal work table, was the commander in chief himself. He rose on Maltbie's arrival and came forward, hand outstretched. "Ah, Mr. Maltbie, welcome aboard."

Maltbie experienced a rapid sequence of conflicting emotions as he looked at Jellicoe for the first time. The man's face had the fussy-looking primness of a clerk in a ladies' shoe store, yet his clear blue eyes appeared almost supernaturally alert as they gazed out from his weather-beaten skin. He seemed, though he was not, much smaller than Beatty, and more circumspect in voice and movements; yet there was about him an air of compelling galvanic energy, of stored up magnetic force flowing outward in carefully measured waves. The net impression he gave was one of purposeful vitality and high intelligence, tempered by remarkable patience and self-restraint.

"You've come at last," he said. "We've been looking forward to your arrival."

"Thank you, sir. I'm pleased to be here."

"You must be a bit weary after your journey. There's a kettle on if you'd like some tea. Or perhaps you'd prefer some cocoa."

"Tea would be fine, sir," Maltbie said, feeling somewhat guilty about the brandy he'd downed with Otley, as if it meant somehow that everything he got now he'd be getting under false pretenses.

"You'll be hungry as well," Jellicoe said. "And I'm a bit peckish myself come to think of it. Will you have a sandwich with me?"

"Thank you, sir. I'd like to."

"Fine," said the admiral, and gave the order to the orderly on duty. "Now then, tell me, how is Captain Sims?"

"Very well, sir. He asked me to convey his most affectionate regards."

"Thank you. He's an exceptional fellow, I've always thought."

"Yes, sir. He certainly is."

There was a moment's silence. "And he thinks very highly of you, it seems."

"He's very tolerant of my shortcomings, sir."

"Then you must have numerous virtues to offset them, as we both know our friend isn't given to idle praise."

"Well," Maltbie said, "I've always found him remarkably sparing in his praise of me."

Jellicoe laughed heartily. "Perhaps he restrained himself from expressing too much approval to your face, for fear of spoiling you. In his letters to me, however, he's been consistently laudatory."

"I'm glad to hear it, sir. I hope I can live up to my advance billing."

"Why, you already have. That impromptu bit of surgery you performed in the *Lion*'s foretop has made you something of a celebrity, you know."

"Surgery, sir? I don't . . ." But then he remembered: the shell splinter in Tredway's shoulder. How odd that an incident as trifling as that one should provide conversational fodder for the wardrooms and mess decks of the Royal Navy at war. What would the men of the fleet say if they knew about his other brushes with valor? That time on his first training cruise in '99, for example, when he'd climbed the rigging of the creaky old frigate *Constellation* in a full gale to bring down a fellow cadet who'd panicked while they were reefing sail. He remembered the boy exactly—Miles Kinkaid from Louisville: white faced, spray lashed, clinging with a death grip to the mainmast topspar, his eyes clamped shut. None of the sailors would go up after him, and neither would any of the cadets. The watch officer had said that he'd seen this sort of thing before, and Kinkaid would just have to take his chances . . . unless, of course, one of his brother cadets had ten demerits he needed to shed. Maltbie had had a good deal more than ten at the time, and as he lived in dire fear of washing out, the watch officer's proposal was like the answer to a prayer. He had scurried up the rigging, pried Kinkaid off the topspar, and brought him down, much to the amazement of everyone on the ship, not least of all the watch officer, who had made his proposal facetiously. He was decent enough to abide by his words, however, and ten demerits were duly stricken from Maltbie's column in the discipline log.

There had been several other occasions since then on which Maltbie had "distinguished himself," to use the phrase in the citations. The most notable one had occurred four years ago, when an afterburn in the fore turret of the old predreadnought *Illinois* had set off powder charges that gutted the whole barbette. Two men had been trapped alive in the still smoldering powder magazine, and Maltbie had led a squad of volunteers down into the fume-filled blackness and brought them up. As it turned out, it was all to less than no avail, because the two men subsequently died of smoke inhalation, while Maltbie himself and most of his squad were hospitalized for weeks with lung damage.

Despite, or because of, this background, Maltbie did not have much admiration for courage per se. He regarded it as primarily a mental trick, an ability to blind oneself to possible consequences by focusing one's attention on the task at hand. He disliked being told he was brave—it made him feel like an impostor—and he was equally unreceptive to accusations of modesty—in this case most especially. After all, the act of pulling a splinter out of Tredway's shoulder was hardly worthy of heroic verse. Only an incorrigible blowhard would give himself credit for *that*.

"There's a simple explanation for my actions, sir," Maltbie said. "The sailor in question was making an unholy racket, and pulling the splinter out of him was the only way I could think of to shut him up."

Jellicoe smiled. "Captain Sims warned me that you had a tendency to hide your light under a bushel. Is your hand healing satisfactorily?"

"Oh, yes sir."

"Surgeon Maclean did all right by you then?"

"He did indeed, sir."

"Splendid. . . . Well; are your quarters to your liking?"

"My quarters, sir? You mean here aboard ship?"

Jellicoe nodded, with just a hint of perplexity in his face, and Maltbie reproached himself for being so dull-witted, blaming Otley's brandy. What other quarters would the admiral be asking him about, for heaven's sake! "I haven't seen them yet, sir," he said.

"You haven't seen them yet?"

"No, sir. Admiral Madden thought you might want to talk to me as soon as I arrived, before you started work on your telegrams."

Jellicoe's eyes twinkled. "Admiral Madden is in league with my wife and with my wife's sister, to whom he happens to be married. He's been under more pressure from them recently to see to it that I get to bed at a reasonable hour than he's been under from me to see to it that the fleet remains in a state of readiness. It is one of the great paradoxes of the war."

They both laughed. "I'm sorry that you were hustled along here so precipitately," the admiral resumed. "And please do let me know if we've neglected to provide anything you might need."

"Thank you, sir," said Maltbie, marveling that an officer with Jellicoe's responsibilities should concern himself with the amenities furnished a not particularly important foreign visitor. The man was rather a unique phenomenon in his experience, and Maltbie allowed as how he was beginning to feel a bit like a disciple himself.

1915, 9TH MARCH—WILHELMSHAVEN

Admiral Hipper's purpose in summoning von Tiel to the *Seydlitz* had been to inform him that he was being promoted to *Kapitän zu See* and transferred to the Intelligence Division of the *Reichsmarineamt*, both the promotion and the transfer being effective forthwith. The promotion was based on merit, according to Hipper, and the transfer on von Tiel's British background and experience, since his new assignment was to direct a specially selected team of experts in discovering whether, and how, the British were learning of German Fleet movements in advance. Dogger Bank had been but the most recent in a series of "coincidences" involving the sudden appearance of British capital units athwart a German sortie's line of operations, and Admirals Pohl, Holtzendorff, and Tirpitz all wanted to know why the Royal Navy was enjoying such a singular run of luck.

Gehlman learned of the promotion and transfer from the countess, who learned of them via a note her husband dispatched to her from the Wilhelmshaven Hauptbahnhof en route to Berlin. (A letter from Facchetti provided Gehlman with more specific details of von Tiel's assignment two days later.) The note had been delivered by von Tiel's shipboard valet, who said he had been instructed to pack the baron's trunks and accompany them personally to Schloss Lutwitz on the Tegler See near Spandau, where the baron intended to establish offices for his newly designated staff.

The news of von Tiel's transfer coupled with the fact of his immediate departure put an end to a confrontation between Gehlman and the countess that had been building in venomous intensity for most of the day. He had stormed back into the house after walking along the beach for over an hour and on reentering his room had ripped the covers off the countess's naked body. He had then reviled her in language that, under normal conditions, he would have balked at using to a man. He accused her of complicity in von Tiel's lecherous behavior, of voyeurism, of criminal neglect. He demanded that Alis be taken away from Wilhelmshaven, that she be examined for evidence of violation, that von Tiel be reported to the police. The countess, in a display of that rueful wounded modesty that Gehlman remembered seeing in other naked women at those times when they did not look their best, reached down and covered herself with a sheet. She then coolly questioned him about what he had seen and contemptuously dismissed his interpretation as juvenile, and probably envious as well. This accusation provoked Gehlman to an almost ungovernable fury, and he would have struck her had she not forestalled him by asking why, if von Tiel's object had been lechery, he had neglected the simple precaution of bolting his door. "Because he's deranged!" Gehlman had shouted, provoking the countess to sneer, "Or obliging, given your own fatherly fascination with his stepdaughter."

This time he did strike her, hard: hard enough to draw blood from her mouth and nostrils. "Try to understand this, you filthy bitch. Your husband's '*object*' is not at issue here. It's his *actions* that matter, and his *actions* speak for themselves."

The countess spat full in his face, flecking him with blood and saliva. "*Honi soit qui mal y pense*, my gallant Pharisee. He did nothing more for her than John the Baptist did for Christ, if it's really his 'actions' you're concerned about."

Gehlman had stood silent for a moment, watching her blood drip onto the sheets. He glanced at his hand, which still tingled from the force of the blow he had struck. He then went into the bathroom and came back to the bed with a wet towel. Sitting down beside her, he began gently to clean her face, and she after several seconds took the other end of the towel he was using and began gently to clean his. "Alis can't remain here," he said.

"I'll speak to Siggy," she replied. "It won't happen again."

"No! You said it wouldn't happen at all."

"Well, '*it*' didn't, whatever '*it*' is."

And they had continued to argue for hours, until von Tiel's valet appeared with the news that the baron had departed for Berlin, thus rendering most of the questions they were disputing instantly, if not permanently, moot.

A period of truce had ensued, or relative truce, for Gehlman still insisted on the need for Alis to be reexamined by Frau Doktor Bauer, and the countess still resisted his urgings. Her position was, first, that as Alis's behavior had not altered since the first examination—and, more relevantly, since the morning of von Tiel's departure—she could not have undergone any trauma that warranted special medical attention. Second, a specific request that Dr. Bauer examine Alis's genitalia would arouse dangerous suspicions, and possibly threaten von Tiel's career and reputation without justifiable cause. Gehlman countered these arguments by pointing out that Alis's unchanged behavior could as easily be explained by the hypothesis that von Tiel had been abusing her for years, and that there was no reason for Dr. Bauer to suspect von Tiel specifically since, given the lure of Alis's beauty, almost any man who'd had access to her was just as likely a candidate for suspicion. The countess retorted that Gehlman's arguments ignored the realities of the situation, and that, in any case, Alis's welfare was none of his business. Gehlman responded by saying that however remote the possibility that Alis had in fact been violated, the mere existence of the possibility was enough to warrant action; and he added that the possible violation of a nine-year-old child was as much his business as would be a possible murder or rape. One did not have to be the relative of a crime victim to interest oneself in his or her welfare; one had only to be a civilized human being, especially in the case of a minor.

The argument had continued back and forth for days, and Gehlman, to his surprise, found that he was gradually getting the better of it. On a certain level, he perceived, the countess felt the prickings of conscience over the careless manner in which she had brought Alis and von Tiel repeatedly together, and it was perhaps because a second visit from Dr. Bauer would constitute, in part, an acknowledgment of culpability that she resisted it with such vehemence. Then too, on a subtler plane of feeling, he sensed that by giving in to his insistent contentions she saw herself as admitting him to a new level of intimacy and collaboration, a level she found threateningly unfamiliar, as indeed did he.

In the end the controlling consideration was one of inescapable logic: the gravity of the consequences if Alis's hypothetical violation

went undetected was vastly greater than the gravity of any consequences that could flow from her being reexamined. And so it was
that Gehlman and the countess now found themselves seated in the
von Lutwitz mansion's library anxiously awaiting the reemergence of
Dr. Bauer from Alis's room upstairs.

At about the time when the servants began closing curtains and
switching on lights in the face of the oncoming dusk, the two of
them heard a door shut and the sound of the doctor's thick-soled
shoes slowly descending the staircase. Gehlman exchanged a quick
anxiety-ridden glance with the countess, then watched as she silently
marshaled her resources of dignity, as if in preparation for a protracted siege.

Gehlman rose as the doctor's squat, middle-aged figure appeared at
the library doors. The woman had a pasty, liver-splotched complexion, spiky gray-black hair tied back in a bun, mournful eyes, fleshy
lips, and an almost comically bulbous nose. She set her black medical satchel down on the floor near the divan and then wearily seated
herself. Gehlman and the countess looked at her expectantly.

She returned their gaze, gave a small sigh, and said, "Your daughter has an intact hymen, your Ladyship."

The countess merely nodded, but Gehlman caught the tiny shudder of relief that went through her body and himself let out an audible breath of discharged tension.

"I will not ask you who it is you suspect of molesting the child,"
the doctor continued in a tone that suggested that an intact hymen
was bad news rather than good. "But I will tell you that the presence
or absence of the maidenhead is of distinctly limited significance."

"What precisely do you mean?" the countess asked in her chilliest
voice.

"I mean, your Ladyship, that what confronts us here is not a medical but a psychological problem."

"What confronts *me*, Doctor."

"With respect, your Ladyship, what confronts *us*, since you have
solicited my professional opinion on this matter, and since your
daughter's sanity appears to me to be in danger."

"Her *sanity?!*"

"Yes, your Ladyship, her sanity. And I must tell you that in cases
like this the danger is very acute."

"What do you mean, 'in cases like this'?"

"Your Ladyship, it is my opinion that your daughter has been subjected to repeated indignities over the course of several years, stopping short of intercourse to be sure, but in many respects more damaging than would have been a single episode of penetration."

The countess's face had gone very white. "On what do you base this opinion?"

"I base it, your Ladyship, on the similarity of your daughter's psychological condition to that which I have observed in over a score of young girls who've been brought to me under comparable conditions over the past fifteen years. I base it on her answers to my questions, on her reactions to various forms of physical contact, on the fact that her severe shyness has intensified since the first time I examined her, on the fact that there are indentations in the form of small scars on the palms of her hands where she has repeatedly dug in her fingernails in the face of what must have been intolerable stress, and on the fact that she has related to me in detail five separate instances of molestation suffered by her during the past two years at the hands of an adult male whom she refuses to identify."

Gehlman sagged into a chair as the countess's hitherto impregnable composure collapsed into an expression of muted shock. "*Five* instances!?" she repeated incredulously.

"Five, your Ladyship, one of which I believe to have occurred since I first saw your daughter three weeks ago. I only wish you had mentioned your suspicions to me then, if, that is, you entertained any."

"We . . . I . . . had vague suspicions."

Dr. Bauer let out a long sigh. "I can imagine the anguish this must cause you, your Ladyship, but my first concern, as yours, is for your daughter, and I hope that you will henceforth let yourself be guided by what is in her best interests."

"Of course," the countess said dully.

"Cases such as your daughter's arise with depressing frequency," Dr. Bauer said in a tone that was somewhat less reprobative than the one she'd been previously using. "What's important now is not to chastise yourself, but to heal and protect your child."

"Yes," said the countess, her voice quivering slightly. "That's what's important now."

"Yes," Dr. Bauer repeated. "Of course, the first measure you must take is to prevent the man responsible from having any contact with your daughter whatsoever."

"Of course."

"If this were a working-class family I would insist on knowing the man's identity," the doctor said. "I have learned, however, that one does not 'insist' with the aristocracy, so I will confine myself to saying that the man, whoever he is, represents a serious menace to other children than your daughter, and should be dealt with, if only with an eye to appearances, before he claims another victim."

"I will take the necessary steps," said the countess.

"Good. Now, you are aware, perhaps, that considerable advances have been made in treating children's mental disturbances over the past several years. Regrettably, cures are neither certain nor easy, and my expertise in this area is more clinical than theoretical. I should have very little expertise at all were it not for the fact that I'm the only woman doctor between here and Bremen who specializes in pediatrics; consequently I've come to have something of a monopoly on cases like your daughter's, either through direct consultations or referrals from other doctors. I can tell you that I've had some success in helping children come to terms with the experiences they've endured. But I've had failures too, and there are several doctors in Munich and Vienna who are much better versed in child psychology than I am. I will supply you with their names, of course, but I would also recommend that you give me several weeks to see what I can do for your daughter. She appears to repose some trust in me, and trust in many cases is more pivotal than any other factor."

The countess nodded her consent. "What will her treatment involve?"

"I shall want to see her every day: to talk."

"And what must I do?"

"I'll be better able to tell you that after I've spent more time with your daughter. For the moment, though, I would simply say: be gentle, be loving, and try to appear cheerful. The most encouraging consideration in matters like this is that children are remarkably sturdy creatures all in all, one might almost say 'self-righting.' I think recognizing the problems, as you are doing, and securing treatment for them, is already more than half the battle. As to the remaining half, well, that, like most things in life, depends a great deal on imponderables."

Gehlman and the countess faced each other in silence after Dr. Bauer had left. "You were right," she said finally.

"Yes," Gehlman responded. "I wish I'd been wrong."

She looked at him imploringly. "You believe me, don't you, that I didn't suspect?"

"I believe you."

"I should have suspected."

"Perhaps, Regina. But it's done now."

"Yes, I suppose it is."

There was a long silence. "You'll help me . . . us . . . Alis and me?"

"Of course. Any way I can."

He saw that she was shivering, went to her, took her in his arms. She began to sob quietly. "Oh, Ben," she said. "Life is all turning out so badly."

1915, 20TH MARCH—BERLIN

Von Müller shifted uneasily, and the medals on his dress uniform clinked like tiny Japanese wind chimes. Beside him Dr. Walther Rathenau of the Allgemeine Elektrizitäts-Gesellschaft and the Prussian Directorate of War Material Distribution was murmuring on and on about "the situation," "the danger," "the potential catastrophe for Germany." Von Müller listened with only half an ear; on the far side of the Hatzfeld Palace's first-floor reception room was the man Rathenau had insisted on his seeing: the President's emissary. He was standing with Ambassador Gerard, looking small and vaguely simian in evening dress. His posture had something of the automaton about it: immobile from the neck down, arms hanging limp, feet close together, knees straight. Rathenau had said that the man had just come from London and Paris, and had arrived from Basle this morning. Rathenau had also said that the man was on a "peace mission," which struck von Müller as absurd: a peace mission at this stage of the war would serve about as much purpose as a broom in a sandstorm.

The admiral took a closer look at this "Colonel" House: the sleepy eyes appeared impenetrable, the small nose seemed to sniff the air, and the prim little mouth beneath the droopy white mustache opened and closed like a ruminant bivalve, only wide enough for the tiniest least significant mites of information to escape.

Von Müller sighed. This was a fool's errand he was running, and a risky one. Rathenau was correct, of course, that American arms sales to the Allies also provided powerful ammunition to the submarine advocates here in Berlin. But what, realistically, could be done about it? America was in thrall to the dollar; everyone knew that—and it certainly wasn't going to refrain from reaping the profits of war, for all Mr. Wilson's high-sounding homilies. Besides, America was well within its rights under international law: it showed no bias, played no favorites—it would do business with any nation that had gold to pay with, it would sell to all comers at the going rate, it would extend credit if the risk was good, it would build to specification, it would deliver on time. It wasn't America's fault that Britannia ruled the waves, nor was America responsible for the existing law of contraband. But it was precisely because Germany had no legal remedy for the wrongs in effect being done it by the United States that Tirpitz and the others were pressing for the submarine. What more harm can America do us than she is doing already? they repeatedly asked. And when you told them they refused to believe you.

Looking across the room at the two of them now, Ambassador Gerard raised a pudgy finger and pointed in what he probably considered to be a discreet manner in the direction of the billiard room. Rathenau tugged impatiently at von Müller's sleeve, prompting the admiral to utter a brief bark of angry laughter. "Good God, man," he snapped, yanking his arm away. "Have you taken leave of your wits?!"

"Forgive me," Rathenau said. "But there isn't much time before dinner."

"Dinner won't start without the host and the guest of honor, Rathenau, and the host and guest of honor won't be available while they're talking to us. So do try to compose yourself a little."

"Yes, yes. You're quite right. I'm sorry. But this meeting is of such vital importance."

Von Müller rolled his eyes toward the ceiling. "I think you exaggerate, Herr Direktor. War and peace are not determined by men of our echelon around a billiard table. And in any case I am not going anywhere with you until you have regained some semblance of your self-possession."

"Very well, very well. I'm not all that agitated, really. Now let's do go along."

Von Müller wearily shook his head. He was too old for this sort of nonsense. Why in God's name had he even come here? To cajole some creature of the American President into an understanding of the German point of view? Bah! It was all the most patent futility. "Let's get it over with," he said to Rathenau. And as they walked toward the billiard room he tried to console himself with the reflection that he had survived other long bouts of futility in the past.

Gerard made the introductions as the four of them stood around the green felt table. Then, addressing himself to the two Germans, he said, "Please pardon this somewhat melodramatic choice of venue, but it was my thought that discretion dictated some place close by the reception room where our presence could be explained, uh, uncompromisingly."

"Then perhaps we should all arm ourselves with cue sticks," von Müller said with just the smallest hint of irony.

Gerard and Rathenau took him seriously and moved at once to the wall racks. House, however, flashed him a quick twinkling of amusement and said, "I seem to recall that a number of balls ought to be in evidence as well, if the subterfuge is to be totally convincing."

"Three, I believe," von Müller responded, trying to keep a straight face. "Of varying shades of white."

"Yes yes. Quite right," said Gerard, handing House and von Müller their cues. "They should be down here," he added, bending to look beneath the rim of the table and reemerging flushed with triumph. "Yes! Here they are," he said, letting the three pale enamel spheres roll across the vivid surface of green.

"So!" said von Müller. "Discretion is satisfied. Shall we proceed to business?" It wasn't like him to be so blunt, but he was still feeling short of patience, and he ignored the anxious glance that Rathenau sent in his direction.

"Business seems to be the bone of contention between our two countries," House remarked. "From what Ambassador Gerard tells me, the feeling here is that every German casualty is directly traceable to an American-made gun or shell."

"No, sir," said von Müller. "We are very much aware that Armstrong-Vickers and Schneider-Creusot are taking as heavy a toll of German lives as are Bethlehem Steel and du Pont de Nemours. It's just that England and France are our sworn enemies, while the United States purports to be neutral."

"Purports, Admiral?"

"Purports, and in many respects is. But the practical effect of your neutrality is clearly beneficial to the Allies, and just as clearly detrimental to us."

"Not as beneficial to them or as detrimental to you as would be the practical effect of our belligerency, which God forbid."

"Which God forbid, indeed. But there is an increasingly influential current of opinion in Berlin to the effect that even as a full-fledged belligerent America could do us only marginally more harm than she is already doing, and England only marginally more good."

"Hence last month's submarine decree?"

"No, sir. Most decidedly no. Last month's decree represents a very close run defeat for that current of opinion, a defeat suffered thanks in large part to the efforts of men like Herr Rathenau here and the chancellor, who recognize the importance of good German-American relations."

"Forgive me, Admiral, but if that decree was a defeat, I shudder to contemplate a victory."

"Well may you do so, sir. For there was intense pressure on the All Highest War Lord to declare a total submarine blockade of England comparable to the total surface blockade in effect against us."

"I don't see, Admiral, how a submarine blockade could ever be comparable to a surface one."

"You refer, no doubt, to the requirements of international law that the presence of contraband cargo must be verified by visit and search, and provision made for the lives of passengers and crew before any vessel may be taken or sunk."

"I refer to those requirements, among others, and to the fact that submarines are unlikely to be able to observe them."

"That is precisely the point. The pressure on the Kaiser came from those who wished him to authorize submarine warfare without restrictions or restraints, even at the cost of noncombatants' lives."

"But that's unthinkable!"

"It is being *thought*, sir, and vehemently espoused as well. And the proponents of the policy grow more numerous and vociferous every month. In the final analysis, it was only the High Command's decision to strike eastward this year that frustrated them. The Great General Staff did not want to give a new enemy time to arm and muster in the west while Germany's energies were concentrated against Russia. But if the eastern strategy does not accomplish its objectives, the submarine question will be raised again, more loudly and more insistently than before. And if America does nothing to dispel the widespread belief that she is showing blatant partiality to the Allied cause, the advocates of unrestricted submarine warfare will get their way."

"But that belief is unreasonable. We are not showing partiality."

"Whether you are or not is more or less immaterial. Most Germans *believe* you are, and they are without much evidence to the contrary."

"That, from all I've heard, is largely attributable to the hostile attitude of your press."

"I admit that many of our newspapers have been intemperate in their criticism of the United States. But I can promise you that any significant demonstration of the bona fides of American neutrality will be fully reported here, and will also be of immeasurable value to the advocates of moderation, such as Herr Rathenau."

"What sort of 'demonstration' did you have in mind?"

"An embargo on the sale of arms."

House grimaced sardonically. "And failing that?"

"A more vigorous denunciation of the illegal British blockade."

"But we've repeatedly protested against their additions to the contraband list."

"Yes, you've 'protested.' Yet when Germany takes similar action, you threaten us with 'strict accountability.'"

"Submarines take human lives, Admiral; blockading ships take only property."

"Blockading ships take lives, sir, when they prevent food from reaching hungry mouths, hungry *noncombatant* mouths."

Looking at the Colonel's face, von Müller judged that he had made a point, but how much of one it was impossible to tell. "I won't belabor the issue," he resumed. "But you can see that those Germans who recoil at the thought of war with America sorely need evidence to show that America is amicably, or at least not inimically, disposed toward us."

"Thank you, Admiral," the Colonel said after an interval of thought. "You've done a great deal to clarify the problem."

And perhaps a little to solve it? von Müller asked himself, much in doubt that the answer could be yes.

March 21st, 1915

Dearest Melina,

What a day we had today! It was the vernal equinox, you know, the official end of winter (though it certainly didn't feel like it), and it was a big holiday for the whole fleet. It's really amazing what Jellicoe does to keep morale high up here, and today was his crowning achievement. First thing this morning he and I and Admiral Madden and Flag Captain Lawson went over to the small island called Flotta just south of where the battleships are moored. On Flotta, if you can believe it, there is a golf course! Every battleship was responsible for preparing one of the holes, that is, for taking a stretch of scrub and thistles and clearing it for a fairway and making a tee-ing area and a putting green. Anyway, we went over there and played the most extraordinary game of golf I've ever experienced in my life. Everyone was in a very great hurry because the regatta was scheduled to begin at ten, and in any case, I'm told, it's frowned on for officers to spend more than two hours on the course and away from their duties. So what happens is you come up to the first tee and hit *over* the people who've just teed off while they're still en route to hit their second shots. And then you gallop away yourself, literally *running*, while the next foursome behind you hit their tee shots over *your* head. The same procedure is repeated on the second and third and etc. shots, and woe betide anyone who hits into the rough as he'll be left behind for sure unless he finds his ball immediately or drops a new one. As you can imagine, it's all a little unsafe, and there are lots of cries of "Fore!" heard at every point on the course, and lots of "give-me's" on the greens (any putt under six feet is considered a "give-me" in fact). But it's great fun and wonderful exercise, and nobody pays too much attention to the scores (which in itself is probably a good thing for morale!). There's a YMCA hut just off the fifteenth fairway, and it takes a fearful pelting every time there's a golf day, but everyone is very cheerful and good-natured about it, and the men visiting the hut like to watch their officers jogging by and acting "daft," as they put it.

Anyway, we got through playing golf at ten and the regatta began. The senior officers competed in skiffs, and the Russian observer, Commodore von Schoultz, came in second, only narrowly losing out to Rear Admiral Arbuthnot of the 1st Cruiser Squadron. The biggest competition was in the rowing, though. The men were terribly excited about it, in fact, and it was all wonderfully organized. Poor Otley was very disappointed because the *Iron Duke*'s boat won the 4th Battle Squadron title only to finish second in the championship race to the boat from *Neptune* of the 1st B.S. Otley had bet a pound that *Iron Duke* would win. He said he didn't mind losing the money so much as he minded giving it to the particular fellow who won the bet, a marine gunner from the *Neptune* whom Otley describes as "a snake of the first quarter."

After dinner and divisions there was a big soccer ("football" according to you people) match between a picked team from the battleships and a picked team from the cruisers and destroyers. There was much ferocious cheering and oath shouting, and the game took on a comical aspect as it was raining very hard and the field turned to mud. In any case, the battleships won, which consoled Otley a bit for the loss of his pound. There were a great many spectators from the Orkneys at the match, and they all acted as if it was a very inferior brand of soccer they were seeing played. I'm so unfamiliar with the game that I couldn't judge for myself, but it looked to me like many of the players were very skillful, and I'd be surprised if any Orcadian team could defeat them.

After tea came the event that Otley said was the most important of the day: the boxing championships. The eliminations had been taking place for weeks, and tonight the champions of the battleships squared off against the champions of the cruisers/destroyers in six weight categories. All the matches were scheduled to be six rounds and were held aboard one of the depot ships, the *Imperieuse* (which, appropriately enough, used to be a transport for frozen meat). The deck was completely jammed with spectators, and two empty colliers were moored alongside to serve as grandstands for the overflow. The matches were tremendously exciting, and the shouting and cheering were so loud that my head's still ringing from them. The best bout was for the middleweight championship, which was won by an extraordinary marine sergeant named Bellmaine, who's only five feet five inches tall, but who looks like a block of stone. He beat another fellow a good half a foot taller than him by taking tremendous punishment about the head in order to deal out worse punishment to the other man's body. Otley was almost hysterical with delight, as he says that Bellmaine is his particular "mate." He would have bet on him—he bets on *everything!*—but had no money left after losing his pound earlier in the day. I offered to make him a loan, but he wouldn't consider it, saying I had no business handing out money to "the likes of us" when I should be saving it to support "your pretty future Mrs." You know, my dearest, I sometimes think I should never have let him see your photograph, as he's become terribly old-maidish ever since and seems to think he has a responsibility to *you* to make sure *I* don't behave foolishly. I think he regards you as some sort of modern-day goddess who's charged him with the task of superintending me. In fact, ever since I showed him the talisman and told him the story behind it, he's been checking on what seems a half-hourly basis day and night to make sure that I've got it on! If it were possible to become cross with him—about this or anything else —I would certainly do so. But it isn't, so I don't, though I often think I'd like to.

Anyway, after supper we all crowded into the *Imperieuse*, as many of us as could fit, and had a fine old sing-along. If there's one thing these sailors are more enthusiastic about than rowing, soccer, and boxing, it's singing—or roaring, which is more nearly what they do with songs. And they know so many—they sang for almost three solid hours! Many of the songs I'd never heard before. There was something called "The Ballad of Wing Kang Loo" about an unlucky Chinaman, which seemed to have about thirty verses. And there was "When You Are in Trouble, John," and "A Rollin' on ther Grass," and "My Little Gray Home in the West," and "Come into the Garden, Maud." They sang "Tipperary," of course, and "Everybody's Doing It," and "Roses of Picardy." And whenever they needed a break from singing someone would stand up and do a recitation, such as "Gunga Din" or "How Bill Adams Won the Battle of Waterloo." It was a wonderful way to end the day, and at ten-thirty Admiral Jellicoe got up and made a little speech congratulating everybody for their accomplishments in the sporting events and complimenting everyone on how well they were performing their duties. And the men cheered and cheered and cheered him, and he waved and gave that shy little smile of his and went back to the *Iron Duke* to do another ninety hours' work. What a man he is!

And so tomorrow, I imagine, we'll go out again on another sweep, or take target practice near the Pentland Skerries, or perform fleet maneuvers, or pay a visit to the Northern Patrol. It's odd that the weather and the monotony of life here don't get people down, but everyone is cheerful and enthusiastic, and you never see anyone moping or acting glum. Then too, since there's always so much work to be done—even for me!—the time seems to pass very quickly.

As for myself, I am well, but I miss you very very much. Every time one of your letters arrives I rush through it in the hopes of finding a sentence about when you're coming back to England to marry me, but no luck so far. If I don't find such a sentence soon I'm going to despair and sicken and go off my food—and maybe even forget to wear your talisman, Otley or no Otley! I don't mean to nag you, dear one, but I do so long to hold you again and I do so want to marry you and spend my life with you. So please, *please*, come soon. It's been so long since I've seen you that I sometimes have terrible fears that you are only a glorious dream I once dreamed and were never really real at all. Thank God I have your letters and your talisman to reassure me. Thank God that you *are* real, and that you've chosen to let me love you, as I have, as I always will, and as I continue to do every minute of every day.

God bless you, my beloved Melina.

Your eternally devoted,
Harry

1915, 22D MARCH—WILHELMSHAVEN

Alis kept her distance: one pace behind him and two or three yards to his left as they walked along the beach. Every so often she would cast a mistrustful glance in his direction, and Gehlman could see the fearful confusion in her eyes, the puzzlement, the trapped-animal anxiety. What does he *want* from me? he could imagine her shrieking to herself, and he could also sympathize with her consternation. It had been over a week now since the countess had departed for Berlin to confront von Tiel and initiate separation proceedings. Every day since she left, Alis and Gehlman had gone through the same unalterable motions: they would have lunch and dinner together, in silence; they would have hot cocoa together just before Alis's bedtime, in silence; and they would take this walk together, accompanied only by the sound of ripples from the Jade Bay washing

up gently on the sand. Gehlman, of course, would vastly have preferred to engage in talk, but Dr. Bauer had explained that the initiative for conversation at this stage had to come from Alis, or not at
all. The doctor was encouraged, so she said, by the fact that Alis was
actually willing to spend time alone with Gehlman in the countess's
absence. When Gehlman said that he thought "willing" was something of an overstatement, the doctor smilingly replied that that was
only because he didn't realize how adamant some children's *un*-
willingness could be.

He looked at Alis walking: the dainty steps, the perfect ladylike
posture. Yet again he arraigned himself on the charge that his motives were no purer than von Tiel's where she was concerned, and yet
again he vigorously protested his innocence. He *knew*, on the one
hand, that he had no sexual desire for Alis. But, on the other hand,
he did most decidedly *feel* something for her, something quite intense. Had she been his daughter—had he ever had a daughter, in
fact—he might simply have construed the feeling as paternal love,
and been done with it. But how was paternal love possible in the absence of paternity? And what other kind of love was conceivable in
the circumstances—other than the inconceivable kind peculiar to von
Tiel?

Aware that he did feel this "something" for Alis, and afflicted as
he was by a vague Hebraic sense of guilt, Gehlman found it impossible to keep his conscience clear. He stood accused, but the bill of in-
dictment was blank; and with no specific charges to refute, he remained in his own mind suspect, beleaguered by the niggling logic
that asserted, if you were truly innocent, you would not be in the
dock.

All these ruminations about himself had been rendered at once
more immediate and more academic by the news Facchetti had
brought with him yesterday from Berlin. Von Tiel, in his new position as de facto chief of naval counterintelligence, had been pressing
vigorously for Gehlman's detachment from the High Seas Fleet. His
argument was that until it was established whether, and how, fleet
operations were being communicated to the enemy, all potential
gaps in naval security should be precautionarily sealed. In response
to resistance from the Foreign Office, which wished to avoid offend-
ing the United States in the absence of substantial provocation, von
Tiel had alleged that certain unspecified features of Gehlman's conduct as an observer were "susceptible of an ominous interpretation,"

and he had threatened to bring the matter to the attention of Admiral von Tirpitz, which was tantamount to leaking it to the press. The Foreign Office had bridled at "this near approximation of blackmail," and had threatened in its turn to invoke the authority of the Kaiser to make sure that von Tirpitz kept silent and von Tiel kept in line. There matters stood at the time that Facchetti's contacts inside the *Reichsmarineamt*—whether under instruction or on their own initiative—conveyed to him the details of the interdepartmental controversy. Facchetti had reported to Gerard, who had consulted with Colonel House on the evening of the Colonel's arrival. House's reaction had been immediate and unequivocal: if Gehlman's presence in Wilhelmshaven was proving to be a source of friction in Berlin, then its continuance would be regarded as a liability in Washington. The Colonel did not want the forces of moderation in Germany— many of whom were concentrated in the Foreign Office—expending their energies over a matter as trivial as the recall of a naval observer. He suggested, therefore, that Facchetti inform his contacts that Gehlman had been summoned back to America for consultations and would be leaving right away. He suggested further that Facchetti himself proceed to Wilhelmshaven, explain the situation to Gehlman, and assist in facilitating his departure.

That conversation had taken place some thirty-six hours ago, and Facchetti had arrived last night at nine. His eyes had widened extravagantly when Gehlman explained why von Tiel might have other motives then naval security for wanting him out of the country, but they both agreed that the existence of such motives had no practical bearing on the need for Gehlman to leave. The countess was due back from Berlin today, so Gehlman, armed with the necessary travel documents that Facchetti had brought with him, could depart for the Netherlands tomorrow. Now, walking along the beach with Alis beside him, he began to think for the first time about what going away actually meant.

It had been barely two months since his arrival, barely six weeks since Alis and the countess had come, and less than four weeks since von Tiel had left. Yet as Gehlman contemplated a return to America and a return to his life in the navy, it was with a feeling unaccountably akin to grief. Loneliness began to seep into his muscles again, and with it came the small jolt of realizing that this loneliness was something new—not new in his life by any manner of means, but new in his life in Germany.

Slowly, unwillingly, he began to acknowledge the form that his feelings were taking. He belonged to a *family* here, a family of his own, for the first time in his adult life. He was part of two people who cared for one another and cared about the other one. Brief as the conjugality had been—carnal, clandestine, sordid, self-serving—it had still been family: a partial reprieve from total involvement with all-devouring self. But now it would be ended, as blindly, as capriciously as it had begun. And he would have to resume his trek across the arctic landscape of his soul, no longer inured to the cold by decades of cynicism and contempt, but exposed, made soft, by a few vagrant moments of warmth.

He looked again at Alis and felt pain, the pain of loss. No, he realized, he did not lust for her—he thirsted. Well, it was a thirst that would just have to go unslaked, he told himself; and it seemed at that instant that every nerve end in his body let go with a scream of anguish. It was intolerable that he would never get to know her. And it was impossible that they should part from one another without ever having exchanged a friendly word. While Gehlman respected Dr. Bauer and was reluctant to disregard her instructions, the sacrifice of silence he was being called on to make was now simply too heavy to endure. He'd be gone tomorrow anyway, so such negligible damage as he might inflict by speaking would heal and be forgotten in a week.

If he *was* going to speak, however, he had to be very careful about what he said. His words might be trivial, or bromidic, or casual, or even jocular. Whatever they *might* be, though, they *had* to be gentle and calm, and they ought not to require a response.

He looked at Alis again. Her maid had dressed her in white this morning, or rather overdressed her, in contemplation of the raw March weather. She wore Hessian boots with red tassels, a woolen cardigan over a ruffled pinafore, and a white fox coat that was gathered at the waist by a belt of spotted ermine. The ensemble was topped by a heavy woolen tam and set off by a scarf of fire-engine red that matched the pompon on the hat. Taken together with the obsidian darkness of Alis's eyes and hair, the total effect was more than memorable, and Gehlman, having arrived at the decision to break the silence, now found himself feeling almost boyishly tongue-tied by her beauty. Why speak to such a creature when simply looking at her was such a joy? It would be an act of boorishness, like disrupting a tableau vivant.

But no; that was irresolution talking. Well then, what was the blandest subject he could think of? . . . Of course! The first resort in any awkward silence.

But gently, he reminded himself, calmly.

"I wish spring would get here," he said, gazing up at the overcast sky.

Out of the corner of his eye he saw Alis snap her head toward him and look at him with an expression of surprise. She immediately averted her gaze again, though, causing him to experience an intense sensation of defeat. He restrained himself from saying more at that moment, deciding to walk on at least fifteen more paces before making a second attempt. On his fifth pace, however, he heard her say, "Spring began yesterday afternoon, at twenty past three."

He had to keep a tight rein on himself to avoid revealing his excitement and elation. He counted off three more paces and in a tone of edified interest said, "*Really.* At twenty past three, you say?"

She kept her eyes lowered, but after several moments responded with a nod. "That's when the sun entered the region of the constellation Aries."

She still didn't look at him, so he permitted himself a broad and exultant smile. She was actually *showing off!*

He decided as a next step to venture an oblique compliment. "There can't be too many people your age who know so much about astronomy."

After seven silent paces he began to reproach himself for having tried to flatter her. Of course it had made her suspicious of him.

But he was wrong; on the eighth pace she spoke again. "Herr Kunitz says that astronomy was the first true science."

There was a vaguely interrogative note in her voice that suggested she might be asking Gehlman to corroborate or dispute her tutor's assertion. He fervently hoped that that was the case, because if she was actually asking him to clear up some doubts she had about Herr Kunitz's declarations, that would be a strong indication that, in one context at least, she regarded him as being provisionally no worse than innocuous. It wouldn't indicate that she trusted him, of course, but it would suggest that her *mis*trust had real and definable limits.

"Which science do you think came first?" he said, risking his first direct question.

Four paces elapsed before she answered, but he could see that the pause resulted from deliberation, not wariness. "Mathematics," she said finally, turning for the first time to look straight at him.

"Well," he said, weighing his words, "I don't think that mathematics, strictly speaking, can be considered actually a science."

Alis's brow knitted. "No?"

"Not really."

"I don't understand."

He noticed with pleasure that she had, perhaps unintentionally, abandoned her custom of staying one pace to his rear and was now walking abreast of him, no more than three or four feet away. "Well," he said, "science, as I understand it, is a branch of knowledge that has to do with things that can be seen—like the stars, or planets, or mountains—and things that can be heard—like thunder or music—and things that can be measured, like the speed of the wind or the strength of a magnet. Mathematics, on the other hand, has to do with numbers and relationships, things we can only think about but can't see or hear or measure. In other words, science has to do with things that our senses or our scientific instruments can detect in the world around us, while mathematics has to do with things that exist only in our minds."

Alis's forehead was now deeply furrowed; as well it might be, Gehlman reflected. This was a fairly deep discussion for a nine-year-old mind.

But not too deep, apparently, because to his astonishment she now asked, "What about God?"

"God?" he repeated dull-wittedly.

"Yes, God," she said, with just the least trace of impatience in her voice. "God can't be seen or heard or detected by scientific instruments, but He doesn't exist only in our minds, does He?"

Gehlman had to restrain the urge to smile. From weeks of silence they had proceeded directly to philosophical dialectic. What was it Regina had said at the beginning? "It seems that you've brought me a metaphysician."

"I really don't know very much about God," he said, ducking Alis's question.

"Because you are Jewish?" she asked guilelessly.

At this he could not keep from laughing. "Very possibly," he said. "Although I must admit that that explanation never occurred to me before."

He was delighted to see small traces of a smile flickering at the corners of Alis's mouth. "I didn't mean to make a joke," she said.

"I know," he answered her. "But you made an extremely good one nevertheless."

Now she did smile, shyly but without trepidation. And to Gehlman's enormous satisfaction she smiled several more times as they walked and conversed with each other, all the way back to the house.

On their arrival the footman told him that a certain Herr Keller had been waiting for some time to see him. Feeling irritated by the intrusion, Gehlman went into the library to confront an elderly stoop-shouldered man in a frock coat. The man's eyes were red, as from weeping, and his manner was agitated in the extreme.

"Commander Gehlman?"

"Yes?"

"I am Adolf Keller. I was the Gräfin von Lutwitz's personal attorney."

The man's use of the past tense struck Gehlman with foreboding. "Yes?" he said again.

The man stood there wringing his hands and glancing anxiously from side to side. He began to speak a couple of times, then suddenly lurched across the room and shut the doors. Turning at last to look at Gehlman, he seemed almost on the verge of palsy, and in a quavering voice he said, "Her Ladyship is dead."

The words hit Gehlman like a sharp slap in the face. "Dead?" he asked stolidly. "What do you mean, dead?"

"I mean, she is *dead*, Commander." There was an angry edge to his words. "She died yesterday morning, of a fall from a horse."

Gehlman sagged into a chair.

"That, at any rate," Keller continued, his tone modulating from anger into contempt, "is what the police have chosen to believe."

"*Chosen* to believe?" Gehlman heard himself repeat.

"She was riding with her husband, Commander. Her horse 'bolted.' She was 'found' with her skull smashed. The rock onto which she 'fell' was no bigger than a man's hand. Her horse had a broken leg and was destroyed by Baron von Tiel before he went for assistance. These facts admit of more than one interpretation, I'm sure you'll agree."

"He *murdered* her!"

"I am convinced of it. Especially in light of the conversation I had with her Ladyship three days ago, during which she explained her reasons for wishing to terminate her marriage and concurrently executed a new will."

"My God! Did you tell the police what she said to you?"

"I wasn't asked to, Commander. And when I learned of her death yesterday afternoon and volunteered the information to the investigating magistrate, I was told very decisively that the case had been closed."

"Closed!? Only a few hours after her death?"

"Seven and one-quarter hours, Commander, to be precise. The baron, after all, is a man above suspicion: a holder of the Knight's Cross, a brave officer, an important functionary of our Naval Staff, an aristocrat. To accuse him of lechery, incest, and murder without solid proof is a step requiring more temerity than one can reasonably expect from a Prussian bureaucrat, especially in time of war."

"But Dr. Bauer can testify—"

Keller shook his head impatiently. "I know about Dr. Bauer, Commander, and there is nothing to which she can testify that will in any way incriminate the baron. I must tell you very honestly that the best we could hope to do, even assuming cooperation on the part of the authorities, is make a plausible case—but not a sufficient one. What you yourself saw in the baron's bedroom, for example, is by no means conclusive on the question of lechery, quite apart from the fact that your government would hardly wish you to involve yourself in a public scandal here, particularly one in which your private involvement is already so far advanced. As for Dr. Bauer and myself, we could give only hearsay testimony, which in any event would most probably be considered privileged. The doctor could, arguably, attest to the fact that Alis had suffered interference, but not to the identity of the malfeasor. As to the very remote possibility that Alis herself might be permitted to name her despoiler, I'm afraid that her late mother's reputation and her status as not only a child, but a child receiving treatment for nervous distress, would tell very forcibly against her credibility. Besides which, the ordeal of recounting, several times at least, the indignities to which she was subjected is not the sort of thing Dr. Bauer, or indeed I myself, would permit you to visit upon your new ward."

"*My* new ward?"

Keller appeared not to hear him. "Your first concern," he continued, "and our first concern must be to see to it that Alis's welfare is protected pursuant to the terms of her Ladyship's will."

"Wait a minute! You mean that *I* have been designated as Alis's guardian?"

"Subject to one or two conditions, yes. Didn't the countess discuss the matter with you?"

"My God!" Gehlman said, feeling a sudden surge of guilty jubilation oddly admixed with a strong sense of loss. "What are the conditions?"

"First," said Keller, "that you take Alis out of Germany, or, if your duties require you to remain here, that you send her to live with her great-aunt in Stockholm until such time as you are recalled or transferred."

"I'm leaving tomorrow for America," Gehlman interjected. "At least, that was my intention."

Keller shot him a mildly interrogatory glance, but merely said, "Good. I should have thought a degree of celerity was indicated in any case, given the circumstances. I can attend to all the details of probate here."

"Yes," Gehlman agreed.

"The second condition is that you keep Alis outside Germany for as long as she remains your ward, which normally would be until she attains the age of twenty-one. The third is that you exercise the greatest care to see to it that, from this day forward, Alis's stepfather learns nothing of her whereabouts."

"Is that all?"

"That's all. I believe her Ladyship was planning to leave Germany herself for Alis's sake."

"Well then, it's settled. Those are conditions I would have come up with myself."

"Good. That makes it just a matter of signing and registering the necessary—"

Three soft raps on the door interrupted Keller's words.

"What is it?" Gehlman called out irritably.

The chauffeur stepped into the room. "Excuse me, sir, but as you said you wished to be driven into town this morning, I thought I should tell you that the baron just rang from the railway station and instructed me to come for him."

Gehlman and Keller exchanged a look of alarm. "He can stop her leaving the country," the attorney said. "Perhaps indefinitely."

Gehlman stood very still for a moment, trying to collect himself. Von Tiel had certainly wasted no time. In fact, if Gehlman hadn't ordered the car this morning so that he could go into town and close his local bank account, the baron's arrival would have taken them completely unawares. Even as it was, he was dangerously close at hand, and Herr Keller's "celerity" was now of the utmost importance.

Gehlman took a deep breath and turned to face the chauffeur. "Miss Alis is unwell, Karl," he said in a clipped efficient tone. "I was just about to send for you. Go and bring Dr. Bauer here immediately."

"And the baron, sir?"

"Send the carriage for him, and have someone request Captain Facchetti to join me in the library."

"Very good, sir," the chauffeur said, withdrawing from the room.

Gehlman and Keller looked at one another. "We have about twenty minutes," Gehlman said.

"Excuse me, Commander, but this Captain Facchetti . . ."

"He's a close friend and colleague, Herr Keller; I'm going to want his advice."

"I see. And what is it you are intending to do?"

"That depends on what you tell me I *can* do. For example, if von Tiel could be temporarily neutralized somehow, would it be possible for Alis to leave the country in my custody?"

"Legally, no, since the countess's will has not yet been registered."

"What if I stayed in Germany and waited for the will to be registered?"

"As I said before—"

Keller was interrupted by a knock on the door and the entrance of a chambermaid. "Excuse me, Commander Gehlman, Captain Facchetti asked me to tell you that he would be down momentarily."

"Thank you, Uta. Oh, and by the way, please tell Miss Alis's governess to pack a suitcase for her as quickly as possible: enough clean clothes and other necessities for a week's journey. And have Josef pack my things as well. We'll want to be leaving in fifteen minutes. Oh, and Uta, tell Karl when he returns with Dr. Bauer that I want him to wait for me with the car *in the garage.* Do you understand?"

"Yes, sir."

"Very well. Thank you, Uta."

"Very good, sir," the chambermaid said, and left the room.

"You were saying, Herr Keller?"

"I was saying that the baron could effectively delay Alis's departure from Germany for a long time. But, far more serious, he could also secure temporary custody of her while contesting the validity of the will."

"Even if we raised the issue of his depravity?"

"In that case she might be provided with a guardian *ad litem*. But von Tiel would still be allowed to see her occasionally, if only in her guardian's presence."

"What would be von Tiel's chances of voiding the new will?"

"That's impossible to say. But as far as the provisions relating to Alis are concerned, he could claim to be her closest surviving relative, and the additional fact that he is a German aristocrat would weigh heavily against the claim of an alien Jew such as yourself, especially since Alis is in line to inherit two important German titles should her brother die without issue."

"And what about her brother?"

"He is a young man of distinctly limited capacities, I regret to say, a lieutenant on the staff of the countess's cousin, General von Lutwitz, the military governor of Brussels. Even if he were awarded custody, he would be in no position to care for her except by proxy through nursemaids and governesses and the like. Von Tiel would still have access to her."

"Then the choices facing us are pretty clear."

"I would say they were, Commander, very definitely."

With a perfunctory tap on the door, Facchetti entered the room. "Morning, Ben," he said in a jovial manner. Then, immediately sensing the mood of tension, he asked, "What's wrong here?"

"I'm going to have to be very brief, Wally. This is Herr Keller, the countess's attorney. He's just told me that the countess has been killed and—"

"My God!"

"—and we both think that von Tiel murdered her."

"*Murdered!*"

"Yes. But according to Herr Keller, the police regard her death as an accident. Either way, the fact is that the countess named me Alis's guardian in a will she executed just before she was killed, and von Tiel is on his way here from the railway station right now. Herr Keller believes that von Tiel stands a good chance of getting custody of Alis for himself, or at least of keeping her in Germany where he can get at her. So, somehow, Alis and I have got to get out of Germany, *now!*"

"How soon will von Tiel be here?" Facchetti asked.

"In twenty minutes or less."

Facchetti went to the couch and sat down, a look of fierce concentration contorting his features. "He's come here to take Alis away with him, you think?"

Gehlman nodded.

"Undoubtedly," Keller declared.

"Then our job is not just to stop him, but to prevent him from stopping you."

"Precisely," said Keller. "Have you any methods of prevention to suggest?"

Facchetti shook his head. "Right off the bat nothing feasible comes to mind, short of assault and battery. But since we have twenty whole minutes to think about it . . . How far is it to Holland from here?"

"About fifty miles," Gehlman told him.

Facchetti stood silent for a moment. "Let's look at a map."

Gehlman crossed to one of the bookshelves and got out a large Deutsche Institut atlas of Lower Saxony. He opened it on the desk as Keller and Facchetti moved to either side of him.

"Look!" said Facchetti. "There: that neck of the Ems just west of Emden; it can't be more than three miles wide."

"Wally! For God's sake, this isn't *Uncle Tom's Cabin*—and I'm no Eliza crossing the ice with little Harry."

Facchetti grinned at him. "Have you ever, by chance, had any experience in the handling of boats or ships in the course of your professional career, Commander?"

"Where do I get a boat or ship to handle, Wally? And what do I say to the Dutch authorities about my unorthodox entry into their country?"

"To answer your second question first, you won't meet any Dutch authorities at night in the harbor of"—he moved his finger over the map's surface—". . . Delfzijl, whence, in the morning, you will depart by train for Groningen and The Hague, like any other Dutch traveler. Once at The Hague, you will find a foreign service type named Kiley—a friend of mine whom I will contact by telegram this very night—ready to assist you at the American consulate. Need I say more?"

"A word about obtaining a boat might be in order."

"I offer you two alternatives: buy one for two or three times its stated value from some poor but dishonest fisherman—or, if that seems too risky a course, engage in outright theft."

"All right then," Gehlman said, beginning to see the potential in Facchetti's plan, "what's my first step? Do I drive to Emden?"

Facchetti again looked at the map. "No. You drive to the village of . . . Knock, about ten miles west of Emden on the coast of the Ems."

"Wouldn't it be simpler, gentlemen," Keller interjected, "to drive close to the border at Bunde and then cross on foot?"

Gehlman saw that the attorney was looking somewhat distraught, and he conjectured that all the talk of stealing boats and stealing across frontiers might not be sitting well with a respectable solicitor's middle-class scruples.

"It would be simpler, Counselor," Facchetti said, "but in fact it isn't, as a glance at the map will confirm. You'll notice," he continued, as they all bent over the atlas, "that this whole stretch of border, from the Ems down to the Rhine, is unbroken lowland and marsh. It would be chancy enough for Ben to try crossing it on foot at night himself, let alone with a little girl in tow."

"But surely," said Keller, "the Ems estuary must be patrolled."

"True enough," Facchetti replied. "But we've got a first quarter moon to work with, so even if the sky is clear it should still be dark enough after midnight to get across the channel unseen."

"Well," Keller said, "I know little of ships or the sea, but isn't there some considerable danger in crossing several miles of water in a small boat in total darkness?"

"I realize it must seem dangerous," Gehlman responded, "but as long as one has one's bearings a small boat is actually safer in narrow waters than a big one. As you can see on the map, moreover, the Ems is sheltered from the more severe North Sea weather by the Frisian Islands."

"Yes, I see that." Keller sighed unhappily. "But I find this whole undertaking extremely worrisome nevertheless."

"It isn't as if we have much choice, Counselor," Facchetti said. "Von Tiel will have every border crossing to Holland alerted inside of the next two hours. In fact, Ben will be doing well just to get as far as Emden without being stopped by the police."

"I suppose you're right," Keller acknowledged glumly. "I only wish—"

The sound of someone knocking on the library door made all three men start.

"What is it?" Gehlman called out.

The chambermaid poked her head into the room. "Excuse me, sir; Frau Doktor Bauer is here."

"Oh, thank you, Uta. Please have her come in—and be sure to tell Karl he's to put the car in the garage and wait for me there."

"Very good, sir," said the maid, withdrawing.

"What do we want with the chauffeur, Ben?" Facchetti inquired.

"I'll explain later," Gehlman replied, as the weary-looking doctor came into the room.

"The child is unwell?" she asked as Gehlman came from behind the desk to greet her.

"For the moment she's fine," Gehlman responded. "But we have an extremely serious problem to deal with, and we'll need your help."

He introduced the doctor to Facchetti and Keller, and then rapidly summarized the situation. "So we have to get Alis out of the country," he concluded. "And I'd like you to explain to her what's happened, and prepare her psychologically to—"

"No!" Dr. Bauer interrupted. "Explanations will have to wait until she's safely out of Germany. We can't risk her becoming hysterical at this juncture. I'll provide you with some mild sedative pills to give her this evening. Meanwhile it will have to suffice for me to tell her that you're taking her to her mother. . . . Now tell me, how do you propose to neutralize the baron?"

"I think the best way would be to let him believe that we're making a run for it straight for Bunde, when actually we'll be on the north road bound for Emden."

"Why should he assume that you're headed for Bunde?" the doctor asked.

"Well, in the first palce, it's the nearest border crossing and the last one south of the Ems. In the second place, I have a plan for making the chauffeur think we're going there. And in the third place, I'm going to mark the route to Bunde on the map in that atlas on the desk, and then leave it lying open, as if by an oversight."

"How will you get him to look at it though?"

"By leaving it near that liquor cabinet next to the door; that's always the first place he goes. He'll notice the atlas right away because he's a stickler about books being left out of the shelves. He'll be annoyed to find it lying around open and he'll be infuriated to see that it's been marked up. The minute the servants tell him that Herr Keller was here and that Alis and I have left, he should immediately make the assumption we want him to make."

"Bravo, Ben!" Facchetti bellowed. "You've got a hidden talent for intrigue."

"I hope so, Wally. But we still don't have a boat, remember."

"I believe I have a solution to that problem for you," Dr. Bauer announced.

The three men turned to look at her.

"My family is from Emden," she explained. "My sister and her husband still live there, and they have a summer house on the coast at Heiselhusen."

Gehlman crossed back to the desk and looked down at the open atlas. Heiselhusen was a good ten kilometers north of the narrowest part of the channel, but still a feasible starting point.

"And they own a boat?"

"They own a five-meter sailboat, Commander. Is that big enough?"

"It's plenty big enough, unless it's still in dry dock for the winter."

The doctor raised a hand to her cheek in a gesture of dismay. "Dear God! I hadn't thought of that."

"Let me suggest to all of you," Facchetti cut in, "that we'd be well advised to concentrate our attention for the moment on the business of getting out of here. We can negotiate the finer points of this flight from Egypt once we're safely under way."

Gehlman glanced at the clock on the mantel; Facchetti was absolutely right.

Despite their frenetic haste, the carriage bringing the baron from the railway station was turning into the mansion's driveway by the time they were ready to leave. The five of them exited through one of the back doors and hurriedly made their way to the garage, where the somewhat bemused Karl was waiting as instructed. It took an agonizingly long two minutes for them to get themselves and their luggage into the large Benz touring car, and Gehlman kept expecting to see von Tiel erupt from the rear of the house at any second, with a Luger flashing in his hand. Fortunately all the servants walked in such fear of the baron that none of them would dare speak until spoken to. Pray God von Tiel was in a taciturn mood!

They drove out of the mansion's grounds without interference, crossed the Wilhelm-Brücke, and were soon moving briskly out of town along the Bismarckstrasse. After five miles they came to the main fork in the highway, and Gehlman, pursuant to the plan he'd contrived, instructed the chauffeur to go left, toward Bunde. A mile or two farther along, on the fringes of the village of Altgödens, he told Karl to pull over and stop. "I believe we lost a piece of luggage back by that farmhouse," he said, pointing. "We'll wait here for you while you go and fetch it."

Obediently, though a bit sullenly, Karl got out of the car and cast a meaningful glance at the suitcases strapped securely to the rear luggage rack. Having made his point, he then trudged off in the direction indicated. After several paces, though, the sound of the car's engine being started caused him to turn around, and he stared in mute incomprehension as the Benz sped away from him toward the west.

From his study of the atlas, Gehlman knew there was a connecting road at Weisede that would get them back on their way to Emden. Karl, meanwhile, would probably make his own way back to Wilhelmshaven and report there that they were en route to Bunde. He might also try to call, of course, but he wouldn't get through, because Gehlman had taken the precaution of cutting the mansion's telephone wire before they left.

They arrived at Emden at 2 P.M., just a little over an hour after abandoning Karl by the roadside. Gehlman's major worry—that von Tiel might ask the police to send out a general alert for the car—appeared to be unfounded. They'd gotten nothing more than cursory glances from the four or five policemen they'd passed. The feint toward Bunde must have accomplished its purpose.

Dr. Bauer's sister lived on the Cirksenastrasse, across from the post office and two or three blocks from the railway station. Gehlman, Alis, Facchetti, and Keller waited in the car while the doctor went inside the house to find out about the boat. Keller made good use of the time, feverishly preparing the papers that Gehlman would need to establish his status as Alis's legal guardian.

Gehlman himself was preoccupied about his new ward. How did she feel about all the strange things that had been going on this afternoon? Her face revealed little. She had sat silent and solemn in the back seat between Facchetti and Dr. Bauer all the waay from Wilhelmshaven. She showed no sign of disbelieving the doctor's assurances that she was being taken to see her mother, but Gehlman knew that, given the circumstances, she was far too intelligent to be free of doubt.

"Do you have enough cash to get you as far as The Hague?" Facchetti asked, bringing him out of his thoughts.

"I have four or five hundred marks, I think; that should be sufficient."

"Here," said Facchetti, passing some banknotes to him from the rear seat. "Take three hundred more. You may have to offer a few bribes along the way."

"Dutchmen don't take bribes," Gehlman said. "Thanks, anyway."

"All men take bribes; it's what distinguishes us from the lower animals. Besides, I want to be able to tell my grandchildren that the son of Oskar Gehlman once borrowed money from *me!*"

"Well, in that case, by all means," Gehlman said, grinning.

His grin vanished abruptly, however, because Facchetti's mention of bribes raised a worrisome issue in his mind: the amount of influence von Tiel could bring to bear on the Dutch authorities. Might the baron demand that Alis be detained in Holland pending adjudication of his claim to custody? He might very well. "Herr Keller," Gehlman said. "Forgive me for interrupting your work, but could you step outside the car for a moment so that we can discuss a . . . private matter."

"Of course," said Keller.

They walked to the rear of the automobile, and Gehlman in a low voice explained what was troubling him. The attorney listened carefully, then shook his head. "No, I don't think the baron would dare contest a custody suit outside of Germany. In a Dutch court he would be just another plaintiff, and enough evidence of his depravity would come out to ruin him several times over. Family law in the Netherlands is far more concerned with the welfare of the child than is family law in the Reich, and a much greater latitude of testimony is allowed on the question of parental fitness. I think that the most the baron could do is delay your departure for the United States for a week or two. Once he consults his solicitor, though, he probably won't even do that."

"He might, however, resort to extralegal tactics, mightn't he?"

"With the baron, there is always that possibility," Keller said, as Dr. Bauer emerged from the house and hurried over to them, looking flushed.

"We're in luck, Commander. They just finished caulking last Sunday."

"That's wonderful. But is your sister aware that she'll probably never see her boat again?"

"I didn't consider it advisable to burden her with the details of the situation. She thinks a Bavarian colleague of mine will be sailing for pleasure up the coastline to Norden."

"I'll arrange through my uncles to have her reimbursed as soon as possible, several times over, in fact."

"Perhaps you could have your uncles send the money to me, Commander; that way I can tell my sister it comes from my Bavarian colleague, along with his profound regrets for having run the boat on the rocks off Pilsum."

"Of course," Gehlman said.

"Hey!" Facchetti called to them, leaning out the car window. "What's the verdict?"

"We have our boat," Gehlman told him.

"Praise be!" Facchetti said, emerging from the car. "In that case I'm going to light out for Berlin. I've got to send a cipher message to friend Kiley at The Hague, and I can only do that from the embassy."

"I should be going back too, Commander," said Keller, whose nerves were by now plainly ragged. "If I am called on by the baron to account for my part in this affair, I wish to be able to prove that I was en route from Emden at the time you left the country. I don't know if that will help a great deal, but at least it will be something."

"Of course," said Gehlman who up to that point had not given any thought to the risks the attorney was running. "He can't really prove anything against you, or prosecute you, can he?"

"He can prove I was in this car with you and probably not much else. As to prosecution . . . Well, he is a man of influence and will certainly do all he can to create unpleasantness."

"I want you to know that you will be fully compensated for all expenses you incur on my account, Herr Keller."

"Thank you, Commander; but your safe arrival in Holland with Alis will be compensation enough for me."

"Then I am very much in your debt, sir," Gehlman said, extending his hand.

"Good-bye, Commander, and Godspeed," said Keller, grasping it.

"Better get a move on, Ben," Facchetti interjected. "Don't want to tempt fate."

Gehlman turned to him. "You've been a life saver, Wally. I can't begin to—"

"Yes yes, we know all about that, Ben. But I would have done the same for any other Academy man."

"Well, I'm deeply grateful anyway."

Facchetti patted him avuncularly on the back. "Go in peace, my boy; the prayers of the Gentiles go with you."

Gehlman laughed and tightly gripped Facchetti's hand. "Thanks, Wally. Take care of yourself."

"A *bientot, mon ami.* I'll keep you constantly informed of developments on every front."

"I don't doubt it. . . . Dr. Bauer?"

"Yes, Commander. I think we should go now," the doctor said, getting into the car's back seat with Alis.

Gehlman gave a half-salute–half-wave to Facchetti, then went round to the driver's side, got in, started the engine, put the car into gear, and drove off out of town toward the coast.

It was a lovely little boat, and it had been lovingly maintained. Gehlman stowed his own and Alis's luggage on board and subjected the craft to a systematic inspection, which revealed no defects whatsoever—unless obsessive neatness, order, and cleanness were defects. He climbed back up onto the small pier and approached the stone bench where Alis and the doctor were making a meal of the bread and liverwurst he'd stopped to buy on the way.

"Your sister and brother-in-law must be very conscientious people," he said. "If I kept up a boat of mine as well as they've kept up this one, I'd never lend it to anybody."

Dr. Bauer gave him a look of wry self-deprecation. "My family, Commander, is in many ways what the textbooks would describe as 'an interesting study in neurosis,' myself not least of all included. And you are quite right; permission to borrow this boat was by no means granted graciously."

Gehlman smiled at her with gratitude and sympathy. "Now I understand why you were inside your sister's house for such a long time. I suppose you'll never hear the end of it, when the boat doesn't come back."

Dr. Bauer shrugged. "My sister and I have never been close, Commander. I can bear her indignation."

Gehlman noticed as Dr. Bauer was talking that Alis seemed to be having trouble staying awake, even though it was only a little past five. Remembering the mention of sedatives earlier on, he gave the doctor a questioning glance and received a barely perceptible affirmative nod in return.

He ate some bread and liverwurst in silence as Alis slowly sagged against the doctor's shoulder. Once she was fully asleep, he carried her onto the boat and tucked her securely into one of the cabin's immaculate berths.

"She was becoming anxious about going on the boat with you," Dr. Bauer said as he stepped back onto the pier. "I gave her enough sedation to carry her through till morning. Do you think you'll have any trouble getting across?"

Gehlman surveyed the sky. The chill overcast of the morning and early afternoon was lowering now, and the northeasterly breeze was stiffening into a gusty ten-knot wind. Isolated raindrops fell at sporadic intervals, and the formerly calm surface of the estuary was beginning to display a quickening pattern of whitecaps. "It won't be a very smooth trip," he said. "But with the wind building like this we should be able to make it across in less than three hours."

Dr. Bauer was scrutinizing him with a skeptical expression. "Please be completely candid with me, Commander."

He sighed, acknowledging the evasiveness of the answer he'd given her. "If the wind gets a great deal stronger, we might have some problem getting in on the lee shore. But the charts in the boat show Delfzijl with a harbor breakwater and a light, so if I don't get too far off course we'll have no difficulty."

"What if you can't find the harbor?"

"I'll reef sail, drop anchor, and wait till it's light enough to see. Believe me, Doctor, I *am* being completely candid when I say there's no danger. My only real concern is that we may be spotted by a patrol. But in that respect the weather certainly favors us."

"Well then, good sailing," the doctor said.

"Thank you . . . for everything. Will you be able to manage the car?"

"It's been a while since I last drove an automobile, but I should be able to get as far as Emden."

"Where will you leave it?"

"Somewhere on the outskirts, near a bus stop."

Gehlman hesitated before speaking again. "I don't know much about being a parent, Doctor. Can you . . ."

She reached up and put a hand on his shoulder. "*No one* knows much about being a parent, Commander. But you, quite obviously, know enough."

"I'm flattered. But what makes you think so?"

"The talk I had with Alis while you were looking over the boat. It appears the two of you had a conversation this morning."

Gehlman grinned broadly, remembering Alis's "Because you are Jewish?" "Yes," he said. "We certainly did."

Dr. Bauer's expression remained serious. "The fact of that conversation is most remarkable, Commander. You have managed somehow to make Alis see the depth and sincerity of your concern for her. I believe, with time, she well might place her trust in you."

"I hope you're right," Gehlman said, exhilarated by the idea of such a possibility.

"I believe I am right," said the doctor.

"What about her mother? When should I tell her about that?"

"I think she already has more than vague suspicions, Commander. She was beginning to question me very closely while we were talking just now—about where her mother was and about why we were making such a complicated to-do about taking her to see her. It would take a child with far less intelligence than she has to miss the general significance of what's been happening today. That's another reason why I sedated her, in fact."

"So I should tell her soon then?"

"It would be preferable if you could wait until she's had a little time to adjust to New York. But if the only way you can avoid telling is by lying to her or refusing to answer her questions, then tell her the truth. It's important that she not have reason to doubt your honesty or your candor."

"I understand."

"If you do have to tell her before you reach the United States and she appears to be taking it badly, you can give her one of the pills I've provided, every twelve hours, until she starts to calm down."

"Very well. But isn't there any other advice you could give me?"

"Only to trust your instincts, Commander. You are really a very good and kind man, you know, and I think caring for Alis will help you to realize that."

Gehlman looked down at his shoes in embarrassment, then

abruptly up at the sky. "I think it's almost dark enough to get started now," he said.

Dr. Bauer laughed softly. "Yes," she said. "Rather face a stormy sea than acknowledge one's own gentle nature."

"Much much rather," Gehlman admitted with a sheepish smile. "Well then . . . I guess I'll say good-bye."

"Good-bye, Commander. God keep you both."

He wanted to respond to her somehow, but nothing came to mind. So he simply said "Good-bye" again and stepped aboard the boat.

The wind grew stronger as they moved away from the shelter of the shore. It was shifting from northeast to north, and Gehlman let out the mainsail boom to catch the full brunt of its power. The jib strained at its stays and the boat heeled just slightly to starboard as he kept its bow on a south-southwest heading. With the mounting wind came steadier rain and lashings of spray. He hoped that Alis would not awaken because in weather like this she would be both scared and sick.

He scanned the dark horizon in all directions. The din of sea and wind would drown out the sound of an approaching patrol boat, but he was powerless to evade one in any case, so the problem was more or less academic. Against such a minor handicap, moreover, could be offset the advantages of reduced visibility and a walloping tail wind. The boat was making five, perhaps even six, knots, and at that rate they would reach the Dutch coast in little more than two hours.

The only real danger now was that they would be blown onto the lee shore in the darkness and wrecked. The night was as black as any he'd seen, and the wind continued to increase in force. Land, sky, and water had long since merged into an undifferentiated pitch-dark stew of noise.

As the minutes passed, he altered course slightly eastward, so that they would not be coming at the shore head on. He strained his eyes and constantly tested the resistance of the tiller, hoping for some advance warning of shoaling waters. Then, far off the starboard quarter, he saw what had to be the Delfzijl light. They had gone past it!

A quick glance at the chart in the beam of a lantern confirmed his apprehension. It was just as well he'd altered to east, because they'd be aground by now if he hadn't! The coastline ran southeast from Delfzijl, however, and it was clear, using the harbor light as a point of reference, that despite the course alteration they were still dangerously close to the shore.

At almost the exact instant he reached this conclusion he heard and felt the centerboard plowing its way into sand.

He moved quickly, bringing the boom whistling around to port at lethal speed and at the same time releasing the jib. The boat was slowing rapidly and the centerboard was still in contact with the bottom. It would be rising up in its slot soon, and he would no longer have any control.

He was about to abandon the tiller and bring Alis topside when the water suddenly deepened. He turned the bow directly into the channel with a little sob of relief and did the best he could to reef the flaccid jib against the buffets of the by now frenzied wind. Then he slowly brought the boat onto a course for the Delfzijl light, plowing into the angry waves that piled up against the starboard beam.

It took him two hours of tacking and anxiety to cover the short distance to the harbor entrance. Shivering and soaked to the skin, he brought the boat inside the breakwater and moored it to the first bollard he saw. It was a few minutes past ten o'clock. Descending into the cabin he found Alis still asleep, her breathing slow and steady. He looked at her as the rain tattooed down on the deck above him and felt a surge of joyful serenity such as he'd never known before. They had made it; they'd come through. He and Alis, the family intact.

BOOK IV

1915, 31ST MARCH—THE NORTH SEA

Maltbie felt a hand gently shaking his shoulder, then heard the soft voice of the wireless officer. "I say, Harry, sorry to rouse you, but . . ."

"What time is it?"

"A bit after four."

Maltbie sat up in his bunk and rubbed his eyes. "Has Red Fleet been located?" he asked, referring to Beatty's Battle Cruiser Fleet, which Jellicoe's Blue Fleet was out hunting on maneuvers.

"No, no, Harry; nothing like that. It's just that it's such a wonderful night for wireless. The atmospherics are at an absolute minimum. We've been picking up all sorts of things. I reckoned you wouldn't want to miss it."

"Thanks a million, John. You're damn right I wouldn't."

He swung his legs onto the deck and groped for his boots in the dim blue light shed by the twenty-four-hour-a-day deckhead fixture.

"I've got to get back," Commander Salmond said. "Come along as soon as you're ready."

"Right, John. Thanks again."

Maltbie switched on his reading light and located his boots. Like most of the other officers, he had adopted the practice when at sea of sleeping in his woolen underwear, trousers, and socks so that dressing in the event of a call to action meant simply donning one's shirt, tying one's tie, and slipping into one's jacket—or, in his case, fastening his collar and buttoning his tunic.

This time the summons was not so urgent, and Maltbie sat for a moment on the edge of his bunk listening to the background roar of the ventilation fans and the far-away thrum of the turbines. Judging by the feel of the vibrations beneath his feet, he estimated that they were making sixteen knots, three-quarter speed, which was a pretty good clip for a one-hundred-ship armada.

He stepped out of his cabin into the perceptibly cooler air of the passage, then walked for'ard to the first ladder. This brought him down to the mess deck, where he went for'ard again, down another ladder across the lower deck, and into the passage leading to the wireless office. He was moving briskly ahead when a small figure emerged without warning from the cipher room just to his right. There was a near collision as Maltbie twisted to his left to avoid running the man down. "Sorry," he said a bit abruptly, and was almost on his way again when he realized he was looking into the twinkly blue eyes of the commander in chief.

"Good morning, Maltbie," Jellicoe said.

"Good morning, sir," Maltbie responded, wondering to himself, Doesn't the man ever *sleep?* He had seen Jellicoe working intently at his desk not five hours before.

The two of them stood facing each other, smiling awkwardly. It occurred to Maltbie that Jellicoe would probably be curious to know what he was doing at this hour in this part of the ship. He would never ask, of course; he was far too polite. But Maltbie had no intention of keeping the information from him.

"I was just on my way to the wireless office," he said. "They tell me it's an extraordinary night: almost no atmospherics, and a good strong air wave."

Jellicoe's eyes lit up. "I thought I was the only officer left who still got excited about voices in the ether."

"Oh no, sir. Salmond came and woke me especially—and he'd certainly have wanted me to wake him if he'd been the one who was sleeping."

"Well, it's gratifying to learn that not everyone is blasé about the wireless nowadays. Perhaps I needn't hide my guilty enthusiasm any longer, especially as you experts aren't concealing yours. . . . I wonder if we can pick up Malta."

"We had Gibraltar for a few minutes last week, sir."

"Really! I think I'll come along and listen with you, if I may."

"Of course, sir," Maltbie said, as they walked the remaining few paces to the wireless office.

The office door swung open as they approached it, rather as if their arrival had been anticipated. In fact, though, a tall thin marine enlisted man was in the process of leaving. Maltbie was more than moderately surprised to see that it was Otley.

"Mornin', sir," the corporal said, flattening himself against the side of the passage to let Jellicoe go by. Just the tiniest flicker of discomposure passed over his features when he registered Maltbie's identity. "And good mornin' to you, sir, as well."

"Good morning, Terry," Maltbie said. Out of simple curiosity he was about to ask Otley what had lured him to the wireless office at such an ungodly hour, or at all for that matter. But given the presence of the admiral and the likelihood that friend Terry was engaged in one of the innumerable and unauthorized wagering schemes that had kept him seven years a private, Maltbie decided that it would be better not to raise the question. "See you after breakfast" was all he said in the end.

"Right, sir," Otley responded, with a wobbly smile that suggested either gratitude or—oddly enough—apology.

As Maltbie followed the admiral into the office, he wondered idly what possible reason Otley could have for feeling apologetic toward him.

Salmond and the two petty officers on duty made to rise when Jellicoe appeared, but he motioned them to remain seated. "I understand the ether is brimming over," he said.

"It is indeed, sir," Salmond replied. "Would you like a quick tour of the tunes?"

"I believe I'd enjoy that very much."

"Done, sir," said Salmond with a grin, handing earphone sets to Maltbie and the C in C.

Maltbie put his on over his head, leaving his right ear free to hear what the younger petty officer was saying as he plugged them in. "We'll listen for Nordeich first," he said. "He's due to transmit in about two minutes."

Nordeich was the German high power station near Bremen. Maltbie had heard its transmissions often. Jellicoe, however, had an expression of rapt anticipation on his face as he listened to the tweetings and buzzings that skittered across the as yet unoccupied frequency.

While waiting for the first few pulses of International Morse to come through the night, Maltbie let his eyes travel over the crowded interior of the W/T room. The senior petty officer was seated in the rear, keeping guard on the Admiralty and ship-to-ship wavelengths. This was the man, CPO Millikan, who had shown Maltbie around on his arrival some six weeks ago. Then the British terminology— "tune" for radio frequency, "valve" for vacuum tube—had been rather confusing to him; now it was the old familiar American words that were beginning to sound a little strange.

On the right-hand bulkhead of the office sat the *Iron Duke*'s two

14-kilowatt transmitter-receivers: service installation Mark IIs calibrated to send and receive twenty-eight frequencies. They were standard spark and crystal sets capable of a daylight transmission radius of five hundred miles, and *Iron Duke* was the only ship in the Royal Navy that carried two of them. On the bulkhead opposite were three 1.5-kilowatt T/Rs, backup sets with a transmission range of one hundred miles. The rear bulkhead of the office looked like a cross between a library and an old curiosity shop. There were bound and loose-leaf manuals, signal logs, binders filled with Admiralty regulations, and a motley collection of books on wireless telegraphy, all freely intermingled with spare valves, disassembled earphones, orphaned dials and tuners, miscellaneous oddments of receiving and transmitting apparatus, and cardboard boxes full of new and used components. The office as a whole had rather a warm and homey flavor to it, due in large part to the fact that its small and crowded confines were occupied and in use twenty-four hours every day.

"Here he is," the younger petty officer said, and in the earphones Maltbie heard the strong deep-voiced pulses: *dah-dit-dit, dah-dit, dah* —DNT: Deutsche Nordeich Telefunken—repeated seven times and followed by a long stream of International Morse.

"He's very punctual, he is," said the petty officer. "Set your watch by him."

"What's he saying?" Jellicoe asked.

"It's the daily news broadcast, sir: lies and slander."

They all laughed.

After they had listened for several minutes to Nordeich, the petty officer switched to the equally strong though somewhat shriller tone of the original Marconi station at Poldhu in Cornwall. This was followed by a succession of British shore transmitters: Rame Head near Plymouth, Culver Cliff at Portsmouth, Roches Point near Queenstown in southern Ireland, Ipswich, Aberdeen, Pembroke Dock, and the new high power stations at Cleethorpes and Horsea Island. Next, much to Jellicoe's undisguised delight, came the somewhat strident call sign of Rinella in Malta. "Ah, Malta!" the admiral sighed. "Back in '93 I was ill aboard the *Victoria* when she collided with *Camperdown* off Tripoli and went under. When they fished me out of the Mediterranean, I was sent back to Malta to convalesce, and my wife came out from England to nurse me. What a lovely summer we had there. I still get nostalgic about it."

"But wasn't it Malta fever that you were ill with in the first place, sir?" Salmond inquired.

Jellicoe's prim features relaxed into a playfully sheepish smile. "I prefer to think of it in its more generic guise of undulant fever, John —and in any case there was some question as to whether I in fact contracted it at Malta. . . . But how do you come to know what it was I was ill with?"

"I was a midshipman aboard the *Camperdown*, sir."

"You don't say so!"

"Yes, sir."

"I thought you did your time as a snotty on the *Trafalgar*."

"No, sir; on the *Trafalgar* I was a sublieutenant."

"Well, well," Jellicoe said, shaking his head remorsefully. "I can't think why I didn't remember that."

"Perhaps you had other things on your mind," Maltbie said in an attempt at respectful banter which, to his ears at least, came out sounding dangerously like familiarity.

Jellicoe gave him a rather dry but for the most part still benign look and said avuncularly, "An admiral should know his staff, Mr. Maltbie. And in any case one should never make excuses for authority; there aren't any, and authority will usually make them for itself."

"There's the Eiffel Tower," said the petty officer, providing Maltbie with a very welcome opportunity to return his attention to the sounds coming in from the night.

The "tour of the tunes" continued. They picked up the C in C of the Russian Navy transmitting from Kronstadt on the Gulf of Finland; they heard Madrid, and then the North Front station on Gibraltar.

"We've never gotten such strong signals from so far away," Salmond said, and the petty officer responded, "Tonight might be the night we pull in St. John's."

"You mean, *Newfoundland?!*" Maltbie asked.

"Yes, sir."

"Now that *would* be exciting," Jellicoe said.

The petty officer slowly rotated the tuner while Maltbie, Salmond, and Jellicoe held their earphones tight against their heads; even CPO Millikan had picked up an extra set and was listening.

Off the standard wavelengths the ether took on the sound of a deep primeval sea; it was an elemental roaring sound unbroken by the usual stray bits of transmissions. Sometimes it grew louder and sometimes softer as the tuner traversed the frequencies, but in quality and portent the sound continued unbroken—mysterious and oceanic.

"There!" Maltbie shouted. "What's that?"

They all strained to hear, except Millikan, who had had to put down his extra set of earphones in order to take in a signal that was coming in on the Admiralty frequency.

"I don't hear anything," Salmond said.

"Half a minute, sir," the petty officer cut in, his face alive with excitement and concentration. "I think Mr. Maltbie's onto something."

He moved the tuner very slowly, no more than a millimeter every few seconds. Then they heard it: a faint high-pitched *dah-dit* followed by a sudden swelling of the background oceanic roar.

They waited.

The roaring subsided a bit, then a bit more. Then the signal came in distinctly, though still faintly: *dit-dit-dah, dit-dit-dit, dah-dit-dah-dit*—USX.

"My God!" Maltbie exclaimed. "That's the new high-power transmitter at Arlington, Virginia!"

"No!" said Jellicoe. "Is that possible?"

"I wouldn't have thought so," Salmond replied, reaching hurriedly for one of the manuals on the rear wall. "But let's have a look."

He set the book down roughly on the table and began riffling through the pages in such haste that several of them tore. In his earphones Maltbie heard the signal beginning to fade, but the *dit-dit-dah, dit-dit-dit, dah-dit-dah-dit* was still unmistakable.

"Here it is," Salmond said in an excited voice. " 'USX: 100-kilowatt Fessenden Rotary Spark Transmitter at 350 kilocycles per second . . .' "

"I'm tuned to 475, sir," the petty officer told him. "Give or take."

"Hold on," said Salmond. "There's a footnote." His eyes ran hungrily over the page. "Footnote footnote footnote footnote . . . *here!* It says: 'Added: USX—35-kilowatt Poulsen Arc Transmitter at 470 kilocycles per second, installed: October 1912; operational: March 1913; operated by U.S. Navy; location: Arlington, Virginia, U.S.A.' . . . *Hurrah!*"

And for some indefinable reason they all started to laugh and shout and shake each other's hands, celebrating this purely happenstantial reception of a few feeble pips of sound. The signal faded away and their laughter trailed off, finally ending in embarrassed smiles. Maltbie was puzzled as to why they had all been so jubilantly excited. But they had, and he still felt it: a sense of discovery, of ascendancy, of mastery over nature, of triumph. It was a wonderful feeling—sparkling and full, like New Year's Eve.

"Here's another message just in from the United States," CPO Millikan said, and there was a huge grin on his face as he handed the piece of paper to Jellicoe. "Cable forwarded *en clair* by the First Sea Lord."

Jellicoe read what was written, and a huge grin came over his face as well. "I believe this is for you, Mr. Maltbie," he said, handing Harry the yellow foolscap.

Maltbie looked at Millikan's handwriting, read the message, and blinked several times in disbelief. How many other wireless receivers had been tuned to the Admiralty frequency, he wondered in embarrassment—in how many different countries.

> RETURNING ENGLAND STOP OBJECT MATRIMONY STOP WILL YOU STILL HAVE ME QUESTION MARK SAILING NEW YORK ONE MAY ARRIVING LIVERPOOL EIGHT MAY LUSITANIA STOP I LOVE YOU STOP MELINA.

So there was laughter and shouting and handshaking once again— with even better cause, Maltbie felt, even better cause by far.

1915, 31ST MARCH—NEW YORK CITY

Gehlman was not, as a rule, subject to spasms of patriotic emotion, but the sight of the Statue of Liberty on this cold and inclement morning had most assuredly brought one on. He had a sense, for the first time in his life, of what the immigrant masses must feel as they crowded ships' railings for their first glimpse of the new country. It was not a joyous feeling, not the warm gladness of reaching some promised land, but a sense of relief, rather, of deliverance from an oppression of the spirit. For Gehlman, of course, the oppression had a face and a name; and even now, with the Atlantic as a bulwark, the specter of von Tiel remained a chilling one.

At The Hague, strong echoes of the baron's fury had started to reverberate through ministries and consulates even as Alis and Gehlman were en route there by train from Delfzijl. Though prevented by Dutch visa requirements and his security-conscious *Reichsmarine* superiors from immediately leaving Germany himself, von Tiel had lost no time at all in initiating legal action through Dutch attorneys. Elwood Kiley, Facchetti's enormously fat and, as it proved, enormously resourceful friend in the consular service, had had his powers of ingenuity put to the sternest test. After listening to the full details of their escape, Kiley had driven Alis and Gehlman to his small house on the Nieuwe Park Laan in Scheveningen, near the seashore. There his comparably large housekeeper had taken immediate charge of Alis, sweeping the still somewhat drug-benumbed child into her beefy arms and carrying her off for a hot bath, some warm milk, and bed. The intensity of the woman's solicitude had been such that Gehlman was a bit put off by it. Alis, however, seemed to accept it as a matter of course, and was soon fast, and to all appearances contentedly, asleep.

After an afternoon of discreet inquiries, Kiley had arrived back home late in the evening and explained to Gehlman the situation as he saw it. He said that Herr Keller was probably correct in thinking the Dutch courts would confirm Benjamin's designation as Alis's guardian. The difficulty, however, was that he and Alis had left Germany and entered Holland illegally, which meant that the Dutch courts would refuse to hear their case and simply send them back across the border. Even if the courts could be persuaded to accept jurisdiction, he continued, Gehlman's quasi-diplomatic status as a naval observer rendered the possibility of a public judicial proceeding undesirable in terms of American foreign policy interests. On the positive side, though, Kiley said that he had learned indirectly from a contact of his in the Ministry of the Interior that neither von Tiel nor the Dutch authorities knew as yet where he and Alis actually were, or even if they had fled to Holland in the first place. He said that von Tiel's attorneys had asked the authorities for assistance in locating the two of them, but had confessed to having no knowledge of their whereabouts beyond the "supposition" that they had entered the country near Bunde. Also on the positive side, Kiley had gone on, was the fact that Gehlman was extremely rich; this was a good thing because it was going to take extremely large quantities of money to get him and Alis to New York.

Next morning Gehlman had placed a call from Kiley's office to Albert Gehlman of the Hamburg Handelsbank. He had asked his uncle to instruct a correspondent bank in The Hague to make ten thousand dollars worth of guilders available to Mr. E. Kiley, immediately. Albert Gehlman had said simply, *"Ja,"* and then added, for discretion's sake in English, "How are you, Benjamin?" "I'm well, Uncle," Gehlman had responded, "though under a little strain at the moment. I'll send you a letter very soon, to elaborate. And I'll send you repayment too." *"Ja,"* Albert Gehlman had said. "I understand. Be careful, Benjamin—and give my love to your father and mother."

It was important to move quickly, because the car abandoned near Emden would provide a clue to his and Alis's route of escape, as indeed would the sailboat abandoned in Delfzijl harbor. Though Kiley had gone off to the bank before lunchtime, it wasn't until well after midnight that he returned to the house in Scheveningen. "Thank God for the Italians!" he'd said on his arrival. "They're the only ones who appreciate an honest bribe."

The *Principessa Mafalda* of the Lloyd Italiano line, bound for New York and Buenos Aires, was due to leave Rotterdam in an hour, he'd reported. Gehlman and Alis were to board her a mile or so off Hook of Holland; traveling first class in a single cabin, the one-way fare for both of them would be $15,000—$7,500 paid that afternoon by Kiley and $7,500 to be paid by Gehlman on docking in New York. (The ship's captain had demanded $20,000 originally, but Kiley had bargained him down.)

Having awakened Alis and, with the housekeeper's help, prepared her for the journey, Gehlman had with great reluctance dissolved one of Dr. Bauer's pills in the cocoa the housekeeper prepared for her. She was sound asleep again by the time he settled her into the back seat of Kiley's car.

The fifteen-mile ride to Hook of Holland had ended at an apparently deserted pier, but a small boat with a well-muffled outboard motor had glided in after two or three minutes. Kiley had paid the boatman five hundred dollars in guilders. Then he'd turned his back to the man and quickly handed Gehlman a small revolver—"To discourage breaches of contract," he'd whispered—and an envelope containing the two thousand dollars that remained of Uncle Albert's ten.

"I can't think of any way to thank you adequately," Gehlman had said as they stood there.

"Any friend of Wally's," Kiley had responded, then waddled hastily away into the darkness.

The air was still and dank as the boatman headed out into the North Sea, and the *Principessa Mafalda* had come into view after some twenty minutes, lights blazing all along her hull to advertise the fact that she was a merchant liner. She was a bigger ship than Gehlman had expected, almost 10,000 tons, and she was crawling along at three or four knots, presumably in anticipation of the scheduled rendezvous. The boatman had maneuvered up to an accommodation ladder near the port bow and thrown a line to a ship's officer who was waiting at the bottom. Gehlman had stepped up out of the boat with Alis nestled in his arms. After hurriedly handing up their luggage, the boatman had cast loose and disappeared astern. Alone now, face to face with the officer, Gehlman had experienced a moment of uncertainty and fear. To what sort of people, he wondered, had he entrusted his own and Alis's safety. The expression of awed reverence that came over the officer's face when he took his first close look at Alis's features provided the hint of an answer. "*Che bellezza divina!*" the man had whispered, bowing Gehlman toward the steps of the ladder as if the Princess Mafalda herself was about to be carried aboard.

The officer's reaction proved far from atypical, with the result that the voyage across the Atlantic became something of a triumphal progress for Gehlman and Alis—or for Alis at any rate, with Gehlman as collateral beneficiary. The myth of Italian child worship turned out to be no myth at all. The two of them dined at the captain's table every night; despite the terms Kiley had negotiated, moreover, they were quartered in luxurious adjoining staterooms, with matrons provided to serve as Alis's full-time maids. The fact that she and Gehlman were fugitives appeared to be of no consequence to the half dozen officers and crewmen who were in on the bribe. The two of them were treated as if they were regular passengers who had purchased ultra-expensive tickets which entitled them to some hitherto unknown category of ultra-deluxe first-class service. In a way, of course—absent the notion of entitlement—that was precisely what they were.

To Gehlman's amusement, he had found himself cast by the ship's officers in the role of his own ward's equerry. Any special consideration shown him, it was clear, was shown him because he constituted Alis's retinue and therefore served an important shipboard purpose, much as a boiler served the purposes of the primary turbine. In addition to being amused, Gehlman had also been fascinated to see for the first time the extraordinary power that resided in beauty as compelling as Alis's. The countess had been right; she *was* a freak— but what was more fascinating even than her power was the perfect equanimity with which she accepted the adoration she inspired. She accepted it not as something she was entitled to, but rather as something that partook of the natural order of things. It was a given that people should adore her, a given like gravity or the motions of the stars. Thus she was able to acknowledge all the attention paid her with a kind of graciously reserved indifference, as if the practice of worshiping her was a silly but innocuous habit that people had to be permitted to indulge in, but which got a bit tedious to contemplate after a while nevertheless. In this regard she had exactly the same air of patiently muted ennui that Gehlman remembered seeing on the faces of royal visitors at ceremonial functions in Washington: they recognized the importance of the forms, but wouldn't it be nice just once if people were to treat them like normal human beings.

As to his own relationship with Alis, Gehlman had been disturbed during the first few days of the crossing by what he perceived to be a regression in the development of their rapport. Alis's renewed, though diminished, wariness could be explained, he knew, by the jarring dislocations to which the child had been subjected. But there was a further contributing factor on the level of their personal interaction: he was deceiving her, and he was sure that she could sense it.

How could she fail to sense it? Gehlman was not an accomplished practitioner of deception; in fact, any sort of duplicity made him distinctly uneasy—not out of moral considerations so much as out of a visceral antipathy to distortions of reality. He had always been a person who needed to distinguish what was real in the world around him from what was merely convention. Perhaps because of the persecution he'd suffered and the systematic pretensions of mental illness he'd been forced to endure with his mother, he was extremely sensitive to any disparity between precept and practice, between what people said they did and what they really did in fact. He was one of those unfortunate sports of nature for whom the emperor's new clothes were not only a fraud, but a threat—and for the simple reason that convention had consistently betrayed him, had repeat-

edly and to his cost gulled him into believing that his own perceptions were not the legitimate starting points for truth. After having
been ambushed and clobbered by experience over and over again as a
consequence of his gullibility, Gehlman the boy had grown into
Gehlman the man: angry, suspicious, and alone. And he had come
to have a fierce antipathy to any sort of tampering with cognition,
his own or anyone else's. Accordingly, on the fourth night out, once
the matron had tucked Alis into bed, Gehlman came into her stateroom determined to tell her the truth.

"Hello," he'd said.

"Hello," she'd answered, her expression—as it had been now for
several days—guarded and a bit mistrustful.

"May I sit down and talk with you for a moment?"

"Yes," she'd said gravely.

"I . . . have to tell you something."

"What is it?"

Gehlman had assessed the wisdom of what he was about to do one
final time, then let out a long breath and plunged. "We aren't going
to New York to meet your mother."

"Where is my mother?" she'd asked him, her voice dull, devoid of
any inflection, almost as if she knew the answer herself and simply
wanted to find out if he did.

"She's . . . dead. She fell from her horse, in Berlin, a week ago,
and was killed." (Her death is what matters, he'd rationalized to
himself, not the real cause of her death.)

She had stared at him for what seemed a long long time as tears
welled up in her eyes. He'd thought she would say something, cry
out, scream, but in the end all she had done was turn over silently
and bury her head in the pillows.

He'd sat there and watched her, waiting for her shoulders to begin
shaking with sobs, waiting for her to moan or wail. But she'd stayed
motionless, silent. Finally he'd become concerned that she might unwittingly be suffocating herself and had gone around to the other
side of the bed to make sure that she could breathe. He had found
her staring out desolately at the far wall of the stateroom, a large wet
blot of tears on the pillow case beneath her cheek. Not knowing
what else to do, he'd seated himself beside the bed where she could
see him and prepared himself to keep vigil with her through the
night.

She'd fallen asleep finally toward morning and had stayed asleep all through the day, though tossing restlessly much of the time. Dozing on and off in his chair, Gehlman had remained with her constantly. She'd awakened shortly after eight in the evening, almost twenty-four hours after he'd broken the news. Seeing him in the chair before her, she had begun to weep again in silent desolation. On an impulse he'd reached out and taken her hand to comfort her. She'd gone rigid for an instant when he touched her, and then she'd begun to sob: great wracking sobs of grief. As the tears fell, she'd gripped his hand tightly in both of hers and hugged it against her chest.

Gehlman was moved by this gesture—moved, as he saw it, out of all proportion.

Now Alis was standing beside him on the promenade deck, grasping that same hand securely in her own. The towers of lower Manhattan stood out against the slate gray sky, and with his free hand Gehlman pointed to the Commercial Guaranty Trust Building, saying, "That's where my father works."

Alis looked up at him with the slightly blank, slightly nettled expression children adopt when presented with gratuitous information of minimal interest. "But we're not going to *live* there, are we?"

"No. The house we're going to live in is five kilometers farther up the island."

"Is your father going to meet us when we land?"

"I certainly hope so," Gehlman said.

With the captain's enthusiastic approval, he had sent a radio message yesterday afternoon to New York, asking his father and the family attorney, Mr. Bograd, to be at Pier 90 at Fiftieth Street at 11:00 A.M. For the sake of caution he hadn't gone into detail, figuring that Oskar would be sufficiently startled by such a cryptic—indeed, by *any* —message from him to assume that a matter of some urgency had inspired it. (The captain, who had seemed at first a little disappointed that Benjamin had not made any mention of money, took comfort when he saw that the message was addressed to the chairman of a bank.)

Now, as Gehlman stood at the railing, he noticed a police launch speeding toward the ship. As it got nearer, he saw to his surprise that the well-dressed gentleman standing just outside the wheelhouse was none other than Mr. Bograd himself.

Bograd handled everything: he took the documents Facchetti and

Herr Keller had provided in Germany and expeditiously got Alis and Gehlman cleared by customs and immigration. He also sent his clerk to the bank in his limousine to fetch the final $7,500 owed to the *Principessa Mafalda*'s captain.

Once all the formalities were concluded the ship's officers lined up at the gangplank to bid Alis—and Gehlman, incidentally—good-bye. One by one they came up, bowed, and kissed her hand. It was a spectacle Gehlman found silly somehow, but oddly endearing nevertheless. Alis's reaction was her standard one of stoical noblesse oblige, leavened just the least little bit perhaps by a bemused sense of pride.

Oskar was waiting for them beside his car in front of the pier exit on Twelfth Avenue. "Hello, Benjamin," he said with a mildly interrogative inflection, his gaze shifting quickly to Alis.

"Hello, Father. This is my ward, Alis von Lutwitz."

"How do you do, Fräulein," Oskar said with a stiff but courtly half-bow.

"How do you do, Herr Gehlman," Alis responded with a curtsy.

There was a moment of silence while Oskar let his eyes rest on the remarkable contours of Alis's face. Then, collecting himself, he said, "Well, Benjamin, shall we go home now?"

Alis's arrival at the Gehlman mansion was memorable for a number of reasons, not least of all the almost instantaneous spark of animation it touched off inside the traditionally cheerless walls. Benjamin took her around the house and introduced her to the servants, who reacted to her with the same sort of rapt veneration he had seen aboard the *Principessa Mafalda*. He showed her several upstairs rooms that he thought she might like for her own; and she indicated a preference for one on the mansion's southeast corner, overlooking the kitchen gardens of the houses on Seventy-eighth Street. Benjamin instructed the housekeeper to get the room ready for her and unpack her things. Then, after checking with Oskar, he took her along to the rooms his mother occupied on the second floor, facing Central Park.

Erna seemed at first not to recognize him, but the moment of distraction passed quickly. "Ben!" she gasped, as he braced himself for a torrent of effusive endearments. As she rose and rushed to caress him, however, she noticed Alis for the first time, standing solemnly by his side, and stopped dead. For several seconds she just stood and stared, but then, in a voice that was unusually strong and lucid, she said, "Hello, my dear. How very, very beautiful you are."

"Thank you, Frau Gehlman," Alis replied with, to Gehlman's considerable surprise, a timid but genuine smile.

He introduced Alis and said that, as his ward, she would be staying for a while in the house. Erna took the hint and postponed asking questions, saying instead to Alis, "We must choose a room for you, then."

She came over to Benjamin and kissed him lightly on the cheek. "What a wonderful surprise to have you home again," she said, then reached down and took Alis's hand. He was about to tell her that a room had already been selected, but as he watched her walk out into the hallway with Alis he thought better of it.

While Alis napped in the afternoon, Benjamin told Oskar and Erna how she had come to be with him. They reacted with shock, anger, and sympathy to the story; and it was the first time in Benjamin's memory that all three of them had shared the same feelings. At dinner Alis was pure charm, conversing with Oskar and Erna in *Hochdeutsch* locutions of the most ultra-correct formality. As Benjamin ate, he found it wonderfully engaging to hear his stiff old father acknowledge that, yes, ocean liners *were* great fun to travel on, and yes, the meat *was* unusually delicious, and yes, New York *did* have an exceptionally good zoo that Alis could visit. At the mention of the zoo, Erna chimed in with a suggestion that all four of them go up to the Bronx in the morning and visit it. To Benjamin's accelerating amazement, Oskar immediately agreed.

Another first: his father skipping a morning's work.

He put Alis to bed after dinner and in his own room sat for several hours sipping brandy and reflecting on all that had happened since their walk on the beach nine days before. Prior to retiring he went to her room to make sure she was in some unspecified way "all right." He found Erna there, gazing at her from the foot of the bed, with great glistening tears cascading down the length of her cheeks. She put a finger to her lips and gave him a soft rueful smile. It was yet another first for him, this one perhaps the most significant of all. Because he saw at that moment that Erna was not the squat bovine caricature of a female he'd always avoided and despised, but simply a baffled, bruised, and timeworn creature like himself. Now to some degree a parent also, he at last found it possible to accept having once been her child.

1915, 23D APRIL—BERLIN

Great mountainous waves of frustration and rage rolled across von Müller's mind as he read through the file that Dr. Rathenau's friends in the War Ministry had somehow managed to put together. Blindness, madness, and stupidity were not merely afoot in Germany, they were rampant—and where was the counterpoise against them?

What *possesses* us? von Müller wondered to himself. How did we come by this tunneled perception that sees the world as a linear progression toward final decreed objectives.

Von Müller shook his head. But it isn't a question of metaphysics, for God's sake! It's a question of simple common sense, which we've been lacking since the very first hour of the war. All right; if *realpolitik* demands that you march through a country like Belgium, whose neutrality you are bound by treaty to protect, then march, and let God defend the right. But having marched, don't then have the Chancellor of your empire attempt to justify your actions by declaring that the treaty you've just broken is nothing more than "a scrap of paper." And having marched, don't take the attitude that the people of the neutral country you've just invaded are criminal *franctireurs* for resisting you. Don't "make examples," don't level six-hundred-year-old cities like Louvain, don't engage in reprisals that bring the odium of an already disapproving world down with redoubled intensity on your head.

And the zeppelin and airplane raids over England and France; what in God's name were they intended to accomplish? It would take a brain very severely riddled by fantasy to assume that a few bombs dropped into city streets might so distress the Allied common man as to send him clamoring to Westminster or the Quai d'Orsay with demands that his government sue for peace. Much more to be expected were the reactions the raids had in fact produced: fury and renewed determination in the Allied camp, disgust and reprobation among the neutrals.

And then, yesterday, the crowning imbecility at Ypres: chlorine gas. This had been no mere political blunder, no mere darkening of the cloud beneath which Germany's honor and renown were now daily withering away. Oh no. This had been a colossal military gaffe as well. For not only had Germany added to her burden of world-

wide opprobrium (despite the fact that the army was totally unprepared to follow up on any havoc the gas attack might have wrought
in the Allied front line), Germany had also initiated a form of warfare that the westerly and southwesterly winds prevailing in Flanders
would make her bitterly regret with each passing month of the war.
Why no one—*no one!*—had considered the implications of the fact
that the attack had been delayed *six full weeks* because of unfavora-
ble winds from the west was surely one of the great conundrums of
military science.

All these things, however—the excesses in Belgium, the senseless
air raids, the criminally stupid introduction of gas—all these things
paled in significance next to the enormity of what was set out in this
file. For here on these flimsy carbon copies was documented nothing
less than a wide-scale, uncontrolled, uncoordinated, and haphazardly
manned program of German propaganda, espionage, and sabotage
inside the neutral United States of America, a program financed to
the amount of 600 million cash goldmarks (or $150 million), which
money was not only being held in the possession of, but being dispersed at the discretion of none other that Count Johann-Heinrich
von Bernstorff, *Imperial Germany's ambassador to the United States!*

Von Müller noticed that he was trembling, and that he actually
felt afraid. It was one form of folly to sponsor covert acts of war
against the one nation whose continued neutrality was vital to your
own country's long-term survival; but it was very nearly certifiable de-
mentia to go further and cast your monarch's personal diplomatic
emissary to that nation in the role not simply of an accessory, not
simply of an accomplice, not even simply of a spy, but in the one role
most utterly and diametrically incompatible with his primary purpose and function: the role of master conspirator.

Was Germany being governed by madmen? Was Germany being
governed at all? Or had it become just a huge steel-enveloped automaton of war—mindless, inertial, and totally unaware of the dangers converging on it from outside its line of sight?

As von Müller turned over the pages of the file, his anger steadily
gave way to depression and a listless apathy. The facts as set out here
simply defied the imagination; the mind went cataleptic in the face
of them, particularly the catalogue of sabotage:

> 3d January: bomb explosion aboard the SS *Orton*
> berthed at Brooklyn, New York, taking on
> a cargo of shell casings bound for the Clyde.

18th January: incendiary fire set at John A. Roebling Sons Company at Trenton, New Jersey, which manufactures steel rope pursuant to contracts with Allied purchasing agents ($1,-500,000 est. damage).

2d February: unsuccessful attempt to blow up the railroad bridge between Vanceboro, Maine, and McAdam, New Brunswick (German Army Reservist Werner Horn arrested same day, now being held for trial, request for extradition to Canada is pending).

9th February: bomb placed in SS *Hennington Court* berthed in New York harbor, preparing to sail for Brest with a cargo of guncotton. (Bomb was discovered by ship's personnel and defused.)

16th February: fire set aboard SS *Carlton* berthed in Baltimore harbor, taking on a cargo of steel plates consigned to Messrs. Armstrong-Whitworth, Elswick, Tynemouth.

1st March: bomb explosion in du Pont de Nemours plant at Haskell, New Jersey, manufacturing smokeless powder. No damage est.

20th March: bomb explosion in Remington Company plant at Alton, Illinois, manufacturing rifle parts. No damage est.

The most recent entries in the file were eminently the most depressing of all:

31st March: Pursuant to instructions from Geheimrat Dr. Heinrich Albert, commercial attaché, German Embassy ["*Lieber Gott!*" von Müller huffed], the New York law firm of Hays, Kaufman & Lindheim has this day secured a charter of incorporation for the "Bridgeport Projectile Company," said company to expend up to $28 million for the purposes of (1) preempting Allied purchases of critical manufactured goods such as lathes, milling machinery, etc., (2) accepting contracts from Allied purchasing agents for the manufacture of various arms and munitions, such arms and munitions to be made defective or not made at all, (3) paying higher wages than comparable arms manufacturers, and in other ways fomenting labor unrest in the U.S. armaments industry, (4) manufacturing armaments in cases where they can be employed in furtherance of German war objectives.

3d April: Confirmed arrival in New York (via Christiania, Norway) of Fregattenkapitän Franz von Rintelen, traveling on a Swiss passport as M. Emile V. Gaché, to serve as director of sabotage activities in the United States and Canada. Fregattenkapitän von Rintelen's mission extends also to establishing and financing various front organizations (particularly among Americans of German, Austro-Hungarian, and Irish descent) for the purpose of mobilizing U.S. public opinion in favor of a comprehensive arms embargo.

21st April: Arrival (not yet confirmed—via Rotterdam) of Army Lieutenant Robert Fay, traveling on a Dutch passport under his own name, whose mission is to employ a new explosive device of his own design for the purpose of destroying the rudders of ships carrying war matériel to the Allies.

Von Müller put the file down and was astonished to note that tears were brimming in his eyes. Old and rheumy! he reflected of himself, roughly wiping away the wetness with the back of his wrist.

But on the other hand, didn't he have ample reason to weep? Here in Germany was such an earnest nation, such a well-meaning, industrious, inventive, hard-working nation, such a *good* nation—yet it was afflicted with this unfathomable blindness. Bridgeport Projectile Company indeed! Twenty-eight million dollars! Why, sums larger than that changed hands hourly on the New York Exchange, and no one even gave it a thought.

Alas, the German eagle: pecking away at the toenails of a dozing rhinoceros and deluding itself that it was thereby impeding the beast's ability to walk. For a little while yet the rhino might continue to doze, but when it eventually awoke . . . ah then, ah then—poor eagle.

And you, old man, von Müller mused, you are merely a speck in the eagle's eye: you can make it blink, but you cannot make it see.

1915, 1ST MAY—KEW

House took Grey's arm as they walked along the sun-dappled pathway by the Thames. They had come to Kew at the Foreign Secretary's suggestion—he had said he always found the park extremely restful—and House had assented readily, for if ever a man was in extreme need of rest, it was his friend Sir Edward. While it was true that Grey had taken a brief vacation at his Fallodon estate earlier in the year and was scheduled to take another at the beginning of June, it was painfully apparent that he had lost more ground than he could ever hope to recover. The change in him just in the seven weeks the Colonel had been away was shocking. His stride had become more uncertain, his posture more bent, his complexion more pasty, and his voice more unsteady. Most alarmingly, the handwriting on the note he'd sent House welcoming him back to England had been a barely legible scrawl, the obvious product of a shaky hand and a fast-failing eye. The only things about him that had not suffered any impairment were his gentleness and his lucidity of thought, which had, if anything, become more appreciable.

It was true that the Asquith government was in serious trouble: there was the munitions shortage, which was blossoming into a full-fledged scandal, and there was the controversial amphibious assault on the Gallipoli Peninsula, which was not blossoming at all. But House suspected that it wasn't these mundane, though important, political problems that were wearing Grey down—it was the endless carnage.

"What's that?" Grey said, stopping abruptly and lifting his head. "A finch, I think. Do you see it?"

House looked up toward a sound of chirping and of fluttering wings, just to his right. "Ah, yes," he said. "A little gold-colored fellow."

Grey squinted toward the bird sounds. "Is he gold all over, can you tell? Or are there markings?"

House looked up again, a bit wearily. Birds had never been one of his consuming passions. "He's got a black cap," he said in a tone suggesting careful scrutiny, "and black markings on his wings."

"No! Really?"

"Yes. Very distinct they are too."

"Well! That's certainly a rare omen—of something or other."

"How so?"

"Because that little bird, my dear Colonel—unless I'm very much mistaken—is nothing other than a male American goldfinch: *spinus tristis*. Though I can't, for the life of me, imagine what it is he's doing in England."

"He doesn't belong in England?"

Grey smiled. "Oh, he's certainly welcome here. It's just that he's not indigenous."

"Perhaps he's on a special diplomatic mission. Shall I ask the State Department to look into it?"

"I would think they have enough to do at present, drafting official protests for your friend to send to us and the Germans."

"Ah ha! Then you do acknowledge that we're evenhanded in our protests."

Grey smiled the smile of a man who has just completed a successful finesse. "Yes, and it is precisely your 'evenhandedness' that I lament."

"Oh? I would have thought you'd have found it laudable in a neutral."

They had come onto a greensward by the river, awash in the heavy fragrances of fresh flowers and alive with the drowsy buzzings of nectar-sodden bees. Grey lifted his face to the sunshine, closed his eyes, and took a long deep breath. "Shall we sit for a while?" he asked.

House felt a warm surge of affection for the Foreign Secretary. Woodrow Wilson, finding himself in such a glade on such a day, would have had exactly the same reaction. In fact, did the world but know it, the stiff and austere American President was one of the most incorrigible sitters-on-grass House had ever encountered. Indeed, on more than one occasion he had even known the Chief Executive to go so far as to remove his shoes and socks!

"That would be very pleasant," the Colonel said.

They sat down side by side, legs folded in, facing the Thames. Grey plucked a few blades of grass and examined them abstractedly as he rolled them between his thumb and forefinger. "Let's posit that a farmer starts for a town to sell his eggs," he said, "and on his way is stopped by a soldier who says the farmer cannot pass because the town is under siege. In such a case the farmer might reasonably feel . . . disappointed."

"Yes." House nodded. "He certainly might."

Grey appeared not to hear. "And let's posit also that the farmer then starts off for a neighboring town, but that on his way there a soldier from another army knocks him off his horse and smashes his eggs—because the neighboring town is under siege too. . . . Now then, when you, as the farmer, confront the contending generals, are you going to be 'evenhanded' in your condemnation of their two styles of siege warfare?"

House pondered a moment, then replied, "No. But I would be evenhanded in my condemnation of the sieges themselves."

Grey shook his head. "That wasn't the question."

"Perhaps it should have been. If the illegal sieges were discontinued by both generals, the styles in which the sieges were managed would become academic."

"I note the introduction of the word 'illegal' without comment," Grey said with a perfunctory smile. "But what I am saying to you is that in a context where sieges are an accomplished fact, the question of *style*, if you will, becomes not academic but pivotal. We both know that there are rules of war that have been rendered obsolete by modern science and technology, and I would be prepared to defend the proposition that the old notions of contraband and close blockade are among them. Why? For the simple reason that one no longer lays siege to towns and cities, but to entire nations. And a siege implies the interdiction of all traffic into and out of the encircled camp."

House listened carefully. Grey was making a very important admission about British policy, though it was hard to say whether he was doing so intentionally or inadvertently. He was admitting that Britain's policy was indeed one of starving Germany out.

"Now a siege, admittedly, is a hard and cruel form of warfare," Grey continued. "But it can be conducted in a manner that comports with civilized standards of behavior. And that is the distinction I am endeavoring to make: between rules of war, which are mutable, and standards of civilized behavior, which are not."

House was silent for a moment. Grey was giving a great deal away. If laying siege to entire nations was admissible, then Germany's air and sea bombardments of unprotected towns in Britain and France were legitimate acts of war. The Foreign Secretary seemed to be conceding that noncombatant status was now no longer possible for the inhabitants of a belligerent state. The rights of noncombatants, he seemed to be saying, were operative only outside the encircled camps; that is, in neutral nations—what few there were—and on the seas, which Great Britain controlled. It was a clever thesis, and House conjectured that Grey was presenting it to him not so much as a statement of the present British policy, but as a blueprint for the evolving diplomacy of the United States.

As they sat together silently in the bright spring sunlight, House let his mind amble forward along this line of thought. It was reasonably apparent to everyone everywhere that with the coming of warm —or "campaigning"—weather, the war in all theaters had begun to build in both momentum and savagery. The past week alone had witnessed the inauguration of a German offensive against Ypres, a French offensive against the St.-Mihiel salient, and a British offensive against the Gallipoli Peninsula. Italy was expected to declare war against Austria-Hungary any day, moreover, and Russia was bracing itself to withstand an imminent assault by no fewer than *twelve* German and Austro-Hungarian armies. Both sides, in short, were aiming for a decision this year: the Central Powers in the east, the Allies and Italy in the west and south. The chances of ending the stalemate appeared remote, however, as it was now fairly clear that the defensive was lopsidedly dominant in modern warfare, and likely to remain so. Thus the long-term prospects were for a continuing war of attrition, and it was in that context that Grey's besieged nations doctrine took on special significance. Because Britain controlled the seas, and the seas together with Anglo-French colonial possessions and the Russian land mass gave the Allies effective dominion over 90 percent of the entire planet's surface.

In a war of attrition, that was a singularly ominous statistic for the Allies' opponents.

Of course, the ranking strategists in Berlin would be aware of this, and their response, on the evidence of the past few weeks, was to dispute dominion of the seas by employing the submarine. Back at the end of March, for example, the British cargo-passenger steamer *Falaba* had been torpedoed and sunk one day out of Liverpool with the loss of over a hundred lives, one of which had been American. Wilson, on House's advice, had not applied the "strict accountability" standard on the theory that an American sailing from a British port on a British ship bound for a British colony (The Gambia) could not reasonably expect immunity from Britain's enemies. Two days ago, however, the American tanker *Cushing* had been attacked, by mistake in all likelihood, and in any event unsuccessfully, by a German seaplane off the Dutch coast. And only this morning reports had been received that another American tanker, the *Gulflight*, had been torpedoed off the Scilly Islands, with probable loss of life. This attack, House guessed, was almost certainly accidental too, but it was a clear portent of a dangerous trend.

It was not simply a question of accidents-will-happen, for if it were, "strict accountability" could probably be satisfied by German apologies and compensation payments. While these, of course, would not bring dead Americans back to life, they would eliminate the aspect of *mens rea* in the undersea attacks, and absent this "criminal" intent, the United States would not be provoked to go to war.

But the problem was not accidental attacks on American ships; it was the possibility of deliberate attacks on Allied ships carrying Americans and American goods. Or say, the probability; because outside of coastwise shipping, America was a trading nation with virtually no merchant marine of its own. It was a queer anomaly, but there it was: better than 90 percent of American trade was carried in foreign bottoms, as were better than 80 percent of American travelers. Now the trade by itself did not represent an insuperable problem, as the vast preponderance was now in exports, and the burden of risk could be placed on the buyers. But the travelers were an altogether different matter. They had a right to cross international waters without thereby imperiling their lives, or at least without having their lives deliberately imperiled by U-boats. Of course, this notion of "the right to travel" put Germany in an extremely difficult position. Because ships that carried people carried cargo as well, and if your only options were to sink the ships or let them pass, you stood to suffer no matter what you did.

Germany, in other words, could act on the basis of Grey's besieged nations theory, retain America as a neutral, and lose the war of attrition. Or Germany could start smashing the farmer's eggs, provoke America into fighting, and lose the war to superior force.

The besieged nations theory, then, was nothing less than a prospective rationale for American belligerency in the event Germany threatened Great Britain's control of the seas. It left England with an impregnable blockade, and Germany with an insoluble dilemma. And the beautiful—or hideous—part of it was the elegant seductiveness of its internal logic. Grey was not manipulating, he was prophesying—and very subtly challenging House to prove him wrong.

The Colonel looked at the Foreign Secretary, sitting there placidly in the sunshine by the river. Yes, the man was tired, perhaps, but he was still up to doing his job.

1915, 1ST MAY—NEW YORK

West Street on the Hudson was in its usual state of bustling turmoil as Gehlman and Alis walked southward in the humid morning air. There were five transatlantic sailings today according to the shipping news page of the *World*: the Anchor Line's *Cameronia*, Cunard's *Lusitania*, the *Czaritza* of the Russian-American Line, the American Line's *New York*, and the Holland-America Line's *Rotterdam*. Also on the shipping page of the *World* was an odd insertion just beside the Cunard announcement of the *Lusitania's* sailing.

NOTICE! [it read]
"Travellers intending to embark on the Atlantic voyage are reminded that a state of war exists between Germany and her allies and Great Britain and her allies; that the zone of war includes the waters adjacent to the British Isles; that in accordance with formal notice given by the Imperial German Government, vessels flying the flag of Great Britain, or

of any of her allies, are liable to destruction in those waters
and that travellers sailing in the war zone on ships of Great
Britain or her allies do so at their own risk.

At the bottom of the notice, in twenty-point capital letters, was the
attribution: "IMPERIAL GERMAN EMBASSY," and below that,
"Washington, D.C. April 22, 1915."

"What do you make of this?" Gehlman had asked his father at
breakfast.

Oskar had leaned over and adjusted the pince-nez he wore for
reading. "Ah yes," he had said. "I saw the same notice in the
Times."

Gehlman had smiled to himself; his father always read the *Times*
out of a sense of loyalty to his friend Mr. Ochs—and out of a sense
of propriety too, of course—even though he found the paper a trifle
dull, and secretly nursed a guilty preference for the *New Yorker Staats-
Zeitung.*

Oskar had reread the insertion while Gehlman held the paper up
for him. "It looks to me like an attempt to scare people away from
traveling on British ocean liners," he had said.

"What for?" Gehlman had asked. "To put Cunard and White
Star out of business?"

Oskar had given an amused grunt. "Nothing so ambitious, I think.
Just for propaganda purposes would be my guess: to make people
think England doesn't really control the seas."

Gehlman had taken the newspaper back and studied the notice
more carefully. "Well, it certainly sounds rather threatening," he
had said finally.

"Yes?" Oskar had responded. "Well, you are a sailor. How serious
a threat could it be?"

"To a fast liner like the *Lusitania,* not very serious at all, assuming
she zigzags properly. A submarine could never get in position to
deliver an attack. But the slower ships could be in trouble, if the
Germans really intend to go after liners."

"But they've sunk a liner already, I believe. The—uh—*Falaba.*"

"No. The *Falaba* was a slow cargo steamer; the submarine was
able to overtake her on the surface and then give her some time to
get her boats out. If she'd been a liner, the sub could never have
caught up with her. It would have had to either fire submerged without warning, or just simply let her go."

"Well, that settles it then, no? The faster liners are too fast to be sunk, and the slower ones could only be sunk without warning, which would be unthinkable."

"Yes," Gehlman had said. "I suppose it would be."

"You *suppose!?*"

Gehlman had sighed. "I've told you, Father: it's a pretty ugly war they're fighting over there."

"Yes, but a passenger ship carrying innocent women and children. Good God!"

"Oh, I agree, Father. Of course. It's just that I'm not as sure as I used to be six months ago about the limits of human iniquity."

"I think you mean the limits of *German* iniquity, Benjamin. Your judgment still seems to be a little biased by your experiences with that von Tiel fellow."

"Yes, perhaps," Gehlman had conceded, not wishing to argue the point. And in any case Oskar was probably right; the memory of "that von Tiel fellow" was still very much upon him.

They were at Fourteenth Street now, approaching Pier 54, the Cunard slip where the *Lusitania,* scheduled for a ten o'clock sailing, was being besieged by a converging horde of taxis and ice vans and limousines and trucks, all struggling to make headway through a milling crowd of several thousand people. So much for the German warning, Gehlman reflected as he watched tearful relatives, blue-clad customs men, hurrying porters, graft-fattened port officials, and burly policemen all participate in their various ways in the embarkation of what looked to be something over a thousand passengers. Gehlman glanced down at Alis—her lips parted, her eyes sparkling with excitement—and felt a little thrill of adoration. What an utterly unaccountable child she had turned out to be! And what an enormous difference she had made in his and his parents' lives. In the Gehlman mansion she was the undisputed sovereign. Oskar and Erna frankly worshiped her, and the competition among the servants to see to her needs and comforts was, so Gehlman heard tell, cutthroat to an almost venomous degree. Of course her beauty explained much of the adulation; just looking at her beside him now, dressed in her navy blue skirt, matching middy blouse, and red-ribboned straw hat, caused him to experience the familiar feeling of constriction in his throat.

He had never had the least presentiment that Alis would make such a wholehearted and successful adjustment to the new life that had been thrust upon her. In the few minutes he and Dr. Bauer had had to discuss her future back in March, they had both assumed that the stress involved in adjusting to a new environment without her mother would seriously deplete her psychic resources. It was now clear, however, that in making this assumption they had failed to consider two highly significant facts. The first—which afforded Gehlman some cynical amusement—was that, apart from the minor incidents of furnishings and faces, Alis's new environment was precisely the same as her old one. The rich, after all, were a far more homogeneous nation than any of those to be found on a map, at least as far as domestic amenities and social usages were concerned. And so Alis had merely changed milieus—from rich German in Germany to rich German-American in New York. In addition—and this was the second significant fact—she had privately, and perhaps unconsciously, at some point come to the conclusion that Gehlman was a person she could trust.

Since their arrival in New York, she had come to trust his parents too. Erna, for example, had summarily taken charge of the task of providing Alis with all the accoutrements of a new life in America. She had interviewed several dozen applicants for the positions of governess and tutor, narrowing the field in each case, and then letting Alis meet the best qualified contenders and make the final decisions on the basis of whom she liked best. Erna had also consulted at length with the housekeeper as to which of the female servants would be best suited to serve as Alis's personal maid, the choice falling at last on a husky young woman named Hannah Beck, who had immigrated two years before from Carinthia and who was good-natured, cleanly, loyal, and uncomplicated. Concurrently with seeing to these staffing questions, Erna had supervised the decoration and furnishing of Alis's bedroom and playroom. She had also—since Alis had arrived with only a single suitcase—taken her downtown every day to shop for clothes. One day they would buy shoes, the next day dresses, the day after, coats and capes for every occasion, then underwear and stockings by the gross, then hats and boots and mufflers for every possible climatic condition, then eight or nine formal ensembles for dinner, then just a soupçon of jewelry: simple gold, simple pearls, for special occasions like the theater or the opera, then the finest bristle brushes and tortoiseshell combs and perfumed bath salts, then riding habits for leisure, for jumping, for show, then bathing costumes and summer parasols in colors to match all the dresses

—and then, on a regular basis thereafter, odds and ends to fill in such gaps in Alis's wardrobe as still, inexplicably, remained.

After Alis had had a couple of weeks to get adjusted to her new surroundings, Erna had called in a doctor to give her a thorough checkup. She had then taken her to see a dentist, a podiatrist, an orthodontist, an ophthalmologist, and the Chief of Pediatric Medicine at New York University Medical School. Satisfied that Alis was in good health, she had enrolled her—with her enthusiastic consent—in riding classes, piano lessons, swimming lessons, and—for some diabolical reason—trumpet lessons as well. She had also co-opted one of Alis's classmates at ballet school, a round and amiable ten-year-old named Natasha Ostlinger, who was the daughter of the German consul, to serve as Alis's sponsor among the other little girls. And when Natasha's good offices proved not quite sufficient to overcome Alis's shyness and hesitancy with English—which she had studied and could speak capably enough with adults—Erna had dragooned a reluctant Frau Ostlinger into cohostessing a lavish party at the consulate for the children of all the more prominent German-American families in New York. Spending money liberally, Erna had secured the services of the famous magician Mr. Houdini (born: Erich Weiss), the famous puppeteer Signor Castaldi (born: Manfred Rupermann), and the famous ventriloquist Mr. Richter (born: Milos Hrabiski). The party was a great success, and Alis, under Natasha Ostlinger's good-natured patronage, was soon giggling and exchanging secrets with three girls her own age, all of whom when the party ended invited her to come the next day and play with them at their homes.

It occurred to Gehlman, seeing his mother thus transformed from a mewling catchment of self-pity into a cheerful and ofttimes formidable *mater familias*, that perhaps the woman's only real problem over the years had been that she'd had virtually nothing to do—or, rather, no one to do anything for. Whatever her problem might have been, though, Alis's arrival had most emphatically resolved it; and Oskar too, with his lighter moods and perceptibly less arthritic step, had joined in the general buzz of reanimation that reverberated throughout the house.

Against this background of almost saccharine well-being (the one sour note having been the split lip and scraped knee Alis suffered in a fall from her horse), Gehlman had been loath to give much thought to the question of whether Alis's mental condition still required medical attention. On a superficial level the answer had seemed to be no, but only yesterday had come contrary evidence on a level that seemed fairly deep.

Gehlman had been summoned to Washington by Assistant Secretary of State Corey, who intimated in his letter that he had instructions for him from Colonel House. This was a positive development from Gehlman's point of view, since he had been in the occupational limbo of "Assignment Pending" ever since his return and had begun to wonder if the navy had forgotten him. Secretary Corey had merely made his limbo official, however, informing him that on his return to New York he should begin preparing a detailed written report on the operations and matériel of the German Fleet, being careful while doing so to discuss its contents with no one but himself or Colonel House, who was expected back from Europe in June.

Gehlman had gone down to Washington on an early train, leaving the house before Alis was awake. He hadn't thought to tell her that he'd be away for the day, especially as he intended to come back on the evening train. Oskar, who always left very early for his office on Broad Street, had dropped him off at Pennsylvania Station and said he would see him at dinner. It had been all quite humdrum and routine. But when Gehlman arrived back at his father's house at seven-thirty that night, he had found it in a state of near-hysterical turmoil. The servants all looked anguished, and Oskar and Erna, recounting what had happened in his absence, were red-eyed and ashen-faced with stress. Alis had simply gone to pieces, they said. On coming down to breakfast she had asked where he was, and when Erna told her that he had gone to Washington, she had seemed to freeze where she sat. After staring blank-eyed in front of her for several minutes, she had suddenly begun to moan and to rock slowly back and forth in her chair. Alarmed, Erna had sought to comfort her and to get her to say what was wrong. But Alis had been oblivious, and had just kept rocking and moaning. Erna had finally summoned Fräulein Beck, and then hurried to send for the doctor. By the time he got to the house, Alis had reached a state of acute distraction. She was wandering blindly from room to room, not moaning any longer, but sobbing convulsively, and wringing her hands with such violence that the skin on her knuckles was beginning to chafe. She gave no sign of hearing or seeing the people around her, and the intensity of her distress appeared to be building every minute. Finally it had become necessary to restrain her and administer a sedative, which after a few minutes had put her to sleep. Erna had called Oskar, who hastened uptown right away. Together they had discussed calling Gehlman in Washington, deciding in the end against it. Alis would probably remain asleep until he got back, they had reasoned, and it would be better for him to conclude his business there today rather than rush back to New York and later have to make another trip.

Alis had awakened an hour ago, they told him in conclusion, acting as if they were afraid he would find fault with their actions or blame them for what had happened. She had awakened, they said, but she hadn't spoken or moved.

Gehlman had rushed up the stairs and along the corridor to Alis's rooms. Fräulein Beck, who was sitting with her, rose respectfully when he came in. Taking the chair she had vacated, Gehlman had bent down and looked into Alis's face. The eyes were a bit swollen, the skin was pale and splotchy, but the forehead, he noted with relief, was cool and dry beneath his hand. "Allie?" he had said in a hoarse half-whisper.

There had been no response.

"Allie?" he had said again, holding his breath as he willed her to respond.

"*Allie!*" he had said a third time, loudly and on the verge of panic.

She had blinked twice, then turned her head slightly and focused her eyes on his face. For ten or fifteen seconds she had simply stared at him. Then, slowly and dreamily, she had sat up, put her arms around his neck, and gripped him hard.

"Silly girl," he had said, feeling almost faint with released tension. "Did you think I'd gone and left you?"

Alis hadn't responded, but had just continued clutching him with what felt like all her strength.

"Try to get some rest now," he had said after a long long while. "I'll stay right here beside you."

He had tried to lean her back onto her pillow, but she wouldn't release her hold on him. "Allie, I'll be right *here*," he had repeated, but her only response had been to tighten her grip.

So he had sat with her, waiting for her to give in to sleep. Almost a full hour passed before he felt the first signs that her fingers were starting to relax. She began to sink back toward the pillow, but then caught herself and restrengthened her hold. For another fifteen or twenty minutes she struggled to stave off oblivion; then, finally, she succumbed.

Sitting there gazing down at her, Gehlman had at first felt remorseful over his failure to consider her possible reaction to what in fact had been their first real separation since they'd met. Then, reflecting on what her reaction had actually been, he had experienced an immense and unexpected surge of fulfillment, which had been followed immediately by a comparably intense pang of guilt, that he should glory in the fruits of her anguish. Flattering as her dependence on him was, it clearly indicated a need for a resumption of medical consultations. He was in the navy, after all, and he could hardly be with her all the time.

Looking down at her, Gehlman had decided to seek a qualified physician. Only gradually did the realization that his career would inevitably separate him from her for long periods of time surface into his awareness. Once grasped, however, the realization sank him very deep in thought. He was still mulling it over now, on this special excursion he'd planned to make up for his thoughtlessness in going off to Washington the way he had.

Apart from the zoo, what Alis liked most was visiting the great ocean liners at their piers on the river. Gehlman rather liked visiting them too, as they were all very beautiful ships. Today he planned to take her across to Hoboken to visit the biggest ship of all: the interned Hamburg-American liner *Vaterland*, measuring over 900 feet in length and 55,000 tons in displacement.

Standing hand in hand with Alis now and watching the *Lusitania*'s passengers go aboard, he caught sight of a petite auburn-haired young woman making her way up the gangplank. Something about the cool and self-possessed way the woman carried herself reminded him of Alis's mother.

He had never really established in his mind what exactly he had felt for Regina von Lutwitz, or how exactly he felt about her death. She'd had courage, he knew, and he'd always admired her for that. But she'd had something more than courage too, something that that vivid little creature with the auburn hair seemed to project. He couldn't name the quality he perceived in the young woman, any more than he could name the young woman herself. It was a quality he remembered, though, and that he hoped to encounter again.

1915, 7TH MAY—SCAPA FLOW TO
QUEENSTOWN HARBOR

Maltbie looked up at the sun and breathed deeply. The warmth streaming down through the hazy air felt good on his face, and the rarefied scent of wild flowers on the breeze bespoke new life, new beginnings. Beside him in the gently pitching barge, Jellicoe and Madden turned their faces sunward too and smiled. Several miles to the south the Grand Fleet rested, released at last from the vault of winter and from the scourge of the equinoctial storms. Spring and hope, and somewhere in the Atlantic a great ship steaming eastward. Maltbie conjured up the image. In a few hours he would be under way himself. And then, tomorrow, in Liverpool . . . fruition.

As the barge glided in to Scapa Pier, Madden instructed the coxswain to proceed next to Stromness and wait. He, Maltbie, and Jellicoe then disembarked and set off westward across the southern trunk of Mainland, the Orkneys' principal island. They walked at "admiral's time," which was a cadence of roughly 150 steps a minute, or five miles per hour. There was nothing official about this pace; it was simply the fastest rate at which one could walk without breaking into a trot. It was the Scapa Flow version of Beatty's "exercise in concentrated form," and there wasn't an officer in the Orkneys who neglected it.

Maltbie, Jellicoe, and Madden took the Finstown Road past Wideford Hill, and then continued west for seven miles to Maes Howe. From the outside it was hard to tell that this enormous mound was man-made. It dated from the Stone Age, when it had served as a family tomb for several generations of tribal chiefs. Norsemen and Crusaders had plundered it and left runic graffiti in the place of its treasure. Nearby were the four remaining Standing Stones of Stenness, and just across Loch Harray was the Ring of Brogar, the Orkney version of Stonehenge.

The three men continued west over Waith Bridge and then turned south for the final two-mile leg to Stromness. They arrived there to find the barge waiting for them; but moored about a mile away, just beyond Outer Holm Rock, the destroyer *Oak* was waiting too. Jellicoe and Madden exchanged a glance. The *Oak* served as the tender to *Iron Duke,* and its purpose in being there could only be to get them back to the battle fleet as fast as possible.

Captain Backhouse, the flag commander, and Maltbie's friend John Salmond, the wireless officer, were waiting on the destroyer's quarterdeck. Salmond's expression was grim, Maltbie saw as he came up the ladder from the barge, and Backhouse, who rarely looked very cheerful in any case, seemed a good deal glummer than usual as he and Salmond accompanied Jellicoe and Madden toward the bridge.

The *Oak*'s engines increased their rumbling almost immediately, and the ship began to move. It accelerated rapidly down the channel between Mainland and Graemsay Islands, and was doing nearly thirty knots by the time it reached Hoy Sound. Maltbie stood at the starboard rail and watched the bow wave curling off the hull. He was curious, of course, as to what the sudden urgency was all about, but he knew his hosts would tell him all they were at liberty to tell him as soon as it was possible to tell him anything. He also knew that he could rule out the possibility that a sortie by the German Fleet was behind the flurry of activity, since in that case Backhouse and Salmond would have looked joyful and excited. Perhaps there was just a priority telegram that had to be answered, or perhaps a collision had occurred, or a ship had struck a mine. At all events, it was pointless to speculate. He would be told what was what in due time.

The *Oak* passed the tip of Cava Island and turned two points to starboard. The dreadnoughts of the battle fleet were visible 3,000 yards on the bow.

Maltbie felt a hand on his arm, and turned to find Jellicoe looking somberly into his eyes. "The *Lusitania* was torpedoed and sunk in the Irish Channel three hours ago, Harry . . . with loss of life."

Maltbie felt himself become strangely calm. To be sure, if a ship is torpedoed there will be loss of life, because torpedoes when they strike explode, and explosions when they occur usually kill the people nearby. But all the other people aboard would have found safety in the lifeboats. Certainly Melina would. Women and children first.

Jellicoe kept his eyes on him and resumed, "Very serious loss of life, I'm afraid. Inconceivable as it seems, the attack came without warning, and the ship sank in twenty minutes."

Twenty minutes! That wasn't enough time to get boats for two thousand people swung out and lowered. *Twenty minutes!* The torpedo must have come straight at the boilers.

"The survivors are being taken to Queenstown," Jellicoe said. "I've wired my secretary to prepare travel documents for you. The *Oak* can take you to Thurso in time for the six-thirty train, and there's a connection at midnight at Inverness for Edinburgh, which should allow you to get a train for Liverpool first thing tomorrow morning. The list of survivors should be fairly complete by the time you get there, and you can plan the next stages of your journey on the basis of the information then available to you."

The *Oak* came alongside the *Iron Duke*. Maltbie saw Otley in the group waiting at the bottom of the ladder and watched in surprise as he jumped aboard the destroyer ahead of everyone else and ran to Jellicoe's side. He had a small sea kit slung over his shoulder and was carrying a sheaf of papers which, after saluting, he placed in Jellicoe's hands.

"Are you coming with me, Terry?" Maltbie asked as the admiral put his signature on the documents Otley had brought.

"If ye don't mind, sir. We've packed some'at to eat and a change of socks and skivvies for us both, and a bit o' soap and such like, as ye might be needin' our assistance what with the confusion and travelin' and searchin' for your intended."

"I believe it's a good idea for Corporal Otley to accompany you," Jellicoe broke in. "I've given you a *laissez-passer* and a special travel permit, but locating one particular survivor quickly may require the kind of assistance for which, so I'm told, Corporal Otley is renowned."

"Thank you, sir," Maltbie said, as Otley beamed.

"And if you run into any snags of any sort because of your foreign uniform, don't hesitate to use my name and say you are engaged on a special diplomatic mission of importance to the fleet. These documents will bear you out."

"I can't thank you enough, sir."

"Just remember me when you send out wedding invitations," Jellicoe replied with a shy grin that gave way to an expression of fatherly concern. "Godspeed," he said, extending his hand; and as soon as he was disembarked, the *Oak* eased clear of the *Iron Duke* and aimed her bows at the Scottish coast.

At Inverness Maltbie and Otley changed from the single-car train that had brought them from Thurso to the single-car train that would take them to Edinburgh. On the way to Inverness, Maltbie had watched the long northern twilight yield by imperceptible degrees to the short northern night. Now, on the way to Edinburgh, he watched the night give way slowly to the dawn. All the while he fingered Melina's talisman through the woolen cloth of his tunic and concentrated prayerfully on the thought that she had to be alive.

He was touched and surprised to find Beatty's secretary, Frank Spickernell, awaiting him at Waverley Station. "Scapa telegraphed that you'd be coming through," Spickernell said. "And Sir David wants you to know that he's completely at your disposal if he can be of help in any way."

"Thank him very sincerely for me, will you, Spick. And thank you too for coming down here to meet me."

"Rubbish," said Spickernell with a gentle smile. "Now, how can we be of assistance?"

"Well, you can get us on the first train to Liverpool . . . and you can tell me if they've released any lists of survivors."

"There's a train for Liverpool leaving in ten minutes, actually," Spickernell said, consulting his watch. "We'll have to shake a leg if we're going to get you aboard."

"And . . . ?" Maltbie prodded as they hurried along down the platform.

"And I'm afraid Miss Bellamy's name is not on any of the preliminary lists."

"How preliminary are they?" Maltbie asked, with dread billowing inside him.

"Very preliminary, Harry: only about a hundred and fifty of an estimated seven hundred and fifty survivors."

Maltbie stopped in his tracks. "*Seven hundred and fifty!* My God, Spick! That ship was built to carry two thousand!"

"I know, Harry," Spickernell said sympathetically. "There may be as many as fifteen hundred dead."

"*Sweet Jesus!*" Otley gasped.

Maltbie stared at Spickernell in disbelief. "*Fifteen hundred,* Spick!?"

"Don't jump to conclusions, Harry. There are some six hundred survivors unaccounted for, and Miss Bellamy, being a woman, is most probably among them."

Maltbie was grateful for Spickernell's words of support, but if fifteen hundred people had gone down in this shipwreck, then survival would have been determined by blind chance, not by sex.

The train arrived at Lime Street Station, Liverpool, shortly after three in the afternoon. Maltbie and Otley walked hurriedly through the concourse, passing half a dozen news vendors whose hand-lettered signboards told the story: LUCY SUNK, ONLY 700 SURVIVE, CREW HERE TOMORROW, HUN RUNS AMOK.

At the nearby Cunard offices there was a large crowd gathered. "Ye check the lists posted out here, sir," Otley said. "We'll go inside and make some particular inquiries."

Maltbie nodded and went anxiously to the bulletin boards that had been set up on either side of the building entrance. Melina was still not listed among the survivors, although the list itself was by now an ominously long one—seven hundred names at a rough estimate.

Maltbie purchased an *Echo* and skimmed the latest bulletins on the sinking while waiting for Otley to rejoin him. When the corporal at length reappeared, there was an uncharacteristic expression of strain on his face. "It's like this, sir," he said. "There's a boatload of mostly crew survivors due here early tomorrow morning and a boatload of passengers that arrives at Holyhead this evening to connect with a special train for London. We checked both manifests for Miss Bellamy, but no go. So we asked to see the list of the confirmed dead, which they wouldn't show us right away, until the sight of Silent Jack's signature changed their minds. Well, the long and short of it is: she's not been found yet. So our best bet would be to make for Holyhead right now, meet that boatload of survivors, ask after Miss Bellamy, and then go on to Queenstown if we're still in the dark."

Maltbie nodded, while a sickening chill of certain calamity crept over his insides.

The steamer from Queenstown arrived at Holyhead shortly after 10:00 P.M., and Maltbie and Otley, as representatives of Admiral Jellicoe, were immediately allowed aboard. None of the survivors they spoke to knew what had become of Melina, although half a dozen of them knew who she was, and two of them remembered having seen her get into a lifeboat.

The steamer started on its return journey at 2:00 A.M. Up on the promenade deck Otley lay snoring on a bench while Maltbie kept a forlorn watch on the moonless star-flecked sky. Lovelier than a summer night full of shooting stars, he remembered having said of her—lovelier than a night like this.

"Dear God . . ." he pleaded silently. "Dear God, dear God . . ."

Even though the port of Queenstown lay glittering beneath the noonday sun as the steamer approached, Maltbie could sense that it was a place of the dead. There was an unnatural hush over the town, as if it had been abandoned to the plague; and as the steamer entered the harbor Maltbie saw that there were pine coffins piled high on the wharves.

Otley sought out the harbormaster as soon as the ship docked, and reported back that the Crown and the Commodore Hotels were serving as hospitals while the Town Hall, the Market Hall, and St. Colman's Cathedral had been set up as morgues. Admiralty House, the headquarters for rescue operations, was only a few hundred yards from the quay. Maltbie went there directly and was immediately ushered in to the office of an elderly Royal Navy captain, who rose arthritically to greet him. "I'm Edward Teilhard," he said in a voice that betrayed extreme uneasiness. "Scapa signaled that you might be on your way."

The captain's obvious tension caused Maltbie to experience an icy crawling sensation on the skin of the back of his neck. "How do you do, sir," he said very quietly.

Teilhard started to speak, then paused and gave a nervous cough. "I—uh . . ." he began at last. "I'm sorry to have to tell you that Miss Bellamy's body has been found."

Maltbie felt as if a million small bubbles had suddenly begun a wild fizzing in his head. He reached blindly behind him for a chair and sat down. "Where is she?" he asked in a choked whisper.

"In St. Colman's. . . . I'm so terribly sorry."

Maltbie stared into nothingness, then stood up trancelike and left the room.

"Oh, no," Otley said softly when he saw Maltbie's face.

St. Colman's was on the West Beach, overlooking the water. Horse carts bearing newly constructed coffins were parked on a small pathway running alongside the outer wall of the nave, and Maltbie's nostrils picked up the scent of fresh-cut lumber as the hexagonal boxes lay there drying in the sun. Just outside the entrance a priest and a port official were conversing in low tones with half a dozen very youthful looking soldiers and bluejackets. Their conversation ceased as Maltbie and Otley approached.

"Can I help you, sir?" the port official asked.

"You . . . you have a Miss Bellamy here?" Maltbie managed to rasp out. "A Miss Melina Bellamy?"

"Yes, sir, I believe so. Are you a relative of the deceased?"

"We were to be married."

The official seemed to quail a little, and hastily looked down at the file of papers he was holding. When he lifted his head again, he did not meet Maltbie's eyes. "Uh, Miss Bellamy was found only this morning, sir," he said. "She was in the water for almost forty hours and there has been some—uh . . . deformation . . . owing to the prolonged immersion . . . you see . . ."

Maltbie nodded weakly, unaware that he had begun to teeter back and forth.

Otley gripped him firmly by the arm. "Perhaps it'd be best, sir, if we didn't . . ."

Maltbie nodded again and let himself be led away.

"As you were engaged to the deceased, sir," the port official called after him in a shaky voice, "would you care to sign for the personal effects?"

"Give us a minute, will you," Otley shouted back angrily as he guided Maltbie past the coffins to the small garden at the rear of the church. "Ye sit here for a bit, sir," he said, indicating the low stone wall separating the garden from the rocks leading down to the water's edge. He went away, returning in a few minutes with a small canvas bag, which he placed on Maltbie's lap. "These are the effects, sir," he said. "We'll go now and inquire about the burial arrangements."

Maltbie nodded, staring out at the sea.

"Will ye be all right for the moment, sir?"

Maltbie nodded again.

"Right then," Otley said, sounding a bit undecided. "Ye stay here, and we'll be back straight away."

Maltbie nodded once more.

For a long while he didn't move. He felt the heat of the sun on his shoulders, tasted the smell of the sea on the incoming breeze. He sensed that a typhoon of grief was raging inside him, but it seemed far away somehow. He couldn't connect it with the nameless sorrow he felt weighing down on his chest, the heavy sadness that was making it difficult for him to breathe. The sadness seemed out of keeping with the sunlight and the gentle wind, and although he knew that it had to do with Melina's death, even that seemed detached from his experience. He was aware that he had loved her, but he couldn't remember what loving her had been like.

After some time he noticed that he was still holding the canvas bag, and he emptied its contents onto his lap. There, held together with a string and wet with seawater, were the letters he had written, along with a leatherbound notebook in the same soaked condition. And there was her passport as well.

He gaped at it stupidly for a long time, then opened it, and turned the front page over to reveal her picture. She smiled her prim little smile up at him, and in one great inundating rush he remembered and comprehended everything that he'd lost. Uttering a prolonged animal-like moan, he toppled sobbing to the ground.

It had been more than two days since he'd had any rest, so as he lay on the grass in the sunlight his sobs gradually subsided into the slow respiration of sleep.

He wasn't sure what woke him, but when he opened his eyes he saw a woman kneeling beside him. She was silhouetted against the waning sun, which made a halo of the hair piled in rich billows above her ears.

"Do you believe that you're awake, Harry?"

He didn't answer, or move, or breathe.

"I tell you that you are awake. Do you believe me?"

"Melina?" he asked in an awed whisper.

"Now listen to me very carefully, my darling Harry. Listen to me with all your power—I . . . am . . . not . . . dead."

He stared at her silhouetted figure, saw its small slimness, glimpsed the hint of auburn color in some loose strands of her hair.

"It's *me*, Harry. Believe what you see. I'm alive. I'm *here!*"

Maltbie sat up, gripped her by the shoulders, and made her turn her body so that the sunlight fell on her face. She reached out and touched her fingers to his cheek. "Yes," she whispered. "Harry, Harry, yes. It's *true!*"

Maltbie took a deep breath; it felt like he was inhaling sunlight.

"Oh, Harry. My adorable Harry. You look like a little boy on Christmas morning."

"Melina," he said in wonderment and gratitude, gathering her to him and burying his face in her hair.

"Yes, yes," he heard her murmur as her arms closed tight around him. "Yes, yes. My darling, darling love."

On the steamer back to Holyhead she spoke about what she had been through. Her lifeboat had been lowered on the port side as the *Lusitania* listed heavily to starboard. As a result, the boat's bottom had scraped against the liner's hull rivets as it descended, and it had begun to leak as soon as it touched the water. Under the supervision of a second purser, who was in command, the half dozen crewmen aboard were able to keep the boat afloat by bailing. But it was painfully apparent that the bottom had suffered structural damage and might not hold together.

"Well, there we sat, up to our shins in seawater, and Mr. McCubbin, the purser, made us a little speech. He said, 'Ladies and gentlemen, it is my sad duty to inform you that the floorboards may give way if we attempt to row.' What he didn't say, of course, was that the floorboards were going to give way in any case—and I'm sure he knew they would, because he proceeded to announce that, thanks to his 'friend and colleague, Mr. McNab,' who was the assistant wine steward in first class, we few, we happy few, in lifeboat number nine were carrying as a special supplement to our provisions a full case of thirty-year-old Napoleon brandy, with which we would, to use his phrase, 'sustain our spirits' for as long as it took to drift to the Irish coast or get rescued.

"Now there were six or seven men aboard, all crew I think, and perhaps three dozen women and a few small children. We were overloaded, in other words, and Ireland was a good ten miles distant. So as soon as Purser McCubbin finished his speech, the crewmen all started exchanging those hangdog our-time-has-come looks, and I knew right away that the boat was going to break up long before we reached the coast. Purser McCubbin had simply been feeding pabulum to the ladies and had decided, wisely I suppose, to feed them some cognac too, on the theory that it might keep them alive longer once they were in the water.

"Well, I certainly wasn't fussy about downing several mouthfuls when a bottle came around to me, but a number of the other women, poor geese, either claimed to be conscientious teetotalers or admitted outright that they couldn't consider drinking directly out

of a bottle in public. Well, you know how tolerant I am of imbecility, Harry, and I was about to make some general observations
of a corrosive nature. But then I looked at those women, and I saw
that it was hopeless. A glance at Mr. McCubbin showed that he saw
it too. It was the queerest thing though. There we were: calm sea,
sunny sky, land in sight, rescuers undoubtedly on the way—and these
women were simply going to give up if their boat sank. I don't mean
that they were intending to give up; they were just absolutely convinced that they would die. So much so that they refused to acknowledge the likelihood that the boat *was going* to sink. They
equated the boat with survival and the sea with death, world without
end, Amen! They were beaten before they swam a stroke. And the
crewmen weren't much better, I guess because all the best seamen
are in the navy now. One fool among them even went so far as to
stick his hand in the water and make some sage observation about no
one 'lasting long in that kind of cold.' Mr. McCubbin yelled at him
to shut his gob, but the damage had been done. He tried to explain
that survival in the water was perfectly feasible under the conditions
obtaining, but all the ladies were now dipping *their* hands in the
water, and pulling them out with expressions of doom on their faces.

"Well, I sat there thinking: Melina, dear girl, you don't know
much about surviving shipwrecks, but survive or sink, how often do
you come by a case of thirty-year-old Napoleon? So I carried on
drinking, and before long I began to feel oddly cheerful and warm—
hot, even. And I looked over at this poor woman beside me, who was
shivering like mad in the frilly frock she must have been having
lunch in when the torpedo hit, and I asked her, would you like my
coat, madam, to keep off the chill? She was so terrified that she could
barely manage an affirmative nod, and I recollect thinking al-
coholically to myself as I helped her put the coat on over her life
jacket that I would have to remember that your letters and my notebook and passport were in the inside pocket. Little did I realize, as
they say in all the novels . . .

"At all events, before too much longer the floorboards gave way,
and I was seaborne. The first shock of the water was unimaginably
dreadful, and the screaming around me was even worse. After a few
minutes, though, the screaming diminished, and the sea, owing no
doubt to my intoxicated condition, seemed to become almost tepid.
A quarter of an hour or so after my immersion, who should float by
holding on to three or four lashed-together oars but Purser McCub-

bin. We exchanged how-de-do's, and he invited me to join his vessel. Once I was aboard, so to speak, he confided that he had been able to salvage a bottle of elixir from the shambles. I asked him rather pertly how much of the bottle was left, as it appeared to me self-evident that his sobriety had been compromised. Happily for me he didn't take offense; he swore in fact that under normal circumstances he *never* drank alone. It was just that when a three-quarters empty bottle had floated near him earlier on, he had felt obliged to drink the remaining contents out of a long-standing aversion to waste. In consequence, the bottle now in his possession was a full bottle, and he very decently offered to share it with me.

"So we sipped and floated along, with Mr. McCubbin pointing out the sights: Old Head of Kinsale, Sevenheads, Galley Head, and far in the distance, Fastnet Rock and Cape Clear. I don't know how long we were in the water, but it must have been quite a while because it was dark by the time we reached land. We were both frightfully drunk, I know, and I remember we did a little dance of celebration on the rocks before curling up under some bushes and passing out.

"Well, I *never* want to feel as sick as I did the next morning—not just alcohol sick, but paralyzingly tired and chilled. Mr. McCubbin was equal to the occasion, however, in that he reached into his jacket pocket and pulled out a half-pint flask. It was Irish whiskey, alas, instead of Napoleon brandy, but it warmed us enough to get us as far as the nearest farmhouse. You can imagine the poor crofter's expression when he saw us: neither he nor his wife had heard anything about the ship, and here were these two dampened drunkards asking shelter from the storm. We explained as best we could, and after some hesitation they took us in, built up their fire, and gave us some dry clothes. We both then proceeded to pass out for something like twenty hours, until this morning, when we went to Clonakilty and got the coach to Queenstown, where we arrived about the time you discovered I was dead."

Maltbie listened, less to her words than to her voice. He held her tightly on his lap and smelled her skin, her hair, and the fabric of the clothes he had purchased for her while she was having a bath at the Crown Hotel. All he could think of was that he would never again let her out of his sight. He had almost lost her this time, and he was determined to run no more risks. So he held her to him and breathed her fragrance while she and Otley gabbled gaily along about the sea, strong drink, and the incomparable benefits of remaining alive.

1915, 14TH MAY–LONDON

House took an almost lascivious pleasure in the feel of his footsteps on the pavement and luxuriated in the sense of undeliberated motion as he strolled northward through Berkeley Square. The May night was unseasonably, but not unpleasantly, cool, and a fine fine mist haloed the street lamps, softening the outlines of trees and house fronts, muting the sounds of traffic.

What a week he had lived through! He felt as if he'd been traveling inside a tornado, or riding one of those new yo-yo toys imported from the Philippines. And how strangely the week had begun—with King George seated opposite him at luncheon in Buckingham Palace and saying, at almost the precise minute the torpedo must have struck, "Suppose the Germans should sink the *Lusitania,* with American passengers aboard. . . ."

He'd told the king the same thing he'd told Grey in response to a similar supposition: chances were the United States would be sufficiently incensed by the atrocity to join in the war. And on Sunday, when the toll of American dead was confirmed to be over a hundred, he had wired Wilson, "America has come to the parting of the ways."

He shook his head now, wondering at how he could have yielded so to the passions of the hour. Partly, of course, it had been the sudden sense of solidarity he'd felt with his British friends: the shared calamity, the shared outrage. But partly it had also been the result of three months' absence from the United States. Absorbed as he'd been in the affairs of Europe, he had lost touch with what he knew to be the fundamentally parochial temper of the American mind, the cheerful insularity that characterized the vast mass of the nation lying outside the Boston-to-Washington arc. This was the America that had elected Woodrow Wilson and to which Woodrow Wilson was accountable, and for this America the *Lusitania* would be cause for indignation and in some quarters even condemnation, but not for war. One tended to lose sight of this America in Europe, just as this America but dimly comprehended the quarrels of the Old World. That was why, House supposed, Wilson's initial reaction to the sinking had come as such a shock.

To begin with, there had been no announcement for four full days after the *Lusitania* went down. Again and again the Colonel had had to explain to his British friends that it was the President's habit, before making any major decision, to turn inward, sometimes for as long as a week, until he had thought all the issues through to the bottom. But then on Tuesday the London evening papers had broken the news of Wilson's Convention Hall speech in Philadelphia:

> The example of America must be a special example. The example of America must be not merely of peace because it will not fight, but of peace because peace is the healing and elevating influence of the world and strife is not. There is such a thing as a man being too proud to fight. There is such a thing as a nation being so right that it does not need to convince others by force that it is right.

This homiletic declaration had been received in England with violent expressions of disdain, and even House had been at a loss for an explanation when he first read it. On reflection, however, he had perceived it to be, at least in some measure, merely an expression of that small-town American temperament with which he'd been so long out of touch. More significant, he had perceived that it was not in fact an official statement of policy, but rather just a stage in Wilson's internal deliberations. The President, he knew, when thinking about a question very deeply, would sometimes—regrettably even in public— do some of his thinking out loud. House concluded that that was precisely what he'd done here. Had he arrived at any concrete conclusions prior to his speech, he would have expressed them specifically rather than indulged as he had in generalities.

Using this line of reasoning, the Colonel had endeavored to convince Grey and the others that the President's formal response to the *Lusitania* sinking was yet to come. But while he and they waited for it he had felt for the first time, and in spite of an undiminished flow of official courtesies, that he as an American was not persona grata.

Then, this afternoon, the text of Wilson's note to Germany had been made public, and the English attitude toward Americans had undergone a sweeping transformation. The note had been startlingly unambiguous about submarine warfare: it could not be carried on against merchant ships, it said, "without an inevitable violation of many sacred principles of justice and humanity." Consequently, the government of the United States was "confident" that the government of Germany would "disavow" the acts of its submarine commanders, make all possible reparations, and prevent any recurrence of such lamentable incidents as the sinking of the *Lusitania*. "The Imperial German Government," the President had concluded, "will not expect the Government of the United States to omit any necessary representation or any necessary act in sustaining the rights of its citizens or in safeguarding the sacred duties of international obligation."

Stripped of its diplomatic gloss, the message was plain as homespun: torpedoing merchant ships is wrong; stop doing it or we fight —and House could not help being thrilled by it. True, it nullified most if not all of his recent efforts for peace, and moreover threatened to embroil America in the war. But it was unmistakably *right*— and courageous and farsighted as well. Sinking merchant ships *was* wrong, after all. It not only compromised the freedom of the seas, which was the indispensable basis of international trade, but also raised the specter of wholesale slaughter on the oceans every time one nation, great or small, made war upon another. True, advances in technology had rendered many old juridical notions about blockade and cruiser warfare obsolete. But what was involved here were not rules of war but principles of humanity. Technology did not alter these principles; indeed, nothing did. They were the bedrock of civilization, and House was proud that Wilson had reaffirmed them. In doing so he'd placed the onus where it belonged: on Germany, while concurrently presenting Americans with a clear picture of the issues at stake. Now, if Germany failed to mend her ways, the nation would see that the times called for war.

Perhaps neutrality and peacemaking had been fond illusions all along, and America's destiny had always lain plainly with the Allies. Perhaps it was past time that the clanking militaristic Germans were called to account. Perhaps, perhaps. Who could tell? That was the way matters seemed to be falling out at any rate, and he couldn't say for certain that things would not turn out for the best. The postwar era would find the western democracies holding sway while a despotic Russia counterbalanced an equally despotic Japan. That really wasn't a bad new order for this millennial century, House acknowledged to himself. No, come to think of it, that really wasn't a bad new order at all.

But at the cost of how many thousand American lives?

1915, 15TH MAY—LONDON

Lord Fisher was not in his office when Reeves-Wadleigh arrived. The rumors had been running broadside for several hours now, and the commander's eyes traveled carefully over the familiar walls and furniture, seeking evidence that might confirm or negate the breathless whispers. The desk was bare of papers, but Fisher had always had the sailor's sense of tidiness, so that wasn't conclusive. The door of the wardrobe was ajar, however, and the freshly pressed admiral-of-the-fleet uniform that customarily hung there was missing, as were the old but always shining half-boots, the naval greatcoat, and the gold-brimmed service hat. Fisher usually wore mufti in London, donning his uniform only for ceremonial occasions, or histrionic ones. Today's calendar was bare of ceremonies, Reeves-Wadleigh knew, so the melodramatic speculation he'd been hearing might very well have a basis in fact.

He walked over to the wardrobe and gazed at his reflection in the mirror on the inside of the door. He had by now gotten used to the fishy gray pallor of his skin, but only this morning had he noticed the initial portents of physical wastage. First had come a small sense of satisfaction over fastening his collar button with unaccustomed ease, then a sudden chill realization that the easiness *was* unaccustomed, then hasty steps to his bathroom mirror, which had told the same story as this mirror here. Looking at the flaccid skin of his throat, Reeves-Wadleigh could feel the sluglike prodding of the cancer and taste the daily more pungent carrion odor that drifted up his gullet from his belly. All at once the unremitting nausea that by now he hardly thought about surged in intensity.

He took a deep breath, steadied himself, looked his mirror image in the eye. Shrinkage, he thought to himself with a sour smile; shrinkage and internal rot. What a dignified way of taking one's leave.

He heard footsteps approaching, and turned to see Fisher, in uniform, entering the room at a brisk pace. The admiral's eyes were shining maniacally and he had about him an air of fevered preoccupation. He was almost to his desk before he registered Reeves-Wadleigh's presence. "Ah, it's you, Monty. Good."

"You sent for me, sir?"

Fisher raised a silencing hand, palm outward. "I'll be right with you, Monty," he said, unlocking a desk drawer and taking out a sheaf of papers.

Reeves-Wadleigh looked at him carefully; the man was obviously overtired and overstimulated. His eyes blinked and blinked, as if the air were full of cinders, and his lower lip hung slack, as if he'd suffered a stroke.

"It's true what you've been hearing," Fisher said as he scanned the papers before him.

"Sir?"

"That I'm going . . . going now, today."

"Oh, I hope not, sir."

Fisher shot him a quick mordant glance. "Others hope not too, Monty, from far less noble motives. But they hope, as you do, in vain. I'm leaving, and that's final. One week from today you shall find me in Scotland, fishing for salmon with the Duke of Hamilton."

And doing what with the duchess? Reeves-Wadleigh wondered with wry admiration, his seventy-four-year-old chief's long-standing liaison with thirty-seven-year-old Nina Hamilton being an unspoken but widely celebrated point of virile pride among British sailors. "What's happened, sir?" Reeves-Wadleigh asked.

Fisher stopped riffling through papers and gave him a fierce look. "Winston has happened, Monty—Winston and his bloody Dardanelles. The man is *possessed*. He's going to keep flinging ships into the teeth of those Turkish emplacements until we're stripped bare in the North Sea. He's going to lose the war for us, *and I cannot turn him aside!* So I'm going, and that's that."

Not quite, Reeves-Wadleigh thought. The admiral's resignation would shake the Asquith government to its foundations, and after the consequent reshuffling of the political deck, Fisher might very well be dealt a stronger hand, if he didn't overplay the one he was holding now. "I'm sure you're doing what's best, sir," Reeves-

Wadleigh said. "Though I don't see how we can get on without you."

"*Nil desperandum*, Monty," the admiral replied crisply. "There'll always be an England."

"Yes, sir," Reeves-Wadleigh said in a neutral tone. It wasn't his place, after all, to intrude himself into Fisher's political machinations.

"And even though there won't always be a Jacky Fisher, do not think that he passes hence without making provision for those like yourself who have fought beneath his standard."

"Sir?" Reeves-Wadleigh asked as the admiral flashed him a puckish smile.

"You are promoted captain, Monty, as of the first of June."

In spite of himself Reeves-Wadleigh felt a small thrill of exhilaration. Apparently one did not simply slough off the conditioned responses born of thirty-two years in the Royal Navy, even when the approach of one's own extinction rendered such responses ridiculously inapt.

"Thank you, sir," he said quietly.

"Don't thank *me*, dear boy; it's a promotion based on merit."

"I presume to be grateful, sir, nevertheless," Reeves-Wadleigh responded, knowing as well as anyone how revered an article of faith was favoritism in the Fisher creed.

"Yes, yes," the admiral muttered, his attention having shifted abruptly back to the paperwork in front of him. "Now look, Monty," he said after a few moments, his eyes still focused downward, "there's going to be a full-scale inquiry under Lord Mersey into the *Lusitania* scandal. I want you to keep me informed week by week, or more frequently if developments dictate."

"Scandal, sir?"

Fisher looked up at him. "You haven't seen the memorandum from the Trade Division?"

"No, sir."

"Well, when you see it you will learn that Captain Turner disobeyed our regulations about zigzagging, disobeyed our regulations about avoiding headlands, disobeyed our regulations about steering a mid-channel course, disobeyed our regulations about steaming at full speed in the vicinity of harbors, and disobeyed our regulations about keeping well clear of Queenstown. Short of stopping dead in the water, he couldn't have cooperated more fully with that U-boat had he been Tirpitz himself!"

"I suppose he just couldn't conceive of the Germans doing what they did," Reeves-Wadleigh said, knowing how fatuous liner captains tended to be.

"Then he's a confounded imbecile!" Fisher shouted, banging his fist down on the desk top. "I tell you, Monty, it makes me *furious!* People just will not look at the truth. I've told them and told them: Marquis-of-Queensberry rules don't apply anymore. But they don't want to know about it—like our fat-headed friend Captain Turner. Tell them that the first rule of war is to kill your enemy and they go all a-twitter. It's *them* I blame for the *Lusitania,* not old Tirpitz. Tirps and I have always seen eye to eye on the nature of warfare. We talked it out the first time we ever met, at Marienbad twenty years ago, and there wasn't a point we disagreed on. The rules of war boil down to the three all-conquering R's: ruthless, relentless, remorseless. Everything else is treacle and window dressing."

"Yes, sir," said Reeves-Wadleigh, who had heard the tirade in one context or another perhaps a dozen times.

"At all events," said Fisher, "the inquiry is going forward, and I want Turner pilloried for the cretinous dotard he is. I rely on you to keep me posted and to warn me if they show any signs of letting him off the hook."

"Yes, sir."

"Good. Now what's this about our American observer?"

"It appears that his fiancée, Miss Bellamy, was a passenger on the ship."

Fisher froze for an instant, then fixed Reeves-Wadleigh with a sly grin. "I'll wager she was one of the survivors, eh?"

"Yes, sir; although our man at Scapa says she was thought to be drowned at first."

Still grinning, the admiral shook his head. "It'd take more than a point-blank torpedo to sink that little lady, Monty. . . . Did her near miss make any impression on her parents?"

"You mean on their attitude toward the war, sir?"

"Toward the war, toward the Germans."

"I don't know, sir. But I'll initiate inquiries."

"You do that. As to other matters, you know what I want to be kept informed about."

"Yes, sir."

"Good. You can reach me here at the Athenaeum Club, and in Scotland, of course, it's Dungavel, Lanarkshire."

"Yes, sir."

"Anything else, Monty?"

Reeves-Wadleigh paused a moment, weighing the wisdom of raising the issue yet again. "No, sir. Only . . ."

"Only, shouldn't we now ask for Maltbie's recall?"

Reeves-Wadleigh sheepishly nodded acknowledgment.

Fisher gave a gruff laugh. "You, my dear Monty, are a worry wart. The Bellamys may be dodoes, but they're *British* dodoes, and in any case, everything we've learned about Maltbie confirms his absolute devotion to our Britannic interests. So just continue to keep an eye on him, and don't be so xenophobic."

"Yes, sir," said Reeves-Wadleigh, concealing a sigh of frustration. Perhaps, he consoled himself, the United States might soon come into the war. He wished it would, because he wouldn't feel comfortable about Lieutenant Commander Maltbie until it did.

1915, 31ST MAY—PLESS

Von Müller glanced around the conference hall at Pless Castle with a sense of unabashedly vindictive satisfaction. Across the table from him Admirals Tirpitz and Bachmann were launching little darts of badinage in his direction, affecting a jocund bonhomie that was as bogus as the easy good humor of his ripostes. There were times, he reflected, when one felt positively *clever*, like Aesop's hungry fox. How sweet it was to stand back and give one's adversaries room to become a little too bumptious, a little too self-important, then watch them crow and strut and overreach so recklessly that the grapes one has long been coveting tumble out of their grasp. He wasn't thinking primarily of the *Lusitania;* that had merely added the necessary hubris to their presumption. He was thinking of the torpedoed American steamer, *Nebraskan,* which had been the Tirpitz faction's defiant response to the Kaiser's May 10 order to avoid any and all attacks on neutral shipping. The submarine advocates had been outraged by this command, claiming that it imposed impossible restrictions on U-boat commanders and hinting broadly that it was merely a sop to the timorous civilian politicians, perforce not to be taken all that seriously. Riding the crest of the German public's acclamation of the *Lusitania* sinking, they had been emboldened to the point of taking matters into their own hands. And thus it was that, five days ago, U-27 had torpedoed the *Nebraskan*, mistaking her for a British ship, or rather, for the sake of operational convenience, *assuming* her to be one, even though such assumptions had been ruled out by the May 10 directive. It had been a clear case of officially condoned insubordination, a plain flouting of the All Highest War Lord's authority. And it had come, with typical political ineptitude, only three days after Italy had joined forces with the Allies.

Von Müller felt profoundly relieved. Woodrow Wilson's patience and forbearance in the face of severe provocation had supplied the time needed for Tirpitz to overplay his hand, overplay it so egregiously as to force Wilhelm into taking a stand. It was now, therefore, a real possibility that the *Lusitania* incident might develop into a *casus pacis* rather than *belli* for Germany and the United States. That, at any rate, was what von Müller and the Imperial Chancellor had been laboring to make of it throughout the last seventy-two hours. And this morning, at this specially convened conference at Supreme Eastern Front Headquarters, their labor seemed sure to have its reward.

At eleven o'clock exactly the Kaiser entered the conference hall with an entourage consisting of the Imperial Chancellor, Bethmann-Hollweg; the Foreign Office representative at court, Colonel von Treutler; and the key man in von Müller's calculations, General Erich von Falkenhayn, Chief of the Great General Staff of the German Army. The Kaiser was plainly nervous, talking nonstop in a loud staccato voice about artillery tactics and gesticulating spastically with his good arm. General von Falkenhayn made a conscientious show of attending to his sovereign's words, but von Müller could see that the general's thoughts were elsewhere—on a few hours' sleep most probably, judging from the man's all too visible fatigue. Chancellor Bethmann-Hollweg looked exhausted too, but also contented, which was an encouraging sign. Von Treutler looked spruce and sleek, an advantage, von Müller reflected, of being a courtier like himself, unencumbered by the burdens of executive responsibility.

The three admirals stood up and inclined their heads deferentially as the Kaiser took his seat. One glance at Wilhelm told von Müller that this meeting was going to be short; the Kaiser had his I-want-no-arguments expression flashing, and for once the admiral liked the sight of it.

Wilhelm called on General Falkenhayn, who declared in a worn-out monotone that the army was stretched to the limit on all fronts and could not at present bear any additional burdens. "Therefore," he said, "the navy must carry on the submarine campaign in such a manner as to avoid the risk of war with any of the neutrals, most particularly the United States, as we could not withstand a war in which America was on the side of our enemies."

Tirpitz leaned forward, his great forked beard sweeping the table-top. "My dear Falkenhayn," he said in an orotund voice, "the only way to carry on the submarine campaign in such a manner as to avoid the *risk* of war with neutrals is to not carry on the submarine campaign at all." The Grand Admiral turned his gaze onto the Kaiser. "Do I understand your Highness to be ordering the cessation of our U-boat activities?"

"I will not be presented with such either-or ultimata," Wilhelm bristled. "Nor will I hear of any abandonment of our submarine campaign. I am most displeased with the navy's all-or-nothing attitude on this matter, and it seems to me I would be wholly justified in reprimanding the entire naval high command for the sinking of the *Nebraskan* in defiance of my orders."

"Pardon me, your Highness," Bachmann interjected unwisely, "but the *Nebraskan* was only damaged, not sunk."

Von Müller felt a warm glow inside as the Kaiser, quivering with anger, glared at Bachmann and hissed, "Do not strain at gnats with me, Herr Admiral. I do not find it at all appealing."

"My apologies, your Highness."

"Had your submarines had any sense of direction," Wilhelm continued, unappeased, "they would have confined their hunting to cargo ships in the first place, and spared us this whole *Lusitania* crisis."

Tirpitz could barely conceal his rage, von Müller was gratified to note. "I am not aware that any 'crisis' is impending, your Highness," the Grand Admiral rumbled.

"That, sir," retorted Wilhelm in a tone of finality, "is precisely what is causing me vexation. I should like, in future, for ministers of state and high military officials to be a little less parochial in their outlook and a little more amenable to supreme authority, whose task it is to consider *all* the factors touching on Germany's fate, and to try to maintain some sort of balance among competing needs."

Von Müller and the Imperial Chancellor exchanged a furtive glance, the admiral finding it hard to credit the distinct impression that Bethmann-Hollweg had actually *winked* at him.

"Your Highness's point is well taken, of course," Tirpitz responded sullenly. "But might not people think it hard that submarine commanders should be castigated for merely doing their duty."

It was extraordinary, von Müller marveled, how Tirpitz managed to converse respectfully with his monarch and still very explicitly convey threats. Such was his influence with the press that Wilhelm would court serious public disapproval by treating the submariners as anything less than heroes. In this case, however, that wasn't the Kaiser's object, though he'd been maneuvered by Bethmann-Hollweg into making Tirpitz think it was.

"Who said anything about castigating anybody?" Wilhelm flared. "Where did that fantastic notion come from?"

"Your Highness's reference to our U-boats' 'indiscretions' in not confining themselves to cargo ships . . ."

"Perhaps," Bethmann-Hollweg suggested mildly, "it would not be out of place to provide our U-boat captains with some additional guidance."

Tirpitz eyed the Chancellor suspiciously, and the Kaiser asked, "Such as?"

"Such as—only as a temporary measure, of course, until the military situation is less strained—telling the U-boats to refrain from attacks on *any* large passenger ships, including those of the Allies. There can't be more than half a dozen still in service, so I'm told, and their silhouettes are supposed to be quite distinctive."

Admirals Tirpitz and Bachmann looked at each other with expressions of frozen horror. "Your Highness," the Grand Admiral exploded, "to further restrict U-boat operations would be an unthinkable—"

Wilhelm, who had been frowning thoughtfully, raised a silencing hand. "The Imperial Chancellor has every right to our support for temporary measures he deems necessary in the light of existing circumstances," he announced, clearly relieved to be able to offload the responsibility onto Bethmann-Hollweg's shoulders. He paused dramatically for a moment, then declared, "The submarine campaign will continue, with all neutral ships and large passenger liners for the time being to go unmolested. . . . I must say I don't see why an Imperial conference was required to resolve such a minor issue."

The Emperor stood up, and his subjects stood up with him. The official line, clear to everyone present, was to be that with respect to the submarine war nothing whatsoever had been changed. Tirpitz would continue to object, of course, and President Wilson, not knowing the extent to which American demands were going to be met, would not be pleased with Germany's reply to his note. But the navy would obey, with the practical result that the United States would no longer be provoked. That was reward enough for one morning's work. So rewarding was it, in fact, that when von Müller caught the Chancellor's eye for an instant on their way out of the room, it was all he could do to keep from winking himself.

1915, 20TH JUNE—CAPE COD

Between the Gehlman estate at Menauhant on Cape Cod and Colonel House's summer home at Manchester on the North Shore lay one hundred miles of reasonably maintained road, stretches of packed dirt alternating with stretches of heat-softened asphalt. Gehlman reckoned it would be about a four-hour drive, all being well, and as he had just recently taken delivery on a new Pierce-Arrow, the summons from the Colonel provided the perfect occasion for a motoring excursion with Alis.

This June Sunday—the eve of the summer solstice—had dawned warm and cloudless, with a lazy breeze blowing off Nantucket Sound. He had roused Alis at six, waking her as he always did now with a soft kiss on the forehead. They had evolved a morning ritual: he would perch on the side of her bed to wake her, whereupon she would sit up and topple sleepily forward into his arms. Then, sometimes for as long as half an hour, he would hold her and rock gently back and forth, letting her make an easy transition from dreams to waking. He was always struck by the strength with which she gripped him in her groggy condition, as if she were reclaiming him after a long absence, like a cherished teddy bear that had just come back from being restuffed and cleaned. As for himself, the quiet interlude with her in the stillness of each new day was a time of undiluted bliss. He had never been aware that such humdrum household routines as getting a child out of bed in the morning could be imbued with such breathless intensity. But holding her and feeling her hold him was an experience as deep and meaningful as any he could remember, with the additional virtue that it could be repeated unfailingly day after day after day.

He suspected, in his more cynical moments, that a good ninety percent of his rapture could be traced to a simple sensation of power. He had become, after all, Alis's entire universe, or at the very least her sun. She had entrusted herself to him completely; she looked to him for sustenance and warmth; and at no time was she more utterly in his keeping than when she relied on him to shepherd her out of subconsciousness into the day. But the power theory didn't hold up, if for no other reason than that there were too many phenomena it couldn't account for. It couldn't explain, for example, why in holding Alis, Gehlman often felt that her trust in him contributed much more to his well-being than his trustworthiness contributed to hers. It couldn't explain his feeling that Alis had in some way *permitted* him to love her, and thereby—as Dr. Bauer had prophesied—allowed him to acknowledge the possibility that there was something to like in himself. Most of all, it couldn't explain his suspicion that it was in fact *he* who had entrusted himself to *her*, as he'd never done with any human being before, entrusted himself in the sense of having pledged his own existence as security for the happiness of hers.

Fräulein Beck appeared in the doorway and smiled at him. He smiled back and put a finger to his lips; cradling Alis this morning felt particularly delicious, and he didn't want to hurry her awake.

"Shall I bring you and Miss Alis some breakfast, Herr Gehlman?" the maid whispered very softly.

Gehlman gave a small affirmative nod.

Alis stirred a bit as Fräulein Beck left the room. "*Morgen, Babbo,*" she murmured sleepily.

"Babbo" was the name of the pet Saint Bernard Alis had had in Berlin, and it was also the Italian word for "daddy"; hence, by some twist of little-girl logic, it had been chosen as Gehlman's *nom de famille.*

"*Morgen, Liebchen.* Did you sleep well?"

"*Ja . . .* yes."

"Are you talking English or German this morning?"

She gave a little groan and snuggled closer to him, which was her standard response when he asked her silly adult questions at this time of the day. He took the hint and held her silently, breathing in the sweet fragrance of her hair and the scent of sea and pine trees that rode in the open windows on the first shafts of morning sunlight. He held her and savored holding her and had no other desire but to keep on holding her. It still astounded him sometimes that he could ever have accused himself of lustful thoughts where she was concerned. Now, of course, he knew what the word was for the feelings he had had, but they'd been unfamiliar feelings then and he hadn't been certain what they were.

His thoughts drifted to the letter Counselor Grew, on leave from the Berlin Embassy, had just recently brought him from Facchetti. Gehlman shuddered a little. To think, as Facchetti's letter reported, that von Tiel was actually trying to get Alis back, that he'd initiated criminal proceedings against Dr. Bauer and poor old Keller for their part in aiding her escape, that he'd sent his attorneys to the American Embassy to protest Facchetti's role in her "abduction," and that he was still energetically spreading the rumor that Gehlman had been a spy in British pay. Gehlman knew what had happened: by taking Alis away, he'd given von Tiel a cause in life and a prime focus for his insanity. Recapture and revenge would be the baron's watchwords now, and Gehlman fretted that the madman might actually try to extend his reach across the ocean. He'd hired Pinkerton men to guard against the possibility of a kidnap, of course, but the Pinkertons wouldn't help if the law was on the baron's side. Oskar's attorneys had been researching the question of whether it might be for over a week now. If it was, Gehlman stood ready to purchase a judge.

Fräulein Beck soon reappeared with breakfast. *"Gruss Gott, meine Damen und Herren,"* she said cheerfully, setting the tray on a small table near the foot of the bed.

"Gruss Gott, Fräulein," Alis responded, disengaging herself from Gehlman's arms and stretching languorously.

The maid bent down to receive a formal but affectionate kiss on the cheek from her charge, then busied herself fluffing up pillows and clearing a space on the bed between Alis and Gehlman for the tray. Alis meanwhile reached over to her night table for her glasses: one unforeseen product of Erna's exhaustive program of medical examinations. The ophthalmologist had detected a slight astigmatism in

Alis's left eye, a condition so minor as hardly to warrant correction. But Alis for some reason regarded glasses as a symbol of grown-upness, and on discovering that her vision was less than perfect had pleaded for a pair with Gehlman for the full fifteen or twenty seconds required to win him over. These well-nigh useless and thoroughly unflattering lenses she now wore proudly during most of her waking hours, even as Benjamin, Oskar, and Erna strove to reassure themselves that this was merely a phase that she would quickly outgrow.

Fräulein Beck set the tray down on the bed and withdrew. Halfway through his steak, Gehlman paused to observe Alis's dainty consumption of a slice of French toast. He loved watching her eat; she went at food with such comically meticulous precision, as if she were making her debut at some elaborate state dinner. It was hard for Gehlman not to find it laughable, especially in combination with the moon-faced rims of those nonsensical spectacles.

"What is funny?" Alis asked in her best state-dinner manner.

Gehlman beamed at her. "You'll be cross with me if I tell you."

Alis shook her head emphatically. "No. I promise I won't be."

"Very well." Gehlman shrugged. "What's funny is that sitting there eating your breakfast with your glasses on, you look just the least little bit like a monkey."

"A . . . monkey?"

"*Ein Affe.*"

Alis's eyebrows rose, and Gehlman couldn't tell for a moment whether she was going to be hurt or angry or amused or something else. Then all at once, with a playfully sly look at him, she snatched her glasses off her face. "Do I still look like a . . . monkey?"

"Why, no!" he answered in mock amazement.

Alis put her glasses back on and laughed delightedly. "I am happy then."

"Why?"

"Because if I looked like a monkey with my glasses *off* I would *be* a monkey, and I would continue to be a monkey even if I put my glasses back on. But because I only look like a monkey with my glasses *on*, that means that I am really myself, and that I can look like a monkey any time I wish to, even though a monkey cannot look like me."

"What would you say," Gehlman asked after a long ruminant

pause, "if I said that I thought you were trying to make a monkey out of *me?*"

Alis giggled impishly and answered, "But only God can make monkeys, Babbo. *Nicht wahr?*"

Gehlman took in her smile and felt a twinge of envy for all the lucky young men she was going to devastate in the years to come.

Gehlman's Pierce-Arrow 48 was a luxury roadster whose 520-cubic-inch six-cylinder engine was capable of up to fifty-five miles per hour. Like all Pierce cars, the 48 featured right-hand drive, on the theory that everybody who owned one would also have a chauffeur to drive it. Custom, of course, placed the chauffeur on the right, and Gehlman felt a bit uneasy about Alis's being on the side of any oncoming traffic. Fortunately, at seven-thirty in the morning only a small fraction of what little oncoming traffic there was was motorized. And in any case, as Gehlman acknowledged to himself while heading north out of Falmouth toward Buzzards Bay, he had to stop being such an old mother hen where Alis was concerned. He looked over at her: apart from the outlandish glasses, a shimmering vision in her frilly white dress, button shoes, and straw hat. Was it possible that he had met her for the first time barely four months ago?

"Who is Mr. House?" she asked all at once, without preamble.

"A close friend of President Wilson."

"Is he a good man?"

"I've only met him once, Allie, but I think he is."

"Do you like him?"

Gehlman smiled to himself. "I don't know him well enough to like him or dislike him."

Alis frowned a little, as if taking Gehlman's answer under advisement, then idly turned her attention back to the sailboats on the bay.

Gehlman stopped in Plymouth to show Alis the famous Rock, and then drove on to Boston for lunch at the Ritz-Carlton. He reflected, as they ate, how little he and she ever said to each other when they were together, and yet how pleasant he found her company, and how equally pleasant she seemed to find his. He was glad now that he hadn't put her back in a doctor's care, feeling that their relationship would not have become so comfortable for both of them if he had. He recognized that her dependence on his physical proximity wasn't healthy, but he believed that she could be weaned from it as she became more and more at home in her new surroundings.

Above all, Alis was happy, truly happy; he was sure of it. And as for himself, well, when had life ever been so good. Even before he delivered his report to Colonel House's New York residence last week, he had pretty much decided to leave the navy. Every last reason he had ever had for joining or remaining in the service had been overridden by Alis's presence in his life. He no longer had anything to avoid or escape from. On the contrary, he now had a great deal to seek out and delight in. And he certainly didn't have to be an officer in the navy in order to indulge his love of the sea. The only thing he would be giving up, in fact, would be his vocational mania for cannons, and that was an easily tolerable sacrifice. It would be a simple matter of resigning his commission, a simple matter he was determined to attend to soon. For as much as Alis found his absences distressing, so was he deeply troubled by the prospect of any long separations from her. He wondered, with just a trace of apprehension, whether Colonel House would understand his feelings.

The Colonel's two-story white clapboard summer home stood in a grove of stumpy pine trees about half a mile from the ocean. Gehlman drove up slightly before the appointed hour of four and saw House descending the front steps from the porch to greet him. The Colonel was wearing a tan three-piece suit, a high-crowned straw hat, and a tightly knotted brown tie. He looked vaguely somnolent: hooded eyes, drooping shoulders, limply hanging arms. And he had retained that air of inert passivity that Gehlman remembered from their previous meeting: that odd lack of animation that could be taken as readily for utter enervation as it could for consummate repose. Seeing him there, standing in such a way that his stiff celluloid collar seemed the only thing keeping his head from lolling onto his chest, it was difficult to believe that he was the likely next Secretary of State. In fact, had Gehlman never been exposed to the sharpness of the Colonel's mind, he would have presumed the man before him to be little more than a burnt-out husk.

The muscles around the Colonel's eyes contracted the tiniest bit when he noticed Alis. Gehlman introduced her to him, and liked him a little for the full bow with which he responded to her pro forma curtsy. Mrs. House appeared on the porch and further introductions were made. The Colonel's wife summarily dismissed Gehlman's suggestion that Alis would be quite content to sit somewhere and read while he met with her husband. "Cook and I were just going out to pick some blackberries," she said to Alis. "You come help us, and I'll send you a quart of preserves as your wages."

Alis turned to Gehlman with a warily questioning expression. "Blackberry preserves would be delicious with French toast, Allie," he said, and Alis a bit reluctantly let the Colonel's wife conduct her into the house.

"Shall we stroll a bit?" the Colonel asked.

"Fine," said Gehlman.

They walked around the side of the house and picked up a grassy path that led in the direction of the ocean. After an initial few minutes of silence, the Colonel said, "Your report was very illuminating."

"Thank you, sir."

"There were sections that were beyond my technical grasp, of course, but my overall impression was that it contained a lot of information that will be of considerable use."

"I hope that's so, sir."

House gave him a vaguely friendly but otherwise inscrutable look. "Now I think it would be helpful if you could tell me something about your relations with Baron von Tiel."

Gehlman had been more or less prepared for this. He had never deluded himself that his involvement with von Tiel and Alis and the countess had been in any way in keeping with House's instructions to remain inconspicuous. He knew that, in strict terms of military obedience, he should have left the von Lutwitz mansion the very night that Alis and the countess arrived, and that his failure to do so had embroiled him in an unseemly, discreditable, and altogether foreseeable scandal, whose repercussions were still being felt. He didn't regret his actions, given the benefits that had flowed from them. But he did feel ashamed of his dereliction of duty.

So he told House everything, from his arrival in Zurich to his recent receipt of Facchetti's letter about von Tiel. He skimped no details and was careful to avoid self-justification. The Colonel listened in silence, walking contemplatively with his eyes on the ground and his hands clasped behind his back. The grassy path they were on curved eastward as they strolled, and joined up eventually with a dirt track running just inland from the beach. Gulls wheeled in the clear ultramarine sky, and the muted rumble of the waves breaking on the shoreline served as a sort of counterpoint to the droning of Gehlman's voice.

The sun was trending north of west when he finally finished his account, and the ensuing silence, in his opinion at any rate, rapidly became oppressive. For what seemed a very long time, however, the Colonel just kept walking along in his semisomnolent manner, putting one slow contemplative foot in front of the other. Finally he broke the silence, though, saying with just the smallest flicker of a smile, "Well, Commander, if the *Lusitania* were still afloat, we'd have good reason to be vexed with you."

Gehlman felt a weight of apprehension being lifted off his chest. Had the Colonel cared to do so, he would have been perfectly justified in referring Gehlman's conduct to the Navy Department for disciplinary action, which action would most probably have taken the form of a reprimand, and a permanent stain on his record. Even though his decision to resign his commission would have rendered such a punishment innocuous from the point of view of eventual promotion, it still would have grieved him to conclude over twenty years of naval service under an official cloud. Thus House's half-humorous tone of reproof was a great relief to him, as was his implication that, in light of recent events, no real harm had been done for which Gehlman ought to atone.

The dirt track petered out at the edge of a tidal marsh, and the two men turned and began to retrace their route. "Would I be mistaken," the Colonel asked after several minutes, "in assuming that you now contemplate resigning from the navy?"

Gehlman was startled by House's acuity of perception, but he responded casually, "No, sir, you wouldn't be mistaken."

House nodded, then lapsed again briefly into silence. "Having met Fräulein von Lutwitz," he resumed finally, "and having listened to your account of her background, I can well understand your reluctance to subject her to any further strain."

Gehlman braced himself. In his experience, statements beginning with "I can well understand . . ." were all too frequently followed by statements beginning with "But . . ."

"I'd like you to defer your resignation temporarily, however," the Colonel went on, substantially confirming Gehlman's premonition.

"For how long, sir?"

For the first time since they'd begun walking House turned to look him in the eye. "I don't know, Commander. But I think I can promise you that any separations from your ward could be kept to a minimum."

To Gehlman's ears those were weasel words, and he had to concentrate on keeping a sarcastic edge out of his voice as he asked, "Could you give me some idea of your reasons for wishing me to defer my resignation?"

The Colonel smiled. "Of course, Commander, though I don't know that they should necessarily be thought of as *my* reasons."

The man was a deft hand at a rebuke, Gehlman reflected irritably. But who the devil did he think he was that such reasons as he might express would not be *his?* Still, he'd been tolerant about von Tiel and understanding about Alis, so without making it sound too blatantly snide, Gehlman managed, "Excuse me: a poor choice of words."

House smiled again, a bit ruefully. "What did you think about Secretary of State Bryan's resignation last week?"

"What did I *think* about it, sir?" Gehlman asked, wondering why House had changed the subject—*if* he'd changed the subject.

"Yes. Did you find the reasons he gave for resigning persuasive? Do you agree with him that the United States is biased toward the Allies and is pursuing an unreasonably rigid policy with respect to submarine warfare?"

Gehlman didn't know what sort of answers to give. Like most people he had been surprised by William Jennings Bryan's resignation earlier in the month, and then mystified when the text of Wilson's second *Lusitania* note—which ostensibly was the source of the Secretary's disaffection—was made public. The President had simply reiterated the sentiments of his May 13 message, as far as Gehlman could tell, so how Bryan could concur with that note and then resign because of this new one amounted to something of a riddle. True, Wilson had brushed aside Germany's allegations that the *Lusitania* had been armed and was carrying troops and ammunition; the issue, he had repeated, was one of humanitarian principles, not legalities. But that part of the note didn't seem so radical a departure as to warrant a resignation. At bottom, of course, Gehlman wasn't really all that interested in the reasons why politicians did or did not do what they did or did not admit they'd done, accepting it as a fairly well verified fact that their motives were muddled part of the time and sordid most of the rest. As to House's specific questions, well, Gehlman, as a student—or, say, a practitioner—of sea power, understood exactly the distinction between Britain's felonies on the high seas and Germany's felonies beneath them: it was the dreadnoughts at Scapa Flow. As long as the supremacy of those ships went unchallenged, Germany's only option in sea warfare was the submarine, unless the seas—and the war—were to be conceded to the Allies. Unfortunately for the Germans, though, their sea weapon was a blunt instrument, incapable of the graduated transgressions of the surface ship. And it was that, a simple divergence of technology—not morality—that made Germany a murderer and England only a robber. If, however, with the prospects for a second term beginning to loom in his calculations, Woodrow Wilson thought it advisable to take a forthright stand against murder, Gehlman could see no harm in his doing so—although while he was at it, why not protest against robbery as well?

But, Gehlman conceded, all this was probably more robust an answer than Colonel House would be wishing to hear, so he said simply, "I think the President is doing the best he can, under difficult and trying conditions."

House acknowledged the empty obeisance with a dry grimace. "Well, my point, Commander, is that Secretary Bryan's resignation is indicative of precisely how difficult and trying conditions really are. He resigned because he feared that unless we acquiesced in Germany's violations of international law, war would be unavoidable. On balance, I believe that he might well be right, but that doesn't lead me to the conclusion that a policy of acquiescence would be correct."

"Forgive me, sir, but how does this relate to the timing of my resignation?"

House gave him a look of sorely tried indulgence. "It relates, Commander, as follows: Germany is unwilling to renounce submarine warfare. We are unwilling to tolerate it. Whatever restraint Germany is exercising at the present time is conditioned on strategic considerations which are by no means immutable. As the war continues and Germany's strategic outlook alters, the pressure to wage all-out war with the submarine will increase. If Germany is losing, the counsels of desperation will be heard; if she is winning, it will be the counsels of arrogance. In either case, as long as we adhere to our insistence on respect for international law, the chances for war will multiply. Now Mr. Bryan's way of dealing with this apparent impasse would be to yield on the issue of international law. An alternative approach, however, is to make the prospect of war with the United States so unpalatable that Germany will shrink from it even in the last extremity. And this can be done only by building up our armed forces to such a level that our allegiance to *either* side in the present conflict would spell certain defeat for the side that provokes us. That is the direction in which American policy is moving, Commander. I think it likely that in the coming months as much as $500 million will be voted by Congress for naval construction alone. I think it reasonable to foresee the navy doubling in size within the next four or five years. And as it grows, experienced officers such as yourself will be in increasingly short supply. There will be ships aplenty, more ships than captains to command them."

Gehlman felt angry and disappointed. Was that all the Colonel's disquisition boiled down to—a recruiting speech? Not that the idea of a ship wasn't still alluring. But it was the first thing he'd considered when he began to contemplate resignation, and it hadn't tilted the scales.

"That, of course," the Colonel continued, "is only a general consideration. As far as you specifically are concerned, there is first and foremost the invaluable knowledge you derived from your sojourn with the German Fleet, knowledge that the various bureaus of the Navy Department will want to share in even greater detail than you've provided in your report."

"Of course," Gehlman said in mounting irritation. "I hadn't planned to resign without first completing my duties."

"No, certainly not," House responded blandly. "And then, too, there is the work to be done with Lieutenant Commander Maltbie."

"Lieutenant Commander Maltbie, sir?" Gehlman asked. He'd heard the name mentioned now and again over the years—it was a small navy—but of the name's bearer he knew virtually nothing.

"Commander Maltbie is our observer with the British Fleet. We hope to get him back here shortly for a month or two of consultations, and while he's here I imagine it would be worthwhile for the two of you to get together and compare notes, so to speak."

"Yes," said Gehlman, who had more or less assumed the presence of a corresponding observer with the British, but still felt a little surprised to discover that one actually existed.

"And finally," the Colonel said, as the roof of his summer house came into view among the pine trees, "there is the fact that if war with Germany should in the end prove unavoidable, the unique knowledge you've acquired will be of immense importance in determining the tactics of both our naval forces and Great Britain's."

So, thought Gehlman, after more than twenty years of abuse and discrimination calculated to drive him out of the service, the navy—or, rather, the nation—had decided to take him into its arms, to cherish and enfold him, just when he wished to take his leave. There was an irony in that too grim for him to find enjoyable. And there was the further irony also: that von Tiel's charge that he'd been a spy for the British might very well prove true.

1915, 4TH JULY—DUNGAVEL, LANARKSHIRE

Maltbie sank back in the seat of the railway compartment and let out a long sigh. It had been a wonderful, even a glorious, day, but he was glad nevertheless that getting married was something one did only once. He looked across at Melina. Her eyes were closed and her hands rested on her lap. But there was a stiffness in her back and shoulders and a slight compression of the contours around her eyes and mouth. She wasn't asleep; he was sure of that. But she wasn't feigning sleep either.

He looked down at her hands, which lay protectively, palms downward, no more than an inch or two above her body's cleft. After some time he lifted his eyes and found Melina gazing into them. It was clear that she had seen where he'd been looking. They exchanged quick nervous smiles, compounded of embarrassment and apology: apology for looking on Maltbie's part, for having seen him look on Melina's.

This was a subtly different Melina from the impulsively passionate creature Maltbie had met in Washington and savored in rose-scented letters. It was a different Melina, even, from the plucky sea sprite who had given such an animated and playful account of her close brush with death. This Melina, the one who existed now, was no less loved, no less cherished, than the Melina of Washington and Queenstown Harbor; she was simply—it seemed—more uncertain.

The change had been gradual but unmistakable, beginning with their visit to her parents. Arriving in Liverpool from Queenstown,

they had parted company with Otley, who was obliged to return to
the fleet, and had proceeded to King's Cross after dispatching a telegram to Sir Lloyd and Dame Margaret in Cambridge, advising them
of their probable time of arrival there (this being supplementary, of
course, to an earlier telegram advising them that Melina was alive).
On the train from London to Cambridge Melina had suddenly
begun to cry. She had stopped in mid-sentence, in the middle of an
anecdote about an encounter with a rattlesnake in Canyon de
Chelly, Arizona, and burst, almost violently, into tears. The spasm
had passed quickly, though, and they had both agreed—and so informed the goggle-eyed young soldier who was sharing their compartment with them—that it was nothing more than a delayed reaction
to her recent ordeal.

Sir Lloyd and Dame Margaret were not the cuddlesome little couple that Maltbie had assumed from Beatty's and Melina's descriptions. Sir Lloyd was a large heavy volcano of a man, verging on the
apoplectic, and Dame Margaret was a frosty, razor-witted dowager-
empress of a woman—hardly the nice white-haired old gentleman
and nice gray-haired old lady that the admiral had referred to nor the
overindulgent "darlings" whom their daughter had extolled. Their
expressions of delight over being reunited with Melina, and moreover being introduced to her fiancé, had been liberally interlarded
with expressions of outrage over the Germans' unmitigated gall in
sinking a ship on which their only child had been a passenger. To
Maltbie's bemusement, they seemed to regard the attack on the
Lusitania as a personal affront, and they told Melina that it had
"obliged" them to "reconsider" their "entire attitude" toward the
justness of the war.

Bemused as he was, Maltbie had also been vastly relieved to hear
them say this: it made his presence in their house a good deal less
compromising from the point of view of the conversation he'd had
with Ambassador Page on his arrival in England back in January. Of
course he had written the ambassador requesting permission to make
the visit as soon as he received Melina's cable accepting him: if he
was going to marry her, after all, he had to present himself to ask her
father's permission. But the reply he got back, though affirmative,
was so ominously formal and remote that he inferred the strain on
Mr. Page's patience to have been extreme. Now, however, with his
prospective parents-in-law reconsidering their "entire attitude," he

could contemplate a full two or three weeks in their company with equanimity.

He had enjoyed Cambridge and the green expanses of East Anglia enormously. He had walked through the richness of the Fitzwilliam Museum and had wept during a performance of the Mozart Requiem in King's College Chapel. He and Melina went on bicycle journeys: to Ely to see the cathedral, to Newmarket to see the horses. They would bring along a picnic lunch, stopping to eat whenever appetite and scenery were compatible. Having eaten, they would lie on their backs and gaze up at the benign puffs of cumulus floating in silence on the gently bracing springtime air, air that had come clear across the Atlantic from the polar regions, been warmed and humidified by the Gulf Stream, leeched dry by the hills of Wales and Cornwall, and then sent along eastward in company with sunlight and the odors of honeysuckle, dogwood, and new-mown hay.

Sometimes, lying there, they would kiss, their lips barely touching, as if the least excess pressure would bruise their mouths. And sometimes, with the most solemn circumspection, Maltbie would reach up his hand to her breast, and feel her clutch it, then not too roughly push it away.

These moments featured little of the strenuous ardor that had marked the embraces they'd shared in Washington. From the eroticism Melina had displayed on those occasions Maltbie understandably enough had deduced that, though a lady, she was a lady of the world and a lady of practiced desires. He discovered in Cambridge, however, that, in the most innocent sense of the word, she was a bluffer. It had been all very well for her to play the scarlet woman as a stranger in a foreign city en route to the remoter parts of a rude new world. But here, in England, with her parents watching and her spinster's membrane soon to be pierced, it was an altogether different matter. For the first time since he'd met her it occurred to Maltbie that there might be some significance in the fact that a woman as lovely as she was had reached the age of twenty-six without ever having wed. So strange was it to think of her afraid of anything that her fear of something he each day ached for more seemed outlandish in the extreme.

But it occurred to him also that he might be fatuous in assuming that defloration was the sole focus of her fear. Hadn't she specifically told him that she was "terrified" by the thought of marriage—and in the same letter added pointedly, "I am not a domestic animal"? And there was furthermore the fact that she must now be thinking, as the soubrette says when pressed for kisses in a fashionable play: "Why, dear sir, we hardly *know* each other!" Their relative lack of acquaintanceship didn't bother him, but then he was addlepatedly in love. And too, he had to acknowledge, he was neither the virgin nor the candidate for domestication in this impending union. Prostitutes and social convention respectively had seen to that.

And so, without thinking of it in those terms, he had been patient with her: taking no liberties and pressing no demands. Paradoxically enough, a lurking suspicion that she was really too good for him helped him to get through those times when she was most ambivalent and reserved. One day, for example, while walking through the Backs along the River Cam, they had crossed paths with a husky young don. He had had anguished eyes in an open and smiling face framed by a fine blond beard. He had also had a pair of crutches to offset the absence of his entire left leg, which he had lost, Melina told Maltbie later, while serving in France with the Kensington Regiment of Princess Louise. It had been clear, though their exchange of pleasantries was scrupulously banal, that the young don, named Eckersley, and Melina had at one time meant a good deal to each other. It had also been clear, simply from listening to the man, that Eckersley was brilliant, accomplished, sensitive, patrician, and from the testimony of his crutches, most likely a hero. Melina had been very quiet after the encounter and had gone to bed early in the evening. Sitting in his own room, Maltbie could imagine fairly well what had gone on between them. They had met here, fallen in love, quarreled about the war when he decided to volunteer, and parted. He, meanwhile, had met Melina in Washington no more than three months later and caught her, it now seemed clear, on the rebound. Well, he had reflected mournfully, how else could he have caught her, radiant and precious as she was? So what if he hadn't been her first choice? He was glad to be the choice that got the prize. It didn't even trouble him—it did actually, but only because it accentuated his unworthiness—that Sir Lloyd and Dame Margaret, although unfailingly polite, plainly regarded his conversation as sadly lacking in the degree of bite and acuity to which they were accustomed. He couldn't blame them for wondering occasionally, as he did himself, what it was that their daughter found so dear in him to love. He was grateful she found something, however, or at least was continuing to look.

Foreseeing how miserable Maltbie would be if he had to continue his observer assignment cut off from Melina at Scapa Flow, and realizing moreover that he would be too diffident and dutiful to request a transfer on his own, Admiral Jellicoe, with characteristic thoughtfulness, had sent a letter to the Admiralty, for eventual transmission first to the Foreign Office and then to the American Embassy. This letter, copies of which were marked for Admiral Beatty and for Maltbie himself, said simply—and untruthfully—that billeting problems up at Scapa obliged the commander in chief to send Lieutenant Commander Maltbie back, temporarily, to the battle cruisers, which action was concurred in by the Vice Admiral BCF. Maltbie's copy of the letter arrived in Cambridge twelve days after he and Melina did, and it bore two handwritten endorsements. The first: "Please don't think of this as an expulsion; it is intended as an engagement present. You are, now and always, welcome aboard the *Iron Duke*. JRJ. P.S. Corporal Otley will join you at Rosyth." And the second: "I've got my lucky confessor back! Hurrah! Will my lucky confessor's fiancée honor us by making Aberdour her home for the duration of your term with us? Please convince her to do so. Beatty."

"You made quite an impression on him three years ago," Maltbie said as he showed Melina the letter and its addenda.

"And you've made quite an impression on him this year, it seems," she replied, flashing him one of her pyrotechnical smiles.

"Did he make an impression on you?"

"Harry! Are you *jealous?*"

"Well, you can't blame a man for wanting to know how his prospective wife feels about her prospective landlord."

"One can too blame him; it's not at all genteel to want to know such things."

"I note with interest that you are avoiding my question."

"I note with disapproval that you haven't answered *mine*."

Maltbie surrendered in laughter, wondering a bit forlornly how much longer the blond-bearded Eckersley would have sustained the verbal joust and how much more enjoyment Melina would have derived from an opponent who more nearly matched her mettle.

He had gone back to Rosyth at the end of May, leaving Melina to spend a few weeks alone with her parents. He would infinitely have preferred her to come with him, but there was the matter of her trousseau, she said, and the need to confer with other scholars before beginning to write up the findings of her fieldwork. Unspoken, of course, was a desire to have time to think, time that Maltbie knew she needed, loath as he was to contemplate what the fruits of careful thought might be. She would feel the need to meet with Eckersley, he presumed—not for a tryst, but for a final survey of their feelings for each other. He dreaded the thought of such a meeting, but didn't doubt that it had to take place. Even if it didn't have to, the last thing he wanted to do was crowd her. If he attempted to force the issue in any way, he might lose her; if he left it to destiny, he might not. But even though he understood this, the month he spent without her at Rosyth proved the severest imaginable trial for his self-control. In writing his letters to her, the self-restraint required to keep from nagging her to come or to write him more frequently or to confirm their wedding date often left him perspiring. And he never opened her letters to him without his fingers shaking and his hands going clammy with sweat. "Dear Harry," he kept expecting to read, "I am so terribly sorry to hurt you, but . . ."

On June 24, however, she had wired from London that she would be on the *Flying Scotsman* the next day and was agreeable to a fourth of July wedding at Aberdour, as they had tentatively planned. The battle cruisers had come in from a two-day sweep on the morning of the twenty-fifth, and Maltbie had received the telegram in the midst of the sooted pandemonium of coaling, whereupon he let out a most indecorous whoop of jubilation that brought quizzical but friendly stares from the several dozen grime-covered sailors in his vicinity.

That evening, waiting freshly scrubbed on the platform at Waverley Station, he had had a flash of sobering insight: he understood, with near clairvoyant certainty, why Melina was going to be his wife. He could picture the scene between her and Eckersley, could hear him refusing with implacable finality—despite her tears—to consider himself a suitable mate for her in his truncated condition. Maltbie knew the English: their hopeless addiction to the noble gesture. And he could imagine Melina, swept up in a passion of love and self-sacrifice, swearing to Eckersley that his lost leg made no difference, that her feelings hadn't changed, and that she was prepared (even just imagined, these words caused Maltbie pain) to renounce her plighted troth, defy convention, and proclaim herself his wife before God in church, though not one cleric could be found to santify their union, nor one friend to witness it.

Too many novels, Maltbie reflected sheepishly; he was out-

Englishing the English with all that imagined nobility and romance. But still, he insisted to himself, one day, when he and Melina were very old and grizzled, he was going to ask her what, if anything, she and Eckersley had said—if, that is, they had actually met. He laughed self-mockingly at the thought; even at the age of eighty she would probably tell him in no uncertain terms to mind his own business.

The wedding had been delightful: a day of dazzling sunshine and cool west winds. Great shafts of moted brightness had streamed through the courtyard skylight at Aberdour, bathing guests and principals in a mellow golden haze. The surface of the tennis court had been covered with Persian and Turkish carpets, transplanted from inside the house. On the bride's side there had been only Sir Lloyd and Dame Margaret plus three or four Cantabrigian worthies. On the groom's side, however, had been Beatty's entire staff—less Flag Captain Chatfield, who was minding the fleet. Otley had been there too, all shiny and beaming in his best dress blues, and Waite had stood up for Maltbie with a minimum display of tongue-in-cheek.

Lord Fisher, decked out in the full regalia of an admiral of the fleet, had looked on like an imperfectly domesticated satyr while the Reverend Mr. Lydall, the BCF chaplain, performed the ceremony. And afterwards, while the band played, Fisher had let no one dance with Melina for more than a minute or two before cutting back in himself. "Good heavens!" she had whispered half seriously to Maltbie as they enjoyed a private moment at the buffet. "That old man is the incarnation of *evil!*" With her eyes shining and her flushed skin contrasting with the lavish white lace of her gown, she again looked to Maltbie like the faerie queen that had roused him from his bed on Christmas Eve in Washington. He had felt his love for her so intensely then, looking down at her, small and exquisite on his arm, that it was like a blossoming sunburst inside him, and he had wanted to fall on his knees and thank her: for being, for being there—and for being his.

There had been telegrams: from Jellicoe and—a touch of gracious urbanity—from Ambassador Page as well. There had been cables also: from Spring Rice and Captain Sims. The one from Sims, read aloud by Beatty, went thus:

SEVEN A.M. JULY FOURTH 1915 STOP YEAR OF AMERICAN IN-

DEPENDENCE THE ONE HUNDRED FORTIETH STOP DAY OF YOUR
MARRIED LIFE THE FIRST STOP HOUR OF YOUR PROFESSIONAL
LIFE AS FULL COMMANDER USN THE EIGHTH STOP CONGRATULA-
TIONS TWICE OVER AND WARMEST REGARDS SIMS

This had brought forth loud hear, hears, and from Beatty: "Ladies
and gentlemen, a toast! A toast to the bride and groom! A toast composed in fond memory of the evening I first met this estimable
young American officer and warned him of his fatal susceptibility to
this beautiful young British lass. Ladies and gentlemen, I propose
this couple's marriage: for the glory of love, and to the honor of us
all!"

Great puffs of gray-white cumulus tumbled eastwards above them
as the Lanchester touring car, driven by Mr. McGough, the Duke of
Hamilton's gillie, labored south toward Dungavel from Hamilton
Station. It was almost ten o'clock, but at these latitudes there was
still plenty of light with which to view the grounds of the estate.
They owed this site for their honeymoon to Admiral Fisher, who had
been a guest there himself until only yesterday, when he had been
summoned out of retirement to serve as chairman of the newly
created Admiralty Board of Invention and Research. In Edinburgh
en route to London Fisher had learned from Admiral Beatty of the
wedding scheduled for today at Aberdour and had promptly had
himself invited to it. At Aberdour, before the wedding, he had
learned from Morrison Waite, the best man, of the meager one-week
honeymoon the bride and groom were planning to spend at Kinross
on Loch Leven. "*Kinross?!*" he had thundered. "What sort of honeymoon is *that?*" Waite had explained that Maltbie wanted to be
close enough to Rosyth to respond to a summons in case the Germans ventured out. "Commendable zeal. But why *Kinross?*" Because, Waite had answered, there was a cottage near there on the
lakeside belonging to Flag Lieutenant Seymour where the newlyweds
could stay for free. Fisher had brushed this aside. No young woman
with the gristle to take a bite out of Winston Churchill on board his
very own Admiralty yacht was going to spend her honeymoon in any
cottage—not while John Arbuthnot First Baron Fisher of Kilverstone
had life and breath in his body. No indeed; she was entitled to nothing less than a ducal mansion. Dungavel was only forty miles from
Hawes Pier; there was a telephone there; and there were three finely

tuned automobiles available for use in an emergency. With the battle cruisers at four hours' notice for steam, Commander Maltbie could make it aboard the *Lion* with over an hour to spare. The estate was fully staffed, moreover, and offered salmon fishing, walking, tennis, croquet, badminton, a bathing pool, a library, a flower garden, a conservatory, and even a small observatory equipped with an eight-inch reflecting telescope. More than that, the place was empty: the duke would be away till the grouse season began in August, and the duchess, well, the duchess wasn't there either. Mr. and Mrs. Maltbie would be very welcome as guests of his, and there was nothing to argue about or discuss, *Dominus vobiscum!* Waite had conveyed the admiral's edict to Maltbie and Melina shortly after the ceremony, and had managed to overcome their qualms about seeming to disdain the hospitality offered by Flag Lieutenant Seymour. Thus had a thirty-room mansion and fifteen-hundred mountainous acres of Lanarkshire become the site of their wedding night assay.

Mr. McGough was not a particularly cheerful yeoman, nor even a locally colorful one. He wore a brown tweed suit, vest, and cap, along with heavy boots and an expression that seemed to mingle fury and grief. His wife, who was waiting at the mansion's front door, looked exactly as one would have expected a woman to look who had lived long years with a husband of such glowering visage. She conducted Melina and Maltbie upstairs, installing them in adjoining rooms that had each a private bath. After she left them they proceeded to unpack, glancing occasionally with self-conscious smiles through the doorway that marked the boundary between their respective keeps. The sky outside had shaded to a dark grudging grayness, and the sound of the wind was lonely and chill. Maltbie stood at the window and looked out at the murmurous silhouettes of the nearby treetops as they waved slowly back and forth in the restless air, like bearded sages nodding their agreement to some ponderous truth.

So his wedding night had come.

All the weeks since that afternoon when he had lost Melina and then found her again seemed to him to have been pointing toward this moment in time, to have been focused on it, as if it were a helmsman's point of reference, like a star. It was only a matter of minutes now, he reflected, until that moment of consummation for which the banns had been published, the vows exchanged, the guests gathered, the toasts proposed. How strange it was that this joinder of the flesh which the marriage institution had been created specifically to sanction was never, even by implication, referred to by any of the parties involved, or by anyone else either, for that matter, within the confines of polite society. One avoided the subject, skirted around it, blushed if it somehow arose—and one did this even though desire for one's intended wife was a plainly necessary, if not always entirely sufficient, condition precedent to marriage with her.

Maltbie, of course, had been exposed to the mid-Victorian Platonic romanticism that glorified the pure communion of souls over the impure junction of genitalia. But with Melina there had never been the slightest doubt in his mind, or body, that he desired her in the most patently carnal way. There were times, in fact, in Washington, when holding and kissing her had become a torment of frustration. He had occasionally deluded himself at such times that all he really wanted to do was lie beside her in a sort of de-sexualized variation on the perfect communion of souls. On reflection, however, he had always been forced to acknowledge the fact that the notion was a disingenuous one. Now, thanks to the fact of marriage, the question before the house was no longer whether or when, but *how*. And not *how* from some simple mechanical standpoint either, but *how* in terms of respect for Melina's maidenly feelings and needs.

The truth, Maltbie admitted to himself, was that he felt more than moderately afraid. With one partial exception, the only women he'd ever known had been women he'd bought and used. With them his duties and obligations had terminated the moment that money changed hands; thereafter he'd been free, within limits, to do exactly as he pleased. He didn't know for certain if his thrusts had ever caused those women pain or if his caresses had ever afforded them pleasure. Some had lain there in a transport of listless boredom, others had uttered moans of bogus arousal so obviously intended to hasten the onset of ejaculation as to have precisely the contrary effect. Still others had jabbered and prated and giggled away as if conversation and copulation were interdependent activities. Only one, eight years ago in Cavite, had shown him some aspects of herself as a woman. Her name—the name she'd used, at any rate—was Estrella, and her age at the outside had been fifteen. Maltbie could not have been her first client, but he was probably her first of European stock, and her small, lithe, brown, and acrobatic body had become for a time an obsession. He had brought her gifts, paid her double her normal tariff, and begged her, ultimately, to teach him how to give her pleasure. It had puzzled him then: the urgent need he'd felt to give and fulfill instead of merely buy and take. But his instinct had been dead on target, because mutuality in that instance had turned the sexual experience into an ecstatic celebration of life. But could one generalize from Estrella to women in general? And could one dare assume that the caresses that had pleased a dark-skinned Filipino whore would not humiliate a genteel and cultivated white woman like Melina? One simply didn't know, and it was one's uncertainty that gave rise to one's trepidation.

"Is it cold in these rooms, Harry, or is it just me?"

He turned from the window. She was standing in the doorway between their rooms wearing a white floor-length nightdress. Her hair was down, a luxuriant tress spilling over each shoulder and coming to rest upon the pillow of each breast. "My God, how lovely you are," he said.

She held his gaze for a moment, then looked down at the floor, immobile. After some seconds a bright silvery tear fell from her eye and struck the floor with a tiny *plock!* He went to her, put his arms around her, felt her shivering as she returned the cradling pressure of his embrace. "Forgive me, Harry," she said into his chest. "I'm behaving like a fool."

"No, no," he answered, kissing the top of her head and adding, to his ears inadequately, "you're not, you're not."

She tightened her arms around him fiercely.

"It doesn't have to be tonight, darling," he whispered.

She pulled a little away from him and looked up into his eyes. "Dear sweet Harry, yes it does. It's what I want, what I've been wanting."

She reached up and brought his face down to her lips, kissing him with passion. After a long while their mouths parted. Melina stood back a little and looked deep into his eyes, almost as if she were looking *for* something. Then, very gravely, she said, "Harry, there was another man, before you."

Maltbie froze for an instant, gave way to the conditioned reflex of shock. But the reflex passed, and he thought to himself how ironic it was that he, newly promoted for his proficiency, should have proved so extremely inept at reading signals. He could feel Melina waiting tensely for his reaction, the smell of her in his nostrils like cool fragrant powder. Who? he thought to ask. When? *Why?* But then he couldn't see the point in asking, because for all intents and purposes he already knew the answers.

So what? Did it matter . . . ?

Yes, goddamnit, it did!

He had an impulse to push her away from him and walk out of the room. But in the same instant he came back to the physical reality of her, waiting there motionless in his arms. There was no justifying it, no excusing it. But hadn't she tried to warn him: "You must believe that I am made of the same base clay as everybody else."

And *why* did it matter so much? He felt hurt, humiliated, duped, manipulated—and angry, angry that she had chosen this night of all nights, this hour of all hours, to confess.

He held her a little away from him and drank in the beauty of her face. He deplored her timing, but he would not mistrust her motives.

"It's the last time I'll ever hurt you, Harry," she said, tears streaming down her cheeks.

She meant that, he knew, unrealistic as it was. And he saw that she was deeply deeply sorry. Not sorry in the sense of remorseful over what she had done, but sorry in the sense of saddened over the pain he had to suffer to come to terms with it. She was telling him, in effect: Here I am; I have made my marriage vows and I will honor them. But I will not deny my past or go back on anything I have done. What I have done is part of me, and what is part of me is part of what you love, part of what you've married. So accept, my husband, please accept.

He looked down at her and managed at some cost a smile. "Well, my sweet Melina," he said finally, "the honors are even between us . . . because there were other women before you."

She smiled back and gently lifted his hand to her lips.

When they returned to Rosyth on July 11, there was a telegram from the embassy in London. DEPARTMENT DESIRES YOUR PRESENCE WASHINGTON FOR CONSULTATIONS, it read. PROCEED WITH ALL DISPATCH.

BOOK V

1915, 26TH JULY—WASHINGTON, D.C.

"Can I give you a lift?" Gehlman asked as he and Maltbie descended the steps of the Army and Navy Building to West Executive Avenue.

The offer seemed to catch the youthful-looking officer by surprise, and Gehlman questioned for an instant whether his assessment of Maltbie had been mistaken. When he'd met him for the first time a week ago, just as all the debriefings and meetings with the General Board were getting under way, he had quickly formed the impression that the man was no bigot. There was something in his face and manner that seemed to rule prejudice out: a kind of humble self-acceptance that didn't appear to depend for its maintenance on an assumption of superiority to others. But Gehlman had been wrong before in his judgments about people's attitudes, and Maltbie's hesitation now triggered a spurt of suspicion and doubt.

"I'd love a lift," Maltbie said, partially allaying Gehlman's uneasiness. "But I'm staying all the way out Massachusetts Avenue, at the British Embassy."

"Oh, of course," Gehlman replied. "Your wife's the ambassador's niece, isn't she?"

"Yes," said Maltbie. "And it's a good thing, frankly, because I certainly couldn't afford to house us in the manner her uncle does."

Gehlman smiled; it seemed that he hadn't been wrong in his assessment after all. "Well, I'd be happy to drop you off," he said.

"Are you staying out near the Naval Observatory too?"

"Well, no, actually; I have a house over at Fourteenth and M. But I'm taking my ward to the zoo this afternoon, so it would be no trouble at all to deliver you to the embassy."

"In that case, sir, I accept with thanks."

The chauffeur Gehlman had brought down with him from New York opened the Pierce-Arrow's rear door as the two of them approached.

"I'm not sure you should be calling me 'sir,'" he said in a friendly tone. "Despite my advanced years, the fact remains that we're both the same rank."

Maltbie gave a shy grin. "It's only been three weeks since I became a commander," he said. "I guess I haven't quite got the hang of it yet. . . . Besides, you become a captain on August first, if I'm not mistaken, so it wouldn't do for me to start indulging in familiarity."

Gehlman grunted. The promotion to captain was a little extra surprise incentive that House had engineered without his knowledge, and he had decidedly mixed feelings about it. "We'll probably be at each other's throats before we finish our work together," he said, motioning Maltbie to precede him into the automobile. "So familiarity is probably an essential first step in the development of our professional relationship."

Alis and Fräulein Beck had been waiting in the car, and Gehlman introduced them to Maltbie. The young officer's reaction to Alis was the standard one of stunned enchantment, but her reaction to him did not run true to form at all. With other people, men in particular, Alis had invariably been reserved and withdrawn on first acquaintance. With Maltbie, however, she behaved much as she did with Gehlman, but right from the start.

"Do you like Fräulein?" she asked the commander pertly.

"Fräulein?" Maltbie echoed, mystified.

"*Fräulein,*" Alis repeated emphatically, gesturing toward Hannah Beck, whose sweet, round farm-girl face was rapidly turning red.

"Oh, Miss Beck, you mean. Well, yes, of course I like her. I think she's lovely."

"She thinks you are lovely too," Alis announced excitedly. "She said so to me when you were coming to the car."

"Well, I'm very flattered," Maltbie said, as Fräulein Beck cringed in embarrassment.

"I don't want to intrude on your matchmaking, Allie," Gehlman interjected, "but I have to tell you that the word 'lovely' in English is not generally used in reference to men, especially married men, like Commander Maltbie here."

Alis looked mildly affronted. "You are *married?*" she asked Maltbie.

"Yes. I have to confess that I am."

Alis sighed, then turned solicitously to Hannah Beck and said, "Don't worry; we will find someone else for you."

The three adults in the back of the car broke into laughter at this, and Maltbie said, "I'm sure someone as *lovely* as Miss Beck will be found by some fortunate fellow long before there's any need for you to do her finding for her."

"Really?" Alis asked. "Is that what happened with you and your wife? Did *you* find *her*?"

"I guess you could say I was lucky enough to stumble on her."

"Stumble?"

"Find her by accident."

"Ah. And is she very lovely?"

"Oh, yes."

"As lovely as Fräulein?"

Gehlman watched with interest as Maltbie hesitated a beat while searching for a tactful answer.

"I honestly don't know if she's as lovely as Miss Beck," he responded finally. "You see, I'm in love with my wife, so it's impossible for me to compare her to other women."

"Why?" asked Alis, who plainly found this topic of conversation to be one of consuming importance.

"Because," Maltbie answered with pensive intensity, "the fact that I love her sets her apart in my eyes from all the other women in the world and makes her special to me in every way. And what that means, for me, is that no other women can be compared to her."

Alis pondered in silence for a while, then asked, "How did she make you love her so much?"

Maltbie smiled. "I'd be much more interested to know what *I* did to make *her* love *me*, even a little."

Gehlman smiled too, as Alis continued her interrogation. He thought he could guess what Maltbie had done to make his wife love him; it would be the same thing he'd done just now to make Alis so impertinently open up to him on first acquaintance. He had been himself—an unremarkable achievement viewed superficially, but a fairly uncommon one in Gehlman's experience. Maltbie was without pretensions, but also without any affectations of humility. He was genuinely self-effacing and genuinely deferential, but he was also well supplied with self-respect and far from indiscriminate in his displays of deference. Gehlman had had occasion to observe him over the course of the week, and he'd seen that the man set very definite

limits. With people he respected—and Gehlman had been flattered
to find himself numbered among them after a day or two—Maltbie
would go out of his way to be ingratiating. But he was never servile,
and with people he didn't respect or didn't agree with, regardless of
their rank, he was tenacious in defense of both his opinions and his
autonomy. He wasn't arrogant or disrespectful, but when he took a
stand he stuck to his guns. He was exactly the sort of officer, in fact,
that Gehlman would have liked to have had as an exec, though Benjamin wasn't sure he'd ever have wanted him for a captain. At all
events, he was certainly the sort of man he'd be happy to work with
—and would be working with at that: for the next several weeks, in
secrecy, at the Naval War College in Newport, Rhode Island.

The Pierce-Arrow turned into the British Embassy driveway at
Massachusetts Avenue and Thirty-first Street. Maltbie said good-bye
to Alis and Miss Beck, and warmly thanked Gehlman for the ride.
As the car started to pull away from the embassy's front entrance,
Benjamin heard a woman's voice call out, "Yoo-hoo! Harry!" He
turned to look out the back and saw a petite auburn-haired woman
run up to Maltbie and give him a kiss. His breath caught in his
throat. She was the same vivid creature he'd seen board the *Lusitania*
for its final voyage!

1915, 27TH JULY—CORNISH, NEW HAMPSHIRE

House leaned back in his chair and regarded the two piles of documents on the table with weary resignation. Here they sat—the President, the Secretary of the Treasury, the Assistant Attorney General,
and himself—face to face, not just with evidence, but with *proof* that
Germany was actively engaged in a form of covert warfare against
the United States. He couldn't shake the sense of unreality that
seemed to pervade this entire business. Sitting on the screen porch of
the President's summer retreat in New Hampshire, with the moths
thumping against the wire mesh and spasms of heat lightning fretting the viscous night air, it hardly seemed credible that the quarrels
of the old world could intrude so blatantly on the domestic tranquillity of the new. But they could, they did—though given the low

comedy ineptitude with which the intruders had exposed their machinations to official view, one couldn't yet feel too anxious about the common defense or the general welfare.

Secretary McAdoo and Assistant Attorney General Warren had both had astonishing stories to tell. McAdoo's tale was of Secret Service operative Frank Burke, assigned since May to shadow German nationals suspected of neutrality violations. Last Saturday, the twenty-third, he had been in New York, following Geheimrat Doktor Heinrich Albert, commercial attaché of the Imperial German Embassy. Shortly after 3:00 P.M., he had observed the Geheimrat leaving the offices of the Hamburg-American Steamship Company on lower Broadway. Maintaining surveillance, he had followed Dr. Albert aboard a Sixth Avenue elevated subway at the Rector Street—Trinity Place station. On the trip uptown, the Geheimrat had glanced repeatedly at his watch in a manner that suggested to operative Burke that the gentleman was late for some appointment. Corroboration of this hypothesis was forthcoming at the Fiftieth Street station, when Dr. Albert hurriedly exited the train, leaving behind him on the seat next to the one he had occupied a large bulging briefcase. Displaying commendable initiative, operative Burke had snatched up this briefcase and sprinted out the front of the car just as the Geheimrat, having apparently realized his oversight, was sprinting back in at the rear. A chase ensued, but operative Burke, blessed with fleetness of foot, retained possession of the briefcase, which proved, when opened, to contain encyclopedic details of an extensive German program of covert political agitation all across the United States. There had been subsidies paid, the briefcase revealed, to newspapers and newspaper correspondents sympathetic to the German cause; there had been generous contributions made to German- and Irish-American pressure groups; there had been concerted efforts undertaken to foment anti-British feeling, particularly in the cotton states; there had even been—outside the realm of the purely propagandistic—the purchase of a large munitions factory in Bridgeport, Connecticut, which purchase effectively denied the factory's entire output to would-be customers representing the Allies.

Assistant Attorney General Warren had had an even stranger story to relate. It seemed that a Mr. Emil Gaché, a purported businessman of purportedly Swiss nationality, had met and fallen in love with a certain Miss Anne Seward over the Fourth of July weekend at Kennebunkport, Maine. Both Gaché and Miss Seward had been guests at the Colony Hotel, and one night, in a moment of intimacy, he had confided to her—unaccountably, in House's opinion—that his real name was Franz Rintelen von Kleist, that he was a commander in the German Navy assigned to the Admiralty Intelligence Staff, and that he was working in the United States as a secret agent. As it happened, Miss Seward was not only patriotically inclined but also a family friend of the new Secretary of State, Robert Lansing, whom she had contacted the morning after Gaché-Rintelen made his revelations. Lansing had immediately sent his assistant, Chandler Anderson, to Kennebunkport to hear Miss Seward's story, and on Anderson's return to Washington, Assistant Attorney General Warren had been brought in on the case and placed in personal charge of a special team of agents working for the Justice Department's Bureau of Investigations. The agents' report, completed less than a week ago, showed that Rintelen was nothing less than the mastermind behind a concerted program of espionage and sabotage carried out by a large well-organized underground organization, an organization that was also engaged in fomenting labor unrest in major industries, hindering the export of American munitions to the Allies, and provoking armed hostilities between Mexico and the United States.

House looked around the table. There was Warren: bland, competent, but certainly, in this company, feeling a bit out of his echelon. There was Secretary McAdoo: hawk-eyed, hook-nosed, every muscle aquiver with ambition. And there was Wilson: plainly infuriated by the Germans' duplicity, his brow furrowed, his eyes narrowed, and his lips pressed tightly together. Inside the house, moreover (and not, small mercy, out here on the porch), was the President's new friend, Mrs. Galt, quite the most banal woman the Colonel had ever dealt with. Unlike Ellen Axson Wilson, who, though no great intellect, had been wise enough to refrain from intruding her opinions when men sat down to talk, this lady—the widow of a jewelry store owner, no less—had no hesitation about giving voice to ideas so pedestrian as to make conversation at the average quilting bee seem sophisticated by comparison. What was worse was the fact that Wilson confided in this woman, showed her state papers, and lapped up her inanities as if they dripped nectar. The President had always had this weakness with regard to women, this tendency to enshrine. Having spent almost all his adult life at the center of a family universe populated by an adoring wife and three adoring daughters, he had developed a psychic dependence on female ministrations. With his

wife dead and his daughters grown and scattered, however, that universe had collapsed, and he was clearly counting on the Galt woman
—though he'd met her only in March—to create a new one for him.

House sighed quietly: Mrs. Galt was an affliction he would have to
suffer in silence. Clearly, she wasn't going to go away, and just as
clearly, the President wasn't going to stop wanting her beside him.
So that was that. Meanwhile there was this vexing matter of Germany's somewhat clumsy version of diplomacy by other means. How
should the President respond to it? He had already grasped the net-
tle with respect to the question of preparedness, having requested
Secretary of War Garrison and Secretary of the Navy Daniels to
prepare large-scale programs for building up their services, these programs to be ready for submission to Congress as soon as it recon-
vened.

What else ought he to do? Expel the German ambassador? Break
off diplomatic relations? No. Now that the Germans had revealed
their true colors and Wilson knew the sort of people he was dealing
with, the next step, plainly, was to use his knowledge to good effect.
As House saw it, there were two immediate objectives: first, to stop
the sabotage and subversion, and second, to give the public some
idea of what the Germans had been up to. Discussion around the
table quickly proceeded to the conclusion that the accomplishment
of the first objective would follow automatically from the accomplishment of the second. The question was, therefore, how much of
the German perfidy to reveal and how to reveal it. If war was going
to come to America—and the powers in Berlin seemed peculiarly
bent on bringing it here—then the people of the country needed to
be educated about the nature of the German threat. "Noninvolvement" was still the rallying cry in most sections of the nation, after
all. On the other hand, the German intrigues, though reprehensible,
were not *necessarily* inconsistent with a desire to remain on what
passed for friendly terms. They were directed not against the country
as a whole so much as against a sector of the country's economy—the
munitions industry—that was causing Germany serious harm. A complete disclosure of the Rintelen file might easily generate such violent public indignation in the United States as to rule out all
possibility of ever reaching an accommodation with the Berlin
government. The Albert material, on the other hand, would be sensational enough to galvanize public opinion, but not so sensational
as to send it spiraling out of control. The President, therefore, ac-

cepted House's suggestion that the contents of Dr. Albert's briefcase should, at some appropriate time in the near future, be conveyed to editor Frank Cobb of the administration's staunch ally the New York *World*. Cobb, it was agreed, could publish as much of the material as he cared to, provided only that he did not reveal from whom he'd obtained it. As to Rintelen, the Justice Department wanted to let him operate a while longer under surveillance so they could be sure they had a grip on his entire organization. At the right time, though, he would be picked up, and a "leak" to the newspapers would inform his masters that the President was on to their game.

It wouldn't take much now, House reflected grimly as the meeting concluded: another *Lusitania*, another Rintelen, and America would be on the brink of war—or over it. It was all up to the Germans. And the auspices weren't good.

1915, 6TH AUGUST—LONDON

Lord Fisher stood looking out the window at Admiralty Arch, his fingers squeezing and interlacing and twisting as his hands rode restlessly on the lumbar region of his back. Reeves-Wadleigh watched him sympathetically; the man, after all, deserved better. He was the father of the modern British Navy; he had brought it kicking and screaming out of the nineteenth century and made of it a sea weapon that kept Britain safe from defeat as long as it remained afloat, regardless of what happened in Europe. (Alas that it couldn't also propel Britain to victory!) It was hard that such a man should be set aside and left to molder in an advisory role. Admittedly, he had overplayed his hand in May, overplayed it egregiously. But that was no reason to cast him out in favor of a mediocrity like Admiral Jackson, his successor as First Sea Lord, or a political acrobat like Balfour, Churchill's successor as First Lord, who knew nothing of the sea or of ships or of seamen. The Board of Invention and Research couldn't command even a tenth of Lord Fisher's energies, and the strain of underactivity was telling on him. He was querulous, often petulant now, and he carried his years like the yoke of subjection. It was a sad spectacle watching him try to make much out of little. All his life he had painted with a broad brush on a big canvas; now he was reduced to pencil sketches on foolscap.

Reeves-Wadleigh shifted cautiously in his chair and withdrew a handkerchief from his trouser pocket. Every week it required more and more vigilance to keep Fisher from suspecting his illness. Not because Fisher was more watchful, by any means, but because he himself was markedly sicker. The last thing—literally, the last thing —that Reeves-Wadleigh wanted was to have his illness discovered. If it was, he would be invalided out of the service and condemned to spend his remaining months staring into the empty eye sockets of extinction, staring while his sister mewled and puled at him, bewailed and whimpered and dragged him down, until his resolve to die with dignity melted away and his life ran out amidst screams and retchings on sweat-defiled sheets.

With a quick economical movement, Reeves-Wadleigh lifted his handkerchief and mopped up the beads of perspiration on his forehead. It was a cool day, despite the season—dark and threatening to rain. It was not a day to be seen perspiring if one could avoid it. He slipped the handkerchief back into his pocket and let out a long breath. The odor of the peppermint candy he chewed did not fully suppress the relentless decaying-meat smell that swelled up like marsh gas from his insides, and he had to fight in silent fury to stave off the impulse to gag. The effort of self-control caused the sweat to break out on his face again.

Why didn't the admiral *say* something! he wondered in exasperation. With so much time on his hands, Fisher had taken to summoning him almost daily now, and the accumulated stress of these frequent audiences was wearing Reeves-Wadleigh down at an accelerated rate. There was one consolation, he reflected sourly: he got to wear brand-new shirt collars almost every month. In fact, he had to. Since the flesh of his neck kept receding, last month's collars would look downright Etonian on him.

"So, Monty," Fisher said at last, "what have you new to tell me?"

"Relatively little, sir. Except, I believe we've found out what's become of Commander Maltbie."

Fisher snapped his head around. "You don't say so!"

"Yes, sir. He's—"

"Tell me, Monty; I'm curious. How the devil do you people manage to come up with such information? I was only half serious about wanting to know when I asked you. And here I discover you've gone and found out!"

Even with his longtime mentor, Reeves-Wadleigh experienced a reflexive reluctance to discuss the mechanics of the intelligence trade, and into the lengthening silence he said, "Are you asking me, sir?"

"Yes, Monty," Fisher responded, a slight eddy of irritation curling over his voice. "I'm asking you."

Reeves-Wadleigh felt the sweat starting to gather in rivulets and flow downward toward his eyebrows. "Well, sir, first we contacted Captain Gaunt, our attaché in Washington, whose duties include naval intelligence. Neither he nor the military attaché could come up with anything. So we contacted the head of our Secret Service in America, and he—"

"Who's he?" Fisher interrupted. He was again looking out the window.

Reeves-Wadleigh felt a violent churning in his bowels. The identity—even the *existence*—of the man in question was on the same level of secrecy as the breaking of the German naval codes. Reeves-Wadleigh himself, his chief, Admiral Hall, who was director of the Intelligence Division of the War Staff, and Colonel Hankey, the secretary of the Cabinet's War Council, were the only people in England outside the War Council itself who had the information. Even Reeves-Wadleigh wouldn't have known the name had not the diplomatically sensitive nature of the inquiries he was making required him to communicate direct. And even on the level of the War Council it wasn't likely that anyone other than the Prime Minister and the Foreign Secretary knew what Admiral Fisher now wanted to be told.

Unthinkingly, Reeves-Wadleigh took out his handkerchief and wiped his soaking brow.

"Damnit to bloody hell, Monty!" Fisher barked. "Why don't you bloody answer me!?"

Reeves-Wadleigh started, and hastily put his handkerchief away. The admiral, he noted with relief, was too irritated to be curious about the perspiration, or even notice it. "I'm sorry, sir," he said promptly. "The gentleman in question is Sir William Wiseman, acting under cover in New York City as the head of a company called W. Wisdom Films, Inc."

"I know Wiseman," Fisher said in a curt tone. "What did he tell you?"

"He said Commander Maltbie and his wife were living for the moment in Newport, Rhode Island, and that the commander was working at the Naval War College."

"Is the War College in session during the summer?"

"No, sir. That's the odd thing. The only other officer in residence there, apart from staff, is a newly promoted captain named Gehlman."

"Who's he?"

"A gunnery specialist, as far as we know."

"What are the two of them working on?"

"We don't know, sir. We're trying to find out."

"What about this Gehlman's service record?"

"We're hoping to get a look at it, sir."

"Well, keep at it. This sounds interesting."

"Yes, sir. Sir . . . ?"

"Yes?"

"Is it still contemplated that Commander Maltbie will be allowed to return?"

Fisher turned toward him and shook his head. "Still fretting, Monty. Well, well . . . if you and Wiseman can come up with anything to convince anybody that he shouldn't be allowed to, I'll take up the cudgels for you."

"Very good, sir."

Fisher took out his watch. "Ah!" he said in a noticeably lighter tone. "I must now go meet Lord Loreburn and start plotting my imaginary return to official prominence. Did you have anything else for me?"

"No, sir. Nothing important."

"Fine, Monty. Come see me again next week."

"Yes, sir."

"And, Monty . . ."

"Sir?"

"Old dogs snarl for no good reason sometimes, even at people they like."

"Yes, sir," said Reeves-Wadleigh, oddly touched.

Fisher gave him a paternal smile. "Get some rest, Monty. You're looking a little seedy."

"Yes, sir," Reeves-Wadleigh answered. And as soon as the admiral was gone he put his head down, let out a long heavy sigh, and gratefully mopped his throbbing brow.

1915, 20TH AUGUST—NEWPORT

"War is hell, Harry," Gehlman said, picking the *Lion* and the *New Zealand* off the tactical table and depositing them in a shoe box marked BLUE FLEET—SUNK.

Maltbie made a small puffing noise as if he'd been punched in the solar plexus and stood there shaking his head.

"I might also point out," Gehlman went on glibly, "that you've lost both your admiral *and* your second-in-command."

Maltbie lifted his gaze from the blue slate surface. "But you still don't know where my main force is," he said with a smile. "And *your* main force is still a long, long way from home."

"True," Gehlman responded evenly, looking back down at the line of tiny boats representing his Red Fleet in the "battle" then in progress.

The slate surface was littered with roughly modeled toy ships, no more than an inch or two in length. Small as they were, they were still too large to conform to the scale of the table, whose ten-by-fifteen-foot expanse was divided by white lines into 150 twelve-inch squares stipulated to be 10,000 yards (or a bit less than six miles) a side. The unusually large scale of 1 to 30,000 was necessitated by the unusually large area of water that forces as unusually large as the Red and Blue Fleets required for their combat maneuvers. The scale's one drawback, a minor one, was that the inch-long toy ships representing destroyers worked out to be four times the length of any dreadnoughts now afloat—and the two-inch toy dreadnoughts worked out to have lengths of nearly a mile!

Gehlman focused his attention. Maltbie was plainly correct about the seriousness of the situation. Although Red Fleet was winning the skirmish, it was also in grave danger of losing the battle. Despite the fact that the Blue battle cruisers were suffering from the salvos of their Red opposite numbers and had lost the *Lion* and the *New Zealand* as a result, and despite the fact that Red's main force was on the verge of "crossing the T" of the Blue battle cruisers—i.e., was about to steam perpendicularly across the Blue line of advance, thereby subjecting Blue to the full weight of its broadside—it was the

Red Fleet, not the Blue, that now faced the threat of extinction. For, some thirty miles—or five squares—to the northwest, well out of sight beyond the tactical horizon, Maltbie's Blue main force was approaching at full steam. And by the time Gehlman's Red Fleet learned of its existence, it might well be too late to turn tail and run back to port.

"What time is it?" Gehlman asked, his eyes still frozen on the board.

Maltbie consulted a piece of paper cluttered with numbers, did a brief series of calculations, and replied, "Seventy-eight minutes until sunset."

"That early?"

"I'm afraid so, Ben."

"Damn!" Gehlman said. "This *is* serious."

Maltbie said nothing, just looked on with a vaguely sympathetic smile.

"If this were a chess game, I think I'd resign," Gehlman muttered.

"Well, here you always have the option of hauling down your flag and giving up."

Gehlman looked up with an expression of calm amusement. "Very droll, Commander. . . . What time is it, in fact?"

"A little after six," Maltbie answered, consulting his watch. "We've been at it for ten hours."

"Really! Well, may we adjourn . . . or are you determined to annihilate me today?"

"Not at all. In fact, I rather like the idea of your having the entire night to contemplate your doom."

"Don't be too cocksure just yet, Harry. You've still got a deployment problem in front of you."

"Too true," Maltbie acknowledged, returning his gaze to the board and then shifting it to the sequential deployment diagrams that had been drawn on one of the blackboards near the far end of the table. The Blue—or British—dreadnoughts were steaming southeast at 21 knots in six columns abreast. In order to fight, they had to deploy from this compact cruising formation into a single line of battle, as the Red—or German—dreadnoughts had already done. Given the fact that the two fleets were converging at nearly fifty miles per hour and would be in range of each other within fifteen minutes if they remained on their present courses, deployment strategy would be critical to the outcome of the battle—especially since a deploy-

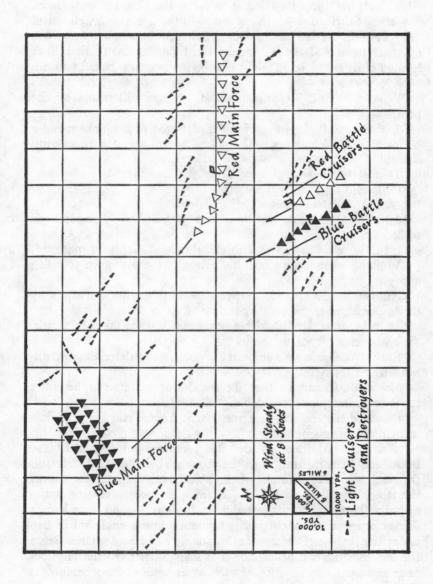

Red Main Force

Red Battle Cruisers

Blue Battle Cruisers

Blue Main Force

Wind Steady at 8 Knots

N

6 MILES
14,000 YDS.
8 MILES
10,000 YDS.
10,000 YDS.

Light Cruisers and Destroyers

ment of twenty-four dreadnoughts would in itself take more than fifteen minutes to complete!

The difficulty was not that Maltbie had too many options to consider, because in fact he had only two: he could deploy left or he could deploy right. The factors he had to weigh in making his decision, however, were manifold, and in many instances of ambivalent weight. If he deployed to the right, for example, the Germans, by altering course toward the south, might be able to cross his T. He would also run the risk of a torpedo attack by the German destroyers, and almost certainly be at a disadvantage with regard to shooting as well, because he would be silhouetted by the sun behind him while the stipulated west wind sent his funnel and salvo smoke toward the enemy like a screen. On the other hand, if the Germans were prevented from turning south by Maltbie's battle cruisers, or were simply so intent on crossing his battle cruisers' T that they skimped on their efforts to detect the possible presence of his main force, then he could cross *their* T with a starboard-wing deployment, and also join up with his battle cruisers and drive the Germans northward, away from their base. Deployment to the left on the port wing was far safer to be sure, but it gave the Germans a chance to turn and head for home with what amounted to a victory, given the already accomplished destruction of the *Lion* and the *New Zealand*.

Maltbie and Gehlman had been fighting battles like this for almost a month now. Day in, day out, six days out of every seven, they had played out scenarios of every conceivable description, using the knowledge gained from their experience as observers with the belligerent fleets. That was the assignment the navy's General Board, in consultation with Assistant Secretary Roosevelt and Colonel House, had given them at the end of July after a solid week of debriefings devoted to the amplification of their previously submitted reports. The Board had also presented them with a sheaf of supplementary technical questions to which they were to return written replies at the conclusion of their war-gaming.

Through its venerable president, Admiral Dewey, the Board in its final session before sending them off to Newport had admonished them to regard their assigned duties as subjects of the strictest confidentiality. As best Maltbie and Gehlman could determine, there was some embarrassment in official circles over the fact that America had placed observers with both belligerent fleets without informing

Deployment from column to line on the Starboard wing—maintaining heading Enemy to Port.

Deployment from column to line on the Port wing—maintaining heading Enemy to Port.

the leaders of either country involved that links had been forged with the naval forces of the other. (Indeed, Maltbie had been a little shocked himself to discover that one of his own colleagues had seen service with the Germans.)

So they had come to this room on the second floor of what had been, until thirty years ago, the Newport poorhouse on Coasters Harbor Island. The current tenant, the War College, was only slightly less impoverished than the building's former inmates, being the long cherished brainchild of its founder and first president, Commodore Luce, but the stingily funded stepchild of its reluctant parent, the U. S. Navy. It bore the indelible intellectual imprint of its late second President, Captain Alfred Thayer Mahan, the near Promethean sailor-historian whom Gehlman liked to refer to—with only token irreverence—as "the Macaulay of the seas." As befitted an institution dedicated to the study of maritime warfare, it faced an ocean inlet, Narragansett Bay, and the war-game room looked westward across that body of water toward the gentle hills of Conanicut Island. In the center of the room, with its surface only two feet off the floor (so that College-designated "admirals" could step up and stroll about among their dreadnoughts) was the tactical table, the focal point of Maltbie's and Gehlman's labors. Ranged around three sides of the table were movable blackboards on which students could list for ready reference the stipulated conditions under which a given battle would be fought, or draw tactical diagrams to aid themselves in visualizing complicated maneuvers. The blackboards also served to keep track of the incidents of an engagement: which ships had been damaged, which turrets had been put out of action, which wireless aerials had been shot away, which crews had been decimated, etc. On the fourth side of the table there was a podium, about three feet high and equipped with a pair of lecterns. Here instructors would stand when the College was in session, observing silently for the most part, but occasionally giving voice to some dour observation such as: "If Blue's admiral does that, gentlemen, he had better resign himself to fighting the remainder of this battle under water."

Maltbie and Gehlman, as it happened, were fully qualified to fight their battles without tutorial supervision. Gehlman had had a year as a student at the College during which he had logged his full measure of "table time," and Maltbie had had the benefit of two years' service on the staff of Captain Sims, who was as inveterate a war-gamer as any officer ashore or afloat. In fact, during Maltbie's tour of duty with the Atlantic Flotilla, Sims had sometimes conducted full-dress simulations on the deck of the *Birmingham*'s wardroom as often as twice a week.

As they were both already competent to wage tabletop battles, it remained for them only to articulate their basic strategies and stipulate the various scenarios in which those strategies could be tested. Then they could commence hostilities.

The strategies were easy; just about any naval officer in the world could have provided them. The key factor in their formulation was that Britain, with the nominal support of France, Italy, Russia, and Japan, indisputably controlled the seas. Offensively this enabled her to place steadily mounting pressure on the economies and food resources of the Central Powers. Defensively it was nothing less than the sine qua non for her survival. As an island, she could neither feed herself nor keep her factories producing without massive maritime imports. Control of the seas depended on the universally acknowledged supremacy of the British Fleet. Without that supremacy, it would be not only German submarines but German battleships seeking prey in the North Atlantic, and not Germany but Britain being strangled by blockade. Thus British naval strategy began with one overriding principle: the Fleet must stay supreme. And the chief corollary was equally unequivocal: *Caution!* Maltbie had heard it first from Morrison Waite and several more times from others of higher station: "Admiral Jellicoe is the only man on either side who can lose the war in an afternoon." One field of mines, one squadron of submarines (Maltbie remembered how the battle cruisers had recoiled at the sight of just a single periscope at Dogger Bank) could eliminate at a stroke the numerical superiority Jellicoe's dreadnoughts enjoyed over the Germans. And from that moment on, the fate of the Allies would hang in the balance. Officers of the Royal Navy might declare to a man that they could contemplate a ship-for-ship engagement against the High Seas Fleet with perfect confidence as to the result. But privately they would be constrained to admit that any battle between roughly equivalent forces was at bottom a lottery, and that even under the best of circumstances one could never guarantee victory, but only deserve it.

So strategy boiled down to this: for the British, keep the fleet concentrated, using the battle cruisers to try to lure the Germans far enough out of their harbors so that they can be intercepted and forced to fight. For the Germans, stay close enough to home to keep from being forced to battle, but also try to locate and destroy detached British squadrons—such as the battle cruisers—thereby whittling away the Royal Navy's superiority in numbers.

The possible scenarios for a fleet action between the British and German navies were, in theory, innumerable. In practice, though, it was possible to narrow down the variables considerably. The British, for example, would always refuse battle at night, and the Germans would always try to avoid a head-on test of strength.

A most critical variable was weather, which could almost always be counted upon to be bad in the North Sea, but bad in a multitude of different ways. Other variables of comparable importance were the number of daylight hours available to the British when contact was made, and the distance of the Germans at that time from the swept channels leading to their ports of refuge. By mixing various ingredients of weather, time, and distance, Gehlman and Maltbie had come up with several dozen battle scenarios, which they had then played out on the tactical table.

The play had by no means been frivolous. For in their simulations they stood in the shoes of the rival admirals; they tried to act as Jellicoe and von Pohl would act in the stipulated circumstances, and were obliged by the rules to live with the consequences of their decisions for as long as a game was in progress. Although the entire surface of the tactical table was clearly visible to both of them, for example, they were limited in their decision making to the knowledge possessed by the admirals they represented. Thus Gehlman as Gehlman could see that the Blue Fleet was menacing the Red Fleet from the northwest, but Gehlman as von Pohl had no idea that the Blue Fleet was anywhere in the vicinity, and he would continue in ignorance until his flagship or one of his destroyer screens got near enough on the table to spot it, given the light and the weather conditions stipulated.

Every decision Maltbie and Gehlman made while commanding their "fleets" had to be articulated, justified by reference to their experience with the fleet in question, agreed on as plausible by both of them, and as a last step meticulously logged. More often than not they would find their battles developing in unexpected ways, and they might spend hours mulling over a crucial signal—a signal, they were aware, that an admiral in the thick of an action would frequently have to make in the space of two or three minutes. The absence of a time limit on decision making was one of two major areas in which war-gaming diverged from reality. The other was the absence of real consequences if the decisions made were wrong.

The results were nevertheless of significant value. The rigorous internal logic of the war games coupled with Maltbie's and Gehlman's unique fitness to play them produced after several weeks a very decided trend. Thanks to their apparent ability to predict German Fleet movements—and, of course, to their numerical superiority as well—the British, when weather, light, and distance from port permitted, almost always inflicted catastrophic damage on the Kaiser's ships whenever a full-scale action was fought. While it was true that the British didn't yet know how vulnerable their turrets were to the kind of cordite flash that had nearly destroyed the *Seydlitz* at Dogger Bank, the ships they lost to magazine explosions were not nearly numerous enough to alter the results of any of the simulated battles.

The conclusion Maltbie and Gehlman were now moving toward with ever increasing certainty was that if the German Fleet ventured too far out from its harbors, there was a very good chance of its being destroyed. The gradual emergence of this conclusion from the vast array of technical calculations that went into the play-out of the various scenarios was an exciting and gratifying result. And although the work they did was intellectually stringent, mathematically exacting, and often time consuming to an almost intolerable degree, it was also, for two avid seamen assigned to play admiral with the two greatest fleets in the world, truly and undeniably fun.

It was such fun, in fact, that Gehlman was at times almost suspicious of its necessity. Colonel House, after all, had jumped him several notches on the seniority list to the rank of captain simply in order to dissuade him from leaving the service. Mightn't he also be capable of presenting him with this intriguing temporary assignment in order to further sweeten the brew? But no; quite apart from being alert to the excesses of his own suspicious nature, Gehlman was also fully convinced of the importance of what he and Maltbie were doing. The intelligence information they were compiling was of well-nigh incalculable value, not simply to their navy, but to the makers of America's foreign policy as well. That Britain was almost certainly going to retain her dominion of the seas throughout the war, after all, was a fact that would be of consuming interest to every highly placed diplomat in the world.

After carefully double-locking the door of the war-game room, Maltbie and Gehlman strolled downstairs. They said good night to the sulky yeoman who had been assigned as the building's charge-of-quarters for the weekend, and went down the front steps, narrowing their eyes against the orange brilliance of the descending sun. This was a favorite time of day for both of them: the gentle interlude toward the end of a summer afternoon when the wind died down and all creation seemed to bask contentedly in the waning radiance spilling from out of the sky. They walked southward along the shore, then east across the causeway connecting Coasters Harbor Island to Newport proper. As they walked they chatted idly, the slightly harsh and commanding quality of Gehlman's voice nicely complemented by the easiness and subtle deference of Maltbie's manner. They turned south again on Farewell Street and walked to the Broadway intersection, where they turned left. Some thirty yards along, side by side, were two frame colonial houses, one gray and one white, the residences of two officers on the College faculty who were away for the summer. The houses faced south, and from their porches one could see the roof of the nearby Touro Synagogue, the first and oldest Jewish house of worship in the new world. On the porch of the nearer—gray—house sat a robust young blond woman in a maid's uniform, diligently sewing; a few feet away from her, on the porch steps, a beautiful ten-year-old girl with shining black hair and odd-looking black-framed spectacles sat bent over an open book. On the farther porch there was a table heaped high with books and papers, and seated at it, her brandy-colored hair piled richly above her neck and ears, was a young woman with a knowing, mordant, and just the least bit rakish smile on her face.

Melina watched Maltbie and Gehlman strolling up the street and reflected yet again on how sinfully attractive she found the Jewish captain—apart from his personality. He was a sour man, she thought, and she had never had much use for sour men. But he *was* beautiful, and his mind had a nice astringent bite to it, whenever he let his guard down sufficiently to indulge his talent for irony. She shifted her gaze to Maltbie, walking along on the captain's left, and felt a great surge of protective love for him. How gentle and innocent he seemed beside the other man's grating good looks—and how endearingly funny too, with his big flaring ears and tiny pug nose. He saw her and waved, and she waved back, feeling the sudden galvanic flexion in the muscles of her underbelly that often occurred when he was nearby. She had thoughts of his body, the clean slenderness of it between her thighs, its stamina, its slavelike dedication, and she wondered yet again how she had ever managed to stay chaste for so many years and at the same time stay sane (though perhaps abstinent rather than chaste was the proper word). She could not conceive of ever again having to do without sexual intercourse in her life, but it continually mystified her that a need that had gone unsatisfied for so long could become so utterly compelling when at last it was met.

Ever since her early teens, of course, she had more than half suspected that she was what was often referred to as "sensually inclined"; and it was perhaps only because she had been raised amidst the echoes of an unabashedly erotic culture that this suspicion had never been repressed. It wasn't just the statues of priapic demons she had seen in her youth, nor the suggestive fragments of Orphic ritual she had studied as the sole pupil in her parents' "school" that had spared her the Victorian fixation on spotlessly clean-minded virginity. It was also the light and the smells and the landscapes she'd grown up with: the wind in the dwarf pines along the Argolid coast that had sometimes seemed to carry with it the wild moanings of the Bacchantes; the hot *meltemi*, blowing through the olive groves near Delphi, that had pushed her dress against her pubic mound like a shamelessly prurient caress; the ruins of Knossos on Crete, bedecked in wild flowers, resounding with the call of the cicadas, and evocative of bare-breasted Minoan priestesses with writhing snakes in their outstretched hands, of bull leapers and lurking minotaurs and doomed children bursting to know each other's bodies before the sacrificial dance.

Melina watched as Alis hopped off the porch steps of the house next door and ran to Gehlman with a little whoop of excitement. She had to acknowledge that the child's devotion to Gehlman was clearly a mark in his favor, just as Maltbie's, she supposed half cynically, was clearly a mark in hers. It was odd, she mused, the rough parallelism between the two pairs of people: herself and Gehlman in the role of adoring parents, Alis and Maltbie in the role of adoring children—with an exception noted so that she and Harry could share the same bed, of course.

From her chair on the porch Melina returned Gehlman's rather formal-sounding "Good evening" with a small nod and an amused smile. Closing the notebook that held the draft of her monograph on her work in the Southwest, she watched as Alis flirted innocently—

and outrageously—with Maltbie, even while clinging to her guardian's neck. How wonderfully predatory the human female, she thought, practicing lisps and smiles at the age of ten, even before knowing to what end.

Alis let Maltbie depart after a few moments, and Melina's eyes followed him as he walked the few paces to their front steps, came up beside her on the porch, and kissed her cheek. "Hello, darling," he said.

"You're early this evening, Harry. I hope you've not grown slothful."

She watched him beam at her by way of response. Really! She thought, it was like taking candy from a baby with him—or rather, giving candy to one. She was habituated to these pert little remarks, these feeble little jests, that even Zuleika Dobson would have found cloying after a while, but he always thought her deliciously witty for them. And the worst of it, she admitted to herself, was that she was going to go on being intolerably precious even though she disdained herself for doing so, and all for the sad and tawdry reason that she doted on his doting.

She leaned over and cupped her hand along his cheek. "You're a goose," she said, alerted by her motions to a slight dampness between her legs. (My God! she thought. Just from watching two men walk down a *street!?*)

"A slothful goose?" he responded, turning his head to kiss the hollow of her palm.

The dampness abruptly increased with her sense of the pressure of his lips. "A delicious goose," she whispered hoarsely. "Harry . . ."

"Yes?"

"There's something I want to discuss with you—upstairs."

She saw an expression of concern come over his features, then a sort of boyish hope. "Of course, darling. Right now?"

"This instant," she answered with mock severity, her heart starting to beat so percussively that she could hardly breathe.

She lay on her back, watching the evening light filter through the softly stirring white lace curtains. He lay next to her on his side, his arm across her stomach and his mouth against her collarbone.

God! she thought; how lovely it was to be worshiped and thought delectable—even if one's deification, and one's delectability also, were predicated on a certain naiveté on the part of one's disciple.

Ah, ego. Such an unfeminine trait, she'd always thought, even as she'd cultivated it like an orchid. And yet, she hastened to reassure herself, she was not unfeminine. Men desired her. She, God knew, desired them.

She reflected that all her feminist principles had foundered on that particular rock. Because men, being desirable, were therefore interesting as well, while women for the most part were a terrible bore. If they were "enlightened," as the style had it, they were also strident and lacking in humor. If they were "accomplished," they tended to fritter away their talents on high society's ceaseless shivaree. And if neither enlightenment nor accomplishment had crossed their minds, they were endlessly petty and trivial—or else manipulative and devious. And, invariably, parasitic too, no matter how they read their lines.

Not that men, apart from their sexual fascination, were made a great deal better: all the fragile male egos she'd encountered, posturing and capering their way across the world like truculent Barbary apes. At least women didn't feel the need to foment wars. At least women were willing, for the most part, to wallow in the squalid banality of domestic life. At least the slaughter they perpetrated was only at their loved ones' expense. But with men it was conquer or die, or rather conquer *and* die, given the modern refinements of military science. And all for the sake of those fragile egos.

She thought of Eckersley: where was that ego now? Sulking like a wounded bear in some cave.

The *fool!*

And yet hadn't she, in spite of herself, once fed his madness? That sultry September night on the Backs, not quite a year ago. That terrible quarrel when, in an altogether unfeminine manner, she'd called him a selfish ass, and worse, only to then give in to that supremely selfish, supremely asinine, supremely *feminine* impulse of love, thereby confirming in an instant all his most fallacious assumptions about honor and patriotism—and her preparedness to forgive them.

Melina ran her fingers along the smooth coolness of Maltbie's arm. It was a terrible thing she'd done, opening her thighs to Eckersley that night. And not just terrible, but vicious. For she'd known— she *must* have known—what he would infer from her submission (if one could call it that). And she must also have known that his inference would be totally wrong. For, surely, her only thought had been: all right, you . . . you *patriot!* . . . if I'm going to lose you, if you're

bent on throwing away our future together in order to protect our little king from the feckless tantrums of his German cousin, then at
least I'm going to know you once before you go.

Surely it had only been that; not any frantic emotional last-ditch
defense against his leaving, not any bribe to keep him with her, not
any overpowering need to hold him to her and feel just for the space
of a minute that he was safe in her protection from any harm the
world could work.

No, no . . . most surely not—not remotely such feelings as those.

Maltbie stirred a little, moved his head, and lightly kissed her
breast. She put her arm around his shoulders and hugged him tight
against her.

And it had all conspired to bring about that terrible scene in Cambridge ten weeks ago, after Harry had gone back up to Rosyth. It was
bad enough to have seen Eckersley at all in his mutilated condition,
but to have seen that the mutilation was internal as well, to have
listened to the self-pity and the reproaches, and at last to the ignominious begging—that had been very like torture. Melina wondered
—and her interest was far from academic—what she would have
done if Eckersley had been stoical and strong. Would she be in bed
in Cambridge this evening, next to a man with a stump for a leg?

Ah men, ah women—a plague on both our houses. What mattered
was this adoring man beside her now. He was hers forever—and in
fifty years they would both be dead. So to perdition with anxiety,
guilt, and doubt for just one evening. She was alive, Harry was alive,
and the summer air was cool and sweet to breathe. What more could
any erring mortal dare to want?

They came downstairs at seven thirty and went next door to eat,
as they did most evenings of the week. Gehlman had a cook, after all
(a superb one, in fact), and Alis needed Harry around in order to
practice her flirting. Then too, the alternatives, in the form of the as-
sorted Vanderbilts, Berwinds, and Belmonts down on Bellevue Avenue, were far too dreary to cope with more than one or two times in
a month. Melina under the best of circumstances had rarely been
able to regard humanity at its leisure as a particularly edifying spectacle, but she very much suspected that these hyperaffluent specimens
of American grandeur would not yield edification even if they were
hard at work. It irritated her that their invitations never went to
Gehlman, that a youthful relative of the British ambassador should

be preferred to a seasoned captain in the United States Navy simply on the basis of creed. England might have more than its share of national warts, she knew, but mindless anti-Semitism wasn't one of them. Thus it was not just the stupidity but also the unfamiliarity of the phenomenon that caused her to find it offensive.

Erna Gehlman was present at dinner, Friday being one of the two days each week that she traveled the seventy miles from Menauhant to see Alis. The main course was fresh lobster served with a sauce made of butter and garlic, so exquisitely delicious that Melina—who was always ravenous after making love—barely listened to the conversation around the table. As it had for five nights running, the talk centered on the sensational revelations the *World* had been printing each day about the activities of the German commercial attaché, Dr. Albert. From the porch came the pleasantly mournful sound of the harmonica being played by one of Captain Gehlman's Pinkerton men, and Melina let her mind drift with the music. Then Erna's voice, directed at Gehlman, jarred her out of her reveries: "Your father thinks the *Arabic* sinking is going to push us over the brink."

"The *Arabic*?" Melina said sharply. "You mean the liner?"

Erna shrank back a little in her chair and nervously touched a hand to the neckline of her dress. Looking around the silenced table, Melina realized that she ought to have moderated the intensity in her voice. They would all—except Harry, possibly—be thinking that she was "sensitive" about torpedoed ocean liners, when her concern, in fact, was far more prosaic. "I'm sorry, Mrs. Gehlman," she said. "I didn't mean to sound so . . . convulsive."

"Oh, don't apologize, my dear. I can imagine how you must feel about it."

"Well, this is the first I've heard of it, actually. When did it happen?"

"Yesterday, dearest," Maltbie intervened. "I ought to have mentioned it, but I didn't see that there was any point in—"

"I know, darling; I don't blame you. . . . Were many passengers lost?"

"They think perhaps fifty," Gehlman said.

"Americans?"

"Well, there were Americans aboard, of course, but as of now only two are . . . unaccounted for."

Melina turned swiftly back to Erna. "And your husband believes that the United States will now go to war?"

"Well, his opinion was that unless Germany very quickly disavows the attack, the United States will be forced to take drastic steps."

Concentrating on the maintenance of a composed demeanor, Melina turned to Gehlman and asked, "And is it likely that a disavowal will be forthcoming, do you think?"

Gehlman shifted slightly in his chair. "I wouldn't say it was likely, Melina. But I wouldn't say that it was out of the question either."

More pabulum for the ladies, Melina thought, cursing herself yet one more time for her folly in having rejected a martial fiancé only to then accept a naval husband, deluding herself as she did so that neutrality was an immutable—or rather, unsinkable—condition.

It was arranged, largely by Alis's calculation, that the two most indulgent adults at the table should walk her down to the Casino for ice cream. She'd been having a running battle—a very genteel running battle—with Gehlman for some weeks over the frequency and immensity of her craving for this particular treat, his position being that too much ice cream would ruin her teeth and make her fat, and her position—only slightly more *a priori*—being that it would not. As for Melina, Alis had perceived very early on in their acquaintanceship that in this lady she was faced with a person who had once been a beautiful little girl herself, and therefore knew and was proof against almost all of the tricks of the trade. Maltbie, however, was completely at Alis's mercy, and Erna, as a grandparent, was ever prone to indulge her.

So Gehlman and Melina took chairs on the porch while Alis and her retinue, shepherded by a Pinkerton, walked into town. Leaning back and puffing on his cigar, Gehlman watched them disappear down the block.

"I think your young lady fancies my husband," Melina said after a while.

"I don't blame her," Gehlman responded. "He's a fine fellow."

Melina smiled. "Yes," she said. "He is."

With two cadenced beats of his index finger, Gehlman tapped the ash off the end of his cigar. "You shouldn't fret too much about this *Arabic* business, you know," he said after some deliberation. "Even if we do come in, it's the army, such as it is, that'll fight the war."

"It's kind of you to say that," Melina replied, thinking that it *was* kind of him, even though he lied.

"I'm not just saying it, Melina. It's the literal fact. If the Germans won't fight the British Fleet by itself, they're certainly not going to take on us and the British together."

"No, I suppose not," Melina said. "But war is always ingenious in devising fresh new occasions for death. It's still safer to be at peace."

"True enough," Gehlman admitted. "But I don't see how it can affect Harry. I mean, as an observer he's already in the war as much as he can ever be. He's been in battle, and the ship he was on took a number of hits. So how much more danger could he be in even if the United States does decide to fight?"

"I suppose you're right, Ben—and God knows I don't much like the idea of Harry sailing around with the Royal Navy. I went a little mad, you know, when I heard about Dogger Bank out in New Mexico. I was really no good for anything for *weeks*, until I got a letter from him. But it's been seven months since that battle, and as you say, the Germans have shown no inclination to chance another fight. So I've learned to live with the situation, if not exactly like it. But if America comes into the war, that will change everything. Harry will want his own ship, won't he? And sooner or later he'll get one. And even if he doesn't, with your fleet added to ours, and all the noise in England about the navy not *doing* anything to help win the war, I'm certain that new life-endangering ways of expending our surplus sea power will be found."

"Aren't you overextrapolating just a bit?"

"Do you think so? I don't know. All I know is that things are fairly stable right now—stable and safe. And I want them to stay that way. I don't want anybody rocking the boat, if you'll excuse the nauticalism."

Gehlman laughed softly. "You know," he said, "I probably shouldn't mention this, but speaking of rocking boats, I'm reasonably sure that Alis and I saw you boarding the *Lusitania.*"

"No! Really? You mean back in May?"

"Yes."

"How very strange. Where was I? What was I wearing?"

"You were going up the gangplank, and I think you had on a dark blue cape of some sort."

"Yes. That's right! I *was* wearing my blue cape."

"That clinches it then. I remember you turned around near the top of the gangplank and said something to someone behind you. I remember thinking that you looked very . . . plucky."

"Plucky? Well, how farsighted of me."

Gehlman laughed again, and in the brief ensuing silence Melina became aware of a feeling of slight apprehension hovering on the periphery of her consciousness. "How did you happen to be at the dock?" she asked.

"Because of Alis. I used to take her down to West Street every week or so, to look at the ships."

"Ah, I see," Melina responded, wondering if Gehlman realized how much he was admitting, and feeling more than a little bit flattered in spite of herself. She looked at him closely. No, he hadn't knowingly been making an overture. Still, it was titillating to learn that she had made such an impression on him, seen only once from afar. And though she warned herself that she would have to step carefully henceforth where he was concerned, she couldn't quite shake off a new perception of him as being somehow . . . endearing.

For the present, however, she guessed that she had better change the subject. "Ben, may I ask you a somewhat personal question?"

He quickly turned his head to look at her and said in a halfway guarded tone, "Of course. What is it?"

"Well, as we're living just a few yards from that beautiful old synagogue across the way, I'm curious as to why you never go there."

Gehlman was silent for some moments, seeming either irritated or ill at ease, if not both. But his voice was casual when he said finally, "I suppose, Melina, for many of the same reasons that you and Harry haven't gone to Trinity Church."

Melina felt an unaccustomed surge of embarrassment. "I'm sorry, Ben. It was rude of me to pry."

For a long time he said nothing. Then, breaking the silence, "It's not anything momentous, Melina. I'm just not much of a believer."

"I see."

"Are you?"

"In Judaism?" she asked in a contrite but playful tone.

He didn't smile. "In anything."

Her first impulse was to go on being flippant, but she suppressed it. "I believe in certain people—Harry, for example."

"He's fortunate."

"Don't be too sure."

"What else do you believe in?"

She thought for a while, then said in all honesty, "Precious little."

"You're a brave woman to admit it."

Melina turned to look at him, and for a very brief instant he looked back. "I don't much mind not believing in anything," she said, wondering why she had broached this of all subjects when she knew—or rather, and yet again, *must* have known—that it would propel their acquaintanceship in the direction of greater intimacy.

"I mind sometimes," he said broodingly. But then he got to his feet and added in a lighter tone, "And then other times I don't mind at all."

He stretched and yawned extravagantly, then turned to her with a smile. "Perhaps tomorrow night we can discuss politics," he said.

And though Melina laughed with him when he said it, she was miffed that it hadn't been she who had brought their talk back to the level of the innocuous.

1915, 2D SEPTEMBER—BERLIN

Von Müller wearily contemplated the penciled annotations his sovereign had applied to President Wilson's latest note. Opposite "The rights of neutrals in time of war are based upon principle, not upon expediency . . ." the Kaiser had written, *Immeasurably impertinent!*

". . . and the principles are immutable."

You don't say so!

". . . It is the duty and obligation of belligerents to find a way to adapt new circumstances to them. . . ."

There you are!

". . . The government of the United States feels obliged to insist upon freedom of the seas. . . ."

Commands!

". . . The government of the United States cannot believe that the Imperial German Government will any longer refrain from disavowing the sinking of ocean liners. . . ."

Unheard of!

". . . Friendship prompts the government of the United States to say to the Imperial German Government that repetitions by the commanders of German naval vessels of acts in contravention of neutral rights must be regarded by the government of the United

States, when they affect American citizens, as deliberately un-friendly . . ."

i.e., War!

At the end of the text, the Kaiser had scribbled what he no doubt intended to be a scathingly definitive critique: *In tone and bearing this is about the most impudent note I have ever read! It ends with a direct threat! W.*

The admiral sighed a little and looked up into Wilhelm's eyes.

"Well, Müller, what do you think?"

The admiral knew from long experience that the question did not pertain to the text of the note, but to the gloss. "It grieves me," he said, sidestepping, "that you should be subjected to such arrant prov-ocation."

"Ha! Wilson is just one out of the dozens of . . . *provocations* I have to contend with."

"I know, your Highness," von Müller responded, seizing the op-portunity to get right to the point. "The navy's action in sinking the *Arabic* has produced a most serious situation for you to rectify."

The admiral could see that he had been successful in jostling Wilhelm off balance by shifting the onus from President Wilson's "impudence" to the Imperial Navy's disobedience. He knew that Wilhelm's foremost concern was to have someone to blame for every problem afflicting him, and while Wilson's note was the immediate cause of his present irritation, the underlying cause was the navy's failure to abide by the rules. Von Müller's statement, therefore, was simply intended to remind the Emperor that chastising a subordi-nate admiral was a far less arduous task than attempting to exact sat-isfaction from a coequal head of state.

"Yes!" said Wilhelm, taking immediate aim on the easier target. "It amounts to gross insubordination, after I specifically forbade them to make attacks on ocean liners."

"*Large* ocean liners, your Highness," von Müller interjected, rais-ing one of the key points the Imperial Chancellor had asked him to discuss. "Admiral Bachmann alleges that as the *Arabic* had only one funnel, it was reasonable for the U-boat commander to assume that she was fair game. Admiral Bachmann points out that the *Arabic*, having been half again as large as any other one-funneled ship on the North Atlantic route, was the *only* single-funneled ship that fell within the large-ocean-liner category specified in your Highness's order, and that—"

"And that now that she's been sunk, the same mistake can never be repeated, so all is well!"

Von Müller made a show of suppressed amusement calculated to indicate that, while laughter in the face of the Imperial wrath would be indecorous, it was still by no means easy to maintain one's gravity in the face of the Imperial wit.

"This is no laughing matter, Müller," Wilhelm said, obviously flattered. "It smacks of a conspiracy to circumvent my authority."

Once the Emperor got started down the slope of taking umbrage, it required only the gentlest of nudges to keep him rolling. So von Müller merely said, "Yes, particularly when I reflect on how patient you've been with Bachmann up to now."

"Well, I'm through being patient with him, Müller. It's time that he was sacked!"

"In his defense, your Highness," von Müller said, wishing to remind Wilhelm that there were other boils than Bachmann to be lanced, "he was under considerable pressure from Grand Admiral Tirpitz."

"Then it's time Tirpitz was sacked too. No doubt we have one of his innumerable offers of resignation somewhere in our files."

"Of course, your Highness," von Müller said, making a series of rapid calculations. The dismissal of von Tirpitz was far too risky a step to be considered. The man was "Father of the German Navy," after all, and had an enormous public following. Vexatious as he was inside the fold, he would be an intolerable irritant outside it. "I only wonder"—von Müller frowned—"where we should find someone of comparable stature to replace him."

Wilhelm responded with gratifying promptness to this light touch of the brakes. "That *would* be difficult, wouldn't it. Still, his behavior demands some sort of censure."

"Unquestionably. Has your Highness considered revoking his privilege of direct access to the throne?"

"I *had* thought of that," Wilhelm said weightily. "And on reflection I think it would carry more of a sting than would asking for his resignation."

"It would certainly be a very graphic demonstration of your Highness's displeasure."

"Yes, yes it would. But don't try to get round me, Müller; Bachmann has still got to go."

"I understand, your Highness."

"Who do you think should replace him?"

"Perhaps Admiral von Holtzendorff, your Highness. He's a cooperative and intelligent officer, as you know, and would certainly be most scrupulous about deferring to your authority."

"Well then, Holtzendorff, by all means."

"Of course, removing Bachmann does not entirely solve the problem of the *Arabic*," von Müller said in a tentative tone of voice.

Wilhelm glared at him. "Well, it's been sunk, Müller. Do you expect me to raise it from the deep?"

Von Müller reprimanded himself for not having disposed of the *large*-ocean-liner issue earlier on, knowing as he did that once Wilhelm had taken action on a matter, he liked to assume that that matter was closed. "My thought, your Highness, was that the phrase 'large ocean liners' suffers from a degree of ambiguity, and that in order to avoid a repetition of an incident like the one involving the *Arabic* it would perhaps be advisable to forbid attacks on *any* passenger ships whatsoever, without distinction as to size or registry."

Von Müller held his breath while Wilhelm brooded. "Agreed!" the Emperor said at last, adding curtly, "Anything else?"

"Nothing at present, your Highness," von Müller said, exhaling in gratified relief.

He first notified the Chancellor, Bethmann-Hollweg, and then Treutler of the Foreign Office. Admiral von Holtzendorff, Bachmann's soon-to-be successor at the Admiralty, was told last, and von Müller informed him at the same time that henceforth *all* passenger ships were to be immune from submarine attack. Holtzendorff readily accepted the new restriction, and added, as von Müller had expected he would, that under the circumstances there would be little point in maintaining U-boat patrols in the Channel or athwart the western approaches. Von Müller quickly agreed that, of course, under the circumstances it made much more sense to recall the U-boats secretly and integrate them into the operations of the fleet.

The only question still worrying him after von Holtzendorff left the room was whether any more liners would be sunk before the recall could become effective.

1915, 7TH SEPTEMBER—NEW YORK CITY

Seated in the study of his East Fifty-third Street apartment, Colonel House looked from Gehlman to Maltbie and back again. He still found it rather remarkable that what had begun as a maverick flotilla commander's impertinent initiative back in November should have become a matter of such momentous potential significance to the United States today. Assistant Secretaries Roosevelt and Corey had reported to him that the corridors at Navy and State were buzzing like sawmills. The buzzing had become so loud, in fact, that Admiral Dewey had felt obliged to lock up the half dozen copies of what was now being referred to as the North Sea Analysis in his personal safe, so that the merely curious and the chronically officious could be kept from the sensitive information best left to those few key bureau chiefs with a bona fide need to know. One unfortunate by-product of a windfall such as this one, House reflected, was that it attracted unwelcome attention.

"My praise is superfluous," the Colonel said, "but I'd like to add it to that which you've already received."

Maltbie and Gehlman thanked him.

"The work you've done, not only at the War College, but overseas with the two belligerent fleets, has been of tremendous value. And I'm told that the way you've done the work has rendered it more valuable still. So on my own and the President's behalf, I'd like to thank you for the contributions you've made, and to assure you, in the unlikely event you are not already aware of it, that your efforts are deeply appreciated."

Maltbie nodded and smiled shyly. The corners of Gehlman's mouth curled upwards perhaps a millimeter.

"I can tell you now that at about the time you commenced work at the College, the General Board under Admiral Dewey submitted to the President proposed naval appropriations for 1917 which comprehend the construction of fully four battleships, four battle cruisers, thirty-odd submarines, twenty-five or thirty destroyers, and several dozen auxiliary ships as well."

Both Gehlman and Maltbie registered amazement.

"The Board also proposed an increase in naval manpower of eleven thousand men and an increase in the class size at Annapolis from three hundred to four hundred twenty-five."

With some small satisfaction House noted that even Gehlman was beginning to look like a farm boy getting his first glimpse of the big city.

"Finally, the Board recommended that the 1917 program be repeated on an enlarged scale from 1918 through 1925, the final objective being the construction of forty-eight new dreadnoughts with all the requisite flotillas and auxiliaries at an estimated final cost of one and one half billion dollars."

Maltbie let out a long, low whistle while Gehlman's eyes narrowed incredulously.

"I probably don't have to tell you that this program, if agreed to by Congress, will raise the United States to the first rank among naval powers. And even allowing for congressional parsimony, I don't think there can be any doubt that by the year 1925 this country will have the largest and most powerful navy in the world."

The Colonel sat silent for a moment to let all he'd just said sink in.

"I tell you this now, in strict confidence," he resumed finally, "because it has a direct bearing on the nature of your next assignment."

Maltbie leaned forward with an expression of eager interest. Gehlman sat motionless in an attitude of guarded mistrust.

"I assume you've seen the newspaper accounts of Saturday's sinking of the Leyland Line's *Hesperian*, and I will confess to you that this latest submarine atrocity seems to signal the final failure of our efforts to come to any sort of understanding with the German government. As far as we know, the liner was attacked without warning and without provocation, and in the absence of some kind of prompt explanation or disavowal—which past experience suggests will not be forthcoming—there seems to be a very good chance that this country will be at war within the space of a very few weeks."

Maltbie's face took on a somber expression; Gehlman's remained impassive.

"None of this is for public consumption, of course," the Colonel continued. "But it is something I felt you needed to know in light of the work I'm going to ask you to undertake."

A frown of suspicion appeared on Gehlman's brow.

"Given the likely imminent rupture in German-American relations, I believe I can prevail upon Sir Edward Grey and Mr. Arthur Balfour to permit *both* of you to serve as observers with the British Fleet."

Gehlman's frown gave way to an expression of undisguised irritation.

"I'm aware, of course, Captain Gehlman, of your deep reluctance to accept sea duty in the face of your—uh—domestic responsibilities. But consider the situation: the United States is approaching the brink of war, and even if we manage to remain neutral for the short term, the long-term prospects remain extremely ominous. It seems all too probable that our navy will be fighting alongside Britain's before too much longer, in which case quick success in coordinating the operations of the two fleets will be in good part dependent on how much knowledge of the Royal Navy's operations you've both acquired. Whether we enter the war or not, however, if the Allies win, our navy and England's are going to be in direct worldwide competition for years to come. I mean amicable competition, to be sure, but that entails rivalry nevertheless.

"Now, battle cruiser operations, I'm told, differ significantly from the operations of a battle fleet, and we in this country are about to embark on the construction of the very first battle cruisers we have ever had. It would be desirable, therefore, for us to have an officer such as yourself or Commander Maltbie available with plenty of battle cruiser experience under his belt. Similarly, it is my understanding that a fleet of several dozen dreadnoughts, such as Britain has now and we shall have in time, is a significantly more complicated tactical unit to command than is a fleet of a dozen or less, such as we have at the present moment. It would, therefore, also be desirable for us to have *another* officer such as yourself or Commander Maltbie available with plenty of fleet experience under his belt."

House shifted in his chair and leaned forward so that he and Gehlman sat squarely face to face.

"All this having been said," he continued in a somewhat lower and more intense tone of voice, "there remains the unique contribution that you alone are capable of making."

Gehlman met his gaze sullenly and asked, "And that is . . . ?"

"That is, the contribution we discussed during your visit to Manchester in June. You are the one man in the world who is in a position to compare British and German wartime naval operations on the basis of personal experience."

Gehlman let out a little puff of exasperation.

"Quite apart from the immense importance of your observations to us as an emerging naval power, their importance to us as a possible ally of Great Britain against Germany would be well-nigh incalculable."

The expression on Gehlman's face was that of a man being backed into a corner and not liking it at all.

"Now I understand that you have special obligations with respect to your ward, but thanks to Commander Maltbie's great success in commending himself to both Admiral Jellicoe and Admiral Beatty, I think we can minimize the hardships you foresee."

Maltbie seemed somewhat puzzled by the mention of his name in this connection, and he and Gehlman exchanged a glance of incomprehension.

"I take it, Commander," the Colonel resumed, "that your wife is welcome to reside at Admiral Beatty's home near Rosyth for as long as you're attached to the Royal Navy."

"That's correct, sir."

"It is also my understanding that Admiral Beatty's forces are seldom if ever absent from port for more than one or two days at a time."

"That's true also, sir."

"Well then, it occurs to me that as your wife and Captain Gehlman's ward have been neighbors in Newport for these past six weeks, it might be possible for your wife to look after Fräulein von Lutwitz during those brief periods when Captain Gehlman is at sea, assuming of course that they have some fondness for one another."

"You mean," Maltbie stammered, "have Alis, Miss Lutwitz, stay at Aberdour with my wife?"

"Precisely," House replied. "Captain Gehlman could visit her for several hours every day when the battle cruisers are in port. And you could make occasional trips down from Scapa Flow to visit your wife."

Maltbie looked slightly dumbfounded, and Gehlman quickly stepped in with, "I think separating Commander Maltbie from his wife just to accommodate a personal problem of mine is rather unfair. We've been operating all along on the assumption that he would remain with the battle cruisers."

"No, Ben," Maltbie said ruefully. "Colonel House is right. This is the only arrangement that permits you to do what's needed without causing Alis to suffer excessively in the process."

"Thank you, Commander," the Colonel said. "I think that puts the case very nicely."

"Well, I think we have to discuss this idea with the other people affected before we make any final decision about it," Gehlman said in an angry voice.

"Of course, Captain," House responded silkily. "Perhaps you could inform me of your conclusions by lunchtime the day after tomorrow."

1915, 20TH SEPTEMBER—WADHURST, SUSSEX

Milky autumnal sunlight drifted down through the leaves like incandescent powder and spattered the dark blue cloth of Reeves-Wadleigh's uniform with shimmering speckles of gold. The trees and meadows of the Duke of Hamilton's estate stretched away northward toward Royal Tunbridge Wells in a dreamy haze that complemented the glow of aberrant serenity inside the captain's wasting body. He was, they had said, "in partial remission," and though they had hastened to inform him that this was only a reprieve and not a pardon, he could not help feeling glad about it. Then too there was the paregoric he'd been taking to relieve his constant nausea. It had been pressed on him by his sister as a specific for the "peptic ulcer" he had affected with her in order to explain away his perceptible loss of weight. At first he had disdained the remedy, primarily because his ulcer was fictitious, but also because he doubted his sister's capacity to make a useful suggestion in any context. A glance at the florid prose on the medicine bottle's label, however, had indicated that the tincture might serve among other things to combat "the distressful enervation secondary to nausea." So he had tried it and had liked the result, liked it so much that he had steadily increased the dose to the point that he was now consuming almost a full pint a day. This particular day he was feeling especially sanguine, not only because he had already consumed the contents of a four-ounce bottle, but also because he had just lunched with a duchess for the first time in his life.

Having at last met Nina Hamilton, Reeves-Wadleigh could understand Fisher's devotion to her. It was difficult to believe that such a pretty, shapely, and youthful-looking woman had already borne her semi-invalid husband seven children. Her tremendous energy and didactic force of personality made her a more intimidating presence than even Fisher himself, who, along with God and vivisected animals, was the chief object of her ardor. She would not rest, she had said in so many words over sherry, until her dear Jacky's genius was once again accorded the recognition of high office in this, the supreme hour of Britain's travail. Fisher had beamed at her, and throughout lunch they had steeled one another to endure the obstinate blindness of those in power with consoling references to the infinite wisdom of the Almighty, with whom they both appeared to be on intimate terms. Reeves-Wadleigh could not remember having ever heard the name of God so often taken otherwise than in vain in the short space of sixty minutes, and it made him proud to share the company of such elevated spirits.

The problem was, however, that he could not stay sufficiently upset. Paregoric and high-minded conversation had left him feeling hopelessly eupeptic, even though God Almighty in His infinite wisdom knew that there was nothing to feel eupeptic about. So rather than follow Fisher and the duchess's example by taking a postluncheon nap, Reeves-Wadleigh had instead taken a walk to review in his mind the catastrophic developments he had come here to discuss with the admiral. Though perhaps "catastrophic" was somewhat overstating things. "Alarming" would be closer to the mark, as indeed would be "preposterous."

On returning from his hike he found Fisher taking tea alone in the rose garden. "Hullo, Monty," the admiral said cheerily. "Will you join me?"

"Nothing for me, sir, thank you," Reeves-Wadleigh replied. The unaccustomed exercise, not to mention the lengthening interval since his last sip of the opiate, had served to put a substantial dent in his well-being. A hint of nausea hovered around his consciousness now like a malign afflatus, while itches and aches he remembered but vaguely from the preparegoric era began wriggling and squirming inside his joints like the larvae of awakening wasps.

There was no longer any impediment in the way of his feeling upset.

"So," said the admiral after taking a sip from his cup, "you have news of Captain Maltbie."

"Commander Maltbie, sir," Reeves-Wadleigh corrected gently.

"*Commander* Maltbie," Fisher acknowledged with a trace of brusque irritation, as if the error had been trivial. "What about him?"

"Well, he's returning here shortly, together with Captain Gehlman; and despite the information we've obtained on them, they are *both* to be sent off to the fleet."

"The information you've obtained . . . ?"

"Yes, sir."

"What information?"

"The information in my report, sir: the one that was sent to you yesterday."

"Oh . . . that," the admiral said. "Refresh my memory, will you?"

"Of course, sir," Reeves-Wadleigh replied, deeply—and disproportionately—dismayed to find that Fisher had failed to read the material. "Our people in America had no trouble finding out what Captain Gehlman and Commander Maltbie were doing at the War College. They were engaged in war-game simulations of possible battles between our navy and Germany's."

"Really," said Fisher with visible interest.

"Yes, sir. Their report, our people tell us, is the talk of Washington. Not its contents, of course, but its existence—and its importance."

"What about its contents?"

"On that we have only rumors, sir. Admiral Dewey has impounded all copies of the report and drastically restricted access to it."

Fisher gave an amused snort. "Well then, what do the rumors say?"

"The rumors say that the report's conclusion is that Jellicoe would almost certainly win if there was a battle."

"I should bloody well think so!"

"Yes, sir."

"Well, that's certainly no cause for lamentation, now is it? Why all the gloom and consternation?"

"Because, sir, we've found out that Captain Gehlman may be working as a spy."

"What? A spy for whom? The Germans?"

"We don't think it's the Germans, sir, though we haven't entirely ruled out the possibility that it might be."

"Well, for whom then?"

"The Americans, sir."

"The *Americans!* Since when do the Americans have spies?"

Reeves-Wadleigh suppressed a sigh of exasperation. "All countries have spies, sir, all the time."

"But what have the Americans got to spy about, for heaven's sake?"

"Quite a bit, sir; that's why I've been so uneasy about this observer business all along."

"Please elucidate."

"It's very simple, sir. The Americans have yet to cast their lot in this war, and before they do so it would pay them to learn as much as possible about the strengths and weaknesses of their potential allies—and adversaries."

"Monty, you're not seriously suggesting that the United States might join with the Germans against *us?*"

"I *am* seriously suggesting it, sir: not as a likelihood, but as a possibility. By the Americans' lights our blockade policy constitutes a serious provocation, so serious that they went to war with us in 1812 to put a stop to it. If we should be obliged by circumstances to adopt harsher measures than those already in force, and if the Germans should yield to American pressure on the question of submarine warfare, we would be left as the only foreign power against whom the United States had a substantial grievance."

Fisher pondered awhile, then said, "I take your point, Monty, for the sake of argument. But what's the basis for your assumption about Captain Gehlman being a spy?"

"Well, sir, when our people in Washington started looking into Gehlman's background, they found an unexplained gap in his service record."

"How do you mean?"

"There is a record on file at the Navy Department of every assignment Captain Gehlman has ever had since his graduation from Annapolis—up until January of this year. From January until this past June, however, there is a blank."

"Go on."

"When our people in Washington couldn't solve the mystery of those missing six months, I at first thought, well, that's that. But then it occurred to me: why was Gehlman chosen to engage in war-game simulations with Maltbie? Possibly for the same reason that Maltbie was chosen to engage in them with him: because he'd been an observer with one of the fleets!"

"Impossible!"

"That's what I thought too, sir, initially. But just to be certain, I asked Admiral Hall for permission to wireless a query to one of our contacts in Berlin."

"And . . . ?"

"And, in a letter smuggled out through Holland, I got back a most remarkable reply."

"To wit . . . ?"

"The Americans sent Captain Gehlman as an observer to the High Seas Fleet in January. He was aboard the *Seydlitz* at Dogger Bank. He lived in Wilhelmshaven as a guest in the home of Hipper's first gunnery officer—"

"Baron von Tiel?"

"Why, yes, sir," Reeves-Wadleigh said in astonishment.

"There's still some life in old Methuselah yet, eh, Monty?" Fisher said devilishly.

"Yes, sir. I mean, of course, sir. But . . ."

"You assumed perhaps that in my capacity as First Sea Lord I wouldn't have troubled to learn the names of Hipper's staff—or that having once learned them I wouldn't have remembered them this long?"

"No, sir. I only . . ."

"Not every old war-horse is ripe for the knackers, you know; not even one as antiquated as I am."

"Of course, sir," Reeves-Wadleigh said, trying to conceal his exasperation. Here he had just revealed what Fisher should in any case have read for himself: that the newly designated American observer had recently seen service with the German Fleet. And all the admiral could do was prate about his undiminished powers of recollection.

"Are you by any chance sulking, Monty?"

"No, sir. Certainly not."

"Then get on with it. What about this Gehlman?"

"He was involved in a rather spectacular scandal, sir," Reeves-Wadleigh replied, trying not to sound aggrieved. "Baron von Tiel accused him of spying, apparently, but our contact in Berlin reported that there was also personal animosity between them because of Gehlman's relationship with the baron's wife and stepdaughter."

"Ah ha! By 'relationship' I assume you intend something . . . amorous."

"With reference to the baron's wife, sir: yes. She and Gehlman were reputed to be carrying on an affair."

"I see. And where does the stepdaughter come in?"

"Well, sir, when Gehlman was recalled to the United States at the end of March, he took the baron's stepdaughter with him."

"*What?!*"

"Yes, sir. The baron's wife died in a riding accident shortly before Gehlman left. There was some speculation that the baron might have murdered her, especially as she had just recently revised her will and named Gehlman the child's guardian. At all events, Gehlman took the child out of the country before von Tiel could stop him, and she's with him now in the United States."

"Good heavens, Monty! This sounds like something out of Dumas *père.*"

"The strangest part is still to come, sir. After his wife's death and his stepdaughter's 'abduction,' as he called it, the baron's notorious heavy drinking seems to have gotten out of hand, and as he was by then in charge of an important intelligence operation of some kind, his superiors began to worry about his fitness. The upshot was that he was relieved of his duties early in August and placed on what was referred to as 'convalescent leave.' Three weeks ago, however, he disappeared completely, without a trace."

For several moments the two men sat silent.

"That, Monty, is quite a story you've told me."

"Yes, sir."

"Now tell me what you conclude from it."

"I conclude that Captain Gehlman should under no circumstances be permitted to serve as an observer with our fleet. First, because he has already served with the German Fleet, which the Americans are concealing from us, and second, because he has been accused of spying, which ought automatically to disqualify him whether the accusation is true or not, and regardless of who made it."

"Hmmmmm," said Fisher. "Did you raise these points with the First Lord?"

"Yes, sir, I did. Or rather, Admiral Hall did, at my request."

"And what was Mr. Balfour's response?"

"His response was that, given the likelihood that America and Germany would soon break off relations, the objections to Captain Gehlman could not be regarded as determinative. He added, though, that the captain should be kept under close surveillance throughout his sojourn with us."

"À la Maltbie?"

"Yes, sir: à la Maltbie."

"And you think I ought to put my oar in to keep Captain Gehlman from perpetrating espionage upon us?"

"To guard against the risk of his doing so, sir."

"Well, I'll do what I can, Monty, which isn't much as things stand at the moment. But I wouldn't get my hopes up if I were you. I think Balfour is going to require something far more substantial before he and Sir Edward Grey will risk a démarche with the United States."

"Something far more substantial!" Reeves-Wadleigh muttered to himself back in his room, having downed four full ounces of paregoric in a single draught. "Something like the loss of a dozen dreadnoughts!"

He gazed dully at the empty bottle on his night table, then greedily swallowed the last few drops of the medicine remaining in his glass. Ah well, he thought as the opiate glow streamed like sunlight through his body, if we're defeated, at least I won't be around long to witness the humiliation.

1915, 26TH SEPTEMBER—NEW YORK CITY

Though the day had been summery, there was a definite nip in the air as the sun slipped behind the irregular crenellations that formed the skyline of Central Park West, and Gehlman shivered at the prospect of the approaching winter. Alis beside him was intently scuffing her feet through the fallen leaves that carpeted the length of the Mall, making more than sufficient noise to attract amused smiles from the people strolling in the opposite direction. There were times

—and this was one of them—when he found her behavior almost uproariously comical. The seriousness with which she did the silliest
things, such as plow her way through a layer of autumn leaves, was
so antic and endearing to him that he often had to restrain himself
from sweeping her into his arms and hugging her to within an inch
of her life. (*Why* he had to restrain himself from giving effect to
that impulse was a question he was only just now beginning to
ask—and the preliminary tentative provisional answer seemed astonishingly enough to be that there was *no* reason, no reason whatsoever. Though deeper reflection, he supposed with resignation, would
inevitably provide one.)

He looked over his shoulder at Melina strolling with Maltbie several paces behind him. Something seemed to have gone out of her
since the three of them had discussed House's "proposal" back at the
beginning of the month, and he sensed that she, as much as he, was
feeling angry and exasperated about being maneuvered by the Colonel into what amounted to an impossible position. Using Maltbie's
naiveté and selflessness as his knight and bishop, House had proceeded to move all four of them around like pawns—and the most
galling part of it was that the four of them left to themselves would
almost certainly have done what House wanted on their own initiative. Gehlman, in the final analysis, would never have turned his
back on what he perceived to be his duty; Melina, forced to confront
the issue, would never have pressed for her own interests to the detriment of Alis's; Maltbie was, if anything, too ready to make sacrifices
for the common good; and Alis, as a child, was obliged to suffer such
trials as her elders put upon her. As House had thus been bound to
win his point in any case, it simply hadn't been necessary for him to
rig the game so cynically, especially since in doing so he had deprived
Gehlman and Melina of the consolation of an honorable capitu-
lation and left them smarting and resentful at the indignity of having been cheated. All he'd done was make everything just that much
harder; or at least that was how Gehlman saw it, not fully acknowledging the extent to which his own stance of intractability might
have dissuaded the Colonel from trusting to his and Melina's better
instincts to produce in the end the desired result.

Though there was a good deal more to Gehlman's intractability
than just his stance; because the more he thought about his projected mission, the more unsavory it seemed to him. He wasn't at all
happy with the prospect of concealing his previous assignment from

his British hosts. To his mind it meant that he was being foisted on them under false pretenses, and that once among them he would be an accomplice—no; a principal—in the perpetration of a fraud. On a more self-centered level, furthermore, there was the fact that he would be serving aboard ships—the British battle cruisers—that both he and Maltbie knew to be dangerously underarmored around the turrets. The near destruction of the *Seydlitz* at Dogger Bank had taught the Germans a vital lesson that the British had yet to learn— but neither Gehlman nor Maltbie would be free to act as tutor for them.

What Colonel House completely failed to understand, in Gehlman's opinion, was that observers almost inevitably took on the national coloration of the fleets and armies with which they served. It was only human nature to form an attachment for men of one's own profession with whom one shared the fatigue, the laughter, the tedium, and the dangers of a wartime existence. Even in Gehlman's case, where he and his German host had developed a violent personal antipathy for one another, there were still vivid memories of kindness, hospitality, and good fellowship. Gehlman felt no less affection for Hipper than he expected to feel for Beatty. And he emphatically resented having been placed in a position where loyalty to one naval service meant virtual treachery toward another, especially since neither of the services in question was the one to which he owed his primary allegiance.

And if his situation was untenable, he reflected, how much worse off was the anglophile Maltbie. For him the difficulty would reside not so much in concealing the truth about Gehlman's previous assignment as it would in concealing what he'd learned from Gehlman about the structural vulnerability of the British battle cruisers. Harry's revered friend David Beatty and all Harry's other friends on Beatty's staff might be blown to oblivion by just one German shell, but Harry was forbidden by what passed for duty from saying the words that might safeguard their lives.

Even to a non-practicing Jew like Gehlman, it was clear that whatever he and Harry did they would both be straying a quite considerable distance from the straight and narrow pathways of the Law.

They left the park at Sixty-seventh Street and continued down Fifth Avenue to Grand Army Plaza to have a look at the just completed Pulitzer Fountain. Then, retracing their route two blocks northward, they arrived before the imposing Renaissance facade of the Havemeyer mansion at 1 East 60th Street.

Gehlman gritted his teeth as they entered the building; he was dreading the next few hours. Louisine Havemeyer, together with her friend Miss Cassatt, was having a private exhibition and benefit auction of the works of some painters whom the invitation alleged to be "French Impressionist Masters." To Gehlman, who had little use for art to begin with, this meant that the artists in question were thrice benighted: as Frenchmen (for whom Gehlman, being Germanic and, more pertinently, Jewish, had the most vigorous contempt), as Impressionists (whatever *that* implied, over and above something insufferably modern), and as "masters" (which Gehlman thought a singularly fatuous term to apply to painters born after 1800).

Another reason he was dreading what lay ahead was the *Tribune*'s (and the *Times*', and the *World*'s, and the *Herald*'s, and the etcet-era's) breathless assertion that "everybody who was anybody" in New York society would be present and accounted for at Mrs. Have-meyer's salon. Normally Gehlman shunned the company of any-bodys with as much enthusiasm as he shunned the company of Frenchmen, Impressionists, and premature masters. But Melina, as a sometime devotee of modern painting, had persuaded him that the pictures to be placed on view were too exceptional to be missed, even if he was sure he wouldn't like them. She said that Alis, at least, *had* to see the paintings, as a matter of elementary education, and that Maltbie and Gehlman would be eager to look at all of them once they'd seen just one or two. She was a formidable advocate by nature, and a passionate one on the subject of these artists; and as Gehlman felt beholden to her for staying with Maltbie at Seventy-ninth Street to help accustom Alis to the living arrangements planned for Aberdour, he forebore insisting on his reluctance to the usual extent. (He also felt a slightly irrational twinge of guilt about contributing—if he had—to the imminent disruption of Melina's married life.) Then too, Mrs. Havemeyer's great event was unques-tionably in an excellent cause: Belgian War Relief; and the auction of several canvases contributed by various collectors might in some respects prove amusing. So here he was: looking resplendent and un-comfortable in his gold-braid dress uniform and feeling in all honesty and sincerity rather put upon and out of sorts. It occurred to him that this was perhaps the first time in many years—at least, in a social context—that he had done something he affirmatively had not wanted to do.

That, he supposed, was what came of having affectionate daily commerce with a child!

As he might have expected from a high society art exhibition, almost no one was looking at the paintings—or rather, almost everyone was looking at, or talking about, one painting exclusively: something called "Picnic on the Grass" by the famous Monsieur Manet. Given the crush around this picture, Gehlman couldn't get much closer to it than ten feet, but its chief asset as far as he could tell was a somewhat chunky naked lady engaged in what looked like a rather effete conversation with two or three fully dressed men. A glance at the catalog revealed that this effort was "an epoch-making masterpiece," which led Gehlman to the conclusion that he should henceforth refrain from consulting the catalog.

As the bar, the buffet, Monsieur Manet's picnickers, and, consequently, just about everybody who was anybody in New York society were on the second floor, while most of the paintings were being exhibited on the first, Melina, Gehlman, Maltbie, and Alis were soon by common consent headed downstairs. Gehlman was surprised on viewing the paintings to find himself liking most of them, except those of Monsieur Cézanne, which looked very flat, and those of Monsieur van Gogh (a Dutch colleague of Cézanne's, Melina explained), which looked very . . . disturbing. He particularly liked the landscapes of Monsieur Monet and Monsieur Pissarro, but much as he liked them he still couldn't see what all the fuss over Impressionism was about.

The last room they entered contained about a dozen works of Monsieur Renoir: several landscapes, several interiors, and five or six informal portraits. The portraits were all of females: a woman reading, a little girl with a bunch of wild flowers, a woman sitting in the sun, a little girl and her nurse, a woman at the theater. There was something about these pictures, an undefined common thread running through them, that held Gehlman's attention. They contained no sharp angles, he noticed, no violent contrasts of color; just soft and harmonious curves, warm flesh tones, gentle contours. And there was that undefined something more as well, that pervasive yet elusive unifying quality.

What was he seeing here? he wondered. These figures weren't people; they weren't even intended to be people. They were something altogether different. But what? Shifting his focus from canvas to canvas, the ghost of an answer came to him: they were *perceptions* of people.

Gehlman felt almost giddy. The pictures before him, he suddenly understood, were what Monsieur Renoir *saw!* In some utterly incomprehensible and miraculous manner, the painter had managed to transfer his vision of the world onto canvas in a way that permitted people who looked at his work to see things not just through his eyes, but *through his mind!*

With this realization, or rather, hard upon it, came the shocking corollary that the reality Gehlman had always assumed to be absolute was in large part the product of his own personal preconceptions. Here he was, after all, looking out from inside the mind of Monsieur Renoir—and the world he saw was a totally different place from the world where he'd always lived. It was a much pleasanter place, if the truth were known: not cramped and crabbed and rife with deceit and predation, but warm and spacious, filled with gladness and with . . . what he felt for Alis.

So the world was not as he had found it, but as he had fashioned it: in his own image.

This was a revelation he would want some time to conjure with.

He was abstracted throughout the remainder of the evening, and all during the homeward walk up Fifth Avenue. Judging, furthermore, by the broad smile on Melina's face when she asked him if the evening had been quite the ordeal he'd been expecting, the degree to which he'd been affected was fairly evident to all concerned. "No," he'd replied with a broad smile of his own (broad but somewhat sheepish), the evening had not by any means turned out to be a total loss.

Later, after he kissed Alis good night, instead of getting up and leaving as he'd always done before, he stayed seated on the side of her bed. He sat there, with her fingers cradled in his palm, until, without forethought or calculation or even what passes for volition, he said, "Listen, Allie, I know things have been difficult for you in the past, and I know you're worried about me being away now and then when we're in Scotland. So I just want you to know that I love you and treasure you as if you were my own daughter, and that I will always love you and treasure you, and that I will never do anything to hurt you or make you sad, and that you mean more to me than anything else in the world."

She gazed up at him gravely from the soft linen recess of her pillows, silent and pensive. "I love you too, Babbo," she said finally, sitting up and reaching out her arms.

And as he held her, it came to him that Monsieur Renoir's world had been a good deal closer than he'd thought.

1915, 4TH OCTOBER—QUINCY, MASSACHUSETTS

Looked at against the background of low cumulus scudding over the Fore River shipyard, the monstrous gray wall that was the hull of the nearly completed USS *Nevada* seemed to Melina to be slowly tilting in her direction, like the swelling crest of some dark malevolent wave. She slowed her pace in the shadow of its inimical presence, pulling back gently on Maltbie's arm.

"Is something wrong, dearest?" he asked, as the tall patrician figure of Captain William Sims, on his right, turned to look at her with an expression of concern.

"No . . . no, nothing," she said, feeling slightly lightheaded and short of breath. "It's just that I never imagined anything so . . . so awesome, so *huge!*" (Or, she refrained from adding, anything so brutal-looking, so ugly.)

"Huge!" Sims said in a bantering tone. "Why, this little darling is just a baby. If you want to see something really enormous, get Harry to take you to Brooklyn and show you the *Arizona*. She's a hundred feet longer, four thousand tons heavier, and two guns meaner than my girl."

Melina noted the odd noun Sims had chosen to describe his new command, an object as unfeminine and unpetite as anything she could imagine. "Thank you, Captain," she said shakily, "but your 'girl' is of more than sufficient size for any purposes of mine."

"Are you sure you're all right, darling?" Maltbie asked. "Perhaps you'd just as soon not go aboard."

"Yes," Sims offered promptly. "There's oil and grease all over the place in there. I'd hate you to get a stain on that pretty dress of yours."

"I'm fine, Harry," Melina said, bridling a bit at what she regarded as Sims's paternalistic presumption. The captain, she suspected, would have preferred it if Maltbie had come up to Boston by himself to look over the new ship. To Harry's credit, however, he was no more willing to subtract two days from their remaining time together than she was to let him do so. Besides, she had never actually visited a battleship, and this one, according to Harry, was very very special. It was America's first "superdreadnought," he had said: the first to be oil-fueled, the first with triple turrets, and the first with something called "all-or-nothing" armor protection. As he'd described the ship, it had sounded remarkably interesting. But face to face with its brute immensity, interest was decidedly not the feeling she felt. Fear was a closer approximation of her emotions, fear and a kind of revulsion as well.

Though perhaps Sims's battleship was not entirely to blame.

The sight of the *Nevada* brought into sharp relief a feeling of apprehension that had been weighing on Melina more and more oppressively as the departure date for England drew nearer. Clearance for both Maltbie and Gehlman had come through from London a week ago, and the American liner *Philadelphia* on which they'd booked passage was due to sail for Liverpool the day after tomorrow. Maltbie was as upset as she was over the prospect of their impending separation, but that at least was something concrete and definable. What troubled Melina more deeply, in a way, was the ambiguous role she seemed fated to play once they all got to Scotland.

By virtue of her marriage, she now held dual citizenship, but in Britain she would continue to be treated as a British subject unless and until she renounced her nationality. If she gave up her British citizenship, which in any case she had no desire to do, she would jeopardize the arrangement that envisioned her living at Aberdour with Alis. If she remained a British subject, however, there were provisions of the Defence of the Realm Act that left her in a highly dubious position. Sections of the Act could be construed to place her under an obligation to inform the authorities that Gehlman had seen service with the German Fleet, even without the authorities' asking her. And though there was little likelihood that that specific question would ever arise, it seemed inevitable that there would be curiosity about Alis. Melina could say truthfully enough that Gehlman, as a close friend of Alis's mother, had on that account been named the child's guardian. But speaking the truth was not the same thing as revealing it, and not revealing it might mean withholding or concealing it, to the detriment of the realm's defense.

All this Melina had heard together with Maltbie and Gehlman on the day after their conference with Colonel House. Mr. Bograd, the Gehlman family attorney, had gone on to say, however, that decisions of the Hague Tribunal clearly protected dual nationals from what the Court had described as "treason by default." Simply stated, the rule was that a citizen of two nations ought not to be held accountable for acts of omission against one sovereign if such acts were the outgrowth of duties of allegiance to the other. In other words, although dual nationals could not legally spy or engage in subversion, neither could they be legally coerced by one country to commit overt acts that contravened the interests of the other.

Of course, it was a very complicated area of the law, Mr. Bograd had said; and of course one could never predict the action of a specific court in a specific jurisdiction in specific cases before the event. But he felt reasonably confident that Mrs. Maltbie would encounter no difficulties as long as she refrained from telling outright lies. It was more nearly a moral than a legal question, after all . . . now wasn't it? Or say, a question of equivalent moral and legal weight.

Quite apart from the fact that she had found Mr. Bograd insufferable personally, Melina resented him for implying that a degree of turpitude attached to a course of action she was prepared to undertake. She had never had much of a penchant for moral introspection, having always gotten fairly satisfactory results from her visceral perceptions of right and wrong. Mr. Bograd's odious insinuation, however, was that she was about to enter a zone of moral twilight, where only a conscience as refined as his could see a person through. Worse than odious, however, was the galling thought that he might be right.

Since that meeting Melina had been unable to escape the feeling that she was being swept along by tides over which she had no control. All at once, it seemed, she was being treated like her husband's wife instead of herself. She felt suddenly subordinate, subordinated, and deprived of the use of her will. How she had come to be in such a position she thought she might know; why she had allowed herself to be placed there, however, was as much a mystery as what she could have done to stay free—and somewhat less of a mystery than what she could do now to escape.

They went up a gangplank into an area that was going to be the mess deck and then up by a series of internal ladders and catwalks to the open spaces of the forecastle. As Sims had warned, there *was* oil and grease all over the place, but aside from smelling worse, the lubricants seemed no more soiling than the mud and dust Melina was used to from archaeological excavations. The din inside the ship was far more disconcerting, though, as welders, riveters, and steamfitters appeared to be striving together to achieve the greatest possible bedlam. The near darkness, too, was disorienting, and by the time they emerged into the daylight Melina had twice barked her shins against the rims of undetected coamings.

Once up on deck she found herself staring at the three outsized gun barrels jutting from the forward turret. Her sense of deep foreboding was confirmed when they went inside. Never in her life had she been in an environment so alien to her. The breeches of the cannon, visible through heavy glass plating, looked like obscene open sores. And there was no *space* anywhere, no room to move or breathe. Yet Sims told her that twenty-seven men served on the gun platform, with sixty more serving on the levels below.

She went down into the chill confines of the working chamber and peered through a hatchway into the magazine rotundas beneath it. As she gazed downward, a terrible feeling of suffocation began to engulf her, and she experienced a violent desire to be outside. Keeping her composure long enough to gracefully decline Sims's invitation to descend to the magazines, she managed in a calm voice to excuse herself and say that she would wait for him and Maltbie up on deck. Once topside, she leaned with her back against the turret wall and swallowed great gasping mouthfuls of air. The guns, the cold gray slabs of armor, the mountainous walls of steel, all spoke to her of leering mad-eyed death. It made her cringe to think that Harry found them beautiful.

1915, 9TH OCTOBER—PHILADELPHIA

The grandstands of Baker Bowl in Philadelphia cast a lengthening shadow across the infield as little George Foster of the Red Sox continued to stifle the Phillies' normally potent bats. House cast a sidelong glance toward Wilson and Mrs. Galt, seated beside him in the presidential box right next to the Boston dugout. It had, he reflected, been quite a week, a week of decidedly mixed blessings, to which a chilly Saturday afternoon at the World Series provided a peculiarly fitting climax. Baseball and matrimony: these, it seemed, were the country's predominant concerns at the moment—and perhaps the President's as well, judging by the expression of exuberant contentment to be seen on Wilson's face. Having made public his engagement only three days before, the President was still enjoying the harvest of felicitations from friends and well-wishers that the announcement had immediately evoked. These first fruits of love's labors won tasted sweet to him, no doubt; the sour fruits took longer on the vine. It was inevitable, House supposed, that the watchdogs of respectability would soon be barking about funeral meats coldly furnishing forth marriage tables and about disloyalty to Ellen Wilson's memory (as if fourteen months of mourning connoted virtual indifference to the deceased). The Wilson-haters, too, would soon be heard from, hawking smears and innuendos about the President's "lascivious nature." Cabot Lodge and Teddy Roosevelt were probably corresponding already, seeking to outdo each other in effusions of scorn for the President; and Hearst and Brisbane could be counted on to start slinging mud most any day.

That remarriage was going to cost Wilson votes was a foregone conclusion, but House was glad to be getting it out of the way a year before the nation went to the polls. It was a necessary evil, given the President's pathetic need for female succor, and while his chosen helpmate was in many respects an unedifying creature, she at least came free of taint or scandal. At the moment, in fact, the only major objection to her was that she made the President too sanguine, when a somber outlook seemed more in keeping with the trend of world affairs.

Paradoxically enough, Wilson was afflicted by a surfeit of good news. On Tuesday evening, only twenty-four hours before he made his engagement public, he and Secretary Lansing had received the letter from Ambassador Bernstorff that announced the almost whole-sale submission of Germany to American demands on the subject of submarine warfare. The letter said that instructions had been issued to U-boat commanders that rendered any repetition of an *Arabic* or *Lusitania* incident out of the question. It also specifically disavowed the act of the submarine officer responsible for the sinking of the *Arabic*, and offered to pay an indemnity for the American lives that were lost.

Wilson, Lansing, and even House himself had been highly gratified by the contents of this letter, but for House at least it raised as many problems as it solved. Getting the preparedness program through Congress, for example, was now going to be a much more difficult proposition. Even before Count von Bernstorff's letter was made public, loud voices of opposition to increases in military ex-penditure had been heard, in Washington and throughout the coun-try as a whole. The loudest voice had been, and still was, Bryan's, who, not content with editorial diatribes in *The Commoner* against "profiteers of slaughter," was now in the midst of a barnstorming tour across the South and West, telling his audiences that "this na-tion does not need burglar's tools unless it intends to make burglary its business."

Bryan's was by no means the only voice of angry dissent, however. In fact, most elements of Wilson's natural constituency were, so to speak, up in arms about the preparedness issue. Progressives, farmers, and labor leaders were all most emphatically disaffected, as ap-parently were women, in near unanimous force. Even Democrats in Congress were making mutinous noises, and Claude Kitchin, the new House majority leader, was plainly in the antipreparedness camp. Increasingly on this question the President was going to be forced to consort with his political enemies: the Lodges, the Roose-velts, the industrialists, the financiers—and this was not going to im-prove his chances for reelection come next November.

The preparedness plan had been in trouble in any case, even be-fore the receipt of Bernstorff's note. The $1.5-billion ten-year forty-eight dreadnought program House had brandished before Gehlman and Maltbie had already been scaled down to half a billion dollars over five years for eighteen capital ships, and even those reduced

figures were under attack. Now, because Germany's diplomatic retreat and the apparent resolution of the submarine controversy had
removed the threat of imminent hostilities, the opponents of military
spending would grow more vociferous still.

House did not for a moment believe that the last shot in the
U-boat battle had been fired. With Bulgaria poised to enter the war
on the side of Turkey and the Central Powers, and with Germany
continuing to dominate the Russians in the east, the scales of decision in Berlin might very likely incline toward a redoubled undersea
offensive before the current year was out. Any country capable of
unleashing a Rintelen and an Albert against a neutral nation with
which it was purportedly on friendly terms was manifestly not to be
trusted, and House was more and more convinced that the United
States and the German Empire would be impelled sooner or later to
a settling of accounts. He didn't know to what extent, if any, the
President shared this conviction, but he did know that Wilson no
longer put much stock in Teutonic bona fides.

It seemed clear to the Colonel that America would be the next target on Germany's list in the event of an Allied defeat, and given that
assumption the so-called *Arabic* pledge transmitted from Berlin this
week amounted to little more than a dangerous inducement to complacency. More than that, it obliged Wilson, in fairness, to resume
the acrimonious debate, which the *Lusitania* sinking had pushed into
the background, over British violations of international law and British infringements of neutral rights. Only this morning, in fact, Secretary Lansing had presented the President with a voluminous draft
communiqué protesting the Allies' illegal blockade practices and
their continuing interference with the conduct of legitimate trade.
The legal scholarship that had gone into the note was impeccable;
every argument made in it was unanswerable; Wilson's obligation to
approve its contents and send it off to London was indisputable . . .
yet from the point of view of America's long-term foreign policy objectives—at least, as the Colonel perceived them—the effect of the
note would be almost entirely counterproductive.

For House was now in possession of a letter from Sir Edward
Grey, a response to a letter he himself had sent with the President's
authorization, that seemed to open the door to decisive American intervention in the cause of peace. Proceeding on the assumption that
Germany had proved itself incapable of conforming to civilized
standards of international behavior, the Colonel had intimated to

the Foreign Secretary that the United States was prepared—if the Allies were agreeable—to issue a sort of ultimatum to all the belligerent powers. The ultimatum would state that, as the neutral nations of the world were being made to suffer because of the war and were being subjected to constant violations of their rights, it was therefore the duty of the belligerents to undertake peace negotiations immediately, basing them on the goal of worldwide disarmament. The Allies, having secretly consented to this initiative in advance, would "reluctantly" go along with the American proposal. If the Central Powers went along as well, House on Wilson's behalf would have pulled off the diplomatic coup of the century. But if, as was more probable, the Central Powers refused to cooperate, the current of world opinion would shift markedly against them, with the likely result that America and the other neutral nations would soon join in the struggle to bring them to heel.

Grey's reply, received only this morning, was not directly responsive to the Colonel's suggestion, but it readily bore the inference that his plan would be acceptable *if* the United States was prepared to participate in a binding postwar security system based on a league of nations, and *if* Germany was prepared to withdraw its armies from Belgium and France. Grey seemed to be saying, in other words, that Britain might be willing to accept a peace based on the status quo antebellum if it could be satisfied that the United States would stand behind such a settlement to the point of using force.

What went unsaid in Grey's letter, but which hardly needed saying, was that House's plan to compel negotiations (complete with its promise of American cobelligerency should Germany prove inflexible) was a step in the right direction from the British point of view. But would America also shed its historic isolation: not simply join with Britain in the prosecution of a war, but join with Europe in the preservation of a peace?

House felt certain that, brought face to face with this vital question, Woodrow Wilson would eventually answer "Yes!" And that was why he regretted the need to send Lansing's note of protest off to London. He didn't want the Anglo-American dialogue on important issues of war and peace to be complicated at this juncture by minor questions of law and trade. He wanted America and England to concentrate on common interests. (If their doing so accomplished nothing else, after all, it would at least ease his conscience about having sent Gehlman off to Rosyth without revealing to the British where he'd been before.)

House glanced again in the President's direction as Wilson applauded the Red Sox' taking a 2–1 lead. He hoped he was serving his great friend well, and prayed he was serving him wisely.

BOOK VI

1915, 8TH NOVEMBER—ABERDOUR

Melina looked out her Aberdour sitting room window into the murky gloom of mid-day on the Forth, and with a small fretful shudder pulled her woolen shawl more tightly around her shoulders. The ruined abbey on Inchcolm Island, barely a mile away, appeared for a moment through the frigid drizzle, then faded from view behind a sluggish miasma of fog.

Melina sighed and noted with a certain bitter satisfaction that her breath had produced a billow of condensation in the air. With its huge rooms and lofty ceilings, Admiralty House was an unheatable barn; and for Melina, who hated being cold almost as passionately as she hated being deprived of sunlight, it was a decidedly uncongenial residence.

Her one consolation for the chill dreariness of the place was the memory of the last night Maltbie had spent there before departing for Scapa Flow. Not knowing how long it would be before they were reunited, they had ravished each other like creatures possessed: with a fierceness and a carnality so extreme that they had had trouble letting their eyes meet in the morning. She had thought then, mistakenly, that a sexual experience of such magnitude might sustain her until Maltbie could be with her again. She had also thought that it must certainly have caused her to conceive with him, and she'd been equally mistaken about that. Indeed, since his departure four weeks ago, neither her menstrual rhythms nor the clawing need to have his body had altered one whit.

Scapa Flow, it turned out, was a good deal farther away than the three hundred miles that were marked on the maps. It was two train rides, a boat ride, and a sheaf of special travel documents away. In fact, allowing for all the hours spent waiting between boats and trains, a round-trip from Scapa to Aberdour could easily consume three days; and Harris Edward Maltbie, for his sins, was not the sort of man to take that much time from his duties for any but the most pressing reasons.

Although she'd thought about it at tedious length, Melina remained at a loss to understand her situation. Almost overnight, it seemed, she had fallen from a state of regal freedom to a condition of abject servitude. For the first time in her adult life she was in a place she didn't want to be, leading a life she didn't want to lead, and yet unable, as far as she could tell, to alter her circumstances to any appreciable extent. For the first time in her adult life she felt badgered and resentful, shoved about by arbitrary impositions, hobbled by vexatious obligations. And the worst of it was that there was no place to lay the blame, no villain to charge with trespass against her self-dominion. Harry was innocent of all crimes except conscientiousness and humility. Gehlman's only transgression was the nagging sense of duty that had kept him from resigning his commission. Alis was guilty only of needing security—and perhaps of being entitled to it. The artful Colonel House, Melina supposed, only had America's best interests at heart—and even she herself was actuated by impulses of a seemingly selfless nature.

So it was a conspiracy of virtue, an immaculate cabal, that had brought her to this cul-de-sac, and a conspiracy of circumstances that now kept her here. The plan for Erna Gehlman to come over and help with Alis's nurturance, for example, had foundered on any number of objections, Erna's uncertain health being foremost among them. She had wanted to come, most definitely, and Alis had fervently wanted her to, but Scotland in winter seemed a forbidding prospect to a frail Germanic woman of sixty-eight. And when Melina found that Admiralty House was well-nigh unfit for habitation, Erna's participation had been conclusively ruled out.

Worse, at least from Alis's point of view, was the exclusion of Fräulein Beck, whose Austrian nationality was determinative, given the nature of Gehlman's duties. She too had had to remain in New York, leaving Melina as Alis's sole source of psychic support apart from Gehlman himself, who could manage a visit of an hour or two only three or four times a week.

Things might have been better, marginally, for Melina if she could have moved to more agreeable, or in any event warmer, lodgings. But the war had packed the Edinburgh region chock full, and housing was not to be had. Even had there been somewhere suitable to move to, there were diplomatic considerations that militated against leaving Aberdour. There were other considerations also, given the fact that Gehlman's friend, Captain Facchetti, had written that Alis's stepfather had disappeared recently from Berlin. The man was mad, Melina knew, and half-English as well. Admiralty House was provided with a full-time guard of Royal Marines, however, and the extra precaution seemed essential, even if the danger seemed remote.

So Melina felt trapped: she couldn't leave Scotland without Alis, who wouldn't leave Scotland without Gehlman, who couldn't leave Scotland without deserting his post or resigning his commission. Up to now she had sustained herself by working on her New Mexico monograph (which meant consulting on a fairly regular basis—sometimes even when consultation wasn't strictly necessary—with friends and colleagues of her parents at Edinburgh University and the Royal Scottish Museum). There were also daily letters to Maltbie, frequent excursions into Edinburgh with Alis, excellent concerts, an occasional visit to the cinema, and now and then what passed for a game of tennis: she and Alis stumbling around the court, knocking balls everywhere indiscriminately, and all the while giggling helplessly at their own ineptitude.

Her relationship with Alis had been another sustaining factor; it had progressed from a rather severe, though affectionate, skepticism on her part and a rather wary though admiring trepidation on Alis's to an almost sisterly camaraderie that in many respects offset the difference in their ages. There was a nice blend of the maternal, the filial, and the sororal in their interactions, with Melina taking particular pleasure in Alis's shyly antic sense of humor.

And so, despite loneliness and underheated living quarters, she had stayed clear of morbidity and depression. It hadn't often been easy, and at times the only thing that kept her from sinking into a morass of self-pity had been the knowledge that things would not continue as they were indefinitely. Even if nothing else changed, the seasons would; and once she got through the winter, she felt, the worst would be behind her.

But today the winter seemed to stretch before her like an interminable cold gray desert. The sun hadn't shone now for fifteen straight days, and to make things worse, Lady Beatty had just concluded a three-day visit. The former Mrs. Ethel Tree was anything but a gay divorcée; in fact, as far as Melina could tell, she was downright neurasthenic. At all events, whether from nervous disorder or from having been raised as the only daughter of a multimillionaire, she seemed incapable of thinking about or discussing anything other than life's consistent failure to make her happy. So convinced was she that her discontentment was the outcome of someone's or something's culpable neglect that Melina found herself constantly braced in a defensive frame of mind. Such defensiveness was alien to her, and she emphatically disliked it, not least of all because it used up psychic energy that she badly needed to keep her own spirits from sagging.

Lady Beatty's departure this morning for the south of France ("There, at least, one can have a decent meal!") had left Melina feeling drained, and the endless chilling grayness of the weather now seemed like a jackboot on her back. Had her leanings toward depression been idiosyncratic, she might have felt more equal to the task of coping with them. But the experience of the last four weeks had clearly demonstrated that it was actually her stubborn striving toward cheerfulness that was abnormal for the world she lived in. Even Scotsmen acknowledged the dreariness of the long Caledonian winter, taking solace in their whiskey and their stout. This year, moreover, on top of seven months of arctic dampness to look forward to, there were fifteen months of prodigal slaughter to look back on, with no end in sight.

Britain's verdant summer hopes of victory had proved unfounded, and Melina had noticed the change of national mood the moment she arrived back in Liverpool during the first part of October. In the less than three months she'd been away, the country seemed to have come to a realization that the struggle it was engaged in bore no relationship whatsoever to nineteenth-century notions of "diplomacy by other means." In fact, the people now seemed perfectly comfortable with the idea that the war was incomprehensible. No conceivable national objective that anyone could point to could possibly be worth the cost that was being paid. Hence, the objective could only be supranational or supernatural. Britain was being tried, being tested, being purged—and the duty of every Briton was to persevere in the face of all adversity and prove worthy of his race. The cry was no longer *Victory!* but rather *Refuse defeat!* The model was no longer valor, but endurance. The goal was no longer to conquer, but to fight through to an honorable peace. Britain, in short, though remaining a nation in arms, had ceased to sing anthems as it marched.

Sounds from downstairs indicated the arrival of a visitor. Given the time, Melina guessed that it was Gehlman, and the characteristic clack of his shoes on the staircase confirmed her assumption. The tempo of his footsteps was always strangely hurried, as if he were seeking to escape from some pursuer but didn't deign to break into a run. She heard him reach the landing and was surprised when the sound of his steps grew louder in the hallway, rather than fading as it usually did in the direction of Alis's room on the other side of the house.

He knocked on her door, and she asked him to come in. His appearance shocked her. "Ben! You look terrible!"

The blanched skin around his exhausted eyes wrinkled slightly as he went through the motions of a smile. "I've always found it odd," he said, "that one of the chief ways of expressing solicitude in our culture is to say something that would normally be taken as an insult."

Melina returned his smile. "Well, you do look terrible," she said. "You're not ill, are you?"

He shook his head. "Only tired. We've just come back from thirty solid hours in a gale—and we're going out again tonight."

"Oh, no! Alis will be so disappointed."

"You're right, Melina, she will be. And that's partly what I wanted to . . . excuse me, may I sit down?"

"Oh, of course, Ben; I'm sorry. Would you like to have some tea sent up, or something to eat?"

"What I'd like is a large cognac, actually, and an extra log on that fire."

"Certainly," Melina said, reaching for the bell cord. She had originally interpreted the fact that he'd come in still wearing his greatcoat as an indication that he'd been in his usual hurry. Now an altogether different interpretation occurred to her, and she had a strong surge of companion-in-adversity sympathy for him. "You were saying . . . ?"

"I was saying . . ." Gehlman responded, settling himself stiffly into an armchair by the fire and stretching his legs out so that the soles of his shoes almost touched the andirons, ". . . that this whole arrangement leaves a lot to be desired."

"I won't argue with you about that."

"I should think not. But you've been a damn good sport about it nevertheless, if you'll excuse the profanity. Really, you've been wonderful."

"Plucky, Ben—wouldn't you say?"

He grinned at her. "Definitely, madam. Plucky *in excelsis.*"

An elderly butler appeared in the doorway. "You rang, mum?"

"Oh, yes, Williston. Would you bring us some brandy please, and also some more wood for the fire."

"Very good, mum," the butler said and trudged away.

Melina turned back to Gehlman, who was staring blankly into the flames. "Ben?"

From the way his head jerked, it almost seemed that she'd awakened him. "Ah! Yes. Where were we?"

"We were dilating on my exceptional strength of character."

"Oh, yes. And with good cause."

Melina inclined her head with mock solemnity.

Gehlman's answering smile was only pro forma. "I've been thinking, Melina," he said in a serious tone, ". . . and doing some reading as well."

"Yes?"

"My thinking's been that the reason I don't like this arrangement isn't just that it's rough on you and Alis and Harry, but that it's dishonest."

"You mean, because of your previous assignment?"

"Because of that. But more particularly because of the position we've put you in."

Melina looked down at her hands. "Well, I really haven't yet been put in a 'position' fortunately."

"That's only because no one has pressed you about Alis. But it's unrealistic to expect—"

He stopped speaking as the butler reappeared along with a scullery maid carrying an armful of logs. While the maid built up the fire, the butler poured two snifters of brandy and presented them arthritically to Gehlman and Melina.

"Thank you, Williston," Melina said. "You can leave the bottle."

"Very good, mum," the butler replied.

When they were alone again, Gehlman resumed, "What I'm saying is that, sooner or later, you're going to be asked a question that you won't be able to answer truthfully without, as the saying goes, 'spilling the beans' in the process. And when you are asked that question, I want you to be sure to tell the whole truth."

"I don't understand, Ben. You want me to . . . 'spill the beans'?"

"Precisely."

"But why? I can always evade unwelcome questions if I want to."

Gehlman looked at her grimly. "I don't think evasion is going to be safe enough in this case."

"That sounds very ominous."

"It's meant to, Melina. You remember when we spoke to my father's lawyer, Bograd?"

Melina nodded.

"Well, didn't that whole discussion make you uncomfortable?"

"Of course it did, Ben. But he specifically said that I would be within the law as long as I didn't tell lies."

"Yes. He was very glib about everything, wasn't he? Well . . . I think he was wrong."

"Wrong! What do you mean?"

"Well, I'm no lawyer, but I thought I could read the Defence of the Realm Act as well as Bograd; so I did read it, very carefully, and it seems to me to say that refusing to divulge information of military value, or deliberately concealing it, can be regarded as treasonable."

Melina was incredulous. It had troubled her at first that she was being asked to keep secrets from her own countrymen. But she had persuaded herself that the nature of the information was too innocuous and that Anglo-American ties were too close to make her silence in any way culpable. She knew, on a certain level, that she was engaging in moral casuistry, but she didn't care to think about that, and had more than enough on her mind to ensure that she didn't have to. Now, however, there was this talk of *treason*, which quite apart from seeming wildly out of place, scared her dreadfully.

Gehlman took in her expression of anxiety. "Melina, please, I didn't want to upset you. All I'm saying is that if anyone asks, answer. The worst that can happen is that I'll be recalled. In fact, Harry could come back to Rosyth in that case—so the worst would in some ways be the best."

For a long moment Melina looked into his eyes. Was he *inviting* her to tell someone about his service in Wilhelmshaven so that he could return to America with both Alis and a clean conscience? But no, she thought: that was unduly cynical and ungenerous of her. All he was saying, really, was that telling was preferable to not telling if and when the question arose.

She looked down for a second, then raised her eyes to look at him again. "What a tangled web we're weaving, Ben."

"Yes," he responded in a tired voice. "I can't help thinking that life on this planet was once a great deal simpler."

1915, 2D DECEMBER—LONDON

Reeves-Wadleigh raised the gleaming steel and glass syringe to the light and carefully pushed in the plunger until a tiny stream of fluid spurted from the tip of the needle. Strange, he thought, that the neglect of this one little mundane precaution could be so instantly fatal —that one harmless fragile bubble of air introduced into the bloodstream could be so much more certainly lethal than a bullet.

Using his right hand and his teeth, he tightened the rubber tubing around his left bicep as much as he could, then probed with the needle in the crook of his left elbow until the point found its way to a vein. This was always a moment of extreme sexual arousal for him: the shaft of his penis would ache urgently and the air he drew into his lungs would take on a tangy sharpness.

With delicious slowness he pulled back the plunger to make sure the needle was firmly seated; blood filled the lower end of the syringe, sending wispy filaments of color through the limpid morphine solution it contained. The excitement of anticipation at this point was nearly comparable to the effect of the opiate itself— although "nearly" in this context was a highly extensible word.

The plunger of the syringe sank into the barrel in response to the pressure of Reeves-Wadleigh's thumb. There was a slight bulging feeling in his eyes and nostrils and a slightly metallic sensation in his mouth as he withdrew the needle from the vein. He glanced at the sweep hand of his watch as he placed the empty syringe down beside it on his night table; he then wetted a small dab of cotton with alcohol and placed it over the tiny puncture in his arm, releasing the rubber constriction when he'd finished.

He sat very still and began to count silently to thirty. At "twenty-four" a warm sensuous glowing sensation became perceptible in his abdomen and began to stream outward through his body like a sunburst. At "twenty-seven" the sensation reached the region of his loins, and the corona of his already distended penis began to expand like a swelling balloon. At "thirty" he experienced orgasm, and when the spasms were over he fell backwards onto his bed from a sitting to a semiprone position and lay there, sunk in the great waves of peace and fulfillment that washed over him in rhythm with the gently persistent cadence of his pulse.

The blessed transition from paregoric to intravenous morphine had occurred almost happenstantially. He had gone to his doctor complaining of severe constipation, and on questioning had reluctantly confessed to "taking a sip" of paregoric several times a day. The doctor, after examining him, had questioned him further, with a cold skepticism that suggested that "taking a sip" was a phrase he'd heard before in this connection. When at length Reeves-Wadleigh admitted to downing nearly two pints on a daily basis, the doctor had bestowed on him a look that mingled resignation and disgust, and had then prescribed a laxative that proved rather excessively effective. Several days later the doctor had summoned him back and told him that the benzoic acid in paregoric would certainly aggravate his condition; in fact, on the basis of his examination, it had most probably done so already. Did that mean that he was no longer in remission, Reeves-Wadleigh had asked. The doctor had been very much afraid that it did. He had six to nine months left, the doctor had said; perhaps a year if he confined himself to a hospital, perhaps three months if he continued with paregoric. Reeves-Wadleigh had replied that he would prefer six months out of hospital to a year in and three months with paregoric to six months without. Only then had the doctor mentioned morphine, not out of Hippocratic compassion, Reeves-Wadleigh felt sure, but out of fear for his professional reputation if one of his patients died prematurely because he'd failed to offer him a nonacidic opiate alternative.

Thus had begun what was in many ways the happiest period of Reeves-Wadleigh's life. The euphoria brought on by morphine was a great consolation for dying of cancer, and though the ratio of opiate to solvent in his syringes continued climbing higher and higher (to compensate for the tolerance his body was building up) he didn't worry about that, or indeed about anything else. He did try, occasionally, to stave off the need for stronger injections as long as possible. But the orgasmic ecstasy he experienced each time he increased his dosage level was a potent temptation he could seldom resist.

Life for him had become an amusing exercise. Where before he'd felt anger, there was now only contempt; in place of anxiety, there was only clinical curiosity; where there'd once been near torrential despair, there were now only the placid zephyrs of indifference. The subject of Captain Gehlman, for instance, which had formerly caused him unending aggravation, was now only his favorite hobby. He was still convinced, of course, that Gehlman was a threat to Britain's safety, but finding him out and chasing him down were no longer matters of consummate urgency; they were merely token spoils in an indolent game of hare-and-hounds.

Reeves-Wadleigh's thinking about the Gehlman matter had become infinitely sharper, he felt, since the introduction of opium derivatives into his bloodstream. In fact, looking back now, he found the slowness of his mental processes in times past almost laughable to contemplate. He didn't know when exactly the truth had dawned on him, but it *had* dawned, most decidedly, and it shone down now like the sun on a midsummer's morning. Of course Gehlman was a spy for the Americans, for what was an observer anyway but a spy spying openly and with the consent of those he spied upon. The whole spy notion, Reeves-Wadleigh now realized, had distracted him from the key element in this whole affair: Gehlman was of German blood and, more pertinent, the nephew of Emil and Albert Gehlman, the German-Jewish bankers. Although Reeves-Wadleigh had been aware of this fact for months, it was not until his early morphinic reveries that the implications of the fact had fully come home to him. Now he saw it all so clearly—all of it, that is, except the denouement. Gehlman had been sent to the German Fleet at the same time that Maltbie had been sent to Britain. As far as Gehlman's American masters knew, he'd had to leave Germany because he'd involved himself in a scandal there. Since his sojourn with the Germans had been kept secret, moreover, his masters decided—with his enthusiastic prompting, no doubt—to send him to Britain after he'd compared notes with Maltbie, for the obvious reason that he would thus be enabled to make direct comparisons between the British and German Fleets. What his masters failed to realize, however, was the same thing Reeves-Wadleigh had failed to realize until recently: that the whole saga of Gehlman's troubles in Germany was a fabrication, or, as Lord Fisher had unwittingly defined it, "like something out of Dumas *père*."

Who stood to suffer if Germany lost the war, after all? German business interests among others, and German bankers, such as Emil and Albert Gehlman, most particularly. What were Emil and Albert Gehlman? Jews. What was Oskar Gehlman? A Jew. To what did a Jew owe his first allegiance? His Jewish God. To what did a Jew owe his second allegiance? His family. To what did he owe his third allegiance? His fellow Jews. To what did he owe his fourth allegiance? His money. What allegiance came after all four of these? Allegiance to country.

And so, what were the obvious conclusions? The Gehlman family was for Germany, Benjamin Gehlman most specifically included, and the entire von Tiel melodrama was a German cover story designed to conceal some kind of plot.

What kind of plot?

Ah, that indeed was the question.

From his long years in intelligence work, Reeves-Wadleigh knew that cover stories most often went wrong because they pointed in exactly the opposite direction from the truth. The Germans were just inexperienced enough in matters of espionage to fall prey to this tendency.

Now, what does the present cover story indicate? That Gehlman and von Tiel are mortal enemies. What truth does that point away from? That they are in league together in pursuit of some as yet unknown objective. On this hypothesis, the baron's wife wasn't murdered at all, but simply died in an accident. And her poor daughter hadn't been abducted, but was simply being used ex tempore to lend credence to the cover.

The giveaway, in Reeves-Wadleigh's opinion, had been von Tiel's relief from duty because of "alcoholism," and his subsequent all-too-predictable "disappearance." That, he felt, showed a really lamentable absence of imagination on someone's part. Since von Tiel had almost certainly left Germany, however—whether he'd disappeared or not—and since he was a valuable intelligence commodity regardless of what errand he was embarked on, Reeves-Wadleigh had requested the assistance of Admiral Hall, the director of the Intelligence Division. The first thing he'd asked for had been precautionary surveillance of the estate in Dorset where von Tiel's widowed English mother lived. The second thing was a QM (or "query message") to British agents in Holland and Scandinavia, von Tiel's most likely points of departure for England. The message had given a physical and biographical description of von Tiel and had asked for data on his whereabouts and movements. No responses had been received from the agents in Rotterdam, Copenhagen, and Göteburg. But from the agent in Christiania—who apparently had access to steamship passenger manifests—there had recently come the news that a purported Dutchman, a Mr. B. S. van Teel, had sailed for New York aboard the Scandinavian-American liner *Bergensfiord* on September 26. The agent had also reported that descriptions of Heer van Teel obtained from the *Bergensfiord*'s officers tallied with the description of Baron von Tiel that had been sent out from London.

Reeves-Wadleigh stared dreamily up at his bedroom ceiling. So von Tiel had gone to America—had arrived there, in fact, the day before Gehlman left. Obviously Gehlman had notified him that he, Gehlman, had been successful in getting his masters to assign him to the British Fleet; and the two of them would have met in New York to concert their plans. Soon, Reeves-Wadleigh felt confident, von Tiel would be coming to Britain too. In the meantime, Gehlman was being watched aboard the *Lion,* just as Maltbie was aboard the *Iron Duke,* while Sir William Wiseman's operatives in New York were searching for von Tiel. Once they found him, they would shadow him and inform Reeves-Wadleigh when he departed for England. Reeves-Wadleigh's men would take charge of his surveillance on his arrival, and when he and Gehlman finally rendezvoused to put their plans into effect, the Royal Navy's counterintelligence section would have them dead to rights.

Reeves-Wadleigh closed his eyes and let himself drift tranquilly toward warm and enveloping sleep. This business of slowly dying wasn't half as bad now as it had been at first. The morphine served to stifle the pain, and the Gehlman–von Tiel plot served to occupy the mind. It seemed wrong somehow, but Reeves-Wadleigh had to admit to himself that as his life ran out he was really having quite a lot of fun.

1915, 19TH DECEMBER—WASHINGTON, D.C.

It struck House, as his eyes wandered over the pedestrian furnishings of Mrs. Galt's gaslit home on Twentieth Street NW that the whole marriage ritual ran contrary to nature. It was, at bottom, the price women exacted from men in return for the delights of copulation, a sordid transaction under the best of circumstances. But mankind seemed comfortable with it—or resigned to it—so who was he to censure? Perhaps, to be honest, his jaundiced attitude was nothing more than a reaction to Mrs. Galt's unworthiness. Perhaps it wasn't really marriage he despised, but only this particular marriage of Woodrow Wilson's.

House looked at his watch; it read seven o'clock. The guests wouldn't be arriving for another hour. He walked into the drawing room, where the ceremony was going to take place. A preposterous floral bower had been constructed in front of the mantel, with orchids and American Beauty roses in vulgar profusion. Framing the bower, whose canopy was lined with white heather, were extravagant hangings of fern. Rose trees and fern bushes littered the floor around the bower's base, with an effect that was rather less sylvan than mortuary. And inside—the crowning banality—was a white satin priedieu on which the smitten couple would kneel. It was all in the most egregiously bad taste, the Colonel thought; and given the ludicrous excess that marked the decor of this wedding, one shuddered to contemplate the appearance of the bride.

The Colonel heard footsteps on the staircase behind him, and turned to see the President's physician, Lieutenant Grayson, descending at a trot.

"Good evening, Cary," House said.

Grayson's face lit up when he saw him. "Colonel! The President just sent me to go find you."

"Well, I'd say you've accomplished your mission with commendable despatch."

"Yes," said Grayson with persistent but now slightly uncertain enthusiasm. The Colonel's deadpan witticisms always seemed to leave him at a loss. "Look, excuse me, sir, but would you mind finding your own way up? He forgot his Bible, so I have to run back to the White House and fetch it. You turn right at the landing, and it's the second door on the right."

"I thought he'd sent you to fetch *me*," the Colonel said playfully.

"He did, sir. That's the reason . . . *one* of the reasons I was so glad to see you just now. I didn't know if I could find you and also go get the Bible and then get back here ahead of the guests. I'm still a bit pressed though, as I said, so if you wouldn't mind . . ."

"No, no, not at all, Cary. You go along."

"Thanks, Colonel. I'll get back as fast as I can."

"Fine, Cary," said House, reflecting mirthfully on the idea that the President's needs at this pregnant prenuptial moment had boiled down to the yin-yang of divinely inspired Scripture on the one hand and his aging unholy self on the other.

He went up the stairs and down the hall. Wilson's door was open. "May I enter?" he asked, knocking gently on the doorjamb.

The President, who'd been standing pensively by the window, turned and smiled broadly. "Edward! Splendid! I just sent out a posse for you."

"I know. I met it head on outside the drawing room."

Wilson laughed and advanced with his arms outstretched, causing House to worry for an instant that the President was going to embrace him. Wilson confined himself to shaking his hand and clapping him on the shoulder, however. "Well," he said, with a glance down at his elegant evening clothes and gleaming white waistcoat, "what do you think?"

"I think you're in danger of outshining the bride."

"Impossible!" Wilson bellowed jovially. "Wait till you see her."

"I'm sure she'll look unforgettable," House said, struggling to keep a tone of irony out of his voice.

Fortunately, Wilson was far too caught up in exuberant anticipation to detect the intrusion of any sour notes. He walked around the room with his hands clasped near his chest, looking, in House's opinion, somewhat like an ecstatically prayerful headwaiter. "You know, Edward," he said, stopping suddenly and turning to face the Colonel, "I feel almost *indecently* happy."

"Hardly appropriate for a ranking world statesman," House observed with a sly smile.

Wilson roared with laughter. "Ah, Edward," he said, "I'm having second thoughts about you going off to Europe again. Ten weeks is a long time to be deprived of your counsel."

"Well, I'd be a bit reluctant about going over myself, if I didn't think it was the only way to make them grasp the significance of our willingness to abandon nonentanglement."

"Yes. At least this time we have something concrete to offer them as an inducement to stop the fighting."

"I only hope it's enough. From what my friends on Wall Street tell me, the Allies are buying so much from us on credit that our neutrality is going to be very seriously compromised if the war goes on much longer."

Wilson frowned. "It's an endlessly bewildering business, Edward.

gle, and that I'm powerless to forestall them."

"Well," said House, lightening his tone, "no man is called upon to even *try* to forestall them on his wedding day. So put the whole business out of your mind . . . and forgive me for having brought it up."

The President smiled at him warmly. "Be sure to telephone me at Hot Springs before you sail."

"Of course, Governor," House replied.

"Good," said Wilson. "And now, let joy be unconstrained."

"Amen," House responded wistfully, hopeful that joy, in his absence, would not become synonymous with Edith Galt.

1915, 30TH DECEMBER—ABERDOUR

Maltbie lay motionless on the bed and stared blankly at the ceiling, half listening to the small rustling sounds Melina's clothes made as she disrobed in the dressing alcove. Until a few moments ago he had been in the process of getting ready for bed himself, but all at once a great nausea-inducing wave of fatigue had rolled over him and almost literally knocked him off his feet. Accordingly, apart from his tunic being unbuttoned, he was in all respects still dressed and ready for duty, right down to the tightly knotted laces of his half-boots. When he'd slept at all during the past ten weeks he'd done so dressed like this, and it didn't seem to matter much that he was now back at Aberdour on leave.

A gust of wind rattled the casements and sent granules of sleet clattering against the windowpanes. Maltbie winced. For him the weather had taken on a character of such purposeful malevolence that he often felt a hysterical urge to scream at it to stop tormenting him. Although Scapa and the Fleet Zone around it were not the coldest regions in which he had ever served, nor the wettest, nor the stormiest, they were nevertheless more consistently cold, wet, and stormy in unison than he would have thought meteorologically plausible.

Service with the Grand Fleet as winter descended differed radically from service when spring was near at hand. The fleet's task, to be sure, was the same one, but the mood of the men who performed the task was altogether different. For one thing there was the darkness. At 59° north latitude Scapa received less than five hours of daylight as the winter solstice approached, and even that meager allotment of radiation was subject to cruel exactions by the perpetual overlay of clouds. Then, of course, there were the gales. Great angry columns of polar air spun eastward by the Greenland low would pick up energy and moisture over the North Atlantic Drift and then smash through northern Scotland on their way to the ice floes of the Barents Sea. To be out on a sweep when one of these furies struck was a harrowing experience, even aboard a ship as massive as the *Iron Duke*. And to be in harbor was only marginally better.

Life amidst the darkness and the storms meant never being warm, seldom being dry, frequently being exhausted, and almost always being bored beyond description. For the officers, particularly those aboard the flagship, exhaustion was so prevalent due to the crushing work loads and the demands of maintaining constant battle readiness that boredom hardly even mattered. For the men, however, boredom mattered very much indeed, so much in fact that Jellicoe devoted what verged on a disproportionate percentage of his energies to combating it. There were the sing-alongs, of course, and frequent amateur theatricals of an occasionally bawdy nature (what with men costumed for female roles) aboard the depot ships *Ghourko, Borodino,* and *Imperieuse.* The boxing competitions provided spectator sport as well as lively intersquadron rivalries, and motion pictures from London and America were shown on a twice- or thrice-weekly basis on the mess decks of every large ship in the Flow. Every fortnight, moreover, a popular music hall performer would make the journey from the south to entertain the wildly appreciative sailors. Far and away the most memorable performance Maltbie witnessed was given by Harry Lauder, who sang and cavorted for three solid hours before the almost four thousand men who'd managed to squeeze aboard the *Ghourko.* He sang "I've Loved Her Ever Since She Was a Baby" and "That's the Reason Noo' I Wear a Kilt." He sang "The Same as His Father Was Before Him" and "The Saftest of the Family." He told outrageous stories in his outrageous Scottish burr, and the roar of the sailors' laughter shook the hull plates. When he broke into "Roamin' in the Gloamin'" the men all joined in with him, and they kept on singing for almost an hour, right through "Bonnie Charlie's Now Awa'." That well-loved song produced a magical final few minutes, as Lauder and the sailors took turns singing the chorus back and forth to one another:

> "Will ye no come back again?
> Will ye no come back again?
> Better lo'ed ye canna be,
> Will ye no come back again?"

Despite Jellicoe's untiring efforts, morale remained a serious concern. The men existed in cramped smelly quarters and were lucky if they got ashore on Mainland for a three-hour march once a week. Fistfights, or worse, became more frequent, and tension on the lower decks was sometimes almost palpable.

The major problem, beyond question, was the lack of action. The war was in its sixteenth month now, and the Grand Fleet had not yet seen an enemy ship. It didn't help that the battle cruisers had been in a couple of fights that the battleships had arrived too late to get in on. It helped even less that the newspapers that arrived daily from the south bore ever more strident headlines on the order of WHAT IS THE NAVY DOING? Thousands of soldiers were dying in France every week, it seemed, while Britain's vaunted dreadnoughts never got close to so much as a scrape. From admiral on down to boy second class, it rankled deeply.

Maltbie knew, as did every officer at Scapa, that what the navy was doing was controlling the seas. The men knew it too, after a fashion, but they didn't really understand why such unaggressive tactics were required, so the criticism in the press became harder and harder to bear. Most civilians didn't really understand either, and on the two or three occasions Maltbie managed a trip with some fellow officers into Kirkwall, he noticed that the welcome the Orcadians gave them became noticeably cooler each time.

He himself, feeling obliged to share to the fullest all the wartime trials of his shipmates, stood watches with them and suffered all their discomforts as if he were British himself. Left to his own initiative, he wouldn't even have taken this New Year's leave, because he hadn't been up at Scapa for the four full months that other officers had to wait before being permitted their first spell of relief. He had become so worn out, however, that Jellicoe—prompted, Maltbie guessed, by the ever impertinent Otley—had intervened in the matter and virtually ordered him down to Edinburgh, securing compliance with a promise that Maltbie could go to sea with Beatty if the Germans should happen to come out while he was there.

The trip south from Thurso had been long, cold, and uncomfortable. Given the exhausted state in which Maltbie had undertaken it, moreover, it was not surprising that now, nearly paralyzed with fatigue, he had fallen dead asleep.

Melina emerged from the dressing alcove in her white silk nightgown, the mist of perfume she'd applied still wet beneath her ears and between her breasts. On seeing Maltbie sprawled insensible across the bed, she at first gasped in fright, but the slow rising-and-falling motion of his chest quickly reassured her.

She walked across the room and looked down at him, helpless and unconscious beneath her gaze. She had planned to make love first and then tell him how unhappy she was at Aberdour, and how she wished he would get away from Scapa more often, and how she thought she couldn't stand much more of coldness and winter and Scotland. Looking at him now, though, his face haggard, his body limp and drained of vigor, her own hardships seemed to shrink to unimportance. She'd been pampered all her life, she told herself, had always gotten what she wanted. So it was high time for some Duty and Self-Sacrifice. Surely she wasn't too spoiled to rise to the occasion. She would suffer in silence and endure, just as did many others. She would *not* behave like Ethel Beatty!

It was odd, however, that even as she made that affirmation she did not feel as she thought she ought to about her war-worn husband. She did not feel the protective love that she had always felt so strongly in the past. She did not feel the desire she usually felt either, nor even her newfound wifely dedication. She felt instead a kind of dead sourness sitting like a lid on a far more bitter feeling that she did not want to and would not acknowledge.

It was anger.

1916, 26TH JANUARY—BERLIN

Von Müller eyed House mistrustfully as the Colonel poured him a cognac. He felt intensely uncomfortable about being closeted alone with the American in Ambassador Gerard's office; the other guests at this embassy dinner in honor of the Houses' arrival in Berlin would certainly misinterpret what was going on. They would think that he had initiated the meeting with the Colonel at the Kaiser's behest, in order to propose some new compromise arrangement with regard to the submarines. They would gossip extravagantly, and the rumors would reach Wilhelm's ear. Then von Müller would have to spend God knew how many hours convincing the Emperor that the report of this conversation he intended to make to him first thing tomorrow morning had been accurate and complete in all respects. Of course, the Kaiser would eventually feel reassured about his loyalty and then apologize with embarrassing abjection for having ever doubted it. The whole business would inevitably be tiresome and depressing; it would also cause von Müller to wonder yet again how much longer he could tolerate his role as his sovereign's favored retainer.

"I'm going to be candid with you, Admiral," House said, walking to the sofa and presenting von Müller with his drink. "Perhaps even foolishly candid."

The admiral met House's eyes and concentrated on keeping his voice free of any skeptical inflection as he said, "Foolish candor? Perhaps you should think twice."

House gave him a comprehending smile. "Very well then. Let's say, calculatedly risky candor."

Von Müller's eyebrows rose. "May I ask why you should wish to take any risks with me whatsoever, calculated or otherwise?"

"Do you know the expression, 'nothing ventured, nothing gained'?" the Colonel responded.

The admiral nodded. "In that case, may I ask what sort of 'gain' you have in mind?"

"A very modest one: ending the war."

"Ah," said von Müller softly. "On whose terms?"

"On humanity's terms."

"Humanity is not a belligerent power."

"No. But it is, you'll admit, an interested party."

"Yes," von Müller responded with little conviction.

"My dear Admiral," House said, "you know I have just come from discussions in London and Paris. What would you say if I told you that my conversations there revealed a genuine readiness to negotiate a peace?"

"I would say, a second time, on whose terms?"

"On no one's terms. Just simply on the basis of a return, with minor modifications, to the status quo ante, together with the elimination of militarism and navalism under the supervision of some sort of league of nations."

Von Müller gazed at his snifter of cognac. He supposed that the Colonel was sincere enough—but *really!* "With minor modifications" was an altogether ludicrous phrase to employ in a context such as this. It begged the very questions that the sentence surrounding it raised.

Lifting his eyes to look at House, the admiral said, "The elimination of militarism and navalism seems rather a utopian objective at this point in history."

House shook his head. "Please don't misjudge me, Admiral. I'm under no illusions about the obstacles in the way of peace. But since the continuing good offices of a neutral United States appear a prerequisite for its achievement, I am concerned that my country's status as a neutral should be secure. I know from numerous sources that you together with the Imperial Chancellor have been instrumental in helping our two nations resolve our differences over submarine warfare. My object now is to get from you some sense of the dialogue going on in your government with regard to that critical issue."

Von Müller shifted uneasily in his chair and began to express an objection, but the Colonel held up his hand. "I am not remotely suggesting anything that might compromise your position, Admiral. Please believe me. I simply want to get some idea of the factors that influence the decision-making process."

"Why?" von Müller inquired bluntly.

"Because if the United States is going to depart from the policy of nonentanglement in European affairs that has guided the country since its inception, I want to make certain that we do everything in our power to support those factions in the belligerent nations whose influence would contribute to the success of our eventual intervention."

"I see," von Müller said, knowing that such an answer, while true as far as it went, went a very short way indeed toward the whole and unvarnished truth. House must have learned somehow of the increased pressure now being exerted on the Kaiser by the submarine advocates, and he naturally enough wanted to know what the chances were that the Tirpitz faction would get its way. If the chances were good, then the political advisability of an overt American peace initiative would be very much open to doubt.

"I promised you candor, Admiral, and I hope for candor in return. So let me tell you what I know about the situation from various sources, and then ask you to advise me on it."

"My advice may not be of much value, Colonel. I feel obliged to make that very clear."

House gave him a poker-faced look of disconcerting duration and finally said, "I'm sure you'll be as forthcoming as your obligations will permit."

Von Müller returned the look, then gave a noncommittal shrug.

"Good," said House with a faintly amused grimace. "Now I will not ask you to confirm or deny any part of what I say. I will simply outline the situation as I understand it."

"Very well," von Müller replied.

"I know, for example, that about a month ago there was a meeting of the army and navy high commands. I believe that this meeting was called in order to discuss the new strategic situation resulting from the German successes in Russia, the Balkans, and Turkey. I know that there is a strong current of opinion among military leaders here to the effect that Germany's chance for victory must be seized this year, before the Allies' strategic advantages in a long-term war of attrition begin to take on significant weight. I know that your government intends—with my government's reluctant acquiescence—to shortly begin unrestricted submarine warfare against enemy merchant ships that carry offensive armament, given that such ships have been instructed by the British Admiralty to attack submarines on sight. I know—as of course do the British and the French—that Germany is massing forces for a major stroke somewhere on the western front. And I know that Admiral von Pohl's illness will momentarily result in his replacement as commander in chief of the High Seas Fleet by Admiral Scheer, whose aggressive approach to sea, as well as undersea, warfare is widely celebrated."

The Colonel paused and gave von Müller a mildly interrogative look. The admiral by way of reply merely nodded, however, in a manner that indicated he had heard what had been said but had nothing to say himself in response to it. He was moderately impressed with the extent and depth of House's intelligence data, but he had no intention of providing the Colonel with any sort of corroborative—or noncorroborative—reaction. House appeared to understand and accept this after several moments, and quite equably resumed his monologue: "Now, what do I infer from all these bits of knowledge? I infer that Germany is bracing for a supreme effort to force a decision in the war, and that the advocates of all-out submarine warfare may soon be exerting the maximum possible pressure on your sovereign to grant them freedom of action, regardless of the repercussions with respect to neutral nations."

The Colonel paused and looked directly into von Müller's eyes. "What I would like to have from you, Herr Admiral, is a rough estimation of the likelihood that you and the Imperial Chancellor will be able to counteract this pressure, and a rough stipulation of the kinds of circumstances in which the Kaiser might be forced to yield to it."

Von Müller frowned and made some rapid calculations. The rough "estimation" and "stipulation" the Colonel was angling for obviously could not be given him without betraying grand strategic designs. Von Müller had to say something, however, or House might very well "infer" that the advocates of unrestricted submarine warfare had already carried the day, and that war between Germany and the United States was only a matter of time.

Colonel House was regarding him with patient expectation, and the admiral finally spoke. "I can say only this: as long as the military situation remains roughly in status quo, and as long as we have a fleet capable of denying Britain a supply route to Russia through the Baltic, it should be possible to avoid unfortunate incidents at sea. If something should happen to our fleet, however, or if the overall strategic situation worsens to such an extent that extreme measures are called for to ward off a defeat, then I can give no assurances that those measures will not be employed."

The Colonel appraised him thoughtfully as he spoke and, when he finished, probed: "I don't suppose there's any chance that you'd be willing to elaborate at all on what you've said."

Von Müller smiled at him, for the sake of diplomacy. "There is no chance whatsoever."

House smiled back. They had said enough.

1916, 14TH FEBRUARY—LONDON

The slate gray winter afternoon was yielding to the deeper chill of a dank and smoky winter evening as Gehlman and Alis walked through Green Park toward the Ritz. Before the war the lamps would have begun to come on at this time of day, but now they stood sightless, like relics of a vanished civilization.

They had arrived early that morning aboard the sleeper from Edinburgh. Maltbie and Melina were supposed to have traveled with them, but Maltbie's train from Inverness had been delayed by a snowstorm, so he and Melina had presumably taken the *Flying Scotsman* this morning and were probably just now disembarking at King's Cross.

The somewhat cryptic telegram from the embassy's naval attaché had been sent to them three days ago: YOUR PRESENCE REQUIRED NLT SIX P.M. FOURTEENTH INST. Gehlman had welcomed the summons with as much enthusiasm as his condition of advanced fatigue permitted. On its face it granted him a needed respite from duty as well as his first opportunity since arriving to spend some meaningful length of time with Alis. On a more significant level, however, it presented him with an occasion for terminating the manifestly unsatisfactory arrangement in which he found himself mired.

He had made the decision during the night as he lay in his sleeping car berth too overtired to sleep. He was not seeing enough of Alis; Maltbie was not seeing enough of Melina; and neither he nor Maltbie was learning enough to justify the personal sacrifices they were both being called on to make. More particularly, there now seemed little likelihood that the German Fleet would ever venture out of its harbors again, and even if it did come out there seemed *no* likelihood that it could be forced into giving battle.

Gehlman wanted out; that much was by now vividly clear to him. Even though Alis—thanks to Melina—had made a splendid adjustment to the new life she'd had imposed on her, that was no reason to go on depriving her of the fuller and richer life she could be living in New York. Erna missed her terribly, Gehlman knew, and Oskar also wanted very much to have her back.

As for himself, he was as worn out as he had ever been in his life. Unlike Beatty and his staff, who seemed to derive extra reserves of stamina from the danger they perceived their country to be in, Gehlman had no patriotic stake in putting up with the hardships and exertions of their wartime life. And while he liked Beatty and the *Lion's* officers well enough, Britain and the British as a whole had never really held much charm for him. Now, moreover, what with massive casualty lists and the introduction of the alien system of conscription, the United Kingdom had become so somber and stiff-lipped a nation as to oppress far more buoyant spirits than his.

Of course, he admitted to himself, there were compensating factors on the professional level. It was fascinating, after all, to be serving aboard the very ship that had almost blown the *Seydlitz* out of the water at Dogger Bank. In fact, the whole experience of serving on both sides in the same conflict was an intriguing one. What was most intriguing of all was the difference in the way each of the contending fleets viewed itself and its adversary. The Germans displayed an exuberant esprit de corps that combined professional pride with an odd sort of guileless enthusiasm. It wasn't that the German sailors were amateurish in performance—far from it—but there was definitely something of the amateur in their attitude toward what they did. They seemed to take a childlike pride in the idea of being a major naval force in the world, and they also seemed enormously flattered by the notion that they were substantial enough a factor in the scales of power to merit an opponent as exalted as the British Fleet. There, in Gehlman's opinion, was the key deficiency in the German naval service: its officers and men stood in awe of their North Sea rivals. Not that they were intimidated by them; they weren't. But they had such respect for the men and traditions of the Royal Navy that they unwittingly gave the British an advantage. Rather than wishing to destroy their adversaries, they were more interested, on a certain level, in proving to them their own worthiness as foes. It was almost as if they wanted the respect of the Royal Navy more than they wanted its destruction.

The British, on the other hand, were models of cold-hearted determination. For them the preeminence of their naval service was a foregone conclusion, as was, in their minds, the outcome of any eventual clash with the Germans. Unlike the High Seas Fleet, the Royal Navy had a vital role to play in the preservation of empire and nation, and the attention of the battle fleet was focused on only one thing: the ruthless elimination of any threat to its predominance. The British viewed the Germans with just a trace of condescension, moreover: Fritz was a game enough fellow, brave and competent in his way, but he was also essentially a parvenu whose presumption would sooner or later get the better of him, at which point he would be quickly and conclusively dispatched.

The essence of the British attitude was embodied in the short blocklike figure of Sergeant Arthur Bellmaine, the fleet middleweight boxing champion, who had been assigned as Gehlman's servant. Any mention of the German Navy would draw from Bellmaine a curt dismissive snort, a sort of nonverbal "Oh, *those* silly chaps." It was clear that, in the marine sergeant's eyes, the entire High Seas Fleet was little more than an irritant, a bothersome enemy diversion that tied down the bulk of Britain's naval power in the North Sea and kept it from concentrating on its proper task of single-handedly winning the war.

After checking in at the Connaught this morning and placing Alis in the custody of the hotel matron, Gehlman had gone around the corner to Grosvenor Square and been shown upstairs to the office of Commander Symington. The attaché had informed him that the summons sent to him and Maltbie had been dispatched at the instance of Colonel House, who was in London and wanted urgently to talk with both of them. That constituted good news from Gehlman's point of view; it meant that he would be able to explain his new intentions directly to the man who was primarily concerned with them; it also meant that his departure for New York might then be expedited. The only ominous note was the fact that House wanted to talk to him and Maltbie *urgently;* but Gehlman could not imagine any matter of sufficient urgency to keep him from going home.

He had gone back to the Connaught in a celebratory mood and whisked Alis off for an overdue tour of London, which she'd seen only *en passant* on the way up to Scotland from New York. He felt almost giddy with anticipation as they crisscrossed the city, taking in the Tower, Madame Tussaud's, St. Paul's, Westminster Abbey, Trafalgar Square, the National Gallery, and finally Buckingham Palace. It had been four full months since he'd last been able to spend an entire day in Alis's company, and the prospect of soon being free to devote most of every day to her filled him with a kind of bubbly jubilation. He wasn't altogether accustomed to such strong surges of emotion, and he supposed that the brief dizzy spells he began to experience as the day wore on resulted from the interaction of keen excitement and well-nigh crippling fatigue.

Now, as they walked through Green Park, a spell of dizziness came over him that did not subside as had the others, but rather intensified with such rapidity that he found himself reeling sideways off the walkway. He reached out as his balance left him, groping blindly for a bench or tree to take the burden of his weight. But there was nothing there.

He fell heavily onto his left shoulder and lay for a dazed instant on the grass without any sense of where he was. Then Alis gave a piercing shriek: *"Babbo!"* and the world around him came back into focus. He sat up to find that she was at his side, tugging frenziedly on his right arm to get him up. "It's all right, Allie," he said hoarsely, more concerned about the terrified look in her eyes than he was about his own sudden incapacitation.

He let her help him onto the nearest bench and sat taking deep breaths as she stood in front of him with tears streaming from her eyes. "It's all right, Allie," he repeated, but his voice broke as he said the words, and to his astonishment he burst into uncontrollable sobs.

The first thing he felt—after the astonishment passed—was a sudden flash of comprehension. He perceived that the sobbing and the dizziness both stemmed from the same basic cause: he was exhausted beyond the point of self-control, or rather, he was exhausted and self-control was no longer required of him, because the decision to leave Britain had been made.

He looked at Alis and smiled through his tears. In many ways, even as he kept on crying, he began to feel more tranquil than he had felt in months. Alis, her own cheeks red and wet, put her arms around his neck. He hugged her close against him. "Poor Babbo," she said, and he answered, "No, no, Allie; I'm fine. I'm all right. . . . We're *both* all right, in fact. We're going home."

"*Really*, Babbo?" she gasped, her eyes widening.

"Really," he confirmed.

Melina was waiting in the Ritz lobby, looking tired and strained. Commander Symington had met them at King's Cross and accompanied them here only ten minutes ago, she said. He had had to hurry back to the embassy, however, and Maltbie had thought he should hurry upstairs to the Colonel. So she had been left alone here to wait until Alis came to take care of her.

Gehlman laughed and suggested that she go with Alis back to the Connaught, where he'd booked a room for her and Maltbie. Melina was quick to agree, saying she badly needed a bath and a nap.

They exchanged weary smiles, and Gehlman said, "I think there are better days just ahead."

She gave him a questioning look.

"I'll explain in detail at dinner," he said, starting toward the elevators. "Alis can give you a good enough idea to lift your spirits in the meantime though."

Colonel House answered Gehlman's knock in person and ushered him into a softly lit sitting room. Maltbie was standing with a drink in his hand. He looked hollow-eyed and pale.

"Enjoying Scapa?" Gehlman asked wryly as Colonel House poured a glass of brandy for him.

Maltbie grinned. "Words fail me," he said.

House invited them both to sit down and then began pacing slowly around the room. In the ensuing silence Gehlman decided that the moment was ripe for him to raise the matter of his return to the United States. Just as he was about to speak, however, the Colonel's voice forestalled him.

"Gentlemen, I've asked you to come all the way down here from Scotland because momentous events are impending in which you could play a most pivotal role."

Gehlman felt a chill run through his body; the word "urgently" started to reecho in his mind.

"I cannot go into detail, of course," House continued, "because of the extreme delicacy of the discussions now in progress. All I can say is that the question of war or peace may depend on my obtaining certain information which you two alone will be in a position to provide."

Gehlman exchanged a quick uneasy glance with Maltbie. House's use of the future tense was the very worst kind of portent.

"Gentlemen," the Colonel went on, "it is absolutely essential for me to have as much advance notice as possible of any eventual fleet engagement in the North Sea. Accordingly, if either of you at any time suspects, for whatever reasons, that there is an increasing likelihood of such an engagement taking place, I want you to inform

Commander Symington by telegram at your earliest opportunity. All you need say in the telegram is, 'Request two weeks' leave commencing such-and-such a date.' The date you name should be your best rough estimate of when the fleet action might occur, unless of course it is about to occur right away, in which case you should say, 'Request two weeks' leave commencing as soon as possible.' Is that clear?"

Gehlman and Maltbie nodded dully.

"Good," said House, taking in Gehlman's morose expression. "Now, Commander Maltbie has told me that his wife finds her situation in Edinburgh increasingly difficult to bear . . ."

Gehlman flashed Maltbie a look of surprise; so Melina's stoical facade had finally given way.

". . . and as she is the linchpin, so to speak, of your arrangements, I take her unhappiness very seriously indeed. If, however, you gentlemen can prevail upon her to put up with her unsatisfactory situation just a few months longer, it may be possible for President Wilson to bring this terrible war to an early end."

Gehlman sagged in his chair, his body leaden with the weight of disappointment. So the bitter cup was not yet empty; there were draughts of duty still to be drunk. And poor Melina: how wrong to have told her that there were better days ahead.

1916, 6TH MARCH–KILVERSTONE, NORFOLK

"Admiral's Walk" at Kilverstone was a grassy avenue of yew trees leading down from the hall toward the River Wittle, and at its far end was a forward-leaning sleepy-eyed figure of Nike framed by a copse of Norway spruce. Reeves-Wadleigh found the presence of this relic of the sailing era almost startlingly incongruous, given Kilverstone's location fully sixty miles from the sea on the Norfolk-Suffolk border. Congruity had never been one of Lord Fisher's major preoccupations, however, as witness the obvious pride the admiral took in having the well-weathered figurehead there on his estate.

"It's from the old two-decker *Calcutta*, Monty," Fisher boomed as they strode down the hill in the teeth of a gusty northeast wind. "My first ship: eighty-four guns."

Reeves-Wadleigh had to exert himself to maintain the admiral's pace, and somewhere beneath the thick coating of morphine that sheathed his nerve ends he could feel his body starting to protest.

"Sixty-one bloody years ago last month," Fisher continued. "*Anno Domini* 1855. I was a ruddy cadet, off to fight the Roosians in the Baltic. But the weather was so bloody horrible that a week after leaving Plymouth we were all the way back at the Scilly Islands, a hundred miles farther from St. Petersburg than if we'd stayed in port!"

Reeves-Wadleigh smiled at the thought of the old-time navy, enslaved to wind and tide. As few as thirty years ago, when he was a cadet himself, sails had still been the preferred, the "appropriate," devices for imparting motion to a ship. Engines—and engineers—were carried on sufferance, and great was the mortification when they had to be employed.

Only thirty years ago.

They came to the bottom of the walk and sat down on a bench that the spruces sheltered from the wind; the Nike loomed before them as low clouds scudded by above the treetops, sending down occasional angry spatterings of rain.

Fisher gazed fixedly at the figurehead, seemingly lost in recollections. After a time, though, he gave a valedictory sort of sigh and turned to Reeves-Wadleigh. "So, Monty; our friend the baron is on his way hither?"

"Yes sir, aboard the Danish liner *Hellig Olav.*"

"Is he still Mr. B. S. van Teel, the doughty Dutchman?"

"Yes, sir, he's still traveling on that passport."

"And he's booked passage for . . . ?"

"Southampton."

"Is that definite?"

"Yes, sir."

"We seem to be on to something, Monty."

"Yes, sir," Reeves-Wadleigh replied with considerable satisfaction. "We certainly do."

"How did Meinheer van Teel spend his time in America?"

"He spent it in what seemed to be a rather peculiar manner, at first glance. During October, November, and most of December he stayed at a small residential hotel on East Seventy-ninth Street, across from the residence of Oskar Gehlman."

"Ah *ha!*"

"Yes, sir. And every day, every single day without exception, he would leave his hotel at seven in the morning, walk across Fifth Avenue to a park bench facing the Gehlman mansion, and sit there until nine o'clock at night."

"What? He sat there every day for fourteen hours, without eating, without relieving himself, without *moving?*"

"Yes, sir, as far as we know. He took breakfast in the hotel at six and dinner at a German restaurant on Eighty-sixth Street at nine. He was always well dressed, and he always carried a pint flask of cognac, which he consumed discreetly over the course of each day."

"So as to keep off the chill, no doubt," Fisher said drily.

"Well, sir, from everything we know it appears that, for him, a pint a day amounted to being abstemious. Although it was actually more like a quart a day, since he also took cognac at breakfast and dinner."

"Good heavens! What a remarkable fellow. Where did the money come from?"

"Well, sir, our people in New York didn't locate him until early December, so we don't know what financial arrangements he made when he arrived. The staff at his hotel and the waiters at his restaurant said he always appeared to have plenty of money though. And since he never went to a bank while our people were watching him, I assume he either brought the dollars with him from Germany or converted a large sum of marks at various exchange banks when he first got to New York."

"You say our people didn't locate him till early December; how did they learn about his activities before then?"

"From the hotel manager and his employees; they were almost more curious about him than our people were."

"How did our people get them to talk about him?"

Reeves-Wadleigh hesitated for a fraction of a second, but then acknowledged to himself that Fisher would eventually compel him to answer anyway. "They presented themselves as American Secret Service agents investigating aliens suspected of engaging in espionage."

Fisher rocked back and guffawed. "Those cheeky devils!" he bellowed. "What bloody nerve! And they pulled it off, did they?"

"Yes, sir. The staff at the hotel talked very freely about von Tiel when our people finally interviewed them in January. Of course, by then von Tiel was no longer there to inhibit them from telling what they knew."

"Oh? And where had our fine friend got to?"

"To Washington, sir."

"Ahhhhhh."

"Yes, sir. He arrived there on December twenty-seventh, took a room in a boardinghouse near the Anacostia Aerodrome, and during the first week of January started taking long daily walks around the Army and Navy Building just west of the White House."

"You mean, he just walked and walked around that one particular building?"

"Yes, sir: very slowly and deliberately, like a sentry."

"I see. And . . . ?"

"And after several days of this, he approached a young junior grade lieutenant named Childress as the man was leaving the place in the evening."

"Who is this Childress?"

"Actually, sir, the question might more accurately be phrased, who *was* he, as he apparently committed suicide about a week ago."

"Really? How very, very intriguing. What else about him?"

"Very little, sir, I'm afraid. He was twenty-six years old, he was a bachelor, he worked in the Bureau of Construction. We don't know where he fits in, really. All we know is that he and von Tiel had dinner together every evening for two weeks or so, that the baron spent the night in Childress's apartment on the night of January nineteenth, and that Childress took a room at von Tiel's boardinghouse on the twentieth, where he was found with a bullet in his eye three days after von Tiel returned to New York to come here."

"Von Tiel didn't kill him?"

"No, sir. Childress went to work on the two days between von Tiel's departure for New York and the day of his own death, and we know definitely that the baron was in New York up to the time he boarded the *Hellig Olav.*"

"Correct me if I'm wrong, Monty, but isn't there a sharp odor of Sodom in this story?"

"We're reasonably certain that there is; yes, sir."

"I see. And what do you make of all these peculiar goings-on?"

"Well, sir, we still have a good deal less information than we'd like to have, but my best guess is that von Tiel camped outside the Gehlman mansion in order to await some kind of signal from Gehlman Senior—perhaps that Childress was prepared to cooperate, or that he had finally obtained some key entrée inside the Navy Department. Whatever the signal was, von Tiel obviously received it at the end of December and thereupon left New York.

"Now, what transpired between him and Childress in Washington is almost entirely conjectural. My own assumption is that Childress probably lost his nerve at some point, and that von Tiel seduced and blackmailed him to prevent him from backing out. Having gotten what he was after, he then left Childress in the lurch."

"And the poor fool promptly killed himself," Fisher concluded.

"Yes, sir. That's my reading of events."

"Hmmmm. Do you think Gehlman and von Tiel are doing whatever they're doing with the knowledge and consent of the powers that be in Washington?"

"No, sir. If they were working for the Americans, they wouldn't have had to go to the trouble of recruiting Childress. He obviously supplied some sort of information that the Navy Department wanted to keep secret."

"Very well; then would I be right in assuming that there is no connection between the plot you're investigating and Colonel House's meeting with Maltbie and Gehlman in London last month?"

"Yes, sir. I believe that assumption would be justified by the facts."

"What about Commander and Mrs. Maltbie? Do you think they're involved in this conspiracy?"

"It seems unlikely, sir, but we can't yet exclude the possibility."

Fisher sat frowning pensively for several seconds, then asked, "What's Gehlman up to now?"

"He's back at Rosyth, sir; though he's been spending much less time on the *Lion* since he returned from London."

"Oh?"

"Yes, sir. He's been spending much more time with his ward and Mrs. Maltbie."

"And what does that signify, do you think?"

"I don't know, sir. I'll just have to keep at it."

"Do that, Monty; you're doing yeoman work."

"Thank you, sir."

"But take a little time off now and then too; you look pretty badly run down to me."

"I feel quite fit, sir," Reeves-Wadleigh lied, excusing himself on the basis that, given morphine, the statement was virtually true.

"Well, take a day's holiday anyway. This war has a long way to run yet, and we'll need men like you to stay the course."

"Thank you, sir. But didn't I hear rumors that Colonel House's mission here portended some progress toward peace?"

"Rubbish!" Fisher snorted. "Oh, people smiled at him and listened earnestly to his ramblings—where would we be without American money and munitions, after all?—but no one in the government took him the least bit seriously. All those peace plans of his are the purest essence of make-believe."

"I'm relieved to hear it, sir," Reeves-Wadleigh said.

"And well you might be, Monty," Fisher replied, lifting a hand toward the Nike. "There's what we're fighting for, dear fellow: Victory! An end at last to the German plague!"

"Hear, hear, sir!" Reeves-Wadleigh responded with enthusiasm, struck for a brief instant by an eerie narcotic sensation that the figure of Nike had actually smiled.

1916, 23D MARCH—LOCH LEVEN

Sun!

The clouds had begun to break up as they drove out of Aberdour after breakfast. By the time they reached Cowdenbeath the gaps between the clouds had become as wide as the clouds themselves, and Gehlman had stopped to put down the top of the Morris-Cowley that Lady Beatty had placed at Melina's disposal. Now, as they headed east along the southern shore of Loch Leven, the sky was a lucid blue, flecked here and there with only the wispiest tufts of white.

Melina lifted her face to the warmth and savored it, indifferent to the bite of the forty-degree air and to the buffeting gusts of wind that curled round the windscreen. In an earlier incarnation, she mused, she must have been a Mithraic priest, a devotee of the sun. How else explain the almost religious exaltation she felt as the light touched her skin? The equinox had come, the long ordeal of winter would soon be at an end; and Melina felt a pagan urge to dance, to gorge herself on living. (Part of her revived sense of vitality, she suspected, was related to the fact that seven weeks had passed since her last flow of menstrual blood.)

She looked over at Gehlman, straight and stern behind the wheel. Sensing her gaze, he turned to look at her, and the sternness left his face. Sitting between them, red-cheeked and bundled warmly, Alis took in their moment of interaction and beamed like a happy imp.

Melina looked back up at the sun and closed her eyes. It was odd, she reflected, how much could be changed by a woman's tears—how much *had* been changed by hers. The week they returned from London, the day after Maltbie left to go back to Scapa Flow, Gehlman had come to see Alis, and Melina in a panic of depression had begged him to stay for tea. He had consented—he could hardly have refused—and Melina in the midst of pouring him a cup had found herself starting to weep. Once she started, it was well beyond her power to stop, and Gehlman's manifest embarrassment made her feel so silly and weak that she cried even harder. He had, of course, asked what was wrong, but in a voice that indicated a concern for her real and strong enough to offset the uneasiness caused by her tears. She had held back for a moment in a last effort to sustain the character of loyal, long-suffering wife, but then it had all poured out. She had recited her loneliness and boredom, her feelings of entrapment and desperation, her hatred of the endless winter cold and dark. He had listened with sympathy, and she had gone on to tell him more: of her anger and resentment, of her mad urges to escape, and of her increasingly bitter quarrels with Harry, whose subservience to duty and blind acceptance of the way things were drove her wild with impatience.

To her surprise, Gehlman had responded with his own outpouring of frustration and discontent. He had said how tired he felt, how sick he was of never being able to spend more than an hour or two with Alis, how he objected to "being used" by the people in Washington, and how he despised himself, not just for coming to Britain under false pretenses but also for enmeshing Melina in the deception. The situation was intolerable for all of them, he had concluded, and now that he knew Melina's feelings exactly matched his own, he was damn well going to make some drastic changes.

In the weeks that followed, Melina had been amused—and disappointed—by the wide disparity between her somewhat self-indulgent notion of what "drastic changes" might entail and Gehlman's highly circumspect forays into actual truancy. The policy he adopted, after much moral agonizing and consternation, was to take a full day off once a fortnight and devote it to Melina and Alis. Though this hardly constituted profligate depravity in Melina's opinion, Gehlman spent his entire first day of what he referred to as "French leave" walking around Edinburgh in a guilt-ridden state of nerves. Melina accordingly proposed to him that they should spend his next day of wicked license far from the sight of the battle cruisers' smoke, and she mentioned Flag Lieutenant Seymour's cottage near Kinross (where she and Maltbie were to have honeymooned) as a sensible place to go. She was to reflect, later, that this suggestion had probably sprung from a facet of her character that she had always preferred to disavow.

It quickly became apparent that Gehlman would not be able to bring himself to ask an officer he was serving with to aid and abet him in his dereliction of duty, but when Seymour showed up at Aberdour with Beatty one afternoon, Melina had no compunctions about making the request herself. The flag lieutenant had said of course: she could use the cottage any time she wished, and he had gone on to give her detailed instructions as to the location of keys, linen, larder—and even nearby golf and shooting. It took some doing to allay Gehlman's persistent misgivings once she told him that things had been arranged; but she finally got him to yield to his baser nature, and this day of sun and freshness was the laudable result.

The cottage was a small affair of gray stone and brown wattle on the northwestern side of the Loch. About a mile across the water on a rocky little island stood Lochleven Castle, where Mary, Queen of Scots, had spent a year as the prisoner of Lady Douglas before escaping in May of 1568 and rushing off to add Langside to her lengthening list of military defeats.

Melina, Gehlman, and Alis ate their picnic lunch on the small wooden pier near the cottage's front gate, and then decided to chance a trip to Castle Island in the old rowboat that was lying under the ell of a nearby woodshed. Gehlman applied his professional eye to the boat's surfaces and judged it prudent to bring along two pitchers from the cottage scullery. Sure enough, on their way back from the island one of the floorboards came loose. Melina had a bad moment as the icy water started to trickle into the boat; she had a terrifying sense of déjà vu, which she quickly realized was not an illusion but a memory. The cottage was barely three hundred yards away, however, and Gehlman was cheerfully shouting burlesque emergency orders in an old-sea-dog tone of voice. "Avast, ye lubbers," he called out as Alis giggled with excitement, "bail or we're done for!" Melina obeyed, saluting Gehlman and Alis in turn, and barking, "Aye aye, Cap'n!" as she bent to the task. Alis joined in with the second pitcher, and after less than ten minutes of not very strenuous exertion they were back on dry land.

The sun was sinking behind Lendrick Hill as they pulled the boat to the woodshed. Back in the cottage Gehlman built a fire while Melina and Alis made tea, and as the twilight waned the three of them sat with their feet dangling from the pier and fished contentedly for their dinner. Alis caught two fair-sized speckled trout, Gehlman caught three more, and Melina caught none, a failure for which she atoned by cleaning and cooking the catch with considerable éclat.

It was dark by the time she finished the washing up, but the oil lamp in the scullery and the firelight in the sitting room provided ample illumination. On entering the cottage's one small bedroom to kiss Alis good night, she found her already asleep, with Gehlman gazing down at her paternally. His face, she thought, had a softness and vulnerability to it as he looked at the child, a quality of sweetness that seldom emerged from behind the ironic mask he presented to the world. She knelt down and kissed Alis's forehead, then stood and without conscious premeditation looked Gehlman squarely in the eye.

Several seconds passed as they examined each other's faces in the muted light that came from the fireplace in the adjoining room. The excitement of being away from Aberdour, of being alone *en famille* with Gehlman and Alis, of sensing spring's immanence in the hills and woods around her, had left Melina feeling skittish and unruly. The day of sun and bracing air had left her feeling sensuously tired as well. Now, for a brief instant, she had a wild impulse to press her mouth to Gehlman's and thrust herself urgently against his body. She hardly thought of her marital status as they stood there; her wifehood seemed part of another world. Back there with the gray ships and the loud guns and the miles of dead men who were piled high around Verdun—that was the world where she was a married woman. But here she was free and wanton, a child of nature who had never lived by rules. She was hungry too, eager to have what she craved, and the embryo she harbored gave her immunity from reaping what Gehlman might sow.

The seconds went by. Melina saw surprise and confusion in Gehlman's eyes, as though the hunger that was there too had never before been suspected or acknowledged.

"We have to get an early start tomorrow."

"Yes," Melina answered, in a way that left nothing resolved.

"I'll take the armchair by the fire," he said equivocally, gesturing toward the second small bed in the tiny room.

"All right," she whispered, not shifting her eyes.

He turned his gaze away from her, evidently struggling to know the right thing to do. "We should think," he said at last. "We should think before we talk or act."

"Yes," said Melina, trembling breathlessly at the thought of how close they'd come. "Yes, we should."

He returned his eyes to hers. "Sleep well."

"Good night," she answered. But as he turned to go she reached up suddenly and kissed him lightly on the lips. "Sleep well, dear Ben."

"No chance of that now," he responded in a gentle voice.

She smiled at him, a full womanly smile that came all the way up from inside her and then persisted, even as Gehlman walked out of the room.

1916, 7TH APRIL—ON THE POTOMAC

A fine mist muffled the street lamps of Alexandria as the presidential yacht steamed easily down the Potomac at her three-quarter speed of twelve knots. Although visibility in the soft evening twilight was two miles or better, House's conversation with Wilson beneath the quarterdeck's awning was regularly interrupted by blasts of the *Mayflower's* foghorn. Evidently Captain Coryell was a bit overawed by the responsibility of having the President aboard. That, at least, was House's interpretation, fostered to no small extent by the generalized sense of irritation that was fretting his nerves.

It was not characteristic of him to be peevish, which made his peevishness all the more difficult to conceal—especially since one of the major causes of his bad temper was sitting not three feet to his left. Mrs. Galt—as he continued to think of her—was a vision of porcine complacency, seated there in her sable-collared coat. In his opinion her very presence constituted an affront, not an affront to him so much as to the dignity of American statecraft, in which he and Wilson were immersed. The woman's inroads into politics and diplomacy had increased to an alarming extent during House's absence in Europe. And his return at the end of February had done nothing to reverse the trend. It wasn't that she intruded her opinions, or even herself; but she seemed to regard her presence at Wilson's side when matters of state were discussed as not simply condoned by social custom, but enjoined by natural law!

House would have preferred some other venue for this conference in any case. He disliked the pervasive dampness that seemed an inevitable feature of life aboard smaller ships (most particularly at this time of year in these waters) and he disliked his cramped stateroom even more. But the documents from London and Paris had arrived yesterday, and given their content, he and the President had had to confer without delay. It was just his bad luck that Lieutenant Grayson had finally convinced Wilson to take a brief cruise for his health at virtually the same instant the pouches came in. The President, of course, had tried to beg off the junket, citing the seriousness of the crisis that impended; but Grayson had argued that the strains of dealing with whatever lay ahead might undermine Wilson completely if they were piled on top of the strains of the previous months without even a token layer of relaxation to cushion their weight.

He had a point, and Wilson knew it. The preparedness campaign he'd waged—barnstorming around the country in the middle of winter—had sapped his energy. The Mexican situation—General Pershing's pursuit of Pancho Villa through the barrancas of Chihuahua state—had brought him face to face with the prospect of another 1846. And Louis Brandeis's nomination to the Supreme Court —the Boston attorney being every businessman's *bête noire*, and a full-blooded Jew to boot—had plunged him into one of the most vicious political alley fights he had ever had to contest. All this on top of the endlessly ominous perplexities of the European situation was beginning to tell on his nerves; so a two-day "working vacation" did not seem an unreasonable concession to make to his flesh.

The consequence, though, for House, was that Mrs. Galt—who in the White House, at least, still kept to her place—was now about to witness the demise of the Colonel's long-nurtured plans for a mediated peace. She was going to be in on his failure to serve the President effectively, in other words, and the thought of that caused him distress that was almost physical in its intensity.

There was no denying the evidence in front of him, however: even if one discounted as biased the reports of the French and British Admiralties, there were still the affidavits of the American passengers and of the special investigators sent to Boulogne by Ambassador Sharp. In volume the evidence was overwhelming and in substance it was incontrovertible: on March 24 at 2:55 P.M. Western European Time a torpedo had exploded against the hull of the London, Brighton and South Coast Railway steamer *Sussex*, 1,353 tons, bound from Folkestone to Dieppe, killing some fifty of the 325 passengers aboard and injuring four of the twenty-five who were American. The ship was unarmed and the torpedo had struck without warning. It was a paradigm case of what Germany had promised *not* to do.

It almost certainly meant war.

"As I see it," House said, "there are only two things to be done: first, we should ask Sir Edward Grey one last time to assent to our demanding a peace conference right away . . ."

Wilson looked at him with tired unhappy eyes. "It sounds like a forlorn hope to me, Edward, but I don't suppose it can do any harm."

It infuriated House to see Mrs. Galt give a small fatuous nod of agreement.

"Second, we must draft an ultimatum to Germany, saying that unless she promptly renounces all submarine attacks on unarmed merchant vessels, we shall immediately sever diplomatic relations."

"What, do you think, will be their response to such an ultimatum?"

"If this attack was deliberate, they probably won't make a response."

"*If* . . . ?" the President said pointedly.

"There's always hope, Governor."

Wilson leaned back abruptly in his chair, as if House's use of the old term of intimacy had somehow affronted him. "Hope," he repeated in a lifeless voice.

"It's getting cold, Tommy," Mrs. Galt said at that moment. "I think we should all go inside."

The Colonel did not look at her.

"Very well, my dear," Wilson replied with a careworn smile, adding to House, "I presume we've covered the necessary ground."

"Yes," the Colonel murmured. "I think I'll stay out a while longer, though, sort things out in my mind."

"As you wish," Wilson responded with a casualness that House regarded as unnecessarily cool.

He walked to the fantail and looked out in the direction of Washington, by now a good ten miles to the north. Small wonder the President was cool, he told himself; his closest adviser had lost him the peace, and his November reelection too in all probability. Although there would be no Bull Moosers this year to split the Republican vote, the Democrats had still hoped to win on the slogan of "Progressivism, Prosperity and Peace," despite being the minority party. The Bryanists and their ilk would never support a platform of "Progressivism, Prosperity and Victory in Europe," however; so the split this time would be in the Democratic camp.

It was all going wrong, the Colonel reflected bitterly. The United States was being pushed into war by external events, instead of marching in under the banner of its national principles. And Woodrow Wilson, the best hope for the continuing progress of mankind, was going to be first on the casualty list.

Why? House asked himself. Why had the Germans done it? The only thing surer now than the death of his own dreams and aspirations was the doom and defeat of the German Empire.

The whole world had suddenly ceased to make sense.

How fitting that its American queen should be Edith Bolling Galt!

1916, 20TH APRIL—BERLIN

Von Müller could see that the Kaiser was flabbergasted—and that was just fine with von Müller. The time for patience, for indirection, and even for tact had passed the moment U-29's torpedo struck the *Sussex*. It may have passed two weeks earlier, in fact, when the Emperor authorized the resumption of submarine warfare against enemy merchant ships. But von Müller had held his tongue, largely because von Tirpitz had not held *his*, and had at last carried out his threat to resign. The Grand Admiral had been pushing for attacks on every ship that entered the war zone, neutral as well as Allied, liners as well as freighters. When he failed to get his way he had stalked out of the *Reichsmarineamt* in the most flagrantly histrionic manner, infuriating Wilhelm to such an extent that the political price of accepting the old sailor's resignation no longer held any terrors for the Emperor. Given the situation, von Müller had stifled the urge to attack from the opposite flank with demands that the U-boats be restrained. True, the resumption of undersea patrols posed serious dangers vis-à-vis the United States, but the instructions limiting the submarines' freedom of action were very precise, and in cases of uncertainty the potential target was always to be given the benefit of the doubt.

Alas, those clear and precise instructions reckoned without the willful stupidity of men like Konrad Pustkuchen, captain of U-29. Indeed, it was the account of the *Sussex* attack in Commander Pustkuchen's log that convinced von Müller to take a stand. That, and the ultimatum that had just arrived from Washington.

The two documents were on the Kaiser's desk, where von Müller had rather emphatically set them down. They represented a nice study in contrasts: muddled incompetence *v*. decisive clarity.

The log, with emphasis and special punctuation provided by von Müller, read as follows:

> The ship resembles a Channel packet vessel, but it has only one stack and a bridge very much like that of a warship. As it does not follow the route prescribed by the British Admiralty for ships of commerce, it cannot be a liner[!]

In view of its strange[?] rear structure, I take it for a
minelayer[!!] It carries no flag and is painted black all
over . . .

The ultimatum required no gloss or embellishments from the admiral:

> Unless the Imperial Government should now immediately declare its purpose to abandon its present methods of submarine warfare against passenger and freight-carrying vessels, the Government of the United States can have no choice but to sever diplomatic relations with the German Empire.

Had von Müller felt obliged to underscore any one word in the message, "immediately" would have been that word. It made clear the fact that President Wilson was no longer disposed to debate the issue; he wanted a "yes" or a "no" from the Kaiser—and he wanted it now!

"Calm down, Müller, for heaven's sake! You are beside yourself!"

"Forgive me, your Highness, but I must insist on being heard."

"*Insist!*"

"Yes, your Highness; insist. I would be remiss in my duty, both to you and to Germany, if I did not make my perceptions known in the most straightforward manner at this critical juncture."

"Really, Müller, your presumption astounds me."

"I very much regret that my actions should appear presumptuous, and of course I am prepared to yield my place in your service the moment I am commanded to do so. But your Highness *will* hear me now, unless you send to have me ejected bodily from your presence."

"Müller! For God's sake!"

"Your Highness . . ."

It was a bit sad, the admiral reflected, how easily bullied was Germany's All Highest War Lord. The vacillation and empty bluster in Wilhelm's expression revealed the man's pathetic sense of inadequacy, his desperate need to be propped up and reassured. Unfortunately for him, however, the number of people in his retinue whom he did not yet despise or mistrust had grown smaller week by week, and the few equerries who'd endured were falling from favor at an ever accelerating rate. For Wilhelm, therefore, to lose his most respected and trusted adviser now would be a personal calamity, and both he and the adviser knew it. There was never any question but that the admiral would have his way.

"Oh, very well, Müller," the Kaiser said sulkily, "speak your piece."

"Thank you, your Highness. I wish to say only that the fact that we have broken our promise to the Americans concerns me less than the fact that we have needlessly incurred their fatal enmity, or are about to. We are, in other words, about to lose the war, despite the fact that we have ready to hand a virtually unused maritime weapon that is far superior to the submarine in all respects and also completely unobjectionable from the United States' point of view."

"You refer to . . . ?"

"The fleet, your Highness."

"The *fleet!?*"

"Yes, your Highness."

"Gad, Müller, is this your momentous utterance? The *fleet?*"

"If your Highness will bear with me for a moment—"

"Do you realize that the British outnumber us in dreadnoughts by almost two-to-one?"

"I am conversant with the relative strengths of the contending navies, your Highness."

"Please don't be sarcastic, Müller."

"Your pardon, your Highness. But if I might resume what I was saying. . . ."

"Oh, of course, of course, by all means. Please don't mind me for an instant."

"As you wish, your Highness. The point I am endeavoring to make is this: if the British lose their fleet they lose the war. So rather than guarantee a British victory by provoking America to join the Allied camp, it seems to me that our submarines would be better employed in sinking British warships in conjunction with our dreadnoughts. Quite apart from the *Aboukir*, *Cressy*, and *Hogue*, destroyed during the first weeks of the war, U-boats have sunk ships like the *Formidable*, in the Channel, and ships like the *Majestic* and the *Triumph* in the Mediterranean off Gaba Tepe. Now if our entire undersea flotilla, including our submarine minelayers, were to withdraw from the western approaches and embark on joint operations with the High Seas Fleet, I believe we would stand a good chance of wresting control of the seas from the British Navy. At all events, I believe we should at least give this alternative a fair test before embarking on the inhuman course which will probably spell *finis Germaniae* in any case."

Wilhelm gazed at him appraisingly; he had aroused the Emperor's interest.

"It's an attractive notion, Müller; I can't deny it. But what about the British capacity to forecast the movements of our ships?"

"I've gone into that, your Highness. They appear to have some sort of wireless monitoring facility at the Admiralty in London which enables them to make educated deductions from our fleet transmissions. They may even have penetrated our naval codes to some extent. The technicians at Telefunken have recently developed a new high-power wireless interference transmitter, however, and it should be ready for use in the next few weeks. It will have to be employed sparingly lest the British suspect something and start shifting frequencies on us. But it will be available for use in critical situations to offset any advantage they may enjoy at present."

Wilhelm, seated behind his massive desk, slowly tapped the butt of a pencil against its shiny marble surface. "Discontinue commerce raiding altogether, eh?"

"For the time being, your Highness; yes."

There was a long silence. "I'll consider it."

"Thank you, your Highness. I would mention only one more thing."

"Yes?"

"The American note says 'immediately.'"

The Kaiser gave him a sourly enervated smile. "Thank you, Müller. I'm sure we're all very much in your debt."

1916, 6TH MAY—EDINBURGH

Reeves-Wadleigh looked down at the body of Sublieutenant Devers and tried without success to feel pity instead of irritation. Irritation prevailed, he supposed, because he was as annoyed with himself for having chosen Devers in the first place as he was with Devers for having bungled the assignment. Youth and ardor, both of which Devers had possessed in abundance, were clearly (in retrospect) not the sort of qualities needed to sustain a mission of secret surveillance —especially when the person being shadowed was as wily and ruthless as von Tiel.

Reeves-Wadleigh could imagine what had happened: Von Tiel had probably suspected nothing for the first several weeks, which was only reasonable given the precautions that had been taken to make him feel secure in his van Teel persona. (One of Reeves-Wadleigh's men, dressed as a customs officer, had even made the "Dutch businessman" pay duty on an unopened bottle of cognac that was found in his luggage at Southampton.) Devers, lulled into overconfidence by the baron's lack of suspicions, would have yielded perhaps a small fraction of his vigilance to boredom, forgetting that surveillance was more a matter of craft and judgment than of doggedness and concealment. Having followed von Tiel from the dock through London and up to Edinburgh, and having spent nearly sixty consecutive days trailing him from his hotel off Balgreen Road to Haymarket Station to Aberdour Station to Admiralty House and back again, Devers would have begun to do things by rote, not fully realizing that von Tiel's predictability was rapidly becoming *his* predictability as well, and not fully appreciating that an alien spy would be far more alert than a loyal native son to patterns of repetition in the environment.

It wouldn't have taken much carelessness on Devers's part. Von Tiel had spent twelve hours every day in a quiet corner of the park abutting the Aberdour Castle complex. From where he sat, he could look through the trees to Admiralty House gate about thirty yards away. He spent his time making notes in a pocket diary, notes that apparently pertained to all traffic into and out of the mansion. Whenever someone arrived or departed, von Tiel would consult his watch and make a diary entry. Perhaps on just one occasion, as he began to write, his eye had registered a vaguely anomalous figure on the Castle walk. He would not have jumped to any conclusions, of course, but would simply have filed the datum in a readily accessible compartment of his mind. Half-unconsciously, however, he would have begun to make visual spot checks of the Castle's battlements as he sat on his bench in the park. Before too long he would have realized he was being watched; and from that moment on, the ardent young Devers was as good as dead.

Devers's body was sprawled in the narrow neck of White Horse Close, off Canongate, where von Tiel had no doubt led him. The sublieutenant lay on his stomach with his hands palm downward on the cobbles. The tip of his left thumb was no more than six inches from his nose; in fact, his staring eyes almost seemed to be focused on it. The fingers of his right hand rested as if preparatory to a manicure in the burnt sienna puddle of blood that had formed at the base of his skull. Two bullets had entered the rear of his brain: one through the parietal bone at about the level of his brow and the other through the occipital bone at about the level of his nostrils. Judging from the character of the wounds and from the powder burns in Devers's hair, Reeves-Wadleigh estimated that von Tiel had fired at a distance of under one foot. The angles of entry suggested that the brow-level shot had come first, sending Devers to the ground, and that the nostril-level shot had been fired as a coup de grace. There was no mystery as to the nature of the murder weapon, since it lay in the puddle of Devers's blood not an inch beyond his fingertips: it was a Mark V Webley .455 revolver, standard army issue. Von Tiel had thoughtfully placed his two spent cartridges in the well of Devers's left ear.

Reeves-Wadleigh let out a long somewhat melancholy sigh. It was hard to get *too* upset, what with his bloodstream full of morphine, but short of outright coma it was just as hard not to feel vexed. Von Tiel now knew that his cover as Meinheer van Teel had been pierced, and there was virtually nowhere in Britain he could not have fled to in the eight or so hours that had elapsed since Devers was killed. If he ever surfaced again, which seemed unlikely, it would only be in order to strike; and the chances of finding him then or earlier were extremely remote. The only option open, as far as Reeves-Wadleigh could tell, was to redouble the surveillance on Gehlman and hope very earnestly for the best. It would be the lamest sort of wishful thinking to imagine that a man like von Tiel would abandon his mission simply because the authorities were on his track. He couldn't be scared off. He could only, one hoped, be stopped.

It was with moderate surprise that Reeves-Wadleigh turned to see Lord Fisher striding forcefully into the Close from Canongate. As a matter of course he had sent a messenger to Dungavel, where the admiral was staying, to inform him of Devers's murder. He'd known that Fisher would be interested, of course, but he hadn't realized how heavily time must have been weighing on the old sailor's hands. When, after all, had the death of a sublieutenant ever been of sufficient moment to compel the presence of an admiral of the fleet?

Fisher gazed down at the body. "Poor laddie," he said.

"Yes, sir," Reeves-Wadleigh responded.

Fisher turned to face him. "So, now they've stooped to murder, eh?"

"Yes, sir," Reeves-Wadleigh answered, thinking that "stooped" was an odd word to use in the context of wartime espionage.

"You know, Monty, I have a feeling that this ties in with everything else."

"Sir?" said Reeves-Wadleigh, mystified.

"Don't be dense, Monty," Fisher snapped, not bothering to conceal his irritation. "First the Germans unleash their onslaught against Verdun. Then they start sticking their noses out beyond Heligoland —for the first time in over a year. Then, not two weeks ago, they steam over to Norfolk and shell Lowestoft and Yarmouth. The day after they do that, the bloody Irish begin a rebellion. And less than a week after *that*, the Germans knuckle under to the United States on the *Sussex* matter and pretend to give up submarine warfare altogether."

Reeves-Wadleigh stared at the admiral, or, rather, tried to look at him without staring.

"And now there's *this*," Fisher continued, all oblivious. "Monty, don't you see the pattern? The von Tiel–Gehlman plot is all part of one grand master-design: the combined use of espionage, sabotage, subversion, diplomacy, military might, and naval provocation for the purpose of knocking us off balance and bringing us to our knees."

"I must say, sir," Reeves-Wadleigh responded carefully, "the possibility you raise had not occurred to me."

"That's perfectly understandable, dear boy. It takes a practiced eye to see the gold beneath the shingle."

"Yes, sir," Reeves-Wadleigh said dully. Even with the morphine in his veins, the spectacle of his aging master was a very, very sad thing to behold.

1916, 14TH MAY—NEW YORK

The library of House's residence on East Fifty-third Street faced a courtyard garden. It was not a "busy" garden, filled with the clamor of noisy-colored flowers or the clutter of fleshy marble *putti* in various stages of mischievous flight. There was no statuary in it, in fact; and the vegetation was a study in the mutest tones of green. There were ferns and well-trimmed hedges, and several juniper trees as well. There was also a solitary oak, a tall and aged tree whose branches creaked painfully in the fresh spring breeze but whose leaves still glistened and danced like a sapling's, blissfully indifferent to the waning life flow in the boughs from which they'd sprung.

A sudden gust of wind set off a murmurous rustling in the old tree's limbs, and House looked up from the speech he'd been asked by his great friend to prepare. He gazed out the second-floor window and took a moment's comfort from the garden's orderly beauty, then brought his eyes back to the peroration he had just begun to draft: "We believe that every people has a right to choose the sovereignty under which they shall live, that the small states of the world have a right to enjoy the same respect for their sovereignty and territorial integrity that great and powerful nations expect and insist upon, and that the world has a right to be free from every disturbance of its peace that has its origin in aggression and disregard of the rights of peoples and nations."

Satisfied with that as an expression of his and Wilson's credo, House picked up his pen again and set down the sentence that was to be the speech's raison d'être. It flowed easily onto the paper, this historic sentence that he'd been picked by destiny to write: "So sincerely do we believe these things that the United States is willing to become a partner in any feasible association of nations formed in order to realize these objects and make them secure against violation."

There it was: the terminus of 120 years of American foreign policy, the first turning in a road that began when George Washington took leave of his countrymen in September 1796, and admonished them: "'Tis our true policy to steer clear of permanent alliances, with any portion of the foreign world."

House leaned back in his chair. On Saturday evening, May 27, at the New Willard Hotel in the District of Columbia, the twenty-eighth President would tell the League to Enforce Peace—and all mankind!—that the strictures of the first President no longer governed the actions of the United States. America was at last going to take her seat in the council hall of nations, and there, God grant, restore the harmony in which humanity had flourished in the century since Waterloo.

What a fine moment that would be, House reflected; a moment that a month before had seemed impossible of realization. But the *Sussex* attack had *not* been deliberate, and the Germans *had* agreed to abide henceforth by the accepted rules of international law. Wilson's patience and forbearance had been triumphantly vindicated. Now, when the Democrats met in Convention at the St. Louis Coliseum on June 14, they would do so as a united party, solidly committed to the man who'd preserved the country from war while at the same time upholding its honor. Now, too, House and the President could press forward in earnest in their pursuit of peace. Never mind that the British and French were being refractory, or that German bona fides was still in doubt; the important thing was that American neutrality was at last firmly established, in fact as well as law. However vindictive and unreasonable the warring parties continued to be, the benign influence of the new world could now, finally, be made to tell on the old.

And not a moment too soon: for on the same desk with the draft of the President's speech was the New York *World* with a front-page article stating that deaths—not casualties, but deaths—on *each* side at Verdun had now exceeded the appalling figure of one hundred thousand!

There were two other important items on House's desk as well, items that the Colonel had pondered over long and hard without a comforting result. One, bulky and squat in its dark blue binder, was the North Sea Analysis. The other, terse and implacable on its coarse yellow paper, was the cable from Commander Symington in London.

House sighed unhappily. He supposed it was only natural that the Germans, having ceased to wage war with their submarines, should now test British sea power with their fleet. Natural or not, their new naval aggressiveness represented a serious threat to the prospects for peace—a serious threat, that is, if the conclusions of the Analysis were correct.

Symington's cable reported that both Maltbie and Gehlman regarded a major clash in the North Sea as an increasingly likely possibility, at least up until the commencement of the equinoctial storms in September. That fact resounded ominously in the Colonel's mind with his distinct recollection of Admiral von Müller's words: "If something should happen to our fleet . . . I can give no assurances that extreme measures will not be employed."

There is so much at stake, House told himself—more, perhaps, than has ever been at stake before. And on that basis, he supposed, it was only simple prudence to have summoned William Corey to New York from the Department of State.

House had left instructions that Corey was to be shown upstairs as soon as he arrived, and promptly at 5:00 P.M. there came a soft rapping on the library door.

"Come in, Billy," House called out, and the Assistant Secretary walked into the room.

The Colonel had always had a special fondness for William Everett Corey. The young bureaucrat had that cool patrician sleekness peculiar to golden boys from Groton who'd gone on to become golden men at Yale. He had also, however, a subtly carnivorous urbanity that worked a nice harmony with the Phi Beta Kappa key on his waistcoat and the Skull-and-Bones self-assurance in his eyes. He was rich, of course—old money—and his wife was richer—older money still—so that an ambassadorship was the very least he might aspire to. Given his brains and his ambition, moreover, one hesitated to place a limit on the very most.

"Good evening, sir," Corey said.

"Good evening, Billy. Have a seat."

"Thank you, sir," said the Assistant Secretary, lowering himself gracefully into an armchair and casually crossing his legs.

"I have an important confidential mission that I'd like you to undertake."

If Corey was startled by House's abruptness, he was careful to betray no sign of the fact. "Of course, sir," he said in a placid voice.

"Have you read this, as I suggested?" House asked, lifting the North Sea Analysis off his desk.

"Yes, sir."

He put the blue binder back down. "How would you summarize its basic conclusion?"

"I would say its basic conclusion is that a fleet engagement between the British and German navies would almost certainly result in a major German defeat."

"Precisely. And how, in your opinion, would Germany react to such a setback?"

"Well, she could concede total control of the seas to the Allies, which would be catastrophic strategically and fatal from the point of view of domestic politics. Or she could devote every resource of her naval establishment to an all-out resumption of the submarine campaign, which would certainly bring us into the war against her, but might also force England out before our power could be brought to bear."

House smiled. "Ten out of ten, Billy."

"Thank you, sir," said Corey, smiling back.

"Now then, what if I were to tell you that a fleet engagement between the British and German navies is likely to occur within the next several months?"

Corey frowned. "Is it, sir?"

"Let's say that it is."

"Well, sir," Corey said, shaking his head sadly, "I would regard that as truly terrible news . . . *tragic* news!"

"Why?"

"Because of everything we've worked for since the *Lusitania* was sunk."

House nodded approvingly. "Now, one last not-so-hypothetical question: what if it were within our power—without in any way endangering British lives or ships—to intervene covertly in the battle that may soon take place and thereby prevent the destruction of the German Fleet?"

Corey uncrossed his legs and leaned forward as if hoping that the Colonel would say something more. He sat that way for a long, long while, with the rustle of the ancient oak's leaves in the courtyard the only sound to be heard in the room. "I would say," he responded finally, "that I stand ready to be of service."

"Thank you, Billy," the Colonel said softly.

"Thank *you*, sir—for your trust in me."

House rose and extended his hand. Corey got up from his chair and crossed the room to grasp it. The Colonel put his left hand on the younger man's shoulder and said, "This is not a pleasant task I offer you."

"No, sir; only a necessary one."

House gently patted Corey's shoulder, then turned and pointed to the North Sea Analysis. "The most likely contingency according to that study," he said, "is that the British will manage somehow to get between the Germans and their base. While it's true that Admiral Scheer has enough speed to avoid battle for a day or two, he's eventually going to run low on coal. When that happens his only hope will be to try to steal his way homeward at night. And if British wireless communications should be disrupted for some reason when he makes his attempt, his chances of getting through will be improved."

"I understand, sir."

"Colonel Squire, our military attaché in London, is home in Washington on leave at the moment. He's something of an electronics wizard, I'm told; so you might wish, without mentioning your mission, to consult with him."

"Yes, sir. I'll do that."

"Thank you, Billy. Work as quickly as you can."

For a long time after Corey left, House sat gazing unhappily out of the window at the oak tree. He felt certain, almost, that he was right to do what he was doing, and that he had no valid alternative to elect. He knew that his motives were of the highest, and that his commitment to peace was genuine and deep.

Still, the sacrifice of personal honor was a painful one to make.

1916, 24TH MAY–LOCH LEVEN

An eerie light suffused the moisture-laden air as billows of fog drifted in silence through the trees on the shore of the lake. Gehlman looked at his watch and, seeing that it read 10:15, held it to his ear to make sure that it was running properly. He still could not get used to the endless twilight that was a feature of these latitudes during the weeks around the summer solstice. The sun, when it was visible, didn't go down so much as it bored laterally into the northwestern horizon, like a buzz saw. Tonight, of course, it had gone down behind an impenetrable shroud of rain and fog; but its light still lingered, lending a ghostly enchanted-forest kind of aura to the pine grove next to Lieutenant Commander Seymour's cottage. Gehlman listened to the evening quiet: the sound of water dripping from the sodden tree limbs, the lonely cry of a loon from across the lake, the barely audible plash of ripples against the pilings of the nearby pier. Inside the cottage, Melina would be luring Alis toward sleep: sitting at her bedside, singing softly to her, holding her hand. It was a scene Gehlman never tired of watching, and would have been watching now but for the strange uneasiness that had impelled him to come outside.

He listened attentively to what sounds there were, trying to pick up any alien element that might have put him on his guard. There was nothing, however; just the dripping and the lake sounds and the odd unearthly light. Suddenly and for no apparent reason he shivered all over his body—a purely animal sensation of danger. He wheeled around and strode quickly back to the cottage, bolting the door securely once he was inside. He took off his boots and placed them in the wardrobe by the coatrack. Inside the wardrobe were three of Seymour's hunting rifles and a Springfield the flag lieutenant had purchased as a teenager during a visit to the United States. Gehlman could see that the old weapon had been lovingly maintained over the years. He picked it up, checked the action, located a box of ammunition, and inserted a round into the chamber. He then laid the rifle flat on the floor underneath the wardrobe and went to make sure the scullery door and all the shutters were properly latched.

He didn't normally give this much credence to his untutored instincts, but then his untutored instincts didn't normally speak to him in such unequivocal terms.

He walked to the doorway of the small bedroom. Seeing him, Melina put a finger to her lips and then extended her hand for him to take. He grasped it, glanced at Alis's sleeping face, and quickly checked to see that the bedroom shutters were securely closed. As he did so, Melina guided his hand beneath the collar of her dress and downward to the aureole of her right breast.

Her forwardness still shocked him, almost as much as it excited him, and he wondered if his spasm of fear had simply been an unconscious expectation of punishment for his sins. He continually surprised himself with his capacity for guilt, especially since—until this affair with Melina anyway—he had always thought of himself as a sophisticate. He could see now, however, that at bottom he was just as hobbled by Mosaic notions of sexual morality as was his father. All the motions he had gone through two months before—the oh-so-noble self-restraint, the "we-should-think-before-we-talk-or-act" disclaimer—seemed now to him the lamest sort of prospective expiation. He had simply been deluding himself that a temptation resisted initially could be credited somehow against all subsequent falls from grace. It couldn't, of course, particularly when the subsequent falls began occurring before the initial resistance really started to pinch, i.e., inside of a week.

Part of the problem in Gehlman's conscience was that this affair was different from all his previous episodes of sex. This was not merely fornication, as with a mistress, nor was it even condoned debauchery, as with Regina von Lutwitz. This was out-and-out adultery: clandestine sexual intercourse with another man's lawfully wedded —and, parenthetically, pregnant—wife. It was clandestine sexual intercourse, moreover, prompted by much more than feelings of lust.

Gehlman didn't know if he was in love with Melina; he did know he was fascinated and delighted by her. Her feelings for him, he could sense, were more restrained. She was clearly not in love with him, but how much less than in love she was was not easy to divine. That she took tremendous pleasure in him was in no way open to doubt; but he had a feeling that much of the pleasure she took derived not so much from what he was as from what he and their relationship represented in her mind. It seemed that their affair had somehow restored the self-confidence and sense of self-dominion that had seeped out of her since her marriage in July. Her commitment to the marriage appeared to be as absolute as ever, though, and references to divorce were as utterly absent from her conversation as were references to Harris Maltbie.

Gehlman moved his fingers caressingly over Melina's nipple. Leaving the door of the bedroom slightly ajar, they moved into the sitting room and undressed one another in front of the fire. Gehlman lay on his back, and Melina ranged herself astride his hips; then, with a convulsive shudder, she sank down upon him. Gehlman shut his eyes and savored the sensations of her inner flesh while his hands ran slowly over the surfaces of her body. Apart from their labored breathing, neither of them made a sound, for fear of waking Alis. Their orgasm, when attained, was celebrated in quivering silence.

As the fire died and Melina lay bathed in perspiration on top of him, Gehlman found that the animal sensation of danger he'd experienced earlier was gradually beginning to return. Perhaps it *was* only guilt, he conceded uncertainly, as from outside the cottage came a furtive rustling of leaves.

Then again, he thought, girding himself to stay wakeful till daylight, perhaps it wasn't guilt at all.

1916, 29TH MAY—LONDON

The Assistant Secretary's expression was one of cool patrician detachment as he said, "I've been sent here with instructions for you that may in some respects seem incompatible with your conceptions of personal honor."

Maltbie stared at Corey in disbelief, and then at Gehlman, who was regarding the Assistant Secretary with a gaze of such mordant skepticism that for a wild moment Maltbie thought the two of them might be engaging in some tasteless form of practical joke.

That Corey should have begun this Monday morning meeting at the embassy with the bland enunciation of such an appalling idea was fully in keeping with the air of unreality that had pervaded the events of the past several days. First had come the urgent summons to London, without any preamble or explanation, and just at a time when a fleet engagement with the Germans seemed most probable. Then there was Melina's strange behavior in conjunction with Maltbie's unannounced arrival at Aberdour on Saturday night. He had never before seen her in such a mood: at once recklessly loquacious and girlishly silly. She had even erupted into laughter several times while they were making love, only to then rearouse him with a carnality so savage and lascivious that he'd thought once or twice that she might actually be unwell. When he awoke yesterday morning, moreover, and got ready to depart for Waverley Station, she had kissed him and burst abruptly into tears. After a few minutes, however, and with as little apparent cause, she had become completely calm again, and had affectionately sent him on his way to catch his train.

The next odd incident had occurred when he confided his perplexity about Melina's behavior to Gehlman on their way south to London. Rather than listening carefully and making a thoughtful response as he'd always done when they'd talked in the past, Gehlman had seemed reluctant to discuss the subject Maltbie had raised, and had finally dismissed it with the pat suggestion that it was probably Melina's pregnancy that had made her so abnormally excitable.

Now, in this morning's papers, there had been the accounts of President Wilson's momentous speech in Washington, and of his unfortunate statement to the effect that, as a would-be peacemaker, the United States was "not concerned with the causes and objects of the war." The anti-American feeling that had been growing rapidly in intensity since the resolution of the *Sussex* crisis had boiled over in response to this expression of fine impartiality, at least in the columns of the *Mirror*, the *Mail*, and the *Express*. The fact that Wilson had committed the United States to participation in European affairs had gone almost totally unremarked, and even *The Times* suggested that the President's break with six generations of American foreign policy amounted to little more than a political gimmick designed to gain votes at home.

Bewildering as all these developments had been, they were as nothing compared to Corey's casual announcement that he had come with orders for them of a potentially dishonorable nature. Maltbie responded immediately with anger: "That's a pretty damned despicable thing to say in such a calm and collected manner."

"Would it be any less despicable if I said it differently?" Corey asked in a gentle voice.

"It would be less offensive," Gehlman cut in.

"Then I apologize to you," the Assistant Secretary responded. "I suppose in bracing my own nerves to perform this mission I may have hardened myself somewhat to its ethical implications."

"That shouldn't have taken very long," Gehlman retorted in an amiable tone.

"I'm sorry you think that."

"I'm sorry I'm right."

There was a loaded silence that lasted for several seconds. Unruffled, Corey finally resumed the conversation: "Shall I proceed with your instructions?"

"By all means," Gehlman answered. "Do we get the iniquity first and the rationalizations second, or do we just get the iniquity and a homily on 'ours-not-to-reason-why'?"

"I think it would be best, perhaps, if I were to begin with the iniquity and work my way up," Corey replied, smiling.

"A statesmanlike plan of action, Mr. Secretary. We who are about to be fed dung salute you."

Corey gave a soundless laugh. "You have an antic sense of humor, Captain."

"The perfect complement to your antic sense of honor, Mr. Secretary."

Maltbie noted with satisfaction that Gehlman's last barb had penetrated Corey's skin. "I believe the word you're looking for is 'touché,' Mr. Secretary," he said.

Corey shifted his eyes rapidly from Gehlman to Maltbie and back again. "Yes, well, without further deferring the subject, I've been sent here to instruct you to help preserve the German Fleet from destruction."

Maltbie was incredulous. "The *German* Fleet, did you say?"

"The German Fleet. You'll recall, no doubt, the conclusion of your North Sea Analysis to the effect that the British were likely to get between the Germans and their bases and thereby force the High Seas Fleet to give battle."

"Yes," said Maltbie.

"You'll recall also the outcome you predicted for such an engagement."

"A German defeat."

"Precisely. And you'll recall further the Germans' one possible hope of escape."

"Evasion during the hours of darkness."

"Correct again . . . well . . . you will find back at your hotel a black leather valise and a small brown suitcase. Each contains a radio transmitter capable of generating interference on any one of five British frequen—"

"*No!*" Maltbie shouted. "That's absolutely unspeakable! Don't say another word!"

"Why not, Commander?" Corey asked sharply. "If you're so sure of your ground, if your integrity is so impregnable, why not hear me out? You can always say 'get-thee-behind-me' when I've finished speaking my piece."

"And another thing," Maltbie retorted, ignoring Corey's gambit, "if you think Ben or I could lug a fifty-pound piece of radio equipment onto a ship without its being noticed, you're sadly—"

"The weight of each bag is less than twenty pounds," Corey interrupted.

"Less than twenty pounds! That's utterly impossible. Why, the batteries alone must weigh thirty or—"

"There are no batteries."

"*What!?*"

"The transmitters are equipped to draw power from any electrical outlet on your ships."

"You can't power a radio directly off a ship's mains," Maltbie said in a tone of disgust. "Current that strong would burn out every tube in the set inside of four or five hours."

"Eight or nine hours, actually, with the partial converter your sets are equipped with. But even if it were only four or five, that would be sufficient for our purposes. All we want you to do is improve the Germans' chances of getting away at night by transmitting for three or four hours on the British frequency used for reporting contact with the enemy. We've given each of you a one-half-kilowatt quenched-spark transmitter with an effective range of ten to fifteen miles. You need only connect it, tune it, switch it on, and then leave it. There's a key-down switch that'll keep the set transmitting continuously even if you can't be there to operate it. It will transmit uncorrelated static signals over a band width of about fifty kilocycles. And since the British—as your report revealed—keep their reporting channel clear at all times, they won't be aware of the interference unless someone breaks radio silence on another frequency in order to ask for acknowledgment of a sighting message."

"Sighting messages aren't acknowledged," Maltbie said sullenly. "They're supposed to be relayed in some cases, but there's too much radio traffic during an action for the C in C to acknowledge all the incoming signals."

"I know," said Corey with a trace of self-satisfaction. "That was in your report as well."

Maltbie glanced over at Gehlman, who was slouched in an armchair with his eyes closed and his right foot tapping out a slow cadence on the floor. He looked back at Corey, feeling a kind of dull anguish. "You've been very thorough, I must say. You seem to have thought of everything."

"I tried to," said Corey.

"Now, perhaps, you could tell us why we're being asked to engage in sabotage."

"You've read about the President's speech?"

"Yes."

"Well, that speech is part of a full-scale American effort to bring the war to an early end. I can't go into details, but I can tell you that the President is on the verge of asking the belligerents to discuss a truce under American auspices. The settlement of the *Sussex* crisis is what made this peace initiative possible. If the German Fleet were to be destroyed, however, unrestricted submarine warfare would be resumed in a matter of weeks. Rather than mediating a peace, the United States would be drawn into the war. That is why we want the High Seas Fleet to escape."

"I see," said Maltbie, feeling slightly less certain of his position than he'd felt before.

"I hope you'll believe me, Commander, when I tell you that the decision to ask this sacrifice of you was reached only with the greatest reluctance, and only after all alternative measures had been considered and found impracticable. I hope you'll also believe me when I say that tens, perhaps hundreds, of thousands of European *and* American lives will be spared if, thanks to you, the President's efforts meet with success. It comes down, essentially, to this one simple fact: you are being asked to sacrifice your personal honor, the one thing that matters most to you as a man, for the welfare of your country and for the redemption of a suffering world. It is as great a sacrifice as anyone has ever been called upon to make."

Maltbie's sense of outrage had by now given way to a pronounced feeling of resentment and confusion. So deeply was he immersed in the tangle of his thoughts, in fact, that the sound of Gehlman's voice momentarily startled him.

"You're *good*, Mr. Secretary," Benjamin said sardonically. "You're really first rate. I see a great future in store for you."

Corey gave him a thin smile, said nothing.

"Of course, I myself have never fully subscribed to the for-want-of-a-nail theory of history. I mean, I've never been altogether convinced that the affairs of men and nations are resolvable into mechanical equations. I *have* noticed, on the other hand, that just about every crime, every depredation, every atrocity ever committed in historical annals was justified at the time by just such an appeal to a higher morality as you so eloquently made just now. I would be interested in knowing, therefore—before I so nobly 'sacrifice' my personal honor—what exactly is the likelihood of an American peace initiative succeeding. I have the impression, for example, that the war involves a great many nations and a great many matters of dispute. I have the further impression that there are so many nations and so many matters of dispute involved as to render a negotiated peace impossible at this point. Now, given these troublesome impressions of mine, don't you think I'm justified in regarding the affecting little sermon you just preached us as being just the least little bit simplistic?"

"The trouble is, Captain Gehlman, that you were never elected to an office of trust wherein your impressions, as you call them, could serve as a valid basis for the foreign policy of the United States. It is Woodrow Wilson's 'impressions' that must be determined in such matters, I'm sure you'll agree."

"Oh, most assuredly. But then—and do please correct me if I'm mistaken—Woodrow Wilson was never elected to an office whose powers included the right to make war without the consent of Congress."

"War making is not the issue here."

"Oh? Then how would you characterize sabotaging the operations of another country's navy? As an act of peace?"

"An act *for* peace."

"Ah ha! The higher morality again."

"If you like."

"It comes down to a question of conscience?"

"It comes down to a question of duty."

"It comes down to a question of horseshit, Mr. Secretary—hot, brown, and steaming."

"If you say so, Captain. The decision is in any case yours to make as best you can. And yours, Commander Maltbie."

"The first truthful statement you've made so far, Mr. Secretary. But let me just leave *you* with something to think about, since you've been so lavish in presenting draconian dilemmas to us. Suppose, for example, that the decision we face isn't simply, do we or don't we do as we are told. Suppose it's also, do we or don't we inform the British of the little errand you've just run."

"That would be treason, Captain Gehlman," Corey said evenly.

"Would it? All right then, let's leave you out of it for the time being and let you continue your slither toward the pinnacles of national office. The question still remains, what do Commander Maltbie and I do about *one another*? I mean, there are higher moralities to consider, now aren't there? In fact, that's the thing about higher moralities: everybody's got one of his own. Now, what if my higher morality says that it's so wrong for us to do what you want us to do that I must not risk the possibility that Commander Maltbie's higher morality doesn't correspond to mine? Or what if his higher morality says the same thing about me? You see, all unwittingly, you've presented us with two distinct questions: to act or not to act, to inform or not to inform. Because after all—and I put this to you in all earnestness—wouldn't it be rather disingenuous of me to refuse my services on moral grounds while knowing that someone else was in a position to perform those services just as well as I could? Of course it would, Mr. Secretary. So you just dwell on that, while Commander Maltbie and I go through the hell you've concocted on our behalf."

"I'm sorry you see things that way, Captain," Corey said.

"I know you are; that's about the only consolation I can salvage from this damnable mess."

Maltbie looked from Gehlman to Corey and back in a state of near shock. He felt as if his entire world had just exploded in his face. He was a signals officer, after all, not an ethical philosopher. How in God's name was he going to come up with the right course of action?

Or was the least heinous course of action the most that he could reasonably hope to discern?

1916, 30TH MAY—BURNTISLAND, NEAR ABERDOUR

Gehlman rubbed his itching eyes and watched the phosphenes dancing on his retinas. He didn't know why he felt so desperately tired. True, it had been nearly 2:00 A.M. when he'd been awakened by Melina, but he'd subsisted on three hours' sleep before without its telling on him like this. It had to be the accumulated psychological strain of the past several days, aggravated by the frantic anxiety he had felt about Alis.

She'd been looking a little pale on Sunday when he'd left to go to

London. And when he returned to Aberdour yesterday evening he had found her in bed with a temperature of 100.5°, complaining of nausea and general achiness. Melina had phoned the pediatrician, Dr. Cleethe, just prior to Gehlman's arrival, and had described Alis's symptoms to him. The doctor had said that it sounded like she might have intestinal influenza, and had promised to come by first thing in the morning to examine her. Around one forty-five, though, Melina had come to Gehlman's room and told him that Alis was suffering severe abdominal pain and had a temperature of 104°. Dr. Cleethe, on being roused out of bed and informed of this, had diagnosed acute appendicitis, and instructed Gehlman to bring Alis immediately to St. Fillan's Infirmary in Burntisland, two miles east of Aberdour. The doctor had been waiting for them when they drove up to the infirmary entrance at two-thirty. A quick examination had confirmed the diagnosis, and shortly after four Alis had been operated on.

Now it was after seven, and Gehlman had just come from Alis's bedside, where he had stood vigil for nearly an hour. Dr. Cleethe had said that all was well, and so had the surgeon. But the sight of Alis unconscious, her hair matted, her skin unnaturally white, was so upsetting to Gehlman that the words of reassurance had sounded hollow. *Look* at her! he'd wanted to scream. She doesn't speak; she doesn't move. How in God's name can "all be well"?

But he hadn't said anything, just wondered to himself how other men and women ever managed to endure the terror of raising a child they loved, or to survive the loss of one.

He felt Melina's hand on his shoulder. "They say she'll sleep till five or six this evening at least. Perhaps we should get a little rest too."

Gehlman shook his head. "You go on. Someone should stay with her, and I'm sure I wouldn't be able to sleep anyway."

"Miss Dyson is going to stay with her, Ben," Melina replied, referring to Alis's governess. "You're not going to do yourself or Alis any good by sitting around here in your present condition."

"What 'present condition'?" Gehlman asked irritably.

"Bloodshot eyes, stubbly chin, general gauntness of demeanor and sloppiness of dress."

He looked at her smiling pertly up at him, and smiled back in spite of himself. "All right, madam," he said. "Let's go back to Aberdour, have some breakfast, and make ourselves presentable. Then, perhaps, a brief walk or drive to clear the cobwebs out of our heads—and then back here no later than noon."

"Done!" said Melina, eyes sparkling and clear.

Having bathed and shaved and changed into clean clothes, Gehlman felt somewhat less tired as he came down the stairs. Melina was waiting for him with a wicker basket on her arm. "Let's have a picnic breakfast at the cottage," she said with meaningful intensity. "It's only three-quarters of an hour's drive."

He found to his irritation that he was instantaneously aroused by the look in her eyes and the tone of her voice. "Melina, really, with Alis in the hospital and . . ."

"You said we had till noon," she cut in. "That gives us ninety minutes for motoring, ninety minutes at the cottage, and thirty minutes for unforeseen contingencies."

"Such as . . . ?"

"Such as, wishing to stay at the cottage for an additional thirty minutes."

They exchanged a look that was unambiguously erotic. "You're a brazen woman," Gehlman said.

"And you're a jaded man," she shot back, smiling up at him with eyes that glowed impishly with anticipation.

"Let me call the hospital before we go," he said, surrendering guiltily and with a keen sense of excitement.

She lay beneath him, small-breasted, slim-waisted, warm-skinned. He could feel her heart hammering against his chest as she uttered little sobs of gratification and ran her hands across his back.

They had never made love with such voracity before. For Gehlman, once he'd entered her, the experience had become almost mystical in its intensity. He had felt an urgent longing to submerge his sense of self in her, to fuse their minds and bodies on a more than physical plane. And in a way he had succeeded; because for the first time in his adult life his reasoning faculties and self-awareness had switched themselves off, and he had existed for an ecstatic interval in a universe of purely sensory impressions.

"My God, Ben!" Melina gasped breathlessly. "My *God!*"

He ran his lips over her face and neck. Her God indeed.

But *his* God; He was another matter entirely.

This affair was getting out of hand. Everything was getting out of hand. Events were occurring far too rapidly to be processed or comprehended. Melina, Alis, that swine Corey . . . and Harry—poor perplexed Harry. How shaky were the pillars on which *his* world rested!

The meeting with Corey had ended in time for him and Maltbie to retrieve their luggage and then make the *Flying Scotsman* at King's Cross. It was clear that Corey's arguments had shaken Harry —and that Gehlman's counterarguments had shaken him even more.

The black satchel and brown suitcase had been waiting in their rooms; if they'd left them there, the ultra-punctilious Connaught staff would simply have forwarded them up to Scotland. No, no; the cup couldn't be passed so easily.

Poor Harry. Poor poor lad.

The alien items of luggage had sat on the overhead rack like ticking bombs. It seemed that Maltbie had actually thought Gehlman was serious about informing. He was pathetically relieved when Gehlman told him his only purpose had been to make Corey anxious.

"Then what *had* we better do?" Maltbie had asked after a long silence.

"About those radios?"

"Yes."

"I can't tell you what to do, Harry. I don't really know what the right thing to do *is*."

"But what are you *going* to do, Ben?"

"What seems right when the issue arises. . . . Look, Harry, it's like courage in battle—you can't tell ahead of time how you're going to react under fire."

"You'll never use that radio," Maltbie had said miserably. "You're too damned *moral!*"

Ah Harry! You poor poor trusting soul.

Melina moved her body against him. "What time is it?"

He looked up at the clock on the mantel. "Ten-thirty."

She gave a carnal little laugh. "Thank God for that extra half hour," she said, twining her legs around his hips and pulling his open mouth down to hers.

This time his mind stayed with him, while his body worked its will. His mind kept picturing Maltbie's forlorn expression as they'd stood yesterday evening in Waverley Station. Harry could have made a connection for Inverness in fifteen minutes or he could have spent the night with Melina at Aberdour and resumed his trip in the morning. "I'd better get up there," he'd said lamely. "It looks like the weather's finally starting to clear, and Scheer's almost certain to come out if it does."

There had been a good deal of truth in that, Gehlman knew, but not enough to explain Maltbie's decision. The weightier truth was that Harry was afraid: Melina's strange behavior had frightened him; Gehlman's reluctance to discuss her strange behavior had frightened him; Corey had frightened him. Gehlman understood his reaction perfectly: it was the same reaction he himself had had thirty years ago to the sordidness of life ashore. Harry had needed to think, just as he himself did now; and life on a battleship was simpler and far less cluttered with distractions.

Damn Melina! Gehlman thought, even as his body sank deeper inside her. Why had she behaved like such a ninny the other night? All right; Harry's arrival had been unexpected. And all right; she hadn't seen him since the start of their affair. But still—to have behaved in such a hysterical manner was inexcusable. She should have been better prepared, more self-possessed.

Like *he'd* been.

Oh, yes; what a brilliant display of preparedness and self-possession *he'd* given when Harry had asked his advice: "It's her pregnancy that's making her so excitable"!

God! What inadequate sophisticates they'd both turned out to be.

Melina's arms and legs tightened fiercely around his body; he felt her stiffen, and then quiver like a vibrating string. He plunged himself deeply inside her, relaxing the muscles that he'd used to hold back. A few thrusts of his pelvis were sufficient—and then she lay whimpering beneath him, breathing out little animal moans.

Well, they'd have to be better sophisticates in the future; that was all. He could think of nothing more wrong, more morally reprehensible, than letting Harry find out what they'd been doing. In a sense, Harry knew already, of course—but without corroboration he would never know he knew.

In a month or two, Melina's pregnancy would end the affair in any case. In three or four months he would be back in New York with Alis. And Melina, with Harry, would be thousands of miles away.

Did he love her? Did she love him? It didn't really matter. Their relationship was finite and had to remain so. She knew it and he knew it too. In fact, it was the one single moral imperative of which he was absolutely certain.

He leaned back and ran his hands over her body, which was slippery and shining with perspiration. "We have to get back," he said.

"Yes," Melina answered.

But his hands, unbidden, kept on moving over her skin.

"Yes," Melina said again in a hissing whisper. "Yes . . . *yes!*"

It was half past eleven by the time they walked out of the cottage. The sun had burned off the morning fog and now shone down brightly as it approached the meridian. Gehlman lowered the Morris's top at Melina's request and then for a long moment just stood and gazed at her with a kind of rapt fascination.

She was in her element: her eyes closed, her face lifted up to the sun; and he could think of few women who could emerge from two hours of passion into the full light of day without paint or powder on their faces and still look more desirable than they had at the outset. That, he judged, was Melina's most compelling quality, the basis of her allure. It was her animal nature: the way she thrived on—and reveled in—the most elemental components of life—and the way she languished and faded without them. She was elemental herself, he decided, élan vital made flesh.

Had things been different, he might easily have loved her very much indeed.

Shortly after they turned east on the Glenrothes road, Gehlman noticed a large black Crossley approaching rapidly from the rear. At a distance of about fifty yards it began to slow down, however, and for a mile or two it just followed them about three car-lengths back.

They turned south toward Cowdenbeath at the Scotlandwell fork, and the Crossley followed suit. Its persistent presence behind them was beginning to make Gehlman uncomfortable, but just after the fork it accelerated and roared past them around a curve and out of sight. Gehlman did not get a good look at the driver, who had on goggles, a duster, a cap, and a scarf. The man's profile reminded him vaguely of von Tiel, though, and a reflexive little shiver ran over his skin.

They drove along southward toward the sun, with the eastern shore of Loch Leven on their right. The road wound upward slightly, till they were about thirty feet above the level of the lake. The speed-ometer read an even forty miles per hour.

"Look, Ben! Isn't it lovely!" Melina exclaimed, pointing out at the lake view and the brown-green hills beyond.

"Beautiful," Gehlman agreed, flicking a glance to his right as he steered around a curve.

The Crossley appeared ahead of them at a distance of some thirty yards. It had decelerated and was now going about thirty-five.

"Damn!" Gehlman said in irritation, braking and shifting down. The Crossley's driver was languidly waving him on, and after check-ing behind him for traffic, Gehlman pulled out to the right to over-take.

As he pulled even with the touring car, he had the impression that it was beginning to accelerate again. His own speedometer read forty-five now, and yet he wasn't gaining ground.

Fortunately the road ahead was clear, but Gehlman gave an angry burst of his klaxons nevertheless.

The Crossley's driver was plainly an incompetent.

Gehlman took his foot off the gas pedal, deciding to abandon the attempt to pass. The Crossley slowed down too, however, and as it did so the driver reached up with his left hand and removed his cap and goggles.

Gehlman froze in horror at the sight of the insanity in the eyes.

"What is *wrong* with that gentlema—" Melina started to say, as von Tiel savagely rammed the Crossley into the Morris's left side.

"*Jump,* Melina!" Gehlman shouted, as the car's right-hand wheels started chewing up the gravel on the shoulder of the road.

But she couldn't jump, because by then the right-hand wheels had gone over the edge of the embankment, and the Morris was tipping onto its side.

He heard her scream as the car rolled laterally into thin air while retaining most of its forward momentum. Then the right front wheel struck a rock, adding a sudden violent end-over-end motion to the sideways rotation. Melina was catapulted out of the passenger seat and hurtled some fifty feet through the air down to the underbrush on the edge of the lake. Gehlman, closer to the point of impact, was spilled out of the car into some bushes about ten feet below the level of the road. He landed hard on his back and rolled for several yards until his momentum was spent, while the car toppled crazily onward and crashed further down. The impact knocked the wind out of him, but he knew as soon as he stopped rolling that he hadn't been seriously hurt.

His first thought was to aid Melina; however, the sound of grinding gears and a revving engine alerted him to the fact that von Tiel would be coming back to finish him off.

He scrambled down the embankment toward a thick clump of heather bushes and dove behind them. Some twenty feet above him and sixty feet to his right he saw von Tiel appear on the shoulder of the road. He had a pistol in his hand.

The baron surveyed the underbrush for what seemed a very long time. Finally, he started to make his way down toward the remains of the car, but it was clear from his actions that he didn't know where Gehlman was. Benjamin felt around for a rock, for *anything*, to use in self-defense. As he did so, though, he caught the sound of an automobile approaching from the direction they'd just come. The baron heard it too, apparently, because he abruptly stopped his search and hurried up the hill. Gehlman felt a ripple of puzzlement in his mind even as he sighed with relief. It wasn't like von Tiel to take flight as he had, just on the verge of achieving his revenge.

The sound of the Crossley's departure was almost exactly compensated by the sound of the other car's approach, and Gehlman clawed his way up the embankment to the highway in order to wave the oncoming automobile down. It was a navy staff car, and at the wheel, to Gehlman's astonishment, was his servant aboard the *Lion*, Sergeant Bellmaine!

"What in God's name are you doing out here?" he shouted, bypassing the amenities.

"Just out for a spin, sir," Bellmaine answered with obvious embarrassment, adding halfheartedly, "As you'd gone off to London, I thought I'd take a few days' leave."

Such a statement was patently nonsensical, given Bellmaine's duties on the *Lion* and the ever increasing likelihood of a full-scale action at any moment. Was it possible that the man had actually been following him? And if he had been, *why* had he? But at this juncture Gehlman had no interest in cross-examining the sergeant. Whatever the explanation for his unexpected appearance on the scene, the important thing was that he'd come when he had and was available to help now.

"You're looking somewhat knocked about, sir," he said. "Have you been having any trouble with your car?"

"I've had an accident, Sergeant, a very serious one, and I'm afraid my passenger may be badly injured. We have to get her to a hospital."

"Of course, sir. Where is she?"

"Follow me," Gehlman said, turning and heading off down the embankment.

Melina was lying on her back amidst some scrubby bushes about ten feet from the water's edge. Her right arm was bent back underneath her body at a sickening angle. There was a livid welt on her left temple, which was beginning to swell, and a deep gash just below her left cheekbone.

Gehlman knelt down beside her and gently touched her forehead. It was cold and clammy.

Her eyes flickered open. "Hello, sweet Ben," she said in a piteously weak voice.

"Hello."

"My arm hurts quite a lot."

"I know," said Gehlman, trying to determine what to do. She was in shock and at the very least had suffered a concussion. The more serious likelihood, however, was that she had sustained internal injuries as well, which meant that he oughtn't to move her. On the other hand, she was in a great deal of pain and needed immediate medical attention of the kind only a hospital could provide.

He would have to move her.

With Bellmaine's assistance, he rolled her as gently as possible onto her stomach so as to get the weight of her body off the dislocated right arm.

"Was that very painful?" he asked her, crouching down to make sure that she was able to breathe in this new position.

"No," she murmured.

"Does the arm hurt any less now?"

"No," she repeated, coughing weakly and bringing up some blood in the process.

Gehlman stripped off his suit jacket and put it over her. As he adjusted it around her shoulders he looked down and saw that her skirt below the area of her buttocks was soaking wet with blood.

The *baby!*

For an instant he was overwhelmed by a feeling of panic, but the sound of Bellmaine's voice close beside him snapped him out of it.

"She looks pretty bad, sir," the sergeant said softly. "We'd better get her to hospital double quick."

"Yes," said Gehlman. "Go bring the car as close as possible, and I'll carry her up."

"Right, sir. Do you think you can manage by yourself?"

"Yes," said Gehlman, feeling a sudden powerful swelling of rage against von Tiel. "She's very light."

They put her into the back seat, with Gehlman holding her head in his lap so as to be able to minimize the effect of the car's motion. Bellmaine covered her with a thick blanket from the staff car's trunk and then eased the vehicle into gear.

They decided on Dunfermline, fifteen miles away, as the nearest town with a fully equipped hospital. Bellmaine took it as fast as he safely could, and the road surface, fortunately, was smooth.

Every so often as they sped along Melina's eyes would flicker open, and she would smile up at Gehlman and say, "My sweetest Ben. My sweetest darling Ben." Then her eyes would close again, and he wouldn't be able to tell if she was conscious or not.

By the time they reached the outskirts of Dunfermline, however, it was clear that consciousness had left her. Gehlman shuddered to contemplate the amount of blood she must by then have lost.

"She's comatose! Get a move on!" the examining physician had shouted at the orderlies as they carried her on a stretcher into the hospital's interior.

"Will she be—" Gehlman started to ask.

"Impossible to say," the physician snapped, turning abruptly and following the stretcher inside.

"Captain Gehlman! Look!" Sergeant Bellmaine shouted to him from the balcony on the south side of the hospital driveway.

"What is it?"

"The battle cruisers, sir."

Gehlman ran over to him. Five miles away, below them and to the south, was Rosyth, and there in the Firth were *Lion*, *Tiger*, *Princess Royal*, *Queen Mary*, *New Zealand*, and *Indefatigable*, all pumping great black billows of smoke into the air. How long they'd been making steam was impossible to tell, but it was clear from the density of the smoke that they were preparing to weigh anchor as soon as they had sufficient pressure in the boilers, which might be very very soon indeed. Damn! Gehlman thought. Why must this happen just *now?* With Melina hanging between life and death, and Alis . . .

"*Alis!*" he shouted out loud, sprinting back to the reception area of the hospital. Now he understood why von Tiel had fled so precipitately from the scene of the crash.

"I'm Captain Gehlman, attached to the BFC," he said to the bilious-looking middle-aged nurse on duty, "and you must connect me *immediately* with St. Fillan's Infirmary in Burntisland."

The nurse looked at him with mistrustful eyes. "It's extremely urgent," he said. "I'll take full responsibility."

"Very well, sir," the nurse said grudgingly. "Would you give me your name again, please."

He had to fight to keep himself from shoving the woman aside and attempting to place the call himself; only the daunting complexity of the switchboard dissuaded him. "Gehlman," he said through clenched teeth. "G-E-H-L-M-A-N."

"Thank you, sir," the nurse said in a disapproving tone, writing it down. Then, with maddening slowness, she contacted the central exchange and made the connection.

"With whom do you wish to speak?" asked the female voice on the other end of the line.

"Dr. MacIlderry," Gehlman said, naming Alis's surgeon, "or Dr. Cleethe. It's extremely urgent."

"I'm sorry," said the voice, "but I don't know either of those names."

"*What?!*" Gehlman shouted. "Is this St. Fillan's Infirmary?"

"Why, no sir; this is—"

But Gehlman didn't wait to hear what it was. He slammed the receiver down, brought his face to within a few inches of the nurse's, and snarled, "There is a child's life at stake in this matter and every second wasted puts it in even greater jeopardy. Now, *please!*—get me through to St. Fillan's Infirmary in Burntisland before it's too late."

"Y-yes, sir," the nurse stammered in alarm, hastily plugging in some lines and attempting the connection again.

This time Gehlman got through to Dr. MacIlderry and began rapidly to explain the situation, leaving out only the fact that Alis's stepfather happened to be an officer in the German Navy. "Yes, Doctor," he repeated, "he is armed and unscrupulous and extremely dangerous. She must be protected from him at all times. I'll defray all expenses, of course—*only you must make sure that she is guarded every single moment!*"

The doctor said he would take immediate steps to protect her, and asked if Gehlman had any special instructions for her governess. Gehlman said he did, and requested that Miss Dyson be summoned to the phone.

"How is Alis?" he asked when he heard her voice on the line.

"Still asleep, sir, but doing very nicely, according to the doctors. They say she'll be pretty groggy for a day or two, but that that's normal."

"Good. Now listen, Miss Dyson, it looks like the BCF's going out any minute now, so I'll be at sea for one or two days. Mrs. Maltbie and I were in an automobile accident and she's in hospital here at Dunfermline."

"Oh, good heavens! Is she all right?"

Gehlman gave a moment's thought as to how he should answer that question. "She'll *be* all right," he said, "but she won't be able to visit Alis while I'm away. So you'll have to hold the fort by yourself, if you think you can manage."

"Oh, of course, sir. I'll see to everything till you get back."

He next asked the nurse to connect him with Admiralty House in Aberdour. Having listened to his conversation with Dr. MacIlderry, she now seemed less reluctant to cooperate.

"Oh, Captain Gehlman, there's been a burglar!" old Williston said as soon as the connection was made.

"When?"

"Just now, sir—in broad daylight, if you please."

"What happened?"

"One of the maids went to change the linen in Miss Alis's room— and there he was!"

"Did he get away?"

"Oh yes, sir. He jumped from the window and ran off."

"*Damn!*"

"Pardon, sir?"

"Nothing. Have you notified the police?"

"I was about to pick up the instrument, sir, when you rang."

"I see. All right, Williston, I'll notify the police myself. In the meantime, please have Mrs. Maltbie's maid pack some clothes and toiletries for her and bring them to Dunfermline Hospital. We've had a bit of an accident with the car."

"Oh dear!"

"Yes, it's very distressing. Arrange to have someone sit with her at all times, will you. I'm at the hospital now, but I've got to get aboard the *Lion* straight away, so I'm leaving everything in your hands."

"Very good, sir. I'll attend to all that's needful."

Gehlman tried to collect his thoughts while the nurse connected him with the police at Aberdour. It was a good sign, he supposed, that von Tiel had gone to Admiralty House; it could only mean that he did not know where Alis was. If anyone was capable of finding out, though, he was.

He gave the constables at Aberdour a description of von Tiel and of the Crossley he'd been driving, having informed them that he'd just in the past few minutes attempted to force his way into Admiral Beatty's official residence. Then, for good measure, he asked to be connected with the Burntisland police station, and repeated all he'd said to the constables there.

Sergeant Bellmaine was by now beginning to display marked signs of anxious impatience, so after checking one final time on Melina's condition—she was undergoing emergency surgery and the prognosis was "guarded"—Gehlman hastened over to the waiting staff car and slumped exhausted into the passenger seat.

His mind was racing: had he done everything he could for Melina and Alis? Was he right to leave them like this and return to the *Lion*? Should he notify Maltbie of what had happened?

The car wound its way down toward St. Margaret's Pier. He *had* done everything possible, he supposed; and there wasn't much more he could do if he stayed ashore. And yet the thought of Melina, broken and alone under the cold surgical lights . . .

But, no. He would go aboard the *Lion*, have a shower, put on a clean uniform—and perhaps even steal one or two hours' sleep.

And there *was* one ironic satisfaction he could salvage out of all this stress: marooned in his room back at Aberdour, a victim of all the crises and the haste, was a small black leather valise.

BOOK VII

1916, 31ST MAY–LONDON

It had been months since Reeves-Wadleigh had last had trouble sleeping. But tonight, with both Jellicoe and Scheer pushing out into the North Sea, not even an increased dosage of morphine could still the turmoil in his mind.

By the sickly predawn light that filtered into the room he was able to make out three twenty-five on his bedside clock. He reached over and picked up the empty syringe that lay next to it. "Morphine," he whispered self-mockingly. "Elixir of Morpheus, son of Sleep, god of dreams, called after *morphe*, Greek for 'form,' because 'the god gives form to our airy night-tide visions.'

"Our airy night-tide visions," he repeated, savoring Ovid's turn of phrase.

He raised the syringe contemplatively into the air, holding the barrel between his right thumb and forefinger. How appropriate for him to have come to read *Metamorphoses* at this stage of his life, or, rather, death—or, rather, dying. Moira's suggestion, of course; the consummate unmarried sister—so plain, so well read.

His hand lost its grip and the syringe fell, landing needle first in the flesh above his left breastbone. It lodged there, upright, and he stared at it stupidly, unable to feel any pain.

How quickly it was happening now; the organism grinding to a halt. The voluntary muscles were no longer responding in a reliable manner. The involuntary ones . . . but why think about them.

He withdrew the needle from his skin and threw the syringe weakly onto the floor. A few more ambulatory weeks at most. Then, when he could no longer get around on his own, a massive overdose; and he would become an airy night-tide vision himself. Morpheus would carry him away.

And yet still the questions nagged at him: *why* had they come down to London? Whom had they seen at the embassy? What had they been told?

And where in God's name was von Tiel?

The fleet had sailed so soon after Gehlman's and Maltbie's return that neither Bellmaine nor Otley had had time to transmit a report to him.

They'd send one along when the fleet came back, of course.

A tremor of anxiety ran over and through his body.

If the fleet came back, that is; and not airy night-tide visions of sunken ships.

BERLIN

Von Müller started awake in his chair as the gold-crusted Louis Quinze clock on the mantel chimed four. Through the half-open door leading into the Imperial bedchamber he could see Wilhelm sprawled across the sheets, half dressed and fast asleep.

Von Müller sighed and reached for the bottle of cognac on the table beside him. The Kaiser had asked that he "stand watch" with him until "my fleet" got safely home. The admiral wondered idly if Wilhelm had ever actually stood a full watch in his life. All in all, he doubted it.

He took a healthy swig of the amber liquid he'd poured into his glass and then loosened the collar of his uniform. Scheer and Hipper should be approaching Heligoland about now, some thirty or forty miles out. In an hour or two they would be making sixteen knots in the swept channel through the main British minefield. Around thirty minutes after that Hipper would increase to twenty-two knots, and —if the British ran true to form—the hunt would then be up.

The Kaiser coughed in his sleep and churned about for a few moments like a man trying to struggle out of quicksand. He was not resting easily on this watch they kept.

Poor Wilhelm, the admiral thought: he has the seaman's hatred of losing ships, but the landlubber's terror of risking them. Two or three times in the last several days, in fact, he'd been on the verge of calling off the entire operation. The only reason he'd finally permitted it to proceed was Admiral von Holtzendorff's ridiculous "promise" that the U-boats lying in wait outside Scapa and the Firth of Forth would decimate the British forces long before any German forces had to contend with them. Of course, the chief of staff had qualified the promise by adding, "unless they come out during darkness," but the qualification had been so offhand and muted that it had passed the Kaiser by.

Naturally the British would come out during darkness—for the exact same reason that Scheer and Hipper had come out during darkness themselves: because to come out at any other time—barring high seas or poor visibility—rendered battleships sitting ducks for submarines, which the Royal, no less than the Imperial, Navy possessed and was using.

Still, the plan as a whole was a good one. Hipper would range north, some fifty miles ahead of Scheer, in order to bait the trap. If luck was with him, he would be intercepted by Beatty while Jellicoe was still far away. He would fight a running battle with the British vice-admiral, drawing him southward into the jaws of Scheer's main force.

If all went well, it would be the beginning of the end of Britain's naval power, which was to say, her capacity to go on waging war. And if all did not go well, there would still be enough sea room to evade battle until darkness, when the new Telefunken interference devices would permit the High Seas Fleet to steal home.

The Kaiser coughed again, then gave a small whimpering sigh.

How wonderful, von Müller mused, to be at sea now, on this great and historic day.

And how much less than wonderful to be here in Berlin with one's sovereign, standing watch in a Louis Quinze chair.

NEW YORK CITY

House sat bolt upright in his bed. A loud report, like the sound of nearby cannon, had jolted him out of his sleep.

He stayed very still, every sense alert; but the only sounds were his heartbeat and the blustery wind in the courtyard outside.

His watch read six fifteen.

He got up, put on his robe and slippers, and peered cautiously out of the window. Above him dark-bottomed clouds boiled and tumbled from west to east, driven along by the lash of the wind.

"What portentous weather!" he murmured to himself, half in jest, as he sniffed the cool wildness in the air.

Could it have been thunder? he wondered, scanning the courtyard for some evidence of recent rain.

Then he noticed the oak.

He trudged downstairs, through the pantry, and out the back door. He slowed to a halt as he got near the base of the tree.

It had been one of the largest branches, about twelve feet up, and the wind had snapped it off like a twig. Before the leafy end came to rest on the ground, the base of the branch had stripped about six feet of bark from the trunk. The wound ended just above the level of House's eyes.

He took a few tentative steps and looked at the tree's exposed flesh. There was no cambium layer that he could discern, just vertical channels of moist-looking dark brown scum bounded by gummy gray striations of fiber. He thought he could detect a movement along the channels: little off-white freckles that scurried up and down in mindless patterns of frenzy.

To think that that proud tower had been harboring such filth and decay.

He would get a tree surgeon in this very morning, he determined. Surely one could localize the rot.

He forced himself to look at the open sore again.

Surely, surely . . . but he was really not so very sure at all.

THE NORTH SEA, APPROACHING JUTLAND BANK

"There's Admiral Jerram now, sir," said the flag commander in the quiet conversational tone cultivated by all of Jellicoe's staff. "Bearing east-southeast."

The commander in chief lifted his binoculars to his eyes, as did Maltbie and the rest of the officers on the compass platform. About five or six miles off the starboard bow the eight dreadnoughts of the 2d Battle Squadron were visible through the light midday mist.

"He's right on time," Jellicoe said cheerfully. "Signal him to pass astern and take station on the port wing."

Maltbie watched as searchlights blinked acknowledgments along the line of approaching ships. Last night's order from the Admiralty was being put into effect. It had come in only minutes after he himself had arrived from Thurso, and it had read, in pertinent part, "Concentrate eastward of the Long Forties, ready for eventualities."

Led by the *Iron Duke*, the 1st and 4th Battle Squadrons had slipped out of Scapa at 10:30 P.M. and passed north of the Long Forties area early this morning; at 11:00 P.M. Admiral Jerram in *King George V* had taken his squadron out of its temporary base at Cromarty on the Moray Firth and proceeded south of it. Now, some thirteen hours later, the two components of the Grand Fleet had met at their prearranged rendezvous, roughly one hundred miles east of Aberdeen.

Maltbie was always thrilled by the sight of the fleet concentrating into full cruising formation, and this day, with all his unhappy thoughts giving way to the majesty of the moment, he relished the spectacle even more.

Two miles to port *King George V* was leading *Ajax, Centurion*, and *Erin* into station at nineteen knots. One mile nearer, *Orion* was steaming a parallel course at the same speed, ahead of *Monarch, Conquerer*, and *Thunderer*. As the two divisions drew abeam of *Iron Duke* they brought their speed down to the main body's sedate progress of fifteen nautical miles per hour.

And now the Grand Fleet was formed.

Maltbie turned to look at *Royal Oak, Superb*, and *Canada*, keeping station two cables apart behind the flagship. A mile to starboard *Benbow, Bellerophon, Temeraire*, and *Vanguard* plowed through the glassy calm. Another mile to the southwest were *Colossus, Collingwood, Neptune*, and *St. Vincent*. And last, three miles distant, was the starboard-wing column, *Marlborough, Revenge, Hercules*, and *Agincourt*.

Any one of these ships, Maltbie reflected, could have confronted the Spanish Armada and instantly destroyed it, could have blasted the *Monitor* and the *Merrimac* out of the water with a single salvo— could even have taken on Admiral Togo at Tsushima Strait and reduced his entire line of battle to a line of blazing debris inside of half an hour.

Any one of them.

To think, then, what a full two dozen might accomplish.

And the most powerful battle squadron of all wasn't even there in formation! The 5th under Admiral Evan-Thomas in the *Barham* had been sent south ten days ago to Beatty as a temporary replacement for the BCF's *Invincible, Inflexible,* and *Indomitable,* which had been sent north for target practice in the Pentland Firth, and which were presently scouting for Jellicoe some five miles off the flagship's port bow. The 5th Battle Squadron had half the ships but fully as much firepower as the 1st, the 2d, or the 4th. This was because *Barham, Valiant, Warspite,* and *Malaya* were all brand-new second generation superdreadnoughts, mounting eight guns of fully 15-inch diameter, powered by oil-fired turbines capable of generating twenty-five knots of speed, and protected by armor that, at thirteen inches, was thicker even than the *Iron Duke*'s. In the wardrooms up at Scapa, in fact, it was widely—and not altogether facetiously—suggested that, with a force as powerful as the 5th BS attached to his flag, Admiral Beatty might be tempted to go after the entire German Fleet!

Through his binoculars Maltbie scanned the horizon to the southeast, but the empty shimmering boundary between sea and sky barely impinged upon his mind. His thoughts were far away: in London with Assistant Secretary Corey, on the train from Scotland with Gehlman, in the bedroom at Aberdour with Melina . . . and in his cabin on the *Iron Duke* with that hateful brown suitcase. Corey, Gehlman, Melina, the suitcase: these component strands of his confusion were so hopelessly tangled as to frustrate all striving toward coherent thought. Yet he had to unravel them somehow, and think, before events usurped his power of choice.

All right; start with the crucial question: should the radio be used?

Why the passive voice, brave Harry? Isn't the proper question, should *I* use the radio?

Yes. All right. That's the proper question.

Good. . . . Well, do you *want* to use the radio?

No!

Don't then.

But the chances for peace, for America staying out of the war; aren't they worth something? Aren't they worth the sacrifice of my honor?

But it isn't just your honor that's at stake here; the Royal Navy has a great deal to lose as well.

What's the Royal Navy to me? My country is the United States, isn't it? I swore to preserve, protect, and defend it, didn't I?

Ah, but is the preservation, protection, and defense of your country likely to be secured by treachery and dishonor?

It would seem so, in this instance.

But how could it *be* so? Aren't treachery and dishonor contrary to what the country stands for in the first place?

It's an imperfect world; questionable measures may be called for to safeguard the least imperfect nation in it.

Safeguard? Is the nation in some kind of danger?

It's in danger of being dragged into the war.

With what result?

With the result that the side we join with will win.

So where is the danger?

All right; the country's survival may not be at issue, but its general welfare is.

You would stoop to treachery and dishonor for your country's general *welfare?*

I've been ordered to.

A feeble response, laddie.

It's not for me to question the decisions of my superiors.

But it is up to you to question the legality of any orders they may give you.

There's nothing illegal about the orders they've given me.

No? Isn't sabotage an act of war?

Yes.

Has Congress authorized anyone to commit acts of war?

No.

Well, if it hasn't authorized anyone to commit them, how could anyone else order them to be committed?

But the chance for peace?

Suppose the Royal Navy destroys the High Seas Fleet, opens up a supply route to Russia through the Baltic, lands an Allied invasion force at Rostock, only a hundred miles from Berlin. Doesn't the chance for peace reside in those contingencies as well?

Maltbie found that he was working his jaw muscles so violently as he conducted his inner debate that his head was beginning to ache from the exertion. He lowered the binoculars from his eyes and leaned against the railing of the compass platform. All around him the excitement and elation of his shipmates seemed almost palpable;

every man was absorbed in the prospect of confronting the Germans, every man had a function to serve, a duty to perform. As never before in his service with the British Fleet, Maltbie felt alone, isolated, out of place. In this supreme hour he had no duties and served no purpose, yet he might nevertheless determine the outcome of the battle. His mind told him that he would be wrong to obey Corey's orders; but that fact that he didn't want to obey them made him doubt his mind's capacity to render an impartial judgment. Even if he declined to act himself, he was still left with the problem that Gehlman had presented: if it was wrong to do something yourself, could it be right to let someone else do it for you? Of course, Gehlman might not do it either—or the situation calling for action might never arise, if God was merciful. . . . Gehlman: why had he been so uneasy about the subject of Melina? And Melina: why had she reacted so strangely to his own unexpected appearance at Aberdour the other night? One ominous explanation hovered over Maltbie's consciousness, but he refused to acknowledge it. Life simply could not be that unfair, it simply couldn't attack him on that front when he was so desperately embattled on this one. No, no. Ben Gehlman was incapable of such a thing . . . even if Melina wasn't.

Even if Melina *wasn't?!*

My God! Where did a thought like that spring from?

His jaw muscles were working again, even more violently than before. He hastily returned his thoughts to the question of the small brown suitcase; it was by far the easier problem to contemplate.

The plan of operations called for Jellicoe to steam eastward to latitude 57°45′N and longitude 4°15′E, a point off the Jutland Bank almost 250 miles from Scapa Flow. Beatty, some sixty nautical miles to the south and steering a roughly parallel course, was to turn toward the Grand Fleet and steam for a rendezvous if he had no news of the enemy by 2:00 P.M.

So far there had been no news.

On the bridge of the *Iron Duke* spirits began sinking shortly after Admiral Jerram had taken up his station on the port wing. The sun was burning off the morning mist, and conditions for a full-scale engagement were ideal. As two o'clock approached, however, Maltbie began to have some hope that the Germans had once again scurried back to port and thereby spared him a decision.

The great ships continued forward in their six stately columns, but as so often in the past, their bows pointed out toward an empty horizon. "Just another bloody useless sweep!" Maltbie heard a signalman mutter as two o'clock came and went.

Then, at 2:18 P.M., over the hitherto silent wireless, came a signal from Commodore Alexander-Sinclair in the *Galatea*, easternmost of Admiral Beatty's light cruiser scouts: "Urgent. Two destroyers, probably hostile, in sight bearing ESE, course unknown."

Gehlman felt the hairs rising on the back of his neck as Beatty signaled a redeployment of his destroyers toward the sound of the *Galatea*'s guns, preparatory to a turn by the battle cruisers themselves. Up to the blocks went the flags for twenty-five knots, and from the stacks of *Princess Royal*, *Queen Mary*, and *Tiger*, churning through the *Lion*'s wake, came doubly thick billows of smoke. Three miles to the east, *New Zealand* and *Indefatigable* acknowledged the call for speed, and five miles to the northwest the massive outlines of the 5th Battle Squadron seemed poised to turn in support.

The aches and bruises that were the legacy of Gehlman's encounter with von Tiel receded altogether from his awareness, and in their place came a new sensation, unexpected and overwhelming. Gehlman was astonished by it. He had passed through the trial of Dogger Bank—even including those pregnant twenty seconds he had counted off at von Tiel's request—with little more than an intense feeling of excitement. Now, however, even before the enemy could be detected on the horizon, his entire mind and body were in the grip of abject terror.

What was he doing here?

The *Lion*, it now seemed to him, was little more than a cordite and lyddite bomb surging through the water toward its point of detonation; the uninterrupted chain of cartridges and projectiles between its magazines and its working chambers was in fact a short fast fuse, ready to be ignited by one well-placed German shell. How could he have run so blindly to meet his death? he wondered despairingly. This imminent battle had nothing to do with him; he had no role to play in it—other than to be numbered among the dead. Why was he here, when the two people he cared for most were back on the north shore of the Firth of Forth, alone and in need of his support. God *damn* you! he shouted to himself: the unthinking, the formula response—the conditioned reflex that had sent him running to battle because his ship was making steam. Madness. Insanity.

Perhaps if he'd brought the black satchel with him there would be less futility in what he'd done. But no, Harry had been right; he would never have used it. Not because he was too damned moral. Because he was too damned spiteful.

His mind jerked and wriggled in panic, like a rabbit caught in a gin. What could he do? Run to Beatty and warn him of the danger? But no: that was ignominious, it would mark him as a coward. More pertinently, it would do no good. There was nothing anyone could do now to make the ships safer except decline battle, which no one would think of doing. It was way too late for warnings. The game would have to be played out, the terror and anguish would have to be endured. And it would all have been so much less frightening, he reflected, if he had never known Alis. Life had been a great deal easier to live in the days when he'd had a great deal less to live for.

At 2:32 P.M. the *Lion* swung into her turn, and the battle cruisers behind and abeam of her followed suit. Three minutes into the turn came a further signal from Alexander-Sinclair: "Urgent. Have sighted large amount of smoke, as though from a fleet, bearing ENE."

Like sparks struck off steel, jubilant smiles flashed around the admiral's bridge as a dozen pairs of binoculars swung to face east by northeast. Gehlman glanced over his right shoulder to the west-by-north quadrant to reassure himself that the 5th Battle Squadron was there close astern in support. Hipper wouldn't dare take on six battle cruisers and four superdreadnoughts at once, he told himself. But the 5th Battle Squadron *wasn't there!*

Gehlman turned completely around and raised his binoculars to his eyes. The four great battleships were now almost hull down on the horizon, a good ten miles away. They must have missed the turn signal and continued north!

Gehlman watched in horrified disbelief as the gap between the two forces continued to widen. Within thirty seconds, however, he saw that the distant silhouettes were beginning slowly to lengthen. After a minute or two they just as slowly began to narrow again. Evan-Thomas had finally made his turn—but he still had a lot of steaming to do before he could provide Beatty with any support or, more important, before he could force Hipper to flee.

Sighting reports continued to come in as the *Lion* swung round to a course of northeast. The light cruiser squadrons were pressing outward at thirty knots in order to establish visual contact with the enemy and determine his strength. Soon the *Falmouth* and the *Nottingham* were confirming the *Galatea's* signals with signals of their own: it was clear that a naval force of no mean proportions lay just over the eastern horizon.

Over an hour had passed since the *Galatea's* initial report, and the smoke of the enemy was now discernible from the bridge of the *Lion* itself. Then, just before 3:30 P.M., Gehlman caught sight of three . . . four . . . *five!* large silhouettes arrayed in line of battle some 25,000 yards to the northeast. Several lookouts spotted them at the same time, and Beatty immediately ordered a southward turn so as to cut off their route of escape.

Gehlman shot a glance westward to see if the 5th Battle Squadron had made up any of the lost ground. It had, but on turning back to face eastward Gehlman saw that Beatty and the enemy were converging at such a rapid rate that the shooting would start long before Evan-Thomas got within range. His fear tore at his insides.

The enemy ships were now clearly visible and Gehlman realized that for the first time in more than a year he was looking at the battle cruisers of Admiral Hipper. Leading the line and recognizable by their superimposed forward turrets were two *Derfflinger* class ships: the newly completed *Lützow* first, most probably, and *Derfflinger* itself second. Next was the old familiar outline of the *Seydlitz*, and behind her the somewhat stumpier silhouette of the *Moltke*. Last in line, with just one turret fore and aft to go with the two amidships, was the older and slower *Von der Tann*.

So it was six against five, at least until Evan-Thomas arrived. The German inferiority in numbers was partially offset, however, by the westering sun, which sharply defined the British ships against the sky, and by the westerly breeze, which was sending British smoke toward the enemy like a screen while Hipper's smoke floated harmlessly away on his unengaged side. It was offset also by the cordite in the British working chambers.

Beatty signaled his ships to form up in line of bearing preparatory to opening fire. *New Zealand* and *Indefatigable* swung round to take station to the rear of *Tiger*, and as *New Zealand* crossed the *Lion's* bows, Gehlman saw that over his uniform her captain was wearing the famous grass kilt that a Maori chieftain had given him when the ship called at Auckland before the war. According to the chieftain, the kilt, if worn during battle, would protect the ship from harm.

Gehlman knew, however, that, given first-class German marksmanship, there was nothing that could do that.

Both Beatty and Hipper were now steaming south on slightly convergent courses, and at 3:45, with the range estimated at 18,000 yards, *Lion* and the ships behind her opened fire. Even as the shells were in flight, though, there came a ripple of answering flashes along the entire enemy line. The British salvos landed a good 3,000 yards long, and the splashes they made were still visible behind the German ships when the approach of Hipper's reply became audible from out of the east. It sounded to Gehlman as if the whole vault of the sky was made of silk being torn to shreds by the hands of angry giants. Then fully twenty shells in tightly spaced patterns of three and four sent the sea around the *Lion* billowing into monstrous black-green geysers that stank of TNT.

Within minutes the British line was taking hits, and Gehlman hardly knew how he kept himself from screaming. By four o'clock the flagship had been struck half a dozen times, and the ships behind her were suffering murderous punishment as well. Perhaps the British dreadnoughts weren't so vulnerable after all.

A heavy explosion on the forecastle sent splinters buzzing onto the bridge; Beatty and his officers did not deign to acknowledge them by ducking behind the blast mats, however, and instead stared down the flying steel shards. (Gehlman didn't duck down either—a stray splinter was among the least of his anxieties.)

Turning to see how the rest of the BCF was holding up under the barrage, he saw something at the end of the line that brought back all his terror in a rush. *Indefatigable*, having apparently been struck a crippling blow, had hauled out of line and appeared to be sinking by the stern. As her dwindling momentum slowly moved her onward in the water, Gehlman saw three blurred hyphens plunge directly onto her forward turret. The explosion of the projectiles was followed instantaneously by a secondary explosion of terrible magnitude, and the great ship heeled over and disappeared beneath an awesome pall of orange-tinged smoke.

There was an instant of mute stupefaction on the *Lion*'s bridge as the *Indefatigable*'s thousand officers and men disappeared into the depths. Oh God! Gehlman thought. The British dreadnoughts were every bit as vulnerable as he'd feared.

But as if to refute this conclusion, there appeared on the bridge at that moment the flayed-looking figure of a sergeant of marines. He was hatless, his uniform was tattered and bloody, and the surface layers of his skin were in many places burned away. With a dazed expression in his eyes he approached the flag captain and said, "Permission to speak to the commander, sir."

Captain Chatfield, whose attention was on the smoking eddies where the *Indefatigable* had been just a moment before, snapped out, "The commander's at his midships battlestation, damnit!" He then lowered his binoculars and turned as if to shower the witless intruder with a few more well-chosen words. But on seeing the sergeant's condition he sucked in his breath and gasped, "What in God's name has happened, man?"

"Q turret's gone, sir," the sergeant replied in a dull monotone. "The crew's all dead, and we've flooded the magazines."

Gehlman rushed to the side of the bridge, with Chatfield close beside him. The roof of Q turret amidships—nine inches of armorplate —had been folded back like the lid on a tin of sardines, and the turret's two 13.5-inch cannon were cocked up at crazy angles toward the sky. Thick yellow smoke boiled up as from a volcano, and here and there round what remained of the gunhouse platform were bits and pieces of crewmen's bodies.

"Was Major Harvey killed as well?" Chatfield asked, referring to the turret commander.

"Both legs blown off, sir. He gave the order to flood the magazines just before he died."

"Damn!" said Chatfield.

Gehlman felt strangely exhilarated. Even as he'd watched the *Indefatigable* explode, the *Lion* itself had been within a few brief seconds of equally cataclysmic destruction. Yet for some reason—or for no reason, more probably—his ship and his life had been spared for the second time in as many battles. Francis Harvey and Sigismund von Tiel had saved it: a dead Briton with his dying breath and a live German who had just yesterday attempted to murder him.

Looking aft beyond Q turret, Gehlman saw that the 5th Battle Squadron had finally gotten near enough to open fire on the rear ships of the German line. He could imagine the consternation aboard the *Moltke* and the *Von der Tann* as Evan-Thomas's one-ton 15-inch shells started splitting the seas around them: no sooner had Hipper's gunners managed to even the odds by sinking the *Indefatigable* than this awesome new juggernaut came bellowing down from the north.

Beatty too saw that the 5th Battle Squadron had opened fire, and he therefore altered course so as to close the range. The shooting at this point attained an intensity that battered the mind, and the scale of the confrontation was even further magnified when both Beatty and Hipper ordered their destroyers to launch torpedo attacks against the enemy line. Within minutes the eight-mile stretch of water between the contending dreadnought forces was aswarm with small ships darting in and out among the geysers and plunging shells. The secondary armaments along both lines of battle erupted into life, creating a din that consumed all the senses. The *Lion* was struck again, and her main wireless was shot away. Then a 4-inch shell from one of the German light cruisers ricocheted off the water and landed with a loud *clang!* between the main funnel and the fiery remains of Q turret. Gehlman watched with oddly detached curiosity to see if the shell would ignite before a damage control party was able to muscle it overboard. The sailors worked quickly, though, and in under a minute the smoking projectile went over the side and sank beneath the *Lion's* wake.

As Gehlman raised his eyes to take in the surviving ships of the BCF, he saw two shells crash into the *Queen Mary*, which was third in line behind the flagship and *Princess Royal*. There was a moderate explosion amidships, but then a huge red gout of flame shot up from her forepart, followed by an even more shattering eruption from her midships turret. The ship all at once broke apart, sending smoke and fire—and even her fifty-foot steamboat—spiraling lazily upward a thousand feet into the sky. The stern rose high out of the water, with the propellers still pointlessly turning; then twelve hundred men and 30,000 tons of the Royal Navy's elite cavalry slid hissing and steaming out of sight.

Tiger had to veer out of line to avoid *Queen Mary's* wreckage, and for a moment she too appeared to be engulfed in fire, while *Princess Royal*, straddled by German salvos, disappeared in a welter of smoke and water. It was at this point, with two, or possibly four, of the six BCF ships destroyed, that Beatty, turning to Captain Chatfield on his right, said in a laconic, almost derisive tone of voice, "There seems to be something wrong with our bloody ships today. . . . Turn two points to port"—i.e., Attack! Even in the midst of his crippling fear, Gehlman had to admire the Admiral's sangfroid.

The range began rapidly to close, but then Hipper, who was beginning to feel the crushing weight of the 5th Battle Squadron's fire, broke off the action and veered away to the east. As he did so, however, a signal came in from Commodore Goodenough in the *Southampton*, which was scouting for Beatty some two or three miles ahead of the fight: "Battleships SE."

"*Scheer!*" Beatty shouted, immediately ordering a change of course toward Goodenough's position.

Every man on the bridge now pointed his binoculars southeastward, eyes straining to confirm that the prize was indeed and at last in sight. After five minutes or so of steadily mounting excitement, the dim shapes of masts and funnels began to materialize on the horizon. At that instant another signal arrived from Goodenough: "Have sighted enemy battle fleet bearing approximately SE, course of enemy N."

There was a moment of fierce jubilation on the *Lion's* bridge—unvoiced but unrestrained. "Let's show them the way to the *Iron Duke!*" said Beatty, ordering a sixteen-point turn toward Jellicoe and the mass of British naval power.

Hipper and the German battle cruisers immediately followed suit, taking up station ahead of the *König* class battleships that formed the leading element of the main force of the High Seas Fleet. It was clear to Gehlman that the German admiral believed he was about to score a coup, with twenty-one dreadnoughts on the heels of Beatty's eight. In less than an hour, he reckoned, the man would be getting the shock of his life—while he himself, he prayed, would finally be safe.

The British guns kept booming and the German salvos kept falling as battle cruisers, battleships, light cruisers, and destroyers careered headlong toward the north. Gehlman guessed there had to be nearly 150 ships churning up the sea within a fifteen-mile radius of the *Lion*; and all 150 of them were on a collision course with the over one hundred more that were heading south.

In the annals of naval history, the moment of Armageddon was now at hand, or so it seemed. But at that moment, off the *Lion's* unengaged bow, there appeared a note of poignant incongruity. It was a sleek white ketch, with the flag of Denmark flying from its stern. Through his binoculars Gehlman could make out the shapes of men and women lounging together beneath the mizzen. They were clad in summer white and had champagne glasses in their hands. Most wonderful of all was their reaction on seeing the dreadnoughts go by. There before them, not 10,000 yards away, the most awesome ships in the world were hurtling through the water with massive enemy salvos falling around them on every side. And how did these idle young boaters respond to the vision? By lifting up their glasses and gaily waving hello!

It was perfectly natural, and also perfectly absurd, Gehlman thought. It occurred to him later that it might also have been perfectly apropos.

Beatty's ships and Jellicoe's were now converging at nearly fifty miles an hour, and the battle cruisers began to bend their course around to the east so as to keep the C in C's approach concealed from the Germans as long as possible. As *Lion* completed her initial starboard turn, the shapes of three large warships became dimly visible far away to the east-northeast. "By heaven, it's Hood and the *Invincibles!*" Beatty exulted; and through his binoculars Gehlman saw that it was indeed the 3d Battle Cruiser Squadron, *Invincible, Inflexible,* and *Indomitable,* steaming full tilt toward the fight. Jellicoe must have sent them on ahead to lend support to their beleaguered brothers in arms.

Gehlman consulted his watch. It was getting on 5:45. Almost three and a half hours had now passed since the *Galatea* sent her first signal. Jellicoe had probably kept Admiral Hood attached to the mass of the battle squadrons until there'd been definite news of the enemy's position. That meant that the *Invincibles,* with their five-knot speed advantage over the fleet as a whole, could not be much more than ten or fifteen miles ahead of the *Iron Duke.*

If that was the case, then the collision of Scheer's ships with Jellicoe's would take place in little more than half an hour.

Coursing toward the southeast at its top speed of twenty knots, the Grand Fleet was magnificent to behold. On the compass platform of the *Iron Duke,* however, there was extreme anxiety. Nearly forty minutes had passed since the last wireless report on the enemy's position, and for all intents and purposes the battle squadrons of the Royal Navy were steaming blind. Somewhere up ahead of them Admirals Beatty and Hipper were trading salvos, with Admiral Scheer a slow but by no means dilatory spectator to their rear. Even if position reports had been coming in from the *Lion* in an adequate manner, the fact that the BCF and the Grand Fleet had been out of sight of land all day and steaming through different tidal currents would have made any estimates of relative bearings unreliable at best. But position reports had not been coming in, and the battle fleet was still in its six-columned cruising formation, virtually impotent until it could deploy into line of battle.

The question was, in which direction should it deploy?—but the answer to that question depended on the enemy's position and heading, which no British ship had so far divulged. Maltbie, no less than Jellicoe, was at a loss to understand why Beatty wasn't transmitting the vital information, and the possibility that Gehlman might have misunderstood Corey's instructions and started jamming in daylight swept over him like a cold wind. He experienced a sensation of terror. Even granted that poor visibility was the most probable explanation—coupled perhaps with overabsorption in the conduct of the running battle and damage to the *Lion*'s aerials as at Dogger Bank—Maltbie was still staggered by the fact that Corey had given him and Gehlman such unconscionably excessive power. Either one of them, succumbing to just a moment's aberration, could wreak havoc on the entire British Fleet by simply flipping a switch. Presenting him and Gehlman with radio transmitters had been an act of flagrant irresponsibility, as Maltbie now perceived it: carte blanche to change history in response to some arbitrary whim. Anger rose in him. He'd be damned if he was going to use that transmitter!

It wasn't a moral question in the final analysis; it was a question of hubristic presumption. Corey's superiors obviously believed that they could tune history to their tastes, filter out the contingencies that weren't compatible with their diplomatic objectives. But Maltbie now felt that he knew better. One couldn't intrude oneself into an event as momentous as an encounter between the two most powerful fleets that had ever existed and expect one's intrusion to have a predictable or delimited effect. Everything that happened today, as well as everything that *didn't* happen, would have a significance impossible to calculate. Corey said peace would be achieved and neutrality preserved if the Germans escaped destruction. Well, Corey and his superiors just simply could not *know* that, any more than Maltbie and Gehlman could know the contrary. Of course, if they *were* capable of knowing it, then, Maltbie presumed, he would be obliged to obey the orders he'd been given. But they *weren't* capable of knowing it, and it was their erroneous assumption that they were that had deluded them. Assuming they possessed God-like powers of perception, it would have been but a short step for them to assume a God-like superiority to conventional notions of honor. This was where their confusion resided: not in ordering a wrong action, but in believing that they were competent to order one. Similarly, Maltbie's confusion up until this moment had not resided in his readiness to obey their orders, but in his belief that their orders had some claim to be obeyed. Morality was not at issue here, he now realized; the question was one of authority. And even though he recognized that his whole process of reasoning might be nothing more than an elaborate rationalization for avoiding what he found repellent, his arguments were still plausible enough to sustain him. They were sufficient unto the day and unto the hour; and he was damned if he was going to subject them to any further analysis.

He glanced sympathetically at the commander in chief, who looked composed but a trifle weary, his old navy Burberry and white silken scarf contrasting with the leathery brown texture of his skin. His blue eyes were keen but just the least bit pinched with tension, and Maltbie noticed with amused affection that the gold leaf of the visor on the admiral's cap was badly tarnished.

Here was the man who could lose the war in an afternoon. But lacking information and forced to deploy on conjecture, he might now well be the man who could lose the war with a single command. Well, fate—not William Corey—would make the decision.

Finally, at 5:52, a message came in from Commodore Goodenough in the *Southampton:* "Enemy battle fleet has altered course to north. Enemy battle cruisers bear SW from enemy battle fleet. My position 56°50′N, 5°44′E at 5:50."

Immediately, as the sound of cannon fire became audible off the starboard beam, the navigation officers bent down to their charts to plot the *Southampton*'s reported position. It worked out to be some twenty-five miles due south, which didn't seem to tally with any of the previous reports that had come in. As if to confirm this discrepancy, *Marlborough* at the head of the starboard-wing column now astonishingly reported, "Our battle cruisers bearing SSW, three to four miles, steering east. *Lion* leading ship."

Now there was real confusion. *Lion*, some six miles away from the *Iron Duke*, was presumably engaged with Hipper's battle cruisers, which *Southampton* had reported to be *to the southwest* of the enemy battle fleet, which was itself reported to be some twenty miles south of the commander in chief.

The sound of guns was growing louder second by second, and still Jellicoe couldn't act. "I wish *someone* would tell me who is firing and what they are firing at," the admiral said with a note of uncharacteristic testiness in his voice.

And at that instant, plunging forward at full steam abaft the starboard bow, *Lion* and her cohorts came surging into view with German salvos falling round them on every side.

"Where is enemy's battle fleet?" Jellicoe signaled instantaneously.

It was during the intolerably anxious wait for Beatty's reply that Maltbie noticed there were only four large ships in the BCF's line. "Dear God!" he whispered to himself, just as he had at Dogger Bank.

"Enemy battle cruisers bearing SE," the *Lion's* searchlights flashed out, and on the bridge of the *Iron Duke* there was an almost audible surge of exasperation.

"Where is enemy's battle fleet?" Jellicoe signaled again, no doubt wishing there were some way to underscore the final word in his transmission.

Even once the order to deploy was given, the transition process from cruising to battle formation would easily take a quarter of an hour to complete. During those fifteen-plus minutes, moreover, perhaps thirty to fifty percent of the Grand Fleet's guns would be masked by the maneuvers involved in forming line of battle. Admiral Beatty was now four miles directly ahead of the *Iron Duke*, steaming perpendicularly across the C in C's line of advance. He was engaged with the enemy battle cruisers, which were probably a maximum of ten miles off his starboard beam. The distance between the enemy battle cruisers and the enemy battle fleet could be calculated to be between five and ten miles at the most. Splitting the differences and doing the sums, the distance between Scheer and Jellicoe would be just about twenty-plus miles. Subtract from this twenty the ten-minus miles at which both fleets would open fire; figure in a closing speed of close to thirty-five knots; load on the fifteen-plus minutes it would take to form a line of battle—and you got an answer that cried out convulsively, You must deploy *now!*

Finally the *Lion's* searchlights flashed again: "Have sighted enemy's battle fleet bearing SSW."

The strain was now so unbearable that Maltbie, free at last to indulge his natural sympathies, could hardly breathe. Beatty's message had neglected to give the enemy's course, and there wasn't time to ask for it. Jellicoe would just have to assume that Scheer was headed roughly north, and that the Grand Fleet was about to pass diagonally in front of it at a distance of twelve to eighteen miles.

Now: did one deploy to the east on the port-wing column led by *King George* V, or to the west on the starboard-wing column led by HMS *Marlborough*?

A deployment to the west would be a deployment *toward* the enemy, a deployment in the Nelsonic tradition of coming to grips with the foe and fighting full bore to the finish—no small consideration when one remembered that the Royal Navy, as well as the British nation, had been waiting for this moment for twenty-two months. Of course, a deployment toward the enemy was also a deployment that might not be completed when the two fleets opened fire. But weren't well-judged risks the key to winning wars?

A deployment to the east, on the other hand, had two great advantages and one grave drawback. Beatty had veered around toward the east, and Scheer, to prevent the BCF from crossing his T, was probably bending his northerly heading eastward as well. If the Grand Fleet deployed on its port wing, it would end up on a heading of east by south, nearly perpendicular to the conjectured line of Scheer's advance. That meant that Scheer's T would be crossed as decisively as any T in the history of naval warfare . . . *if* the estimates of his course and bearing were pretty nearly correct.

The second major advantage of a deployment on the port wing was that the visibility, which was deteriorating rapidly in all directions, was deteriorating *least* on the westerly bearings. If Jellicoe deployed eastward, accordingly, he would have significantly better shooting.

There remained, however, the one grave drawback. If the Grand Fleet deployed to port, away from the enemy, there was a serious danger that Scheer, realizing his desperate situation, might break off the engagement and flee west into the gathering mist and haze. Of course, if he did do that, it was open to Jellicoe to turn southward and cut off his route back to Kiel. But the sea was wide, and there were now only two hours to sunset.

After all these months, to find the German dreadnoughts only to lose them again would be unthinkable. It was a real possibility, given an eastward deployment, however, and the one man who could lose the war in an afternoon had to look that possibility squarely in the eye.

Maltbie watched as the commander in chief walked briskly over to the magnetic compass, the steel strips on the heels of his shoes clicking on the platform's iron grating. For some fifteen seconds he looked down into the binnacle, his features pensive and composed. The rumble of the guns outside, the hum of the *Iron Duke*'s turbines, the whistle of the wind through the waiting signal halyards, all seemed to diminish out of deference to this moment of decision. Then Jellicoe looked up, and in a calm voice said, "Hoist equal speed pendant southeast."

Deployment would be on the port-wing column.

Instantly the fleet signal officer called over the rail to the boatswain at the halyards: "Hoist equal speed Charlie London!" Within seconds *Benbow* and *Orion*, starboard and port, acknowledged the order. *Colossus* and *King George V* would acknowledge next. But Jellicoe wasn't waiting. "Dreyer, commence the deployment," he said to the flag captain, who immediately blew two short blasts on the siren and ordered the helm put over. The leaders of the adjacent columns followed suit as did the outer column leaders seconds after.

The battle squadrons had waited so long for this moment and practiced so often for this maneuver that preparative, acknowledging, and executive signals could only slow them down. "Deploy east!" they'd been told—and eastward, at flank speed, they moved.

The question now was, where would the German dreadnoughts appear—and how soon? Eight minutes into the deployment the first hint of an answer arrived in the form of Hipper's battle cruisers, which emerged out of the mist about 10,000 yards due south of the *Iron Duke*. Before the guns of the Grand Fleet could open fire, however, the German ships were obscured by drifting smoke. Fortunately, Maltbie saw, Beatty's ships and Admiral Hood's, which were 3,000 yards closer to the enemy, continued to have Hipper in view; the concentrated fire of the seven remaining British battle cruisers would be nothing short of withering at a range of 7,000 yards.

Invincible was steaming at the head of Beatty's line, and gaps in the mist and smoke revealed that she was shooting brilliantly. It seemed, though, that at least four of Hipper's five ships were concentrating their fire on her alone, perhaps because from their position she was the only large ship to be seen. As Maltbie watched, a German salvo struck *Invincible*'s midships turret. There was an explosion, a pause, and a series of terrible, firecrackerlike bursts of flame. Then, with one huge concussive blast, the ship literally broke in two, buckling inward until only her bow and her stern could be seen above the waves.

"Enemy battleships bearing south!" one of the lookouts shouted at that instant. Maltbie snapped his head around toward the horizon off the starboard beam. There they were: just barely visible in the uncertain light—*König* class battleships, the van of the High Seas Fleet! Maltbie shot a look astern; the deployment was not quite complete yet, but it was complete enough . . . and what must it look like to the captain of that leading German ship: a seven-mile-long phalanx of British dreadnoughts with its broadside of two hundred heavy-caliber cannon staring him right in the face!

All up and down the British line the great ships opened fire. There was no question of coordination or distribution of salvos; the visibility was far too poor for that. It was just fire at what you can see for as long as you can see it.

The pulverizing cannonade lasted five or six minutes, then gradually petered out into comparative silence.

The Germans had disappeared.

Maltbie scanned the southern horizon through his binoculars but saw nothing other than smoke and mist. From his work with Gehlman at Newport, he remembered the maneuver that "Red" Fleet had employed once or twice when confronted with this kind of situation. It was called the *Gefechtskehrtwendung*, or "battle about-turn," a rapid 180-degree change of course similar to the one Sims had made use of from time to time in maneuvering the Atlantic Flotilla. It was a difficult maneuver to execute, though, especially under heavy fire, and Maltbie didn't feel certain that it was the tactic Admiral Scheer had chosen now.

Neither did Jellicoe, apparently. Having lost visual contact with the enemy, the C in C ordered the fleet to a course of south, athwart the Germans' route back to Wilhelmshaven and Kiel. Although he couldn't find Scheer in all the haze and funnel smoke, perhaps Scheer would be obliging enough to find him.

For over half an hour the Grand Fleet moved southward through seas that were eerily quiet. The battle squadrons had been virtually untouched by German shells, and even the battered ships under Beatty's command were reported still steaming and ready for action.

Maltbie was surveying the sky to the westward when the sound of salvos came rolling toward him from the rear of the British line. "Battleships bearing southwest!" two lookouts yelled simultaneously, and within seconds *Iron Duke* and the ships around her had opened fire.

Scheer was heading due east, it became apparent, perhaps in the hope of passing behind the British line and racing homeward. But he had blundered into the Grand Fleet's center instead, and was being buried beneath the concentrated fire of almost three dozen ships.

Maltbie watched in awe as the British salvos crushed in the head of the German line. Then in astonishment he saw Hipper's battle cruisers surging out from the van of Scheer's force. They were steaming at full speed, and directly at the heart of the British line! It was nothing short of a death ride, calculated no doubt to give the German main force time to escape. Right behind the battle cruisers came a swarm of destroyers, eight or nine of them laying smoke to cover Scheer's retreat, and twenty or thirty others coming straight at the Grand Fleet's broadsides. It was going to be a massed torpedo attack, all out.

Hipper's battle cruisers were now less than 8,000 yards from the compass platform on which Maltbie stood, and the sea around them was a playground of giant fountains. With the destroyers launched, however, Hipper's badly clobbered ships finally turned southward, then westward and away.

In support of the several British flotillas that were already sprinting toward the enemy on their own initiative, Jellicoe ordered light cruisers out to join in the attack on the oncoming destroyers. The German boats were too numerous to be warded off, however, and they managed to launch their torpedoes at a range of some 7,000 yards. With manifest reluctance, the C in C ordered the battle squadrons to turn away eastward from the approaching menace, and as they did so the fleeing German dreadnoughts made good their escape in the opposite direction.

Once again the firing died down, and with the torpedo threat past Jellicoe again turned south and west in search of Scheer. The Grand Fleet was still astride the German admiral's route home, but sunset was fast approaching, with total darkness less than an hour behind it. No one seriously contemplated a night action against the High Seas Fleet. British searchlights were notoriously inferior to those of the Germans in just about every respect—and in any case, the larger fleet always lost the advantage of numbers in the confusion and hazard of darkness.

As the light dwindled, Jellicoe ordered the fleet into night cruising formation. The three battle squadrons formed columns of eight in line ahead with the *Iron Duke* at the front of the middle column. The 4th Light Cruiser Squadron was sent forward to guard against possible frontal attacks; the 2d Light Cruiser Squadron was sent west to search for the Germans; and the 11th, 4th, 13th, 9th, 10th, and 12th Destroyer Flotillas formed a rearguard against torpedo attacks. The flotillas, not incidentally, were also charged with the duty of detecting any German attempt to steal eastward behind Jellicoe's back. Beatty's force steamed a course roughly parallel to the C in C's but ten miles to the southwest.

Maltbie watched as Jellicoe and his staff pored over the charts in order to assess Scheer's most likely next step. There were three different routes around or through the British minefields in the waters outside the German ports. It wasn't possible to cover all of them, but Jellicoe disposed his forces so as to permit a rapid response in whichever direction the High Seas Fleet might elect to move. All that remained now was to stay intact through the hours of darkness and hope for good shooting at dawn.

The night hours passed quickly, with frequent though short-lived eruptions of gunfire dotting the blackness to the north and west. Aside from one sighting report from the destroyer *Garland* shortly before ten, the wireless provided little news. Maltbie again speculated as to whether Gehlman had actually decided in the end to do what Corey had asked. He was still fairly certain that he hadn't, but the unexplained flare-ups of shooting far astern—presumably encounters between stray destroyers or scouting light cruisers—generated a trace of doubt. It was remarkable, he reflected, how closely the actual battle had conformed to the specifications set out in the North Sea Analysis. He remembered that the report had rated the Germans' chances of regaining their bases once cut off from them extremely remote, absent some kind of unforeseen contingency. But he still began to experience an anxious feeling of premonition as the night wore on and the radio receivers remained silent.

As 2:00 A.M. approached and the first traces of dawn began to tinge the horizon to the northeast, yet another outbreak of cannon flashes fretted the sky to the north, again with no wireless transmissions to explain the cause. It looked like the day would be clear and breezy, and among the officers in Jellicoe's retinue there began to be much optimistic talk of another "Glorious First of June," Lord Howe's famous victory over the French in 1794.

At 3:09 the upper limb of the sun's disc rose out of the sea. Jellicoe ordered the Grand Fleet into line of battle preparatory to the encounter that would certainly soon begin. Lookouts on every dreadnought scanned the water and sky in all directions.

Shortly before four the blow fell. Maltbie saw the terrible pain in Jellicoe's eyes as the Admiralty telegram placing Scheer thirty-five miles *east* of the *Iron Duke* was read out by a signalman. The High Seas Fleet had squeaked through, and no amount of steaming could now overtake it.

The atmosphere on the compass platform was leaden with anguish, and Maltbie, feeling a nagging spasm of remorse, headed below to his cabin. The moral question he had neglected to answer had come home to roost, it appeared. He saw now that his assumption about Gehlman's incorruptibility might have been little more than a convenient excuse for inaction. But was it really possible that Ben had used his transmitter? Even now it still seemed an outlandish idea.

For a long time, back in his cabin, he sat on his berth and pondered. No, he decided finally, there had to be some other explanation, even if he couldn't for the moment imagine what it might be.

Feeling very tired all at once, he pulled his sea chest out from under his berth and unlocked it, thinking as he did so that he would have to find some discreet way of disposing of the brown suitcase, which he'd hidden inside. He opened the chest and began looking for a pair of pajamas, thinking that this day, for a change, he had earned the privilege of sleeping in something more comfortable than his uniform. Perhaps five or ten seconds elapsed before he came up with his pajamas; it was only as he lifted them from the sea chest that his tired mind registered the fact that the brown suitcase was gone.

1916, 4TH JUNE—DUNFERMLINE

Reeves-Wadleigh regarded the two Americans with a feeling of vague uneasiness; even now neither one of them was behaving in a manner that comported with a consciousness of guilt, and that was perplexing given the weight of the evidence against them. Admittedly, a few pieces of the puzzle still were missing, but there was nothing equivocal about those radio transmitters—or about the report Reeves-Wadleigh had received from the Signals Branch.

It had only been seventy-two hours ago, while the fleet was steaming home from what was now being called "the Battle of Jutland," that Corporal Otley had reported in special cipher on the Admiralty frequency that he'd discovered a wireless transmitter hidden in Maltbie's cabin. He'd reported further his decision to confiscate the transmitter immediately, even at the cost of alerting Maltbie to the fact that he'd been found out. Reeves-Wadleigh had approved of that decision; Maltbie had nowhere to run to aboard the *Iron Duke*.

In response to Otley's report, Reeves-Wadleigh had sent a coded message to Sergeant Bellmaine aboard the *Lion*, instructing him to conduct a thorough search of Gehlman's cabin and to report immediately by telephone when the BCF got back to Rosyth. Bellmaine's call had come in the following day; he reported that there was nothing of consequence in Gehlman's cabin. Reeves-Wadleigh told him to make a search of Gehlman's quarters at Aberdour and to keep the American under redoubled surveillance at all times, pending further instructions. When Bellmaine reported finding the transmitter in the black satchel, Reeves-Wadleigh had issued orders for both Maltbie's and Gehlman's arrest.

Maltbie, it had turned out, was by then hurrying south, accompanied by Otley, in response to a message from Gehlman stating that Melina Maltbie was in serious condition at Dunfermline Hospital. Reeves-Wadleigh had been irritated by Otley's apparently unilateral decision to let Maltbie leave Scapa, and he had been still further irritated to learn that the stolid Bellmaine had known all about the accident involving Gehlman and Mrs. Maltbie, but simply had not gotten around to reporting it. When he taxed the sergeant about this

apparent lapse, Bellmaine had responded blandly that he hadn't regarded the incident in question as pertinent in any way to the issues
of espionage and sabotage. From the lameness of this explanation,
and from the barely detectable undertone of resentment that had accompanied it, Reeves-Wadleigh had deduced two things: first, that
Bellmaine, like Otley, had come to like the man he kept watch on
and was, therefore, increasingly uncomfortable in the role of spy; and
second, that Benjamin Gehlman and Melina Maltbie were having an
affair.

Gehlman had been arrested yesterday morning at St. Fillan's
Infirmary in Burntisland, where his ward was recovering from an
emergency appendectomy, it seemed. Reeves-Wadleigh was by that
time en route north from London, conjuring with the preliminary report of the Signals Branch. The branch, as was customary after any
major fleet operation, had cross-checked the signal logs of the ships
involved to verify that no serious errors in transmission or reception
had occurred. None had, but the cross-checking turned up a discrepancy far more significant than any transmission error. At 1:45 A.M.,
June 1, the 12th Destroyer Flotilla leader, *Faulknor*, had come upon
the dreadnoughts of the High Seas Fleet. After first making sure that
it was German ships he had in front of him, Captain Stirling of the
Faulknor had radioed on full power to Admiral Jellicoe: UR-
GENT. PRIORITY. ENEMY BATTLESHIPS IN SIGHT. MY POSITION TEN MILES
ASTERN OF FIRST BATTLE SQUADRON. He had repeated that message at
1:56, and at 2:08 had signaled: URGENT. AM ATTACKING. At 2:13 he
sent his last message prior to losing contact with the Germans:
URGENT. COURSE OF ENEMY IS SSW. Had Jellicoe received those messages, it was apparent, he would have immediately realized what
Scheer was attempting to do, and he could have accordingly turned
east and forced the High Seas Fleet to give battle. The point, however, was that he had not received the messages—not one of them,
despite the fact that a post-battle check of the *Faulknor's* wireless apparatus had revealed it to be in perfect working order.

Needless to say, the *Iron Duke's* receiving equipment was also
found to have been functioning properly. Even if it had been subject
to some freakish malfunction, however, the fact remained that there
had been fifty-seven other British ships keeping guard on the reporting frequency, and of these exactly *one*, the destroyer *Marksman* of
the *Faulknor's* own flotilla, had picked up the messages that Captain
Stirling had transmitted. During the entire course of the battle only

two other messages addressed to the C in C had failed to reach the flagship directly, but in both cases no fewer than a dozen other ships had monitored the transmissions, and each of the messages in question was eventually relayed to Jellicoe.

Otley's cipher report of June 1 gave the time of his discovery and confiscation of Maltbie's transmitter as 3:15 A.M., approximately one hour after Captain Stirling's final unheard message. True, the transmitter had not, when found, been operating, nor had its crystal been tuned to the reporting-of-the-enemy frequency. Given that the transmitter was equipped with a key-down switch, however, it would have been a simple matter for Maltbie to absent himself from the compass platform during the night, switch on his wireless, tune it, and then make a second trip to his cabin before sunrise to detune it and switch it off. His brief absences, under the circumstances, certainly would not have been noticed, and indeed, the hypothesis of Maltbie's culpability was, in Reeves-Wadleigh's opinion, the only one that could conceivably account for what had happened.

Well, perhaps not the *only* one; there was another hypothesis, a farfetched and unsubstantiated one to be sure, but one that could not be conclusively ruled out. This hypothesis was that German jamming had blocked the *Faulknor*'s transmissions, and the reason it couldn't be ruled out was a disturbingly simple one: of all the destroyer and light cruiser and even dreadnought captains who had sighted elements of the German main force during the hours of darkness, *none* except Captain Stirling had attempted to report their sightings to the commander in chief. Why they had not attempted to do so was a question of stunted initiative and mistaken assumptions outside the scope of Reeves-Wadleigh's official competence. The fact that they had failed to do so, however, left him with an uncorroborated theory and an uneasy sense that he might be overlooking some vital point.

The question uppermost in Reeves-Wadleigh's mind when he arrived in Edinburgh concerned Baron von Tiel. The German's involvement in the plot was still problematical, and the uncertainty about it had to be resolved.

And resolved quickly. Lord Fisher, who'd been waiting for Reeves-Wadleigh at the North British Hotel, had expressed himself forcefully, after being briefed, on the imperative need for immediate and definitive answers to *all* the questions pending, including those pertaining to von Tiel. He was going to contact Churchill, he said, as

Churchill had ready access to the Prime Minister. Also, given Churchill's relative obscurity in Parliament since his ouster from the Admiralty, he could act for Asquith confidentially and in total secrecy. What the Prime Minister would rightly say when Churchill apprised him of the situation, Fisher had continued, was that Maltbie and Gehlman could not be kept in custody and incommunicado for more than another day or two at most. They would have to be either exonerated and set free or proven guilty and officially charged within the next forty-eight hours. Already the American Embassy would be asking for news of them in light of the mounting public excitement about the battle; and telling Ambassador Page that his two naval observers had been arrested on charges of sabotage was a step of such grave consequence that only absolute certainty as to the truth of the allegations could justify doing it. If Maltbie and Gehlman were truly guilty, the chips would have to fall as they might; but it would be far better for everybody, Admiral Fisher had admitted ruefully, if they turned out somehow to be innocent. Reeves-Wadleigh had been glad to note that, if nothing else, the prospect of an actual break with the United States had at least enabled Fisher to regain some sense of perspective.

After taking leave of the admiral, Reeves-Wadleigh had lost no time getting down to work. He was so absorbed in the urgency of his task, in fact, that he forgot to administer his customary mid-afternoon syringe. He was surprised, afterwards, that he had been able to work so efficiently in spite of that.

His first step had been to summon Otley and then Bellmaine to his room at the North British Hotel and to question each of them closely in search of significant fragments of information. Bellmaine had reluctantly confirmed Reeves-Wadleigh's supposition about Gehlman and Mrs. Maltbie; the increasingly ill-concealed scorn with which the sergeant yielded to Reeves-Wadleigh's demands for further information about their relationship, moreover, confirmed the captain's supposition about Bellmaine himself: the man had clearly developed serious doubts about the propriety of keeping watch and informing; he was just not cut out for intelligence work.

Lord Fisher had telephoned toward evening to say that Churchill would be coming up from London to conduct an inquiry on Asquith's behalf. He instructed Reeves-Wadleigh to meet the former First Lord at Waverley Station in the morning and give him a full briefing on the way up to the Dunfermline wireless station, which

Fisher had selected as a peculiarly appropriate place for the proceedings contemplated. "How's your investigation going?" the admiral had asked before ringing off. "Satisfactorily, sir," Reeves-Wadleigh had responded, forebearing out of ingrained habits of secretiveness—and also, perhaps, out of something a little like shame—to tell Fisher of the tactics he intended to use to get at the truth.

It had come as no surprise to him when he found Commander Maltbie adopting an attitude of intransigence. The young officer had stated quite bluntly that he had refrained for reasons of conscience from using his transmitter, though he did admit having brought it aboard the *Iron Duke*. He had done nothing to harm the Royal Navy or Great Britain, he said, and he therefore did not feel obliged to provide Reeves-Wadleigh with any further information. His foremost concern at the moment, he had added, was his wife's serious medical condition, and he demanded the right to be beside her at all times until she was out of danger. Reeves-Wadleigh had replied with a casual shrug that Maltbie might be allowed to visit his wife, but only if he cooperated fully with the investigation now in progress. For a moment he thought that the American might actually attack him with his fists, but in the end Commander Maltbie had simply stalked out of the room. Reeves-Wadleigh had signaled the guards at the door to take him back to the marine barracks in Edinburgh Castle, where he was being held; he then prepared himself to play his hole card with Captain Gehlman.

To his considerable surprise, it had appeared at first that the hole card might not even be necessary. For Gehlman had immediately opened the interview by telling him that there was a dangerous German naval officer running loose somewhere in the Edinburgh area.

"Really?" Reeves-Wadleigh had responded, affecting skepticism. "That sounds highly unlikely, if you'll forgive my saying so."

Gehlman had agreed without hesitation that it did indeed sound unlikely, but he had then proceeded to tell a tale of such garishly detailed depravity that Reeves-Wadleigh would have been half inclined to believe it had he not already been familiar with its general outlines. He was convinced, however, that the only reason that Gehlman at this point had volunteered the information about von Tiel was in order to dissociate himself from complicity in a plot that involved a German national. Of course, if Gehlman were actually telling the truth, on the other hand, then Baron von Tiel would fall completely out of the clandestine transmitter equation—and Reeves-

Wadleigh's actions over the previous few months would end up looking just the least bit foolish. Gehlman's professed reason for raising
the von Tiel issue unilaterally had been his mounting concern over
his ward's safety, now that he himself was in custody; but though
that reason was consistent with his story, it was by no means conclusive as to the story's veracity.

Given his ever dwindling life span, the prospect of looking foolish
didn't particularly alarm Reeves-Wadleigh. Even though he was still
more than ninety percent certain that Maltbie had blocked Captain
Stirling's four messages, that Gehlman would have blocked them
had Maltbie for some reason missed the battle, and that von Tiel
had supplied both men with their transmitters, he was still conscientious and professional enough to accord his ten percent modicum
of doubt a respectable weight. He had been designated judge and
jury in this case, not prosecutor; his task was to find the truth, not
confirm his preconceptions. It was possible, just possible, that Gehlman was telling the truth, that the baron was simply a madman.
And though that fact by itself did nothing to vindicate the two
Americans, it did most decidedly alter the complexion of the case
against them.

"Let me understand you, Captain," Reeves-Wadleigh had said
after Gehlman had finished speaking. "It is your assertion that this
hypothetical Baron von Tiel—a senior officer in the German Navy—
somehow made his way undetected into Britain solely in order to
avenge himself on you and then carry off your ward."

"That is precisely my assertion."

"You are suggesting, in other words, that a German naval officer
would come here at the risk of his life in the middle of a war for
reasons having nothing whatsoever to do with the struggle between
his country and Britain."

"That is what I know to be the fact."

"Well, forgive me, Captain, but here we have a situation where
the German Fleet miraculously escapes destruction because four
messages intended for Admiral Jellicoe never reach him, where a
transmitter capable of blocking the reception of those messages is
found in Commander Maltbie's cabin aboard the *Iron Duke*, and
where an identical transmitter, presumably a backup, is found in
your own quarters at Aberdour. Now, doesn't it seem reasonable for
one to suppose that a captain in the German Navy, if he'd bothered

to come to Britain at all, would have come here expressly in order to provide you with the transmitters that were found?"

"It seems reasonable, yes; but it isn't what happened in fact."

"Well, that leaves me at something of a loss then. If the possession and presumptive use of these transmitters cannot be explained in terms of some objective of our enemies, then where did the transmitters come from, and whose objectives were they intended to serve?"

Gehlman had regarded him narrowly. "It sounds to me as if you're not as dubious about the existence of Baron von Tiel as you pretend to be."

Reeves-Wadleigh had been impressed with Gehlman's acuity, but he'd also been prepared for it. "I am not at all dubious about the existence of a German agent somewhere in Britain who has played a role in the plot under investigation. I am *quite* dubious that his name is Sigismund von Tiel, however—though such a personage may actually exist—and equally dubious about the motives you ascribe to him to explain his presence here on other than, shall we say, official business."

Gehlman had gazed at him for a long time, saying nothing.

"My problem, Captain," Reeves-Wadleigh had resumed eventually, "is that without the hypothesis of a German agent in this scenario, I have no way of explaining what Commander Maltbie did or how he was enabled to do it."

"How do you know he did anything?"

"He has confessed as much," Reeves-Wadleigh had replied, poker-faced.

"Please forgive me if I say that *I* am dubious about that."

Reeves-Wadleigh had smiled his cadaverous smile. "Very well, Captain; let's say that I'll take everything you've told me at face value, and also that I'll take steps to guarantee the safety of your ward. I'll even put Scotland Yard on the trail of Baron von Tiel if you like—"

"Oh, yes!" Gehlman interjected. "You can also check with the police at Aberdour and Burntisland, come to think of it. I reported his presence in this area to them on Tuesday, just before I boarded the *Lion*."

"Did you?" Reeves-Wadleigh had said, thinking that Gehlman might well have done such a thing, but only because von Tiel would by then have outlived his usefulness and because betraying him to the police would be a mark in Gehlman's favor, should the transmitter in his quarters be discovered. "Well, thank you, Captain. I will certainly follow up on that lead . . . but I still remain very much in the dark as to what you and Commander Maltbie were doing with those transmitters, and how you came to be in possession of them."

Gehlman had been silent for some seconds. "All I can tell you," he had said finally, "is that I never used mine, and that I'm reasonably certain Commander Maltbie never used his."

"That really isn't good enough, Captain."

"I'm afraid it's the best I can do."

Reeves-Wadleigh had gazed at him steadily. "That's your final word, is it?"

"I'm really not at liberty to say anything more. And even if I were, no good purpose would be served by my speaking."

"Is there nothing I can say to persuade you to reconsider?"

"No; I'm sorry, but there isn't."

"Very well." Reeves-Wadleigh had sighed, preparing to lay his hole card on the table. "Then I must regretfully inform you that Commander Maltbie will now have to be given the details of your relationship with his wife."

Gehlman's features had set instantaneously into an expression of icy fury. "There aren't any details to give," he said tightly.

Reeves-Wadleigh had sadly shaken his head. "You've been under constant surveillance since your arrival in Britain, Captain. There's no point in feigning innocence."

Gehlman had glared at him. "To say anything to Commander Maltbie about my relationship with his wife would be a pointless cruelty."

"Not necessarily. It might shock him into telling us who supplied those transmitters, and why."

Gehlman had continued to glare.

"Consider the question, why don't you, for the rest of tonight. Sleep on it. There's to be an inquiry tomorrow. You can indicate then whether you are prepared to speak, or whether we shall be obliged to."

Reeves-Wadleigh had leaned back and rubbed his eyes after Gehlman left the room. He was pleased with the way he had handled things and confident that the next day would bring him the answers he sought. He was also, he had noticed, extremely overtired. He had

had barely enough energy left, in fact, to prepare a solution for his syringe, plunge the needle home, and collapse in tranquillity on his bed.

Now, however, with the inquiry under way and Admiral Fisher saying to Commander Maltbie, "Just tell us whatever you feel you can," Reeves-Wadleigh found himself becoming distinctly uncomfortable. Reviewing in his mind the interviews he'd conducted with Maltbie and Gehlman, and seeing the two of them standing there in front of him now, he felt a chill and sudden certainty that neither of them was responsible for the *Faulknor*'s four lost messages. He noticed now what in his exhaustion of the previous evening he had failed to notice: that something was missing in their behavior, a subtle shading he had learned to look for over the years in people suspected of wrongdoing. It was consciousness of guilt, a quality whose presence in most malefactors produced a strong and ineradicable impression. Innocence could be feigned, after all; Gehlman had tried to feign it when confronted with his affair with Mrs. Maltbie. But feigning an absence of guilt was a far more complicated matter, one well beyond the capacities of even the most impassioned pretenders to innocence. Gehlman, for example, though affecting outrage over the allegation of adultery, had not even begun to project an impression of absence of guilt.

He was projecting such an impression now, however, as was Maltbie; and both of them had projected the same impression last night. That was why Reeves-Wadleigh was anxious. For if Maltbie and Gehlman were honestly convinced that they had done nothing wrong, then his chances of compelling them to reveal the source and purpose of their transmitters would be very slim indeed. He looked at Maltbie: although the commander was plainly overwrought and consumed with anxiety about his wife, the tactic of keeping him from her bedside clearly did not provide the leverage needed to pry the missing information from him. The success of the inquiry therefore appeared to depend entirely on the hole card he had played with Captain Gehlman. Gehlman's expression of disdainful amusement did not give him much cause for hope, however.

Well, he'd briefed Fisher and Churchill; they understood the situation. The matter was effectively out of his hands. It all came down to the extent of Captain Gehlman's concern for Commander Maltbie's feelings.

"I'm not suggesting that you should betray a trust, Commander," Fisher said coaxingly. "I'm simply asking you to give us as much information as you possibly can, consistent with the dictates of personal honor."

"I understand, sir," Maltbie responded, "and I wish to say three things: first, that I regard the fact that I've been kept from my wife's bedside as despicable—"

"Your wife is in a coma, Commander," said Fisher. "And while we recognize your urgent desire to be near her, the seriousness of your case coupled with the fact that she would derive no benefit whatever from your presence at her bedside has led us to err, if you will, on the side of caution."

"Then why did Captain Reeves-Wadleigh give me to understand that I could see her if I gave you the information that you're seeking?" Maltbie demanded in an accusatory tone.

"Because," Fisher replied easily, "once we know the true dimensions of your case we shall no longer be obliged to guard against the multitude of unknown contingencies which arise from our lack of knowledge. Now, what is the second thing you wish to say?"

"Only that I've told you everything I am in good conscience free to tell you, and that my telling you anything more would not be in anybody's best interests."

"And the third point . . . ?" Fisher asked, not deigning to acknowledge the second.

"The third point is that I have a way of proving to you that neither I nor Captain Gehlman ever used the transmitters you discovered."

"Oh?" said Churchill, who'd been uncharacteristically quiet up to that point. "Please elaborate."

"It's fairly straightforward, sir," Maltbie said. "The transmitters were built to operate off batteries, but also off ships' mains. It was understood that the current would burn the sets out inside of eight or nine hours; but they were designed to be used only once, so that didn't matter."

Churchill leaned forward ponderously. "Go on, Commander."

"Well, sir, if you were to operate the transmitters, I'm sure you'd find that they would continue to function for the full time period specified. If either Captain Gehlman or myself had operated them, they'd last only five or six hours at most."

"But only twenty-one minutes were required to block the four missing messages," Fisher interjected.

"I realize that, sir," said Maltbie. "But we had no way of knowing when signals would come in. If we'd been intent on keeping Admiral Jellicoe cut off, we'd have been obliged to keep transmitting throughout all the hours of darkness."

For some seconds there was silence. But then Churchill said, "Well, the test that you're proposing wouldn't be conclusive, Commander, though it would provide pertinent information. Even if the results confirm your contentions, however, we should still insist on knowing where the transmitters came from and why they were given to you."

"I'm sorry," Maltbie said into a lengthening silence.

"Thank you for your candor, Commander," Fisher said finally. "It now seems that we must repose our hopes in Captain Gehlman."

Gehlman looked over at Reeves-Wadleigh, who shifted his eyes toward Maltbie for just a fraction of a second and then returned his gaze, meaningfully, to Gehlman himself.

The room was very quiet for a long long while. "Well, gentlemen," Gehlman said at last in a tone of resignation, "I'll tell you what I know—but I doubt you're going to like it."

1916, 6TH JUNE—DUNFERMLINE

Shafts of sunlight poured into Melina's hospital room, brazen and inappropriate as blaring trumpets. In his chair at the foot of her bed, Maltbie drifted from wakeful exhaustion to dreams of himself dozing in his chair and coming awake again, which he always did after a minute or two of sleep. Every so often he would stand up, stretch, and look down with a sort of fugitive hope at his wife. There was never the slightest movement. The swollen and battered left side of her face still showed no signs of healing, the obscene tube they'd inserted into her right nostril betrayed no evidence that she continued to breathe, the plaster-enclosed right arm lay like a dead weight on the bedcovers, grotesquely disproportionate to the outline of the small body it abutted.

They were very much afraid, the doctors had told him, that the question was no longer would she live or die, but, rather, would she die without regaining consciousness. She had lost too much blood, they said, and in addition to the miscarriage had suffered a punctured lung and ruptured spleen.

He looked down at her left hand where he had placed the talisman she'd given him. He had laced the chain loosely through her fingers, so as to give himself the illusion that she was consciously holding the medallion. The boy on the dolphin rode joyfully over the sea, free and whole, forever young. Maltbie liked to pretend to himself that if Melina's soul did indeed leave her body, it would flow down her arm and fingers into the body of that golden child.

There was a soft knock on the doorjamb, and Otley said, "Captain Gehlman's coming up, sir."

Maltbie gave a faint nod of acknowledgment. The anguish he felt over Melina was not much more intense than the sense of betrayal he felt in connection with Otley. Despite everything the corporal had done since the receipt of Gehlman's message at Scapa to demonstrate that his affection for him and Melina was as genuine as his faithful-retainer persona had been spurious, Maltbie still could not bring himself to forgive his long-protracted duplicity. While he appreciated the risk Otley had taken in letting him come south to Dunfermline in response to Gehlman's telegram, and while he knew that the corporal was almost as desolate over Melina's condition as he was himself, he still could not and would not speak to him. On a certain level he knew that such a sanction in this case was petulant and cruel, but with all the troubles he had to contend with at this juncture, he lacked the energy needed to bring charity to bear.

Maltbie scanned Gehlman's face as he came into the room. Since the trip up from London they'd had barely five minutes' conversation together; in fact this was the first time they were seeing each other in private, though the muffled voices of Otley and Sergeant Bellmaine just outside the door rendered their privacy something less than total.

"How is she?" Gehlman asked, crossing to the bed.

"The doctors say not good—but I don't believe them."

Gehlman shot him a look of approving encouragement. "I don't either," he said.

"And what's your news?" Maltbie asked.

"Well, it seems they tested our transmitters. Mine lasted nine and a half hours and yours lasted a bit over ten."

"Fine workmanship," Maltbie said with an edge.

But Gehlman was looking down at Melina again, his jaw muscles working. "What? . . . Oh, yes; nothing but the best for our kind of work."

They exchanged grim smiles.

"Anyway," he continued, "they're apparently satisfied as to our bona fides, or, say, our lack of specific culpability."

"Where do you think the specific culpability lies, Ben?"

"You're the wireless expert; you tell me."

"I'm stumped, frankly. With you and me out of the picture, it comes down to either atmospherics or German jamming. But the atmospherics weren't all that bad at the time, and any Telefunken interference on the reporting frequency ought to have been detected immediately—unless the Germans have come up with something we don't know about."

"I heard some talk in Wilhelmshaven about experimental work on new jamming devices. Perhaps they did come up with something."

"Do you think we ought to mention the possibility to Reeves-Wadleigh? It might help remove any doubts they still have about us in London."

Gehlman shook his head. "I'd leave well enough alone at this point. My impression from Reeves-Wadleigh is that the foremost desire at 10 Downing Street is to be rid of us. In fact I'm supposed to leave for America as soon as Alis is fit to travel."

"How is she, Ben?"

"Mending well. . . . I haven't told her about Melina."

"No, of course not," said Maltbie. "Any word of her murdering stepfather?"

"Well, I have the feeling that Reeves-Wadleigh still thinks you and I and von Tiel may be in league together. He refuses to discuss him."

"Good God!" Maltbie said in exasperation. "How can he still think *that*, with Melina lying here . . ."

"He apparently doubts my contention that it was von Tiel who forced us off the road."

"Christ!" Maltbie said.

Gehlman once again returned his gaze to Melina, and as Maltbie looked over at him a small chill of remembered suspicion washed

over his body. He banned it though; now was certainly not the time.
"What do you think they'll do about Corey, and Colonel House?"
he asked.

Gehlman turned to look at him. "I don't know, Harry, but I imagine they'll try to capitalize somehow on what I told them."

Maltbie hesitated before saying, "You know, Ben, I don't blame
you for what you did at the inquiry . . . but I do wonder why you
did it."

Gehlman gave him a tired smile. "Simple enough, Harry: I
thought the truth might make us free—as it in fact appears to be
doing."

"Only that?"

"*Only*, Harry? . . . Well, perhaps I was feeling just a shade vindictive too. I don't know. But I don't at all regret what I did. Not
one little bit."

They talked for a few more minutes, then Gehlman made to leave.
Maltbie accompanied him downstairs, with Otley and Bellmaine a
discreet few steps behind, no longer manservants and informers, but
escorts—even bodyguards.

Outside in the sunlight the two Americans shook hands. "Come
again tomorrow," Maltbie said, "if you can."

"I'll come by in the morning," Gehlman responded.

Maltbie nodded and looked around the sun-filled courtyard, empty
except for a solitary figure reading a newspaper by the south-facing
balcony. "God, but the weather's been beautiful. It's almost like a
cruel joke, somehow."

"I know what you mean," Gehlman said as, with Bellmaine in at-
tendance, he started walking across the driveway to a waiting navy
staff car.

Turning to go back inside, Maltbie caught sight of the man with
the newspaper. He was walking briskly away from the balcony in
Gehlman and Bellmaine's direction, and Maltbie, on some primal in-
stinctual level, sensed immediately who he was. "Ben!" he called out,
starting down the steps with Otley close behind him.

Gehlman stopped and turned.

"It's him, Ben," Maltbie shouted, pointing, as the man, now less
than twenty paces distant, reached into a pocket of his coat.

Sprinting toward Gehlman, Maltbie saw him turn and look, then
freeze as a revolver appeared and was pointed at his chest.

Courage is a mental trick, Maltbie remembered as he crashed into

Gehlman, knocking him to the ground at the instant von Tiel pulled the trigger. It was the last thought of Harry's life; the bullet from the revolver shattered the entire right side of his skull.

1916, 8TH JUNE—BERLIN

Von Müller sat at his desk, bent beneath the weight of his despair.

The fleet had done so well, he'd thought: three dreadnoughts sunk for the loss of one, an estimated 6,500 casualties inflicted as against 3,000 sustained, the success of the interference devices. And yet here, from Admiral Scheer himself, from the commander in chief's personal report to the Kaiser on the battle, were these unfathomable assertions:

"A victorious end to the war within a reasonable time can only be achieved through the defeat of British economic life—that is, by using the U-boats against British trade. In this connection, I feel it my duty to strongly advise Your Majesty against the adoption of any half measures . . ."

Von Müller slowly shook his head. Just because the fleet had had a narrow escape, the Tirpitz supporters were arguing for its virtual internment! We tried to fight on the surface, they were saying now, and we got away by the skin of our teeth. We dare not risk another such encounter. It is *beneath* the oceans that Germany must wage her naval war.

"Dear God, dear God," von Müller whispered to himself. If the fleet had been crushed, Tirpitz's partisans would have clamored for all-out submarine warfare in response. But the fleet had not been crushed; it had won a measure of victory. Yet they were saying that it could not again be risked.

They wanted the argument both ways.

And with a feeling of fatigue and dread, von Müller acknowledged to himself that all too soon they might have it.

1916, 9TH JUNE–DUNFERMLINE

Now Gehlman kept the vigil by Melina's bedside, though how much longer the vigil might continue had become strictly a day-to-day proposition. She was losing ground, the doctors said, her vital signs were growing steadily weaker.

She was, in a word, dying.

Even before Harry's funeral Gehlman had formed the resolve to stay with her. If she did by some chance regain consciousness before she died, he wanted to make certain that she did not awaken to the faces of strangers. Sir Lloyd and Dame Margaret had been informed of her condition, of course, but both of them were incapacitated by severe summer influenza and unfit to travel. Gehlman thought that was just as well, in a way. If she awoke at all, Melina would probably think it was still May 30 as long as only he was there. Gehlman wanted to sustain her in such a misconception; he wanted her to think that Harry was alive.

As he had many times before, Gehlman looked out the window and gave himself up to remembering that moment in the hospital driveway: von Tiel coming toward him, the pointed gun, the shock of the gunshot simultaneous with the shock of Maltbie's barreling into him and knocking him down. Harry had made a noise when he tackled him, a brief agonized *nnnnngg!* sound that Gehlman kept hearing in his thoughts and in his sleep. He had landed hard on the ground, with Harry's already lifeless body on top of him. Twisting his head around, he had seen Otley and Bellmaine swarming over von Tiel. Otley, in fact, had gone a little berserk, and it had finally taken Gehlman and Bellmaine's combined strength to drag him off the baron, who was by then unconscious and bleeding heavily from Otley's maniac kickings and punches.

At first Gehlman had found it impossible to understand what Maltbie had done. Even now the mentality behind the act remained mysterious to him. He knew that Harry had not meant to sacrifice himself; he sensed that he had acted simply out of . . . conditioning. Indeed, for a day or two Ben had even flirted with a feeling of contempt for Harry's action. It had been the self-consciously heroic deed of an incorrigible knight-errant, utterly inappropriate to the twentieth century, and something Gehlman never would have done himself. But at the brief and simple Royal Navy funeral—organized by Spickernell and attended by Beatty and others, all of them ignorant of the transmitter imbroglio—Ben had finally realized that his contempt for the act was merely a last-ditch defense for his cynicism, to which Harry had forever given the lie. He understood, or began to understand, that it was possible for some people to act unselfishly for unselfish reasons, that there was such a thing in life as unpremeditated goodness. He began to understand, also, why Melina had chosen Harry rather than one of innumerable others.

Because Harry had believed in and actually practiced the conventional virtues, Ben had always had to resist a temptation to condescend to him. He realized now, however, that it had been precisely this about the man that had made him uniquely *un*conventional. It had been so easy to discount him, even despise him for his goodness. Only now did it begin to be apparent to Gehlman that such an attitude was merely the terrified reaction of the erring Pharisee come face-to-face with his first true Christian.

He stood up, stretched, and peeked out into the corridor at the cot where Alis lay asleep. His decision to maintain Maltbie's vigil had of course meant confronting Alis with Melina's condition. The only other option would have been to leave her with Miss Dyson at Aberdour, but a separation at this time was something that neither of them would have tolerated well. Her reaction on seeing Melina had been the same as her reaction when Gehlman told her about Maltbie: she had looked up at him through her tears with an expression of incomprehension and reproach, as if wanting to know why such a thing had happened and, more particularly, why Gehlman had permitted it to happen. He had cringed a little beneath that accusatory gaze, but his baffled silence in each case had in the end seemed answer enough.

He adjusted Alis's covers, then went back into Melina's room and looked out at the pale blue early morning sky. Unselfish for unselfish reasons: that was something he believed beyond his ken. He was glad he hadn't used the transmitter, for example, but in good part because he would not have cared to be responsible for the anguished torment in Admiral Beatty's eyes on the morning of June 1. He would also, of course, not have cared to have been caught out and shot as a saboteur. And telling the inquiry about Corey and House:

the ludicrous aspect of that had been that he hadn't really cared a damn about keeping silent; and when they offered silence about his affair with Melina in exchange for what he knew, his biggest problem had been pretending that he found the choice a hard one to make, especially as it gave him the opportunity to visit nemesis on those who were really at fault.

Well, he had survived, and he had Alis; selfishness was not altogether without its rewards. Though neither was it altogether without its punishments, as Melina had reason to know. And as he had reason to know himself, but for his crushing fear of unlocking the psychic cellar in which he'd tried to bury all his sorrow and guilt.

There was a sound, a movement, and Gehlman hurried to Melina's bedside.

"Hello, Ben." Her voice was piteously, almost inaudibly, weak.

"Hello," he whispered, placing his hand very gently on hers, realizing with a shock that it still held the talisman that Harry alive would have had round his neck. But then, there wasn't much chance she would notice it.

She closed her eyes, then after a long while opened them again. "You're weeping, Ben. Does that mean you truly care for me?" Her inflection was one of self-mockery.

"Yes," he rasped out.

She smiled weakly. "It's all right for you to care for me, you know. One can never be too well cared for in this life."

"You're right," he replied, roughly wiping his eyes with the cuff of his left sleeve.

"I care for you, my sweetest Ben," she said in a fading whisper. "But we mustn't . . . mustn't ever . . . hurt . . . our sweetest Harry."

"No, we mustn't," Gehlman agreed.

But her gaze became fixed as he said it, and he doubted she ever heard.

1916, 15TH JUNE—LONDON

Reeves-Wadleigh shakily placed the syringe on his night table, next to the note he had written to his sister. The morphine solution in the barrel was five times the strength he was accustomed to; it had been a job getting all the crystals to dissolve, in fact. If, however, one was determined that the outcome should be absolutely guaranteed, then one couldn't afford to work on narrow margins.

He leaned back against the pillows and let out a long, deep breath. Well, he allowed, he'd done all right on balance; he'd had his innings. Of course that last important matter, the Gehlman–von Tiel business, had turned out rather sloppily—but then that couldn't really be charged to him. His instincts had been right, even if his working hypothesis had been slightly wide of the mark. And the whole thing had turned out fairly well for Britain, all things considered. Even though Maltbie and Gehlman had been exonerated of personal blame for the Germans' escape, the fact that they'd been directed to help effectuate it—and been provided with the means to do so, moreover—gave Asquith a good-size club with which to beat down future American impudence and intermeddling.

Still, Reeves-Wadleigh reflected, he would like to have established definitely why Captain Stirling's signals went awry. He also wished that Gehlman and Bellmaine had been able to pry Otley off von Tiel a little sooner, before the enraged corporal had kicked in the baron's skull and left him an empty-eyed vegetable. (Yes, Reeves-Wadleigh admitted to himself, he very much regretted, from hindsight, having let von Tiel roam free; the lives of Commander and Mrs. Maltbie did not weigh lightly on his conscience.) And the final and most interesting question: Gehlman. Why had the paltry threat of revealing his sexual peccadilloes caused him to become so wholeheartedly cooperative—even to the point of incriminating someone as highly placed as Colonel House?

Ah well, some questions would remain unanswered—unanswered by *him* at all events. The Gehlman–von Tiel file in its entirety, along with all the notes on the Dunfermline inquiry, had been safely consigned to Churchill's keeping. Despite the former First Lord's unending panoply of faults, he could still be depended upon to use the documents to Great Britain's best advantage.

As for Reeves-Wadleigh himself . . .

The surface veins in his arms had long since collapsed under the onslaught of repeated punctures, so this final syringe—like the others during these final days—would have to go in near his groin.

He felt no fear as the plunger sank down; morphine was his old and trusted friend, even his salvation.

He was a captain in the Royal Navy and the sea beneath the keel at last was calm. The fires were banked, the crew was paid off, and the cannon were cocked blindly to the sky. No wind, no steam, no current, no tide—just the ocean stretching endlessly before him.

He took his place on the bridge, looked one final time toward the misted shore, and then slowly . . . slowly . . . slowly . . . drifted away.

1916, 19TH JUNE—NEW YORK CITY

House sat on a stone bench in the sunlight, not far from the broad flat stump that was all that remained of his once majestic oak. From House's point of view, that stark remnant of dead nobility and grace was the one somber note in this otherwise limpid June morning. Certainly he had nothing to complain of in the daily papers. It was with a sense of real satisfaction that he read the dispatches from St. Louis. The party had proved itself to be not simply united, but uplifted. Bryan was back in the fold, Champ Clark was noisily contented, money for the campaign was rolling in, and with every step toward the nomination had come the stirring, vote-getting chant: "He Kept Us Out Of War!"

No matter that Teddy Roosevelt had healed the schism in Republican ranks. No matter that Charles Evans Hughes would mount a potent challenge. With a record like Wilson's on foreign and domestic matters to campaign on, the Democrats would surely keep the President ensconced in power.

Even more gratifying than the news stories, in a way, were the reports from the naval attachés in London and Berlin on the recent battle in the North Sea. It appeared now that the painfully difficult decision he'd made to intercede on the Germans' behalf had turned out to be a true act of statesmanship. Were glory what he sought in life, he might regret the fact that posterity could never be told what he'd done.

Of course the German Fleet's salvation had so far done nothing to make the warring nations of Europe more amenable to the mandates of reason. The British, oddly enough, seemed more intractable than ever.

House sighed. Thinking of the British, he thought also of Commander Maltbie and his wife. How tragic their deaths were, how senseless and how tragic.

His secretary appeared at the back door. "Excuse me, sir. Captain Gehlman has arrived."

House glanced at his watch. "Ah yes. Have him join me out here, will you."

After a few moments Gehlman strode out into the garden. The Colonel rose and started to extend his hand, but the expression in the other man's eyes made him think better of it. He limited himself to saying, "Good morning, Captain Gehlman. Welcome home."

"I hope by now it's 'Mr.' Gehlman, Colonel. I've asked to resign my commission."

"I see," said House, not liking Gehlman's manner. "I'm sorry to hear that."

Gehlman reached into his jacket pocket and brought out a small white envelope with a red wax seal on its flap. "Mr. Churchill asked me to give you this letter from Prime Minister Asquith," he said, placing the envelope on the bench next to which they stood.

House felt a sudden shudder run over him, along with anger at Gehlman's studied insult in refusing to hand him the letter directly. "Thank you," he said coldly.

"I just want you to know," Gehlman continued, "that neither I nor Commander Maltbie had anything to do with the German Fleet's escaping. We never used the transmitters. We had no effect whatsoever on the outcome of the battle."

House, with an effort, kept his composure. "Why, may I ask, are you so eager to have me know that?"

Gehlman gave him an arid smile. "For purely patriotic reasons, Colonel; so that you'll have the information available for future reference."

He turned and left without saying anything more.

House watched him go, then reached down with a sense of dread and picked up the small white envelope. His fingers trembled a little as he prised off the Prime Minister's seal. Inside there was a single piece of paper. He pulled it out and with a pang of humiliation read:

10 Downing Street
1916, 10th June

My dear Colonel House,
> *We know.*
> *We understand.*
> *We hope, in turn, for understanding.*
>   *Asquith*

EPILOGUE

In the privacy of the study of his Hyde Park Gate home, Winston S. Churchill, MP, sat feeding a thick file of papers one by one into the cheerfully burning fire. On the desk to his right the morning editions proclaimed the long-awaited news:

THE YANKS ARE COMING
AMERICA JOINING THE FIGHT
USA DECLARES WAR ON GERMANY

It was a momentous day for Britain, though its coming had been easily foreseeable ever since the Germans declared unrestricted submarine warfare at the end of January.

It was a momentous day for Churchill too. He was half American, after all, and his ties with the United States were such as to give his friend Prime Minister Lloyd George an additional excuse to bring him back into the government.

Meanwhile it was important to consign this file on Maltbie and Gehlman to the flames. Of the three men in Britain besides himself who'd known the whole story behind the affair, Reeves-Wadleigh was dead, Lord Fisher was old and ailing, and Herbert Asquith was deposed and stripped of power. Now that America was in the war, no good purpose could be served by allowing the documents to survive.

Watching the papers burn, Churchill felt a considerable sense of relief. If he was any judge of history, the United States and Great Britain had many a long mile to travel together in this violent twentieth century, and trust between the two countries would have to be kept at the highest possible level.

Let the flames consume the sorry record, therefore; let the truth be expunged by the fire. It was, perhaps, a serious disservice to history, but good Anglo-American relations would have to take precedence over fidelity to the muse. The English-speaking peoples would have enough problems to contend with in the coming years, after all. It would be best for them and for Western civilization as a whole if the historical record were purged of all traces and cleansed of all memory of this sordid episode, this shameful and grievously misguided affront to the British nation, and to the honor of the fleet.

Robert H. Pilpel was born in Manhattan in 1943 and attended New York City public schools. He received his Bachelor of Arts degree in history with highest honors in 1963 from Stanford University, where he was elected to Phi Beta Kappa. After graduating from Yale Law School and being admitted to the Connecticut Bar in 1966 he enlisted in the air force. He left the service in 1970 and moved to Rome, having been awarded a Fulbright fellowship to study comparative criminal law. He began writing professionally in 1971 and now makes his home in New York City.